THE
FELON'S DAUGHTER.

BY THE AUTHOR OF THE "DAUGHTER OF MIDNIGHT."

WITH TWENTY-THREE ILLUSTRATIONS,
DRAWN BY W. H. THWAITES.

LONDON:
JOHN DICKS, 313, STRAND; AND ALL BOOKSELLERS.

THE FELON'S DAUGHTER;

OR,

PAMELA'S PERILS.

CHAPTER I.

SHOWS HOW JACOB SHARPLES HAD AN INTERVIEW WITH THE WHITE RAT IN OLD FLEET DITCH, AND WHAT HAPPENED THEREUPON.

"CRUSH him! Smash him! Down with him! Life for life! His own child, too! Hit him again!—don't leave life in him! A rope—a rope! Hang him to the bars! Yah! whoop! brain him! Hold the door fast! Silence in the crib! Death to Jacob Sharples! Death—death! No, no! Save him till to-morrow, when the poor girl is to suffer. Hang him at the end of a pole, and carry him before the cart! Down with him! Smash him now! Death to Jacob Sharples!"

Such were the cries, and shouts, and imprecations which greeted the sudden and most unexpected appearance of a man, with marks of blood upon his face and his apparel torn and disordered, who presented himself in an apartment, so enveloped in clouds of tobacco, and so crowded with men, women, and lads, that it was a wonder any new arrival created any sensation whatever.

This apartment was on the ground floor of a house in old Fleet Lane, by Holborn Bridge.

The hour was midnight.

Suspended from the ceiling by rough twisted wire was an iron hoop, to the rim of which some half-dozen candles were tied clumsily.

Some of those candles were off the perpendicular sufficiently that when they burnt they sent the ho tallow, drop by drop, on to the heads of the persons below.

Those persons might be about thirty in number, and now that they were all on their feet—now that they were all yelling, shouting, and gesticulating at the man with the torn and disordered apparel and the blood upon his face, they presented a terrible spectacle of human passions.

"Kill him! Smash him! Crush him! Down with him at once! Yah! yah! Down with Jacob Sharples!"

The man turned and staggered towards the door again. There was an awful look of consternation on his face. His eyes seemed to be protruding from their sockets. He tried to speak, in the vain hope of quelling the storm of indignation that roared about him.

"Pals! pals! I—a—pals!"

A yell of rage drowned what he would fain have said.

Pewter pots—wooden measures — glasses — tobacco pipes—shoes—a knife or two—a three-legged stool—a heavy bludgeon—all these articles began to batter the head and shoulders of the forlorn looking, blood stained, ragged man, as they were flung with reckless confusion from every hand.

He cowered down before the storm.

"Pals! pals!"

Another yell stopped his utterance.

A pint pewter pot struck him on the brow.

The wretched man staggered beneath that blow.

"Give it him again! Down with him! Kill him! kill him! Death to Jacob Sharples!"

"Mercy! mercy!"

He made for the door—his hand was upon it; he might possibly escape. Whatever he had done to make him in such bad odour with the assemblage in that house, it was quite evident was all-sufficient to arm their most angry passions against him.

There was no prospect but death in staying.

"Mercy! mercy! Let me go!"

There was a rush to get at him. The throng of persons impeded each other. The wretched being surely had a chance of escape. No—he falls! It is but to one knee. He is up again—he opens the door—again he stumbles! Yells and shouts resound in his ears.

There seems a chance of his escape, for no one now means to pursue him.

Then he suddenly gives up all hope—for the door is pushed open wide from the outside—and a young man, a little past the age of boyhood, his long, black hair dashed partially over his face, which was of a death-like paleness, appears.

It was almost with a scream that this new comer welcomed the sight of the man who was in such bad odour in that old house in Field Lane.

"Jacob Sharples!" cried the young man.

The wretched being looked up into the pale, young face for a moment.

"Dick—Dick Doubleday!" he gasped.

He then made a desperate attempt to fly—to force his way from the room, past this young man; but Dick Doubleday caught him by the throat, and held him as though he were in a vice.

Then, while the dilapidated, bleeding man shrunk down and cowered before that boy, whom, to judge from their relative sizes and strength, he could have annihilated, Dick Doubleday spoke in a high, excited tone.

"Pals, and dear friends all! I came to ask you—to—to—try—to—to—save—save——"

He seemed choking. There was a name upon his lips—a name in his heart—a name in every fibre of his brain—which it almost killed him to attempt to utter.

"You mean Pamela!" said a voice from the furthest end of the dingy apartment.

"I do—I do! Oh, my Pamela!"

Nothing could exceed, nothing could come near, the tone of heart-breaking anguish in which those words were pronounced. No description, no power of language, can paint the pathos of their utterance.

"Oh, my Pamela!"

The persons present in that room were outcasts of society—highwaymen, housebreakers, footpads, thieves of every variety and description. The house itself was a well-known fence and lodging-house for gentlemen who took the shortest route to other folks' pockets.

But yet these persons were human.

Yet they belonged to the great human family, and had not shaken off their connexion with humanity. Every voice was hushed as Dick Doubleday spoke. Every heart responded to that terrible request, which was more in the tone than in the words he uttered.

Jacob Sharples groaned.

"Oh, my own dear Pamela!"

Dick Doubleday let go the throat of the wretched man, who was crouching at his feet, and clasped both his hands over his own face.

The silence continued for the space of about half a minute.

During this time, if you had been able to look in upon that strange assemblage, you might have supposed that some singular death had visited them all, and struck them into statues, in the attitudes in which it found them.

It was a female voice that broke the silence.

"Don't take on so, Dick. It's soon over, and she can't suffer but once!"

Dick Doubleday removed his hands from before his eyes, and the expression of them was awful to see.

"Suffer!—suffer! My Pamela suffer!"

Jacob Sharples tried to crawl past him.

"Stop him! Stop Jacob!" cried a voice.

Dick looked down.

With a cry of rage he sprung upon the trembling wretch.

"Villain!—sneak!—wretch!—murderer!"

"Help!—help! He will strangle me!"

The two rolled to the floor together.

A dozen hands separated them.

Dick Doubleday was calmer when he rose up from that brief struggle.

Jacob Sharples was whiter and more ghastly.

And now that the spell of silence which had sat on every heart was broken, every one appeared to wish to speak at once.

"Settle him! Settle Sharples! He has been the death of the girl!—his own child, too! Down with him! Kill him off-hand, Dick! Nobody will peach! Kill him!"

"Help! help! Murder!"

"Pals, hear me!" cried a voice, which was above all the tumult.

A tall and stalwart man had sprung upon the table in the middle of the room.

"Hurrah! hurrah! Hear Handsome Jemmy! Hear him! He'll tell us what to do, and how to do it! Now, Handsome Jemmy, what's it to be?"

"Pals all," said Handsome Jemmy, as he adjusted his cravat and pulled forward the "love locks" of his hair,—"pals all, I think Jacob Sharples must have had a jolly bad opinion of us all!"

"We have of him, Jemmy!"

"Yes. But if he hadn't had a bad idea of us, he would hardly have shown his face here on this Sunday night, knowing what happened on Friday, and what's going to happen to-morrow!"

"It's Monday now!" said one.

"Why, so it is, Ned—so it is! One o'clock, I declare!"

Dick Doubleday had turned from the trembling Jacob Sharples, and closed and locked the room door. For a few moments he had listened to Handsome Jemmy, as the man on the table was named, and then he got impatient, and in a voice of entreaty he called out, "The night flies — the morrow is coming! Pals all, will you let her die? Pamela! Pamela!"

A loud and general "No" came from every lip; and then one said, in quiet tones, "If so be, Dick, you will only show me how to prevent it! That's all, my boy!"

"The cart," said Dick Doubleday, speaking in choking accents,—"the cart that to-morrow morning will carry my dear Pamela to Tyburn passes the end of the lane. They say that she is to be—or they mean her to be—the last who will be carried to Tyburn to—to suffer! Pamela!—my Pamela!"

The effort to speak connectedly of the fearful facts to which he alluded was too much for Dick Doubleday. He burst into tears, and sobbed aloud.

"That will do him good!" said a woman, who made her way through the throng, and carefully dabbed Dick's eyes with a handkerchief.

"Good—good! Oh, dear—oh, dear! nothing will do me good!"

"Now, Dick," said Handsome Jemmy, "there's time enough to think if we can do anything for Pamela! It's about Jacob here, her old rascal of a father, we want to talk!"

"She is only sixteen!" sobbed Dick.

"Come, come, be a man!"

"And so—so—pretty—so good—so——"

"Hem! Well, it is hard, Dick!"

"She—she is the prettiest, dear girl in all London; and only to think that this wretch, who calls himself her father, might have saved her by a word!"

A yell of indignation at Jacob Sharples burst forth now again from the assemblage.

"Well, now," added Handsome Jemmy, "that's all true, Dick! We all knows it, and we are all sorry for it. Poor Pamela Sharples was tried before Chief Justice Holt on Friday last, and cast for death!"

"And all for what?—all for what?" screamed Dick Doubleday, holding both his arms above his head excitedly. "All for what? For going into Mr. Welton's, the draper's, on Ludgate Hill, with a bad guinea! Oh, cruel laws —oh, blood-stained laws! And what did the Chief Justice say when—when my Pamela spoke, and said that she did not know the money was bad, and that the other gold and silver she had with her was all bad—what did the Chief Justice say?—'If any one will come forward, and own to giving you the money to change, and that you did not know it was spurious coin, I will direct the jury to give you the benefit of the doubt.'"

Jacob Sharples, at this point in what Dick Doubleday was saying, uttered a cry of despair.

"And this wretch—this father," added Dick, as once again he grasped Sharples by both the hair and the collar—"this man who calls himself her father was at the back of the court, and when he heard what the Chief Justice said, he hung down his head and slunk away."

"Down with him! Tear him to pieces! Knock his head off! Kill him!"

"And left my Pamela," screamed Dick Doubleday, "to the cruel law!"

"That's about it!" said Handsome Jemmy.

"Hear me—oh, hear me!" gasped Jacob Sharples.

A yell of execration followed the appeal.

"Hear me!—only hear me! If I had stepped forward—if I had said so much—I, too—I, too, would have suffered, and Pamela would not have been saved. I know them too well—too well!"

"You shall know me too well!" cried Dick Doubleday.

"No, no, Dick; let him alone," said Handsome Jemmy. "It seems that Jacob Sharples, the coiner, thinks, if he had stepped forward like a man to save his daughter, he would have been put on his trial."

"I am certain of it—I am certain!" cried Sharples.

"Well, pals all, suppose now we try him; not for coining—not for passing bad money—but for leaving his own child, Pamela, to death, when he might have saved her!"

"Try him! try him! Hurrah! try him!"

"Very good. Who prosecutes?"

"I!" shouted Dick Doubleday—"I!"

"Good! Let me have a chair up here; I will be the judge."

"And we the jury!" yelled every voice.

"Stand up, Jacob Sharples!"

"Up with him! Up with you! Oh, you don't like Well, then, we must make you. There you are! Guilty, or not guilty, eh? Ha! ha! Rare sport this! Hold him up—knock him down! I say, Jemmy, what is to be done with him if he is brought in guilty?"

"I shall propose that he be introduced, then, to the White Rat."

The self constituted judge pointed significantly downwards as he spoke; and it would seem that those words, however obscure they may at present be to the reader, were not only fully comprehended by the assembled members of "the family," but by the prisoner Jacob Sharples himself.

He uttered a yell of dismay, and shook in every limb.

The wretched man saw his fate. It was to be a terrible one!

CHAPTER II.

DETAILS HOW A VERDICT OF "GUILTY," AND A SPEEDY JUDGMENT, BROUGHT VENGEANCE, BUT NO HELP TO PAMELA.

THE night was waning fast, and whatever might have been the object of that concourse of persons in the gloomy room of the fence in Field Lane, they readily enough fell into the suggestion of resolving themselves into a court of inquiry into the conduct of Jacob Sharples.

It must have been some positive hallucination that induced that wretched man, under the circumstances, to show his face in that place.

Even at the entrance of the house he had received some personal ill-usage, the marks of which he brought with him to that apartment, so that he must have been to a certain extent prepared for the indignation which would burst over his head.

But probably he thought that that indignation would expend itself in words; and as he was a member of the large community the first principle of which is to prey upon their neighbours, he felt that to cut himself off voluntarily from all association with what was called "the family," would be intolerable.

Hence, notwithstanding he might be well aware of an amount of unpopularity that might take some dangerous form, he had ventured to show himself on that Sunday night preceding the execution of the last person whom the vindictive laws of that period consigned to death for a commercial offence.

Pamela Sharples, a young girl sixteen years of age, had been tried and convicted of passing a spurious guinea at the shop of a draper on Ludgate Hill.

More money was found upon her; and unhappily for her, the whole of it was base.

The trial lasted thirteen minutes.

From life to death—from that bright dawn of existence to a fearful destruction, did that young girl seem to pass in a brief period of time.

The judges of the land at that period were, with few exceptions, men with hard hearts and stern brains.

The vindictive character of the criminal law warped their better feelings. As advocates, they had pleaded for convictions, and their sensibilities had become indurated, so that as judges they carried them out with little mercy.

But there was something so entirely innocent—something so artless, simple, and interesting about this young girl, Pamela Sharples, that the stern Lord Chief Justice was melted to pity.

Bending over his desk, he had addressed her in a few brief but emphatic words.

"The law is so clear," he said, "as regards this offence, and the facts against you are so conclusive, that neither I nor the respectable persons who occupy the jury-box could sit in this court another hour if we failed to convict you. You say your father gave you this money, with directions to call at different shops, and make various purchases to small amounts, and bring him the change—always tendering in payment the most valuable coin in your possession?"

"Ah, yes! it was so," sobbed Pamela.

"And you say you knew not that the coins were spurious?"

"Before heaven I say it!"

"Then if that father will come forth and depose to as much, I will direct the jury to give you the benefit of the doubt."

Then it was that a man, muffled in an overcoat, and who had kept his head low upon his breast during the trial, slunk out of the court.

That was the father.

The young girl was left to die.

Sadly and mournfully she turned her beautiful eyes from face to face, in the hope that she would see that father among the throng, who alone could snatch her from destruction.

She was condemned.

The law must have its victim.

Such were the circumstances under which Jacob Sharples, the coiner, had sacrificed his daughter; and from that time to the midnight hour on Sunday night, when he ventured to show himself at the fence, in Field Lane, he had not addressed a word to human being.

Maddened by solitude, and perhaps by remorse, and yet not having the courage to take the only step which might arrest the doom of his daughter—namely, the giving himself up to the authorities—he had, perhaps, hoped to drown reflection amid the wild riot which he knew, on that Sunday night, would take place in that house of ill repute.

We have seen his reception; and now, with these few words of explanation, we again look into the staring eyes and on the livid countenance of the baffled villain who finds that he has reached a depth of criminality which makes ordinary felons his accusers—his jury—his judge, and his executioners.

"Now for it!" cried Handsome Jemmy; "let's make short work of it! How long did the trial of Pamela Sharples last, Dick Doubleday?"

Dick had to place his hands against his breast before he could speak, for his heart on that night of terror and despair seemed to have grown too large for the space it occupied.

"Thirteen minutes," he said; "but thirteen minutes!"

"That'll do!" said Handsome Jemmy. "Somebody lend me a watch. I had two yesterday; but somehow or other they didn't go as I liked, so I let old Aaron in the Minories have them."

"Here's a watch, Jemmy," cried one. "I don't know whether it keeps good time or not, but if it don't, it's the fault of the old cove I took it from in Pall Mall. Little Rufus was with me—he's a clever boy that. He puts down his head, and runs bang into the stomach of any old feller who seems to have a good watch in his fob; and then I runs forward and boxes his ears, and helps the old chap up; for in nine cases out of ten he sits down on the pavement, as if he'd come out on purpose to do so; and then, after he has thanked me ever so much, and I've walked off, he finds his watch has walked off likewise!"

"Hold your row!" said Handsome Jemmy, the self-appointed judge. "You'll get that boy Rufus into trouble some day! But now to business. It's ten minutes past one. What's the charge? Speak, Dick Doubleday! What have you to say?"

There was a careless, ribald sort of style about the highwayman, who was called Handsome Jemmy, in commencing this mock trial of Jacob Sharples, which was little in accordance with the deep affliction and anguish of the heart of Dick Doubleday.

But Jacob Sharples, who had stolen several furtive looks at the face of Handsome Jemmy, saw something in his eyes which had for him an awful seriousness.

Beneath the jocund, careless air of the handsome highwayman, there lurked a fearful meaning.

Jacob Sharples detected it.

Dick Doubleday did not.

But then Jacob Sharples was by far the older man, and his perceptions at that moment were sharpened by his fears.

Poor Dick Doubleday's, on the contrary, were blunted by his grief.

And yet he stepped forward, and raising his right arm, he cried in accents which struggled with tears and with despair, "I accuse this man, Jacob Sharples."

"Of what, my lad?"

"Murder!"

Handsome Jemmy's eyes half closed, and a bright light seemed to dart from them as he replied in the same careless tone in which he carried on the proceedings, "A serious charge, that Whose murder is it, my lad?"

"His own daughter, Pamela. She is condemned for his crime, when a word from him would save her."

The handsome highwayman turned slowly towards Jacob Sharples, and amid the profound stillness of all present—for the thieves and reprobates who were in that apartment were immensely interested in this mockery of a judicial proceeding—he said coldly and calmly, "Guilty or not guilty, prisoner at the bar?"

Jacob Sharples licked his parched lips and gazed about him.

"Prisoner at—at the bar?" he said.

"Oh, he objects," said the highwayman, "that there's no bar. Make him one."

A heavy, long, rough knotted bludgeon was produced, and being stretched across the breast of Jacob Sharples, his two arms were dragged over it, and he looked a helpless hideous wretch as he leant heavily upon the extemporised bar.

"Guilty or not guilty?" said Handsome Jemmy.

"It is not I. It is the law—the law—the cruel, wicked law! I have not condemned her. Blame the law, dear pals—blame the law, comrades and family men—not me."

"Guilty or not guilty?" said the highwayman again.

"Let me go! Let me go! I—I will do what I can to save her. I did not think you'd all take it up in this way. I—I—I did not think, Dick Doubleday, that—that you thought so much of the girl."

"Pamela! Pamela! My Pamela!" moaned Dick Doubleday.

"He won't plead," said Handsome Jemmy. "Now hark you, pals all, of every degree. In older times than these—but still not very long ago—when a gentleman of our profession was had up to the Bailey, and would'nt plead, they used to press him—not politely, as you'd ask a pal to take a drop of something, but with a plank upon him, and with a few hundred pounds weight upon that again; and that's why a particular part of the old Stone Jug, you see, pals, is still called the press yard."

"Jemmy, Jemmy," cried one, "you ought to have been a lawyer or a judge, or some other blessed big wig of a rogue or another, instead of being what you is, Jemmy, and no mistake. You'd a been a hornament, you would, to will any in high places. Perhaps a Parliament man—who knows?"

"Hold your row!" said the highwayman.

"All's right, Jemmy!"

"Well, pals, the prisoner won't plead, and we can't press him; but we can find out something else instead; so just be so good, somebody, as to hit him on the head with a quart pot, till he says 'Guilty,' or 'Not guilty!'"

"Murder!" cried Jacob Sharples, "I see you're intent upon my murder!"

Bang! came the quart pot on the top of Sharples' head; and it was evident that that mode of inducing a prisoner to plead was quite as efficient as pressing, for he yelled out, "Not guilty!" in a voice that echoed through the room.

"That'll do," said Handsome Jemmy. "Now you go on, Dick Doubleday."

"For more than a year," said Dick, "I have known and loved Pamela Sharples."

Dick's voice faltered as he spoke.

"Go on, Dick!" screamed a female voice from the further end of the apartment "There's no harm in that, my boy. It will be hard lines when a smart lad don't see something to touch his heart in a pretty face!"

"Bravo! Bravo! Hurrah!"

"Ladies and gentlemen of the jury," said Handsome Jemmy, "will you be quiet? Go on, Dick?"

Dick Doubleday swallowed his emotion, and proceeded.

"I'm quite sure—sure as that I stand here—that Pamela Sharples never knew the trade her father carried on. He's a coiner—we all know that; and we all know that it isn't so difficult to make the base money as it is to pass it. Look at him. Would any one change a guinea for that hang-dog face? But when he gave it to his daughter Pamela, and sent her with her pretty looks and innocent ways to change it, nobody suspected her. They were, perhaps, looking at her eyes instead of at the guinea, and so she brought him home the plunder—innocent as a child—and knowing nothing of it. And now what's come of it? He leaves her to die!—to die for his offences, and hadn't the courage to step forward and say—'I did it!'"

Dick Doubleday ceased speaking, but there was a flush upon his face which showed how his own words had stirred up every feeling of his heart, and how deeply, dearly, and tenderly he loved the girl whose fate seemed to be decided, whatever might become of Jacob Sharples, her abandoned father.

"Prisoner," said Handsome Jemmy, "what have you to say?"

Sharples looked despairingly about him. He saw contempt, hatred, and condemnation on every face.

"What was the use," he said, gaspingly,—"what was the use of two victims?"

"That is untrue!" exclaimed Dick Doubleday. "The judge distinctly said that upon any proffered testimony in proof of what Pamela asserted, she should have the benefit of the doubt. We all know what that means."

"To be sure we do!" said Handsome Jemmy. "Chief Justice Holt is not the worst of his sort. He wanted to get the girl off if he could, and it's possible enough"—here the highwayman bent his eyes upon the countenance of the trembling Jacob Sharples—"it's possible enough that if the prisoner here before us had stepped forward like a man to save the girl they would have pulled him through the affair likewise."

Jacob Sharples groaned.

"But now it's too late," added the highwayman, "for we all know what King George the Third is upon these matters—whoever is cast for death, dies!"

"No—no—don't say that!" shrieked Dick Doubleday. "Don't kill me outright by taking away all hope from me!"

"That's not the question, Dick, just now. It's this man we have to deal with. Ladies and gentlemen of the jury, what say you? Is Jacob Sharples guilty or not guilty?"

The shout of "Guilty!" came so quickly from every lip in reply, that it seemed like an echo of the question addressed by the handsome highwayman.

"No! no!" cried Sharples. "Spare me! This is a mockery; you have carried this jest far enough, all of you. I have been frightened—you see I have been frightened. Let that suffice."

"Jacob Sharples!" said Handsome Jemmy, assuming, with admirable gravity, the manner of a judge about to pass sentence,—"Jacob Sharples! you have been tried, and found guilty of the offence laid to your charge. It is not for me to aggravate, by any words, the unhappy condition in which you find yourself. My duty lies plainly and clearly before me. It is to pronounce upon you a sentence, but—as I have been ably assisted by the intelligent jury I see about me—I am open to any suggestions from them, in regard to what that sentence shall be!"

"*The White Rat!*" cried everybody as with one voice. Jacob Sharples looked too terrified to scream.

There was an awful stillness in the apartment; and then Handsome Jemmy, in a deep, sonorous voice, spoke.

"Jacob Sharples,—the sentence of the court is that you be consigned to the White Rat. I have no doubt whatever—from your looks, as well as from previous knowledge of you in this place—that you know perfectly well what that means."

"No!—no!—no!"

JACOB SHARPLES MEETS HIS DESERTS AT THE "FENCE."

"You do not!"

"No; I did not mean that! I mean mercy!"

"Oh, very well. But as for mercy, that is neither here nor there. You are aware, Jacob Sharples—as we are all aware—that beneath this room in which we now sit, and which will be for ever respectable as a court of justice, is a spacious cellar. In the floor of that cellar there is a trap-door, which, when opened, enables you to hear the gurgling rush of water—in plain language, Jacob Sharples, that no doubt once translucent stream which is now called Fleet Ditch runs beneath this house."

"Ah, Jemmy!" cried a voice, "you are a rum 'un. You should have been a lawyer."

"Be quiet; you said that before. Don't interrupt the court. Where was I?"

"In Fleet Ditch, Jemmy; which you said were a trans—trans something—oh! ah!—a transporting stream, awhile ago!"

"Silence! silence! Don't you see the prisoner is impatient, and waste of time is very important to him; because, at two o'clock this morning—at two o'clock, I say——"

"What—what?" gasped Sharples.

"The tide turns."

"The tide? What tide? I have heard that people die at the turn of the tide. What do you mean?"

"Just this. That portion of Fleet Ditch which runs beneath this house acts as a sewer, and drains out into the river by the side of Blackfriars' Bridge. When the tide's low, if you ain't choked on the way——"

"Choked?"

"Or eaten up by the rats—you may get out into the stream; but when the tide flows, the rush of water is this way, and then all is over."

"Mercy! Mercy! Mercy!"

"So you see, Jacob Sharples, the necessity of wasting no time. It is, moreover, known to you, as to us all, that that sewer is inhabited by a hideous reptile."

"Yes, the White Rat, a creature of hideous dimensions, of patriarchal age, and of unknown ferocity; so that it has become a common saying, when anything is dropped through the trap-door into the Fleet Ditch, that it is given to the White Rat. Sometimes a valuable bit of swag, that is too much hunted after, that cannot be concealed or altered in appearance, has been dropped down there, for fear of compromising the gentleman who found it in somebody else's house, or in somebody else's pocket. Now, Jacob Sharples, we consider you compromise us all; therefore, we mean to give you to the White Rat."

"No, no; better to kill me at once; better shoot me, brain me, hang me, than that!"

"No—that is the sentence. You have your chance. Delays are dangerous. The tides rise quickly. Jacob Sharples, I would advise you to take your departure as soon as possible."

The highwayman made an impatient gesture and sprang to his feet. Half a dozen of the strongest men in the apartment rushed upon Jacob Sharples.

Screams, yells, shouts, and imprecations filled the air He fought like a madman. A chair had to be brought—a heavy chair, to which he was securely fastened. He was mounted, chair and all, upon the shoulders of his judges—of his executioners.

A narrow, slippery staircase, composed of large blocks of stone, embedded in earth, but many of which had slipped out of their places, led to the noisome and terrible cellar below, beneath which rolled again the fetid stream of the Fleet.

There was a trap-door—or, rather two trap-doors—for it was composed of two flaps.

One of those flaps, by withdrawing a bolt, fell downwards on its hinges, as far as two short chains would permit it.

Those chains were useful for drawing it up again.

The other trap-door opened towards the cellar

"Lights—lights here!" cried Handsome Jemmy, the highwayman. "We must have torches in this underground crib. A link, here!—a link!"

There was a flare of light—red, flaring, and unequal. It shone on a crowd of angry faces, and upon the distorted, terrified visage of Jacob Sharples, as he was securely pinioned in the chair.

He no longer appealed to those men about him for mercy; but, in a screaming voice, which sounded scarcely human, he shouted "Murder! murder!"

Those cries were too keen and ear-piercing to be other than dangerous to the general safety, even in that locality.

"Quick! quick!" cried the highwayman. "Away with him!"

They placed the chair upon that half of the trap that opened downwards.

The bolt was withdrawn.

With one wild, unearthly scream, the wretched man fell into the black abyss. still tied to the chair.

He who carried the link darted forward and held it for a moment over the orifice.

All who could crowd round the spot gazed down for a moment.

There was a black heaving tide, upon which the chair floated, and then there sprung upon the chair, and upon Jacob Sharples, a hideous object.

A rat! A rat that might once have been white, but which was now of some strange nondescript colour that could not be defined Of enormous size, the reptile might almost be supposed to belong to some other genus, as it crouched upon the breast of Jacob Sharples, who the next moment, with rat, chair, and all, was washed from under the trap-door by the tide of the Fleet.

CHAPTER III.

DETAILS HOW THE KING'S PHYSICIAN WAS AROUSED AT AN EARLY HOUR, AND HOW DICK DOUBLEDAY AND HANDSOME JEMMY TRIED TO SAVE PAMELA.

GONE!" said Dick Doubleday, as he shrunk back from that dismal opening in the floor of the cellar in Field Lane.

"Close the trap," said Handsome Jemmy, the highwayman. "And now, pals all, this is a matter which it will be wise to keep to ourselves."

"Listen! Listen!" exclaimed several voices in concert

"What is it?"

All who were present in that dismal cellar listened intently.

Strange sounds came from the black muddy stream that ran beneath it—gurgling sounds, as if the water had met with some obstruction—smothered cries—and once—once they all thought they heard a shriek, that seemed as though it came from mortal lips.

A shudder passed through every heart.

"It's the tide," said one.

"So soon, think you?" asked the highwayman, as he glanced by the light of the link at the watch that had been lent to him. "So soon? It wants, even now, ten minutes to two."

"Come away! Oh, come away!" said Dick Doubleday. "I feel that this is justice—I feel that we have done no more than we have a right to do, because it is justice. But, yet—yet——"

"Ah, Dick!" interrupted Handsome Jemmy, as he laid his hand on the lad's shoulder—"ah, Dick! you cannot surely regret the fate of such a man as Jacob Sharples?"

"No—no! It is not that."

"Yet you look dissatisfied?"

"I may well do so. Sharples deserved the fate, dreadful as it is, that has come over him; but if he had deserved it, and met it ten times over, that would not save my poor dear Pamela"

"By Jove! that's true, Dick."

"What shall I do? Tell me Jemmy, what I shall do?"

The highwayman shook his head, as though unable to do so.

"You cannot advise me? You cannot give me any hope?"

"Poor girl! Poor girl! I would give my best horse; I would give all the booty I am likely to get on Bagshot Heath for the next twelve months, if I could only save that young creature from Tyburn Tree to-morrow."

"And I," said Dick Doubleday, as he clenched his hands, and spoke in a high, screaming tone of voice that was painful to hear, "I would give my life!"

"Hush! hush, Dick!" exclaimed Jemmy. "Come this way."

The party had left the cellar with more haste and precipitation than they had sought it; for those strange subterranean cries rang in their ears, and filled them with a thousand superstitious fears.

There was quite a struggle on the slippery disorganised stone steps, to see who would get out of the place first.

Or rather this struggle was to see who would not be the last.

Handsome Jemmy and Dick Doubleday did not make their way into what might be called the common public room again, but the highwayman took Dick by the arm, and led him into a smaller room at the back of the house.

"Dick," he said, "you have a good heart, and some day I should not wonder at all but you will make a figure in the world.

"No, no, no!"

"Don't say no. A light, good-looking, handsome, fellow like you may do anything."

"What do you mean?" inquired Dick Doubleday, of his companion.

"Why, look you here, Dick! It is not might or strength that does work on the road or on the common. It is quite another thing."

"What?"

"Dash! That is the real secret. Dash! Courage! A certain sort of something, Dick, that takes people by storm, and makes them give up purses, pocket-books, watches, and rings, before they have time to know what they are about."

"Yes, yes! I daresay that is all as you say; but what is it to me?"

"Everything, Dick."

"Not now—not now! There will be no 'dash' in me after to-morrow."

Dick Doubleday shuddered as he spoke, for that dreadful morrow was each moment nearer and nearer at hand.

Oh! had he possessed but the power to make the night, which was now slowly but surely passing away, eternal, how freely and how gladly he would have exercised it, and so saved, for ever and ever, his dear, dear, Pamela!

"Tell me—oh, tell me!" he half shrieked—"you, who are a man of judgment, courage, and experience, tell me of something that I can do to try to save her, or I shall go mad."

"Come, come! Don't talk in that way. I tell you now what I will do."

"Yes, yes!—oh, yes!"

"I will go now to the stables in Finsbury, and get my best horse. By the bye, do you know if Pamela can ride?"

Dick shook his head.

"I should think not."

"That's a pity. But still, I can but try it. I will ride up to the cart, just as it gets to the corner of Fleet Market, and try to take her out of it."

Dick groaned.

"They will kill you, Jemmy."

"Perhaps!"

"No, no! That won't do. I will go now—now at once, I will go!"

"Where, Dick? where?"

"To Newgate!"

"Newgate?"

"Yes, I will go there at once, and I will ask to see the Sheriff, and they must send for him; and I will say to him, 'Sir, you are about to take to death an innocent and fair young girl. I, sir, only, am the guilty party. I, sir, gave her the base money to get changed, and persuaded her it was good. I give myself up, sir, in her place, and am quite content—quite happy to die for her.'"

"Stop!"

The highwayman placed his hand heavily upon the shoulder of Dick Doubleday.

"Stop, Dick! That won't do at all. They will just lock you up, and then the execution will take place all the same; and you will beat yourself to death against the walls of some cell, like a wild bird against the bars of a cage."

"Oh, what else—oh, what else, then, can I do?"

"Come with me. You have heard of old Mother Bendydykes?"

"That witch?"

"Well, that is just what they do call her. But you have often, no doubt, heard of her?" returned Handsome Jemmy.

"I hear she tells fortunes to the girls, and the men and lads too; and they do say she knows things that you may fancy are quite locked up in your own heart. Why—why it was only the other day that I saw her in the Market."

"Fleet Market?"

"Yes, Jemmy! She laid her skinny fingers on my arm and said, 'Love her—love her well, lad; and she will never then have a heart seared and shrivelled like old Mother Bendydykes'.'"

"And what did she mean, Dick?"

"Why, of course she meant Pamela; and it was very strange, for I had only been looking after the dear, dear girl a few minutes before."

The highwayman laughed.

"And you know, Jemmy, nobody could tell just by my looks that I loved her with all my heart—with all my soul! Pamela, Pamela—dear, dear, dear Pamela! when shall I look into your sweet eyes again? Oh, Jemmy! you don't know how much I love her!"

"Yes, I do. Come along."

"Where? Oh, where?"

"To Mother Bendydykes. She will advise what to do, if anything at all can be done. I have been kind to her before to-day."

"Day! day! Oh, do not say it is day!"

"No! no! It is night yet—it is night enough yet. Come at once, and no doubt we shall find the old dame at home, at her house in Whitefriars. I wonder often the crazy old crib don't fall down, and crush her and her cats to death. Some folks will have it she is mad, but I tell you what it is Dick—mad or not mad, there is no person's advice I would sooner take than old Mother Bendydykes', if I were in any fix I could not see my way out of."

"Come, then! Any hope is better than none. It is very kind and good of you, Jemmy, to take so much trouble about me and one whom I love."

"Pho! pho! Who would not try to save a pretty little girl like Pamela Sharples from such a death?"

Dick Doubleday was pale and haggard, as if sleep had been a stranger to his eyes for many a night, as he stepped out of the "fence," in Field Lane, with his friend, the handsome highwayman.

"Ware hawks, Jemmy!" said a voice.

"Ah! Who is that?"

"Nobbling Ned."

"What's the row, Ned?"

"I hardly know, Jemmy; but there are a couple of suspicious-looking fellows, pretending to drink deep, at the 'King's Head.'"

"Thank you, Ned—thank you! I had a slight idea I was dogged. Dick, we will go out of the lane the other way, and get on to Holborn Hill by Hatton Garden. It won't take us much longer."

The highwayman and Dick Doubleday accordingly turned their backs upon that well-known ancient public-house, that had stood for a century and a half at the Holborn end of Field Lane. They soon took the round Jemmy had suggested, and then crossing Holborn Hill they drived down Shoe Lane, and made the best of their way to Whitefriars, at the back of the Temple.

St Paul's clock had boomed forth the hour of two, just as they left the fence in Field Lane, and each sound of the clock seemed as if it struck upon the heart of Dick Doubleday.

There was a narrow court leading out of one of the oldest streets in Whitefriars

At the end of that court was a dilapidated-looking house, that was so absolutely grimy, and broken down, and neglected, nobody could have expected it to be the abode of any living thing, save and exc pt the water rats that might come up from the Thames.

"Halt!" said Handsome Jemmy.

"What is it?"

"Did you hear nothing?"

"I thought I heard a strange cry."

"Then I am sure I did; and it came from the house of Mother Bendydykes. Who knows but some one has broken in, and, with the idea of plunder, may try a little in the murder line to-night? Come on, Dick; we may be in time to do the old woman a service, for all we can say."

The highwayman darted down the narrow court, followed by Dick Doubleday; and in another moment they both stood upon the door-step of Mother Bendy-dykes' house.

That house no doubt at one time had been a man-sion of some consequence—probably the town residence a hundred years ago of some prosperous bencher of the old Temple.

It was of considerable size, and had a sort of strag-gling, weedy garden, which went right down to the Thames, and at the bottom of which there was a little stone paved slanting landing-place actually belonging to the house itself.

It had not happened, however, for many a long year that the keel of any wherry had grated upon those old stones.

All was still in the house.

There was no knocker—no bell; indeed, there was no means whatever of making the presence of a visitor known, except by kicking at the door or rapping at it with some hard substance—or perhaps breaking a win-dow, if there were such a thing as a whole one in the whole front of the house to break.

Handsome Jemmy had on his riding boots, so he was very well prepared to salute the door with any amount of kicks that might be requisite.

Somewhat to his surprise, however, the moment he raised his foot to commence operations, the door was flung open.

A low, growling noise came from the hall.

"Hilloa! hilloa!" cried the highwayman. "It is I, mother; it is I—Jemmy! You know my voice, I fancy?"

A huge black cat darted past both the highwayman and Dick Doubleday, and disappeared down the court.

"That's one of them!" said Jemmy.

"One of what?"

"One of the cats!"

"Has she more than one?"

"More than one? Why, she has twenty at the least! But come on! I know where we shall find her! It's the second door on the right hand side of the hall."

By some means, the outer door closed of itself so soon as Handsome Jemmy and Dick Doubleday were fairly in the passage.

The highwayman felt along the wall for the door he had mentioned, and in a few moments Dick Doubleday saw a red glare of light, and was conscious of a strong odour of burning wood.

"This way," said Handsome Jemmy; and, taking Dick Doubleday by the arm, he led him into rather a large room on the ground floor of the house.

This room was divided into two portions by a cur-tain of black cloth—at least, so it seemed—that hung from the ceiling to the floor.

A few miserable old articles of furniture were in that half of the room which was next to the door from the passage; but the only light that was there came from some wood which was smouldering upon the hearth, and which occasionally shot up a small blue flame.

Crouching over this fire, with her long, shrivelled fingers spread out fan-like, was an aged woman. Some old garment, which, upon close inspection, would have been found to be the remains of a costly dress of quilted satin, was drawn like a hood over her head.

It was fastened round her neck by a piece of common rope.

The straggling white locks that hung down over her face nearly hid it; and, as she crouched over the fire, two cats might have been seen sitting partially on her back and partially on each shoulder.

The cats began to hiss, and make that noise which is commonly called swearing.

"What now?—what now?" screamed the old woman. "What want you with Martha Bendydykes? Hang-dogs, I daresay, who want to take some advantage of a poor, lone, old woman! Spit!—spit, my pets!—spit! There's venom in it, pets!—spit!"

The two cats reared their backs, and spat at the in-truders.

"Why, mother," said Jemmy, "don't you know me?"

"And me, too?" said Dick Doubleday, in a mournful tone. "Oh, Martha Bendydykes! if it be true that you know what people think, and can look into the future, tell me—oh, tell me how to save my own dear, dear girl, Pamela!"

The old hag sprang to her feet.

The two cats were nearly dislodged from their po-sition on her shoulders, and only hung on for a moment by their claws.

From the other side of the black curtain there came a deep and awful groan.

"Peace!" cried the hag—and she rapped a walking-stick, which it appeared she had been leaning on, sharply on the floor. "Peace! peace, I say! It is coming out! It is all working out! It was sure and certain! It is fate! fate! fate!"

CHAPTER IV.

CONDUCTS DICK DOUBLEDAY TO OLD BUCKINGHAM HOUSE, AND BRINGS THE DAWN OF A NEW DAY.

It was not the sudden excitement of old Mother Bendy-dykes nor the anger of her cats, that startled Handsome Jemmy, the highwayman; but it was that deep and awful groan that had come from the other side of the dismal-looking black curtain.

Handsome Jemmy stepped back a pace or two, and laid his hand upon one of his pistols.

"What's the meaning of this, mother?" he said. "It seems to me that you are not alone here."

"Never alone! never alone!"

"Ah! say you so?"

"I do say so. Those, however, who have once passed the portal can do no harm to living mortal man."

"What portal? Of this house?"

"No; of the grave! He! he! You start, bold heart as you are. Look here—and here—and here! That's what does it. They don't like it. You see this?"

From the pile of old decayed wood with which Mother Bendydykes had evidently been feeding the fire, she lifted several pieces which it did not require a second glance at to recognise the character of.

They were pieces of coffins.

THE VISIT TO MOTHER BENDYDYKES.

No. 2.—FELON'S DAUGHTER.

Dick Doubleday shuddered.

"And this!" added the hag, as she laid hold of the black curtain. "This, too, attracts them!"

"Attracts what?"

"The shadows. It is made, piece by piece, of the cloth torn from the coffins you see. I made it He! he!—I made it—I, Martha Bendydykes, made it!"

Dick Doubleday regarded the old woman with horror.

"Never mind her odd whims and fancies," whispered Handsome Jemmy; "she will perhaps be useful, for all that."

"Peace! peace! Peace! and listen!" said the hag now, as she struck the black curtain with the stick on which she had been leaning.

Another groan came from the other side of the curtain.

Dick Doubleday became anxious to get out of the ill-omened place as quickly as he could; but, since one whom he knew felt so warmly for his grief and perplexity as Handsome Jemmy, the highwayman, had brought him there he resolved upon questioning the hag upon the subject nearest to his heart.

"Mother Bendydykes," he said, "perhaps you know that Pamela Sharples is condemned to death?"

"To-morrow."

"Yes, alas! Oh, tell me, if you can tell me, how can I can save her?—how can anybody save her? Only point out to me, if you can, any means by which I could even give my own life for hers, and I will so gladly give it! And then, if it be true and possible that the beings of another world can revisit this mortal life, I will be ever near you, to bless and protect you."

"Hush!"

Dick paused.

"Wait!"

The old hag disappeared behind the curtain; and so suddenly and mysteriously did she do so, that whether she had passed between it and the wall, or through some slit in it, or it had yielded before her like a vapour, it was impossible to say.

"Is there any hope?" whispered Dick to the highwayman.

"Hush! she returns."

Mother Bendydykes was absent not more than two minutes, and then she made her way to the portion of the room again where her visitors awaited her, as quickly and mysteriously as she had been absent f om it.

Then she tapped nine times, carefully counting the strokes upon the floor.

At the ninth rap the curtain opened to a width of about two feet, and standing exactly in the opening was a tall figure, completely enveloped in some drapery which covered it up from the top of the head to the feet, so as to present nothing but the general outlines, and the suggestion, from the shape, of a human form.

A strange, blue light threw this tall, gaunt-looking semblance of humanity into bold relief; although where the light came from, neither Dick Doubleday nor his friend Handsome Jemmy could see.

"What is this?" asked Dick, as he shrank back.

The highwayman was silent, but he was not quite so imaginative as Dick Doubleday, and he kept one hand upon the butt of a pistol.

Handsome Jemmy had faith in flesh, and blood, and bone, but he had very little in the immaterial world.

"Speak to it," said Mother Bendydykes, in a low earnest tone; "it will answer you!"

There was something awful and suggestive in the merely calling this form "it." That mode of expression served at once to imply that it was not of this world.

But even then it is possible that Dick Doubleday might have hesitated to speak to the seeming apparition if, at that moment, the clock of the Temple had not struck the hour of three.

Those sounds reminded him of how that night, that once stood between his Pamela and death, was fleeting away.

All other considerations were lost in the one absorbing desire to attempt something to save her.

Dick advanced a step towards the mysterious figure. He clasped his hands convulsively

In a voice, then, that sufficiently betrayed the anguish of his heart, he spoke.

"Tell me—only tell me whether you be of this world or of some other beyond the grave. Tell me, I pray you—beg of you—beseech of you—tell me of some mode by which I can save the life of one dearer to me than my own existence. I will tell you who and what she is. A fair young girl, as innocent as the day. She is condemned to death—most unjustly condemned to death. My heart yearns to save her. It will break if I do not save her, and there will be two deaths—one murder, and one broken heart!"

"Pamela!" said a low, deep voice

The voice came from amid the folds of that drapery which so completely enveloped the mysterious figure.

"Ah! you know her name!" exclaimed Dick Doubleday; "and, knowing her name, perhaps you know all that I can tell you. Save her!—oh, save her!"

"Pamela? Pamela?"

"Yes, it is of her I speak. Tell me how she is to be saved from death."

"Back! back!" said the hag. "You don't know your own danger!"

In the eagerness and excitement of the moment, with his arms outstretched before him, Dick Doubleday had advanced, step by step, until he almost touched the drapery in which the mysterious figure was wrapped up; but at this admonition from Mother Bendydykes he shrank back again.

Then the mysterious figure spoke.

The voice was low and trembling as if that being, whether of earth or of air, struggled with some terrible emotion.

"You will go—you—you only—you will go to the King's Physician, Doctor Haslem, of Bedford Square, and you will ask him to intercede with the King for the pardon of Pamela Sharples The Princess Amelia lies at the point of death, and the royal brain is troubled, and there is but one hope, and one faith: it is in the skill of Doctor Has'em. Who shall ask a favour of the bleeding heart, of the despairing father, but the man who stands between death and his child? It is enough! it is enough!"

The black curtain closed.

The mysterious figure seemed to have vanished into the gloom of the night, and with a creeping terror at his heart, Dick Doubleday turned to the highwayman, and then clasped his hands for a moment over his eyes, as though he would assure himself he was not dreaming, and that all he had seen and heard were not the visions of his own troubled imagination.

The old hag crouched down by the fire again.

The two cats began to spit and snarl at the visitors.

Handsome Jemmy drew a long breath.

"Well, Mother Bendydykes," he said, "I've been here before on one careless, foolish errand or another, but I never heard or saw anything like th s "

"Spit, my pets, spit!" said the old woman.

The cats grew more demonstrative in their anger.

"Well, mother," added the highwayman, "if this turns out all right, and Pamela Sharples escapes death, by your advice or that of the mysterious being behind that curtain, I will not forget you."

"Spit! spit, my pets! Drive them hence!"

The cats looked enraged, and Mother Bendydykes herself began flinging pieces of the old coffins, with which she fed her fire, recklessly at the highwayman and Dick Doubleday.

"Come away," said Handsome Jemmy, "she's in one of her queer humours—come away, Dick; and in sober seriousness, I must say that the advice we've had here is not at all bad. I know for certain that the Princess Amelia, the King's favourite daughter, lies desperately ill—folks say at the point of death. The King himself is at Buckingham House, just across the Park; and if

Doctor Haslem really chose to ask him such a favour as a reprieve for Pamela, I know of no man so likely, or one half so likely, as he to get it."

"I will go to him at once," said Dick Doubleday.

"And I with you."

"Nay, Jemmy; did not that mysterious figure say that I was to go alone?"

"Never mind that, Dick. Who knows but this Doctor Haslem may be restive. You know I'm a fellow of some resolution; and when I make up my mind to a thing, and say it shall be, why I don't stand upon trifles. And now I say Doctor Haslem *shall* go to the King, and shall ask him for the pardon of Pamela, or else I'm not the man folks take me to be!"

Almost the first ray of hope that had illumined the heart of Dick Doubleday now found a home there, as he pressed both the hands of Handsome Jemmy.

They had got clear of the house in Whitefriars, and were in Fleet Street. The distance to Bedford Square was as nothing to the speed they could make, and it wanted yet some time to four o'clock when the highwayman and Dick Doubleday stood upon the doorstep of Doctor Haslem's house.

But there was a faint flush in the eastern sky.

The dawn was coming—that terrible dawn which was to bring death or safety to the innocent young girl who was almost sobbing her heart away in a cell in Newgate.

There was a light in the physician's hall, and without the hesitation of a moment, Handsome Jemmy knocked at the door.

There must have been considerable excitement and wakefulness on the part of the household of the Court Physician on that night, for the door was opened on the instant by the hall porter, who seemed remarkably wide awake for such a functionary.

"Doctor Haslem?" said the highwayman, inquiringly.

"Not at home. An express, I suppose?"

Dick Doubleday felt faint at heart, and was about to speak, when Handsome Jemmy pressed his arm to keep him silent; and at once adopting the mistake and suggestion of the hall porter, he replied, "Yes, as you say, an express. When do you expect him in?"

"Every moment. Her Royal Highness lies at the White Lodge, Richmond, and the Doctor had only to go round by Buckingham House to give his report to the King. But you know all that better than I do, for I suppose you come from the White Lodge?"

"Certainly. We will wait a few moments."

"That's lucky, for here he is."

A carriage dashed rapidly into the square.

Amid the profound stillness of that hour of the early morning, the tramp of the horses, and the rapid whirling of the wheels, seemed to involve the noise of half a dozen carriages in one.

The lights of the vehicle flashed upon door after door, until, with a grating sound upon the curb of the pavement, the carriage stopped.

"That's him." said the porter.

"One moment, if you please," said Handsome Jemmy. "It may save the Doctor a deal of trouble if I speak to him before he gets out."

The footman had alighted from behind, and the door of the carriage was opened. The steps were flung down with a rattle, and the Doctor's foot was on the first one.

In two strides the highwayman crossed the pavement, and placed his foot likewise on the carriage step.

"Doctor Haslem!"

"Sir!"

"A word with you."

"An express from the White Lodge," cried the porter from the door-step.

"Ah!" said Doctor Haslem, as he sunk back into his carriage. "An express so quickly after me? Then all is over, I presume?"

"Not quite," said the highwayman, as he sat down beside the Doctor on the back seat of the carriage.

Dick Doubleday, pale and excited, scarcely knew how to act; but Handsome Jemmy made him a signal, and he sprung into the vehicle.

Doctor Haslem looked a little suspicious.

"What is the meaning of all this?" he said. "I don't half like it."

"Sir," said Dick Doubleday, "you are an eminent physician; doubtless you have saved many a life; and it has warmed and cheered your heart in the still hours of the night, if you chanced to awaken, to feel that you had done so. But now, sir, the fairest, best, and dearest life that you can possibly save, lies at your mercy."

"Well said, Dick — well said!" cried Handsome Jemmy. "I scarcely know you, my lad, to hear you talk in that fashion; but true love, I suppose, sharpens the wits and refines the understanding. Doctor Haslem, order your footman to close the carriage door, and then take one quiet drive round the square, and we will explain to you what we want."

Curiosity, perhaps combined with a certain apprehension of the consequences of refusal, induced the Court Physician to assent to this arrangement.

The carriage was driven slowly round Bedford Square.

"Now, Doctor," commenced Handsome Jemmy, "the life you are called upon to save is that of a young, charming, and innocent girl."

"Then you don't come from the White Lodge at Richmond?"

"Certainly not."

"And you are not an express?"

"Oh, yes; quite an express. But look you here, Doctor — you are attending now upon the Princess Amelia In you the King puts his last faith—his last hope; and there is no man in this country, or out of it, who at this moment, on this particular night, has such influence with his Majesty George the Third as yourself."

"But, sirs——"

"Hear me out. It is nearly four o'clock. Ah! it's quite four—there it goes by old Bloomsbury Church. To-morrow morning—or rather I should say this morning, a few hours hence, a young girl named Pamela Sharples will be taken forth from Newgate by strong, hardy, well-armed men, in cool blood, to be judicially murdered. You can save her."

"I?"

"Yes, Doctor. Here we are in your carriage. Your horses are fresh. There is ample time. The afflicted King keeps watch and ward, no doubt, for news of his sick daughter. He has been persuaded, as all the world knows, to leave the White Lodge, and remain at Buckingham House—for nothing otherwise would keep him from the chamber of, perhaps, the dying Princess. You understand now, Doctor Haslem; you have but to give the order to drive to Buckingham House, and you will see the King at once. Tell him that as his daughter hovers between life and death, another young girl—as pure, as fair, as innocent as that daughter—asks but for a scrawl of his pen to give her life. O Doctor! believe me, the King has it in his power to write a prescription for Pamela Sharples, which he would give one half the world, were it his, you or he could write for his own child!"

"I can't do it," said Doctor Haslem.

"You will do it."

"I cannot do it. Such an intrusion—especially at such a time as this—would be contrary to all propriety, all etiquette. What right have I to interfere in these affairs? And how do I know who and what you are who come to me with that story? You may be a highwayman for aught I know."

"That's just it! I am!"

"What?"

"A highwayman, Doctor, at your service."

"Help!—help! Thieves!—thie——"

"Quiet, Doctor—quiet!"

Handsome Jemmy placed the muzzle of a pistol exactly between the Doctor's eyes.

But the Doctor's voice had been heard: and although, perhaps, amid the tramp of the horses and the rattle of the wheels, precisely what he said may have escaped the ears of the coachman and footman, still the vehicle was stopped.

"That will do," said Handsome Jemmy. "Now, Doctor, if you please, you will be so good as to order your coachman to drive to Buckingham House. Speak loud!"

"To Buckingham House!" said the Court Physician.

The carriage was in motion again in a moment; and Bedford Square was rapidly left behind by the singularly assorted party in that luxurious and well-appointed vehicle.

"You're an impudent rascal," said Doctor Haslem.

"I always was," said Handsome Jemmy; "but still it is not becoming in a gentleman to use bad language; and, what's more, I appeal to you as a man with a human heart, with life-blood in his veins, and surely with something like tenderness and pity in his composition!"

"Let me speak to him—let me speak to him," said Dick Doubleday. "Sir!—sir! Tell me, did you ever truly, fondly, dearly love?"

"Watch!—watch!" cried the physician.

The carriage was just at the door of Bloomsbury Round-house, from which, for some reason, a posse of constables at that moment emerged.

CHAPTER V.

HANDSOME JEMMY HAS AN INTERVIEW WITH THE KING, BUT FAILS IN HIS MISSION.

THE highwayman who was so well known by the flattering name of Handsome Jemmy saw all the danger of his position in a moment, when Doctor Haslem called out for the assistance of the watch at the door of Bloomsbury Round-house.

Dick Doubleday saw it likewise.

"Lost!—all is lost!" cried Dick.

"Not at all!" responded Jemmy.

The coach stopped.

A couple of constables had rushed to the horses' heads; and the alarmed coachman, who this time had heard most distinctly the cry of "Watch! watch!" in his master's voice, pulled up sharply.

The footman held on behind the vehicle, with an expression of growing fright in his face.

Handsome Jemmy looked Doctor Haslem sternly in the face.

"Why, sir," he said, "do you force me to commit an act that I would gladly leave undone? Nevertheless, I will be as humane as I can!"

The Doctor felt an uneasy sensation in his left ear.

That was the side on which Handsome Jemmy sat.

An oblique look in that direction let the Court Physician see what it was that produced the uneasy sensation.

It was the barrel of a very small pistol, the remainder of which was hidden in the hand of the highwayman.

The Doctor turned pale.

"This is the second time you have risked your life," whispered Jemmy. "I think you are gone!"

"Gone!—gone! What?"

"Anything amiss, sir?" said a constable, blocking up the window of the carriage with a large, red face that Handsome Jemmy knew quite well as belonging to one of the most daring of the police of that district.

"Yes," said the highwayman. "But he is quiet now."

"Who, sir?"

"That unhappy young man."

Jemmy pointed to Dick Doubleday.

The constable looked as if he would be glad to know what Jemmy meant; and Dick Doubleday was himself in a similar state of mystification.

"My friend," added Jemmy, keeping out of the glare of light from the carriage-lamps as well as he could, and speaking in a feigned voice—for he was afraid the constable might recognise him,—"my friend, this is Doctor Haslem."

"Oh!"

"Speak."

Handsome Jemmy gave the Court Physician a hint with the muzzle of the pistol.

"Yes, yes," he said; "I—I—am Doctor Haslem!"

"And this young man," added Jemmy, alluding to Dick Doubleday, "is just a little—eh! you comprehend?—not much—but just a little——"

Handsome Jemmy touched his forehead with a finger of his disengaged hand.

"Oh, I see!" said the constable.

"Of course you do! Well, the Doctor here is taking him to a place of safety, and he wanted to put himself out of the coach head-foremost, which made the Doctor cry, 'Watch! watch!' Did it not, Doctor?"

Another impulse of the minute pistol-barrel induced Doctor Haslem to speak.

"Oh, certainly! Yes, yes!"

The constable looked from one to the other of them rather suspiciously; and then suddenly withdrawing his head from the carriage window, he looked up at the coachman, and cried out sharply, "Whose carriage is this?"

"Doctor Haslem's!"

The reply of the coachman was by far too prompt to be doubted for a moment.

"Very well, gentlemen," said the constable; "I daresay it is all right."

"I wish it was," said Handsome Jemmy.

"What, sir?"

"I say, I only wish it was; but I am afraid this poor young man will give us some trouble yet."

"Oh! is that all? Good night, gentlemen."

"Drive on!" said the highwayman.

"Yes, drive on!" added the physician, with a groan and a plunge of his foot.

The carriage proceeded.

"Sam! Sam!" whispered the footman, over the roof, to the coachman.

"What is it, Chawles?"

"Master's got a mad fellow inside. I heard it all."

"No?"

"Yes, he has; and he don't seem half to like the job neither."

"Now, Doctor Haslem," said Handsome Jemmy, "all this is very foolish on your part."

"I will not be coerced to anything," replied the Doctor.

"But, sir, you refused, by fair means, to aid in saving an innocent young girl—almost a child! Oh, Doctor Haslem, Doctor Haslem! I know one thing of you without your telling me!"

"What is that?"

"You have no daughter of your own. You have no dear, dear little girl to put her sweet arms round your neck, and lay her soft cheek to yours, and tell you that she loves you!"

"Oh, heaven!"

Dr. Haslem clasped both his hands over his face, and the tears trickled through his fingers, while his whole frame was shaken by the sobs that came from his heaving breast.

Handsome Jemmy was astonished.

Dick Doubleday uttered a cry of sympathy.

The highwayman had hoped that his words would produce some effect; but he had had no idea they would have stirred the Doctor's heart as they did.

"Sir—Doctor Haslem," he said, "you feel, after all, for this young girl. You have pictured to yourself the kiss of affection from some loving child, upon your cheek?"

"Oh, no, no! Cease! Do not torture—torture! In mercy, say no more!"

"I will not."

"Why, oh, why is this wound, that I thought healed,

JACOB SHARPLES IS RESCUED FROM THE FLEET DITCH.

so tender—so sensitive, still, to the most casual words? Oh, heaven, where is—is——"

" What, sir?"

The Court Physician seemed to be choking.

" Air! air!" he gasped.

" Sir, the windows are both open. What can I do?" The Court Physician wrung his hands, and sobbed.

" Where, oh, where is my child?"

" Your child, sir?"

" Yes. Where is my dear child? Where are the sweet arms that should clasp me?—where is the soft cheek that should be laid confidingly to mine?—where the tender velvet lips that should leave the kiss of fond affection upon mine? Where is the dear child that will call me father—father—father?"

Despair—agony—the very desolation of the heart, seemed to come over that man, who was, in the high and aristocratic society in which he moved, noted for a cold, passionless, rigid exterior.

But the chord of passion and feeling had been touched; and Doctor Haslem's heart expanded with the wild, fitful strains of human agony.

" Sir," said Dick Doubleday,—" sir, sir, if you can feel in this way for the imaginary want of a child to love you, surely you can pity Pamela!"

The highwayman touched Dick with his foot, as he said, in low tones, " Let him alone, Dick."

Handsome Jemmy felt that there was no longer any occasion for the use of that small pistol he had placed in such uncomfortable proximity to the ear of the Doctor. He calmly waited until the storm of feeling had passed away.

The Court Physician leant forward, with his face resting upon both his hands, while he either rocked himself gently to and fro, or the motion of the carriage made it seem as if he did so.

The vehicle then came to an abrupt standstill.

" Ah! what's that?" said Jemmy.

" The King's physician," said a loud voice.

" Pass, the King's physician!" replied another.

There was a rattle, as of military accoutrements, and the carriage rolled through a gateway, and then under a dark, gloomy arch.

" Ah, I see!" said Jemmy. " We go through the Horse Guards."

" It is over," said Doctor Haslem.

He looked up, and spoke calmly and firmly.

" It is over. The story would not interest either of you, but I had a dear little child once; and—and——"

" Dead?" said Jemmy.

" No, no! If I could think that, I should not suffer. She was stolen from me."

" Stolen?"

" Yes. Stolen by some fiend who had no mercy for a poor father's heart. But we will speak of that no more. I cannot speak of it. You wanted me to do something—what is it?"

" We wanted you, Doctor, to speak to the King, to get a reprieve for a young girl."

" Ah! yes, yes! How one's own awakened griefs and emotions throw aside all other matters. To be sure—to be sure! I recollect all now. It is a young girl who has been convicted of passing base money."

" Yes, yes."

" And she is left for execution."

" To-morrow—to-morrow!" said Dick Doubleday. " Oh! gracious heaven, no! To-day—to-day!"

The Horse Guards' clock had struck five.

" I will do it," said Doctor Haslem.

" You will, sir? You will ask the King to save my Pamela—my own dear, dear Pamela?"

" I will."

" God bless you!"

Dick Doubleday seized the Doctor's hand, and left both a kiss and a tear upon it.

" Hush! Here we are at Buckingham House."

The porch of the old house—that abode of royalty, that stood upon the site now occupied by Buckingham Palace—was reached. The carriage of the Court Physi-

cian had been too often there not to be known in a moment, and it was admitted into the quadrangle in front of the house without hindrance or question.

" Come with me, both of you," said Doctor Haslem; " we may have all to plead with the King."

Handsome Jemmy and Dick Doubleday said not a word, but they followed the physician into Buckingham House, which was, from the circumstances we have already narrated, the then temporary abode of the King.

A gentlemanly looking man met them in the first apartment they reached.

" Ah, Doctor!" he said. " Since you are back so soon, I am afraid you bring us bad news."

" No, Mr. Mitchell,—no; but I want to see his Majesty for a few moments."

" And these gentlemen?"

" Friends of mine."

" Belonging to the faculty, Doctor?"

" Oh, yes," said Handsome Jemmy; " we are both professional men."

Mr. Mitchell, who was the confidential valet of King George the Third, looked suspiciously and with some surprise at Handsome Jemmy and Dick Doubleday.

They neither of them had exactly the outward appearance of members of the faculty of medicine.

Handsome Jemmy had a fashionably cut coat of invisible green, with gilt buttons. He wore top-boots and white leathers.

Dick Doubleday was in a suit of dark maroon, and he wore what were called afterwards Hessian boots.

But, certainly, they neither of them looked like members of the medical profession.

The confidential valet of the King might well hesitate a little when he looked at the companions of Doctor Haslem.

But all hesitation, and trouble, and discussion about who or what Handsome Jemmy and Dick Doubleday were was suddenly put an end to in an unexpected way.

A door was flung open, so rapidly that it struck sharply against the corner of a console table; and a man whose dress was in disorder, and who, with one hand, held around him a dressing gown, while his greyish white hair was scattered in confusion about his brows, rushed rather than walked into the room.

" What? what, eh? What, Doctor? Good heavens, what?"

" The King!" said Mr. Mitchell, as he made a low bow.

Dick Doubleday and Handsome Jemmy were startled, as well they might be by this sudden and unceremonious introduction to royalty.

" Well, Doctor; what is it? Soon back, eh? What—what? How is she now? Better? Worse, eh? What?"

" Your Majesty is so gracious that I feel a hope that your pardon——"

" Eh? what?"

" That's it," said Handsome Jemmy.

" What—what, Doctor? Speak—speak, man! Have you a tongue? What of my—my daughter?"

The King lifted his arms above his head; and, at that moment, one of the first gleams of that insanity which for so long sat as a blight upon the mind of the aged monarch, showed itself in the eyes that glared from face to face.

It was a terrible look.

" Speak—speak! Are you all dumb? Did three of you come with one voice to tell me my child was dead —my Amelia? A Princess, gentlemen, I tell you! Why do Princesses die?"

" Your Majesty," said Doctor Haslem, " will, I hope, never have to mourn such a calamity. I am here, first, most humbly to crave your Majesty's indulgent pardon for this intrusion."

" Intrusion! What—what intrusion?"

" I am quite sure that many persons this night pray for the recovery of the Princess Amelia. Oh, your

Majesty, there is one who will put up a prayer so fervent that it must needs reach the ears of heaven, if you will spare her breath to do so."

" One—one—one who? One what?"

" A young girl—one who is condemned to die—one who alone can owe life to your Majesty's royal mercy. I come to beseech your Majesty for a reprieve for Pamela Sharples, who now lies in Newgate, condemned to death for passing base money."

" What? What? What?"

The Court Physician bowed low.

Handsome Jemmy stepped forward.

" Save the poor young thing, your Majesty," he said, " and you will make some grateful hearts in England, who will never forget it."

" Save her, O King!" cried Dick Doubleday. " She's so young—so beautiful—so innocent! Oh, in mercy, spare her life!"

" Bad—bad—bad!"

" No, no! Good, and true, and fair! My Pamela!"

" Bad money! Pass bad money! Brass! brass! brass, eh? Lead! lead! Tin, eh? Might take it ourselves! Pass bad money! Cheat, rob! Bad money! Can't do it! No—no—no! A good example for bad money —good and bad—a bad example—no, a good example. Pass a good guinea—I mean a bad guinea and a good example! Let her hang!"

The King wrapped his dressing gown about him, and left the room as abruptly as he had entered it.

CHAPTER VI.

SHOWS HOW JACOB SHARPLES GOT ON IN FLEET DITCH WITH THE WHITE RAT.

HUMAN life hangs upon threads.

The merest accidents will save it or destroy it.

Jacob Sharples would have given the wealth of worlds, had he possessed it, to be free from the cords that bound him to the chair, that held him so securely when he was let drop down the trap into the black, muddy stream of the Fleet.

It was that chair that saved him!

But for it, he would no doubt have made furious and frantic struggles to make his way through the terrible tide. Those struggles would have exhausted him, and long ere he could have reached the opening of the sewer at Blackfriars Bridge, he would have sunk to rise no more.

But the chair kept him still.

He could not move hand nor foot.

And the chair floated.

Floated on the black, thick, muddy water; just floated sufficiently to keep the head, the face and the breast of Jacob Sharples above the horrible, pestiferous, gurgling, seething tide.

A yell of agony had burst from the throat of the wretched man when first he was precipitated into the Fleet, for at that moment he sunk, chair and all, beneath the tide.

The physical laws of matter, however, would be obeyed, and the chair, with its half dead burden, slowly floated to the surface.

Jacob Sharples breathed again.

Then the white rat sprang upon his chest.

And then Jacob Sharples uttered another cry more fearful than the previous one.

There is a limit to human suffering—to fear—or that agony of the heart and of the brain, which else would produce madness.

The wretched man had reached that limit.

Jacob Sharples became insensible.

But the chair floated.

And the white rat sat upon his chest.

The tide of old Fleet River was gently flowing towards the Thames. The ebb of the great stream is the flow of its tributaries: that is to say, they flow into it;

for then the waters from those numerous sources come on an incline to feed the one great stream.

Therefore it was that the old, thick, heavy, wooden chair—clumsy and rough, but all the better for Jacob Sharples as it was—floated down the tide of the Fleet, and would continue so to float until the turn of the tide of the Thames.

Then the rush of the larger volume of water in the Thames would obliterate the tide of the Fleet.

The flow would be upward.

If Jacob Sharples encountered it, death was certain, for the whole of the arched way, which had converted the Fleet into a sewer, would be filled, and then, float or not float that chair would be of no use to him.

At present, it was a ship—a raft—a life-raft to the coiner, Jacob Sharples.

But the tide turned at two o'clock.

One!—two!

Yes!—it is two o'clock!

One!—two! One!—two!

The great clock of old St Paul's has given forth the sounds, and the City churches echo it.

There was a strange washing to and fro, hesitating sort of aspect about the surface of the Thames.

It seemed as if the water had all suddenly become partially stagnant, and was acted upon by a thousand strange and different impulses.

Now it goes one way in huge rolling masses—then another, with a light froth upon its surface.

It was the turn of the tide!

Then, in a few minutes, if you had dropped a cork or a straw into the river, you would have seen it eddying round perhaps, as if in some mimic whirlpool.

Then it would have moved slowly westward with the flow of the river, as the pure fresh waters of the Channel and the North Sea came in that direction, and stemmed the descent of the river tide into the salt ocean.

The chair to which Jacob Sharples was tied struck against the sides of the sewer.

Then it stopped.

It floated in one spot.

A strange noise came from towards Blackfriars. It was the first check of the descending Fleet—the first rush of the ascending tide!

The white rat leaped off the breast of Jacob Sharples, and fled upwards before that advancing tide. No doubt it had hiding-places far beyond where the river flow would reach.

The chair still floated, but it floated higher—higher —and higher still, for the depth of water in the sewer was now each moment on the increase.

The confined air swept by with a rushing sound as of a mighty wind.

Perhaps it was that artificial rush of air upon the face, the brow, and the eyes of Jacob Sharples that recovered him, but certain it is that the swoon into which he had fallen passed away.

He opened his eyes.

Where was he? What a terrible question to ask of the half awakened mind as he oscillated there gently to and fro on the surface of the heaving tide!

And yet it was the question most likely to arise to the mind of Jacob Sharples. For that period of insensibility through which he had passed might well have the effect for a time of obliterating recollection, and of chasing from him for the moment those terrible events which had placed him in his present position.

Such a state of things, however, could only last for a few brief seconds, and then—as if that rushing wind which was making its way through that confined place over the rushing tide brought with it in a full volume a remembrance of the past—Jacob Sharples not only recollected where he was, but how he came to be there.

He remembered how that thirst and craving for human companionship which had come over him had induced him to seek the "fence" in Field Lane, despite the disapprobation, the contempt, and the possible danger that would surround him

He remembered how that danger had become each moment more formidable, until, fanned by the despair of Dick Doubleday and the indignation of Handsome Jemmy, the highwayman, it had assumed to him a fatal aspect.

Then he remembered the mock trial—the mockery in its institution, but a reality to him.

The chair to which he was bound—the fight and the struggle, in which one man was so impotent against many—then the being carried down to the cellar—the trap-door—and the hideous fetid tide of the Fleet beneath.

And then he remembered the white rat.

All these events became present again to the imagination of Jacob Sharples with awful rapidity; and at the last thought—at the imagination that the hideous reptile might still be sitting on his chest—he screamed aloud.

There was air enough now in that place to fill his lungs, although it would soon all have rushed out of the narrow sewer; and the most fearful form in which a death by drowning could present itself would soon rapidly approach him.

As it was, however, in that rush of air, the cries and shouts of Jacob Sharples were fearfully distinct and appalling.

As yet, the chair which floated him—that ark of safety which had hitherto preserved him—had made but little progress in the contrary direction from that which it had at first taken.

But now it began to obey the upward impulse of the tide, and to float back again towards Field Lane.

Jacob Sharples fully realized his situation. He looked upon himself as a doomed man, and what doom could be more horrible than accident and circumstances had then and there consigned him to?

What a tender and gentle piece of humanity it would have been to have put him to any death whatever—even in the cellar beneath that apartment—provided the process were speedy, in comparison with the fearful fate that now awaited him!

No hope—no chance of succour!

There he floated, higher and higher still each moment; and as with glaring eyes he looked upward, he fancied that even in the intense darkness he could see, within a few inches of his face, the arched brick covering of the sewer.

What could he do but faint or scream?

While there was air left he would yell for mercy, but with no hope that any miracle—for such it would seem to require—would take place in his favour.

Then there came a glare of red light.

Surely that was the commencement of dissolution, and yet it was not painful.

It dazzled his eyes and confused his senses and then he heard a harsh, loud voice.

"Hilloa, there! What's the racket down below? Who's in the sewer?"

"Help! help! In mercy, help! If you are human, save me!"

"A rope! a rope! Slip a good noose in it. Come here, Dainty Diamond, and hold on. There's a big fish in the sewer!"

"A stranded mud-lark, I fancy," said another voice.

Confused and bewildered, Jacob Sharples felt that a rope was cast about him. To be sure, it was round his neck, which was a little awkward; but the very pressure of it beneath his chin, as he was dragged upwards by its means, was pleasant, and not at that moment suggestive of the kind of fate he had all his life looked forward to.

He was half strangled, but the situation was momentary; and then Jacob Sharples found that, along with the chair to which he was tied, he had been dragged through a somewhat similar trap-door to that through which he had been plunged at the "fence" in Field Lane.

He was in quite as gloomy a cellar as that one which, on his descending from it, had appeared to him to be the most terrible place on earth.

Two men only were present; they were both of ruffianly aspect, and the looks they bent upon the trembling, wretched being whom they had rescued from death were anything but reassuring.

"Who and what are you?" said one. "Keep the trap open, Dainty Diamond, till he answers, and gives an account of himself that may please us Perhaps we shall see good reason to put him down again."

"Oh, no, no!" screamed Jacob Sharples; "not that—anything but that! I will reward you—indeed. I will. I have money, which I can find as soon as I am free to seek for it. Have mercy—have mercy upon me!"

"Who are you?"

"My name is—is——Perhaps you know my name? I—I—my name is—Fleet"

"Look at him, Dainty Diamond. Do you know him? Bring the lantern."

The dismal place into which Jacob Sharples had been fished up from the Fleet was lighted by a lantern that hung on a hook from one of the walls. The man who was called Dainty Diamond took it down, so that the full glare of its light fell upon the convulsed and terrified face of Jacob Sharples.

His first immersion in the stream of the Fleet Ditch had left long streaks of muddy water upon him, and his hair was a tangled mass, presenting no trace of colour as it hung about his eyes.

The rough usage he had received had left both blood and bruises upon him; and take him for all in all, a more ghastly, repulsive object than Jacob Sharples presented as the light of that lantern flashed upon him, could scarcely have been conceived.

"He's a beauty!" said the man with the lantern.

"Kind sirs," whined Jacob, "have pity upon me! I don't mean to say that you would sell your mercy to a poor fellow-creature; but whether or not I will pay for it, for I'm a great deal richer than anybody knows of or believes; and you shall have all—all for my life!"

"Who are you?"

Jacob Sharples looked from one to the other, in doubt which it would be most prudent to do—to pretend to be an honest man, who by some accident had fallen into his present position; or to admit that he belonged to the great family of depredators, of which it was more than probable those two men were members.

"In with him, Diggles," said Dainty Diamond: "he's some bad 'un, and not worth a rush. And who shall say it isn't a 'plant,' after all, and that this fellow would peach upon us before we know where we are?"

"Plant" and "peach!" Those were delightful words for Jacob Sharples to hear, for if he had had any previous doubt upon the matter, they assured him that he had fallen among congenial spirits.

But still his experience of the "fence" in Field Lane made him hesitate to declare exactly who he was, in the fear that these men—rough and brutal as they looked—might have heard something of his cowardly desertion of Pamela, and might possibly take a similar view of it to that of Handsome Jemmy, the highwayman, and Dick Doubleday. To be sure, the aspect of Mr. Diggles and of Dainty Diamond, as they called themselves, mutually did not much resemble either the highwayman or the lover of Pamela.

But Jacob Sharples was not a man to draw very nice distinctions, nor were his perceptions at that moment so clear and apt as usual.

"Gentlemen——" he said.

"Down with him!" said Dainty Diamond; "he's a gammonin' of us now!"

"No, no! I will be candid and sincere. I am—I am a coiner!"

"Ah! Then you belong to the family?" cried Diggles.

"Yes," added Dainty Diamond; "and now I know who he is. I thought I'd seen him before. His name's Jacob Sharples."

"No, no! You're wrong—you're wrong! I've often been mistaken for Jacob Sharples, but I'm not that man; because he, you see—he—that is to say, I—

CAPTAIN SANG OFFERS TO SAVE PAMELA.

No. 3.—FELON'S DAUGHTER.

if I'd been Jacob Sharples I should not have left my daughter Pamela to death, when a word of mine, they say, would have saved her."

"Stuff!" said Dainty Diamond; "who's goin' to put his own neck into a noose, to get somebody else's out of it? I heard all about that. If Jacob Sharples had come forward to Chief Justice Holt, and told him he gave the girl the base money to pass, he'd have been nabbed and carted off to Tyburn to a dead certainty. They wanted to grab him, you see, and that's why they convicted the g'rl. She'll suffer because they're aggravated; but wouldn't Jacob Sharples have been a hundred fools rolled into one to make his throat a present to Jack Ketch?"

"That's about it," said Diggles.

"Then I am Jacob Sharples—I am Jacob Sharples! I am Sharples, the coiner; and I've made a good enough trade of it to be able to give you a hat full of guineas for picking me out of that noisome sewer."

"Bad 'uns, you mean," said Dainty Diamond.

"No, no—real gold! On my life, real gold—real gold! These cords cut me to the bone. A knife—a knife!—haven't you a knife, my friends, to cut me loose? Such sensible men as you are, too, taking such a proper view of things."

Diggles cut the cords that tied Jacob Sharples to the chair; and, stiffened and benumbed as his limbs were, it was with a feeling of intense relief that the coiner found himself able to move his arms and feet, and to look around him with something like a sensation of freedom.

He tried to raise his hands above his head, to utter an imprecation upon the heads of those who had tried and condemned him at the "fence" in Field Lane; but he had not power to do so, although the circulation was returning to his veins now that the pressure of the cords was removed.

But his tongue was free, and no temporary paralysis affected it.

The torrent of vituperation he poured forth, and the curses, loud and deep, that he levelled at the heads of Handsome Jemmy, the highwayman, and Dick Doubleday, astonished even Diggles and Dainty Diamond.

CHAPTER VII.

THE KING'S VALET GIVES TO HANDSOME JEMMY A PIECE OF INTERESTING INFORMATION.

"That's over, then," said Handsome Jemmy, the highwayman, as the little party in the apartment of Buckingham House was left to make what they could of the rather extraordinary conduct of the King.

Dick Doubleday was in despair.

Mr. Mitchell, the valet, looked distressed.

When the King left the room, he, the valet, made a movement to follow him; but he checked that, and only executed a low bow, as the door swung shut after George the Third.

Then Dick Doubleday spoke in a high, excited tone of voice.

"There is no mercy but in heaven! There is no strength but in one's own heart and hand! Pamela, my Pamela, I will yet save you, although all the kings the earth ever saw should leave you to die!"

The Court Physician looked at Dick with eyes of sympathy. He shook his head sadly.

"All is over—all is over!"

"No, no, sir, do not say that! Good bye to both of you, and may you both prosper. Good bye, good bye!"

"Dick, where are you going?" asked the highwayman.

"To Tyburn!"

The King's valet looked from one to the other of them in silence for some few moments, and then he said, "I suppose it is about that young creature who is condemned for passing base money, and who is left for death by Lord Chief Justice Holt, that you came?"

"Pamela Sharples," said Handsome Jemmy, "that is the girl!"

"Ah! the Chief Justice has been here himself about her, but the King was—was firm."

"You were going to say obstinate, Mr. Mitchell," said the physician.

The valet coughed.

"Come with me, both of you," added Doctor Haslem. "I will consult with you upon the possibility of doing something."

Dick Doubleday, with his hands clasped together, and a look of despair upon his face, followed the Court Physician and Handsome Jemmy from that apartment in Buckingham House where they had had so strange an interview with the King.

The valet came after them.

"It's to be lamented," he said, "that his gracious Majesty is so—so—very—rather—that is to say——"

"Pig-headed," said the highwayman.

"Oh, dear no—oh, no! But you see, sirs, his most gracious Majesty has a will of his own. Now, there is a man of the name of Bolt, who is cast for death for horse-stealing; and what do you think, now, the King said to the Lord Chief Justice, when he came to ask for a reprieve for this Pamela—Pamela—a—a——"

"Sharples."

"Yes, Pamela Sharples. 'No, my lord,' he said. 'No, Holt, no. But, as you want a reprieve, take one for the horse man. What's his name—same as yours? Eh, eh? Holt or Bolt, or something of that sort.'"

"And my Pamela was left to die!" murmured Dick.

"That was hard," said the highwayman.

"And what said Chief Justice Holt?" asked Doctor Haslem.

"Oh, he went away, and did not say another word. But, as soon as he was gone, the King made a great fuss about being, as he said, as good as his word; and he wrote himself a reprieve for Bolt, the horse man, as he called him."

"Indeed!"

"Oh, yes! I have it in my pocket now, and am about to send it to Newgate."

"You have?"

"It is here!"

They had reached a small octagonal hall on the ground floor of Buckingham House. It was lit by a beautifully painted lantern hanging from its centre, and as the light streamed through the different sides of coloured glass of which the lantern was composed, the reflected colour on the walls of the hall looked very curious, as well as very beautiful.

It was exactly beneath this lantern that the King's valet paused, and took from his pocket a strip of paper, which he allowed them all to see.

There were but a few words upon it:—

"Buckingham House.

"Reprieve and pardon for Bolt, the condemned horse man.

"GEORGE REX"

That was all.

A peculiar look came over the face of Handsome Jemmy, the highwayman.

Right into the eyes of the valet he cast that peculiar look, and Mr. Mitchell was slightly alarmed at it.

"What—what, sir?" he said, as he began to fold up the paper again—"what, sir is—the—a—matter?"

Handsome Jemmy placed his hand on the wrist of the King's valet.

"I want that paper."

"This—paper? This?"

"Just so. I want that paper; and I feel sure that, as a sensible man, you will see the propriety of letting me have it at once, and of making no fuss about it."

"But, sir——"

"Well, sir?"

The grasp of the highwayman's hand tightened upon the wrist of the King's valet. The pressure became almost painful.

The Court Physician turned pale.

A bright flush of hope came over the face of Dick.

For a few seconds, then, Mr. Mitchell and Handsome Jemmy looked at each other in silence.

Then the highwayman spoke.

"Do you understand me, sir?" he said

"I think I do. You want this—this pardon?"

"Exactly."

"In order that you may use it in some way for the release of—of Pamela Sharples?"

"You have said it."

"But the name of Bolt is in it."

"Leave that to me."

"Oh, heaven, there is hope! hope!" half screamed Dick Doubleday.

"Be quiet, Dick," said Handsome Jemmy. "Don't you see I am busy?"

The valet turned very white. He looked imploringly at Dick, and at the highwayman, and then at the Court Physician.

"It's as much as my place is worth," he said, "to let you have this paper. But I was about to hand it to one of the messengers of the Palace, to take to Newgate. I think he will go through the Park, and out by the Horse Guards, and I think he will be alone I—I don't want to say anything else."

"That's quite enough," said Handsome Jemmy. "I think that we will go, Dick."

"Yes, yes!—oh, yes; and in the Park——"

"Dick, will you be quiet?"

Handsome Jemmy took the hand of the King's valet and gave it a squeeze, as he said, "I shall not forget that you have a good heart, and no blame can attach to you, whatever may happen. Now, Doctor Haslem, I fancy you have done all you can for us, and we ought not to trouble you any further in this affair."

"I will see the end of it," said the Court Physician. "My carriage is at your service to go to Newgate."

"Which is just where I don't want to go," said the highwayman, with a laugh.

"But—but——"

"Nay, Doctor, I have two good reasons for not going there. One concerns myself, and the other poor Pamela Sharples. I suspect that if I were to show myself within Newgate wicket, they would press me to stay; and this paper we have seen with the King's signature, being a pardon for Bolt, would hardly serve Pamela."

"Then it would be useless even if you took it from the royal messenger in the Park."

"Not so. In the crowd and the confusion at Tyburn Tree it will pass muster. It is there it will have to be used."

"You are right—you are right, Jemmy!" said Dick. "Oh, dear friend, you think of everything!"

"Come on."

The highwayman hurried, now, out of Buckingham House into the Park, but before he parted from the physician he spoke in a low tone to him.

"Doctor, there is no occasion to compromise you any further in this business. Thank you for what you have done. I think you have saved the young creature, for if you had not brought us here we should never have known of this chance."

"You have my best wishes. I will be at Tyburn to see how you get on."

"You will?"

"If I live, I will. I want to see this young girl who has engaged so much of my attention to-night. Be assured I shall be there."

The Court Physician stepped into his carriage.

"Home!" he said.

The vehicle drove rapidly off, and at the same moment a man in the scarlet livery of the royal family, and with top boots, and a riding whip in his hand, emerged from the gate of Buckingham House.

This man wore a courier's leather wallet, which hung by a broad belt of white leather over his shoulder

It was the royal messenger, with the pardon of Bolt the horse stealer.

The courier took the route along the principal mall of the Park, towards the Horse Guards. He did not hurry himself, but strolled carelessly, like a man who knows that, although the duty he has to perform is important, there is plenty of time in which to do it.

He might have got to about the middle of the mall, when from behind a tree, a few paces in advance of him, there emerged Dick Doubleday.

"Stop!" he said.

"Ah! thieves!"

"Stop!" said another voice.

That other voice was behind him. It was the voice of Handsome Jemmy, the highwayman; who, at the moment he spoke, took such a clutch at the back of the neck of the King's messenger, that he stood as if caught in a vice.

"Help! Mur——"

"Another word, and it is your last! Be quiet, and no harm will come to you!"

The messenger was silent

Dick Doubleday, in pursuance, no doubt, of some instructions he had received from Handsome Jemmy, had disappeared behind the tree again as soon as he had brought the King's courier to a stand-still. The highwayman was quite competent to manage all the rest of the business.

He still held the beleaguered man in that vice-like grasp as he spoke to him.

"Hand out the paper you were conveying to Newgate!"

"I—a—yes—no!"

"Hand it out, or——"

Something cold touched that portion of the neck of the messenger which corresponds to the top of the spine.

He gave a shudder.

"It is only the muzzle of a pistol," said Jemmy. "The shot will be fatal in an instant. You won't suffer."

"Have mercy upon me! I don't want to suffer at all!"

"You are a sensible man! The paper!"

"Here! here!"

"Hand it over your head!"

The courier did so.

"Moggs!" said Handsome Jemmy.

"Here!" replied Dick, in a feigned voice, from behind another tree to the right.

"Blinks!" added the highwayman

"Here!" said Dick, again, in a different voice, from behind another, to which he had darted.

"Grout!" said Jemmy.

"Here!" said Dick, again, in a tone that sounded somewhere else.

"Good gracious!" said the courier. "How many of you are there? A fellow may well give in, when he is surrounded in this kind of way! No, no! Don't do that—don't! Let me see! Don't murder me, with my eyes blinded!"

The highwayman had cast a handkerchief over the head and face of the courier, which he proceeded to tie round his neck in such a way that it was out of the question for him, in the dim night-light of the Park, to see.

"It's for your own good," said Handsome Jemmy. "Take my word, that if you make no resistance to what is required of you, no harm will come to you. I want your red coat."

"My coat?"

"Yes Off with it!"

The courier took off his coat, and with it the courier's wallet that hung by the leather belt.

"Now," added Dick, "you will be so good as to get up one of these trees."

"I can't"

"But you must. Up with you! It's to save your life; for if you cannot climb into one of them, it will be necessary to put an end to you, and fling you into the canal, over the palings yonder."

The courier commenced climbing a tree, assisted by Handsome Jemmy; but Dick Doubleday then came forward, and took the highwayman's place, and helped the royal messenger up the tree, which he made, with his eyes bandaged, a very clumsy attempt at climbing.

"There you are!" said Jemmy, as soon as Dick had safely lodged the courier in the tree. "Now see to his hands."

Dick tied the royal messenger's hands by the wrists to a branch of the tree. It was quite impossible he could in any way escape from the odd position in which he was—for although the dawn was rapidly coming, the silk handkerchief that was over his head and eyes confused objects very much.

Then Handsome Jemmy spoke in a voice of command.

"Moggs, Blinks, and Grout," he said, "you will keep your eyes fixed on this man in the tree. Should he give any alarm, or attempt to escape, bring him down with a bullet at once, and then meet me, you know where."

Handsome Jemmy having given these imaginary instructions to the imaginary guards of the belated courier, beckoned to Dick to follow him; and they at once struck off to the left, to the side mall of the Park, which was then very shadowy and overgrown by the tall old elm trees.

CHAPTER VIII

CONDUCTS THE READER TO THE CONDEMNED CELL AT NEWGATE, AND INTRODUCES HIM TO THE FAIR PAMELA.

In one of those gloomy, condemned cells of Newgate now abandoned to the reptiles that make their way from the banks of the Thames and the shambles of Newgate Market, moaned, sighed, and wept a fair young girl.

The midnight hour had struck.

The morning—that morning so terrible to her—was fast approaching; a morning upon which death seemed to be awaiting her, arrayed in all its terrors—for this young girl was Pamela Sharples.

It was sad—it was agonizing—to think of death in the spring-tide of that young existence; and yet what else could she now look for? What hope could she nourish at her young heart? Who could save her? Who would stir hand or foot in her behalf? Ah, yes! there was one—one who loved her—Dick Doubleday. He, she knew, would gladly give his own life for hers. But would such a sacrifice be accepted?

Ah, no!

Poor Pamela might well despair.

How beautiful she was!

Slender, tall, and fair, she looked like the personification of some of those beautiful creatures of fancy which the brain of artists conceive, but which is in vain sought amid the world's throngs.

Her fair hair was now all disordered, and hung about her face, her neck, her shoulders, like a veil of sparkling tissue.

And there, in that cold, damp cell of Newgate, with no company but the rat, the spider, and the newt, that condemned young girl rests her head upon her hands, and sobs, and waits, and waits for death.

"Oh, father! father! Can that bad, cruel man be my father? Would a father desert his child in this way, to die? Oh, cruel laws!—oh, cruel father!"

There was a heavy, dull sound outside the door of the cell.

Pamela uttered a scream of terror.

It was surely morning before she had expected it, and she was about to be dragged forth to death!

That dull, heavy sound was the fall of an iron bar that secured the door of the cell.

Then there came the rattle of a key in the massive lock, and a gleam of light from a lantern shone into the condemned cell.

"No!—no! Oh, no!—not yet! Oh! save me!—save me! I am too young to die!"

Pamela half rose from her crouching position on the floor, and kneeling, she wrung her hands and wept bitterly.

A tall man of ruffianly aspect stood upon the threshold of the cell; and placing the lantern he carried at his feet, he folded his arms across his breast, and in harsh, grating tones he spoke to the condemned girl.

"Pamela Sharples, do you know me?"

Pamela dashed aside the clustering, dancing ringlets of her beautiful hair, which impeded her vision, and with looks of terror she regarded this man.

"Know you?—know you? Heaven, yes! It is you who have so often followed and persecuted me! It is you who once tried to seize me in the public streets, with the assistance of some associates who were in waiting with a hackney coach; but my cries brought to my aid one who loved me!"

The visitor to the condemned cell made a gesture of rage and impatience.

"Do not I love you?"

"You!—you love me!"

"Yes! and most gladly would I shield you in these arms from the death that awaits you!"

Pamela shuddered.

"The arms of that death were preferable!" she said. "Come it slow or come it fast, it is but death that comes at last!"

"You rave, girl!—you rave! Listen to me! I can save you! The mere fact that I am here ought to convince you of my power! I can save you, and I will save you, if——"

"If what?"

"You will be mine!"

"Never!—never! I cannot well tell you how I loathe you! Death was terrible to me; but now I contrast it with you, and it looks a sweet refuge!"

"Hold!—hold! Say no more in that strain! You don't know me, but you shall know me! I am a gentleman!"

Pamela made a gesture of disdain.

"I say I am a gentleman! You may not know that it was one day about three months ago that I saw you, and from that moment I was maddened with love of you! I have given the Governor of Newgate a hundred pounds for liberty to pay you this visit. It is in my power to add sufficient to that sum to save you entirely from the fate that awaits you on the morrow. Only say that you will try to love me!"

"Never!"

"Reflect!—death is terrible to all, but it has different shapes and aspects, and it is more terrible to the young than to those who have seen the end of many of the bright dreams of youth! I do not ask you to absolutely love me. All I ask of you is to try and do so, or to pretend to do so. With the trial—with the pretence—will come the reality. Pamela! Pamela! I have come here because I have pity upon you! Let me hope that you will have some pity upon me, for you do not know the pangs of despised love!"

"No!" replied Pamela, as she clasped her hands together. "No, I do not—for he loves me whom I love!"

"Perdition! Girl, do you want to drive me mad?"

Pamela smiled through her tears—her thoughts at that moment were with Dick Doubleday.

"Once more, listen to me!" said the visitor, after a few moments of silence. "You do not know who I am?"

"I do!"

"Ah! say you so?"

"Yes—you are one who was indifferent to me until you made me hate you!"

"And you are content, then, to die?"

"Rather than be saved by you!"

"Infatuation! Listen to me, Pamela! My name is Sang—I am called Captain Sang. You may have heard that name before?"

Pamela trembled.

"I have heard of such a man. I have heard him who calls himself my father speak of such a man as one who neither spares age, sex, nor youth! You rob on the highway, and on the least resistance, you murder! There is a reward of a thousand pounds for you. You are a criminal—one whom it would only be right to denounce! Help! help!—oh, help, here!"

"Your cries are useless. I have told you who and what I am; but here, in this prison, they think me a totally different personage. Were you to collect all the officials of Newgate about you, and to declare to them that I was Captain Sang, they would not believe you."

Poor Pamela uttered some mournful sobs.

"And now," added Captain Sang—"now that you know me, I ask you once again to save yourself and me!"

"You?"

"Yes. It is you who can save me, if you please, from myself. By your influence I could become anything! Try but to love me. Promise to be mine, and in an hour from now you will be free; and whatever you dictate to me, as my life for the future, I will promise."

"No—no—no!"

"Pamela—Pamela! Listen!"

One, two, three, four, five, six, seven!

Even to the depths of that condemned cell, the deep, solemn tones of St. Paul's clock, striking the hour of seven, reached. Captain Sang had closed the door of the cell, and as the sounds of the hour died away there came a sharp knocking on the outer side of it.

"Sir—sir!" said a voice; "you cannot stay any longer; the Sheriff will be here."

"Help—help!" cried Pamela.

Captain Sang made a rush towards her, and for one half moment he clasped her in his arms, and kissed the long silky hair that was dashed over her face.

"I love you—I love you! I madly love you!"

Pamela screamed aloud, and burst from him. The door of the cell was opened, and, looking pale and scared, the Governor of Newgate appeared, with a lantern fastened to his waist and a bunch of keys in his hand.

"Sir John—Sir John!" he said; "oh, forbear! This is not in the bargain. It is seven o'clock, and the Sheriff will be here in a quarter of an hour."

"Sir John!" exclaimed Pamela. "This is no Sir John, but Captain Sang, the robber and murderer!"

"The girl is mad," said Sang.

"I'm afraid so," replied the Governor. "My dear, this is Sir John Pope, a goodly gentleman, who keeps a fine house in the Birdcage Walk, by the Park. He has taken a fancy to your pretty face, that's all."

"Heaven help me!"

"Help yourself!" whispered Captain Sang, *alias* Sir John Pope. "Say but the word, and you are free!"

"No, no—oh, no! Death rather than one touch from your arms! Death rather than the pollution! Oh, horror, horror! I do—I do——"

"You what?"

"I do hate you!"

"No, no, Sir John!" said the Governor, as Captain Sang, in a threatening attitude, now advanced towards Pamela. "No, no—let her alone. If she likes being hanged better than all your kind offers, she must take her choice."

"Perish, then!" yelled Captain Sang, as he dashed out of the cell, followed by the Governor, who hastily put up the bar as he called out, "Stop, stop, Sir John—stop! You will run against some of the turnkeys, and they may make disagreeable remarks. Stop a moment, and I am with you. Remember, Sir John, that you are a benevolent gentleman, who has come with some spiritual counsel to the poor condemned souls in Newgate. Stop—stop!"

Captain Sang did stop.

Out of breath with scampering after him along a couple of long, narrow passages, the Governor reached his side, panting.

"Well, sir," he said, "the girl is obstinate."

"Let her hang!"

"Oh, yes; she will hang fast enough, you may depend, Sir John Pope. I can't help her obstinacy, but you must admit that I have dealt fairly with you, sir."

"Yes—yes."

"And all I can say, sir, is, that you are right welcome to come to Newgate as often as you like; and if you see a pretty girl you take a fancy to, I shall not say a word about any more money, but only wish you better luck than with this one, who evidently would rather be hung than have anything to say to your worship."

"Peace—peace!"

The vestibule of Newgate was reached, and Captain Sang dashed out into the street.

The Governor laughed.

"Well," he muttered to himself, "of all the mad freaks I ever heard of, this is about the maddest. Sir John Pope, a most respectable gentleman, keeping a good house in the Birdcage Walk, takes a wild, mad-headed fancy for that girl, who will be hanged this morning, and gives me a cool hundred pounds for leave to speak to her in the condemned-cell, and she, it appears, won't be commonly civil to him, even to save her life! It's an odd world—a very odd world!"

The Governor of Newgate was well enough pleased with his morning's work: he had made a hundred pounds by it; but he was not aware that he had missed a thousand by not crediting the statement of Pamela, that the pretended Sir John Pope was no other than the infamous Captain Sang, a highwayman, for whom there was that reward, and who, by some extraordinary means, had for years baffled justice.

And now Pamela was alone again—alone in that dreary cell.

Eight, nine, ten o'clock came.

The cell door was thrown open.

There was a glare of torches and a crowd of people. A short, pompous-looking man, with a gold chain round his neck, was prominent among the throng. The Governor of Newgate bowed whenever he spoke to him, for that was the greatest man who ever crossed the threshold of the prison. It was the Sheriff.

"Pamela Sharples," said the Governor, "it is my painful duty to inform you that it is ten o'clock, and that I here formally deliver you to his worship, the Sheriff."

Those were a set form of words which the Governor always used on similar occasions.

A couple of turnkeys advanced, and one stood on each side of Pamela.

She shrieked and wrung her hands.

"Oh, this is the bitterness of death! Father!—father! Have I a father, and does he desert me now?"

The Chaplain took one of her hands in his.

"Hush!—hush, my poor girl! Be calm!—be calm!"

"Calm, sir?—calm? Oh, you are all calm, but none of you are going to death!"

The Sheriff kept his handkerchief oscillating between his eyes and his hand. He was a good-hearted man, and his tears flowed just at the same time that he did not wish to lose a word that Pamela said.

"My dear, believe me," he said, "I have done all I could to get a reprieve; but his gracious Majesty—bother him—I mean, bless him—that is to say, the obstinate pig—no, dear, dear me—I mean his gracious royal mind—that is to say—bless us, I mean—he wouldn't do it."

Pamela held out her hand to the Sheriff

"God bless you, sir, and thank you!"

This was too much for the worthy Sheriff; and he was compelled to walk some distance from the spot, sobbing aloud.

"Mr. Sheriff," said a soft silky voice. It was the clerk of Newgate who spoke.

"Well, what?"

"Do you like the—the marrow puddings with sherry sauce?"

"The what, you villain?"

"The marrow puddings that are always one of the dishes of the lunch after the execution."

"D—— the marrow puddings and you too, sir! How dare you speak to me of marrow puddings when a poor young thing like that is about to be put to death? I have a child of my own—my little Nancy. I don't say she is so pretty as this young girl; but—but she is my child, for all that; and—and it seems as if I saw her about to die when—when I look into the face of that poor girl. Oh, dear—oh, dear! If his most gracious—obstinate—kind, good—pig, old brute—no, no!—amiable Majesty had only pardoned her! Ah! here she is!"

Pamela was in the vestibule of the prison.

The cart was at the gate.

"I understand Mr. Sheriff, your worship," said the Governor, "that after this session nobody will be taken to Tyburn; but the little affairs will take place here, before the Debtor's Door of Newgate."

"I don't know—I don't know! Keep up a good heart, my dear! Do, now—do, now! Bless you, do, now!"

A wild yell burst from a thousand voices as Pamela was helped into the cart at the door of Newgate.

"Shame—shame! A reprieve! Shame! Yah! Let the girl go! Quite a child! Let her go!"

A volley of stones, mud, and every missile, soft or hard, that could be collected in the street, was hurled at the Sheriff's coach and the party of officers who were to form the escort of poor Pamela to Tyburn.

Then a small wiry-looking man, with a face like a fox, and a head of hair that looked like pieces of red wire sticking up on end, appeared, and began to climb into the cart.

That was the hangman.

The yell of execration which burst from the throats of the mob was enough to strike terror into every heart.

The small foxy-looking man cowered down by the side of Pamela, as if imploring her protection.

"Forward!" cried the chief officer, who was mounted on a powerful black horse.

The terrible procession started.

From the courts and alleys of Newgate Street—from the pestiferous haunts of crime and vagabondage, by the banks of the river—from Fleet Market, and from the district in and about Field Lane, there came hordes of people; and by the time the procession reached the middle of Snow Hill, as far as the eye could reach there was nothing but upturned faces and yelling throats.

Pamela trembled.

"Oh! this is horrible—most horrible!"

Then she uttered a shriek, for projecting over the parapet of a house-top she saw a face.

It was the face of Jacob Sharples!

CHAPTER IX.

PAMELA IS RESCUED FROM DEATH AND FINDS A REFUGE BEHIND A PICTURE IN THE HOUSE OF THE COURT PHYSICIAN.

THE bright sun burst through the clouds of that sad and terrible morning, and a broad, beautiful gleam of sunlight, like some dazzling and radiant path from earth to heaven, fell upon the dismal procession that was conveying the young, fair, and innocent Pamela to death.

It fell upon the upturned faces of the yelling, roaring, hooting crowd.

It fell upon the fair hair and the gentle child-like face of the prisoner in the cart, did that broad and beautiful sunbeam.

It fell upon that man who was crouching down by her side—that man who looked more like a fox than a man, or something like what one would have supposed a man to look like who, in accordance with the wild fancies of some of the old fables, had once been a fox.

He sought and found refuge by the side of Pamela most effectually, for of all the missiles which came singing through the air at the officers—at the Sheriff—

at the ordinary of Newgate—at everybody and everything connected with the procession, none came even sufficiently near to Pamela to touch that shrinking man.

That executioner!

"Pull him out! Out with Jack Ketch! Pull him out of the cart! Don't let him creep down so close to the girl—we cannot hit him! Out with him! Brain him! Smash Jack Ketch! Hang him on the old lamp post at the corner of the market! Bring him along!—out with him!"

The foxy-looking executioner uttered a yell of terror.

A terrible assault had been made on the cart. The powerful horse that drew it was stopped by twenty hands—the sides of the cart were seized—a tall and strong man got hold of the executioner by one leg!

It seemed as if he must now either come out of the cart or the leg be dragged off!

Horrible idea!

The executioner's leg was surely being pulled from his body. It visibly lengthened—longer, longer still. Then the tall strong man fell backward into the crowd with the boot of the executioner in his hands, which coming off by degrees, had suggested the strange notion that the man's leg was being pulled out to an indefinite length.

"Help—help! Mr Sheriff—Mr. Grogrum! They will murder me!"

The executioner prayed and shrieked for aid.

"Sir! If you please, Mr. Sheriff," said the chief officer of the escort, riding up to the door of the Sheriff's carriage—for that functionary was, after all, close to the dismal procession,—"sir, will you be so good as read the Riot Act?"

"The what?"

"The Riot Act, sir; for then I and my mates will soon settle this little affair by cutting down some of the foremost of the crowd."

"Then I will do no such thing!"

"But, sir——"

"I won't, I say; and, besides, I have no Riot Act here, and if I had, I wouldn't read it."

"There they go!"

"Who go?"

"They are about to make a compact rush at the cart, sir, and they will, in my opinion, rescue the prisoner."

"Do you really think so, Mr. Grogrum?"

"I do, your worship."

"Then I am delighted to hear it."

The Sheriff drew up the window of his carriage shortly and sharply in the officer's face.

"Oh! that's the way the wind blows, does it!" said Grogrum. "A pretty go, indeed, to have the girl taken out of our hands on the road to Tyburn! I do believe everybody has gone mad about her, just because she has a sort of doll's pretty face! Why, Mrs Grogrum, who was always counted a beauty, and used to be called the Belle of Whitechapel, would make four of her."

It was quite evident that the chief officer's ideas of feminine beauty were very different from Dick Doubleday's.

But the danger was to the full as great as he had represented it to be to the Sheriff.

The death procession had fairly reached the valley of the Fleet.

Then, just before the ascent of Holborn Hill, it was quite a common thing for a riot to take place if any one who was popular with the crowd was being taken to Tyburn to die.

The necessary slowness with which the cavalcade must ascend the hill, and the contiguity to that spot of so many thoroughfares, the whole of which were then in possession of the lawless portion of the community, made that particular spot most favourable for a popular demonstration.

A wild and appalling yell burst from the multitude, and then a rush was made upon the cart.

Had Handsome Jemmy or Dick Doubleday been there

to lead the attack, it would no doubt have been eminently successful; but they were not on that spot, and the mob acted too individually and without a proper leader

The officers, on the contrary, were a compact body of armed men.

"Now, mates," said Grogrum, "this won't do! If we once get separated, I wouldn't give a yard of hemp for any of our lives!"

"It's all up. Mr. Grogrum!" said one.

"No, it aint! Fall on them! Use your hangers, and you will make short work of it!"

The force of a certain sort of discipline and regularity of movement were never more sufficiently testified as against a mob than in the present instance.

There were but eight mounted constables in addition to Grogrum.

The mob probably numbered two or three thousand.

And yet these eight men—or rather nine men—rode right round the cart, and cut down everybody who tried to lay a hand on it.

There were shrieks, and cries, and groans, and vows of vengeance, and a terrible surging to and fro of the mob, and cries, particularly from those who were the furthest off, to "Give it them;" but the officers got the best of the affair, for all that.

And the cart was again in progress.

The foxy executioner had, by this time, stooped so low that his head was completely hidden in the straw at the bottom of the cart.

Poor Pamela was pale as a sheeted spectre.

The tumult—the wild cries—the attack on the cart—the blood that she saw shed—all terrified her beyond expression.

From the moment that she had seen the face of Jacob Sharples over the house-top close to Fleet Market, it would seem that some fearful apathy had come over her, and that all hope of averting her dreadful doom had disappeared from her heart.

Perhaps she thought that he might be making exertions to save her? Perhaps she thought it impossible that that man, who called himself her father—although she could not recollect that she had ever had a father's tenderness from him—could leave her to die.

She might have had some vague, indistinct idea or hope that at the last moment there would be a shout in the crowd, and that some one would say, "Jacob Sharples has confessed all, and given himself up!"

Then she would surely be saved.

But when she saw that face—that cold, terrible, selfish face looking down upon her as she went to death, all hopes of that character fled.

Then poor Pamela felt that the man who called her his child was content that she should perish for his crimes, provided he kept himself out of danger.

Then came a gush of tears to poor Pamela's eyes; and when she could look through them and cast another glance at that house-top, Jacob Sharples was gone

Then Pamela thought she would cry out that he was there, and that she was innocent; but the cart went on. The opportunity was lost.

The shadow of death seemed to fall upon that young girl's heart, and to wrap her up as in a pall

The cavalcade reaches the top of the hill—it passes its worst danger—the officers try to get to a trot, but the mob is still too dense to permit them to do so.

The cart is just opposite the narrow end of Leather Lane, when some twenty men make a simultaneous rush at the vehicle, and without uttering a single word, without a shout, without a cry, or adding of themselves in any way to the tumult around them, they seized upon the foxy executioner and tossed him out of the cart as though he had been some insensible bale of goods.

The officers were taken by surprise.

The unearthly scream that the executioner gave was almost the first intimation that they had of the fact that he had been at last successfully dragged out of the cart.

"Don't hurt him!" said a loud voice.

"Hurrah! hurrah!"

The wretched man was kept afloat, if we may use the expression, upon that awful angry sea of heads and faces.

Over the surface of the compact mass of people he was tumbled, dashed, rolled, and flung until he reached the pavement, and then—with a crash that for the moment was above every other sound—he was sent bodily through the window of a linen-draper.

No more was seen of the foxy-looking executioner.

"This won't do," said Grogrum,—"this will never do. Here's a pretty go! The Sheriff will have to hang the girl himself when we get to Tyburn Tree."

"Not a bit of it, Grogrum," cried a man, who scrambled into the cart. "I'll officiate!"

"You?"

"Yes, to be sure; and whatever has to be done I'll do as neatly, I hope, as possible."

"Who the deuce are you?"

"Simon Patch."

"Patch! Patch! I fancy I have heard that name before."

"To be sure you have. I'm the Jack Ketch of Portsmouth, and fucked up Jerry Abershaw on Portsea Common, I did. Bless you, I am a first rate hand at it. I came to town to see my friend Foxy, as we call him, the administrator of Tyburn; but as he has gone into that shop yonder, why I'll do this little job for him."

"You are just in time."

"I think so."

"And the very man for us."

"That's my own opinion, too."

"But what do you wear that horrid, half green, half black-looking patch over your right eye and one half of your face for?"

"A kick."

"Oh!"

"An elephant, at a wild beasts' show, gave me a slight kick in the eye; and, as my name's Patch, I thought in truth it looked rather in keeping for me to wear one."

"Forward!" shouted the officer.

The cart went on again.

It was remarked, however, by the officers that it was rather a singular circumstance that not a single missile of any description was now thrown at the cart

Patch, the hangman of Portsmouth as he styled himself, was a tall, slender man. He had a common dark-brown great-coat, a good deal the worse for wear, buttoned up to his chin.

The skirts of that coat reached half-way down to his ankles from the knees, and what could be seen of his feet consisted of some pieces of dirty oil-cloth, by way of boots.

The disagreeable-looking patch of greenish-black silk, or plaster, that covered his right eye and a good half of his face, prevented much of his countenance from being seen, and gave him a most sinister aspect.

Grogrum, the chief officer, raised himself in his stirrups and looked about him.

"Bates," he said to the constable who was next him, —"what's going on?"

"I can't imagine, Mr. Grogrum."

"The mob is not half so noisy."

Bates shook his head.

"What do you think of it?"

"Why, Mr. Grogrum, it seems to me as if those fellows who pulled 'Foxy' out of the cart were a great deal too busy. I can see them going through about among the crowd like so many eels, and everybody they speak to seems as pleased as possible. There, don't you see them flinging up their hats and caps? We shall have the whole lot of 'em down upon us afore we get to the Oxford Road, you may depend on it, Mr Grogrum!"

"I think so, too. Close up!—close up! If it's to be a fight, we can't help it!"

The cart now stopped at Holborn Bars.

It was the custom, then, for the clergyman, who up to

that point had occupied a seat in the Sheriff's coach, to take his place by the side of the condemned person in the cart.

It was always considered that if a reprieve did not reach the City authorities in time to overtake the cart on its route towards Tyburn, before or by the time it got to that limit of the City, all hope and chance of the condemned person being respited was over.

The clergyman, therefore, alighted from the Sheriff's coach.

The mob had no ill-will towards him. They did not associate him in any way with the execution; and he had no difficulty in making his way through the people in his gown and bands.

While the cart, however, stopped for this purpose, and just as the clergyman was half-way towards it, there arose a strange, wild kind of shouting in the direction of the City.

It was a fine and yet a terrible thing to look back and see the mob that was now in the rear of the cavalcade, for it would seem as if the principal portion of that mob had stood still from the moment that the new executioner had taken his place in the condemned cart.

And now, as the officers looked back, and as the Sheriff looked from the window of his coach, and as the ordinary of Newgate likewise paused and looked back, that strange roaring shout, like some advancing cataract, came from the City.

Hundreds of hands—thousands of hands—were uplifted; with hats, caps, bonnets, sticks, handkerchiefs, umbrellas—children were uplifted to people's shoulders—and the shout that came rolling onwards evidently had some origin about the foot of the hill.

What it was the officers could not divine.

Then, while all eyes were directed towards the City, Patch, the "Administrator of Portsmouth," approached Pamela.

He spoke in a low voice, not looking at her as he spoke, but affecting to turn his attention, like every one else, towards the City.

"Don't be alarmed, my dear! It's all right! You didn't think, did you, that a pretty girl like you would be let swing at Tyburn to oblige a rascal like Jacob Sharples?"

"Oh, heaven!"

"Hush! Hush, now!"

"Mercy!—mercy!"

"Come—come! Don't look at me. Say what you like, but don't look at me just yet!"

"Shall I be saved?"

"Of course you will."

Pamela burst into tears.

"Oh, heaven—oh, mercy! Who—who—tell me, who are you?"

"I ain't vain, and didn't give myself the name, my dear, but they call me 'Handsome Jemmy.'"

CHAPTER X.

DICK DOUBLEDAY HAS TO TRUST TO A GOOD STEED FOR HIS LIFE.

"Now, my good girl," added the highwayman, "don't be crying in that kind of way. I think I ought to cry!"

"You—you? Oh, no, no! I have heard of you!"

"You have?"

"Yes, Dick—my Dick Doubleday——"

"Oh, he spoke of me, did he? I suppose he told you what a rascal I was!"

"No—oh, no! He said that you were so generous and so brave, that if ever I wanted a true friend, and he himself should not be able to aid me, to find you out and depend upon you!"

"So Dick said that?"

"Indeed, he did."

"Well, Pamela. I can only say that I don't think Dick has made a mistake in the part of the business

which implies that you may depend on me! But listen to that! Do you hear that?"

"Oh, yes!"

"There, again! Did you ever hear such music?"

"Never—never! Oh, heaven, never!"

"A reprieve! a reprieve! a reprieve!"

The sounds arose from every throat. It commenced deep down in the valley of the Fleet—it rolled up Holborn Hill, being caught by every throat that was not previously hoarse with shouting and hallooing, until, in one swelling chorus, it was echoed round the cart in which was Pamela and Handsome Jemmy, the highwayman.

"A reprieve! a reprieve! a reprieve!"

The Sheriff fairly sprang out of his coach.

The ordinary of Newgate began to think it was no use his troubling himself to go any further.

The officers reined in their horses, but they looked incredulous, and perhaps a little suspicious.

The cry of "A reprieve!" had been raised by the crowds attending executions before that day, and had turned out to mean nothing.

Or if the cry had meant anything, it had been the rallying shout for a riot.

"Do you think it, Mr. Grogram?" asked Bates.

"No."

"No more do I. The King, they do say, never will save any one for coining or passing bad money!"

"A reprieve! a reprieve! a reprieve!"

The shouts were louder—the waving of hats and sticks more wild and exciting.

And then there came up the brow of Holborn Hill a horseman, tall and distinct above the heads of the mob, and pressing his way forward through the narrow lane which was made by the people, and which opened before his horse's head as though the creature had had the capacity to melt the people in its path.

Rising from the low ground below the top of the hill, that horseman seemed as if he came up out of the solid earth.

And his progress through the people resembled what one might suppose would be presented by the red-hot prow of a ship, if such a thing were possible, driving through ice.

In that strange way did he appear.

And in that magical manner did the compact mass of people melt before him.

As this horseman passed the corner of Hatton Garden, a broad golden sunbeam fell upon him.

He then was dazzling to look upon, for he wore a bright scarlet coat, and his hat was trimmed with gold lace.

The horse he rode upon was one of uncommon size and beauty.

A dark bay, with one white foot, and a small white star in the centre of its forehead.

And now and then, as this mounted man in the scarlet coat came onward towards the cart, he raised one arm, and waved something that looked like a piece of paper.

"By Jove!" said Mr. Grogram, "it is a reprieve."

"No doubt of that," replied Bates. "That's a royal messenger."

"I see! I see! I tell you what it is, Bates, the sooner we all draw off now the better, for if there is one plank of this cart holding on to another in five more minutes, my name is not Grogram."

"A reprieve! a reprieve! a reprieve!"

With one last terrific shout of welcome, the mounted man was heralded to the Sheriff's carriage.

The Sheriff was standing close to the door of the highly ornamented vehicle which his state demanded, and he held up both his hands as the messenger in the scarlet coat approached him.

"Now, sir! Now, sir!" he said. "What is it? I'm the Sheriff. Tell me it is a reprieve for that poor girl yonder, and you shall have the best bottle of wine in my cellar, whenever and however often you like to come for it."

THE FLIGHT OF DICK DOUBLEDAY AND HANDSOME JEMMY.

The horseman was flushed in the face, but as he reached the Sheriff, he turned ghastly pale, and every one could see that he shook from head to foot.

"Yes, Mr Sheriff, it is a reprieve for Pamela. For—for the girl—the prisoner—for Pamela Sharples."

"All's right, young man."

The Sheriff held out his hand for the paper, but the young man in the scarlet coat crumpled it up in his hand, and glared wildly about him.

"Good gracious!" said Handsome Jemmy. "What is the boy about?"

Pamela stretched forth both her hands and uttered a shriek of joy.

In that man on that tall and beautiful horse, with the scarlet livery of the King upon him, she recognised Dick Doubleday.

And then, for the first time, Pamela began to suspect that her escape from death only hung upon the chances of success of some daring scheme that had been got up, and was being carried out by Dick Doubleday and his friend Handsome Jemmy, the highwayman.

No wonder that with that conviction her heart sank within her.

For a few seconds she remained in that attitude she had assumed, with her arms extended, and a look, half of joy, half of despair, upon her fair face.

Those moments were important ones.

Dick Doubleday it was, indeed, who was playing the part of the King's messenger; but, at the last moment, he dreaded that the Sheriff would look too closely at the King's pardon, which was for the horse stealer, and not for Pamela Sharples.

"By heaven! the poor fellow in his agitation will spoil all!" said Handsome Jemmy. "I wanted to play that part myself, but he would do it."

"It is—it is the heart that loves me," exclaimed Pamela. "I see him now so well and clearly, and the mystery now of who and what he was is unravelled. He is in the service of the King; he has influence—for who can help loving him?—and he has used it to save me."

"Humph!" said Handsome Jemmy. "I rather think you know less of Dick Doubleday than before. There's an old saying, that 'the cowl don't make a monk;' neither does a red coat make a King's messenger, my dear."

Pamela did not hear a word that Handsome Jemmy said to her. Her eyes were upon Dick Doubleday, and her whole attention was strained to catch, if it were possible, the slightest tones of his voice.

And Dick felt that he had mismanaged in some manner that mission of life and death upon which he had come.

It was the sight of Pamela that had bewildered him, and driven from his recollection all that he meant to do or say.

Audacity, a sort of swaggering insolence, and an announcement that he bore a pardon for the prisoner—rather than a trembling, hesitating product on of it—was the style in which he ought to have proceeded.

But he had caught the glance of those eyes so dear to him.

He had seen the bright morning sun shining upon the fair hair of his Pamela.

And so Dick Doubleday forgot all the instruction that had been carefully instilled into him by Handsome Jemmy the highwayman, and at the last moment felt compelled to hazard a much more dangerous mode of proceeding.

He stooped low upon the saddle of the horse, and while his whole face was convulsed with emotion, and his lips quivered to that degree that he could scarcely speak, he addressed the Sheriff: "Sir, for the love of heaven—for the love of mercy—for the dear hope that in your dying hour you will think of this moment, and find it such a consolation that it shall seem to you like a glimpse of happiness in the midst of the darkest shadows of death——"

The Sheriff was a rather matter-of-fact individual,

with very little imagination; and these words, coming from a King's messenger, with a reprieve for a condemned person, where it would have been so much easier for him just to have handed it out, and said, "Here it is—a reprieve for Pamela Sharples," filled the Sheriff with astonishment.

"Bless me, my good sir! What do you mean?"

"I mean—I mean—— "

"Well, sir; what?"

"I mean that I am sure—that is, that I hope—you know the King's signature well."

"Perfectly."

"Then, sir, be content, and behold it here."

With trembling hands Dick Doubleday unfolded the paper sufficiently for the Sheriff to see the King's signature; but as Dick was on horseback, and looked down, so the Sheriff, being on foot, looked up, and Dick was not aware that the Sheriff saw a little more of the paper than he could.

The last words which the King had written when he signed the pardon for the horse-stealer met the Sheriff's eyes.

"'The horse man!' 'George Rex!' What's the meaning of the horse man?"

"Be content—be content. Be—be deceived, sir, and save her!"

"Oh!"

A new light broke in upon the mind of the Sheriff.

A cadaverous tint spread itself over his face.

"I—I begin to see—to suspect—to fancy, young man, that there is something wrong—some trick in all this."

"There is," said Dick Doubleday.

"You actually own it?"

"I do, sir; and at the same time I leave you to be the murderer of Pamela Sharples. I say, her murderer, because it is in your power to save her. Oh, Mr. Sheriff! think for a moment that it is a small matter for you to be accused of a want of suspicious sagacity, in comparison to the judicial murder of that—that—— There, I need not describe her—look at her!"

The Sheriff turned, and without another word got into his coach.

The conference which we have recorded, as between Dick Doubleday and the really kind-hearted civic official, had not occupied a quarter of the time that we have necessarily taken to relate it, and it was just over when Grogram, the chief officer, impatient even at the slight delay, forced his horse up to the carriage window.

But it was upon the other side to that where Dick Doubleday was that Grogram made his appearance, so that they did not actually meet face to face.

If they had done so, the experienced eyes of the officer might have doubted if, in the trembling, anxious youth on that magnificent horse, in the royal livery, he really beheld a King's messenger.

"Mr Sheriff," said Grogram, "is this really a reprieve for Pamela Sharples?"

The Sheriff did not speak, but he nodded his head.

That action, however, scarcely seemed to satisfy the chief officer, and he stooped still lower in the saddle, as he said, "Reprieve for Pamela Sharples, worshipful sir?"

"The girl is saved!" replied the Sheriff; and then he added to himself, with a groan, as he leant back in his carriage, "What my wife will say about it when she comes to know all the particulars I don't know, for I shall be struck off the list of sheriffs, and she'll lose the chance of being 'my lady' if his gracious Majesty should come to dine in the City."

The peculiar movement which the Sheriff gave to his carriage as he flung himself back in it was considered by his coachman as an order to "move on."

"Hi! hi! Look sharp, now—look sharp! Clear the way! Do you want to be trod on? Is 'osses 'oofs so pleasant? Can't you let me turn? There ain't to be no hanging, don't you hear, all of you? Hi! hi! woa! woa!"

The coachman thus expostulated with the crowd as he turned his horses Citywards.

Grogram waved his hand, and made several gestures to his men to keep close together and follow him in the wake of the Sheriff's carriage; for he had nothing to do now with that cart and its contents.

His eyes happened to fall upon Handsome Jemmy, whom he still identified with his assumed character of Patch, the Portsmouth hangman.

"I'm sorry for you, Mr. Patch!" he cried. "You've lost your job, and I rather think you'll come off second best!"

"Oh, don't mind me!" cried Handsome Jemmy. "I shall do very well. Look to yourself, Mr. Grogram!"

Grogram and the officers shrunk down low in their saddles before a complete shower of missiles of every description which were hurled at them from the crowd, as though at the instigation of some one who had given the word of command to make the attack.

The two footmen at the back of the Sheriff's carriage came in for their full share of this assault, and the sharp stones, with which the mob must have been plentifully provided, rattled upon the back panels of the carriage like so many musket shot.

Dick Doubleday, with a bright flush upon his face, now spurred forward.

His Pamela was saved, and he was at peace with all men. He could almost, at that moment, have forgiven Jacob Sharples; and, raising one arm, he cried out, in a loud voice, "Forbear—forbear! This is needless! Provoke no quarrel when all is saved and all is gained!"

Dick Doubleday was by the side of the cart in a moment and, stretching out both his arms, he almost shrieked the name of Pamela as she flew into his embrace.

And now the reader will recollect how, when first Dick Doubleday had made his appearance in the valley of the Fleet, and proclaimed his purpose to the excited throng of people yelling, shouting, screaming, and hooting after the death cavalcade to Tyburn, the sudden revulsion of feeling he had produced had a strange, electric effect upon the swarm of human beings through which he had to make his way.

A waving commotion, as when the sea is about to be agitated by some tempest which is to curl its waves with foam, then swayed the mob to and fro; and from mouth to mouth—commencing as though in a whisper afar off, and then deepening to a present roar—had come the indications of his approach.

Transpose these sounds, O reader, and suppose them, now, to come from the other direction.

Suppose the mass of people who had by this time impacted themselves in the upper part of Holborn—right up the Oxford Road, as it was then called—to be agitated and acted upon in a similar manner, although from a different cause.

The stillness which reigned about the cart, and the mob upon that spot, and the stillness which induced the officers, holding their arms over their eyes in case of another shower of stones, to half face their horses about and still linger behind the Sheriff's carriage, was the stillness of expectation.

Everybody was listening.

Remaining in the attitudes which they had assumed at the moment, everybody strained his attention to discover what it was that agitated the crowd to the west and which produced the strange roaring cry, which from a good half-mile off surged onward until it swelled into a shout as it reached Holborn Bars.

It would be difficult to comprehend the various cries and exclamations, each one of which was intended, no doubt, to give some warning or some explanation of what was about to take place.

"No reprieve!—no reprieve! The light horse! Save your lives! A sham messenger! He's been in a tree all night! A pardon for Bolt, the horse-stealer! The light horse!—the light horse! Down with 'em!—down with 'em! Take the girl away! They'll hang her yet! Kill the Sheriff! The light horse!—the light horse!"

That cry of "The light horse" was well understood in those days. They consisted of an unpopular regiment of Light Dragoons, named "The King's Light Horse," who were too often, on occasions of public effervescence, brought into collision with the people.

Far away up Holborn, and pressing their way through the crowd at a canter, a party of cavalry might be seen dealing flat-bladed strokes with their sabres at everybody that impeded them, while in their midst rode a hot, bewildered-looking man, without either coat or hat.

"Dick," said Handsome Jemmy, coolly, "I rather think that's our friend we left in the tree, in St. James's Park."

"Lost!—lost!" exclaimed Dick Doubleday.

"Gad—no! He seems to have been found. The fun's not over yet."

CHAPTER XI.

PAMELA IS HIDDEN WITH THE MEMORIALS OF PAST DAYS, AND DICK DOUBLEDAY PURCHASES A HORSE.

THE excitement of the crowd in Holborn was momentarily on the increase.

Some tried to escape, for they knew that the "King's Light Horse" were not particular in their operations when they were let loose in a mob.

Others, with a curiosity that over-mastered all sense or fear of danger, pressed forward to "see what would come of the whole affair."

These two contending parties of the mob swayed the vast assemblage to and fro, and produced in a few more minutes a scene of riot and confusion that threatened the most serious consequences.

The Light Horse were rapidly approaching.

In the midst of them, mounted on a troop horse, which had been lent to him, was the man without coat or hat.

That was in good truth the King's courier, who had been captured in St. James's Park the night before, by Handsome Jemmy and Dick Doubleday, and accommodated with a roost in a tree.

"Jemmy," said Dick, as he laid his hand tremblingly on the arm of the highwayman,—"Jemmy, what is to be done? In two minutes more we shall be surrounded by the Light Horse."

"Two minutes, Dick?"

"Certainly not longer."

"Then there's lots of time. Do you think you can take care of yourself somehow, and find your way to Bagshot Heath to-night?"

"How and why? What is it you want me to do?"

"Dismount, and let me place Pamela on my horse, which don't seem as if he would put out his paces so well with you as with me. I will give her the saddle, and ride behind her; and if in one minute we don't leave those troopers a good distance behind us, don't put faith in me."

"Yes! Oh, yes! They can but take me!"

"Hem! I didn't mean that. But I don't see any other way just this moment, Dick. Mind when you get to the heath, whistle the old Scotch tune, named, 'Whistle, and I'll come to thee, my lad,' and that will soon get you some news of me."

"Ah, Jemmy, it is too late."

"Not a bit!"

"See—see! The Light Horse cut down the people! There is blood upon their sabres."

"Oh, no, no! not for me let there be bloodshed," moaned Pamela.

Dick Doubleday almost flung himself off the horse that Handsome Jemmy had lent him, and the highwayman's foot was in the stirrup, when the officer in command of the Light Horse was seen to point at them with his sword, and then he issued some orders, and the troop of dragoons that was with him commenced clearing their way towards the cart, by a savage onslaught upon the people who were in their way.

Handsome Jemmy was on his horse's back in a moment, and then leaning from the saddle over the side of the cart, he said, "Pamela, it is your only chance. Spring up before me, and you are saved."

"No, no! A thousand times, no!"

Her eyes were upon Dick Doubleday. Her hands were stretched towards him. She knew his danger, for bit by bit by bit she had come to a comprehension of the whole truth of the case, and she felt that although she might escape, he would inevitably be taken.

What kind of penalty he would have to pay for his share in the deception by which her freedom had been obtained she did not know, but she could not—she would not leave him.

"No, no!" she cried again. "It is kind and generous of you to do so much to save me; but rather would I perish with him, than leave him to a fate that he so little deserves. Dick—Dick, you have risked all for your Pamela, and she will try to be worthy of you!"

Handsome Jemmy saw now that upon the next half-minute depended the fate of Pamela. He spoke in a high tone of command, as at the same time he stooped a trifle lower from his horse, and was enabled to fling his left arm around the slender waist of Pamela.

"Dick, leap up behind me. For once my good horse shall carry three. You and Pamela are light weights. Quick! Quick! For life's sake!"

The highwayman had Pamela out of the cart and on the saddle before him by the time he had uttered one half of this speech.

The mob raised a wild shout of exultation.

Dick Doubleday was hoisted on to the tall horse behind Handsome Jemmy by a dozen eager hands.

Screams came from the wounded people, for by this time the Light Horse had got as far as the westward end of Middle Row.

"Good bye!" cried Handsome Jemmy, as he lifted his hat for a moment a couple of inches above his head, and glanced towards the Light Horse. "Good bye!"

One of the troopers took a pistol from the holster of his saddle, and fired it at the highwayman.

The aim was a rapid and a random one, but the bullet hit the hat, and dashed it out of the hand of Handsome Jemmy.

"Ah, that was not a bad shot!" he said. "If I had time I would return it; but as it is, good bye, once more!"

A great clapping of hands arose from the crowd, which in such a vast assemblage had a curious effect.

The horses of the dragoons had stood every sort of excitement, and every sort of noise but that; but the sight of the forest of hands and the noise of the clapping was so new to them, that they shied, and their riders had difficulty to control them.

Handsome Jemmy galloped down the Gray's Inn Road.

The people moved out of his way as if by magic, and then closed up again in a dense mass at the narrow top of the road.

There was then a wild rush at the cart, which was upset and torn to fragments. The horse that had drawn it escaped likewise down Gray's Inn Road; and then the riot that took place, during which the dragoons in vain sought to disentangle themselves from the crowd, was something fearful to contemplate, as it was contemplated by people at every window of every house.

All that had taken place in regard to the escape of the prisoner and the sham King's messenger had been clearly seen both by the military, and by Mr. Grogrum and his party of constables.

The situation of the police, however, had been for the last five minutes rather humiliating.

They were captured.

As completely captured by the mob as any men could possibly be.

It was done in this way.

The special friends of Handsome Jemmy had seen that his, and Pamela's, and Dick Doubleday's escape might be managed before the Light Horse reached the spot, but since the mounted party of constables was already there, they might be a serious hindrance.

On to the crupper, then, of each horse, a man had sprung, and seizing the constable who rode the steed round the body, he was held securely.

Two more men held the horse by the head.

And in this manner the officers were completely harmless, and were merely spectators of all that had taken place.

The tall, powerful steed of the highwayman made nothing of the treble weight that was on his back.

Pamela was light, and so was Dick Doubleday.

Handsome Jemmy laughed.

"We don't find out till the last moment what we can do, Dick," he said. "It did not strike me that you and Pamela together would not be much more than another equal to me on the horse's back."

"Oh, Jemmy, Jemmy—listen!"

The blast of a cavalry trumpet came upon the morning air.

"What—where is that?" said the highwayman.

"It's our fate, Jemmy?"

"What do you mean?"

"Don't you know that we are rapidly approaching the cavalry barracks, down this road?"

"Oh, by Jove, yes! A little before we come to Battle Bridge?"

"Yes, Jemmy. There is a trumpet call again! Some alarm has been given, and we shall have foes both before and behind us."

Handsome Jemmy reined in his horse for a moment or two.

The clatter of horses' feet was heard in their rear, and the braying notes of a cavalry trumpet in advance of them.

"Very good," said the highwayman.

"Good, Jemmy, do you call it?"

"Yes, Dick. It seems to me that so long as our foes are good enough to make so much noise, we shall always be able to know where they are."

The highwayman, as he spoke, abandoned the high road to Battle Bridge, as the modern King's Cross was then named, and turned up a street to the left.

That street was one of the then new streets that led up to Bloomsbury Fields.

A carriage came from the opposite direction at a quick pace.

"Hold, Jemmy, hold!" cried Dick Doubleday. "Don't you know that carriage?"

"Eh? Know it? By Jove, yes! It's Doctor Haslem's carriage."

"It is, Dick."

The carriage was now stopped so suddenly, in obedience to a sharp and peremptory order from some one riding in it, that the horses were nearly upon their haunches.

The door of the carriage at the same moment opened, and Doctor Haslem himself sprung out.

"Stop! stop!" he cried to Handsome Jemmy. "I was at the corner of the Oxford Road, and heard that you had fled with the condemned Pamela Sharples down the Gray's Inn Road, and hoped to intercept you by coming this way. Trust her to me, and I will save her!"

"On your life, sir, will you do so?"

"On my life, I will! I have a means of so doing that none of you know of. It will be far better than that she should be pursued over the country, as she will be. Pamela Sharples, will you trust yourself to me?"

"Ah, yes, sir, with all my heart!" replied Pamela as she looked into the face of the Court Physician, in whose eyes stood tears, and on whose whole countenance were traces of deep emotion.

"Dick, what do you say?" asked the highwayman.

Pamela replied for Dick Doubleday.

"No, no! Oh, how ungrateful I am! Dick, I will not leave you. No, no! Your fortunes shall be my fortunes—your danger, my danger!"

Dick Doubleday could not speak for a moment or two; but he stretched his arm past Handsome Jemmy, and held the hand of Pamela in his.

"Come with me, I implore you," added Doctor

Haslem. "I have no doubt but that I can still procure a pardon. In my house you will find a refuge that will not fail you."

Then Dick Doubleday was about to say something but Handsome Jemmy interrupted him.

"Let me speak."

"Yes, yes!—but Pamela?"

"Let her go to the Doctor's house, Dick. It will be far better than with us, just now. You and I can shift for ourselves somehow; but the slightest accident might place her at the mercy of the officers, who are provoked enough for any mischief."

Dick sighed.

"Doctor Haslem," added the highwayman, "I don't know how you mean to protect this young creature against the law that threatens her life, but you say you can do so?"

"I can and will."

"Then I advise her to trust to you."

"Dick, Dick!" said Pamela; "what shall I do?"

"Trust to Doctor Haslem, dear, dear Pamela!"

"There's not a moment to lose," exclaimed Jemmy, as he sprung from his horse, and lifted Pamela to the ground.

Dick stooped, and placed both his hands on the fair young head.

"Heaven's blessings on my Pamela!"

"And on you, Dick!"

"Dear, dear girl!"

She stretched herself upon her tip-toes, and Dick stooped low from the tall horse. His lips touched the delicate fair, soft cheek, and a delirium of joy shot through the heart and brain of the young lover.

"That will do," said Handsome Jemmy. "Don't mind me, Dick; it's the first time and the last."

As he spoke, the highwayman gave Pamela a much more pretentious salute than Dick had done.

Another moment, and she was in Doctor Haslem's carriage, which drove off at speed.

Dick Doubleday looked after the vehicle with a deep-drawn sigh.

"Don't," said Jemmy.

"Don't what?"

"You will blow me off the horse if you sigh in that fashion. Oh, here they are!"

With a shout of exultation, the party of Light Horse joined to the constables, who had been let loose by the mob, reached the corner of Guildford Street.

"Thank heaven!" said Dick, "Pamela is safe."

"So are we. Off we go again!"

Dashing up Guildford Street, and through the partially-built Russell Square, went the tall, powerful horse; and then, turning to the right, Handsome Jemmy sought the green lanes just beyond Tottenham Court Road.

"It looks suspicious, Dick," said Jemmy, "for you to be riding with me on the same horse, and with that red coat on."

"I will leave you."

"Not at all. Look ahead."

"Yes, yes."

"What do you see?"

"A mounted man."

"Yes; and, on my reputation, I can tell you, Dick, that the horse that man rides is as pretty a bit of bone and muscle and blood as any one would wish to have. I propose, Dick, that you buy that horse."

"I buy it?"

"To be sure!"

"Alas! I have no money."

"I have. Hoy! hoy! You, sir, on the bay horse! Hoy! hoy!"

The horseman, who looked like a gentleman, although not a very wise one, halted, and putting an eye-glass to one eye, he looked, with a vexed expression of countenance, at Dick Doubleday and Handsome Jemmy.

"Aw—aw! What is it—aw—my good fellows?"

"What will you take for the horse?"

"Take—take! Aw—my horse is not for sale—aw—fellows—aw!"

"Oh, but it is, though!" said Jemmy, as he laid his hand upon the bridle. "And, now I think of it, you want to exchange that coat of yours for a red one."

"Are you mad?"

"Not at all, unless the wind goes to the north-east, and then I'm as mad as blazes."

"Aw—aw! Murder!"

"If you prefer it, certainly," said Handsome Jemmy, as he at once clapped the muzzle of a pistol to the eyes of the horseman. "Now, sir, will you sell that horse, or not?"

"Aw—yes, yes! Oh, don't—it may go off!"

"Will you take half-a-crown for your horse?"

"Half-a-crown?"

"Two shillings, then, and the odd sixpence for your coat?"

"Odd sixpence?"

"Well, eighteen pence, then, for the horse, and sixpence each for your coat and hat?"

The exquisite on the horse was getting bewildered at Handsome Jemmy's arithmetic. He put on a look of hopeless stupidity, and glared in the face of the highwayman as though he were seeking for ever to engrave his features on his memory.

"Now, Dick," said Handsome Jemmy. "Look sharp, will you, and let us be off. Your coat, sir."

The horseman took off his coat.

"Your hat, sir."

He took off his hat, which Jemmy put on; and Dick, not without some misgivings that the adventure might have calamitous results, exchanged coats and mounted the horse.

"There, sir," said the highwayman—"there is your money. Two shillings, you know; I don't want a receipt. Good day. If you ever want to see me again, you may find me on Bagshot Heath or Wormholt Scrubbs, and now and then on Putney Common. Good day! good day!"

"Aw—aw! It's a dweam—it's a dweam! I am not a bit awake! It's all a dweam—it's all a dweam!"

CHAPTER XII.

JACOB SHARPLES HAS A MYSTERIOUS VISITOR AT HIS "CRIB" IN CLERKENWELL

THE day had passed away—that day on which, but for the gallantry that had been displayed in her cause, and the series of accidents which had occurred in her favour, poor Pamela Sharples would have suffered death.

A cold wind whistled over London.

The biting rain which, when it does accompany a north-east wind, comes like points of steel, dashed in the face of a solitary pedestrian, who, crouching down before the blast, made his way along a gloomy, dilapidated thoroughfare of the oldest part of Clerkenwell.

That solitary man was Jacob Sharples.

Jacob Sharples, the coiner.

He seemed unable to stand upright. The events of the previous night had aged him considerably—the positive suffering and the terrible fright that the adventure in Fleet Ditch had inflicted upon him, had left their obvious traces behind them.

And now Sharples was facing that keen blast of wind, and the sharp-pointed rain, on his road to his house—his "crib," as he called it, at Clerkenwell.

His escape from the sewer had been little less than providential, but he felt that he had to pay for it.

The two gentlemen who had assisted him in that emergency of his fate were not likely to let slip his offers of ample remuneration.

Jacob Sharples expected them on that night.

Perhaps the groans, and sighs, and strange noises that came from his lips as he struggled onwards against the rain and the wind on that night, had some reference to the expected visit of the personages who had dragged him out of the Fleet.

But it was not until he had produced a key and

opened the door of the most squalid and dingy house in all that dilapidated street, that Jacob Sharples uttered any articulate words.

Then, as he made his way along a narrow, dark passage, he muttered his fears, his anger, his many apprehensions, and his hatreds.

"What will become of me now?—oh, what will become of me now?" he moaned. "What will become of me now? It's all very well to make the money : but who's to pass it? I daren't do so myself—it isn't that I'm afraid, only I don't like the danger ; and Pamela, too, knows all the secrets of the crib, and she isn't hanged, after all. Oh, dear! oh, dear! what shall I do, and what will become of me?"

Jacob Sharples stopped to groan and strike his breast. This he did like a man in the last extremity of despair.

Then in the same grumbling querulous tone he spoke again.

"It's very hard—it's very hard indeed! The girl was very useful to me, for nobody suspected her innocent face ; and many's the bad guinea and bad half-guinea she got off that nobody else would have had a chance of passing ; but now she's lost to me, and I'm alone—alone—alone!"

Jacob Sharples had reached the end of the narrow passage, and opening a door he entered a wretched apartment which was in the profoundest darkness, and to step into which seemed like making way into some damp, unwholesome cavern.

"Ah! the fire's out—the fire's out," he said ; "of course it's out. It's four-and-twenty hours since I was here, and a pretty wretched time I've passed. It seemed a week that that horrid trial lasted at the fence, and then a month—a whole month of agony in the sewer. Oh, dear! oh, dear! what—what will become of me?"

Jacob Sharples only thought of himself in all his groanings and grumblings : there was not one word of pity or commiseration for the young girl whom he would have left to die.

That wretched room in that dilapidated house must have been very familiar to Jacob Sharples ; for, intensely dark as it was, he stumbled over nothing, and soon the flickering flame of a match was hovering about the grate.

Jacob Sharples was lighting a fire.

And much he needed it, for he shuddered, and every limb was tortured with cold.

But the bright blaze which was soon dissipating the darkness and the coldness of the room, failed for a time to warm the half congealed blood of Jacob Sharples.

He shook, groaned, wept, and cowered over the fire he had made—holding out his thin shrivelled hands almost into the very flame, and still ever and anon muttering his discontent.

"She knows all now—she knows all now, and who knows but she may betray me? Oh, dear! oh, dear! when people know other people's secrets, it's just as well they should be hanged, and then they can't tell them."

Sharples then rose from his kneeling position from before the fire, and crawling to a cupboard in the room, he produced a small flask of ardent spirits, which he partook of in a very peculiar fashion.

He slowly poured the spirit on to some bread, so that it was soaked up before it had time to be lost upon the floor ; then he ate the bread, and it was evident that a stimulant thus exhibited revived him considerably.

As Jacob Sharples revived, he got more vicious.

At all events he expressed himself more vehemently and viciously.

"What do people mean by interfering with the law? Nobody would interfere and make a disturbance if I were taken up and about to be hanged. No, I'll warrant me they wouldn't. No Dick Doubledays nor Handsome Jemmys would risk life and limb for me. I might be hanged ten times over for all they'd care—ten times over. Yes, I've said it—ten times over!"

Bang! came a heavy knock at the street door.

Jacob Sharples dropped to the floor of the room as if all power of self-support had suddenly forsaken him.

"What's that? what's that?" he whispered ; "who's that? Has the girl betrayed me—peached—told all the secrets of the coiner's crib?—and have they come to drag me away to death—death on the scaffold—death on the Tyburn Tree? Mercy! Mercy! Have some mercy upon me. I know nothing about it. I'm not a coiner. Bless you, my Lord Judge, I'm a poor man—I'm a poor hard-working man ; and it's that girl Pamela who makes all the bad money, and then passes it, and spends it among highwaymen, and raffs, and bullies, my lord."

Bang! came the knock again.

Jacob Sharples crawled on all-fours into the passage.

He heard voices in the street.

A feeling of relief came over him as he did so ; for in those voices he recognised the voices of the two men who had fished him up from the Fleet Ditch.

Jacob was free of his fear that the officers of justice were on his track ; but the visit of those men was almost as bad, since they came for money for the reward he had so liberally promised them not to cast him back again into the noisome stream of the Fleet, from which in so awful a condition they had hauled him forth into the night cellar.

"More misfortunes—more misfortunes!" groaned Sharples. "Everything goes wrong. These wretches will never be satisfied. They will come again and again, and where am I to get money to give them when my own little store is exhausted? I've no Pamela now to pass the bad guineas and half-guineas, while people are looking at her pretty face instead of the coin."

The knock came a third time.

Jacob Sharples felt that he must open the door, for these continued demands for admission would excite more attention than was consistent with his safety.

He hastened along the passage and opened the door at once, for he had no doubt at all about the character of his visitors.

"Holloa, old Sharples!" cried one ; "have you been asleep? What do you mean by keeping two such gentlemen as we are waiting on your doorstep?"

"Ha, ha!" laughed the other. "So this is the old mouldy crib, is it? You must make a pretty good thing of coining, Sharples, or you would never be able to live in this style."

The two housebreakers burst into a hoarse laugh at this sally ; and Jacob Sharples, if he had had the courage to attempt such an act, had all the inclination at that moment to take both their lives rather than hand them over a single farthing of his ill-gotten wealth.

"I'm a poor man—I'm a poor man!" he said—"a very poor man! and you're disposed to be merry, I see."

"Why didn't you say that when we fished you out of the Fleet? We could easily have put you in again. But that's all stuff, you know! We've come for our money ; and we mean to have it, don't we, Dainty Diamond?"

"In course, Diggles, we does, or else we'll know the reason why!"

"Oh, certainly—oh, certainly, dear, kind friends! I'm sure the few guineas I can give you, you're welcome to."

"Few guineas? Stuff! A hatful, man—a hatful! Didn't he say a hatful, Dainty!"

"In course he did, and he's only jokin' now."

"Jokin'!" screamed Sharples—"jokin'! I jokin', that never joked in my life! Jokin' about money, too! Ha! ha! ha! ha! I've an idea—an idea!"

"What?" cried the housebreakers.

"I've an idea. Come this way. There's a fire here. I hope you'll take some refreshment,—that is to say, when you leave, for I've none here to offer you ; but I've an idea. Follow me—follow me! I wonder I didn't think of it before."

Sharples, with considerable alacrity, now made his way down the passage, and flung open the door of the room in which he had lit the fire.

He was closely followed by Dainty Diamond and Diggles, who could not imagine what the idea was that had so suddenly put him into good spirits.

They were not kept long in suspense.

"Listen to me," said Sharples, as the flame of the fire played upon his pinched-up, eager countenance,—"listen to me—listen to me. I can make any amount of bad money you like to name, and you shall both pass it, and we'll— we'll—— Well, come now, we'll share the profits. Murder!—help!—don't!"

The reply of the two burglars to this proposition was very practical.

Dainty Diamond seized Jacob Sharples by the scanty hair of his head, and Diggles produced a long clasp-knife, which he opened with wonderful speed and dexterity.

"Settle him!" cried Dainty Diamond.

"I mean to."

"No, no! Mercy—mercy! Good, kind pals, have mercy! I was jokin', after all! I do make a joke sometimes! I was only jokin', after all! You shall have the gold—real gold—good honest gold! You shall have it—you shall have it. But you can't get it without me, for it's hidden; and you'd never find it in a twelvemonth's search."

"Be quick about it, then."

"I will—I will—I will—I will! Don't be so impatient. I must leave you here a little while."

"No, you don't."

"I must—I must!"

"But I say you don't. How do we know, Diggles, but there's some trap or another in the cellars of this house, that leads to the sewers? He's used to that sort of game No, old Sharples, if it's any comfort to you to know, we don't mean to lose sight of you!"

"I'm ruined! I'm ruined!"

"What do you mean?"

"Kill me! kill me!"

"Oh, very well! We ain't nice to a shade or two, are we. Diggles?"

"Not a bit of it, Dainty."

Jacob Sharples stretched his arms above his head, and in a despairing voice cried out, "They will know all—they will know all, and I shall be at their mercy. This house and the next one are very old, and are both uninhabited except by me. The next one is condemned, and no one ever crosses its threshold. This one I pay a trifle to be allowed to live in; but I've established a connexion between the two, and that's where I carry on my operations, so that when the traps have come here to nab me, they've found nothing—nothing—nothing!"

"What's all that to us? what do we care where you carry on your sneaking business? It's the money we want."

"Follow me, then—and you shall have it. I have trusted you with all now You can ruin me if you like, but it will do you no good—not a bit of good."

"Who said it would? Do you think everybody's as bad as you are? We haven't left our daughters to be hung, have we?"

"Hush! hush! Follow—follow. I will get a light The condemned house shakes a little, and two stairs in the middle of the first flight are gone. Its an ugly hole. I will get a light—a light."

From the cupboard where he had so recently procured the stimulant that had given him new life, Jacob Sharples produced a small hand-lantern, which having lighted by the fire, he carried before him; and then uttering sundry groans, he left that miserable apartment, closely followed by the two housebreakers, who, as they went, exchanged glances with each other expressive of caution.

They had a tolerably clear conception on their minds that Jacob Sharples would not hesitate at any means by which he could get rid of such troublesome creditors.

They had abundant confidence, however, in their own cunning, which they thought was fully a match for that of the coiner; and they had that appreciation of

his cowardice which assured them they had nothing to fear from downright violence.

The door of the room, in which there was a fire, swung slowly shut—making a whining, creaking noise upon its hinges as it did so.

The flickering flame in the grate was subsiding as the wood which Sharples had flung upon the fire became nearly burnt through.

But still there was a flickering sort of radiance which fell upon the dingy, grimy walls of the apartment—showing where long strips of what had once been a fancy sort of paper had peeled off from the damp plaster; and showing, too, that the wretched home of the coiner boasted but of one table and two ricketty chairs—while a dark mass of frowsy-looking blankets and linen in a corner might represent a bed.

All this the flame of the fire flickered upon for a few seconds, and then there was another low creaking sound of some door upon its hinges.

But it was not the door by which the coiner and the two burglars had left the room.

Another door in one of the side walls had slowly opened, and with a gliding motion a tall figure entered, and made its way to one side of the fireplace, where it stood gaunt and erect, and still as a statue.

If Dick Doubleday and Handsome Jemmy, the highwayman, had seen that figure with the face entirely concealed by the hood of an ample cloak, the skirts of which swept the floor, they would have recognised it as the same that had excited their surprise at Mother Bendydykes'.

CHAPTER XIII.

THE COURT PHYSICIAN MAKES A CONFIDENTIAL COMMUNICATION TO PAMELA.

PAMELA strained her eyes from the coach window, after she had entered Doctor Haslem's carriage, in order that she might see the last of Dick Doubleday, as he and Handsome Jemmy, the highwayman, galloped off in the direction of Tottenham Court Road.

She stretched her hands out of the coach, as she cried out through her tears, "Never again, perhaps!—never again! and they have saved me! Oh, how much have they risked for me!"

Pamela then leant back in the carriage, and relieved her overcharged heart by a plentiful flood of tears.

Doctor Haslem looked pale and agitated.

It was some time before he could command voice to speak, and when he did so it was in a tremulous fashion, which betrayed deep emotion.

"My dear girl," he said, "I wish to ask you some few questions."

"Sir?"

"But I do not wish you to reply to them if they should distress you."

Pamela looked with so much innocence and beauty into the face of the Court Physician, that he could not stand the gaze, but, sighing deeply, he cast down his eyes as he said, "Your name is Pamela Sharples?"

"Yes, yes."

"And—and your father—is—your father ——"

"He never loved me, and he left me to die!"

"He is a coiner?"

"They say so. I hardly know what it means. I did not know at all what it meant until I was told in that dreadful prison of Newgate."

"Is it possible?"

"What, sir?"

"That you could reside with your father, Jacob Sharples, and not know the sort of business he carried on?"

"It is so, sir. My father lives in a very old house in Clerkenwell He seemed poor—very poor; and yet we never wanted for anything actually. He always had gold, with which he would send me out to purchase what was wanted, and I did so, bringing him the change. I was not happy, though!"

" I fancy not. Do you remember far back ?"

" Yes—oh, yes !"

" When you were a little—little——" The Doctor seemed half choked before he could pronounce the word " child."

" Oh, yes !—quite well."

" But Jacob Sharples was not then your father ?"

" Yes, yes—always Jacob Sharples and old Martha."

" Old Martha ? Who was she ?"

Pamela shook her head.

" I don't know, sir. I never knew. But when I was a little child I remember her; she lived with us—with Jacob Sharples, my father, and me—but one day she left us, and since then I have never seen or heard of her."

" Was that long ago ?"

" Oh, so long—so many years !"

The Court Physician sighed, and a shadowy smile crossed his face to hear one just on the very threshold almost of life, as Pamela was, talk of something as many years ago, in which she had herself been in any way concerned.

The carriage had by this time reached Bedford Square, and drew up at the door of the Doctor's house

There came a look of extreme care over the face of the physician, as the carriage door was opened for him to alight.

" Do not speak to any one," he said, " but follow me!"

" Yes," replied Pamela.

She stepped from the coach, and keeping close to the Doctor, she entered his large, handsome hall.

The servants looked at each other, and wondered what all this could mean. The footman whispered to the coachman, and the hall-porter ran out to hear what they both had to say about it

Pamela, in obedience to a side-long glance from the Court Physician, followed him into a spacious room on the ground floor.

The walls of this room were covered with bookshelves. Indeed, there did not seem to be the least available space that had not volumes upon volumes of books crowded into it.

A thick, soft Turkey carpet covered the floor, and heavy curtains shaded the windows

The library had, take it for all in all, a dark, sombre look about it.

The day was young, and yet but few of its beams penetrated into that apartment.

A gloom fell upon the spirits of Pamela as she crossed the threshold.

Doctor Haslem had paused to allow her to follow him; but when she had done so, and reached some dozen paces into the library, he passed her, and closed the door himself, making it fast by a small brass bolt that was beneath the ordinary lock.

Pamela looked a little surprised, but there was not the smallest taint of alarm in her manner as she looked at the Doctor.

Then the Court Physician took her by the hand, and led her to a chair.

" Rest, my dear girl," he said, " while I speak to you."

Tears were in his eyes.

" Ah, sir !" said Pamela, " you suffer ! Are you in pain ?—or, alas, alas ! do you regret what you have so kindly done to save me ?"

" No, no—a thousand times, no !"

" But you weep !"

" A moment—only a moment. Give me a moment and I shall be myself again."

The Court Physician paced the room, and wrung his hands as he did so; and then he struck his breast, and in a low, moaning voice he said, " The same date—this day twelve years ago—twelve long years. Oh, what suffering !"

" Sir—sir ! You are unhappy !"

" Unhappy !"

The tone in which Doctor Haslem uttered the word was such as to let Pamela feel at once she was far from

expressing the depth of misery and wretchedness that found a home in his heart by the word unhappy.

" Ah, dear sir !" she said, hastily. " Pardon me; I fear that it is my presence here that adds to your unhappiness."

" No, no! Oh, no !"

" Because—because if it be so, I will go at once, and find what shelter I may."

Pamela shuddered as she spoke.

" Not with Jacob Sharples," said the Court Physician, in a sharp, pained voice.

" Oh, no, no! Never again !"

" That is well—that is well. No, my poor girl, you shall not be thrown upon the wide world. You shall find comfort and safety here."

" You are too good, sir !"

" Hush! hush! Do not say that."

" But it is very good and kind of you. I did not think any one would love me but—but——"

" But who ?"

" Dick Doubleday !"

" That is the young man who played the part of the King's messenger ?"

" Yes."

" And brought the seeming pardon ?"

" Was it not signed by the King ?"

" It was, but it was a pardon for another—not for you. I don't think, however, that all the world can harm you now."

A clatter of horses' feet in Bedford Square at this moment attracted the attention of both the Court Physician and Pamela.

She sprung to her feet.

The Doctor turned paler than before.

" Hush! hush !"

" Oh, sir, what is it ?"

" I will see in a moment."

Doctor Haslem quietly approached one of the windows, and glanced out.

Mr. Grogrum and his party of mounted officers were at the door of the house.

" Pamela," said the Court Physician, " will you trust to me ?"

" I will, sir—I do."

" By some means, the constables have——"

Bang—bang—bang ! came three heavy knocks at the outer door.

" Discovered that you are here," continued the Court Physician, paying no attention whatever to the interruption of the knocks.

Pamela clasped her hands together.

" I am lost !"

" No !"

" They will drag me to death, for I was not pardoned."

" No !"

The tone in which Doctor Haslem said " No," rather surprised Pamela; but she kept her eyes upon him, and she saw that while he was as pale as death itself, and while his hands trembled painfully, he approached the chimney-piece of the room.

Low down on that kind of iron-work which goes by the name of " fire dogs" there burnt in the grate, or rather on the hearth, some odoriferous wood.

The heat given forth was but slight, and only now and then a slight flickering flame curled up the ample chimney.

Above the chimney-piece was a curtain of crimson velvet, which reached up to the ceiling, and then ran upon a rod of gilded brass.

This curtain hung in heavy plaits or folds, and its lower edge touched the chimney-piece, while its surface rested close to the wall.

Raising both his hands, and uttering a cry as he did so—a cry that seemed to come from the depths of his heart—the physician seized the curtain, and with a sudden jerk ran it on one side.

The full-length portrait of a lady was disclosed immediately behind the curtain.

JACOB SHARPLES AND THE CLOAKED FIGURE.

This portrait occupied the whole of the panel from the top of the chimney-piece to the ceiling of the room.

It did not form the actual panel, for there was a gilt frame about it; and yet it seemed, by the way in which it was fastened there, to be a fixture, and perfectly immoveable.

There was a fascinating grace, a beauty of expression, that was irresistibly winning about the features and general expression of this portrait.

A profusion of beautiful fair hair hung in disorder about the neck and shoulders, and the lady seemed to be looking out of the panel right into the eyes of the spectator.

The dress was such a costume as a lady might wear who was walking in a garden

A hat, in which there was a long drooping feather, hung by one of its strings to her arm.

A hooded cloak of fair blue silk was her outer garment, and there were trees and flowers in the background of the picture.

The Court Physician clasped his hands so tightly together, after he had removed the curtain that concealed this portrait, that the white, rigid knuckles stood in bold and painful relief.

He shrunk down—he cowered down before the eyes of the picture, as though it had been a living thing that could reproach him.

He uttered a half-scream of mental agony, and then, rocking to and fro, he clasped both his hands over his brow, as he spoke mournfully : " The wound rankles still—rankles still. I can never, never forget!"

A tap came at the door of the room.

Pamela heard it.

But Doctor Haslem had raised his eyes, and was looking at the portrait: he heard nothing, saw nothing, but that painted likeness of one whom he had not looked upon for twelve years in life.

The tap came again at the door.

Pamela spoke.

" Sir, sir!—some one!"

He did not heed her.

She touched him on the arm.

He started to his feet.

Then the tap at the door came a third time, and he heard it.

" Quick! quick!" he said in a whisper; " quick, and you are saved!"

There was a massive old arm-chair close to the fireplace, and upon it the Doctor stood in another moment, and with both his hands he pressed on the lower part of the frame of the portrait.

To the surprise of Pamela, who had never dreamt of such a thing, the whole panel, portrait and all, with the gilt frame, revolved on its centre.

There was an opening on each side of the picture, which now only presented its edge to the view.

" Fly! fly!" said the physician; " you will see some steps. They go upwards, through the thickness of the wall, to the floor above. When you reach the top of them, wait for me."

Pamela shrank back, more in surprise than in fear; but the Court Physician thought it was from the latter feeling.

" Be not afraid," he said; " there is no danger. The way is perfectly safe. I will account for your absence in some way; but this is the only means to save you."

The confused sound of voices came from the hall of the house.

Then there came a rap at the door of the library, that was of a very different character from those that had preceded it, and which had been, no doubt, produced by the Doctor's own servants.

This sharper rap, however, was from the hilt of the hanger of Mr. Grogram.

" In the name of the law," cried Grogram; " in the name of the law, open this door!"

" Quick!" whispered the Doctor.

Pamela felt her danger. She knew the voice of Grogram, and she was certain she had no pity to expect from him.

With that intuitive quickness of perception which was a feature in her character, she saw what she had to do instantly.

She sprung on to the chair, on to the chimney-piece, and then passed like a spirit through the opening that was nearest to her past the face of the portrait.

A narrow, dark-looking flight of stairs were before her to the right

" Away! away!" said the physician.

The panel was closed—the curtain was drawn over the portrait again.

The door of the room shook from a kick that Mr. Grogram gave it, and then Doctor Haslem went and drew the little bolt.

Grogram fell headlong into the room.

He had happened, just at the moment that the Court Physician drew the bolt, to have stepped back a few paces, in order to come against the door with all his force, and burst it open; and the suddenness with which it gave way before him precipitated him half-way to the middle of the floor.

" What outrage is this?" said Doctor Haslem.

Mr. Grogram rolled completely over ; and it was a wonder he did not severely hurt himself with his own hanger.

" Help!—help! Come on, comrades!—come on!"

The other constables made a rush into the room ; and Mr. Grogram, scrambling to his feet, glared about him like an enraged tiger.

" You will have to answer for all this, Doctor Haslem," he said, " as sure as my name is Grogram."

" I am very glad, sir, that I do know your name is Grogram," replied the physician; " for I am determined I will make you answer—and that to some purpose—for this outrage "

Grogram looked puzzled as he turned round twice upon his heels, and saw no one but the Doctor in the library.

" It's no go, Mr. Grogram," said Bates.

" Hold your noise!"

Bates shrunk back.

" If you are police-constables," said the physician, " may I ask the cause of this intrusion?"

" Yes, sir."

" Well, sir?"

" We want Pamela Sharples, and we will have her!"

" Who?"

" Pamela Sharples "

The physician shook his head; and then, assuming a puzzled look, he said, " My good fellow, you don't take me for Pamela—what's her name that you mention?"

" No, sir, but you took her up into your carriage in Guildford Street, and brought her here; and Tyburn Tree waits for her, I can tell you, for all her pretty face, that seems to bewitch all sorts of people."

Grogram looked significantly at the physician, as he considered he gave him rather a hard hit then about the pretty face of Pamela, which might be supposed to be the inducement for the interference of any one in her favour.

" Oh! I know who you mean now."

" That's satisfactory, sir."

" You mean a young girl?"

" I do."

" With fair hair ?"

" Just so, Doctor."

" Oh, then, she paid me my fee, and I showed her out of this room myself."

" Your fee ?"

" Yes She had a fancy that her chest was affected; but I think not; so she has gone away more contented, I suppose, and happy than she came. She has been gone some time."

" Confound it, Doctor! Didn't you know that was Pamela Sharples, the young girl who was to suffer this morning for passing bad money, eh?"

Doctor Haslem shook his head with an assumption of

great gravity, as he calmly sat down by his writing-table.

"It is nothing to me," he said, "as a physician, who or what people are who come to me for advice. My consulting-room is perfectly free; and it is a piece of etiquette in my profession not to ask any unnecessary questions. All I have to do is with the health of people who call here—their morals are quite another matter."

Grogrum looked provoked.

He still glared round the room, for his suspicions that the Doctor had by some means secreted Pamela were by no means allayed; and if nothing else had awakened those suspicions, the length of time that he had been kept at the door would have been quite sufficient to do so.

But where could any one hide in that library?

Books—nothing but books—books everywhere! From the ceiling to the floor, nothing but books!

Grogrum paced the whole length of the apartment, for the express purpose of casting his ferret eyes behind each heavy window-curtain.

No Pamela was there.

Doctor Haslem rose with an air of offended dignity.

"If, Mr. Goggles, or whatever your name may be," he said, "your business here is over, I shall be particularly obliged by your leaving my house; and you may be assured that I shall ascertain exactly who and what you are, so that I may make a complaint of you to the proper authorities."

"Do as you like, sir," said Grogrum, insolently. "I'm doing my duty."

Flinging open, then, the library door, he called out to the hall-porter.

"Hillos, you fellow! When did you see the young woman pass out that the Doctor brought home in his carriage, for he says she didn't?"

"No more she didn't," said the hall porter. "No young woman has passed out of here."

"Ah, Doctor!" said Grogrum, turning round with a triumphant grin to the Court Physician; "what do you say to that?"

Doctor Haslem walked into the hall, and looking the porter in the face, he said to him, with calm asperity, "This shows how you invariably neglect your duty; for if you had not left the hall you must have seen me come to the door myself with the young person in question, and let her out."

"I—I did, Doctor, now I recollect. If you please, sir, I did see you. I was unmindful at the moment, but I recollect it perfectly now."

The Court Physician looked full in the face of Grogrum, the constable, but he did not condescend to utter a word.

A ghastly grin was upon Grogrum's face as he made a bow of the most mock solemnity and reverence; and then, without a word, he left the house, closely followed by his myrmidons, who were rather abashed at the whole proceeding, for their veneration for a Court Physician was much greater than Mr. Grogrum's.

CHAPTER XIV.

JACOB SHARPLES IS COMPELLED TO RELATE AN EPISODE IN HIS EARLIER CAREER.

THE spectral-looking figure that had taken up its station by the hearth of Jacob Sharples, while he so unwillingly accompanied his new acquaintances, Dainty Diamond and Diggles, to the condemned house, moved neither hand nor foot, but stood tall, gaunt, and shadowy in the flickering light that occasionally shot up from the wood fire.

The hood of the cloak in which this figure was enveloped must have had two small apertures in it, for now and then the gleaming light of two eyes was visible.

And then the folds would fall again over the glittening orbs, and all would be still, blank, and motionless.

Once, and once only, did one of those deep moaning sounds which the figure had uttered, when discovered by Dick Doubleday and the highwayman at Mother Bendydykes', come apparently from the depths of its afflicted heart.

It was quite evident that whether this appearance were human or belonging to a world beyond the grave, it still had the faculty of feeling.

But it was only once that this mortal moan came from beneath the heavy folds of that robe or cloak which took so much of the character of a monk's habit, with which it was enveloped.

Five minutes—ten minutes—a quarter of an hour passed away, and the figure was still alone.

Once, and once only, a low rumbling sound came from the next house.

Something that might have been considered a half-stifled shriek immediately followed that sound.

All was then still again.

Still as death.

Then the door of the apartment opened—that same door through which Jacob Sharples had left it with the two burglars—and the coiner staggered into the room.

He was alone.

His hands were clenched; his hair was in wild disorder about his face.

There was a spot of blood upon his cheek.

Staggering like one under the influence of potent stimulants, Jacob Sharples reached that apartment, and then fell prostrate on the floor.

In the dim, uncertain light from the fire, which had nearly smouldered away, he had not observed the visitor that was waiting for him; but as he fell, it was at the feet of the spectral-looking person in the cloak, and his head nearly touched the hem of the long garment which enveloped the seeming apparition.

Jacob Sharples lay as if dead, or as if some swoon, which bore so close a resemblance to death that it might be considered its twin-brother, had swept over him.

There was a slight gesture upon the part of the cloaked figure—a gesture of impatience; and then it spoke.

"Jacob Sharples—Jacob Sharples—Jacob Sharples!"

The coiner's head rose a little from the floor.

The seeming apparition spoke again.

"Jacob Sharples—Jacob Sharples—Jacob Sharples!"

The coiner supported himself on his hands, then upon his knees; and in that posture, flinging his head and body as far back as possible, he saw and faced the cloaked figure.

He uttered a shriek of dismay.

"Jacob Sharples, as you value the poor remains of that life which men like you cling to as a chief possession, answer to that which I shall ask of you, as you would answer to that Providence which will one day ask a question of you, which will appal your shrinking soul to answer."

The hair bristled on Jacob Sharples' head. His face became livid with fear, and his teeth chattered together.

"Jacob Sharples, where is Lavinia Haslem?"

Another cry came from the lips of the coiner, but it was inarticulate.

"Where is Lavinia Haslem?" repeated the figure. "Speak, wretch! or you may count the fevered pulses of your heart; for, perchance, one minute more, and then the computation ceases."

Jacob Sharples found his voice. The prospect, the dread, the promise of death appalled him.

"I will tell all—I will tell all!" he screamed. "Only spare me, and I will tell all! The child lives—the child lives! No, I cannot say that it lives, and yet—and yet—there are those who love her, and who have sworn to save her. She lives! she lives! But there is one guiltier than I! You—you—if you come from that world where all things are known that human beings lock up in their secret hearts, while those hearts beat—you know that there is one guiltier than I!"

A deep groan came from the figure.

"Jacob Sharples, you are asked one question. Were you the man who, twelve years ago, on a night of storm and tempest, put off alone in a wherry from the Bishop's Walk, at Lambeth?"

"I was—I was—I—I was that man."

"Did you wait while the tide of the Thames rushed in eddying whirlpools through the old arches of Westminster,—did you there wait for another boat, in which there was a woman and a child?"

Jacob Sharples seemed choking; but by a great effort, he managed to say, "I did—I was that man!"

"Well?"

"You—you want to know—you do know, but you want me to say—that is, you ask me to confess what—what became of that woman and that child?"

"I do."

"She—she lies deep! It is twelve years now; and the body——"

"Wretch! is it of the child, or of its companion, you now speak?"

"The woman—the woman! She had gold—jewels; she—she slipped—slipped! The night was dark, and the wind howled. The blinding rain was baffling and terrible. She found rest in the rolling, heaving tide. She —she lies there still!"

"Murderer!"

"There is one guiltier than I—guiltier than I!"

"Murderer!"

"Mercy, mercy!"

"For your soul's sake—for the conservation of that one atom of mercy which may be extended to you, answer what I shall ask of you."

"I will, I will! I swear I will! By—by——"

"You cannot say it. The word 'heaven' sticks in your throat, Jacob Sharples. But you will answer; fear, and not devotion, wrings the truth from you."

"I will answer."

"Is Pamela Sharples, as you name her, the child whom, on that night of terror and tempest, you met in that boat upon the Thames?"

"She is."

"And no daughter of yours?"

"Mine?—mine? I never had a daughter."

"It is enough."

A yell burst from the throat of Jacob Sharples, for at that moment, as if the words spoken by the mysterious visitor had been the signal for the act, a violent explosion took place among the smouldering embers of the fire.

The remains of the rusted grate were blown into the apartment—a volley of soot descended the chimney— and half-blinded, and burnt in many places by the dull red embers of the wood that flew out upon him, Jacob Sharples ran shrieking into the passage of the house, and from thence gaining the street, he awakened the echoes of the night by his wild cries; and many a sleeper, awakening terrified, wondered what maniac was abroad, howling, yelling, and spreading consternation in his path.

Jacob Sharples fell.

A soft rain was descending, and it not only quenched the particles of glowing embers that had lodged in his apparel, but it brought coolness to his brow, and, after a time, something like peace and composure to his heart.

The monotonous patter of the rain had so careless and composed a sound, that it insensibly exerted its influence over the shattered nerves of the coiner.

He slowly struggled to his feet

"A dream—a dream!" he said. "Surely this is all a dream?"

Some clock struck twelve.

Jacob Sharples counted the sounds.

"So late—so late! A dream—surely it was all a dream! And yet—and yet—that terrible figure—that awful visitant! Yes, it was twelve years ago that some one came to me, and told me that if I took a wherry at the Bishop's Walk, at Lambeth, and went out

upon the Thames, I should meet, coming through the third arch of Westminster Bridge, another boat, in which would be a woman and a child. I—I was to carry them to shore, and then to receive a handful of gold for my pains. But the woman had costly jewels on her. I saw the rubies glow like flame—I saw the diamonds glitter like dew-drops in the sun. I—I took all, and the Thames kept the secret! But the child— the little child, clung to me, and I could not—I—I— could not drown the child! It lived—lived with me, Jacob Sharples—in want, in misery; and it grew in beauty—but it never loved me—never! never! never!"

The coiner was shuffling and staggering through the streets, towards his house again, as, with many moans, he whispered this confession to himself.

"No, no! she never loved me, but she called me 'father;' and from the name of a book that I saw in a shop-window, I called her Pamela. But I found a name upon her clothes, and that name was Lavinia Haslem. Haslem! Haslem! Fear has kept me as yet from mentioning that name!"

CHAPTER XV.

HANDSOME JEMMY ADVISES DICK DOUBLEDAY TO TRY HIS FORTUNES ON THE ROAD.

"DICK," said the highwayman, after he and Dick Doubleday had gallopped some distance from the spot where the horse had been purchased of the exquisite so decidedly a bargain,—"Dick, what do you mean to do?"

Doubleday drew rein, and looked Handsome Jemmy in the face, as he replied, "In what, dear friend?—in what way?"

"Can't you guess?"

"Ah, yes!—Pamela. It is in regard to Pamela you mean?"

The highwayman whistled.

"Is it not so?"

"I confess, Dick, it was not. I did not at that moment think of the dear girl. You don't mind me calling her a dear girl?"

"Not a bit!"

"Then it was not of her, but of yourself, Dick, that I was thinking."

"Of me?"

"Even of you, Dick. What do you mean to do? How do you mean to live?"

Dick Doubleday sighed.

"What have you been doing?"

"Nothing, Jemmy."

"Well, you couldn't do much less; but I suppose you have lived somehow?"

"Yes; my uncle Zachariah has supported me, and I suppose you know who and what he is?"

"The most notorious old—— Well, Dick, I won't hurt your feelings by abusing your uncle. He calls himself a diamond merchant, don't he?"

"He does"

"And he deals in whatever he can get hold of, of any portable value, preferring gold and pearls, of both of which he is a capital judge. He keeps an old smoke-dried looking shop in Long Lane, close to Smithfield— a shop that no one would go into willingly, it looks so dark and so dreary; and there, like some old, brown, hairy spider, at the end of a web, he catches all the game he can."

"It is true!"

"And there, Dick, you vegetated—there you had a life of darkness and misery."

"Yes—until——"

"Until when?"

"I saw Pamela."

"Ah, that indeed! But you don't mean to tell me, Dick, that that pretty creature ever crossed the threshold of old Zachariah's house? House! why do I call it a house?—den, I mean!"

"I will tell you, Dick. Oh, well do I remember the

PAMELA AT THE PHYSICIAN'S HOUSE.

day! It was a morning of gloom in the bleak month of March. The wind whistled through the pens of old Smithfield, and there was a threatening mist in the air when the sun broke and dazzled me!"

"Eh?"

"I was in my uncle's shop, all alone, when the door opened, and two diamonds came in."

"Two what?"

"They were the eyes of Pamela."

"Oh, go on!"

"I was fascinated. From that moment I loved—I adored her. She came with a message from her father to my uncle Zachariah. Jacob Sharples had met with an accident in some of his processes for making base metal look like real gold, and was compelled to remain at home half blinded, so he had sent Pamela on a message to my uncle."

"So! so! The coiner and the old diamond merchant transacted business together?"

"It would seem so, Dick, although until then I did not know it. Pamela looked at me, and the triumph of her beauty was complete. I hardly heard what she said, but I suppose she asked for my uncle; and I suppose, too, she saw what a state of maze I was in, for she laughed in that happy, gentle way, which I fear I shall never, never hear again!"

Dick Doubleday pressed one hand over his eyes, and sighed.

"Nonsense!" cried Handsome Jemmy. "Nonsense, Dick! You will see her, and hear her laugh many a time, yet. Keep a light heart. Hang care. It killed a cat; and it would kill all the cats that old Mother Bendydykes ever kept. Cheer up! What happened next?"

"I don't know."

"Ha! ha! ha! You don't know I suppose you told her you loved her?"

"No! no! But she left the shop, and I recollect I snatched up my hat, and went after her; and then she stopped and asked me if I had any message to Jacob Sharples; and I suppose I said I had, for I walked to his house with her. It's in Clerkenwell."

"I know."

"And then I saw him for the first time; and the message he gave me was to the effect that I was to tell my uncle Zachariah that he thought he should be able to do what he wanted."

"What was it, Dick?"

"I never knew. I had no curiosity. From that day I had no eyes but to look at Pamela—no ears but to listen to her. I was living, breathing but for her. Dear—dear Pamela!"

"Well, Dick, your uncle is an old rogue, no doubt, and deals with the 'family' whenever they have anything of uncommon value to part with. I daresay he and Sharples, the coiner, understood each other perfectly well; but that sort of work don't suit you."

"No—oh, no!"

"You are a lad of spirit."

Dick smiled.

"You have a good horse now, and you will want money. Come, now, what say you, Dick, to the highly honourable course of a knight of the road? Suppose we hunt in couples? It's dreary work on a common all alone by oneself. Suppose you and I cry 'Stand and deliver!' in partnership? What say you, Dick—is it a bargain?"

Dick Doubleday hesitated.

"Come, come! Don't spoil half a mind!"

"Jemmy, what will Pamela say?"

"Say? Oh, she will say what any girl in the world, who is a real girl and has a real girl's heart in her bosom, would say—that she prefers a bold fellow who gets his living on the highway, to a sneak who only deals in other folks' plunder, like your old uncle Zachariah."

A flush of colour came over the face of Dick Doubleday.

"Jemmy, do you think I could carry on your trade, and Pamela not know it?"

"She need not know it till you tell her."

"And I might get money enough to enable me some day to call her my own."

"To be sure!"

"I will do it!"

"Bravo! bravo! You are well mounted, and all you want is some little alteration in dress and a couple of pairs of pistols, and you are equipped for the road, and will look as gallant a fellow as ever cried 'Stand!' to a traveller, or politely requested a bevy of fair ladies in a coach to 'lend you' their rings and trinkets."

There was a look upon the face of Dick Doubleday which had something of pride in it, and something of perplexity. It was not exactly the sort of trade he would willingly have taken up, that of a knight of the road.

But the cogitations of Dick were suddenly cut short by Handsome Jemmy in a very summary manner. He took hold of the arm of Doubleday, and turning his own horse's head to the right, where the road they were on was bounded by a thick hedge, he cried aloud, "Jump, Dick! jump!"

"Where? what? how?"

"Leap!"

"The horse? the hedge?"

"Just so. Your horse will take the leap easily, if you can keep your seat. Did you ever try that sort of thing?"

"Never!"

"Hold, then! hold!"

Dick Doubleday was resolved that in the opinion of Handsome Jemmy he should not suffer from any accusation of timidity; and, although a leap on horseback was a thing that was perfectly new to him, he resolved to take it.

The horse, however, seemed to be an adept at such business, for he took the hedge in good style.

Dick was half off and half on the creature's back when they reached the field which was on the other side of the hedge.

"Well done! well done!" cried Jemmy. "Now, Dick, you see the reason."

"What is the reason?"

"There—behold!"

A heavy old lumbering coach was being drawn down the narrow by-road which Dick Doubleday and Handsome Jemmy had been quietly pursuing at a trot.

The coachman was fat, plethoric, and idle-looking. The horses were starved and lean, and there was no footman behind the vehicle.

In fact, there was an unfitness and incongruous look about the whole affair, which made Handsome Jemmy look at it with some surprise.

But Dick Doubleday uttered an exclamation when he saw this ancient coach with its two lean horses, and its fat driver.

"What's the matter, Dick?"

"I know that coach!"

"You do?"

"Yes, Jemmy. It belongs to old Sir Moss Bond!"

"And who the dev——I mean, who may he be, Dick?"

"A friend of my uncle's."

"Ha, ha!"

"Yes; but how or why they are such good friends, I never knew. Sir Moss Bond, as he is called, lives in one of those big, old red-brick houses on Kennington Green; and he comes about once a month to my uncle's place in London, and they have together a long consultation in a room, the door of which they lock on the inside."

"Two old rogues!"

"Well, Jemmy, I should not wonder."

"I am sure of it, Dick. Do you feel inclined now to try your hand upon an adventure?"

"How do you mean?"

"Go and stop that carriage, and make the two old rascals within it deliver to you all that they have about them of any value. Take one of my pistols—take this mask of crape: it's a pretty one, with an edge of lace to it. Ha, ha! I took it from before the pretty face of a fair lady at Vauxhall, at the last masquerade. You have still the red coat of the King's messenger, and if you pull your hat down over your brows, who will know you?"

A bright flush of colour came to the cheeks of Dick Doubleday.

"You will do it?"

"I will."

"That's right; I shall make a man of you yet. We shall find a gap in the hedge, I see, a little lower down, through which you can make your way. All you have to do is to rest your pistol barrel on the window-ledge of the carriage, and make your demand. But since you are rather new at this sort of thing, Dick, I will look after the coachman for you."

"Do, Jemmy, do."

"Come on, then."

The bright flush of colour faded from the face of Dick Doubleday, as he followed Handsome Jemmy towards a gap in the hedge.

"Halt, Dick; this will do! The old concern they call a coach will be opposite to us in another minute."

"Yes, yes."

"Cool and steady, Dick—keep cool!"

"I will—I will!"

Dick Doubleday adjusted the mask to his face. He buttoned the topmost button of the scarlet coat he wore, so that it was quite close beneath his chin, and he pulled down to the very top of his eyebrows the hat he had on.

The old lumbering coach swayed to and fro on the somewhat jagged and uneven road; and Handsome Jemmy had almost the word upon his lips which he was about to cry out to the coachman, when to his surprise, as well as to that of Dick Doubleday, a loud shouting voice from the field over the hedge on the other side of the way, entirely took, so to speak, the word out of Jemmy's mouth.

"Halt! Stand, or a bullet in your brain!"

"Cuss you!" said the fat coachman. "What do you mean?"

The reply was conveyed in the sharp report of a pistol, and the fat coachman rolled off the coach-box, first head foremost on to the backs of the two lean horses, and then executing a surprising summersault, he alighted on his back in the road.

Handsome Jemmy was astonished.

Dick Doubleday was confounded.

It was by the impulse of the moment that they both drew back their horses under cover of the thick, unbroken part of the hedge, so that they were, to a certain extent at least, out of sight of the person who had apparently shot the coachman.

"By Jove!" said Handsome Jemmy, "this is what may be called taking the bread out of a fellow's mouth!"

"We are too late," said Dick.

"It looks like it. Who the deuce can that fellow be? It's true that I am out of my own track here; but I did not know that another gentleman of our profession made this green lane his haunt, and in broad daylight, too."

The horses in the coach did not attempt to move on after the fall of their driver. They were poor, spiritless creatures; and with the reins partially hanging on their backs, and partially trailing on the ground, they quietly rubbed their heads against each other, and stood still.

Then over the top of the thorn hedge on the other side of the way there appeared a head and face.

The head wore a three-cornered black beaver hat, tied round with dark red cord.

The face was covered with a mask of pasteboard, which was of a bright scarlet.

The effect was very strange.

It looked as if that face had been steeped in fresh shed blood.

Handsome Jemmy named the owner of that face then at once.

"Captain Sang!" he said.

"Who is he?"

"A great scoundrel, as well as a highwayman."

There was no time for further explanation, for Captain Sang, the owner of the blood-red face—and of whom the reader has already heard and seen something in a certain condemned cell in Newgate—began active operations.

"Fling out to the road your watches, purses, and anything of value you have about you!" he roared, in a voice of bullying vehemence.

A cadaverous-looking old face appeared at one window of the carriage.

"Have mercy upon us good Mr.—a—a—highway gentleman! I have no watch, no money; nothing valuable but my life—my life!"

"That's Sir Moss Bond!" whispered Dick.

At the other coach-window there appeared another old, wrinkled countenance, the white hair surrounding which fluttered in the morning air.

"I'm a poor old—old pauper, without a halfpenny in the wide world!"

"That's your uncle Zachariah!" said Handsome Jemmy to Dick.

"It is—it is!"

"You will have it, then!" said Captain Sang; and even as he spoke he fired another pistol. There was a yell mingling with the echo of the shot, and the door of the carriage, on which old Sir Moss Bond was leaning, swung open, and he rolled into the road.

"No, no!" cried Dick Doubleday. "I cannot stand by and see murder done!"

Perhaps Handsome Jemmy would not have tried to prevent Dick from doing what he did if he had had the opportunity; but even as he spoke, Dick Doubleday levelled the pistol that Handsome Jemmy had given him right over the top of the carriage at the scarlet face of Captain Sang, and fired.

The cry that old Sir Moss Bond had uttered was echoed by such a yell that it must have been heard for a mile or two round the spot.

Captain Sang was hit.

How, or by whom, no doubt he was puzzled to think.

He half fell upon the neck of his horse, and in that position the animal carried him off at a rapid pace over the fields.

―――

CHAPTER XVI.

DICK DOUBLEDAY AND HANDSOME JEMMY CARRY OFF THE TROPHIES OF THE FIELD.

"BRAVO!" said Jemmy.

"I hit the villain?"

"Oh, there's no doubt about that! No, no—don't take off your mask, Dick, now that you have the field of battle all to yourself. Go and see what you can make of it."

Dick Doubleday, without reflecting that by so acting he would probably get the discredit of all Captain Sang's ferocity, dashed through the gap in the hedge, and was in another moment by the side of the carriage.

He found his uncle Zachariah down among the straw which was at the bottom of the vehicle, making frantic and unavailing attempts to get under one of the seats, the space there not being more than sufficient to have hidden a child of three years old.

Zachariah, however, had his head fairly under the seat.

"Your money, or your life!" said Dick Doubleday, who began to enjoy the fright he was giving that uncle who had been but a cold and harsh friend to him.

"Murder! murder! Oh, good, kind, gracious Mr. Highwayman, I am a poor old man—a pauper, who will soon be on his parish! Spare my money—I mean my life! Take all, but spare my money—my hard-earned money!"

On the seat of the coach, just opposite to where the old diamond merchant was, Dick saw a small tin box tied round with two strips of leather, and that he at once laid his hands on, without old Zachariah seeing that he did so.

"Surely," thought Dick, "this tin box will contain a something of value; and as regards what my uncle may have in his pocket, I am well convinced that will only be a few shillings—and some of them, perhaps, bad ones that he gets from Jacob Sharples."

Dick was disposed to be content with the tin box; and he faced about towards the field where Jemmy was waiting for him, and held it up as though he would say, "Will this do?"

Handsome Jemmy made him a sign to come away, which Dick was nothing loth to do.

"This way!—this way!" cried Handsome Jemmy. "I hear horses' feet upon the road, and I don't want to lead the life of a hunted hare while daylight lasts. Follow me!"

Over the fields close at hand—those fields which now form the Regent's Park, and upon which are built those lines of palatial residences which the Londoner of the present day is so familiar with—Dick and Jemmy made their way; and, after going at speed for some couple of miles, they found their way into one of those shadowy green lanes which lie between Highgate and Hampstead.

"Halt!" said Jemmy.

Dick reined in his horse.

"What have you got, Dick?"

"I don't know—this tin box."

"It's light."

"Why, so it is, Jemmy."

"And, therefore, valueless to us, I am afraid. No matter; we could not stay longer. Let us see what really is in it. What's this, eh? 'The last will and testament of John Richard Doubleday.'"

"My father!" exclaimed Dick.

"Ho, ho! This may be interesting to you, Dick. Perhaps more interesting than money. Who knows but there has been some villany on the part of your old uncle Zachariah? Let us read it."

"Do so, Jemmy; and yet it surprises me to find such a document, since my father died a poor man."

"Who told you that?"

"My uncle Zachariah, often, and others."

"And you believed him? Ah, Dick Doubleday, that was uncommonly simple of you!"

"I am afraid it was."

"Well, listen to this. What do you think of this clause in the will? 'I give and bequeath to my brother Zachariah, in trust for the use of my son Richard, whatever the seed pearls and the uncut diamonds before-mentioned may produce, feeling convinced that my brother Zachariah will religiously fulfil the intents of this my last will and testament.'"

"Good heavens!" said Dick.

"Well, how much did your fortune come to?"

"Not a groat!"

"Of course not. Well, Dick, I don't think you have done a bad morning's work. Armed with this will, you can make your uncle account for your father's property, I fancy."

"Pamela!—my Pamela!"

"Eh?"

"Oh, Jemmy, Jemmy! why should I not now declare to all the world that I love Pamela, and make her my own—my own dear, dear bride? Why—oh, why should I be so happy?"

"Hem! It seems like enough, Dick, that your first entrance on the road will be your last, considering that you have made such a good thing of it?"

"Jemmy, you shall share!"

"Share what?"

"My fortune—if I really and truly have one."

"Not I, Dick—not I! In the regular way of plunder of course it was all right, and we should have gone share and share alike; but this is quite another matter, and I have nothing to do with it."

At the moment Handsome Jemmy was speaking, they emerged from the shadowy lane on to the high road, and found themselves most unexpectedly face to face with Mr Grogram and his party of mounted officers.

But what happened to Handsome Jemmy and to Dick Doubleday in consequence of this most mal-apropos meeting, we must defer to the consideration of another chapter, while we reconduct the reader to Doctor Haslem's house in Bedford Square, and to the presence of the fair and gentle Pamela, whom we left in the secret recess behind the portrait over the chimney-piece of the library.

Pamela was constitutionally brave, but she could not help feeling some terrors at finding herself in total darkness, and in so strange a place

Her impression, for a few minutes, was that if she attempted to stir from the exact spot on which she stood, she would fall down some dangerous place, and be seriously hurt.

But a few minutes' reflection banished that natural enough idea.

She recollected that she had seen the narrow flight of steps in the wall before her; and stooping, she felt that they were there still, and that they rose in regular succession.

Then commending herself to the care of heaven, which the pure spirit of Pamela could do, although the sacred name had stuck in the throat of Jacob Sharples when he had tried to do so, she slowly moved onwards.

By a natural impulse so to do, although she had no object in the enumeration, Pamela counted the steps.

There were only nine.

Then she was compelled to come to a standstill, for she felt what seemed to be the solid wall before her, and could get no further.

But the small, delicate fingers of the young girl, with their exquisite sense of touch, wandered over this seeming wall before her in the darkness, and she became conscious that she felt a slender bar of some metal, for it was cold to the touch.

And scarcely did Pamela place her hand upon this metal bar, when she heard a slight sound as if some small lock had been opened, and a gleam of faint daylight fell upon her eyes.

She was in a kind of recess over a chimney-piece in another room of the house, precisely similar to that in the library, to which she was indebted for her escape from the constables.

She had touched the spring, which caused another picture set in a panel to revolve; and there she stood—a much finer picture than the pencil of artist ever fashioned — looking down into the apartment with curiosity and surprise in her eyes.

The room was a small one.

The blinds of the two windows were drawn down closely, and the shutters were closed, with the exception of one hinged leaf.

That seemed as if it had opened by accident; and afterwards—some time afterwards—Pamela was led to the opinion that it was the slight movement of the stagnant air of the room she had made by opening the recess in the wall which had caused that leaf of the shutter to fall back.

But for that accident, though, the room would have been in absolute darkness.

Pamela was light and active as a bird.

The leap from the chimney-piece to the floor of the room did not present any terrors or difficulties for her, and she took it at once.

But Pamela was amazed at the quantity of dust that rose up from the floor as she alighted upon it.

It seemed to her incredible.

But there it was, rising in clouds about her, and half choking her.

Then when Pamela looked about her, she saw that this dust was everywhere—lying upon every object, like dingy, strange snow.

Upon the floor—upon the chimney-piece—upon the

THE DEAD HORSEMAN.

No. 6.—Felon's Daughter.

tables—the chairs—the couches—everwhere that it could lodge on.

And then Pamela began to come to the conclusion that surely that room could not have been visited by any human footstep for a long period of time—perhaps for years—for that dust, which seemed to her the dust of ages, could scarcely have accumulated in such abundance.

There was something very peculiar, too, about the general aspect of the apartment: and gradually, as Pamela looked about her, a dreamy kind of consciousness began to come over her that she had stood within its precincts once before.

And yet how could that be possible, so young as she was?

How could Jacob Sharples have ever made his way to the house of that Court Physician?—and if he had, was it likely that he would have brought her with him, even as a child?

And yet, as Pamela looked about her, the strange idea strengthened, and grew into consistency and force.

It was that kind of sensation with which one might awaken in some strange apartment, a casual examination of which only had been made upon retiring to rest; but which examination had been sufficient to leave an impression on the mind that would deprive the room and its appointments of absolute novelty.

Drawn up near to the fire-place was a small table.

On this table was a dingy-looking cloth, reaching nearly to the floor; and to the first observation of Pamela this cloth looked of a brownish slaty colour, utterly destitute of attractiveness.

But she laid her hand upon it, and then she found that the cloth was damask, and had been white, and that it owed this seeming dull and uninviting colour to the thick dust which lay upon it.

Upon the table was an untasted repast.

Some shrivelled bread, a silver cover lying on its side, and on the dish from which it had been removed there was a something which had the dim outlines of a fowl.

A tall flask, with some amber-coloured wine.

One overturned wine-glass, which lay in fragments, and another standing in its proper position—but into which the dust seemed to have settled and eddied, for it was slantwise, half full—pointed to the conclusion that that meal had been laid for two persons.

A pair of gloves lay likewise upon the table.

They looked small and soft; one was flattened, both covered with dust, but the other still took the shape of the hand from which it had been drawn.

A handkerchief lay upon the floor.

And up n the walls of this apartment hung some half-dozen rare pictures.

Shadowy and gloomy did they look—landscapes, figures, and what, no doubt, was bright and sparkling colour—all seeming as if seen through a mist.

And as Pamela looked one by one at these things, as now she faced in one direction and then in another, she was *sure* that she had been there before.

There was one picture—she could not see its subject, it was more specially covered with dust than its fellows—but as she slowly approached it, she murmured to herself, "There would be the mill, and there the stream."

The heavy dust lay lightly, and the breath of a visitor in that neglected room, together with the very passage of her garments through the air, stirred it sufficiently to make it fall in heavy flakes from many of the objects which had harboured it for years.

Such was the case with the special picture which Pamela approached.

It was immediately opposite the leaf of the shutter which was open; and as she laid her hand timidly and gently upon its frame, the collected dust of many years rolled from its surface like a curtain.

Pamela clasped her hands.

She uttered a half-shriek of recognition of that picture.

"The mill!—the stream!" she cried. "This is not

new to me; or do realities that we have never seen before rise up in dreams to mock us, and baffle recollection?"

CHAPTER XVII.

HANDSOME JEMMY AND DICK DOUBLEDAY LEAD THE OFFICERS A CHASE THROUGH OLD ISLINGTON, AND MAKE A CLEVER ESCAPE.

"WE are lost!" said Dick Doubleday, as he and Handsome Jemmy, the highwayman, came so suddenly and unexpectedly into the presence of the party of officers.

There were no less than six of them.

"We are lost! We are lost!"

"Found, I think, rather," said Handsome Jemmy, as he reined in his horse so suddenly that for a moment or two its fore feet were off the ground.

"Surrender," cried the chief officer. "Escape is impossible. Your little game is over, my fine fellows!"

"Is it?" said Handsome Jemmy. "Dick, if you are a man, or want to be one, follow me!"

"I will!"

Jemmy touched his horse with the spurs, and at the same time gave a peculiar shake to the bridle, and the creature dashed forward like an avalanche.

There was no resisting the impetuosity of the shock; and as Handsome Jemmy's boot caught that of the chief officer, the latter was unhorsed on the instant, and lay on the road.

Perhaps Dick Doubleday would not have been able to make so energetic a movement forward as the highwayman, but as it was, he followed in his wake.

A scene of confusion ensued that lasted about ten seconds.

That was all.

The officers were scattered right and left.

Their chief was unhorsed.

Dick Doubleday and Handsome Jemmy had got through their foes, and were on the full gallop along another lane, which looked pretty and shadowy, to the right of where this little battle of cavalry had taken place.

Dick Doubleday was in a state of great excitement.

This kind of life was wonderfully new to him.

Shall we say, too, that it was wonderfully fascinating?

Perhaps it was.

The escape of Dick and his friend was aided now by an accident.

The chief officer had been half-stunned by his sudden flight from the saddle of his horse, but he retained recollection enough to be terribly angry.

He sat up on the ground, and yelled out to his men: "Take them!—take them, dead or alive! I will hold you harmless! Take them, dead or alive!"

This was easier to speak of than to execute; but the chief officer was so infuriated by his tumble, that he thought he would make an attempt to carry out his own behests.

He drew a pistol from his coat pocket, and fired it at Handsome Jemmy.

It was an awkward shot.

The officer was confused by his fall, and the sitting attitude was not favourable to his taking a good aim.

He shot one of his own men!

The bullet entered the brain of one of the constables, who uttered such a yell as it did so, that his horse took fright, and galloped off with him at a mad rate.

"By Jove, Dick!" said Jemmy, as the wild clatter of this horse's heels came after them, "one of those fellows is not only well mounted, but he has some courage."

"We shall be overtaken," said Dick.

"But it's only one."

"The fellow must be mad."

"I think so, too, Dick. Halt—pull up. Don't let you and I gallop all our horses' wind away for one man."

Handsome Jemmy drew bridle gently as he spoke, and brought his horse to a stand-still.

"Woa! woa! Woa, old fellow! That will do. Pull up, Dick."

Dick Doubleday had more difficulty in bringing his steed to a stand-still.

Perhaps he was not so accomplished an equestrian as the highwayman, or perhaps the horse was scared with the knowledge that he had a strange rider on his back.

The result was, that Dick Doubleday, when he did come to a stand-still, was about a hundred feet in advance of Handsome Jemmy.

The officer's horse came tearing on.

It carried a dead rider.

By some means, the dead officer kept his seat in the saddle. Perhaps it was the actual speed with which the frightened horse tore along that prevented the dead man from falling.

But, be this as it may, on came the ghostly rider, looking fixed and rigid, with nothing to indicate what had happened but two small streams of blood running down the face.

There was something truly horrible about the fixed, glassy eyes of the dead man; and even Handsome Jemmy, with all his recklessness, felt a cold shudder came over him as his glance fell upon that awful face.

"Let him pass, Dick!" he shouted—"let him pass! By the heaven above us, it's a dead man!"

These words had hardly time to pass the lips of Handsome Jemmy, when the frightened horse swept by like a whirlwind.

Another moment, and it had passed Dick Doubleday.

Then there was a turn in the road.

The horse and its dead rider were lost to sight; but the clatter, hard and fast, of the horse's feet could still be heard for a short time.

Handsome Jemmy drew a long breath.

Dick Doubleday looked flushed and excited.

"Did you see him, Dick?"

"I did."

"Well?"

"You want to know what I thought of him; and I will say that I never saw anything so horrible in all my life."

"Nor I—nor I."

"We did not kill him, Jemmy?"

"Certainly not. You did not fire, nor I. It has been some chance shot among themselves. But what is that now that I hear?"

"Horses' feet."

"Then the others are coming on our track, and as it is possible enough that they may be alive and have the control of their horses, I fancy that the sooner we push on the better."

"Agreed."

The highwayman and Dick Doubleday put their good steeds to the gallop again; but the officers were not far behind them, for the slight delay had enabled Grogrum to remount and direct his men; and the party, now reduced to five, were speedily on the track of Dick and his friend.

And now Handsome Jemmy, although he could easily have gone on considerably in advance, and left Dick to bear the brunt of the battle, kept his horse neck and neck with the one Dick rode.

He spoke with difficulty, for that rapid locomotion and the beat of the horses' feet were not favourable to conversation.

"Dick," he said, "this lane will soon be past, and then we shall get into the Lower Road of Islington, as it is called."

"What are we to do?"

"I am thinking."

"Think quickly, then, Jemmy, for there they are!"

"Oh, the officers?"

"Yes. Look over your shoulder, and you will see them, Jemmy."

"I can hear them, and that is quite enough for me. A stern chase, you know, Dick, as they say at sea, is a long chase; but the danger is that they will raise a hue and cry in front of us."

"Yes—yes."

"So, Dick, I want to ask you can you leap?"

"Leap? How?"

"I mean can you leap your horse, and keep your seat at the same time?"

"I fancy I can, although I am not an adept at that sort of thing."

"Well, let me get a couple of lengths in advance of you. We shall soon be out of the lane, and then, Dick, whatever you see me do, imitate as well as you can."

"I will."

The officers were well mounted.

To be sure, they would have had no chance as against the hunter that Handsome Jemmy rode; but Dick's horse was either not so fleet, or he had not the skill to put forth its full powers.

The consequence was that the distance between the pursued and the pursuers continued down the lane very much the same.

But the lane was not interminable.

The end that communicated with the high road was close at hand.

Then, by turning either to the right or to the left, Dick Doubleday and Handsome Jemmy would be out of sight of the party of officers—at all events, for a short period.

It was during that short period that Handsome Jemmy meant to make some attempt to throw the officers off the scent.

He turned to the left.

That was towards the north, or country-ways.

The road was much less built upon than it is now, as may be imagined, although country houses and garden walls were abundant enough.

"Now!" said Handsome Jemmy

There was a hedge some four feet high, in which grew almost every wild hedge plant and flower that could be brought together.

On the other side there was a little paddock, and beyond that there was a garden wall with an open gate, apparently leading direct to an orchard.

"Leap after me!" cried Jemmy. "Your horse will do it, seeing the other."

Over went Handsome Jemmy, leaving a good six inches between his horse's heels and the top of the pretty hedge.

Dick Doubleday was not deficient in courage, and he put his horse to the leap at once.

The feat was not executed perhaps quite so neatly as the highwayman had done it, but it was sufficiently successful, for all that.

"Good!" said Handsome Jemmy, as he flung himself from his saddle, and took his horse by the bridle.

Dick hesitated only a moment, and then he remembered he was to do exactly as Handsome Jemmy did, and he, too, dismounted.

The highwayman led his horse through the open gate in the brick wall, and Dick Doubleday at once followed him.

They were in a very pretty mixed garden—one of those gardens so truly English, where the fruit and the flowers, and the bright, brilliant grass, and the exotic shrubs, all mingle together, to make up one pleasant, charming whole.

"Hark!" said Jemmy.

Dick listened.

They both heard the tramp of the officers' horses as they went past the hedge, still keeping to the high road, on which, no doubt, they wondered they did not see the fugitives.

"There they go!" said Jemmy. "And bad luck go with them."

"We are safe!" said Dick.

"I don't quite know."

"Hoy! hoy! hoy! Who be you? Hoy! You musn't bring 'osses in here! Hoy! Who be you?"

These cries came from a stupid-looking lout, half

man and half boy, who, holding a garden rake in a threatening attitude as though it had been a musket, advanced upon Dick and Jemmy.

"Ah, Ben! how are you?" said Jemmy.

"Anan?"

"I say, how are you, Ben?"

"My name bean't Ben; it be Samuel."

"Well, that's all the same, is it not?"

Samuel looked perplexed.

"And now," added Jemmy, with all the calmness in life, "how do you find yourself, eh, Sam?"

"I be right well. Who be you?"

"I'm glad to hear it. How is your master?"

"I bean't got no measter."

"Well, Sam, I didn't say you had. How is your mistress, eh?"

Sam shook his head.

"Come, come, Sam! you don't mean to tell me that you have neither a master nor a mistress? That won't do, you know! This old red-brick house, that looks so pleasant through the trees, is not yours, Sam, is it, eh?"

"Anan?"

"The fellow is a desperate fool," whispered Handsome Jemmy to Dick; "but if we can delay the time for some few minutes more, we shall be all right, and can sally out again, and—— Oh, here is some one else!"

An aged female approached the party. She was of the class of really respectable and confidential servants—such an one to whom might be entrusted life or treasure—one of a class that, alas! seem now to be fading away from the land.

There was no pretension of the lady about her; but yet it was with a feeling of involuntary respect that Handsome Jemmy lifted his hat a little above his head as he said, "I am afraid we are sad intruders here?"

"That depends upon the object of your presence. Pray, what is it?"

This was coming to the point at once; and the highwayman was, for a moment, puzzled what reply to make.

The old servant, with a look of suspicion in her eyes, waited patiently.

"Why, you see—you—a—comprehend," said Jemmy, "that we shall be off directly."

"I comprehend nothing.——Samuel!"

"Yees."

"There is a violent ringing at the gate-bell by the front lawn; see who it is."

"Hold!" said Jemmy. "One moment."

He, too, had heard the violent ringing at the bell, and it occurred to him that, possibly, some busybody might have seen him and Dick Doubleday leap the fence, and have informed the officers of the fact.

"Madam," added Jemmy, "before you send Samuel to the gate, let me speak to you a moment."

"No, sir."

"But really now! Pardon me, we are pursued—it don't matter why or wherefore; but, as you are a woman, we throw ourselves upon your kindness."

"Pursued! Then you are——"

"No better than we should be, I daresay; but yet—— Ah! who may this be?"

"Oh, madam! dear madam!" exclaimed the elderly domestic, as a lady, still young, still beautiful, but with the traces of deep affliction upon her face, and that tearful look about the eyes which is so sadly indicative of tears that have come direct from the heart, suddenly appeared from a side walk of the garden.

The lady—and an unmistakable lady she was—wore a veil upon her head, something after the fashion of a nun; and, from the first words she uttered, it would seem that she had overheard what Handsome Jemmy had said.

"Martha! Martha!" she said sadly, "do you forget?"

"Forget, my lady?"

"Yes. Do you forget that I, too, have known trouble, doubt, and suspicion. Let this place still be called a refuge."

"Oh! madam, I thought you were not so well to-day, and I fear now you ought not to be in the open air."

"You are ever thinking of me, Martha, and I know you are good and kind; but if the poorest wretch, upon whose head the whole world had set a price, were to cross my threshold, I would strive to hold him harmless with my life."

Martha dexterously slid behind the lady, and, with looks of entreaty, made gestures to Handsome Jemmy and Dick Doubleday, to indicate that the lady with the veil was not quite right in her head, and that, consequently, she implored them to go at once.

But the ringing at the gate continued.

There might be danger.

Samuel showed a disposition to sidle off in the direction of the front of the house; and, from his looks, Handsome Jemmy had no doubt whatever that he would at once betray their presence.

"Sam!" he cried.

"Ye-e-es."

"Stay where you are."

"Ye-es. But——"

"Sam, stay where you are."

As Handsome Jemmy spoke, he lifted from his saddle one of the pistols, and held it towards Sam, who immediately fell flat on his back in an asparagus bed, and fenced with the rake in a most ridiculous fashion, as though he hoped, if the highwayman did fire at him, he would have the good fortune to catch the bullet on one of its prongs.

CHAPTER XVIII.

DICK DOUBLEDAY AND HANDSOME JEMMY PAY A VISIT TO THE OLD LAPIDARY, DICK'S UNCLE.

"I WILL go," said the lady with the veil. "Let the pardon of heaven sanctify an evasion of truth which is in the cause of its creatures."

"Stop, madam," said Dick Doubleday. "If you really mean to carry out your kind intention of misleading our pursuers, you shall at least be verbally correct. We will remove to the outside of the wall, and then you can say that no such persons are in your garden."

"Dear madam," said the old servant, "I will go to the gate."

"Do so, Martha; but oh, remember the refuge!"

"I will! I will! Indeed, I will! You have nothing to fear from me."

These last words words were addressed to Handsome Jemmy and Dick Doubleday.

The old domestic went at once on her errand, and then the lady with the veil turned to Jemmy and Dick, and spoke in a voice of unutterable grief.

"You are both young—you have both all the world before you; but if by chance you are beloved—if you find that some gentle human heart bestows upon you the priceless treasure of its affection, grapple that heart to you, as you would the breath of life. Believe nothing, dream nothing, think nothing, listen to nothing, which shall shake your faith, but welcome death rather than the cold desolation of blighted affection!"

The lady with the veil clasped her hands over her face, and moans and sobs came from the bottom of her heart.

Handsome Jemmy was touched.

But Dick Doubleday was deeply affected. He could not account for the strange fact that every word this lady with the nun-like veil uttered to him, seemed like the remembrance of some voice he had heard before.

A voice too, that was to his ears the sweetest of all sweet music.

It was the voice of his Pamela that was recalled to him by the accents of the veiled lady.

She turned aside into the path from which she had made her appearance, and they heard her sobs as she slowly passed away from before their sight.

"What can all this mean?" said Dick Doubleday, as he clasped his hands over his eyes, as if by shutting out the external world, he should be able to come to some clearer idea of the mystery of the voice of the veiled lady which was so like his Pamela's.

"I don't know, Dick, what it all means," said Handsome Jemmy; "but between you and I, the sooner we get on to the road again the better."

It was quite evident that Handsome Jemmy did not feel absolute faith in the good intentions of Martha, the old servant, for there was a listening attitude about him, and he kept his hand upon one of his pistols, while the other was upon the saddle of his horse, as though he expected at any moment the necessity for some action might arise.

This state of suspense, however, did not last many minutes. The clatter of horses' feet was heard, and when the sounds died away, the highwayman quietly replaced the pistol in the holster of the saddle as he said, "I think that's over Dick, and we've given those fellows the slip; so now again I say, the sooner we get out of this place the better."

"I am ready," said Dick Doubleday with a deep sigh; "but it is very strange."

"What is strange?"

"Is it possible, Jemmy, you did not notice it? Did not the tones of that lady's voice strike upon your ear as wonderfully similar to those of my poor Pamela?"

"By Jove, Dick! now you mention it, it must be so I was puzzling myself to recollect when and where I had seen that poor melancholy-looking lady before, for all the while she spoke it seemed as if I had a sort of acquaintance with her. But come on, Dick. That's right; stoop low in the saddle. I think the coast is clear; but those fellows who have been after us have as many tricks and doubles as a hunted fox, and they may still be lurking about, for all I know to the contrary."

Dick Doubleday did stoop low upon his saddle, but he seemed hardly to attend to what his friend Handsome Jemmy was saying, for his eyes were directed through the trees, at the old red-brick house, to which that melancholy-looking lady with the nun-like veil had made her way.

A thousand strange conjectures flitted through his mind, and yet the next moment he could almost have blamed himself and accused himself of imaginative folly, in striving to build up any theories or conjectures from the mere similitude of one voice to another.

It was quite evident, though, that old Martha had obeyed her mistress, notwithstanding the pains she had taken to intimate to Dick Doubleday and his friend, the highwayman, that that mistress was not in a mental condition to be much regarded.

Upon looking over the hedge, they saw that the road was perfectly clear; and Handsome Jemmy, turning to Dick, with a smile, said, "Will you take the leap again, Dick? It will give you a little practice; and a good jump over a hedge or a gate will sometimes be the worth of a man's life."

"I'm willing, Jemmy."

They both took the leap again back into the road, and this time Dick Doubleday certainly did it with greater ease and precision.

"Practice makes perfect," said Handsome Jemmy; "and now, Dick, let us make our little arrangements If we are to hunt in couples, let us lay out the sport properly. Or have you seen enough of life on the road to retire from it? By Jove! too, I was forgetting you may now make old Zachariah, your uncle, render such an account to you as may make you an independent gentleman!"

"He shall render an account!"

"Bravo! I should like to see the old boy's face when you show him the will!"

"There's a little difficulty," said Dick.

"Indeed!"

"Yes. It is true that the will gives me a power over him; but unfortunately the circumstances under which I have become possessed of it give him a power over me."

Handsome Jemmy turned fully round on his saddle, and looked at Dick.

"There is something in that, my boy," he said, "and we must proceed with caution. The old rascal is quite equal to any villany, and would, I fancy, just as soon hang you, who are his own kith and kin, as he would me."

"Most decidedly."

"That's awkward. We shall have to compromise the matter in some way, Dick. And I'll tell you what we'll do. To-night I have an appointment on Barnes Common —a general sort of appointment, you know, Dick, with whoever may pass that way, and to whom it may be worth while to cry out 'Stand and deliver!' I shall put up my horse in the old 'Angel Tavern,' in Barbican— you cannot do better than accompany me; we shall be as safe there as two diamonds in a box of cotton; and so soon as the evening comes, what is to hinder us from walking over to Long Lane, and having a few words with Zachariah?"

"I should like to do so, Jemmy."

"Then it's agreed. And I'll tell you how we will manage it You shall go inside, and see what terms you can make with the old rascal, while I stay without and keep my eyes about me; for he may take it into his head to send to Giltspur Street for a couple of grab-hards and hold-fasts—constables and bracelets—handcuffs, you know, Dick; but if I'm outside, I can intercept the messenger. Who has he to send, by the by?"

"I think he lives alone now, since I left him—with the exception of an old woman, who is stone deaf, and who calls herself Miss Giblets."

"Very good. Then that's settled, Dick? On we go again!"

Handsome Jemmy and Dick Doubleday made a considerable detour round by Newington Green and Hoxton Fields, to make their way into the City; so they came into Barbican at the further end.

The "Angel Tavern" was one of those ancient hostelries which time and modern innovation have swept away.

It was worth a pilgrimage to see it at the period when Dick Doubleday and Handsome Jemmy rode up to its ancient porch.

You went down two steps to enter it; and it was so mysterious, and so dark, and so inconvenient, and so gloomy, and the windows were so small, the framing so large, and the little bits of glass like small eyes striving through difficulties to look out upon the day,—that that old "Angel Tavern" would have been the delight of lovers of the antique, and was a capital specimen of the taste of our ancestors in the matters of light and ventilation.

And yet, somehow or another, those ancestors contrived to live just as long as we do.

There was a sort of stable-yard, no two square inches of which were on the same level, adjoining the old inn; and after a cursory glance about him in the old street, Handsome Jemmy, with Dick Doubleday close by his side, trotted into this stable-yard and gave a peculiar whistle, which, in a few moments, brought a grinning specimen of the ostler tribe to attend to his wants.

"Lor,' Captain! is this you? Why, the sight of you is good for bad eyes. I thought you'd been and forgot the old 'Angel.' This is a friend of your'n, I suppose, Captain?"

"Yes. Look to the horses; and you ought to be obliged to me for bringing a friend who is quite as ready with his guineas as I am with mine."

"You was always a real gentleman, Captain, and no doubt pay your way; but if you was to come here with never a guinea in your pocket, you'd be as welcome as— as welcome as——"

The ostler looked in vain around him for a comparison, and then added, "As welcome as nothing; because you'd be quite sure to give two the next time. But I suppose dark's the word, Captain?"

"To be sure. We shall stay here till nightfall; and if anything goes wrong, it's your fault, not ours."

The "Angel" was most emphatically a house of call for gentlemen of the road.

The officers knew that fact perfectly well, and they were frequently to be seen at the old dingy bar of the ancient tavern enjoying a dram from some of the bottles that Joe Marchus, as the landlord was named, kept for special customers and occasions.

But we have little to do with the Angel or its frequenters. Suffice it that Handsome Jemmy and Dick Doubleday found there a refuge, a dinner, and a bottle of rare, old, choice Canary wine, in perfect safety; although at any moment the landlord or any of his dependan's would have nothing to do but to walk calmly over to Newgate, and put in a claim for a certain hundred guineas as the price of the surrender of the notorious Handsome Jemmy the highwayman to any two or three officers who would come to effect their capture.

"Now, Dick," said the highwayman, "when it is dark outside as well as inside the old 'Angel,'—for the latter condition took place a good hour before the former,—"now, Dick, suppose we pay this visit to old Zachariah?"

"Yes," said Dick; "and I have another visit to pay before I leave London to-night. I cannot accompany you, Jemmy, until I feel quite sure of the safety of Pamela. Doctor Haslem certainly would not play us false, and has by this time found some refuge for her, the secret of which he will not hesitate to entrust to us, since we were certainly her original preservers."

"All right, Dick—it shall be done. A light heart sits the saddle well; but care is heavy behind the horseman. I wouldn't have you come on to the Common to-night, without an assurance that all is well with that charming girl. Come on then, Dick; let it be Zachariah first, and the Doctor afterwards; although, if you have no objection, we will come back to the 'Angel' after visiting your uncle, and get our horses, which we can ride to Dr. Haslem's, at Bedford Square, and then lose no time in making our way to the Western Road."

Dick Doubleday shrunk a little from the free and easy manner in which Handsome Jemmy seemed to conclude that he was about to become a confirmed highwayman; but he did not like to dispute the matter at that present moment, inasmuch until he had had that interview with his uncle he could not tell what his resources might be.

Dick was but young, or he would have felt that whatever those resources might turn out, the worst step he could possibly take would be to seek a precarious subsistence by life on the road, the results of which might separate him from Pamela for ever.

Long Lane, Smithfield, is not an enlivening thoroughfare at the present day; but at the period of our story it was, if possible, dirtier, grimier, and more forbidding in its aspect than it is now.

And that is needless.

How truly time is counted by events rather than by its own progress!

It was in reality but a week or two since Dick Doubleday resided with his uncle, Zachariah, not content, but putting up with all the hard usage he met with, and only in a dreaming sort of way thinking of some future which would be more bright and beautiful.

But now he seemed to have stepped at once from the condition of a dependent boy to that of a self-asserting, self-relying man.

Long Lane looked to his eyes dirtier, narrower, and more gloomy than ever.

The ricketty-looking house and shop occupied by his uncle seemed to be smaller, more obscure, and wretched than ever. It seemed to lean more on the one side than it had ever done before.

These apparent changes were strange to Dick Doubleday; and he could hardly believe that they were not real, and only consequent upon the great step he himself had taken forward in life.

The shop was closed. Zachariah never kept open after sunset; but the initiated knew of a means of tapping for admission which would soon bring the old man to his door.

Of course no one knew better than Dick Doubleday the peculiar kind of knock which would inspire confidence in old Zachariah, and induce him to believe that a customer was at hand.

"Wait here, Jemmy," said Dick; "I will rejoin you as soon as possible; but if you see any one leave this house before I come out, you may conclude I am in some danger."

"I'll look after the 'any one,' Dick, be they he or she or whom they may."

Dick Doubleday tapped at his uncle's door, which, after a delay of about a minute, was opened by the old man himself; and by the glance he took of his nephew in the dubious light, it was quite evident to Dick that he was not at all recognised; for Handsome Jemmy had lent him a long roquelaire cloak, which he had unstrapped from the back of his saddle, and a portion of which Dick held up in such a manner that its flaring scarlet lining met the old man's gaze.

"And what, sir, might you please to want?" said old Zachariah.

Dick spoke in a deep, disguised voice.

"Half a dozen watch-cases, sir, and two edged with brilliants——"

"To sell?" said the old man, eagerly.

"Yes, and at your own price, provided you pick out the stones, and put the cases in the melting-pot as soon as possible."

"My good young man, am I a fool—a dolt—a superannuated old donkey? They'll be in the melting-pot within a hour; and as for the stones—why who can swear to stones? Come in—come in! You seem a nice, proper sort of young gentleman. I think you said at my own price, didn't you?"

"I did."

"That's the way to do business—that's the way. I always give more when anybody leaves it to me—always more. Wait a moment, my dear young gentleman, and I'll get a light. Ah, me! ah, me! I ought to have a bargain now and then. Not that I want one from you, my dear, proper young gentleman, for I mean to give you the full value, and a little more; but to make up for a dreadful robbery—a dreadful robbery."

"A robbery, sir?" said Dick, as he made his way after his uncle into the house, every twist and turn of which was quite familiar to him—"a robbery, sir?"

"Yes. I was stopped on the highway—the King's highway—his Majesty's highway, by two cut-throat thieves, who took from me no end of property. I'll get a light in a minute. Ah, me! ah, me! candles are expensive, and this one's broken. What shall I do? Stop till I put a bit of paper round it, and a pin. That'll do! —that'll do! Now, young gentleman, where are the watch-cases? I think you said my own price, didn't you?"

Old Zachariah had succeeded in lighting the rushlight, and he held it up now between his own face and that of Dick Doubleday, shielding it with his hand from his own eyes; and then, as the light fell upon him, Dick called out, "Don't you know me, uncle?"

CHAPTER XIX.

HANDSOME JEMMY SAVES JACK DOUBLEDAY FROM THE CONSEQUENCES OF HIS UNCLE'S DUPLICITY.

OLD Zachariah dropped the rushlight in a very reckless manner, as he uttered a cry of anger and fear.

"You—you!" he shouted; "you graceless wretch! I suppose you come to rob and murder your old uncle—after all he has done for you for years and years? And there goes the candle! my foot's upon it! Get out—get out; you shan't stay here! You said you wouldn't, and you shall not! A bad penny—a bad penny! You come back like a bad penny, but I won't have you! Get out—get out."

"No, uncle—I won't get out; I have taken too much pain to come in; and I must and will have some talk with you about my poor father's fortune."

"Fortune? Fortune? Beggar that you are! Ha! ha! A pretty legacy! Your father — who was a fool ——"

"Beware, Zachariah! Beware, Uncle Zachariah!"

"Beware of what?"

"If you speak another disrespectful word of my father, I'll knock you down."

"The murderer! The—the parricide! For haven't I been a father to him? The—the—the unclecide, if there is such a word! He wants to take my life! Thieves!"

"Be quiet, uncle."

"Quiet?—quiet? You abominable wretch!—and to come at this time of night, too, and hurt my feelings by saying you had some watch-cases to sell at my own price. You'll come to no good, Dick; you'll be hanged, Richard; and a good job, for you take a delight in hurting your uncle's feelings. You make me cry, but I won't weep for you. Get out! get out, wretch that you are."

"Uncle," said Dick, calmly, "I was tolerably well prepared for a bad reception, but that shall not deter me I would advise you to get another light, for I must and will speak to you about my father's will."

"Will? will? There was no will."

"Then, uncle, you must permit me to contradict you. I am informed there was a will, and I should like to see it."

Old Zachariah, at these words, uttered an exclamation that almost alarmed Dick Doubleday

"The tin box! the tin box!" he cried—"the little tin box! I see it all now! I'm a ruined man! Yes, I see it all! You're in league with villains—robbers—plunderers; but I'll have you hanged! The law is strong, and reaches a long way. It gathers in all sorts of criminals—those who do the deeds, and those who share the profits."

"And yet you escape, uncle?" said Dick.

"I escape? I escape? What do you mean?"

"I mean, uncle, that you share the profits; for where could you possibly suppose those watch-cases came from, that you were so eager to buy of me a little while ago, at your own price?"

"Villain!"

"A hard word, uncle."

"Vampire!"

"Oh, I don't care about that at all. But, in a word, I have come here with a determination to bring you to an account. What became of the rough diamonds and the pearls, seed and otherwise, which my father placed in your hands for my benfit—leaving them to me expressly by will, and to you in trust for me."

"It's false, boy—it's false! You are mad!"

Old Zachariah had lit another rushlight by this time, and placed it on a ricketty-looking table, which Dick knew well, between himself and his nephew.

"It's false, I say. There was no will."

"Uncle," said Dick, "it makes me shudder a little to hear an old man speak so unblushingly what is untrue. I have a sort of disdain to hold this conversation further. I am in possession of my father's will, which formed part of the contents of a certain tin box you lost this morning in a lane near to Newington Green. I am not grasping, uncle, although you are. Give me at least sufficient of my patrimony to lift me above the present necessity of doing that which I would fain avoid for a subsistence, and I will trouble you no more."

"So, so!" said the old man. "Our Dick has turned a highwayman, has he?"

"Uncle, uncle, why parley with me? Take a step half-way towards honesty for once. Give me one-half of what my father left me, and you shall never see my face again."

"A delusion—a delusion! The rough diamonds were worthless—seed pearls were a drug in the market. Boy,

you have eaten and drank—for you always had a dreadful appetite—double the value; and if you do go on the road, you ought to bring me all the bargains you can, Dick, and make it up to me."

"This is trifling with me, uncle. I will have a settlement, or I will find a means to enforce one."

"You will?"

"Most assuredly."

"Well, Dick—well, Dick—there needs no passion—no anger. You shall have a settlement. Come, now, what sum will content you? Where is the will? Let us see it."

"You have seen it, Zachariah, often enough; but tell me at once what you propose to give me."

"Two hundred—that is, I mean one. Tut! tut! what am I saying?—fifty pounds, Dick."

"In the name of heaven, give me the fifty pounds, and let me be gone."

"I will get the money, nephew—I will get the money. I am sure you don't want to be hard upon your poor old uncle. It's all I have in the world, but you shall have it. Wait a few moments—wait a few moments. You have so flurried me, that I am not so quick as usual; but I will get the money. It's upstairs—no, I mean down stairs."

Old Zachariah shuffled from the room, and Dick Doubleday in three strides reached the door after him.

A dark passage was beyond, into which Dick projected his head, and, with his young ears on the alert, listened.

"Giblets! Giblets! Spawn of evil!" he heard his uncle whispering. "Giblets, I say—old snake—do you want a new bonnet—new ribbons—gin—snuff—old beast?"

There was some inarticulate answer from Miss Giblets.

"Then go," whispered Zachariah—"go at once—run—rush—go to the Compter, and tell them to send a couple of officers; there's a highwayman in the house. It's forty pound when he's hanged; and who shall say a word against old Zachariah Doubleday when he gives up his own nephew to the law? Run, you tadpole—run!"

Miss Giblets again made some inarticulate reply, and there was a terrible scuffling in the passage, from which a door opened to the shop, in addition to that one which had admitted Dick Doubleday and his uncle into the back parlour.

Miss Giblets rushed into Long Lane, something after the manner of an infuriated bull, head foremost, without looking where she was going, and she fell right into the arms of Handsome Jemmy.

"Now, old 'un," said Jemmy, "whither so fast?"

"Murder! Thieves! Gin! A new bonnet! Constables!"

"What?"

"Two highwaymen—a constable—a bottle of bonnet and a new gin!"

"What on earth do you mean?" said Handsome Jemmy, close to the ear of Miss Giblets; for he recollected Dick Doubleday had told him his uncle's attendant was as deaf as a post. "What—do—you—mean, old Tabby?"

"A highwayman—a constable wanted!"

"Oh! that's it, is it? You're lucky"

"What? I can't help it—the place is so dirty."

"I say you're lucky, for I'm a constable."

"A Dunstable? I'll have a Leghorn, if I die for it He said a new bonnet, and surely I may have what I like!"

"Listen. I'm a con-sta-ble!"

"Well, go then."

"Go where?"

"To Barnstable. I comes from Barnstable. Do you know the Giblets?"

"This old woman will be the death of me," said Handsome Jemmy; "but I don't mean to let her get any further, for all that; and I must make her take me into the house as a constable."

Jemmy laid hold of Miss Giblets by the head, and placing his mouth to her ear, with the intervention of his doubled-up hand as a trumpet, he bawled, "I'm a Bow—S reet—runner!"

"I've no objection!" screamed Miss Giblets.

Handsome Jemmy gave it up in despair, but he had recourse to some expressive pantomime.

He suddenly seized Miss Giblets by the throat, then by the back of the neck and one wrist, in which attitude he handed her along for a few paces; then he clapped her two wrists together, and went through the pantomimic process of putting on handcuffs.

"He's a _hossifer!_" said Miss Giblets—"he's a _hossifer_ of _polis!_"

Handsome Jemmy nodded.

"I knowed it from the first," added Miss Giblets.

"Then why the deuce didn't you say so?" responded Jemmy.

Miss Giblets thought that the "_hossifer_ of _polis_" she had thus by chance encountered in Long Lane was a kind of dispensation of Providence, and she at once escorted him into the house.

Old Zachariah was in the shop.

"Hist! hist!" he said; "who is there?"

"A runner," said Jemmy, "when he's obliged. What's the row?"

"Hush! are you alone?"

"Yes. What is it?"

"Can you manage rather a desperate young fellow all by yourself—eh?"

"Of course—I'm used to them."

"Come in, then; and—and—do you hear, Mr Officer, —I don't mind paying you handsomely if you rid me of the rascal; and—and—Mr. Officer——"

"Well, what?"

"What do you do if this sort of gentry makes any great resistance—eh?"

"The best I can."

"Ah, yes! Well, well! if that should be the case, and you are forced to kill him, I will hold you harmless, you know, and give such an account of the matter that no one shall blame you, and there will be ten guineas for you. Do you comprehend all that, Mr. —a—a——"

"Brown."

"Yes, Mr. Brown. Do you comprehend all that?"

"I rather think I do; so lead the way."

Old Zachariah did lead the way, muttering to himself as he went, "Ten guineas from fifty leaves, at all events, forty clear gain, and Dick would have fifty; but if this officer, who seems to be a tall, strong fellow, will get rid of him for ten, I shall be better off; and I may slip a couple of Jacob Sharples's bad ones among the ten —perhaps three. Ha! ha! who knows that he would notice even four, or—or five? This way, sir, if you please—this way."

Old Zachariah, who would have murdered one half the human race for a guinea a head, and thought it a charming speculation, led the way for Handsome Jemmy, not through the shop to the back parlour where Dick Doubleday was listening, but out into the dark, dismal passage.

Then he whispered to Jemmy, as he made him stop at the door leading from the passage to the parlour, "Stop one moment—only a moment; and when you hear me say 'Now we will come to a settlement,' you can walk in."

"I will."

Handsome Jemmy was alone in the passage, but it was only for a few seconds that he had that passage to himself.

Miss Giblets was curious.

She wanted to see exactly what was going on, if envious nature had placed a veto upon her hearing all about it.

So Miss Giblets, who had disappeared into the lower regions of the house, now appeared again with a marvellously old candlestick, in which was a tottering rushlight.

Zachariah did not allow any other species of illumination than such as could be afforded by a rushlight in his little establishment.

The feeble light fell upon Handsome Jemmy, and he bestowed a wink upon Miss Giblets, which much confused the ancient maiden.

Then Jemmy, who thought her absence desirable, drew one of his pistols from his coat-pocket, and pretended to be taking deliberate aim at the snuff of the rushlight.

Miss Giblets uttered a cry of alarm, and dropped the candlestick at once.

She missed her footing then on the stairhead, and as the candlestick went clattering down to the kitchen, Miss Giblets slid after it in a very undignified fashion, but then, as she said afterwards, "the only person below was the cat, so it didn't matter much."

This noise, however, did not escape the observation of old Zachariah, and he called out in rather a loud and nervous voice, "Now we will come to a settlement."

"With all my heart, uncle," replied Dick Doubleday.

"And with all mine, I'm sure," said Handsome Jemmy, as he pushed open the door and walked coolly and composedly into the room.

CHAPTER XX.

OLD ZACHARIAH SETTLES WITH HIS NEPHEW, AND THE SCENE CHANGES TO DOCTOR HASLEM'S HOUSE, IN BEDFORD SQUARE.

"SEIZE him! seize him! Thieves! thieves!" cried Dick's unscrupulous uncle. "There's your prisoner, Mr. Constable! Seize him! I give him in charge for stopping myself and Sir Moss Bond, a most respectable and worthy gentleman, on the King's highway this morning."

"Oh, that's it!" said Jemmy.

"Yes, yes; that's it! He is going to resist, too. He is going to try violence. Look to yourself, Mr. Officer; he is capable of any villany—of any treachery."

Handsome Jemmy gave Dick Doubleday a look, which let the latter know that either for the mere fun of the thing, or for some other motive, he, Jemmy, did not wish Dick to recognise him.

So Dick spoke to his uncle in a reproachful tone.

"Is this possible, uncle? Have you betrayed me?"

"Stuff! I harbour no highwaymen here."

"But, uncle!"

"I won't hear a word. Ah, you are chicken-hearted, and won't resist!"

"Resist? Certainly not. What, uncle! would you have me resist an officer—which, I suppose, this gentleman is—in the discharge of his duty? Oh, no, no! Perish the thought!"

Old Zachariah looked savagely disappointed.

"Officer," he said, "do your duty."

"Young man," said Handsome Jemmy, "you will have to come along with me."

"With pleasure," said Dick.

"Stop!" screamed Zachariah; "I must have my property first. He has about him a will—a—a certain will which he stole from me, and which it is proper, you see, Mr. Officer, and necessary I should have possession of."

"It is mine!" said Dick.

"Hold, now, a moment, both of you!" said Handsome Jemmy. "Did he take it from you, old gentleman?"

"He did—he did!"

"And anything else?"

"Plenty of things else. Money—jewellery;—no end of property!"

"Then after the trial——"

"What?"

"After the trial, you can apply to the judge at the Old Bailey for your property back; but you can't have it before—so it's no use your saying a word about it."

Zachariah groaned.

HANDSOME JEMMY FRIGHTENS MISS GIBLETS.

No. 7.—Felon's Daughter.

"Now, young fellow," said Handsome Jemmy to Dick Doubleday, "you had better confess what you have done—eh? Have you taken anything from this respectable old gentleman? If you have, you know, I must take possession of it, and keep it till after the trial."

Dick smiled. He saw Handsome Jemmy's drift, and he replied, as he walked to a corner of the room, "I take this desk."

"Good!"

"I take this key, and I open this cupboard."

"Good again!"

"Help! Help! Thieves! Murder!" shouted Zachariah.

Dick Doubleday dashed the desk down on to the floor with a noise that made Miss Giblets, who was in the kitchen below, and who had just gathered herself from her fall, at once subside within the fender among the ashes; for she thought that the old house was surely coming down about her ears.

The desk fell to pieces, and some heavy bags of gold rolled from it.

Old Zachariah sprang upon them with shouts of dismay; he strove to cover the pieces of the broken desk and the little bags of money with his body, as he stretched himself out on the floor flat over them, and yelled for help and mercy.

Zachariah began to suspect that there was a better understanding than was good for him between his nephew and Mr Brown.

Upon sight of those bags of money, Dick threw away the key of the cupboard which he had then possession of, and cried out. "I will take my father's patrimony and be content. Rise up, uncle, for you hide from me that which I feel assured is my own!"

"No—no! Thieves! Thieves! It is my money; it is mine—mine only! I will not part with a stiver of it! It is my own—my life—my blood—my soul! Help!—oh, help!"

"Come up!" said Jemmy.

The highwayman lifted up old Zachariah Doubleday very much after the manner of the clown in a pantomime when he assists the prostrate pantaloon to his feet.

Then, by a very slight exercise of strength, Handsome Jemmy flung the old man into a corner.

"Take your money, Dick," he said, "and let's be off."

"Ah!" yelled Zachariah. "I am cheated—deceived! —they know each other!"

Dick picked up the four bags of gold and put them in his pocket.

"Uncle," he said, "did I not feel quite sure that I was entitled to this money, I would not take it; but I have my father's will, and at any time you are disposed to properly account for the property he placed in your hands for me, I will properly account for this gold that I now take from you!"

Old Zachariah sunk back into the corner where the highwayman had flung him, and, hitting the back of his head a hard rap against the old wainscot, he seemed to give up the idea of any further contest on the subject.

"Come on, now, Dick!" said Jemmy. "I fancy we have done all we can here, and you don't want to stay any longer in this den?"

"Not a moment."

Dick Doubleday took a last look about him at the wretched habitation in which his uncle resided with all his wealth, and then a more lingering look at the miserable bundle of humanity crouched up in the corner of the room, after which he strode after Handsome Jemmy, with a resolution that nothing but some main force should ever bring him again beneath that roof.

"Now, Dick, what do you intend to do?"

"Give you half this money, and then go to Bedford Square to Doctor Haslem."

"Yes and no! Yes, to the last, and no to the first proposition, Dick. I don't want the money."

"But you ought to have it."

"No, I say, again! What do I want with your money, while I have a good horse that never shies or stumbles with me, and will stand fire—while my pistols are those that never flash in the pan, and while I have a stout heart to say, 'Stand and deliver!' to the King's lieges on the highway?"

Dick Doubleday was quite convinced that the highwayman meant what he said, and he forbore to make an affectation of pressing him to the acceptance of what he had declined.

The old "Angel Inn" at Barbican was soon reached again; and within twenty minutes of Dick Doubleday's last look at his uncle crouched in the corner of the dingy parlour in Long Lane, he and Handsome Jemmy were both mounted and going at a hard gallop towards Bedford Square.

Dick Doubleday never doubted but that the Court Physician would be as good as his word, and find some means of enabling Pamela to escape from the pursuit of the baffled authorities.

But he was nervously anxious to know exactly where she was.

Both Dick and Jemmy alighted at the door of Doctor Haslem's house, and the highwayman held the two horses while Dick Doubleday applied for admission.

The most accessible of men are physicians; and Dick Doubleday was at once shown into a reception room, where, in a few moments, he was joined by Doctor Haslem.

The Court Physician was very pale, and looked as if he had passed through some scene of violent emotions.

Dick Doubleday advanced towards him with eagerness.

"Sir," he said, "to you I owe so many thanks, that I have no language in which to frame them; but you will imagine all my gratitude on my Pamela's account, and excuse the haste in which I implore you to tell me that she is well and safe!"

"I have no reason to doubt that she is both."

"No reason to—to—doubt?"

"None whatever! Of course this house would be anything but a safe asylum for her; so after taking her in my carriage past immediate pursuit, I left her."

"Left her?"

"Yes—to do the best she could; which I feel quite sure would be better than anything I could do."

"Sir?"

"And well, sir?"

The Court Physician had not dared to look Dick Doubleday in the face as he spoke; but now he seemed to think it was necessary that he should make an effort to do so; and he, so to speak, wrenched round his head, and met, as best he could, the fiery and indignant gaze of the young man.

"And, sir," said Dick Doubleday, in a voice that rang through the apartment, "do you mean to tell me that you have cast that young creature upon the world, with all her danger about her, and a price upon her dear, innocent head?"

Doctor Haslem looked ghastly as he licked his pale lips.

"What—what else could I do?"

"What else could you do? Coward!"

"Sir!"

"Coward, I say! You might have let her cling to you for a few hours of safety, till I came to claim her as my own—as all my own. My Pamela! my Pamela! where, oh, heaven! where are you now?"

"Perhaps she has sought her father's protection," faltered the physician.

"No, no—never!"

"Nay, it is surely likely."

"Never! That father!—but why do I call him her father? He is not, cannot be, the father of my Pamela! She must have some other father; or, if she has not on earth, she has one in heaven, who knows how dearly I love her, and how content and happy I was to be to her, father, mother, brother, sister—all human loves and all human relationships in one—and that I could hold her to my heart and call her mine for ever, and for ever!"

Poor Dick Doubleday held by the back of a chair, and bowed his head as this storm of passionate feeling swept over him.

The Court Physician slowly rubbed one hand over the other, and shook in every limb.

He was evidently playing some part that shook him to the heart's inmost core.

But he had made up his mind to play it.

Then poor Dick Doubleday looked up, and spoke to him words of bitterness and despair.

"Let it be ever present to you," he said, "as a grief that cannot be quenched, that you have basely deserted that young, fair girl, when she was entrusted to you surely by heaven to save her. Sleeping or waking, should she come to wrong—to death, may be—may her image ever be before you It is my mission now to seek her, and I leave you the recollection of her gentleness, her beauty, and her innocence. to haunt you along with the conviction that if you have not actually betrayed her, you have abandoned her probably to those who will."

Without another word, Dick Doubleday turned on his heel, and left the house of the physician.

The moment he was gone, Doctor Haslem sunk into a chair, and clasping his hands over his eyes, he moaned out, "What am I doing? What is it that raises this commotion at my heart? Who and what is this young girl to me, that I should so dread to part with her as to lie and forswear myself to that noble young spirit who loves her so well? Who, oh! why is it that I dread she should look, smile, at another? Why is it that the thought of her leaving this house is to me a madness—a despair?"

Dick Doubleday passed through the hall of the Doctor's house like a man in a dream.

He reached the street, and he almost flung himself into the saddle of his horse.

"Dick! Dick!" cried Handsome Jemmy, as he, too, mounted—"Dick, what is the matter?"

"Pamela!"

"What of her?"

"She is lost!"

"Lost! What do you mean?"

"Lost!—betrayed!—abandoned!"

"Explain, Dick—explain. I won't stir a step, nor shall you, until you tell me what that look of despair upon your face means."

Handsome Jemmy kept his own horse well in hand, and he held the bridle of Dick's.

Then, in a few words, Dick Doubleday told him what had happened.

"So! That is it! Well, it was shabby, by Jove! but it shall come home to him in some way. Left her in the streets, poor young thing, to run into any danger, after all the pains we took to save her, and after his promise to be careful of her! No, no!—I don't believe it!"

"What?"

"I say, Dick, I don't believe it."

"What, then, has happened? What worse—what more terrible supposition would you put into my head? Oh, Jemmy, Jemmy! do not tell me that my Pamela is again in the hands of those who seek her life!"

"No, Dick, I don't think that, but there is more in all this affair than meets the eye just at present, and we must manage to ferret it out somehow. I suppose now that you have plenty of money you don't intend to go with me to the Common?"

"I think not, at present, Jemmy. But if, on the other hand, I could only persuade you——"

"To what?"

"To stay in town for a few days, if only to help me to search for poor, dear Pamela. I—I——Oh! Jemmy, you I can trust—you I can rely upon, stay with me for the love of heaven and that sweet girl!"

"Dick, what can you think of me?"

"Think of you?"

"Yes. Do you think I am a stick—a stone—a brick—a piece of hard clay, with no spark of human life or human sympathy within it? Stay with you, my boy?—of course I will!"

"God bless you!"

"Pho, pho! Don't say another word about that, Dick. We will look for Pamela together; and if you and I don't find her, Dick, it will be a hard case indeed."

"Already, Jemmy, my heart feels lighter!"

"To be sure it is! But it won't do for us to be seen about just as we are. We must make some alteration in our appearance, Dick, and we must house our horses somewhere."

"Yes—oh, yes!"

"Well, that's not difficult when once it's determined on. There's nobody in the world will look after the cattle better than old Will Sykes at the ken in Field Lane and there, too, we can fit ourselves out in any way we think proper; so come on, and let us set about it!"

Dick Doubleday felt hope springing up in his breast, now that the highwayman had promised to assist him in the search for Pamela.

More than one-half of the desolation of spirit that had come over him on the statement of Doctor Haslem vanished, and he rode off with Handsome Jemmy to the house in Field Lane in better heart

It was that same house where we first made acquaintance with the reader at the opening of this narrative, and from the cellar of which Jacob Sharples had been compelled to make that unceremonious descent into the territories of the White Rat.

Dick Doubleday had some repugnance to visit that house again; but he did not like to interpose any fanciful objections to the wishes and arrangements of his friend Handsome Jemmy, so they walked from Bedford Square to Holborn Hill without a word of objection on the part of Dick Doubleday.

Doctor Haslem, so soon as he could recover from the state of agitation which his self-accusations had cast him into, rose from the chair in which he had sat rocking himself to and fro in grief and in agitation.

He carefully then locked the door of the room.

Then he mounted to the chimney-piece, even as Pamela had done, and, touching the spring, he opened the cavity in the wall and passed through it

He was seeking the young girl whom he had certainly saved, and whom he was now so loath to part with.

And Pamela was alone in that mysterious room which she had reached as a place of refuge, in the Doctor's house.

That room which to her had been a mystery, and yet not a mystery, inasmuch as it was at the same time a recollection.

Long and earnestly she gazed upon that picture on the wall, which she felt certain she must have seen before.

Or else she had seen in nature the scene which it was the representation of.

She could not decide which of these conditions was the case, but each moment the conviction grew stronger and stronger upon her mind that one or the other of them was a truth.

"Oh, who and what am I?" she cried, as she clasped her hands, and her eyes filled with tears—"who and what am I in reality?—for I feel now convinced of what my heart has always told me, that Jacob Sharples is not —cannot be my father."

There was a deep sigh in the room.

Pamela uttered a cry of surprise.

The Court Physician was by her side, but he was pale as death itself.

CHAPTER XXI.

DICK DOUBLEDAY MEETS WITH AN ACQUAINTANCE,
WHO VERY INCONVENIENTLY RECOGNISES HIM, AND
RAISES A HUE AND CRY.

HANDSOME JEMMY and Dick Doubleday had no difficulty in disposing of their horses in safety at the "fence"
in Field Lane.

" You must know, Dick," said the highwayman,
"that the safest place for such cattle as ours is anywhere but a stable. There's a back room here, well
littered down; and they do say that the celebrated Dick
Turpin—who ran his race a little before our time, Dick
—kept his mare, Black Bess, in this very room for a
fortnight."

" I've no doubt of it, Jemmy; it looks safe enough "

" And it is, my boy; but I won't trouble you with
such things. Your head is heavy, and your heart is
wandering in all the streets, squares, and alleys of
mighty London, in search of one fair face, that, please
heaven, you shall soon look upon."

The keeper of the fence took the visit of Handsome
Jemmy and Dick Doubleday quite as a matter of business.

" Oh, of course," he said; " the horses will be quite
safe as long as they choose to leave them there. Handsome Jemmy knew the terms—a guinea a day for each;
and cheap, too, for heaven only knows what they might
have to give to some prying officer from Newgate or
the Bailey!"

Dick Doubleday was in good condition to be heedless
of any terms of a pecuniary character which might be
suggested, and after he and Handsome Jemmy had become equipped in very sober suits of black, Dick thought
it would be as well to ascertain the exact amount of his
wealth; and as Handsome Jemmy suggested, with his
usual off-hand liberality, that twenty guineas should be
at once handed 'to old Will Sykes, the fence-keeper,
Dick opened one of the pretentious little bags he had
brought from his uncle's, and produced a handful of the
gold that was within.

" That will do, Dick," said Handsome Jemmy. "Why,
you're set up for I don't know how long! You're quite
a man of fortune, Dick! You are——Hilloa! What's
the matter with you, Will Sykes?"

The fence-keeper had suddenly started from a very
lethargic attitude he had been in, and commenced an
aggravated kind of war-dance about the room.

" Why, what's the matter?" shouted Handsome
Jemmy. " Have you taken leave of your senses?"

" The idea!" shouted Sykes, — " the idea! I'm
blessed if it ain't too bad! The idea, now, of trying
that dodge upon an old hand like me—a family man of
thirty years' standing, who's up to all the traps and rigs
you can mention! It's too bad—I'm blessed if it ain't
too bad!"

" What's too bad?"

" Why, to try to put 'em off upon me! Do you
think I don't know Jacob Sharples' work when I see
it?"

" Jacob Sharples' work!" echoed Handsome Jemmy.

" Jacob Sharples' work!" exclaimed Dick Doubleday.

" Why, yes, to be sure! You've got a pretty lot there
of his sham ones! They're a goodish bit too bright for
use, and will go much better with a bit of tarnish on
them!"

" A bit of what?" cried Dick Doubleday.

" Oh, it's all very well," said Will Sykes, " for you
not to know anything about it; but I am surprised at
you, Handsome Jemmy—a gentleman—a real right
down knight of the road—a man as knows what's
what, and never does a mean thing, but cries, ' Stand
and deliver!' and takes what he wants! Oh, Jemmy,
Jemmy, I am surprised at you!"

The highwayman flung himself back in the chair on
which he was sitting, and burst into a roar of laughter.

" I see it all, now," he cried,—" I see it now! Dick,
Dick, your old uncle is one too many for you and for me

too! By Jove! it's clever! I see how it is! These bags
are full of some of Jacob Sharples' handy-work, and
we are just where we were, Dick, before our visit to
Long Lane!"

Handsome Jemmy seemed wonderfully amused at this
climax to the affair between Dick and his uncle. He
laughed again uproariously, and all the more so as a
look of intense chagrin came over Dick Doubleday's
face.

" Then he has still deceived me!" cried Dick; " and
my patrimony——"

" Don't—don't, now," laughed Handsome Jemmy—
"now, don't say any more about that patrimony. The
old fellow has done us as cleverly as possible; and I, for
one, forgive him, and advise you to do the same, Dick.
Here, Will Sykes, you may believe us or not, as you
like; but, on my life, we thought these little bags were
full of the genuine article."

" We did, indeed," said Dick Doubleday, gloomily.

The fence-keeper shook his head.

" They're regular Sharples's." he said. " There's
none of the family that wouldn't know 'em in a moment."

" Pshaw, man—pshaw!" cried Handsome Jemmy;
" we didn't look at them, or we should have known
them. Say no more about it—you can trust me. We're
off on business."

" Certainly, Jemmy," said the fence-keeper, " your
word's good; and these bits of spurious, too, are worth
something. You came by 'em somehow or another, and
may as well have what they'll fetch. I know a customer for 'em."

" Very well," said Handsome Jemmy, as he moved
towards the door, accompanied by Dick Doubleday; " do
the best you can with them, Sykes, and we'll square accounts when I see you again."

" There's only one man," said the fence-keeper,
" who will buy such a lot at once, and that is old
Zachariah, in Long Lane "

This was too much for the gravity of Handsome
Jemmy. The idea that Will Sykes should take to
Dick's uncle the very bags of spurious coin that had
been so recently in his possession, to sell to him again,
was a combination of events that tickled the highwayman's fancy hugely.

" Do, Sykes, do," he said. " That's the very man I
should like you to sell them to. He will be quite delighted to buy them, no doubt; for Dick here and I
happen to have private information that he's very much
in want of such a little stock. Come along, Dick.
Hush! don't say a word. It will be fine sport, and I
only wish I was there to see it But we shall hear of
it. I shouldn't wonder if Sykes and old Zachariah
had a fight over the bags. Come on, Dick—come on.
Don't say a word."

Dick Doubleday did not say a word, but his heart was
too heavy, on account of his uncertainties concerning
the fate of Pamela, to join in the merriment of the highwayman.

" Jemmy," he said, " now that we have all London
before us, what are we to do, and where are we to seek
that dear girl?"

" I can't help thinking." said Handsome Jemmy,
" that, in this dress, and if I can but get a different
coloured wig anywhere, Doctor Haslem wouldn't know
me."

" You wish to see him? Alas! he can tell you nothing."

" I'm not so sure of that. See him, I will; for, to
speak quite plainly, Dick, as I said before, I don't
believe but that he knows perfectly well where Pamela
is."

" Can that be possible? What motive——"

" Oh, men have many motives. Who shall say
but the Doctor himself may become enamoured of a
pretty face, and think that he might look long before he
saw a more charming one than that which is the property of your Pamela?"

" The villain!"

"Nay, Dick, a man is not a villain exactly because he is not insensible to the charms of Pamela Sharples."

"Hush, Jemmy, hush! Do not call her by that name, if you love me. But you fill me with a thousand fears, and rack my heart with the most terrible surmises I can now see, or seem to see, that there has been something suspicious in the physician's conduct all a'ong. You recollect, Jemmy, how averse he was to helping us in the slightest degree, and then what a change came over him, and how enthusiastic he seemed in the cause of Pamela. You should have seen him, too, Jemmy, when I spoke to him only one short hour ago. He seemed like a man upon the brink of the grave—like one already sentenced. It was conscious guilt that shone from out his eyes. Oh, why did I not see it then, and feel assured that he held in his guilty heart the secret of where Pamela was to be found?"

"It's better as it is, Dick Leave him to me. Let me try my hand upon him. Let me see! No, no! Well, I thought I had! That's awkward! Oh, yes, here's one!"

"One what?"

"A guinea, Dick. I'm going to ask the Doctor's advice, while you wait for me in Bedford Square. I'll not only get a prescription for myself, but one that shall likewise be serviceable to you, and it shall be contained in but one word."

"One word?"

"Yes; cannot you guess it?"

"My brain throbs and is bewildered. I cannot."

"The one word will be 'Pamela.'"

"Ah, yes; I should have guessed that, for what other word can heal this wounded heart?"

"Cheerily, cheerily, Dick. I have a hope, and trust that all will be well. Wait for me here. I'm going to consult our physician, and, by fair means or by foul, Dick, I'll get such an opinion upon the case that we shall not have all London before us, as we have now, and not know whether to turn to the right or to the left to search for Pamela. Wait here, my boy—don't be impatient, and I'll come back to you as quick as I can. I'm afraid I must chance matters without the wig — No, by Jove! that's the very thing."

"What's the very thing, Jemmy."

"Why, don't you see? There goes an old fellow with the very article I want—a shabby old snuff-coloured concern of a wig, that would spoil the identity of any man. Wait a moment, Dick. Sir!—sir, if you please!"

Handsome Jemmy ran after an old gentleman with a spencer and a gigantic umbrella, which, by some infatuation, he would hold by the ferule, with the handle downwards, and caught him at about twenty doors from Doctor Haslem's.

"Sir! sir!—if you'll oblige me with your wig, I will compromise matters with you, and leave you your brains—few or many, as they may happen to be—at your own disposal."

The old gentleman turned briskly round with a snarl, but Handsome Jemmy stepped up close to him and caught him by the sleeve, as he added, "Sir, I'm a highwayman—or, rather, a footpad at present. I want a wig to conceal my identity for a short time, since, in a few moments, I have every reason to believe that pistol bullets will be whistling about this square like hailstones in April. Lend me the wig, and pray get out of the way, for those same bullets are not the least respecters of persons."

Handsome Jemmy lifted off the old gentleman's hat, and twitched the wig from under it, as he spoke.

Then, in the most reckless manner, the old gentleman flung down his umbrella, and set off from Bedford Square at a speed he had not accomplished for many a long year before.

Handsome Jemmy smoothed back his own luxuriant hair, and fitting the wig on, he adjusted his neckcloth over the end of his chin; and certainly his disguise was sufficiently perfect that even Dick Doubleday, knowing him so well as he did, might have passed without recognising him.

Handsome Jemmy gave Dick a nod, and then knocked at the physician's door.

Dick Doubleday kept his eyes upon him until he disappeared into the hall.

The door was closed again, and Dick was alone in the square.

He turned round with a sigh, and then started to find himself face to face with a man who was looking curiously at him through an eye-glass.

"Egad!" said the individual with the eye-glass—"egad! Sink me, if it isn't the very man—aw—aw!"

Dick Doubleday might well start, for in this finikin-looking personage he recognised the extremely fashionable gentleman whose horse he had made free with in the green lane so very short a time before.

Nothing could be more *mal apropos* than this encounter, and poor Dick Doubleday felt as if an avenging fate was determined to be down upon him, on account of his first, and possibly his last, highway robbery.

"Egad—aw—it's the very man!"

"What do you mean, sir?" said Dick.

But he spoke faintly. Conscious guilt was at his heart, and he was too young in the profession, which boasted of such an ornament as Handsome Jemmy, to be able to carry off such an awkward position as that adroitly.

"Sink me, it is the very man—aw! You demmed rascal, where's my horse?"

"Your horse, sir?"

"Aw—yes! Where's my horse?—and, egad! my coat? Aw—I forgot the coat. Sink me, sir! you rode off on my coat with my horse on your back! Aw—I don't mean that; I mean the other thing. Egad, sir! I want my coat; and—aw—I want my horse—aw!"

"I don't know what you mean."

Dick Doubleday was puzzled, confused, confounded.

He could not take the life of the man, or inflict upon him some great injury which would rid him of his importunities; and as to freeing himself from him in any other way, there was a steady, cool pertinacity about the manner in which he asked, "Egad! for his horse and his coat," which showed that he was not to be shaken off.

Then Dick Doubleday did the worst thing he possibly could.

It struck him that if he ran through three or four streets he might easily distance his troublesome persecutor, who was probably only passing through Bedford Square, and then return still in time to meet Handsome Jemmy, as he might emerge from the physician's house.

Off set Dick.

"Off! Egad! he's *wunning* away; but I can *wun* —aw! Sink me! it's about the best thing I can do. I can *wun*—aw—beau-ti-ful! I like a *wun*."

The exquisite certainly did not give himself the character for being able to run upon light grounds.

He was swift as an antelope.

Keeping the figure of Dick Doubleday in his eyes, he dashed after him.

"Stop thief! Stop thief! A highwayman— aw! Egad, my horse! Egad, my coat! Stop thief!"

The fearful cry rung in the ears of Dick Doubleday.

A burning flush came to his brow and cheeks—his eyes seemed bursting from his head.

His heart beat violently, and one-half his youthful strength seemed to pass away at the moment that terrible cry first sounded in his ears.

He was not very familiar with that part of London, and all he could do was to dash somewhat blindly forward, taking such turnings as presented themselves to him, judicious or injudicious.

The exquisite followed close upon his heels.

Keeping that provoking and abominable eye-glass by muscular contraction still at his eye—notwithstanding all the speed he made—he never for one moment lost sight of Dick Doubleday.

And every idler in the street—for the evening was yet young—took up the cry, and took up the chase.

Dick Doubleday found himself engaged, for the first time in his life, in a hunt.

A hunt in which, as usual, human beings were the hunters, but in which no wild animal of the woods or plains was the hunted; but, on the contrary, a human being like themselves; and it is well known with what a zest a chase of that character is pursued.

Dick Doubleday had but a poor chance.

A yelling mob was at his heels.

His brain was confused and dizzy.

A strong, stout man flung himself in his path, and grappled with him.

"Now, my fine fellow, I'm your man!"

Dick Doubleday summoned the energy of despair.

He dashed the strong man aside, as though he had been a child, but in the effort he overbalanced himself, and fell.

That fall was fatal.

A dozen hands were upon his throat.

A mass of hot, excited people swarmed around him; and then, as he was held past all power of resistance, he saw the exquisite, with that provoking eye-glass at his eye, glaring in his face, and saying coolly, "Egad, I want my horse! Egad, I want my coat—aw!"

"A horse-stealer, sir?" cried a man in top boots, who had flung his arms from behind round Dick Doubleday's waist. "A horse-stealer, sir, did you say?"

"Aw!—yes—and a coat-stealer, egad! My horse and my coat, sink me! on the highway."

"All's right, sir! I have him—I am an officer. My name's Smithers. Get out of that, young fellow, if you can!"

Dick was a prisoner.

Escape from the astonishing clutch that Mr. Smithers took of him at the back of the neck was quite hopeless.

Indeed, Dick Doubleday, now that the chase was over, and he was fairly in the toils, became much calmer and more able to look his situation in the face. He felt that a struggle would now be as futile as it would be absurd, while it would probably result in some personal injury to himself that would place the possibilities of his release or his escape immeasurably distant.

He turned and looked in the rather good-humoured face of the officer as he said, "I cease to resist you—I submit as your prisoner."

"That's sensible," said Smithers: "give us your arm, young fellow. It's all in the way of business, you know, so there's no need to bear any malice. Now, sir, if you please, we'll get this bird caged, and book the charge. Highway robbery of a horse and a coat, I think you said?"

"Egad, yes! I've had quite a good wun. I like a good wun He thought he'd wun away from me. But I can wun ever so fast. I used to win all the wuns at school, and the last wocce I wun was for a wooden top, and I made that out of my own head."

CHAPTER XXII.

RETURNS TO PAMELA AND DOCTOR HASLEM IN THE ROOM OF THE FORSAKEN REPAST AND THE MYSTE-RIOUS PICTURES.

PAMELA could not forbear a slight cry of surprise and alarm upon finding that she was not alone in that dust-covered apartment where she had found a refuge.

It is true that at the first glance she recognised the Court Physician; and as she had every reason to believe that he was one likely to befriend her, as in truth he had done, the tone of alarm quickly subsided.

But he had either come into the room so silently, or she had been so completely absorbed in her contemplation of the pictures which spoke so forcibly to her memory of the past, that she had not heard him

"Oh, sir!" she said, "pardon me for being terrified at your presence. It was only the surprise of the moment."

Then it appeared that the Court Physician tried to speak, but found the effort too much for him.

He appeared to be choking—gasping for breath; deep groans burst from his labouring breast, and then he fell huddled up to the floor, like a man who has at once and for ever given up the world and all that belonged to it.

Pamela was shocked and terrified.

"Oh, sir! Dear sir!" she cried; "what does all this mean? Tell me, I pray you. Am I the cause of this suffering and emotion?"

Still he could not speak.

"Ah!" added Pamela with a sigh, "I am afraid that my presence is an embarrassment that produces all this suffering. But I will go, sir; I will go at once. Think not of me further but as one whom you have kindly befriended, and who will ever be grateful to you, let her fate be what it may."

At these words of Pamela's the Doctor made a great effort to utter a word.

"No! Heaven, no!" he gasped.

There came then tears to his eyes, and the burning sensation at his heart began to subside.

He touched his eyes with his hands, and in a voice of deep anguish he said, "Blessed tears! Oh, blessed tears!"

Pamela was much affected. She took one of the Court Physician's hands in both her own, and while her tears flowed in sympathy, she spoke gently to him.

"Dear sir, I still cannot but think that it is my presence here that has afflicted you. It may be that the wish to hide me from those men who would drag me to a terrible death has forced you to visit this room, which, I can well perceive, has not witnessed the presence of any living being for a long, long time."

"Oh, heaven!"

"Only see, sir!—the marks of my footsteps, and of yours, lie upon the dust of the floor, as though they were imprinted upon strange-coloured snow."

Such was, indeed, the case.

The physician looked like a man who looks at something without observing it.

He shook his head sadly.

"Nearly fifteen years——" he said.

"Since when, dear sir?"

"Since—since—I was in this room."

"Ah! then it is full of some sad recollections?"

"Oh, heaven!"

"Nay, I will not pain you by speaking of them. You have come to tell me that I am a charge and a danger to you. Oh! believe me, dear sir, I will go forth, ever blessing, ever thanking you!"

"No! no! A thousand times, no!"

"Indeed, sir, do not on my account suffer."

"And what," said the Court Physician, through his tears,—"what should I not suffer now if you were to leave me?"

Pamela could scarcely comprehend what these words meant, but the physician slowly gathered himself, so to speak, from the floor; and Pamela was amazed and shocked to see how much older a man he looked than when she had held the last brief dialogue with him in the library below.

His body was bent; lines of age and care seemed suddenly to have seamed his face; and but that that she thought could surely not be, she would have believed that his hair had whitened, and that decay of an ordinary twenty years had swept over him at once.

"Oh, sir!" she said, "you are ill. I feel assured that you are very ill."

"No, no!"

"Indeed and in truth, you look——"

"No; I am better—much better. Perhaps I am nearer to—to the end! Perhaps so. I think I feel that; but I am better here."

He pressed both his hands upon his heart as he spoke.

Pamela looked at him tearfully

"My dear, good girl," he said, "bear with me for a short time while I accustom my eyes to look about me at this room and the objects it contains."

"Yes—oh, yes!"

"They are all so familiar to me, and yet so strange—so very distant and strange—it seems as if only in some other state of being had I become accustomed to them; and that ages, countless ages had rolled over me since these eyes beheld them."

As he spoke, the physician turned slowly round with his hands clasped, and gazed about him.

No pen could possibly describe the soul-absorbing interest that was in that gaze.

And the eyes of Pamela followed his, as if she, too, felt to the full as much interest as he did in the old, faded, and mysterious contents of that apartment.

And so she did.

But it was a different kind of interest.

The agony of the past was not brooding at her breast.

She had nothing to regret.

He had—a lost life.

He looked at the old, dust-covered pictures on the walls.

He looked at the faded hangings and the mirrors all dimmed by damp and by neglect.

He looked then at the table.

That table on which lay the untasted repast.

Then deep sighs and moans came from him, and he tottered towards it.

He lifted one of the gloves.

His tears fell upon it like rain, and he sobbed as though his heart would break.

It must have broken but for those tears.

"Lost! lost! lost!" he moaned; "lost for ever!"

Pamela would fain have asked him to what he alluded, but there is a sacredness about such deep, real grief which forbids all questioning, and she was silent.

It was a strange sight then to see how Doctor Haslem looked at the shrivelled viands that were upon that table; how he seemed to speculate upon their conditions even in the midst of his heartfelt emotions; as people will attend sometimes to trivial things when the whole soul would seem to be swallowed up and overwhelmed by the rushing tide of some mighty and uncontrollable feeling.

Pamela thought he was calmer.

And so he was.

She spoke to him gently.

"Sir, it does seem so strange to me, but as I look upon this picture with the cottage and the mill, some recollection comes back to me, as if I had seen it once before and knew it well."

"Gracious heaven!"

The Court Physician approached the picture.

He looked at it through his tears.

With a trembling hand then he strove to dash, by the aid of his handkerchief, some of the dust from its surface.

He partially succeeded.

"Yes—oh, yes!" cried Pamela. "Now I know it better still."

The Court Physician looked inquiringly into her sweet eyes.

"What makes you know this picture?" he said; "and why are you so like one who—who——"

A sob choked his utterance.

"One who what, dear sir?" asked Pamela.

"One who is—is long since with the dead."

"And I will guess that it was one whom you loved."

"Loved? loved? Too well—too well by far; and yet not well enough."

This was rather an enigmatical speech to Pamela; but she felt it must mean something that had been a cause of great suffering to the physician, and with the delicate instinct of her feminine nature, she forbore to probe the wound she could not heal.

But the Court Physician took her gently by the hand, and led her to the chair which was drawn close to the table.

"Sit—sit!" he said. "I shall think that she has returned, and that all the past is but a dream."

Pamela sat down in the chair by the table in obedience to his wishes.

Doctor Haslem then, at a few paces distant from her, held by the back of another chair, but he did not sit down. He spoke to her in a voice thick with emotion, and he swayed gently to and fro as he spoke, as though the movement gave some slight ease to his tortured heart.

"I feel," he said, "that it is to you, young as you are, that I ought to tell the story of the past I feel that your young, unworldly spirit can best comprehend the sad history that belongs to this chamber."

"I would fain hear it," said Pamela.

"You shall—you shall. I will obey the instinct that prompts me, and I will tell you all."

"Is it very sad?"

"Oh, so sad!"

"Then it will pain you."

"No, no! It will, I think, remove some portion of the weight which is here in my breast. I have felt for nearly fifteen years now as if the point of some barbed arrow or lance-head had been left in a wound in my breast, which had healed over the jagged steel, leaving it as a lasting torment"

"Then tell me all."

"I will—I will. Nearly fifteen years ago I was a young, proud, prosperous man. My health was high—my spirits good. I seemed immortal in the pride of my health and my strength."

"Alas! alas!"

"Yes, you cry alas! because you look at me now, and you see the wreck."

Doctor Haslem did, indeed, look like a wreck.

But it was principally since he had come into that room that he had fallen into almost decrepitude. He had not looked so before.

"Fifteen years ago," he added, "I was what I tell you; and there was one who loved me, and whom I, in my proud way, loved and cherished, too. My wife—she was my wife and I was proud of her beauty—vain of her love, which fed my own vanity of heart."

"Was she very fair?"

"You have seen the picture which conceals the panel in the room below—that is her portrait. Look, too, at yourself—faintly as you may be able to see your own lineaments in that dust-covered mirror—and you will see her living image."

"I like her?"

"Marvellously like her!"

"And she—she is no more?"

"No more!—no more!"

The agony of tone in which Doctor Haslem spoke those words touched the feelings of Pamela acutely, and she could hardly restrain her tears.

"Ah, dear, good sir!" she said; "if in truth and indeed it will relieve the full heart to tell me of that fair young wife, let me know the sad history."

"I will!—I will! I did love her, but there came a demon into this house—a fiend!"

"Who? What?"

"Its name was jealousy!"

"Alas!—alas!"

"I thought her kindly glances and gentle winning ways betrayed a levity of heart that threatened my peace; and then week after week I received a letter which bade me beware of jealousy, at the same time that it lit up its most baleful fires in my soul. The writer said that he, jealous of my honour, inasmuch as he loved me, was keeping watch and ward over the frail heart of a thoughtless woman. He said—that is, the letter said—that should anything occur which I ought to know, he would warn me."

"Who was 'he?'"

"I never knew."

"And not now?"

"Now no more than ever."

"What happened then?"

"Then, after some three months of that silent agony,

there came one letter to say that if I would pretend to leave London for a few days, and then return at the hour of eleven at night, I should find that the fair and gentle young wife would be in this apartment, with a festive board, well spread, before her, waiting the arrival of one who had persuaded her he loved her better than the husband of her choice, to whom she had ever appeared to be such a marvel of affection."

"That was base."

"Hush! hear all. The letter further stated that she would deny all, and by some specious tale seek to circumvent the discovery of her wickedness; but that if I looked beneath the silver cover of one of the dishes on the table, I should find such confirmation as should dissipate all doubt if an angel should come down from heaven to testify to her innocence."

"Oh, no—no!"

"Yes, I found the proof I burst into this room unawares at half an hour to midnight. I found her here—my fair young wife, with a repast laid out for two persons—this repast that you see here now. It has lain here for fifteen years. She rose from that chair on which you now sit, with a smile, but I scowled her down, and raised the cover of the dish."

"Oh, heaven!"

"I found a letter—a letter from a lover! I could not identify the amorous name with which it was signed. They were too cunning for me, and so he escaped me. He went free!"

"But you did not——"

"Not what?"

"You did not kill her?"

"No And yet I was nearly mad enough for that. Behold! There is the letter still."

The Court Physician raised the silver cover of one of the dishes on the table; and bright and fresh beneath it, as though it had only been placed there yesterday, was an open letter.

"Behold! Oh, behold!"

CHAPTER XXIII.

DOCTOR HASLEM COMPLETES THE RELATION OF THE WIFE'S TRAGEDY AND HIS OWN DESOLATION.

THE voice of the Court Physician, as he proceeded with his recital, had acquired a high tone of grief and despair, which, to so sensitive a heart as Pamela's, was inexpressibly painful to listen to.

Each moment she feared that he was about to confide to her some terrible secret which it would burden her pure spirit to keep.

But such was not the case.

It was rather an episode of suffering than of crime that he had to relate.

"I was mad—mad!" he added. "But you shall read the letter."

He took from the silver dish on which it lay the bright, fresh-looking bit of paper, and handed it to Pamela.

Some fascination seemed to fix her eyes to the writing, and she read as follows:—

"MY LAVINIA,—

"Yes—a thousand times, yes—I will be with you, wafted on the rosy pinions of love. And so the tyrant is away, although but for a brief space. Ah, my Lavinia! let the real heart's passion bask in the sunshine of its own joy to-night.

"Yes, I will come You summon me, and I will come, dearest and best.

"These, from your own   "LOTHARIO."

Pamela read these lines with a shudder. The tone of reckless, heartless libertinism which was in and about this note, like an atmosphere of corruption and guilt, shocked her.

She let the letter drop from her hand as she would have shaken from it some venomous thing.

"What—what happened?" she asked faintly.

"Lavinia—that was my wife—tried to speak, but I scorned to hear her. I struck her once—only once—I saw the red spot upon her cheek. Oh, would that the blow had rather been upon my own heart!"

Pamela shrunk back in the chair.

"Yes, I struck her; and without a word I turned and left the room—this room "

"And then?—and then? Oh, what then?"

"I sat the whole night long upon a door-step in the square—the next door-step to my own, I was watching—watching."

"Watching?"

"Yes, for Lothario!"

"Ah, yes!"

"But he never came. The night was one of storm, the rain beat down upon me, and the wind howled about me—but he never came. No one went into my house. One of the servants, as I thought, left it, with some bundle in her arms, and passed me, but I heeded her not. I was waiting—I was watching for Lothario."

"Good heavens!"

"Murder was my impulse. I watched, I prayed, and I waited for the ribald fiend who had assumed that name, but who would, in his own proper person, feel my vengeance. But during that live-long night no footsteps crossed my threshold as a visitor, and in truth no one left the house but my brother once, and that servant, with a bundle. Yes, I forget; my brother Matthew left twice—once, and he came back again, and then he left again. Poor Matthew! I thought to call him, but I did not. And so the night of squally tempest, of rain, of cold, and of desolation, passed away, and there was no Lothario."

Pamela seemed to feel that this was not all, although the Court Physician clasped his hands over his face, and rocked to and fro, and moaned as though he had got to the end of his story.

"What happened then?" she said, quietly.

"I will tell you. At the first dawn of day I rose and tottered to my own doorstep. My servants scarcely knew me, so worn, so old, so haggard did I look."

Pamela shuddered.

"I staggered, rather than walked, over my own doorstep, and the first person I met was my brother Matthew; and he looked—I remembered since how he looked, although I did not notice it then—he looked scarcely less haggard than myself. He spoke to me kindly, and asked me where I had been. He had no notion that I had been so near at hand"

"And then—and then?" asked Pamela—"what then happened?"

"Better thoughts had began to come over me, and I began to think that she, my wife, might be innocent. I longed to look into her eyes by the daylight, and read there some justification—some explanation."

"Oh, yes, yes!"

At this stage of his narration the Court Physician wrung his hands and sobbed bitterly.

It seemed that he dreaded to approach the climax of his history, so sad and so mournful was it.

Pamela, too, trembled to hear what happened then after the night of terror and despair, and she shrunk from again questioning Doctor Haslem.

It was well to leave him to himself for a while and he was then able to speak to her more calmly.

"I sought this room," he said—"this room in which we are now, for I had seen her here last, and I had a notion that she would be here still."

"You—you——"

Pamela was about to say, "You found her not?" but she abstained, and the physician added—

"She was gone, gone, gone!"

"Alas!—alas!"

"Gone with our child—our dear little one—gone for ever, for ever!"

"A child?"

"Yes. Did I not tell you? Perhaps not; I scarcely know what I put into words and what I only think, but

ASTONISHMENT OF WILL SYKES.

No. 8.—Felon's Daughter.

there was a little child named after its mother, Lavinia. It was then scarcely two years of age, and that unhappy mother had taken her child in her arms, and in the midst of the storm, the tempest of that night, she had gone forth, and I was desolate!"

Pamela was deeply affected.

She could feel for that broken-hearted man in the midst of all her sympathy for the wronged mother and the little one whom she had on that fearful night taken with her.

There did not seem to her for a single moment any question on the mind of Pamela that the wife of the physician was entirely innocent.

Perhaps Pamela, with her few experiences of the world, might have found it difficult to expound any theory upon the subject of that innocence, but she felt it all the same.

It was faith that she had in the purity of the wife of the physician, and to her mind no argumentation was required on the subject.

But she was full of interest in the sad history that had been imparted to her.

"Tell me, dear sir," she said, "have you never, with all your anxious inquiries—and no doubt they have been great and frequent—obtained any news of wife or child?"

"Never—never!"

"That is very sad."

"This room," added the physician, "I found just as it was when I struck that blow which had at once, and for ever, seemed to sever all ties between Lavinia and myself. The untasted repast was upon the table—everything just as you see it. I passed a day and a night here, and then I had it closed up; and I sent to a friend I had in Holland, to send me over a clever artificer; and he did send me one who, under my direction, contrived the secret route to this chamber in the thickness of the wall of the house."

As the physician got to this point in his narrative he became aware that there was a repeated knocking at the outer door of his house.

He tottered to his feet.

"I must go back again," he said, "into the world. I must put on a calm face, and all must seem to be still and serene at my heart. Can you bear to be alone here for a time?"

"Yes, most certainly. There is a something in the room, in the very air of it, that seems homelike and grateful to me."

"That is well—that is well. I will return when I can."

"But stay one moment," said Pamela, "and tell me what place this picture represents?"

She alluded to the picture with the mill and the mill-stream that had excited such strange recollections in her heart.

"It is a view of a country cottage that I have on the road to Edgware," replied Doctor Haslem. "I used to visit it with Lavinia—my wife—and the little one; but since that night of terror I have never looked upon it. You may see the cottage nestling among the trees."

"I do—I do."

The interest with which Pamela looked at this picture increased each moment; and Doctor Haslem, with a deep sigh, left the mysterious apartment by the opening in the wall as he had entered it, so noiselessly, that it was only when she glanced around that Pamela saw he was gone, and that she was alone again in that silent room so full of sad reminiscences.

It was then that the Court Physician had had the interview with Dick Doubleday which had resulted so unfavourably for the physician's reputation for kindliness of heart.

Perhaps Doctor Haslem could hardly have defined to himself why it was that it seemed death to him to part with Pamela Sharples, or to permit any eyes but his own to look upon her.

As yet, he had not evidence sufficient to enable him to look upon her as his long-lost child; but yet there was a something—an indefinable feeling at his heart and brain—which told him she was the little Lavinia who had been carried away on the night of storm and tempest, fifteen years ago, by the outraged wife.

He had, however, such a terror of making a mistake on such a subject, that often, as he had been upon the point of opening his arms and calling out aloud, "My child—my child! come to your own father's heart!" he had restrained himself.

But hour by hour—minute by minute—the conviction was growing strong within him, that in this young girl whom he had helped so materially to snatch from a terrible and ignominious death, he beheld his own long-lost child.

And now letting some few hours pass away, we reach that time at which Handsome Jemmy, the highwayman, knocked at the door of Doctor Haslem, leaving Dick Doubleday waiting for him in the square.

What happened to Dick on that occasion we already know, and we follow now Handsome Jemmy into the house of the physician on that errand which he had set himself, of discovering, if possible, what had become of Pamela.

Handsome Jemmy inquired for the physician in a quiet, business-like manner, and was shown, as a matter of course, into the usual reception room.

But the Doctor was not to be found, and a tall, dignified-looking gentleman, some few years older than Doctor Haslem, entered the room, and said courteously, "My brother is from home, and therefore, sir, if you will kindly say when you will call again, or where he can wait upon you if your visit is professional, I will take care that he is made aware of it."

Handsome Jemmy started at the sound of the voice of this gentleman, who announced himself as Doctor Haslem's brother. He felt certain not only that he had heard that voice before, but that it was very recently that its tones had struck upon his ears.

Where was it?

It was quite in vain that the highwayman asked himself that question.

It was an inquiry that baffled him.

The Doctor's brother, Mr. Matthew Haslem, looked surprised at Handsome Jemmy's silence, and he respoke his words.

Then the highwayman felt more convinced than ever that he had heard the voice before, although he was quite certain that was the first time he had ever looked upon Mr. Matthew Haslem.

But that conviction only made the recollection of the voice more mysterious and inexplicable.

"Sir," said Jemmy, "I did indeed wish much to see Doctor Haslem."

It would appear that by this time Mr. Matthew Haslem had come to the conclusion that it was not as a patient that the visitor he saw before him wished to consult the Doctor, and along with that conviction there came an expression of anxiety into his face almost amounting to terror.

CHAPTER XXIV.

HANDSOME JEMMY, THE HIGHWAYMAN, MAKES AN IMPORTANT DISCOVERY, AND INVOLVES HIMSELF IN A PROMISE.

MR. MATTHEW HASLEM fixed his eyes upon Handsome Jemmy with an expression of nervousness that he strove in vain to wholly combat and subdue.

"Sir," he said, "have you any objection to tell me what your business is with Doctor Haslem?"

"None in the least!" said the highwayman, with whom excessive candour was rather a failing. "None in the least! I want to know where Pamela Sharples is."

"Ah!"

The exclamation uttered by Mr. Matthew Haslem showed that that was just what he had feared.

"Well, sir," said Jemmy, "I cannot help a fancy that

you are as well able to answer me that question as the Doctor himself."

"No, no! Oh no! But you will perhaps tell me why it is you ask, and what interest you have in the question?"

"No. As a friend of Pamela Sharples, I have the right to require of Doctor Haslem some account of her. If you know this, I require the account of you."

The highwayman began to think it was rather a fortunate coincidence that he had first encountered this brother of Doctor Haslem's, because it might enable him to compare together the account of the brothers separately, before, perhaps, they might be able to concoct some story on the subject that would look possible on account of the accord that would be about each of their recitals.

"No, no! I know nothing," said Mr. Matthew Haslem—"I know nothing; and therefore, sir, I leave you if it be your determination to wait until my brother returns."

"One moment, sir."

"Well, sir?"

"Is the girl here, in this house? Has she ever been here?"

Mr. Matthew hesitated a moment, and then he said in a low tone, "She is not here—she has not been here."

"Then, sir," said Jemmy, as he stepped between Matthew Haslem and the door of the room—"then, sir, I will trouble you to stay with me till your brother, the Doctor, returns; for, once to-day, he has given rather a different reply to that same question!"

"What insolence is this?"

"Oh, you can say what you like; but, for all that, I do not mean to let you go."

"Help! I——"

"Stop, sir! stop one moment. No alarm, if you please. I have come here to get some news that shall be true, and authentic, and available of Pamela Sharples, and I will have it. Do not run into danger, sir."

Jemmy, as he spoke, took one of his pistols from his pocket, and flinging open the pan, he settled the priming in its place, and coolly motioned Mr Matthew to a chair, as he added, "You had better sit down, sir; I don't know how long it may be before the Doctor comes home, but ——Ah! that's the game, is it? Why, sir, you have no more chance with me than a child!"

Mr. Matthew had made a sudden dash forward at the highwayman, with an evident intention of snatching the pistol from his grasp, and so getting either the better of him, or at least being on equal terms with him.

But he little knew the calm and cool courage of the man he had to deal with—as little, indeed, as he knew of the strength that was opposed to him.

Handsome Jemmy put him aside with the greatest ease; and, in truth, the principal anxiety of the highwayman was that the pistol he had produced only as a threat, should not go off in the slight struggle that took place.

It was this anxiety that prevented Handsome Jemmy from so rapidly and effectually, as he otherwise would have done, freeing himself from the grasp of Mr. Matthew, for he had to hold the hand with the pistol in it above his head, to keep it out of danger; and the consequence was, that Mr. Matthew snatching at Handsome Jemmy's throat, and being foiled a little, got hold of his vest and tore it open.

A small locket, edged with pearls of no great value, and suspended round the neck of the highwayman by a very finely made Venetian gold chain, was torn from beneath Handsome Jemmy's vest.

That locket was dashed rather violently over the arm of Mr. Matthew Haslem, and then, in a very strange manner, alighted on to the back of his hand, exactly before his eyes.

What basilisk power had that little golden trinket, with its edge of pearls?

What Medusa-like glance came from it, that it should so affect Mr. Matthew Haslem?

The moment his eyes fell upon it he uttered a half-suppressed shriek, and fell to the floor like a dead man!

The highwayman was amazed, and, to tell the truth, a little terrified.

But he did not for a moment attribute the state of Mr. Mathew Haslem to the sight of the locket. He thought some sudden sickness had come over him, which at his age, for he was not a young man, had been produced by the excitement of the brief struggle between them.

"It is no fault of mine," said Jemmy; "and now I suppose I must summon assistance?"

"No!—heaven, no!" gasped Mr. Matthew, as he made a feeble attempt to grasp Handsome Jemmy by the foot, to prevent him from stirring.

"I don't want," replied Jemmy. "If you feel better, let me help you to sit up. There, now! Perhaps you will have less disinclination to answer me about Pamela Sharples!"

The highwayman helped Mr. Matthew to a chair; but the Doctor's brother made an impatient kind of gesture with his hand at the sound of the name of Pamela Sharples, as though some far more important subject had arisen in his mind.

"Tell me—oh, tell me——" he said, faintly.

"Tell you what?"

"Who—what—what—who you are?"

"Oh, that's it! John Smith is my name, and my occupation, idleness."

"John Smith? No, no! That—that locket!"

"That what?"

The Doctor's brother pointed with a trembling hand to the locket that still hung loose and free from the breast of the highwayman.

"Ah!" cried Handsome Jemmy. "I would not lose it for a thousand pounds!"

"Stop—stop! Do not—do not!"

"Do not what?"

"Do not hide it! Let me look upon it again! Have—have you ever opened it?"

"I have!"

"And—and you found——"

"Nothing! It is empty! But what do you know about it—if, indeed, it be possible that you know anything?"

Mr. Matthew looked wistfully into the eyes of the handsome highwayman, as he said, faintly, "Who shall say that heaven may not, in its own good fashion, yet preserve me for much mercy? Tell me how and when you came by the locket?"

Handsome Jemmy would perhaps have answered the question of the Doctor's brother freely enough in his off-hand, heedless way, but his attention was much attracted by seeing the tearful man open the locket as he (Jemmy) had indeed often opened it, and then proceed to touch a small concealed spring, which opened an inner case which he (Jemmy) had never discovered, and from which there rose up, half floating out from the compressed prison in which it had lain as though it were a living thing, a small lock of fair hair.

The highwayman was surprised.

"Ah, sir!" he said; "it seems to me that you know more of the locket than I do."

Mr. Matthew approached his lips with the lock of fair hair as though he was about to kiss it, or to let some tears fall upon it, but he did neither. He dropped the locket with a moan and a shudder.

"I dare not!" he said; "I dare not!"

Handsome Jemmy caught the lock of fair hair as it was slowly descending to the floor, and then as he held it on the palm of his hand he said, "Tell me, sir, what you know of this locket, and of this spray of hair, which for the first time has met my sight. Tell me, I beg of you!"

"I will. But do not—oh, do not be angry again if I ask you first to tell me something!"

Mr. Matthew spoke in such imploring, sad accents, that it was not possible to refuse the request.

"Speak, then," said Jemmy. "What is it you want to ask of me?"

"When and how came you by this locket?"

"I will tell you freely. It was round my neck, I am told, when I was found, at about the age of two years friendless, destitute, and deserted on a door-step."

"Oh, heaven!"

"I was taken to the nearest workhouse, where there was no resource but to keep me, however grudgingly that was done. There I stayed till I was put out as an apprentice to a man who worked me like a slave. I ran away when I was sixteen years old, and from that time to this I am—well, I am——That's my business, however."

"And the locket?"

"Oh, it is a thousand wonders it was ever in my hands; but the only person who ever spoke a word of kindness to me in the workhouse was an old woman, who was a kind of servant and housekeeper to the master; and when I was on the point of leaving, to be an apprentice, as I have told you, she sought me out in the middle of the night, and said to me, 'Jemmy Jemmy, take this locket: it was round thy neck, my poor boy, when thee was brought here; and the master himself took it off, and has kept it ever since, and wants to keep it still; but it is thine, and may some day help thee to know who and what thou art.'"

Mr. Matthew sighed deeply.

"So," added Handsome Jemmy, "from that day to this I have worn the locket round my neck; but I never suspected that inner case to it, which you seem to have known well enough, since you opened it in such a moment."

"Then you—you do not know who you are? No father?—no—no mother?"

"Neither."

"And you—you——"

"Well, in plain language, sir, I may say that, for all I know to the contrary, I may have dropped from the clouds on to that door-step, and——"

Bang came such a violent knock at the door of the residence of the fashionable physician at this moment, that it startled both Handsome Jemmy and the Doctor's brother.

It was so very unusual a knock to come at such a door, that Mr. Matthew sprang to his feet in surprise, and turned paler than before. There was perpetually that look upon this man's face which indicated a mind ill at ease—an expectant, cautious, half-scared expression—as though he felt, in any moment, something might happen which would involve him in difficulty, danger, and distress.

When, therefore, this unusual and startling summons for admission to the Court Physician's house came at the outer door, it was the respectable and well-to-do Mr. Matthew Haslem who seemed to be full of fears, and not Handsome Jemmy, the highwayman.

Such a knock was not likely to be required to be repeated; and, in fact, in the apartment where the Doctor's brother and Handsome Jemmy were, they could hear the sound of loud voices in contention in the hall.

Leading the kind of life he did, the highwayman might well suppose that some accident might have betrayed his presence in that house to the constables.

Turning, therefore, to Mr. Matthew, he gave him a new idea, as he said, "It is possible there is some danger. I don't know if my possession of this locket, which has excited your feelings and your attention gives me any claim to your good offices; but, if it does, I ask you plainly, can you hide me anywhere? If it does not, I must even take my chance, and fight my way clear as best I can."

"Are you in danger?" cried Mr Matthew Haslem, as he tremulously caught Handsome Jemmy by the arm and looked imploringly in his face—"are you in danger?"

"I am."

"Are you obnoxious to to the officers of justice?—are they on your track? Oh! speak to me—speak to me! What have you done? What new terror is this that is to mingle with the strange sensations the sight of

that locket has conjured up in this repentant and agonized brain?"

"Hush!" said Handsome Jemmy; "do you not hear?"

There came the tones of a loud voice from the hall.

"Let us see Mr. Matthew, then," said the voice. "It is our duty, and we must and will search the house."

"That means me," said Jemmy. "I don't blame you, sir, or suspect you in the slightest degree; but I have made up my mind to one thing—and that is, not to be taken while I have my hands at liberty, and this pair of little barkers at my disposal."

The highwayman held both his pistols in his left hand, and glanced towards the door of the room, but Mr. Matthew Haslem clung to him with a half entreating, half affectionate kind of action.

"No, no!" he cried; "I can and will hide you As yet, all is chaos and confusion in my mind, and I know not how to call you or how to address you; but I can and will hide you from your enemies, were they ten times in number what they are, and more diligent and skilful in their search for you than probably consists with any of their intellects. I will trust you with a secret, which you will promise me, on your faith and soul, not to betray."

"I will promise, certainly."

"There is a hiding-place in this house, which no ordinary search, be it ever so stringent, can discover. But you must solemnly promise me that, whatever you see, or whatever you hear in connexion with that hiding-place, you will keep secret for ever and ever, unless I should absolve you from the oath."

"I promise," said Handsome Jemmy: "there can be no difficulty about that."

"Step this way."

Mr. Matthew Haslem opened a door that led from that apartment into the library—that library over the chimney-piece of which was the portrait covered with its heavy velvet curtain.

The Doctor's brother locked that door which led from the reception-room into the library on the inner side; and he did so only just in time, for scarcely had he turned the key when a sharp rapping at it from the side of the reception-room showed that one or more persons had already entered there from the hall.

Handsome Jemmy, the highwayman, turned round twice upon his heels and looked about him in that spacious and well-adorned library; but he saw no place of concealment—unless he could manage to stow himself away horizontally upon the book-shelves, with a row of folio volumes before him

Mr. Matthew Haslem, however, placed his finger on his lips, to signify the necessity for silence, and then he carefully drew aside the velvet curtain from before the portrait on the chimney-piece.

Handsome Jemmy could not but observe the peculiar manner in which the Doctor's brother averted his eyes from that portrait, so that in fact he did not look at it, and only by the sense of touch sought to find the spring which would cause the panel to open, and reveal the recess in the wall.

This, however, he succeeded in doing, and then Handsome Jemmy said, in a cautious whisper, "I see, now—I see, now! By Jove, sir! I don't think they'll find me here, as you say; but, be assured, I avail myself of such a place as this rather from my disinclination to put a bullet into any of their stupid skulls, than because I had any real doubt about escaping. May I ask, sir, where this leads to?"

"It matters not," replied Mr Matthew; "let it suffice for you that it will keep you in secrecy and in safety until these men leave the house. You need not pursue it further than will accomplish that purpose; and perhaps it would be better that you should not—for if you do, you will find yourself burdened with a heavier secret than the mere existence of this secret channel in the wall, and one more difficult to keep."

"Very well," said Jemmy. "Be that as it may, there

MR. MATTHEW HASLEM AND HANDSOME JEMMY.

is no time to lose, for my friends on the other side of that door are getting clamorous "

With very slight intermission, the knocking at the door leading into the reception-room had been kept up.

It was evident that the officers—for such indeed they were—felt some reluctance in such a house as that to proceed to violence; but all their suspicions were aroused on finding that room locked up for Mr. Matthew had likewise turned the key of the only other door which led into it—so that the constables, detecting that keys were in the locks on the inner side, could come to no other conclusion than that some one was there.

"Open! open!" cried a loud voice,—"open, in the King's name, or we will force the door!"

"Ah!" said Handsome Jemmy, as he mounted a chair and got on to the chimney-piece. "I know that voice perfectly well. It belongs to Sylvester, the Bow Street officer—a most indefatigable fellow; but I think I shall foil him now!"

"Quick—quick!" said Mr. Matthew Haslem, "or you are lost!"

"All right, sir—all right!" said Jemmy, as he disappeared behind the panel, and closed it after him. "By Jove! I feel as though I were being lost getting into this place; but I suppose I shall be found again some of these days!"

Mr. Matthew Haslem turned the key hastily in the door of communication between the library and the reception-room.

He confronted the officers with a look of calmness and composure, as he said, "Is this proper conduct in the house of a private gentleman, and one of the physicians to his Majesty?"

———

CHAPTER XXV.

HANDSOME JEMMY, THE HIGHWAYMAN, OVERHEARS THE CONFESSION OF DOCTOR HASLEM, AND IS JUST IN TIME TO SAVE PAMELA.

"WELL!" said Handsome Jemmy, when the secret panel over the chimneypiece in the Doctor's library was fairly closed, and he was in the narrow, dark recess,— "well, here I am, very much like a rat behind the wainscot. I wonder what I am to do next?"

The voices of Mr. Matthew Haslem and the officers came to his ears confusedly.

That panel, with the portrait on one side of it, and some thick cloth on the other, effectually smothered the tones of the voices, so far as regarded their intelligibility.

But Jemmy felt very uncomfortable.

"A pretty thing," he said to himself—"a pretty thing I have here dropped into—shut up between two walls, when I pass the most part of my life on horseback, with the free air of some wild heath or common blowing about my ears! I don't like it at all!"

The narrow channel in the wall seemed each moment to be more stifling to the highwayman.

He stretched out his hands, and found that the space about him was even less than he had thought it.

The soft, uncomfortable feel, too, of the velvet with which the passage was lined gave Handsome Jemmy the sensation of being buried alive.

Gloomy thoughts took possession of him.

"I can't stand this," he said; "I must try and get out of it in some way. How the dence did that Sylvester find out I was here, and what, by this time, has become of poor Dick Doubleday?"

These were both questions that perplexed the highwayman, but it was the latter one only that gave him much concern.

Little, however, did Handsome Jemmy expect that Dick Doubleday was in the hands of the constables, and not waiting for him any longer in Bedford Square.

Then Jemmy finding that the brother of the Court Physician did not come to his rescue, bethought him of the fact that that channel in the wall led somewhere, and that probably it had an opening at its other end.

He recollected, too, that Mr. Matthew had intimated as much to him, by the ambiguous sort of advice he had given to him, not to seek to penetrate all the secrets connected with that place.

But the highwayman did not see any great necessity for complying with such an injunction.

Curiosity, as well as the feeling of irksomeness that had come over him in that place, urged him forward

"I will find out where this odd passage in the wall leads to if I die for it," said Jemmy.

As he spoke he commenced making slow progress in the way that Pamela had taken when she had been introduced to that secret recess by Doctor Haslem.

Step by step, carefully feeling his way, the highwayman went on until he was suddenly arrested by a cry which sounded in his ears like some effort of a heart full of grief and misery to find a temporary relief.

Jemmy listened with all his might.

"What was that? and where was it?"

Those were the two questions he put to himself without being able to answer either of them.

But then he felt quite certain he heard the sound of sobbing, and he found that by placing his right ear flat against what seemed to be the side of the wall on that side he could hear those sounds of sobbing much more distinctly than he could before

Nay, after a few seconds, he could hear a voice, and could distinguish the words.

Those words surprised him not a little.

"Tell me, oh, tell me, where I can find that man; for I must question him before again I eat, drink, or sleep!"

The tones were those of the Court Physician.

But if Handsome Jemmy was surprised to hear Dr. Haslem speak in such a fashion, he was still more astonished to recognise the voice of Pamela in reply.

"Sir, you terrify me; I know not what to think, or what you mean; but if you would, indeed, seek Jacob Sharples, you will find him at his own home."

"Where? where?"

"The street is a wretched one, in Clerkenwell, and it is named Rose Street. The number is four."

"Yes, yes," said Doctor Haslem; "I will seek that man out; and, oh, Pamela! Pamela!—for by such a name I will still call you—let me here confess to you that you are so near to my heart—so dear to me——"

"Oh, no, no!" interrupted Pamela. "Sir, you must not say that to me. All my affections belong to my dear, dear Richard Doubleday."

"My poor, dear girl," sobbed the physician, "you do not yet comprehend the kind of love that I would bestow upon you, if—if—the dictates of my heart are true ones; but you shall remain here, dear girl, in peace, and in safety. I myself will wait upon you, even as a father would wait upon his darling child."

"Alas! I never knew a father's love!"

"Yes, yes, you did know it, but have forgotten it. Oh! what am I saying? What am I daring to say? Let me have proof—proof abundant. Yes, I will seek out this man, this coiner, Jacob Sharples, and I will wrest the secret from his guilty heart."

Handsome Jemmy was puzzled.

"What does all this mean?" he asked himself.

But the highwayman had not much time to waste in reflection.

A period of action was coming.

A dull, heavy sort of sound was in the house—a sound as of trampling feet. The officers were continuing their search, and it seemed as if they approached very near to that apartment where he, Jemmy, heard the voice of Pamela.

The highwayman was fully impressed with the belief that the room in which Doctor Haslem and the fair Pamela were, was, as a matter of course, one of the ordinary apartments of the house.

He had no idea that it was an apartment entirely concealed—walled up, in fact, by the cunning artisan from

Holland, and that the only mode of access to it was by the passage in which he, Jemmy, then was.

As those dull, heavy sounds, indicative of the activity of the constables' search in the house, came upon his ears, his anxiety for the safety of Pamela became excessive.

He heard her speak again.

"There are strange sounds in the house," she said; "is there danger?"

"None to you, dear girl," replied the physician.

"Oh, he is mad!" said the highwayman. "Does he think that the officers will be so foolish as to leave that one room unlooked into?"

"I will then believe there is no danger," added Pamela, "since you say so, sir."

"You may, indeed, dear girl."

"But I don't," said Jemmy.

In his anxiety to make the physician and Pamela aware that the mansion was being searched by what he. Jemmy, called the Philistines, he rapped sharply at the side of the wall, where he had placed his ear to listen.

Both the physician and Pamela uttered exclamations of alarm.

"What is that? What does that mean?" asked Pamela, nervously.

"It must be my brother," replied the Doctor, "for he alone, along with myself and you, dear girl, knows of the secret channel in the wall."

In another moment the Court Physician had opened the panel.

At sight of Handsome Jemmy, who was quite delighted to be free, and who put one foot upon the chimney-piece, so that the panel might not be closed again, the Court Physician uttered a cry of alarm.

Pamela echoed that cry.

"Hush!" said the highwayman. "Do you not know that the t aps are in the house?"

"The what?"

"Good heavens! who are you?" exclaimed the physician.

Jemmy jumped on to the floor.

"Don't you know me?"

"Know you! Oh, heaven, all is lost!"

"And you, Pamela," added Handsome Jemmy: "don't you know me?"

Pamela looked confused. The voice was familiar to her, but the highwayman at the moment quite forgot that he had taken a good deal of pains to disguise himself.

That fact, however, flashed across his mind in another moment.

"To be sure! To be sure!" he said. "How should you know me? There? Now you do?"

"Ah, yes! Dick's friend!"

"The same."

"And the highwayman!" said Doctor Haslem, who as soon as Handsome Jemmy threw off the wig, he at once recognised,—"and the highwayman, or all this is a dream!"

"No," said Jemmy, "it's no dream; but you yet don't seem half awake to the fact that the constables are in the house, and that Pamela is in danger."

"Constables?"

"Yes. A good party of them."

Pamela clasped her hands together, and burst into tears.

"They will drag me to death again," she sobbed. "Oh, better that I had died yesterday, than lived but to suffer all the pangs of hope deferred!"

"Pho! pho!" said Handsome Jemmy; "you don't suppose, my dear, that you are in any danger, do you? It is not likely that that should be the case while Jemmy the Highwayman is here."

"Hush!" said Doctor Haslem.

There was a confused murmur of voices on the outside of the wainscoting which concealed the existence of that small room.

Jemmy was silent.

The voice of Sylvester, the officer, could plainly be heard.

"I am quite certain," he said, "that the man we seek has not left this house; and if we don't find him, I shall feel assured that there is some secret hiding-place in it, which I will find out, if it costs me a month's trouble."

Then the voice of Mr. Matthew, the Doctor's brother, was heard in reply.

"You contemplate an outrage," he said, "which the warrant you have shown me does not authorize."

"I don't care."

"But you will be made to care."

Doctor Haslem turned very pale while this little conference was going on.

Pamela trembled in every limb.

Handsome Jemmy looked thoughtful.

"It is true," added Sylvester, the officer—"it is quite true that we have been over the house and not found him; but one of my men, on whom I can depend, saw the man we seek come in here, and he has never lost sight of the door, so that he is quite sure he has never left the house again."

"You reason badly," said Mr. Matthew. "The house has a back. I nor my brother keep no watchful eye upon any one who may come hither. Who shall say that such a man as you mention might not come here, and while we thought he had left in a legitimate way by the front door, he might slip out by the back, and so, by scaling a wall or two, get into the gardens of Montague House, and escape?"

"No!"

"It is easy to say 'No!'"

"I say no, however, because one of my men is on duty in the gardens of Montague House."

"Do as you please, then, constable!" said Mr. Matthew. "It is not the King's Physician who will dispute the King's warrant!"

A strange tapping sound commenced on the wainscot which specially hid the room which was so hidden, and which contained the two fugitives, Handsome Jemmy and Pamela.

Terror took possession of the young girl.

"My time has come!—my time has come!" she moaned. "They will drag me away to death! Oh, heaven, help me! Richard!—Richard! where are you? where are you?"

The highwayman stepped up to Dr. Haslem, who had been with a confused look regarding him almost as an apparition, so surprised was he at his presence there at all.

"Sir," said Handsome Jemmy, "I can well understand now that this apartment is boarded up in some manner so that there appears to be no entrance to it."

"It is so," said the physician, faintly. "But——"

"But what, sir?"

"Those men—those officers! The suspicion once aroused, and the secret is discovered!"

"That's about what I was thinking," said the highwayman. "And although I am in some state of confusion as to finding Pamela here, and why she is denied to her best friends, yet it seems to me there is but one way to save her!"

At this juncture the voice of Sylvester, the officer, was again heard.

"I feel certain," he said, "that there is some space between this wainscoting."

"Lost!—lost! I am lost!" said Pamela.

She covered her fair face with her hands, and sunk to the floor.

A look of terrible despair came across the face of the doctor.

It was the highwayman alone who preserved anything like composure.

"Listen to me, Doctor," he said, "and answer me what I want to know."

"I will!—I will!"

There was so much strong hopefulness and power about the tones of Handsome Jemmy, that they had a great effect upon the enfeebled mind of the Doctor.

" Tell me," added Jemmy, " do you fancy the constables know of Pamela being here?"

" No!—no! I have no such idea!"

" Then they are after me."

" It may be so."

" Good! Dry your tears, my poor girl! You are in no danger—I will take care of that!"

" You will save me?"

" Indeed I will!"

" But how—how can you do so?"

" Why, my dear, it seems to me that I—and I only—am the person with the power to do so; and as I happen to have the will likewise, why it will be all right."

" You may have the will twenty times over," said the Court Physician; " but I cannot see what power you have."

Handsome Jemmy smiled.

He stepped up to Pamela, and gently kissed her forehead.

" The first kiss and the last, my dear!" he said. " I am the friend of Dick Doubleday, and am not forgetful that he loves you, and that you return his affection. I am now going to save you!"

" Going to save me? What?—what?"

" Why, look you here, my dear! The officers are after me, and there is no occasion that they should find you as well."

" Ah!"

Well, you begin to see. But fear nothing for me! I have a thousand chances of escape. It is not the iron doors nor the stone walls of old Newgate that will keep me in durance! Let them take me, and then they will no longer feel any curiosity in regard to the house."

Pamela sprung to her feet.

She held Handsome Jemmy tightly by the arm.

" No! no!" she said; " I perhaps could not be so generous, so noble as this, but I can be just. You shall not sacrifice yourself for me!"

The Court Physician, with a look of great excitement upon his face, glanced from one to the other of them.

" Pamela! Pamela!" he cried, " remember, oh, remember your danger!"

" There!" said Jemmy, with a smile; " you see the Doctor approves of the plan."

" And I will exert my utmost influence," added the physician, " to be of service to you. Heaven knows how you came here; but being here, if you do what you say——"

Pamela cast a reproachful look at the Court Physician,

" Sir, sir!" she said, " is it well to purchase even life at the sacrifice of a friend?"

" Girl! girl! you know not what you say."

" Enough!" said the highwayman; " my mind is made up. Listen to that!"

" Now set to work on this panelling," said the officer Sylvester, on the other side.

" Good-bye," said Handsome Jemmy.

He disengaged himself from the clinging arms of Pamela, and with one bound, by the aid of a chair, reached the chimney-piece, and disappeared through the spring in the wall.

CHAPTER XXVI.

DOCTOR HASLEM VISITS SHARPLES THE COINER, AND MEETS WITH A TERRIBLE ADVENTURE.

THERE came a creaking noise on the other side of the partition, which had been so artfully put up for the purpose of hiding the existence of that chamber that contained so many gloomy memorials of the past.

Sylvester, the officer, had had his suspicions fully aroused, and he had sent for a workman, who was now directed to get down a portion of the panel.

The sending for that workman had been the cause of that delay in the operations of the constables that had enabled Handsome Jemmy to declare his intentions to Pamela.

But now the man was at work.

Soon that panelling would give way, unless some circumstance should occur to put a stop to the proceedings.

Then the cherished secret of the Court Physician, which for fifteen years had been hidden from the public gaze, would be revealed.

But the interposition that was to put a stop to the operations of the constables was at hand.

The highwayman made short work of the passage from that long closed-up room to the library.

On to the floor of that latter apartment he sprung with a light heart.

And yet he knew that he would soon be a prisoner, and that his life would appear to be in the hands of the law.

There was not a chance of escape, for in order to save Pamela—in order to put a stop to the operations at the panelling that concealed the secret apartment, he must show himself.

Otherwise, there would have been a chance of his yet escaping by the front door.

The two constables who were left in charge of the hall of the Doctor's house would not have been able to successfully oppose the exit of Handsome Jemmy had he chosen to force it.

But that would have defeated his object.

Pamela would have been lost!

So Handsome Jemmy, with a slight flush upon his face, for the occasion was somewhat exciting and unusual, walked out of the library and reached the hall.

The two officers who were there made a rush towards him.

But Jemmy did not intend that they should be his captors. He preferred encountering the stronger party in the hands of Sylvester, the Bow Street runner, who were at work on the panelling.

Therefore the highwayman darted up the stairs three at a time.

The two officers from the hall pursued him, shouting out to their comrades above.

" What's the row?" said Handsome Jemmy, as he came in sight of Sylvester and his party.

" Ah!" cried the Bow Street runner, " I rather think that's my man."

" You don't mean me?" said Jemmy.

" Yes, I do. Come, Jemmy, your time is up, and the very best thing you can do is to give as little trouble as possible."

" Well, Mr. Sylvester, I might take a life or two, but if you must have me, I don't know a better man than yourself to do the job."

" That's sensible. Mr. Carpenter, you need not go on with your work. There is half-a-crown for you. You can pack up your tools and go. It don't matter to me how many cages there are in this house so that I have the bird I came to catch."

Sylvester laid his hand on the highwayman's shoulder.

" Look you here, Mr. Sylvester," said Jemmy: " I suppose you will take me to the old Stone Jug at once?"

" Yes; to Newgate."

" Well, I have, in a manner of speaking, given myself up to you?"

" You have, Jemmy."

" Do me a favour in return. Keep as close an eye on me as you like, but—but——"

The highwayman's voice faltered a little.

" But what, Jemmy?" said Sylvester.

" Don't put the bracelets or darbies, as you call them, on me. I don't like that."

" Hem! It's my duty. But still Jemmy, if you promise me, on your word——"

" What?—what?"

" That you will play me no tricks, but go to Newgate, and let me get rid of you, I don't mind."

" I do promise you."

" On your word?"

" May I never see Bagshot Heath by moonlight again! —may my horse fail me at a leap that is a matter of life

PAMELA.

No. 9.—FELON'S DAUGHTER.

and death!—may my pistols miss fire, and all sorts of ill-luck attend me, if I break my word to you!"

"I am satisfied! Come on. Jemmy; you are a gentleman, and always will be! I'm sorry for you—on my soul, I am!—but it was all the same who took the warrant."

"Quite!—quite!"

"Come on, comrade; our business in this house is over."

It was quite a relief to Handsome Jemmy to find that Sylvester at least had no suspicion that Pamela might be in that house, and no intention of searching for her.

Jemmy was anxious to get into Bedford Square, for being still ignorant of the fate that had overcome Dick Doubleday, he thought that Dick would surely be still waiting for him, and would see what had happened to him.

It was quite a disappointment, therefore, for Jemmy, when he walked out of the Doctor's house in Bedford Square to see no Dick Doubleday.

Sylvester saw the eager glance he cast around him, and he said, "Jemmy, you are looking for some one?"

"No matter!"

"Shall I tell you who?"

"You can try, Mr. Sylvester, but I don't think it at all likely you can."

"Yes—it is Richard Doubleday!"

"Ah! how came you to make such a guess as that?"

"Because he has been apprehended for stealing a horse from young Lord Malvern."

"No!"

"Yes, it is quite true; and as the Round-house to which he was first taken was not thought secure enough, he has been walked off to Newgate."

"Humph!"

"I suspect, Jemmy, that you, too, had something to do with the affair, or else how should Lord Malvern know you were here in Doctor Haslem's house?"

"The deuce!"

"He saw you go in, and knew you at once, in spite of a wig you had on, that made a great difference in your appearance."

"A plague take him!"

Sylvester laughed.

"Tell me," said Jemmy, "what sort of a man is this Lord Malvern?"

"Oh, he is one of the greatest bucks upon town. He pretends to be quite helpless and half stupid—but that is only his way—a sort of affectation. He can run like a greyhound, and leap like a cat! He looks through an eyeglass that he holds on to his eye by screwing up his cheek; but, bless you, he can see a great deal better without it."

"Hem! Then, I fancy, Dick and I caught a tartar, after all."

"If you caught young Lord Malvern, you did. He is a droll fellow, and as full of whims and fancies as possible. It was just a chance whether, when he saw you and Dick Doubleday, he would not ask you to come and have a bottle of claret with him, or give you both into custody for stopping him on the highway."

"Indeed!"

"Yes; he is so eccentric that you never know what he is going to do next."

"I wish," said Handsome Jemmy, "that he had kept his confounded eccentricity out of Bedford Square to-day."

Mr. Sylvester fully relied upon the promise of the highwayman to let himself be delivered at Newgate; so he discharged his comrades, and hired a hackney coach for himself and Handsome Jemmy merely.

And soon the shadow of the dismal walls of the prison fell upon the vehicle; and they fell, too, for a few seconds, upon the heart and spirits of Jemmy.

He was, however, not the sort of person to entertain gloomy ideas for any length of time, so he whistled carelessly as he was conducted up the steps of Newgate.

"Now, Captain," said Sylvester, "I will introduce you to Mr. Dobbs, and then I have done with you."

"Who is Dobbs?"

"The chief warder."

"Oh, very well! Glad to see Dobbs or any friend of yours, Sylvester. Ah! Dobbs, old boy, how are you?"

"What impudent rascal is this?" said Dobbs.

"That's Handsome Jemmy, the highwayman," replied Sylvester.

"What? The bird that was so wild that it was said nobody would ever cage him? The fellow who scattered his guineas about so freely that there was not a 'grab' or a 'nab-'em-all" between here and I don't know where who would lay hands on him?"

"That's the man," added Sylvester.

"Then I am glad to see you; and how may you be, Captain, eh?"

"Quite well, Dobbs—how are you?—and how is Mrs. Dobbs, and all the little Dobbs's—eh?"

"Confound your impudence! How do you know that Mrs. Dobbs has bolted with a corporal—eh?"

Dobbs was enraged.

"My dear fellow," said Jemmy, "I did not know anything of the sort; only you looked so like a family man, that I thought there must be a Mrs. Dobbs, and all that sort of thing. But—hem!—hem!—you have a young fellow here named Richard Doubleday?"

There was the pleasant music of some gold which went quietly from the hands of Handsome Jemmy to that of Mr. Dobbs.

"Yes, we have, Captain."

"Just come in?"

"Only an hour ago."

"That's the man! He is a young friend of mine. You can put me with him—eh, Dobbs?"

"Couldn't."

The clink of gold sounded again as Jemmy transferred some more guineas from his own pocket to that of the chief warder.

"Captain, you are an insinuating man."

"Always was."

"But it's agin the rules!"

"Why so?"

"'Cos you see, Captain, pals ain't to be ever put together. You comprehends?"

"But this will be an exception; so lead the way at once, Dobbs."

"Well, well, I don't know who could resist you, Captain—you have such a way with you."

"A golden sort of way?"

"Yes—yes! That's it."

In less than five minutes Handsome Jemmy was introduced into a cell of Newgate, in which he saw some one sitting on a low stool, supporting his head between his hands, rocking to and fro, as he uttered low moans.

"Leave me! leave me! At least let me know the solitude of my own cell."

The door was closed and barred.

"Dick!" said Handsome Jemmy.

Dick Doubleday sprung to his feet with a shout of pleasure, and fell upon the breast of the highwayman.

But we must now leave Dick and his friend Handsome Jemmy to make the best of their position in a cell of Newgate, while we turn our attention to certain proceedings of Doctor Haslem.

The impression that in Pamela Sharples he had found the long-lost daughter who on that night of terror and despair, when his wife had left his house, had been taken from him, was strong.

But he wanted to make assurance doubly sure.

For that purpose was it that he projected a visit to Jacob Sharples, the coiner, at his wretched house in Clerkenwell.

At about ten o'clock on the same night which had witnessed the arrest of Dick Doubleday, and the voluntary imprisonment of Handsome Jemmy, the highwayman, Doctor Haslem, enveloped in a roquelaire cloak, which he found hanging in the hall of his house, and which was in truth his brother's, set out on foot for Clerkenwell.

A thick rain was falling.

Occasionally too, loud gusts of wind would catch the Court Physician at the corners of the streets, and almost whirl him round.

But that state of the elements was more congenial to his feelings than a serene night would have been.

He often paused to utter deep sighs, and press his hands upon his heart as he made his way onwards.

CHAPTER XXVII.

JACOB SHARPLES THINKS HIMSELF STILL HAUNTED BY A SPIRIT.

WHEN Doctor Haslem reached the wretched street in which Jacob Sharples, the coiner, resided, he felt doubly glad that the weather was so propitious

Had it been otherwise, he feared that he would not have found that gloomy place so still and destitute of life as it was.

The fast-descending rain, however, had forced to what shelter they could find, the squalid inhabitants of that pestiferous region.

Occasionally, as the Court Physician took his way, he could hear the half drunken shouts from the cellars which were used as kitchen, and parlour, and hall, by whole families of the vagabondage of that district.

But he heeded not those cries and shouts.

Once, too, the yell of " Murder ! murder !" came upon his ears.

But he only shuddered, and passed on.

Doctor Haslem's mind was too full of his own affairs, and too intent upon the object with which he had come abroad, to have permitted him to turn aside, if one half the human race had been murdering the other half.

He had a dim sort of idea, by having consulted a map of London, of his route.

He wished to reach the house of the coiner, if possible, without making any inquiries ; and at length he was enabled to feel certain that he was at the corner of the street he sought

The name had no doubt once flourished in fair white letters on the bricks of the corner house, and there was still a faint indication of its presence, which the Doctor could clearly perceive by the reflection of a lamp which was close at hand.

He could not read the name, but the length of the word corresponded to what it should have been, and Doctor Haslem took his way down the street.

From the time of reaching that wretched neighbourhood, the Court Physician had found it wise, despite the mud, to walk in the roadway.

The cellars, in some cases, were so many pitfalls and traps for the unwary.

He would not trust to them.

But he had great difficulty in finding Jacob Sharples' house.

Truly, Pamela had told him the number was four, but as the numbers in that street had long since parted company with the doors, he was rather puzzled how to act

A squalid-looking object, that might be called a child, came out of a house, and, with a half-broken jug in her hand, came creeping shrinkingly past him.

" Stop !" said the Doctor.

" Wot's the lay ?" asked the child.

The voice was that of a girl. She could not be above eight years of age, but she spoke in the slang dialect of the neighbourhood.

" I don't know what you mean," said the Court Physician ; " but here is a sixpence if you will tell me which of these houses is Jacob Sharples's ?"

" A bad 'un ?"

" Well," replied the Doctor, " I am afraid he is no great good !"

The physician thought the child alluded to Jacob Sharples, the coiner.

She really alluded to the promised sixpence.

" Well," she said, " give us hold of it ; I'll try to pass it somehow or another, and they can but nab me, and give me a month, and that I can do on my head any day ! That's old Sharples's house !"

The thief-child pointed to a dismal-looking abode— unquestionably the most dismal in the street ; and the Physician, who still was hardly able to comprehend what she meant about trying to pass the sixpence, handed her the coin.

She went on her way to the public house to get something in the half-broken jug.

Doctor Haslem ascended the old, worn, moss-grown sloppy steps of Jacob Sharples's house.

To his surprise, he found the door open.

But all beyond it was so profoundly dark, that he did not venture to cross the threshold with any degree of boldness.

He felt on the door for a knocker.

There was none. The knockers of that district had long since found their way to the marine store dealers'.

Then the physician kicked at the door

The sounds echoed with a dull reverberation through the house, but they produced no response

By this time, however, Doctor Haslem's eyes were getting a little accustomed to the dark atmosphere of the passage, and he could see that at all events the floor looked solid and even.

He cautiously and slowly made his way into Jacob Sharples's house

Then, when he fancied he must have got about half the length of the passage, he paused, and cried out aloud, " Jacob Sharples ! Jacob Sharples !"

Was it a groan that he heard upon the night air ?

He could not be certain.

It might only have been the wind moaning, and making its way up the dismal old staircase.

He called again.

" Jacob Sharples ! Jacob Sharples !"

Yes : he was quite certain, now, that he heard a deep groan.

But whence it came from, and from whom, he had not the least idea

It seemed to be in the air above him.

It might come from the upper part of the house, or from the lower, or from outside, indeed, for all he could decide.

Notwithstanding the character of that sound, however, it was a positive relief to Dr. Haslem to hear any indication whatever of a human presence in that dismal habitation.

" Speak," he cried, " whoever you are ! Utter some articulate word, that I may know where to seek you : and, if you are suffering, it may be that heaven itself has sent me to your relief !"

The physician's voice faltered as he pronounced the name of heaven—for, deep in the recesses of his own heart, he knew that it was a recollection of no heavenly acts that had brought him to that wretched place.

He listened intently, to endeavour to catch some word in reply to the appeal which he had just made.

But all was still.

It might be that that groan he had heard was the last effort of expiring nature.

It might be that he had taken great pains to find himself alone with the dead.

It might be that the only man who could give him a distinct account of the life and fortunes of Pamela Sharples, had breathed his last on that tempestuous night, and the mystery which seemed half revealed to the aching heart of the Court Physician might never be wholly discovered.

Perhaps there was some thought in his mind that he was deserving of such retribution ; but be that feeling what it might, the terror, the dread of finding that Jacob Sharples was no more, came so strongly upon him, that he seemed to forget all the dangers of that place.

He no longer heeded the creaking of the boards,

which seemed ready to give way beneath his footsteps.

The feeling of insecurity with which he had entered the house seemed to be forgotten, and he strode along the passage, feeling hurriedly the cold, damp wall as he went, with the hope of discovering a door which would lead him into some of the apartments on the ground floor.

The physician did discover such a door.

That door yielded to his touch; but he little knew how near to death he was, and the dangers he was surrounded by in that dismal house.

Had he, by any accidental impulse, been induced to take but one step backwards, he would have fallen the great depth into the long disused kitchens of the house for the balustrades at the stair-head had rotted away.

Doctor Haslem stood for a few moments, without knowing it, on the brink of a dismal precipice.

But the door yielded to his touch, and he advanced forward.

The danger lay behind him, and each step he now receded from it. A few paces brought him to the centre of that apartment in which Jacob Sharples might be said to live, but where he had of late endured so many terrors, that nothing but an utter prostration both of body and mind could account for his still being within its four walls.

He was there.

A faint flickering blue light came from a fast expiring bit of wood on the hearth. It lasted but for a moment, that feeble illumination, after Doctor Haslem stepped into the room, but it was sufficient to enable him to cast one hasty glance about him, and see where he was.

A figure lay upon the floor.

It was human, and there was life in it.

It was either that the faint glimmering light deceived the Doctor's eyes for a moment, or the limbs of this figure quivered as with a convulsion.

But if he were mistaken in that appearance, he could not be so as regarded the low moan which he recognised at once as being precisely of the same character as that which had startled him so recently before he found his way into that apartment.

Doctor Haslem was wonderfully reassured.

His notions and feelings as regarded the danger of his position changed rapidly.

All he wanted was now to know that the figure he saw before him was really that of Jacob Sharples, the coiner; and surely by his art he could keep sufficient life still in the prostrate form to enable him to make the confession that would set his, Doctor Haslem's, heart at ease?

To give him heart's-ease, at least, upon one point in connexion with the fearful tragedy that had darkened his domestic life.

To banish from his mind the dread that, by some fortuitous train of circumstances acting upon his own excited brain, he might be taking to his heart and his arms the child of a criminal, instead of his own long lost daughter.

But the glance that the Doctor had had of the apartment was very transient, and the sudden darkness again was confusing and perplexing in the extreme.

He must have light.

Without light he could do nothing.

But how was it to be procured?

The little wretched fire was almost at its last gasp. The few red embers would only now and then, in a fitful kind of fashion, blow into a bright spark or two, as the cold, vital night air came careering down the chimney, and then they would seem to subside into utter dissolution.

Doctor Haslem felt nervously in his pockets.

He had letters there—letters from the high and noble —delicate little epistles, with professional secrets contained in them, and one even signed by royalty itself.

He cast them without scruple, one after the other, upon the expiring embers of the fire.

What a strange fate for those letters written to the Court Physician, that they should become food for the miserable fire in the den—for it could scarcely be called a house—of Jacob Sharples, the coiner!

A faint blue smoke came from the heap of letters.

The edge of one of them began to burn, but not with a flame—it only smouldered; but the Doctor stooped and blew that one with his breath. Another moment, and there was a bright light.

Everything in and about the coiner's room was as plain as in daylight.

Then Doctor Haslem stepped over the prostrate form of Jacob Sharples; and, collecting hastily such fragments of wood as he saw about—and, indeed, every small article he could lay his hands on that promised to feed the fire—he succeeded, before the flame from the burning letters had subsided, in building up perhaps a far better fire on Jacob Sharples's hearth than it had ever known for many a long year.

That was not the apartment in which the coiner had his furnaces and his crucibles, and all the appliances and apparatus of his art.

That was where he lived.

Lived in wretchedness and poverty—in squalor and in suffering; for, whatever hidden stores of wealth he might have acquired by his well-appreciated skill in the imitation of the current coin of the realm, the wretched coiner had long since lost the hope or the capacity of enjoying it.

And yet he worked on with the terror of the law ever by his side.

How strange an hallucination!

An objectless criminal!

But Jacob Sharples had not commenced in such a state of mind his career; that had grown upon him— partly by success, which had awakened all the cupidity of his nature, and partly from a diseased state of mind, which had been produced by the constant dread of detection, apprehension, conviction, and death.

In those days, a man like Jacob Sharples would have made but a short cut for the gallows—provided he were once fairly laid hold of on the charge of manufacturing base coin.

But Jacob Sharples never passed any himself; and it was to that circumstance he owed his immunity from the terrors of Tyburn Tree.

Doctor Haslem was gratified to see that there was, at all events, no chance of his being left in darkness, for another half-hour at least.

The smoke that came from the various articles he had heaped upon the fire was wayward, and occasionally came in puffing volumes into the room; but the fire itself burnt briskly—perhaps rather aided than otherwise by the few rain spots that found their way down the chimney.

The Physician was about to kneel by the side of what may be called his patient, when he saw that the flicker of the firelight, and probably its warmth, were beginning to have a sensible effect upon Jacob Sharples.

The wretched man opened his eyes and glared about him.

Doctor Haslem drew himself up, and stood by the chimney side so exactly, as accident would have it, in the same place and in the same attitude that had been assumed by the mysterious figure which had produced so terrible an effect upon the nervous system of Jacob Sharples, that attired as he was in the roquelaire cloak he had taken from the hall of his house, he might well, to the disordered eyes of the coiner, be mistaken for that terrible spectral form.

The first glance of Sharples fell upon the Doctor.

He uttered a scream of terror.

"Not gone!—not gone!" he cried. "Still here! Am I never to look up but I see you?"

"He raves," said Doctor Haslem.

"Oh, leave me—leave me once and for ever! I have told you all I can say no more."

This mode of addressing him was perfectly inexplicable to the Doctor, except upon the supposition that Jacob Sharples's wits were deranged.

THE COURT PHYSICIAN AND JACOB SHARPLES.

But as a physician, he had tact sufficient to fall into the humour of such a patient.

"Do you know me?" he said.

"No, dread being," said Sharples; "I do not know you, although you have uncovered your face now, and let the firelight shine upon it. Still I do not know you. You are not the man."

"Not what man?"

"Have I not told you all?" moaned Sharples. "Is this my torture? Am I again and again to be thus visited, and forced to tear my heart out in the recital of the dreadful past?"

"You are Jacob Sharples?" said the Doctor—for he was determined to be secure in the identity of the man he sought.

"Why ask me?—why ask me, you, who know all? I am that wretch—I am Jacob Sharples."

"You had a daughter?"

"There again—there again!" yelled Sharples. "I have told you—I have confessed to you that she is no daughter of mine."

"Pamela not your daughter?"

"Oh, you know it—you know it! How well you know it!"

"Speak, wretch!" cried Doctor Haslem, as he darted forward and caught Jacob Sharples by the throat;— "speak, wretch, and tell me at once whose child Pamela is, and how she came into your possession. Speak! or this moment shall be your last!"

It might be the substantial character of the clutch which the physician took of his throat, or some increasing differences in tone or manner; but Jacob Sharples, excited and bewildered as he was, began to come to the conclusion that, after all, this person who seized him so roughly was not the same spectre who had stood by his hearth and nearly driven him to madness.

"Mercy! mercy!" he gasped "Do not kill me—do not murder me, and you shall know all"

The physician let go his hold upon the throat of Sharples, but he still bent forward, looking into his eyes, as though by doing so he would be able to test the truth of what he might utter.

A feeling of fright crept over the countenance of Sharples, as he said faintly, "You—you are a police officer?"

The Doctor debated with himself for a passing moment whether to favour this delusion or not, and he came to the conclusion to do so, as well that it might conceal his own identity, as perhaps frighten Sharples into a full confession of what he wished to know.

"I am," he said; "but if you answer me truly and freely what I shall ask of you, I shall leave you undisturbed; but upon the least attempt to prevaricate, or to deny me the information I seek, you are a lost man."

"I will answer—indeed, I will answer!"

CHAPTER XXVIII.

DOCTOR HASLEM HAS ALL HIS DOUBTS RESOLVED AND POURS HIS JOY INTO A TREACHEROUS HEART.

DOCTOR HASLEM drew a long breath before he could speak again, and then it was in tremulous accents, which ought to have betrayed to Jacob Sharples how deeply personally he was interested in the questions he ask-d, that he spoke.

"Pamela—that young, fair girl—tell me of her? She was reputed to be your daughter. How came that about? and how came she, indeed, ever in association with such a man as you?"

"It is fifteen years ago——"

The physician groaned.

"It is fifteen years ago since a man came to me, and hired me to convey a woman and a child to the Bishop's Walk at Lambeth. I was then living by the river side, and occasionally rowed a wherry. He gave me gold as an earnest if I would solemnly promise to keep secret

and silent in regard to them, and so, according to his own words, '*let one link be lost in the chain of their escape*'"

"A woman and a child! Go on."

"The child was young—the woman was fair, but she wept bitterly. She had jewels on her wrists, round her neck, and on her fingers. The night was dark and squally; some demon tempted me—perhaps the same that had given me the gold; but I could not let those glittering gems pass by me as if things of no value, and not attempt their possession."

"Wretch!"

"I am—I am! Never sure was wretch like Jacob Sharples!"

"Murderer!"

"No, no! I did not mean to kill her. The night was dark; she thought I meant mischief to the child! She lies deep—deep amid the black mud at the bottom of the Thames!"

"And the child?" shrieked the Doctor.

"The child was saved."

"And Pamela—she was called Pamela Sharples?"

"She is that child."

Doctor Haslem for a moment seemed about to rush upon Jacob Sharples and sacrifice his life; but then checking that fell purpose, he raised his arms above his head, as he cried out in despairing accents, "I—I—oh, heaven, 'tis I who am the murderer! Deeper guilt— deeper guilt still! Oh, why have I sought this revelation, since it but drags down my soul to a fathomless abyss? Murder — murder — murder! and I the true murderer!"

The physician fell heavily to the floor, and as he did so Jacob Sharples, the coiner, seemed to gather fresh strength.

With a yell he sprung upon him, and twining his long skinny fingers in his cravat, he seemed to feel a diabolical pleasure in the thought that his visitor's life was at his mercy.

And so it was for the moment.

And in that moment the life of the Court Physician might have been sacrificed, had not the eyes of Jacob Sharples fallen upon a glittering chain attached to Doctor Haslem's watch.

He forgot then everything in the desire to become possessed of such valuable plunder.

And so he let the substance—which might be called the Doctor's life—go, while he caught at the shadow, which the watch and chain might be likened to, and lost both.

Doctor Haslem was, under ordinary circumstances, a strong and vigorous man; and although, overcome by the mental agony of the moment, he had seemed to be at the mercy of Jacob Sharples, such was scarcely the case.

Certainly, it was not the case so soon as the fingers of Sharples were taken from his throat.

The Doctor sprung to his feet.

He had a dim kind of perception of the mischief the coiner had intended, and with one blow he sent him stunned and bleeding to the floor.

"Murderer!" he cried; "you will take my life, likewise; but it shall not be at your mercy, although to me so sad a possession."

Jacob Sharples was perfectly quiescent for a few moments, and then, with a bewildered look, he again lifted his head

"If," said the physician, "you would still spare that wretched life of yours—if you would induce me to leave you to the pangs and terrors of your own conscience— find some means of convincing me of the truth of what you have stated, and I will seek no vengeance, but strive as best I may to balance the account of criminality between us."

"I have the jewels."

"What jewels"

"Those I took from the lady in the boat—nay, she gave them freely in her terror. I did not strike her."

Doctor Haslem's face turned livid at these words.

They were accidental on the part of Jacob Sharples, but if some fiend had whispered to him at that moment how to strike a fearful blow at the very heart of the Court Physician, he could not have better succeeded.

Well did Doctor Haslem recollect, as those words rang in his ears, that first and last blow which he had struck, and which in its consequences had made his home a desolation and his heart a despair.

"Yes," added Jacob Sharples, "I have the jewels, and if—if you will say no more—if you will let me go—if you will spare me, you shall have them; that is, you—you shall see them."

"I must have them," said the Physician, faintly.

"But they are costly—of great value. You do not mean that you would take them from me?"

"You have kept them for these fifteen years: of what value have they been to you?"

"None—none! I dared not sell them, but I felt I had them."

"Quick, wretch! surrender those jewels, or our compact is void, and justice shall have its way."

"No, no! you shall have them—you shall have them! I will get them; they are here—secreted here—beneath this broken corner of the hearthstone. Here—here!"

"Quick! on your life, quick!"

"But you—you will give me compensation?"

"Another word of that kind, and I will give you to the gallows!"

Jacob Sharples groaned, and moaned, and sighed, as he took from his pocket an old, well-worn clasp-knife, with which he easily succeeded in raising a triangular portion of the broken hearthstone.

Beneath was a cavity, which seemed at first filled up with some old dirty cloth, but upon that being removed, Jacob Sharples produced a small bag, and from it he slowly took a ring which was of peculiar manufacture, inasmuch as it contained six rubies set parallel to each other, in the plainest possible gold.

The light of the fire flashed upon the beautiful gems.

Doctor Haslem uttered a shriek, and, snatching the ring from the hand of Jacob Sharples, he stopped not to see more or to utter another word in that dismal house, but making his way into the street, he rushed through the blinding rain towards his own home, calling out in his agony as he went, "Murdered—murdered—murdered!"

Chance passengers crept into the doorways to avoid him.

The watch even got out of his way, for they thought that some maniac, with all a maniac's powers, was loose in London streets.

And on he sped, as if by a blind instinct, crossing the various roadways, and taking his way with frantic speed down the different streets that led from the wretched quarter of the town he had been visiting, to what was then the highly aristocratic region in which he resided.

And ever and anon as he went he uttered still that cry. "Murdered! murdered!"

It seemed to him as if he must have choked, if he had not uttered that word in all its fearful significance.

And perhaps it was well for Doctor Haslem, on that occasion, that he had so far to go; for if anything could even have a tendency in the slightest way to assuage the mental agony he endured, it certainly was the physical exertion of flying at such speed from Clerkenwell to Bedford Square.

And this had its effect.

Doctor Haslem leant against a lamp-post, and felt a little calmer, and strove to reason himself into being calmer still before he actually made his way on to his own doorstep.

But he felt like a heart-broken man; and that henceforth he had but to wait until the welcome grave should close over him and all his sorrows.

He began to think that reflection might persuade him that he was less guilty than his imagination had at first dictated; but no reflection could ever light up again the pure flame of happiness in his heart.

He was drenched with rain.

His apparel was in disorder.

But Doctor Haslem had, so to speak, got back from the world of imagination into the world of realities again.

And along with those realities came the proprieties of life.

He put himself to rights, as well as he could, before entering his own house; and he was grateful to find that he had his own private pass-key in his pocket, which would enable him to enter much more quickly than as if he had had to knock and ring for admission.

In the midst of all his troubles, however, there was one bright glow in his bosom.

That was associated with Pamela.

He could no longer doubt now that she was his own child. Time, place, and circumstance, all led to the irresistible conclusion that this fair young creature, whom he had been instrumental in rescuing from an ignominious and dreadful death, was, indeed, his own child, who in that moment of despair, fifteen years ago, had been taken by his murdered wife from that very house in Bedford Square.

It seemed to him as if she had come back to him from the dead.

And then he remembered, with a shudder, how flatly he had refused at first to interest himself in her deliverance; and how, in fact, he had only by main force been compelled to those acts which had saved her from death.

What unspeakable horror filled his mind as he reviewed the events of that night on which he had been assailed by the highwayman and Dick Doubleday in his carriage!

What if he had been armed, and resisted to the last?

What if he had succeeded, as they passed the door of St. James's Watch-house, in giving them into custody?

The thought was terrible.

It seemed to him as if the life of Pamela—of his own daughter—had hung upon some slender thread that night, which he had made the most reiterated and vigorous attempts to snap asunder!

But she was saved now.

He had her in safety, had he not, in that secret apartment which had been closed for so long—only, after all, to receive her again on the first occasion that a human foot had trodden on its dust-covered floor.

How strange that was! Her infant footstep had, perhaps, been the last to leave its impress upon that tapestry-covered floor, and the first, after fifteen years had elapsed, again to set foot within the deserted and gloomy precincts of that chamber so full of terrible recollections.

Thronging in troops came all these thoughts to the Court Physician, even as he stood upon his own doorstep.

Then he opened the door and let himself in.

He always kept that key, which he was on this occasion so glad to find he had with him, in some pocket of his clothes.

The clock in the hall struck the hour of one.

Doctor Haslem was amazed to find he had been so long from home.

He had not calculated time as he had held that agitating interview with Jacob Sharples, the coiner.

There was grief at his heart, and there were tears in his eyes, but that house seemed to him to have a different atmosphere within it now that he felt quite certain it was his own dear child who breathed its air.

A holy calm was about the very air which encompassed her.

And so quietly had the Doctor opened his door, that the hall-porter, who, of course, was fast asleep, was not aroused.

For once in a way, the physician did not want to arouse him.

By the lantern in the hall he saw that the ruby ring was still on his finger, where he had placed it as he left Jacob Sharples's house.

His tears fell upon the beautiful crystals.

How well he knew them!

Had he not purchased them himself? Of course he had. It seemed but yesterday that he had bought that ring home as a gift to his young wife; and now—where was she now?

"Oh, where is she now?" moaned the Doctor.

Then his thoughts took him to the deep, cold slime at the bottom of the Thames, and it seemed to him as though he could still see a cold form lying there, the fair proportions of which fifteen years of death had failed to touch.

What an awful thought was that!

The physician expected he would dream of it.

It was more than likely that he would.

Stepping lightly across his hall, he made his way to the library, where he expected to find a fire, even late as it was.

He thought then that he would take off there some of his wet upper clothing, and then—then he would try to sleep.

Perhaps dream!

In fact, the mind of Doctor Haslem was in so confused and chaotic a state, that he could hardly be said to come to rational conclusions about anything as yet.

But he opened the library door and went in.

The red embers of a good fire burned still in the grate, and the air of the room was warm and soft.

A couple of candles were still alight, although burnt low down in the silver candlesticks.

And in the recesses of a large chair, which was drawn close to the fire, slept Mr. Matthew Haslem, the Doctor's brother.

It would seem as if the whole house had retired to rest but Matthew. No doubt he waited the return of his brother.

"Poor Matthew!" said the Doctor. "I am right glad he is up, for I will send him to rest at least happier to-night, since he shall know the fact that in Pamela he is to look upon a much-loved and long-mourned niece."

CHAPTER XXIX.

HANDSOME JEMMY, THE HIGHWAYMAN, AND DICK DOUBLEDAY ESCAPE FROM NEWGATE, AND ASTONISH THE GOVERNOR.

NEXT to his actual release—next, too, to the sight of his own dear Pamela, was certainly to Dick Doubleday the presence of his friend the highwayman in that wretched cell of Newgate.

At the moment, Dick did not ask himself if he, Handsome Jemmy, were a prisoner or not.

To him it only seemed as if that true-hearted and warm friend, so full of courage and so full of resources, had dropped down from heaven to succour him.

"Oh, thank heaven—thank heaven!" cried Dick Doubleday; "I see a face that I can love once again!"

"Well, Dick," replied the highwayman, "here I am, and no mistake!"

"Yes—yes! I am so—so very glad to see you!"

"Much obliged, Dick!"

"Eh?"

"I say I am much obliged. How do you find yourself, Dick—eh?"

"Oh, Jemmy, I begin to dread——"

"What, my boy?"

"That you no longer feel towards me as you did."

"Yes, I do," said Handsome Jemmy, with a smile, as he took Dick's hands with a friendly pressure,—"yes, I do, Dick. I was only jesting with you, because you expressed so much gratification to find that a fellow was locked up in this infernal Stone Jug."

Dick uttered a cry of despair.

For the first moment, it had struck him that Jemmy was a prisoner, and not a visitor to him in that dreary cell.

"Oh, Jemmy, Jemmy!" he said,—"I feel it all now! You are taken, and in some way I am certain that I am the cause of your capture!"

"Well, Dick, I can't deny either the fact of the capture or the cause of it."

"Alas, alas!"

"Why, what's the matter now?"

"I shall never forgive myself!"

"Stuff! Do you think that I care a straw, Dick, what the special causes are that enabled the nabs to trap me as they have? Come, come!—don't trouble yourself on that score."

"But I cannot help it!"

"Nonsense! How do I know what one hour from another may bring forth in such a career as mine? It is true enough that it was all owing to my going to Doctor Haslem's house in Bedford Square that I have been pounced upon; but I went there with my own free-will, and would do the same again, even were I certain it would be followed by the same result!"

"Jemmy, you have a noble heart!"

"Bosh!"

"But indeed you have!"

"Will you be quiet?"

"Yes, yes—I will. But dare I, under these distressful circumstances, ask you if you have any news of—of my dear Pamela?"

"To be sure you may! She is quite well and safe at the Doctor's house."

"Is that possible? Are you sure of it, Jemmy?"

"I ought to be, for I have seen her and spoken to her. And, by the by, Dick, you were blaming yourself just now about being the cause of my capture, while, when I come to think of it, it is that little Pamela, with her bright eyes and pretty face, who has in reality given me over to the traps!"

"Pamela?"

"Ay, Pamela!"

"My Pamela?"

"To be sure; and if you will have patience for a few minutes, you shall hear the full and the interesting particulars, as the fellows say, when they call out the last dying speech and confession of some gentleman who is going to take a drop too much at Tyburn Tree."

Dick listened eagerly to the recital of Handsome Jemmy, and when he had told him all, he cried out, "Oh, Jemmy, Jemmy! I do indeed begin to think that the mystery of the birth of my Pamela will find a solution in Doctor Haslem's house, in Bedford Square."

"I think so too, Dick."

"And I am here — caged up here, and waiting, perhaps for death! I fancy, Jemmy, I am certainly waiting for death. Do you not think so?"

"No, Dick!"

"No?"

"I say 'No!' again, because I hardly suppose you mean to wait here at all."

"But, Jemmy?"

"But, Dick, do you now suppose for a moment that I intend to stay an hour longer in Newgate than I can possibly help; and do you likewise suppose that the prison is yet built—let it be what it may, and let them call it what they will—that can hold me?"

"You will escape?"

"I will!"

"Hush, Jemmy, hush! I hear footsteps in the passage close to this cell."

"So do I. Tell me one thing, Dick. Did they search you when they brought you here?"

"Yes."

"That's good!"

"Nay, Jemmy! I thought it any thing but good, and felt inclined to resist it, as the greatest indignity that I had ever suffered."

"Never mind that, Dick. It was a good thing, because they won't repeat the process; so take care of these pistols, and this small case of leather, which is more valuable still."

"Money is it, Jemmy?"

THE ESCAPE FROM NEWGATE.

"No! Some pick-locks, and two good files, and a small, but rather compact and powerful, namesake of mine."

"Namesake?"

"Yes, to be sure, a crowbar, which the family call a 'Jemmy.' Hide the goods, Dick, anywhere you can; for although the chief warder don't often get such garnish as he has had from me this day, he will still feel it to be his duty to see what I have got about me."

Dick Doubleday had just time to bestow the articles which Handsome Jemmy had handed to him about his clothing, when the rattle of a key in the lock of the cell door was heard.

"Mum is the word," said Jemmy. "Don't speak more than you can help, Dick."

Dick Doubleday had some difficulty about getting the leather parcel into any of his pockets, for, owing to having the small crowbar in it, it was about eighteen inches in length; but he managed to put it out of sight, although he feared that the process of searching might be gone over as regarded him a second time, since it must be evident that his fellow prisoner had had the opportunity of handing anything to him.

But the turnkeys of Newgate did not feel so deeply interested in this duty, as to reflect much about the best way of performing it.

Their lives consisted of a dull, heavy routine of daily duty; and whether a prisoner remained in the prison or escaped from it, really mattered to them very little indeed.

It was Mr. Dobbs and one of his assistants who appeared at the door of the cell.

The assistant carried a lantern.

The cell, however, was not a dungeon. It was, after the eyes got accustomed to it, far from being dark; for the passage from which it opened was tolerably light, and there was a grating above the cell door which permitted some good portion of that light to penetrate to it

Coming, however, from the vestibule of Newgate, no doubt those gloomy internal passages of the old gaol were dark to the officials, and so it was the custom always to carry a lantern.

"Now, Captain," said Mr. Dobbs, "duty, you know, is duty, and must be done."

"What's the matter now?" asked Jemmy.

"Oh, it's nothing! A mere trifle, Captain! But, you see, I've got to make my report to the Governor, and it won't do for me to say I didn't search you."

"Won't it?"

"Not a bit, Captain; and I'm sure, as a reasonable gentleman, as is a gentleman, and you is, and no sort of mistake about it, you are just the sort of gentleman as won't object."

Mr. Dobbs looked in quite an imploring manner at Handsome Jemmy, who, pointing to Dick Doubleday, said, "What's meat for the goose should be meat for the gander, Dobbs. What do you mean by searching me when you didn't search my pal here?"

"Oh, Captain, don't say that! We did—we did! Didn't we now, Crow?"

"I believe you, we did!" growled the assistant, who did not by any means like his name, for he spoke like a crow, and a crow, too, who had caught a bad cold.

"Yes," said Dick Doubleday, who divined the object of Handsome Jemmy, which was to fix in the minds of the officers the fact that he had been searched; "yes, I was searched on my entrance to the prison."

"There, Captain!" said Dobbs, with a triumphant look; "there, Captain! What do you say now?"

"Nothing; I give in. Search away, Dobbs"

"Ah, Captain! you is a gentleman—a reasonable gentleman, you is! Hem! Humph! A pocket-book! A purse! Another purse! A gold watch! Another purse! Three purses! Ah, Captain! I'm afeard you got these purses at a cheap shop!"

"Well?"

"Oh, it's nothing to me—nothing to me in all the world, Captain."

"Yes, it is; because, you can keep which of them you like, and the contents will please you; while the purse itself will do for you to give to the first pair of bright eyes that take your fancy, Dobbs."

"Ha! ha! Well, I will say, Captain, you are a light-hearted one, you are! That will do; come along, Crow. Nothing suspicious found on the Captain, and we don't take away people's money, you see, Captain; 'cos, if we did, how would a gentleman, as is a gentleman, manage to live in Newgate, and where would be the wails I should like to know, of the officers?"

"When, indeed?" said Crow, as he held out his hand to Handsome Jemmy, for Mr. Dobbs had duly pocketed one of the purses and its contents, leaving his subordinate to get what he could himself.

Handsome Jemmy laughed as he placed some guineas in the open hand of Crow, for it was his policy to be on good terms with every official in Newgate.

"Nobody is permitted," said Dobbs, "to take money of any prisoner, and if any officer sees such a thing a going on, he's bound to report it"

Dobbs looked up at the ceiling as he spoke, and that enabled Dick Doubleday to comprehend why it was that Crow looked industriously into one corner of the cell, while Dobbs pocketed the purse which the highwayman gave him.

Neither of the officials of the prison saw the other get anything.

"Good-bye, Captain," said Dobbs, "and good luck to you. The sessions is on, and if all goes well and regular, you will see the end of it next Monday; so keep up your spirits."

"Thank you—thank you!" said the highwayman. "Good night, Dobbs."

The door of the cell was closed.

Jemmy made a motion to Dick Doubleday to be silent for he was listening intently.

"Once—twice! A bar—two bolts—that's all."

The highwayman was counting up the various fastenings of the cell door, as, one after the other, Crow made them serviceable.

Dick was then about to speak, but Jemmy again motioned him to silence, and whispered to him.

"Whatever you say, let it be close to my ear, and in a low tone. It's a dodge of the turnkeys of Newgate, that I was put up to by a knight of the road, to listen at the doors of the cells always for a few minutes after leaving one."

Dick Doubleday thought it better to be silent altogether for some time, so he and Handsome Jemmy did not exchange a word for about five minutes.

Then they both felt certain they heard a stealthy footstep going away from the cell door down the passage.

"He's gone, Dick," said Jemmy.

"And what can you do, Jemmy?"

"Get out!"

"Out of Newgate?"

"Ay, Dick, to be sure—out of Newgate Do you think I mean to stay in it? No; it would stifle me. Tell me, Dick, can you work well with a file, or are you quite unused to use tools?"

"Oh, I can work very well," replied Dick Doubleday. "I was not in old Zachariah's workshop in Long Lane all those years for nothing. What do you want me to do?"

"I want you to stand on my back, and file a passage through that iron grating over the cell door. I would do it myself, you see, Dick, but I am about double your weight, and if I were to stand on your back you'd feel it; but I shan't mind you standing on mine a bit."

Dick Doubleday felt the full force of this reasoning, and he opened the leather case which had been given into his charge by Jemmy, and took from it one of the files.

In a few moments more Dick was securely stationed on the back of Handsome Jemmy, from which place he could manage to reach the grating above the cell door perfectly well.

The iron bars were let deep into the stonework, and

crossed each other at right angles, so that it was a work of some time and some difficulty to get rid of a couple of them.

But the file that Handsome Jemmy had handed up to Dick was a good one, and it bit into the iron bars with speed and ease.

Rust had done a good deal to destroy the tenacity of the outside of the iron, so that it was not in reality above one-half of the original substance of the bars that presented any real labour.

"How are you getting on, Dick?" asked Jemmy.

"Capitally."

"That's right."

"One bar is cut through."

"Bravo!"

"And there goes the other!"

"Can you work out the ends?"

"I am trying."

One of the iron bars fell upon Handsome Jemmy's back, but the only notice he took of it was to cry out, "Below, there!"

"I hope you are not hurt, Jemmy; it slipped out of my fingers."

"Not a bit."

"Then I think that job is done."

"And well done, too. It won't be quite so easy, though, to get through, I'm afraid; but where there is a will there is a way, Dick."

"I hope so," replied Dick Doubleday, rather mournfully; "but I must confess I don't see, Jemmy, how you are to get through. I could easily enough, from my present position, on your back; but whose back have you got to get upon, to raise you high enough?"

"I'm glad to hear you say that, Dick."

"Say what?"

"Why, that you can get through easy, from where you are, because I want you to do it."

"Can I help you then, Jemmy?"

"You can."

Dick Doubleday had the most implicit reliance upon the highwayman and his resources, so with great dexterity he contrived to get through the hole or opening he had made in the grating above the cell door, and alighted safely on his feet in the stone passage outside it.

"Now, Dick, look out," said Jemmy, "and lay hold of the sleeve of my coat, when you see it."

"Yes, yes!"

Handsome Jemmy made two throws of his coat at the opening in the grating, and then he got the sleeve so far through, that Dick could get hold of it.

"Keep it fast," said Jemmy.

"I will—I will!"

One-half the coat was on what might be called Dick's side of the door, and the other half on the cell side, and as Dick Doubleday held it tight, Jemmy was able to climb up on the other side, to the grating.

"That will do," said the highwayman, as he managed to get his legs through the opening.

Dick helped him, and they were soon together in the passage.

"Now," said Jemmy, as he put on his coat, "I mean to astonish the Governor of Newgate!"

CHAPTER XXX.

DICK DOUBLEDAY AND THE HIGHWAYMAN GET THEIR HORSES, AND MAKE THEIR WAY TO EALING COMMON.

AT the period of our story, the authorities of Newgate, and, in fact, of every prison in England, relied upon bolts, bars, and locks, for the safety of the prisoners.

That system has now entirely given place to one of personal superintendence.

Escapes under the old plan were frequent.

They are now almost impossible.

The warders and turnkeys of Newgate used to go about the prison with at the least fifty pounds' weight of keys.

Now, a couple of small, firmly-made, highly-polished, patent keys, to fit a patent lock, suffice.

The world improves.

"Now, Dick," added Handsome Jemmy, "we have began, by force, to get out of Newgate—that is, by physical force!"

"Yes, Jemmy."

"The next force we must use will be the force of assurance!"

"Assurance?"

"Yes. I don't think anything of the chance of getting out by the vestibule, and it's a world of trouble to get out any other way; so what do you say to paying the Governor a visit in his own house?"

"You astonish me, Jemmy!"

"Well, never mind that—I think it can be done; and if so, the sooner the better He, and he only, has the power to take us out of Newgate, and I think if we can get at him he may be persuaded to do so."

"Persuaded?"

"Yes, Dick. After a particular fashion, you know!"

"I think I comprehend you."

"I think you do, Dick. Now, the genius of impudence assist us, for nothing else but that commodity, in a very large dose indeed, will do us any good!"

Dick Doubleday did not want for courage. No heart could be more full of real bravery than his; but he could not believe that there was any probability in the present plan of his friend the highwayman.

"Do not be rash, Jemmy!" he said "I cannot help feeling that a great deal of what you are now doing is for my sake; but a failure would be a most calamitous thing!"

"Calamitous, Dick? By Jove, the most calamitous thing I can think of is Tyburn Tree!"

Dick Doubleday shuddered.

"Come on," added Handsome Jemmy. "I know, from the observations I took when I was brought in here, that if we put our backs against the door of this cell, our faces are towards the Old Bailey, and that is guide enough."

"Guide enough for what, Jemmy?"

"Why, for our purposes, Dick. Are we not going to visit the Governor? and so, if we stand in Newgate with our faces to the Old Bailey, that distinguished individual's house must lie at the right hand, and all we have to do is to make our way in that direction as best we can."

There was something very cheering and heart-stirring about the bold and fearless manner of the highwayman; and although Dick Doubleday could not, in his own heart, feel persuaded that there was much chance of safety or success in Handsome Jemmy's scheme, yet there is always so much that is enticing, and, so to speak, contagious, about bold actions, that Dick Doubleday was pleased at the whole proceeding, in spite of the doubts that his judgment suggested

The stone passage in which they were run right and left—apparently for a considerable distance—parallel with the length of the prison.

In fact, it was one of the main arteries of the building, and was more than likely, if pursued in the direction Handsome Jemmy had suggested, to bring them close upon the residence of the Governor.

The passage, however, was profoundly dark now, and both Dick Doubleday and the highwayman would have given something for a lantern.

There was something awful and solemn too about the stillness of Newgate at that hour, and it would have required no great stretch of the imagination to make them believe that they were the only living beings within that gloomy pile of rough-hewn masonry.

But if this supposition did find a home for a moment in the breast of Dick Doubleday, it was soon dissipated.

The silence of the prison was broken by a heavy

clanging blow being struck, apparently with some iron substance upon iron itself.

The sound echoed in dreary reverberations along the passage, and it had the effect of at once bringing Dick Doubleday and Handsome Jemmy to a stand-still, for they could not but conjecture that some danger to them would be likely to grow out of that sound.

Nay, it might be already a token of alarm which might produce a general search, that would necessarily be fatal to all their hopes.

Then the sound came again, but this time it was a great deal nearer.

Dick Doubleday was puzzled to know what it could mean, and so indeed was his friend the highwayman, for a few seconds, until suddenly uttering an exclamation, he caught Dick Doubleday by the arm, and said, " I know now all about it. I have had every particular of the inner life of Newgate described to me over and over again by an old pal of mine, who stayed here one month before he could effect his escape."

" Is it possible, Jemmy, you can explain those terrible sounds?"

" I can. At a particular hour of the night it is the duty of one of the warders to take the round of the inhabited cells; he strikes a blow upon the door, which it is considered the duty of the prisoner to answer, which he usually does; for should he be obstinate and decline to do so, the cell-door is opened, and the disturbance to him is much greater, so that he gains nothing by his silence. Hark! there it is again!"

" I understand it now," said Dick Doubleday; " but my senses tell me at the same time that it approaches."

" It does."

" And our cell, Jemmy?"

" Will be found empty, you would add."

" It will so, and then there will be a discovery which stops us on the very threshold of our escape."

" I'm not quite sure of that. Leave all to me, Dick. Stand close to the wall, and don't interfere. I think I know a way of managing this matter which may do us more good than harm."

" Heaven send you may!"

" Hush! he comes."

It was quite evident that the warder was proceeding down this passage on the very duty Handsome Jemmy had explained to Dick Doubleday.

A number of cells opened from it, but they were all on one side; and by the irregular intervals at which the warder made his application to the doors, it was evident that he knew perfectly well which cells were inhabited and which were not.

He had a lantern with him, but it hung carelessly by a hook to the belt round his waist; and not having the remotest notion that any one was in the passage but himself, this warder did not even avail himself of the dim light his lantern sent around him.

With a dogged persistence, and perhaps with a mischievous desire to be as great a disturbance as possible to the unhappy prisoners confined in the cells, he took his way, striking heavily at the doors, and pretending sometimes not to hear the feeble voice cry out " Here!" in order that he might have an excuse for striking another blow, which, for all he knew, might vibrate through every nerve of some miserable wretch, weakened mentally and bodily by a long confinement within those dreary walls.

But this was one of the refinements of Newgate.

One of its little tortures.

As the man approached nearer and nearer, both Dick Doubleday and Handsome Jemmy were able to see him, and they simultaneously recognised Crow, the subordinate officer who had come with Mr. Dobbs in his late visit to the cell.

Had this man been not so intent upon his own amusement in disturbing the prisoners by the blows he gave to their cell doors with a massive key that weighed at least ten pounds, he must have seen the two crouching figures of the highwayman and Dick Doubleday in that passage, where there was no means of escaping him.

He seemed to recollect that there were two persons in the cell so recently vacated by the friends, and he dealt the door two blows with the key, as an intimation that they were both to proclaim their presence, or he would know the reason why.

Of course there was no response.

" Oh, you won't speak, won't you?" said Crow. " You pretend to be asleep do you? But I'll wake you up!"

Bang, bang went the key again.

It was by striking the lock that Mr. Crow produced the metallic sound which accompanied his irritating progress through the prison.

" Still you won't answer!" cried Crow. " Very well Captain, you shall pay for this, for I'll report you to the Governor!"

Mr. Crow put down his lantern on the floor of the passage, after making a cursory survey of the fastening of the door with it, and then untying an enormous bunch of keys from his girdle, he selected one, and put it into the lock.

Then he lifted down the bar and shot back the bolts.

With a savage sort of growl he opened the cell door a short distance and called out, " Now, Captain, if you please—garnish! garnish! Nobody gives extra trouble in Newgate for nothing! Garnish—garnish, I say!"

" Take it!" said Handsome Jemmy; " and much good may it do you!"

As he spoke, he stepped exactly behind Crow, and dealt him a blow on the back of the head so straightforward, stunning and decisive, that Mr. Crow flew into the cell, and was only brought up by the wall at the other side of it, as though he had been some missile discharged from the narrow passage through the open doorway.

" I think that'll do," said Handsome Jemmy, as he coolly locked the door and possessed himself of the keys.

" You have not killed him?" said Dick Doubleday.

" Not at all: those fellows' heads are uncommonly thick; but it strikes me he will remain quiet for a little while, and perhaps he may think it good policy to make no noise at all, but let himself be quietly released by one of his comrades in the morning, so as to avoid all troublesome explanations of how he came there."

" You have great presence of mind, Jemmy, and your resources are infinite."

" My dear Dick, what else could I do? But here we are, ever so much better off, I take it, than we were before, since we have now a lantern and a bunch of keys. So come on, Dick, since we are favourites of Fortune, and see what else she will do for us!"

Handsome Jemmy led the way along the passage in the direction of the Governor's house, and coming to a door that barred their progress he had no difficulty in finding among the keys which Mr. Crow had left behind him one that fitted it.

That door was in reality the one which communicated from the private or dwelling part of Newgate to what may be called the prison proper.

At about two paces from it was an ordinary wooden door, such as might be found in any private house.

This wooden door was locked likewise, and Handsome Jemmy had some little difficulty in getting it open, because the key was in the lock on the other side, so that he was baffled in the use of the picklock he had with him, in the handling of which he declared likewise to Dick he " was no great adept."

The little crowbar, however, settled the difference with the lock in a few seconds; only it made some noise, which might have been of importance if the room beyond that door had not been vacant.

But as no one was there, that was of little consequence; and the two fugitives from the cell found themselves in a comfortably-furnished apartment, which certainly formed a portion of the Governor's house.

They neither of them spoke a word upon reaching that room, because they had no sooner stepped fairly into it than they heard the murmuring sound of voices some distance off.

A solitary candle was burning on a table in the centre

HANDSOME JEMMY SHOOTS CAPTAIN SANG.

of the room, but Handsome Jemmy immediately extinguished it.

It was not one moment too soon that he accomplished this feat, for the door of an adjoining apartment was opened on the instant, and some one called out. "Who's there? who's there? Is that you, Mr. Wilkins? Who's there?"

Dick Doubleday and Handsome Jemmy scarcely breathed, so profoundly still did they keep.

"I thought I heard somebody," said the voice; "but I suppose, Sir John, it was nothing?"

"Oh, of course not," cried another voice impatiently from the second room. "If you are not free from intrusion in Newgate, I wonder where you would be. But now about this girl, Mr. Governor. What, in the name of all that's abominable, can have become of her?"

"On my life, Sir John, I cannot tell you."

Dick Doubleday whispered to Handsome Jemmy, "Is it of Pamela they speak?"

"I've not a doubt in the world!" replied the highwayman; "and I've likewise not a doubt but that the Sir John who is speaking to the Governor is no other than Captain Sang, whose conduct is a perfect discredit to knights of the road!"

CHAPTER XXXI.

HANDSOME JEMMY BRINGS CAPTAIN SANG'S CAREER TO RATHER AN ABRUPT TERMINATION, AND DICK DOUBLEDAY FINDS HIMSELF AT LIBERTY.

THE announcement from Handsome Jemmy that the person who was even at that moment conversing with the Governor of Newgate was no other than the villanous and sanguinary Captain Sang, filled Dick Doubleday's heart with a perfect commotion of excitement.

Pamela had found time to inform him of the visit which Captain Sang had made to her in Newgate, and now to hear her name profaned again by the lips of the atrocious ruffian, was almost more than Dick Doubleday could bear.

It was only the strong grasp that the highwayman took of his arm that prevented Dick from rushing at once into the room, and assailing Captain Sang.

"Hush!" whispered Jemmy. "Don't do anything rash, Dick, but remember where we are!"

Dick Doubleday felt that he ought to be guided by his friend; and, in a few half-articulate words, he intimated to him that he would be so.

"That's right!" whispered Jemmy. "And now, Dick, let us listen to what these two rascals are planning and plotting."

The Governor of Newgate, when he had opened the door that led into the inner room, in consequence of hearing some sound in the outer one, had not closed it again perfectly.

There was a triangular gleam of light which found its way into that outer room; and moreover, the opening of the door, narrow as it was, yet permitted the two fugitives to hear distinctly every word that was said by Captain Sang and the Governor.

It was the latter who spoke first.

"You need not look so alarmed, Sir John," he said. "There is no one there, and the candle has gone out."

"Oh, I am not alarmed!" replied Captain Sang, *alias* Sir John Pope, in a blustering tone. "I am not alarmed in the least!"

"That is well, sir! And now, as you were saying, about this girl?"

"Yes, Mr. Governor. I have already paid you one hundred pounds on the chance of persuading her to leave Newgate with me."

"But she would not, Sir John, and therefore our bargain ended at that point."

"It did. If she had consented, you were to let me take her away, and to get up, for the use of the Sheriff, some well-concocted story of her escape."

"Well—well, Sir John?"

"Do you deny it?"

"Not at all. But I don't see what use there is in repeating it."

"Good! We will let it pass. Now tell me what hopes have you of capturing her again?"

"No hopes!"

"Perdition seize you! I thought you had strong ones!"

"Hear me out, Sir John! When I say no hopes, I mean that I have certainties!"

"Ah!"

"Yes! She will assuredly fall into my hands!"

"You think so?"

"I know it! One of the most active officers—Mr. Sylvester—has taken the affair in hand. I am quite sure that you will authorize me to be liberal to him, and I am equally sure that you will be liberal to me; so that I don't see why your wishes, whatever they are, should not be consulted."

"Can you not guess them?"

"Hardly, Sir John."

"You know my house in the Birdcage Walk?"

"Perfectly."

"Then my wishes are just these: that so soon as Pamela Sharples is caught, she be conveyed to me there; and the man who brings her shall receive a couple of hundred guineas of the new coinage."

"A couple of hundred! Hem! And what may I promise Mr. Sylvester?"

"Perdition! I thought a couple of hundred would have settled the job altogether; but say another fifty, and I will pay the sum cheerfully."

"It's a bargain, Sir John."

"Done, then!"

"Done!"

"I don't know how it is," added Captain Sang, as he rose from the chair on which he had been sitting in this private room of the Governor,—"I don't know how it is, but that girl fascinates—charms me. I seem as if I were mad—furious after her. I cannot live without her. For the first time in my life, and I am not a young man, I feel all the force—all the agony of a passion that engulphs all other feelings. I am nearly mad, I tell you, Mr. Governor, and you must find her for me."

"Make yourself quite easy, Sir John; you shall have her at your house."

"You give me new life."

"Dick," whispered Handsome Jemmy, "take one of these pistols."

"Yes—oh, yes!"

"Follow me!"

"To the world's end or to death, dear friend, if needs be."

Handsome Jemmy pushed open the door that separated the two rooms, and walking coolly before the astonished eyes of Captain Sang and the Governor, he said, "I should like to have something to say to that little arrangement."

The Governor uttered an exclamation of despair.

Captain Sang did something much more practical, for he drew a pistol from his breast pocket, and presenting it full in the face of Handsome Jemmy, he pulled the trigger.

It was a thousand mercies that the career and the life of Handsome Jemmy, the highwayman, did not then and there end together.

But it was not to be so.

The pistol flashed and flared for an instant in the pan, but did not explode.

"Perdition!" cried Captain Sang.

But Handsome Jemmy was not the sort of person exactly to stand still and allow himself to be made an animated target for the pistol practice of Captain Sang.

He returned the shot.

The difference was great, for the pistol of Handsome Jemmy did go off.

Captain Sang uttered a yell, and fell heavily on his face to the floor.

" Murder !" cried the Governor.

Dick Doubleday sprung upon him, and grasping him by the throat with one hand, he held the pistol that Jemmy had handed to him to his head with the other. Dick did not utter a word, but the action spoke for itself.

With his mouth wide open, as though prepared for the escape of some shout for assistance, which would have alarmed the whole prison, the Governor stood transfixed and motionless.

" That's right, Dick !" said Jemmy.

A sharp knocking came at some door.

It was not the door at which Handsome Jemmy and Dick Doubleday had made their way from the prison into the outer room, but at another door opening from that outer room.

The knocking continued, and rather increased in vehemence than otherwise.

"Mr. Governor," said Handsome Jemmy, " it will be well for your health to answer truly and promptly what I shall ask of you."

" I—I——Spare my life ! I—will."

" Who is that ?"

" Knocking ?"

" Yes ; who is that knocking ? Tell me, if you know."

" Wilkins."

" Who is he ?"

" My clerk—the clerk of Newgate."

" Very well No doubt he has heard the pistol shot which has rid the world of one of the greatest scoundrels who ever was permitted to breathe its air. So, Mr. Governor, you will be so good, if you value your own life, to make some excuse for the noise, and send Wilkins about his business. But if you have objection, you know —— "

" Ob—jec—tion ?"

" Yes If you would rather die a martyr—if you would rather be one of the glorious band of martyrs——"

" D— the martyrs !" said the Governor, with emphasis. " My life is of more consequence to me than anything else I know of, I should think."

" Go, then, and settle matters with Wilkins. But remember I am here."

Handsome Jemmy took good care that the Governor should feel the cold muzzle of a pistol just at the back of his neck, about the junction of his neck with his spine

The sensation was anything but pleasant.

" Is that you, Wilkins ?" cried the Governor.

Yes, sir."

" What do you want ?"

" I thought I heard a noise, sir."

" Be off with you about your business. I am busy, and don't want you."

" Yes, sir. But I thought——"

" Tell him," said Jemmy, " that if he ever presumes to think again, you will discharge him."

" If you presume to think, you rascal, I will discharge you !" cried the Governor.

" I won't, sir."

The retreating footsteps of Wilkins were heard, and the Governor, turning to Handsome Jemmy with a sickly smile, said, " And now, Captain, what can I do for you ? I see that you have played your game well, and got out of the cell. You don't want to do any mischief, I'm sure—that is to say, more than you have done; for you have shot Sir John Pope."

" Sir John Fiddlestick !" said Handsome Jemmy. " Is it possible you do not know who that is ?"

" A most respectable gentleman, who lives—I ought to say now, who lived—in the Birdcage Walk "

" No, Mr. Governor. That pretended Sir John Pope, the most respectable gentleman, is, or was, no other than Captain Sang, the highwayman."

" What ? The notorious Captain Sang ?"

" Just so But you asked me a little time ago what you could do for me, and I will tell you. It is to let me and this friend of mine out quietly into the Old Bailey, by the private door of your own house."

" No, no, Captain ! If you must needs leave, let it be done in some way that won't compromise me. I will help you through the chapel, and out on to the roof, and we can break a lock or two and——"

" Peace, peace ! I won't do any such thing !"

" But, gentlemen !"

" Hold still !"

" Still ! What?—what ? You don't mean to say you will murder a man in cold blood ?"

" I can't help it."

" Stop ! stop ! Good gracious ! I didn't say I wouldn't do as you wanted ; and if it must be so, come this way, and I shall be glad to see the last of you both."

" The pleasure will be mutual," said Jemmy, as he followed the Governor.

Dick Doubleday took good care to keep close to Handsome Jemmy, so that the Governor and his two most unwelcome visitors reached that little pine, doll's-house looking door, which opens into the Old Bailey, in very close proximity.

" Good night," said the Governor ; " we shall have the pleasure of your society here again soon, I have no manner of doubt."

" That may be," replied Jemmy ; " but I cannot consent yet to deprive myself of the pleasure of yours, Mr. Governor ; so, if you please, put on your hat and come a little way with us—or come without it, just as best suits you."

The Governor bit his lips with vexation, but he saw that there was no help for it, so he took his hat from a peg in the hall, and accompanied Handsome Jemmy and Dick Doubleday down the steps of his house, into the Old Bailey.

At that moment a bell began to toll in the prison.

" Ah ! the alarm bell !" cried the Governor.

" I fancy," said Jemmy, " you have played us some trick."

" No, on my soul I have not ! I have not the least idea of how or why the alarm-bell is ringing, for I have taken no means to make it ring."

" I cannot say that you speak falsely," said Jemmy, " and so I will do nothing ; but I suspect you. Come along !"

With rapid strides, Handsome Jemmy conducted the Governor up Giltspur-street, and when they got right across Smithfield he said to Dick, " I leave you in charge of this man for a few minutes, while I get our horses. Shoot him on the spot if he is troublesome, and then you know where to look for me."

" Yes, Jemmy."

The highwayman did not want the Governor of Newgate to know exactly where their horses were, so he adopted this plan of leaving that functionary in charge of Dick Doubleday while he went for them.

" Look you, young fellow," said the Governor to Dick ; " you may make a good night's work of this if you like."

" How ?"

" I will undertake that you go free from the charge against you, and get a good slice of the reward, if you will give up your friend Handsome Jemmy."

" I have half a mind," said Dick, " to shoot you at once for the proposition ; and if you say a word more about it, I'm quite sure the other half mind will come to me, and I shall do it."

The Governor was silent.

A few anxious minutes more elapsed, and then Handsome Jemmy appeared with the two horses.

" Mount, Dick ! mount !" he cried, " and let us be off. Good night, Mr. Governor !"

CHAPTER XXXII.

THE DOCTOR AND HIS BROTHER HOLD A TERRIBLE CONFERENCE TOGETHER, AND THE GUILTY HEART BETRAYS ITS SECRET.

IT is necessary now that we should again repair to the house of the Court Physician, in Bedford Square, to which Doctor Haslem has so recently returned from that agitating visit he had made to Jacob Sharples, the coiner.

It will be recollected that the physician had let himself into his house with the master-key he always had with him, and had made his way to the library.

Then he found his brother Matthew sleeping a disturbed sleep in the recesses of a large library chair by the red glaring embers of the rather large fire that was in the grate.

The two candles were burnt low in the sticks, and threatened to go out in the course of the next quarter of an hour.

But the fire cast a ruddy reflection upon the rich gilding on the backs of many of the books and upon the massive curtains of green silk which were drawn closely over the windows.

The soft, warm atmosphere of that room was very grateful to the physician, after his exposure to the inclemency of that night of squall and tempest.

But he sighed deeply—a sigh that almost partook of the nature of a sob, as he half-staggered into the room calling out, "Matthew! Matthew! brother! I have some terrible revelations to make to you."

Matthew did not awaken, but only moaned in his sleep.

"Ah!" said Doctor Haslem, "it is sympathy with me that has made my brother suffer so much; and, no doubt, even in the sleep that has now come over him, his imagination is haunted by thoughts of my afflictions."

Matthew spoke inarticulately. At least, it was only now and then that he pronounced a word sufficiently plainly for Doctor Haslem to comprehend it.

"No—no! Die! Ever since then—oh, the agony! Wretch! wretch! If you will not love me you shall, have cause to hate me!"

That was a whole sentence spoken intelligibly; and the Doctor wondered what his brother could mean by it.

But he was still more startled and shocked by hearing Matthew moan out the name which was one of terror and despair, although he believed it to be fictitious, to him, the physician.

"Lothario! Lothario! Oh, heaven, Lothario!"

That was the terrible signature to the letter which had worked such madness in the brain of the Court Physician fifteen years ago.

It was with a sort of shuddering horror that he now heard that name pronounced by his brother Matthew in his sleep.

But that horror gave place to pity.

"How much he feels for me!" said the Doctor, in deep, low tones. "Often and often have I wondered what made Matthew seem prematurely drooping from health, and strength, and life. He is an old man for his years, and even by this light I can see what traces tears and grief have made upon his face. It is something strange, though, that sympathy, be it ever so genuine, should last so long."

"Save her — save her!" gasped Matthew. "Oh, heaven! save her, and save me!"

He sprung to his feet with a cry of terror.

"Matthew! Matthew!" said the physician. "You are dreaming! Matthew—Matthew, awake!"

"Help! mercy! I am not dead yet! I know that then I shall be judged; but till then—I—I——Oh, brother, is—is that you?"

"Good heavens, Matthew, what is the matter?"

"The—the—a—matter?"

"Yes; what can be the meaning of those terrible words? Was that all a dream?"

"All—a—dream?"

Matthew was evidently not quite himself yet, and he sunk back upon the chair where he had been sleeping with a deep groan.

"Matthew! Matthew! compose yourself!"

"Yes, yes—I——All a dream!"

"Matthew! Matthew! you think too deeply, and your sympathetic nature suffers too acutely. Shake off these visions that still cling to your imagination, for I have

realities to speak to you of which far transcend them Oh, Matthew, my brother! this has been a night of terror and yet a night of hope!"

The Doctor's brother was now fully awake, and although there was still a look of undefinable terror upon the countenance, he was no longer in the land of dreams, but had got back to the realities of the world again and to his own position.

"I am afraid, brother, I was dreaming," he said; "and upon subjects which affect my feelings deeply. I am afraid I utter strange disconnected sentences in my sleep, for it has happened sometimes that I have been awakened with the sound of my own voice, and started up in alarm, fancying I was not alone."

"You did speak, Matthew."

Matthew avoided his brother's gaze, as he asked faintly, "What did I say? What did the vexed imagination dictate to the lips."

"You uttered a name, Matthew, which has ever been one of horror to me. A name often used, and passing lightly from lip to lip—a sort of generic name for one who holds honour as a mere word, and who believes that reputation and feeling are but the delusions of the fancy. I do not wonder that that name has clung to you as it has clung to me; for long ago, as you well know, I have felt that it was used by the fiend whose object it was to mar the joy of this dwelling, but as some romancists might use a name to answer the fleeting purpose of the moment."

"Yes," said Matthew, hesitatingly, "that—that name has likewise clung to me."

"We need not pronounce it."

"No, no; we need not"

"And now, brother, I have that to tell you which I think will cause the same struggle in your mind between joy and grief that it has caused in mine—a struggle that nearly killed me—that nearly this night killed me."

The Court Physician forgot his wet apparel, and sat down on a chair opposite to his brother, resting his head upon his hands and rocking to and fro with that despairing motion which shows that when a joy and a grief come together, it is more than probable the latter will achieve the mastery over the imagination.

And now one of the candles expired; it had reached its termination before its companion, but neither the Doctor nor his brother heeded the circumstance; and so white, and wan, and ghost-like was the countenance of Matthew Haslem, that even the ruddy tint which the fire-light cast upon almost all objects in that apartment was scarcely sufficient to redeem it from absolute whiteness.

"Listen to me," added Doctor Haslem;—"you, my brother, who have been the depository of all the secrets of this overburdened heart, listen to me now."

"I listen."

"You know it was on the fourth of September, fifteen years ago, that this house, from being an abode of peace and happiness, of serenity and many hopeful, tender emotions, became a desert in which evil passions roamed about like wild creatures seeking their prey."

"Yes, I know," said Matthew, faintly.

"It was the fourth of September, and a night of tempest such as this."

"Brother!" said Matthew, with a shudder.

"What would you say?"

"This likewise is the fourth of September!"

The Court Physician started, for amid the tumult and the excitement of the last two days he had forgotten completely that circumstance, and that the dismal anniversary had arrived of an event which had cast a cloud over his human existence.

"Gracious heaven!" he cried; "it is so, and this night I have had revealed to me the awful truth as regarded the events which happened fifteen years ago, and which have been the subject of daily useless conjecture, day and night, for that terrible period."

"The truth!" gasped Matthew Haslem. "What truth?"

"I will tell you. From the first moment that I looked

PAMELA IN THE HANDS OF CAPTAIN SANG.

No. 11.—FELON'S DAUGHTER.

upon that fair girl, Pamela Sharples as she was named, an unknown feeling took possession of me. It was surely the voice of nature crying out aloud in my heart, 'Behold your child!'"

"Yes," said Matthew.

"Brother—brother, is it possible that you can receive a communication of this description so tamely? Can I believe my ears to hear you calmly say 'yes' to a statement that I thought would have awakened your liveliest emotions?"

"I—I was mentally stunned for the moment," said Matthew. "Oh, wonderful—wonderful! And so this young girl whom you have saved from death is in truth your long-lost child? This is indeed surprising."

The depression of spirits that Matthew was suffering from must have been very great, for he acted the part of surprise and pleasure so badly that the Doctor looked at him with perfect astonishment.

"Truly, brother," he said, "the perplexities of this night are never to cease. For you receive a communication which almost took away my breath of life as though it related to some indifferent affair."

"No—no! Oh, do not say that!"

"Then I fear that you are ill, brother."

"I fancy I do suffer, but I shall be glad to hear all you have to tell."

"You shall. The rest is of Lavinia!"

Matthew uttered a groan.

The other candle went out.

The ruddy light from the fire was dying away, although there was still sufficient of it to rescue the room from darkness; and almost immediately upon the expiring of the second candle a slight movement took place among the heavily caked embers in the grate, which permitted some little pent-up jet of coal-gas to escape; and, at intervals, that little jet ignited, burning with a white and brilliant flame, which, in its flickering and uncertain radiance, sent the shadows of the Doctor and his brother in dancing grotesqueness on the walls.

Doctor Haslem could not but be struck by the attitude his brother had assumed. It was one of such utter prostration and despair.

"I fear me, Matthew, you are very ill," he said. "I advise you to retire to rest. Recollect that I am your physician as well as your brother. To-morrow, Matthew you can hear all I have to tell you; and as for myself, in good truth. I cannot rest to night until I have looked upon my darling child again, and clasped her to my heart."

"No—no! To-night! tell me all to-night!" said Matthew. "This is the fourth of September!"

"Be it so, then. Without even communicating to you, Matthew, my intention, I went on an expedition in search of the reputed father of that girl."

"Jacob Sharples, the coiner?"

"Yes, brother; and by rare good fortune I found him in his own wretched home, so weakened in mind and body that he was not in a condition to resist the superior force of both which I brought to bear upon him. And so you see, brother, I got from him a recital of all he knew in connexion with the poor, lost Lavinia, and such a confirmation of my own heart's suggestions in regard to Pamela, that I can no longer doubt her identity with that little one who, fifteen years ago, was justly taken from me by the outraged wife and mother."

"He told you all?" asked Matthew.

"He did. The story is strange and terrible. A man, with a boat upon the Thames, was to meet a fugitive woman and a child. He was to row them to Lambeth, landing them there in safety; but the woman had bright jewels about her, which awakened the cupidity of this man. Oh, brother, the story is very dreadful!"

Matthew Haslem seemed to settle deeper into the chair on which he sat, but he spoke not.

"Tempted by the jewels," continued the Doctor, "the man who rowed the boat assailed the helpless woman. He gave me but dimly a recital of what passed, and as each word was like a bolt of fire in my brain, I could not question him very calmly or judicially. I only feel,

brother, that by what he said he brought the scene before me as one might see a picture through a faint mist that would obscure some of its outlines, and yet leave all its main features clear and palpable."

Matthew seemed to recede still deeper in the chair.

"I only know, brother, that there must have been a struggle—that the robber possessed himself of the jewels—and that, perchance, in that struggle, the boat was left to the mercy of the rushing water, and the squally winds. Perhaps it is a mercy, and will ever be one, that I do not know more; but the imagination leaps at once to the conclusion Lavinia found a home beneath the waters; but the child was saved, and that child is Pamela! Brother—brother, do you listen to me? I have proof of what I say—such cold and reasonable proof as might convince the most sceptical. Do you hear me, Matthew?"

"I do," said Matthew, faintly.

"Behold this ring! Your eyes will recognise it, Matthew, even as mine did. Do you not remember you were with me when I purchased it? You will know these rubies again. Behold them, Matthew! Another moment, and we shall have that friendly little light again, which at one moment dazzles our eyes, and then leave us in semi-darkness. There, Matthew! now you can see the rubies. Do you not know the ring?"

The little jet of flame flashed up again in the fire, and the Doctor was perfectly alarmed at the bloodless look in the countenance of his brother.

He thought for a moment that either death had claimed him, or some swoon had come over him; and he uttered an exclamation of grief, which it appeared Matthew heard, for he was neither dead nor had he swooned.

But some fearful tumult must have been taking place in his brain, to reduce him to the state in which he was.

He made a slight movement of one arm and hand, as he said, "I am better; but you see, brother, how strangely this news affects me. I recognise the rubies."

"I was sure you would, Matthew. The murderer had the other jewels, but I paused not to possess myself of them. What were the jewels to me? I only sought the recognition of some one of them, to feel certain of the truthfulness of his story. Proof sufficient lies within the compass of these small, sparkling gems. Lavinia is lost—lost—lost for ever, but my child lives!"

"Lives!" repeated Matthew.

"Yes, brother; and I too, live now, for a new object. In my grief and despair, hitherto, I have turned my whole attention and the whole energies of my mind to a discovery of the fate of my wife and child. That pursuit is over—I know all—but a new one commences, which I pray to heaven I may live to carry out."

"A new one?" said Matthew, faintly.

"Yes, I have now to discover the fiend in human shape, who, envious of my happiness, played with my peace, and wrecked my heart and home for ever. Convinced of the innocence of Lavinia, as I have been for many a long year, I have yet to discover who wrote that letter, signed 'Lothario,' and in the discovery of that person I shall discover another!"

"Another?" gasped Matthew.

"Yes, another, brother. Can you not guess who that other is?"

"But vaguely."

"That other, then, is the man who hired Jacob Sharples to row the boat."

"Oh, yes—yes; you are right—that is the man."

"I must discover that man, if he be yet in life, and I believe he is."

"You believe he is, brother?"

"I do. You may call it a superstition, if you please, Matthew, but I believe he is; for I cannot think one man could commit such a crime against another, and escape from the world without meeting his accuser, face to face, and being told—'Thou art the man!'"

"You are right, brother."

"You think with me, Matthew—you feel for me?

You will aid me in this search for this Lothario, who drove me to madness, and in one moment made me commit the act which banished the sunshine, and withered up the joy of an existence?"

"You are right, brother."

"And now I insist, Matthew, that you retire to rest. You are ill, and I have agitated you with this recital; and in so doing I have acted selfishly. But there are feelings and impulses which we cannot control; and one of the uppermost in my mind, so soon as the truth was known to me, was to seek you out and communicate it to you. It seemed to me as though I could not sleep until I had informed you of all I had learnt."

"Sleep!" said Matthew, in low tones,—"what a blessed thing is sleep—if dreams would not come to vex the sleeper! Ah, brother—brother! you have drugs that do produce the semblance of repose, but none that will ensure its reality!"

Matthew made a dreamy attempt to rise from his chair as he spoke, but his brother hastened to lend him the assistance of his arm.

"My poor Matthew," he said, "you are indeed ill! I was in hopes you would have been able to consult with me on these matters."

"To-morrow," said Matthew.

"Yes; to-morrow—to-morrow! We will then hold counsel, brother, as to the motives of the wretch who played this awful game against my life, and through those motives who shall say that we may not find the man?"

"Yes—yes; to-morrow."

"And what could possibly induce," added the Doctor, as he fully rose to his feet, and leant heavily upon his arm,—"what could possibly induce the villain to employ Jacob Sharples, the coiner, to carry those poor fugitives across the river?"

"Perhaps," said Matthew, dreamily,—"perhaps to *lose one link in the chain of their escape!*"

Doctor Haslem staggered back, and leant heavily on the table for support.

The two brothers were face to face, and the little jet of flame in the fire shot up to wonderful brilliancy.

Doctor Haslem looked in the eyes of his brother, and the expression with which he looked was one of agony and fearful suffering; but while Matthew still leant upon his left arm, he raised his right hand, and pointed with his fore-finger in his face.

"*Thou art the man!*"

CHAPTER XXXIII.

PAMELA IS IN GREATER PERIL THAN EVER OF SUFFERING FOR THE GUILT OF SHARPLES, THE COINER.

MR. MATTHEW HASLEM made no reply whatever to those terrible words from his brother, the Court Physician.

Still leaning on the arm of the man whom he had, for some reasons that the physician could not conceive, so fearfully injured, Matthew looked into his brother's face with that cold, stony gaze that had characterized him during the whole of that strange and agitating interview.

The little boisterous jet of gas in the fire had done its work.

It was no longer in existence.

A sudden darkness fell over the room.

The Court Physician could only see dimly the outline of his brother's face.

But he could feel that he leant heavier upon the arm that supported him.

There was a strange sound then from the lips of Matthew.

Half a sob—half a moan—an attempt to say something, probably; but what it was the physician could form no idea.

Then he could no longer support the weight of his brother Matthew with that left arm.

He felt compelled either to let him fall to the floor, or to take the other arm likewise with which to support him.

The Court Physician instinctively embraced the latter alternative.

There was something fearful about this continued silence of Matthew Haslem.

Something that overcome the indignation—the rage—the storm of vengeful feeling which had begun to make itself felt at the Doctor's heart.

"Speak—speak!" he cried. "Let me hear the voice of the man—of the brother who has betrayed me!"

Matthew did not speak.

He swung round helplessly in the arms of the physician, and fell half upon the chair from which he had risen, and half on the floor.

It was a professional instinct that then told the physician what had happened.

Matthew Haslem was dead!

"Lights—lights!" cried Doctor Haslem. "Help! help! Lights, I say!"

The hall-porter was awakened by the cry, which he recognised as in his master's voice, and he opened the door of the library, letting into it a stream of faint light from the hall.

But in the darkness of the room—for the fire had collapsed, and its dying embers no longer gave out the red reflection—in the darkness, then, of the room, that light from the hall, faint as it was, made a great change.

It fell upon the face of Matthew.

One glance was sufficient for the practised eyes of the physician.

It was the face of the dead.

"Good heavens!" cried Doctor Haslem. "Will these horrors never cease? Lights! Lights, here! Quick! A light!"

The terrified hall-porter soon procured a light, with which he came tremblingly into the library.

"Oh, sir!" he said. "If you please, sir, what has happened? Is it Mr. Matthew, sir?"

"Dead!"

"Dead, sir? Good gracious!"

Doctor Haslem had had time to think. What now would be the use of filling the ears of public rumour with the special circumstances of Matthew Haslem's death? Why hand over his memory to the small scandals of society? The Doctor turned from the dead body with a sigh.

"My brother has died suddenly," he said: "heaven receive and pardon his immortal spirit."

The physician, then overcome by the throng of emotions which the events of that fearful night had created, sat down opposite to all that remained of that brother, and wept bitterly.

The hall-porter was alarmed at this grief on the part of his usually cold and rather stern and stately master, and he shrank back out of the room.

But he left the light.

By that light, when Doctor Haslem had got over the first gust of grief and tears, and looked up through them at his brother, he saw that the last action of his life had been an attempt to draw forth from a breast pocket in his apparel, a letter.

The dead hand still rested on the edge of the epistle.

The physician was too familiar with death to have any weak fears of it, and he at once possessed himself of the letter.

It was addressed in these words.

"To my brother."

Then Doctor Haslem knew that it was for him, and he opened it.

He drew the candle, that the hall porter had brought, closer to him, and making an effort to be composed and more calm, he read the letter.

"BROTHER,

"I have not resided so long with you, and occupied often a place in your laboratory, without making myself acquainted with some of those chemical modes of sapping the springs of life, which are only known to those who are able to arrive at some of the grand secrets of the physical world.

"I have concocted for myself a poison, which according to my calculations ought to produce my death about a quarter past two o'clock on the night of the 4th of September next."

When Doctor Haslem had read thus far he glance at the time-piece on the chimney-piece.

It was five-and-twenty minutes past two.

And that was the 4th of September.

Doctor Haslem shuddered.

But he read on without remark :—

"I have chosen that anniversary and that hour for my death, because it was on the fourth day of September fifteen years ago, at a quarter past two in the morning, that your wife, oh, my brother! your wife Lavinia, left her home, carrying with her your infant child.

"The night was one of storm and tempest; and he who had produced the circumstances that caused her so to leave her home, watched the young mother and the wailing babe through the rain, the gale, and the wild turmoil of the elements.

"She took her way towards the Thames, and it is possible that dark thoughts of self-destruction crossed the mind of that poor wanderer, but her path was crossed by one who spoke to her kindly and in a contrite spirit.

"That one had cause to speak humbly to her, although in his heart there existed towards her feelings of the blackest rage and revenge.

"It was he who advised her to cross the river, and 'drop a link in the chain of her escape.'

"Brother, that man was Matthew—your own brother.

"I am that man.

"It needs not now to tell you why it was that I cherished hatred and vengeance against your wife Lavinia, and against you, and against your child: suffice it that such were my feelings, and that they drove me to a pitch of frenzy, which resulted in the action that made your home a desolation.

"I am the guilty man!

"I, your brother!

"I wrote that letter signed Lothario, which was to act upon your sensitive spirit, and drive you to some act that would form the subject of a life's repentance.

"Curse me—call down the maledictions of heaven on my memory, for I shall be but a memory by the time these words reach your eyes.

"I deserve all your hatred—all your anathemas!

"I had hired a man, by name Jacob Sharples, who, with a boat, was to take the fugitive wife across the Thames. He told me that he did so, and that he had landed them in safety—that is, your wife and your child—at the Bishop's Walk, by Lambeth.

"I believed him.

"For a long time I believed him; until, one day, I saw him in the streets of the City with a young girl—she was almost a child still.

"But I knew her.

"She was your child—your Lavinia's child!

"And from that moment, O my brother! I watched over her, for my heart was full to the brim of remorse for what I had done.

"I found that Jacob Sharples called her his daughter, and that he named her Pamela. I found, too, that he was carrying on the trade of a coiner, and that he sent out this fair, innocent, unsuspecting young girl on the hazardous errand to pass off spurious gold pieces at shops.

"More than once I met her, and to save her from the risks of that day's work I gave her good gold for all the spurious coin she had with her; and she was so artless, so innocent, so utterly ignorant of the ways of the world, that she never suspected the part she was playing; but, because I addressed her gently, and gave her coin of a different denomination to that which she

had of a spurious character, she was satisfied, and went home well pleased.

"I found, too, that she was followed occasionally by a man, who I ascertained was Sir John Pope, who had become enamoured of her rare beauty.

"I assailed him once, and left him senseless at the foot of Holborn Hill.

"Then I found that there was another who loved her, and I saw her eyes brighten when she looked on him, and I knew the light of love was then in her heart.

"His name is Richard Doubleday.

"I did not interfere with him.

"Brother, I mention these things to you, to let you see that I was ever watchful over your child. But I had not the moral courage to come to you, and tell you all, and restore that child to you.

"At length came a catastrophe.

"The young girl, your child, was apprehended for passing bad coin.

"She was tried, sentenced, and left for death.

"I was maddened at the thought, and knew not what to do. I was resolved to save her, but the means did not readily present themselves; and I sought the advice of a woman who had known me well, and who went by the name of Bendydkes, having an evil repute as a kind of witch and fortune-teller.

"While asking her—for well I knew her ability to advise me what could be done to save your daughter from death—there came strangely enough, for the purpose of consulting her on the same subject, two persons.

"One of those persons was a highwayman. The other was the Richard Doubleday who so truly, and so despairingly now, loved your child.

"A brief conversation with this woman Bendydkes got from her a suggestion which I delivered in as mysterious a manner as I could—wrapped up in an old cloak and hood, that had been the property of a monk, and brought from abroad—to the highwayman and to Richard Doubleday.

"The suggestion was that you, as the favourite physician to the King, and at that time the only hope that he had of saving the life of his daughter, the Princess Amelia, should be solicited to ask the pardon of Pamela Sharples of the monarch.

"You know what followed all that.

"And now, O my brother! I have told you all that you need know.

"Pamela Sharples is, in truth, Lavinia Haslem—for you recollect that your little one was named after her mother.

"Your poor wife sleeps in peace at the bottom of the Thames.

"Oh! that I, her virtual murderer, could ever know such peace!

"Acting upon the fears of Jacob Sharples, I have from his own lips gathered a confirmation of all this that I here write to you.

"Brother! brother! Can you forgive me?

"MATTHEW HASLEM"

The Court Physician read the latter part of this strange epistle, with eyes half blinded by tears.

It was quite evident that his brother Matthew had never intended him to know of his guilt until he should be no more.

It was quite an accident that had brought the brothers face to face in life, the one as the accuser, the other as the criminal.

But now, in truth, Doctor Haslem felt that he knew all, and he turned his sorrowing gaze upon the dead body of his brother, as he said, "Matthew! Matthew! I could forgive you better and easier if you had, after all, told me the cause of all this sad misery and revenge!"

It was singular that upon that point Matthew Haslem was silent in his letter, containing, as it did in all other respects, so full a confession.

The Doctor was still left to the wildest conjectures as to the cause of Matthew's conduct.

But soon another thought wholly engrossed him.

His child!

His own dear daughter!

His little Lavinia, whom he had mourned for, as surely with the dead, for so many many years, was now, without a doubt, restored to him.

Proof was now accumulated upon proof that Pamela was no other than his own dear child. And she was in that house! She was safe beneath that roof! Oh, blissful thought! And he, her father, had but to seek her, and fold his arms about her, and bless her, and worship her with a tenderness that would know no limit!

As these thoughts came thronging through the mind of Doctor Haslem, he turned towards his dead brother, and cried out, "Yes, Matthew; yes, I can—I do forgive you, as I hope myself to be forgiven!"

But there was nothing sentient in that poor still form now to hear the words of forgiveness.

The physician, with a sigh, lifted the corpse of his brother, and laid him gently upon a couch that was in the room.

He flung over it a tapestry table cover, and as the rich flounced shroud shrunk to the still proportions of the dead, the Doctor again spoke in accents of deep emotion.

"Yes, brother, I do forgive you, even as I hope to be forgiven!"

Then he turned towards the chimney-piece, and mounting upon it, with the assistance of a chair, he withdrew the velvet curtain from before the face of the portrait.

The portrait of his lost wife Lavinia.

Tears gushed to his eyes.

He held out his arms imploringly to the painted likeness.

"Can you, oh, injured one—can you ever forgive me, on earth or in heaven?"

Then the physician, with many sobs and short spasmodic sighs, opened the panel.

He was about to seek his child—his own dear, long-lost little one; and he told himself that the time had come when she ought to hear the sequel of the narrative which, by the mysterous promptings of nature, he had been urged to tell her already so much of.

He passed out of the library.

He closed the secret panel behind him.

Along the narrow channel in the wall he took his way; and the sunshine of a new joy filled his breast as he told himself that amid all the wreck of his heart and home, one precious jewel had been preserved to him.

His own dear child?

Had he not now something yet to live for? Was there not still the strongest ties that ever heaven forged for man to bind him to the earth?

"Lavinia! Lavinia! My own dear, beautiful child! Let me hear your voice—sweet music to a father's heart! I am your father, my dearest, best beloved, ever, ever darling child—my own Lavinia! That is your name, loved one. Let me hear you speak, for my tears blind me, and I cannot see you!"

All still!

No sound!

No word to cheer the heart of the man who had known so much sorrow!

The physician stood on the chimney-piece of that boudoir which, to him, was so full of terrible recollections, but which he believed now contained one joy that would obliterate them all; and he called aloud to his daughter to speak to him.

One word—if it were only one word!

He did not expect her to say "Father!" yet. If she had, it would have overpowered him—it would have been too much; he only hoped to hear that word from her lips in time to come.

But that silence was getting painful.

It was getting frightful.

The Court Physician dashed the clustering tear-drops from his eyes, and leaped down from the chimney-piece into the room.

"Lavinia! Lavinia! My child! Speak to me!"

All still!

All dark!

He hardly knew how he did it; but, with a quickness and a precision that he could in no wise account for at the time, Doctor Haslem made his way back again to the library for the candle that was there burning, and brought it back with him to the dust-covered and deserted boudoir in an incredibly short space of time.

A glance was sufficient.

The room was empty!

Pamela was gone!

A scrap of paper lay upon the table on which was that untasted repast. The eyes of the Doctor fell upon some writing in pencil.

He approached with the light.

The words seemed to eat into his brain as if they had each been a dart of fire, which penetrated his eyes:—

"I cannot remain here, and know as I do know—for I heard the words from one of those officers who threatened to break into this room—that he who loves the poor orphan Pamela is a prisoner! Richard Doubleday is consigned to a prison, and I must and will seek him, for something seems to tell me that it is on my account. Dear, kind friend, forgive me that I leave your house, and pray for your poor, persecuted, and grateful Pamela!"

Doctor Haslem fell to the floor in a swoon.

CHAPTER XXXIV.

PAMELA FALLS INTO THE HANDS OF A WORSE FOE THAN THE LAW, AND INVOKES THE PROTECTION OF NEWGATE.

THE Governor of Newgate was incensed beyond all description by the manner in which he had been completely out-generalled by Handsome Jemmy.

He gave his own head several deliberate punches when he saw the laughing highwayman and Dick Doubleday ride off, after making him wait in the street for their own good time and convenience.

"Ah!" cried Jemmy, as he took a last look at the Governor. "It's a capital plan for a man to punch his own head when he dare not do so to the head of any one else!"

The enraged Governor, however, did not repeat the process, but he made his way back to Newgate in anything but an amiable mood.

What complexion was he to put upon the whole affair?

What excuse was he to make to the authorities for the escape of two prisoners placed in his custody on capital charges?

That was a little difficulty.

And all for nothing, too!

If he had been paid a good round sum for conniving at the escape of a couple of prisoners, the affair would have been very different.

Then, whatever trouble he might encounter in the matter, would have the set-off of the good round sum to make it endurable.

But all for nothing.

That was, indeed, provoking.

And then again, what was he to do about Sir John Pope, who lay dead in his private apartments? How was he to account for his presence in Newgate? How was he to account for his death?

The Governor was in anything but a happy state of mind, as he ascended the steps leading to his house.

He had an idea of discharging, right and left, every turnkey and every warder who might come across him.

A wholesale eviction of that kind he felt would be assuaging to his wounded feelings; but upon second thoughts, he considered such a measure would be dangerous.

There was not a warder or a turnkey in the whole prison that did not know of some malpractice or evasion of duty on his, the Governor's part, and who might not be dangerous accordingly.

So he reached his own private rooms in as great a rage as any man could be in, while he had no means of venting it upon any one.

He opened the door that led into the outer of the two rooms, where Handsome Jemmy and Dick Doubleday had surprised him and Sir John Pope, *alias* Captain Sang.

He was close to the inner room, when he almost fell back with surprise, not unmingled with terror, to hear a voice cry out, "Who's there?"

The voice of Sir John Pope, too!

The dead Sir John Pope—the shot Sir John Pope! What could it mean? Was it an apparition? No. The Governor was not superstitious, and he did not give way to that idea for more than the passing moment.

"Who's there?" cried the voice again.

The Governor put his head into the room.

"Good gracious, Sir John, are you dead or alive?"

"Alive, to be sure!"

"But—but——"

"You mean that I ought not to be."

"Yes—I—a——"

"Oh, it was easy enough. The bullet passed harmlessly through my cravat, and I thought it prudent to seem dead, as another one might have done some real mischief."

"Hem!"

"Why, Mr. Governor, you don't seem at all so well pleased to find me alive, as I fondly imagined you would be."

"Sir John, I think if you had, instead of falling down to the floor on your face as you did, assisted me, we might have captured those two men."

"Oh, dear, no!"

"But I am sure we might; and you lead me to the conclusion, Sir John Pope, that you—you are——"

"What?"

"A coward!"

"I know I am!"

"You know it?"

"My dear friend, of course I do. I always take care of myself. I know that fellow they call Handsome Jemmy a great deal better than you do. If I had brought him down by my first shot it would have done very well; but after that failure there was no chance for me so long as he thought I was in life. Come now, Mr. Governor, what has happened, and where are they both?"

"Off and away!"

"Of course—that was to be expected. But I stick to my original proposition; and you shall have the money we agreed upon, if you will but find for me Pamela Sharples."

Sir John rose as he spoke, and took his cloak from the back of a chair.

"One moment, Sir John," said the Governor. And he turned a little pale as he spoke.

"What is it?"

"That highwayman, Handsome Jemmy, as he is named, said that you had another name than Sir John Pope."

"True."

"You admit it?"

"I do. I am Captain Sang. You see, I make quite a confidential friend of you, Mr. Governor. I know perfectly well that the reward for me is about three hundred pounds; but the two or three letters that you have written to Sir John Pope, informing him that you will only be too happy to deal with him as regarded any young female prisoner you may have in Newgate, are

worth more to you than such a sum, because they are worth your situation. And, moreover, I am only a coward now and then."

Captain Sang cast a strange, villanous, blood-thirsty look right into the eyes of the Governor.

"Go, then, Sir John, or Captain Sang, or Old Nick himself, for all I care! Go in peace."

"Ah! now you are a reasonable man. Remember, I have promised two hundred and fifty guineas for Pamela Sharples; but for fear you should be unhappy at the thought of losing anything by Captain Sang, why, Sir John Pope will make the two hundred and fifty three hundred. Ha! ha! Will that suit you?"

"It will."

"Then, good night; and I hope when next I meet Handsome Jemmy, he may have as bad luck, and I a great deal better."

Captain Sang fastened his cloak round his neck, and giving the Governor a familiar nod, he left the room just as a warder arrived to say, "If you please, sir, Mr. Dobbs wondered what had become of Silas Crow, and he went the rounds to look for him, and found he was shut up in No 8. So he rang the alarm bell, as Handsome Jemmy and Dick Doubleday were both gone; but nothing has been seen of either of them. And, if you please, sir, Mr. Dobbs thinks they are somewhere in the prison yet."

"Tell him to find them, then," said the Governor, roughly, "or he may run the chance of losing his place."

"Yes, sir."

Captain Sang stepped out into the Old Bailey with quite an easy air.

The Governor's assurance that, as a matter of course, Pamela would be in his power again, had been a great comfort to him; but he hardly expected that his wishes were to be crowned with such sudden and complete success as they were.

Scarcely had Sir John Pope, *alias* Captain Sang, taken a dozen steps from the door of the Governor's house at Newgate towards Ludgate Hill, when, from the shadow of one of the abutments of the old wall, there darted a slight female figure.

"Sir," she said, "I saw you come out of the Governor's house, and you do not look like a warder or turnkey of the prison; so perhaps you will, from gentleness and pity, tell me if you happen to know that one Richard Doubleday is a prisoner there?"

Captain Sang could hardly believe his ears.

The soft, musical, bird-like accents were most unquestionably those of Pamela Sharples.

He stooped and let the light of one of the oil lamps that was nearly opposite shine upon her face, as he said, in his harsh, croaking accents, "The fair Pamela, by Jove!"

Then Pamela—that unfortunate Pamela for addressing a stranger so heedlessly in the gloom of the Old Bailey —knew him at once.

She uttered a shriek, and fled.

But Captain Sang was prepared for that.

He felt certain, of course, that she did not know him when she spoke to him; and he felt as certain that the moment she should recognise him she would attempt to fly from him.

He caught her by the sleeve of her dress.

It ripped up in an instant, and a fragment of it was left in his hand.

But poor Pamela stumbled slightly on the kerbstone of the pavement, and Captain Sang caught her again.

"Ah, my little popinjay!" he cried. "You don't escape me this time!"

"Help! help! Murder!"

"Confound you; be still! Do you know where you are, girl?"

"Help! Oh, help!"

"Silence, I say! The shadows that are around you are those of Newgate; and if once you get within its walls again, good-bye to life, for it is not in reason that you should escape the gallows a second time!"

But Newgate was preferable to Captain Sang; and

Pamela still called out aloud, " Help ! Oh, help ! Save me from this man ! Murder ! murder ! murder !"

These cries could not fail to reach the ears of the warders and turnkeys on duty in the vestibule of the prison.

A couple of them came out.

One carried a hand-lantern.

" What's all this about, eh ?"

" Nothing, my good fellows !" replied Captain Sang. " This girl is a runaway, and I am her fond uncle taking her home; that is all. There is a guinea. Divide it between you, and get me a hackney-coach."

Captain Sang, despite all the resistance of poor Pamela, had managed to unclasp his cloak from around his own neck, and to cast it over the head and face of the terrified girl.

Pamela could not now cry out. She could scarcely breathe ; and Captain Sang, as he flung the guinea on to the pavement, and the turnkeys began to look for it, raised her in his arms, and went at a rapid pace towards Ludgate Hill with his nearly insensible burden.

" Ha ! ha !" he laughed as he went, in low, hideous, chuckling tones,—" ha ! ha ! my little beauty ! I rather think you are my property now, and no mistake ! Who would have thought of such a chance as this, and all for nothing too ? Ha ! ha !"

It was in vain that Pamela strove to disentangle herself from the cloak.

She felt faint and weak from the small quantity of vital air that reached her, and the horrible idea became present to her mind that she was the prisoner of the odious Captain Sang, without even the power of calling upon any one for aid.

Ludgate Hill was thus reached.

" A coach ! a coach ! A guinea for a coach !" shouted Captain Sang.

Such a cry was not likely to remain long unheeded, and from St. Paul's Churchyard a lumbering vehicle soon came down the hill at the disposal of Captain Sang.

" A guinea, my good fellow," said Sang,—" a guinea will be your fare to the Birdcage Walk with me and this young person, who is out of her mind."

" All right, your honour."

Captain Sang sprang into the coach with Pamela, and as he did so, he removed to some extent from before her face the heavy folds of the cloak, and whispered, " Girl, if you value the life of Richard Doubleday, you will be still."

Poor Pamela did not see how the life of her Richard was involved in her being still ; but the spell was effectual, and she only wept bitterly.

CHAPTER XXXV.

DOCTOR HASLEM VISITS NEWGATE IN SEARCH OF PAMELA, AND RECEIVES A PRESENT OF A TORN SLEEVE.

THE Court Physician lay for four hours in that swoon that had come over him in the long shut up boudoir in Bedford Square.

When he opened his eyes it was morning.

Bright and beautiful morning.

A slant sunbeam even made its way into the long deserted room, and it fell with a mockery of cheerfulness and beauty upon the table where that untasted repast had been for fifteen years.

Doctor Haslem was some few minutes before he could quite convince himself that all the events which crowded upon his remembrance were not dreams that had visited him in that apartment.

So sacred to the past was that room, that he thought it not at all surprising a sleep there, if it were a sleep, should be visited by strange visions.

But he felt ill.

As a physician, he could not mistake the sensation that was creeping about him.

There was fever in his veins.

But yet he felt that he had only to go down to the library to satisfy himself whether what he thought had happened was real, or but the suggestions of a distracted imagination.

With giddy steps he was about to leave that secret room.

Then his eyes fell again upon the writing in pencil which Pamela had left for his perusal.

Pamela, his own child !

And that was the first written communication he had had from her ; and what a communication it was !

All other considerations, however, merged in an intense and eager desire to follow her and save her from the consequences of the heedless act she had committed in leaving the sanctuary of that house.

Holding the scrap of paper on which Pamela had written those few words to him, the physician mounted the chimney-piece of that room, and took his way by the mysterious channel in the wall to the library.

Upon leaving the library on the night before, he was sure he took the precaution to lock the door leading into the hall, as well as that which communicated with the common reception rooms.

Upon opening the panel that allowed him to look into the library, the Doctor was convinced at once that no dreams had filled his mind with the distressful images that possessed it.

One glance was sufficient.

There, on the couch where he had left it, was the dead body of his brother.

A sad and awful spectacle.

Sad and awful, even to the physician, who was accustomed to behold death in all its varied aspects.

He stepped down from the picture panel with that air of reverence which the presence of death generally produces in human nature.

" Yes—oh, yes," he said gently. " Yes, with all the fulness of forgiveness and of sadness, I do forgive you, my brother !"

The dead body heard him not.

Matthew Haslem was past either censure or forgiveness now.

Then Doctor Haslem unlocked the door and looked out into the hall.

Several of his servants were there discoursing in whispers, as though they knew something had happened beneath that roof that should be suggestive of death.

At the sight of the Physician, they paused and looked at him as though he had been a ghost.

He was so pale, so wan, so old-looking.

But he had not had the opportunity of looking at the reflection of his own face, and he knew not the change that had come over him.

He beckoned to the hall-porter, who approached him hesitatingly.

" Tell me," said the Doctor, " did a young—young lady leave this house ?"

" Oh, yes, sir ! This time I did see her ; and I took good notice of her, sir, as I think she was crying."

" When ?"

" Soon after Mr. Sylvester, the officer, was here, sir, if you please."

Doctor Haslem sighed deeply.

" My brother, Mr. Matthew," he said, " has died—suddenly died. Let no one disturb his remains."

The Doctor pointed to the library, to signify that it was there that those remains were to be found, and then as surprise and consternation sat upon his face, he left his house.

" Newgate ! Newgate !" he said. " I must and will see her, if they have hidden her in one of their cells ! My child ! My own dear girl ! My Lavinia !"

Making strange gestures, and speaking half aloud, so that the passengers in the streets turned round to look after him in surprise and curiosity, Doctor Haslem made his way to the City.

He did not, at the moment that he reached Newgate, reflect that his best plan would be to go to the Governor's house, and ask for the Governor, the Chaplain, or the medical officer, from either of whom, on declaring who he was, he could have no doubt got all the information he required; but in the distraction of his mind, he went to the common entrance, and tapped at the wicket gate.

Doctor Haslem had not changed those clothes which had suffered so much from the rain in his visit to Jacob Sharples, and he presented rather a dilapidated appearance.

That perhaps accounted for the more than commonly rough reception he met with from the warders.

"What now?" asked a big burly man, as he glanced at the visitor over the gate.

"I want to see some one."

"What do you mean?"

"A prisoner!"

"What?"

"One who I am afraid is a prisoner here. But perhaps you will kindly inform me at once if one Lavinia—No, no—Pamela——"

"It ain't the visiting hours! Be off!"

"Stop! stop! I must!"

"Got a order, eh?"

"No!"

"Bother you, then, why don't you take a civil answer, and be hanged to you? You can't see nobody. I tell you, and there's a end of it; and if you kicks up a row here, you'll get into trouble, you will!"

Doctor Haslem was tasting some of the bitter fruits of his past errors. But the brutal manner of the turnkey aroused a latent spirit in his breast, and he replied angrily, "How dare you speak to me in such a tone? I must and will see the Governor! I am Doctor Haslem, one of his Majesty's physicians!"

"Now, you just be off!" said another officer. "I know you well enough! You have been convicted often enough! I can swear to you anywhere! You come to see Jerry Ablewhite, who is in for burglary, I daresay; but you won't, I can tell you. And if you do come at the proper visiting hours, I'll take good care you don't bring in any spirits or tobacco, for that's what you come for! Oh, I know you!"

What a drop for the Court Physician!

Suspected of trying to smuggle into Newgate spirits and tobacco!

"If you want to see the Governor, why don't you go to his house?" said a voice on the step behind Doctor Haslem.

He turned and beheld a young man, with a much more kindly expression of countenance than the turnkey's, although he was one himself.

"Thank you—thank you!" said the Doctor. "I ought to have thought of that before."

The physician, upon declaring who and what he was, got instant admission to the Governor's house; but he began to comprehend how ill-judged his visit was to Newgate in the fashion in which he made it.

He ought to have changed his apparel, and gone in his carriage, looking like what he was in reality, and then he would have met with every attention.

The Governor, however, made his appearance, and it was with as much composure as he could command his nerves to assume, that Doctor Haslem spoke to him of Pamela.

"I wish to ask, sir, if you have in the prison a young girl named Pamela Sharples?"

"Oh, dear, no, sir! She escaped—or, rather, I should say, was got off somehow by some trickery on the very road to Tyburn."

"Yes—I know; but since that I thought it possible that—that she had by some accident fallen again into your custody?"

The Governor shook his head.

"No, sir—not yet."

"Not yet? Then you think that—that she may?"

"It's more than likely, sir. We generally find that nine out of ten of the escapes come to nothing, and that we have them back again soon."

"Sir, sir!—you—you are human?"

"Human, sir?"

"Yes. I mean you have human feelings, sir; and I

pray you, if that young girl should fall into your hands here, to—to let her be given up to me; and, sir, I don't wish to offend you, but if a thousand pounds——"

"A thousand?"

"Yes; if a thousand pounds would be of any service to you, they will be most heartily at your disposal."

The Governor drew a long breath.

"This beats——" he said, and then he added the remainder of the sentence to himself, which made it up into "This beats Sir John Pope!"

The Court Physician looked keenly into the eyes of the Governor of Newgate, for he had all the gentleman's repugnance to a proposition of bribery or subornation to any one; but he needed not have been at all scrupulous in this case, for the Governor added, "I need not say, Doctor Haslem, that I am your most obedient servant, and accept your terms at once, sir."

The Doctor breathed easier.

"What you gentlemen can see in that little girl, I'm sure I don't know," added the Governor. "We do at times have really fine women here, and nobody—that is, no real gentleman—offers me a sixpence for them. Why there's Nelly Flybynight in now for highway robbery; she's the regulation height for the Grenadier Guards, and can knock down a man with one blow! That's what I call a fine woman; but as for Pamela Sharples, the coiner's daughter, she is positively little, and I'm sure Nelly Flybynight could put her in her pocket!"

Doctor Haslem scarcely heard what the Governor of Newgate said, as he gave utterance to this dissertation upon female beauty, but the conference was at that point interrupted by no less a personage than Mr. Dobbs, the chief turnkey, who, as he placed what looked like a thin silk rag in the governor's hands, said, "If you please, sir, there was a sort of a skrimmage in the Bailey last night, atween a man and a woman, and one of our fellows picked this up on the pavement."

"What is it?"

"It's a sleeve of some woman's dress, sir."

Doctor Haslem uttered an exclamation of surprise and terror.

He caught the torn piece of silk from the hands of the chief warder, and held it tremblingly before his eyes. Could he believe this evidence? If he could, he felt certain that piece of torn silk had formed part of the dress of Pamela.

"What can this mean?" he said. "How could this be found on the pavement of Newgate, or of the Old Bailey? What man—what woman was there, sir?"

The Governor of Newgate began to have quite a different notion regarding Doctor Haslem to what he had had before.

Now the idea struck him that this out-of-sorts, agitated looking man could not possibly be the King's Physician, but was some madman who in his lunacy assumed the character.

With this thought, the gorgeous and glittering prospect of the thousand pounds that had been offered him vanished at once from the imagination of the Governor.

"What do you mean?" he said; "and why do you look at that rag of clothing so earnestly?"

"Alas! alas!"

"Well, it was a lass," said the chief warder; "because I heard her call out for help, and the voice was that of a young one, I should say."

"For help?" cried the Doctor. "You heard my child cry out for help, and you afforded her none?"

"Oh, he is mad as a March hare!" said the Governor.

Now the Governor, of course, meant Doctor Haslem, but the Doctor thought the words were a reply to his, and he said sharply, "Then, Mr. Governor, you should not keep in responsible situations about Newgate men who are in such a state."

"Come—come!" added the Governor. "Be quiet now —be quiet, sir!"

"Lie down!—lie down!" said Dobbs, who took his cue from the Governor, and fully believed that the Doctor was a madman.

PAMELA SAVES CAPTAIN SANG FROM THE GUILT OF MURER.

No. 12.—FELON'S DAUGHTER.

The physician was getting bewildered

" In the name of common sense." he said, " what does all this mean? Is Pamela Sharples, as you name her, in Newgate or not?"

" Certainly not!"

" Then I will seek her, if I have to roam the wide world in search of her."

Doctor Haslem, still clutching to his heart the bit of the torn sleeve of Pamela's dress, hastily descended the steps of the Governor's house, into the Old Bailey.

" Ah !" said the Governor, when he was alone, " Sir John Pope is my man   This fellow is mad—mad as he can be ; and yet in what a rational sort of way, to be sure, he did offer that thousand pounds for Pamela Sharples. But I'll stick to Sir John Pope. His money is safe and sure ; and what is it to me if he is Captain Sang, so long as I make a good thing out of the whole affair. But what they can all of them see in that baby-faced girl, who is decidedly little, I can't make out !"

Doctor Haslem had the world before him to choose what route he might please, in his search for Pamela, and he was utterly at a loss what to do.

At one moment he thought he would visit Jacob Sharples, in the forlorn hope that she had gone there.

But the Doctor gave up that idea almost as soon as it suggested itself to him.

" No, no," he said ; " she would not again place herself in the power of that man."

Then the Doctor thought that if he could find Dick Doubleday or Handsome Jemmy, the highwayman, they would be able to be of effectual assistance in tracking the route of Pamela.

But were they not both prisoners in Newgate? Surely, yes. And he had, in the absorbing feelings of his heart for Pamela, forgotten their very existence, after all that they had done for her.

Had not the highwayman actually allowed himself to be taken into custody rather than that Pamela should be dragged from her place of refuge in his, the Doctor's house, in Bedford Square?

Had not Richard Doubleday contributed so largely to save her on the occasion of that terrible departure from Newgate to Tyburn?

Now that Pamela was lost to him, the physician began to have a much keener perception and appreciation of all that the highwayman and Dick had done for his daughter than he had before.

And feeling now so helpless as he did, standing at the corner of Newgate Street, looking about him and knowing not which way to turn to look for his lost child, how gladly would he have hailed the appearance of either Handsome Jemmy or Dick Doubleday !

But they were far away.

Doctor Haslem, however, thought that he would make an attempt to see one or both of them, if, as he thought, they were in Newgate.

The cool and easy manner in which the Governor had signified his acceptance of the bribe that had been offered him, opened the eyes of the Court Physician to the way business was transacted at Newgate.

He felt in all his pockets until he found a couple of guineas, and with them in his hand he went once again to the wicket.

" I want to know if either Richard Doubleday or a highwayman, named Handsome Jemmy, are in Newgate?"

The hand of the turnkey closed upon the two guineas like a vice.

" They was." he said, " but they gave us the slip last night as Lever was."

" Escaped?"

" Yes ; that's about it."

" Can you tell me where I am likely to get any news of them?"

" Yes ; Cole's, in Field Lane."

Bang went the little wicket shut in the Doctor's face. No doubt the turnkey thought the questions had been quite enough for two guineas.

CHAPTER XXXVI.

CAPTAIN SANG CONDUCTS PAMELA TO HIS OWN HOUSE IN THE BIRDCAGE WALK, AND ORDERS SUPPER FOR TWO.

" HARK you now, my little ladybird !" said Captain Sang, as the coach rumbled along—" hark you now ! You may make matters worse by being troublesome, but perdition take me if you can make them better !"

" Help ! help !"

" Oh, you won't be quiet ! Well. then——"

" No, no ! Do not touch me ! Monster !"

" Be reasonable, then. Why, what, in the name of all that's infernal, have you got to complain of ?"

" Oh ! if you have one grain of pity in your heart, I pray you to let me go !"

" Go ? where ? To Newgate ?"

" Anywhere !"

" And then to Tyburn ! Ha, ha ! I tell you what it is, little one. But for me you would be now in a cell of the Stone Jug again. What mad trick was it that brought you to that quarter of the town ?"

Pamela was in despair.

She wrung her hands and wept. She was afraid again to cry out for help, for when she had last done so the hideous Captain Sang had attempted to fling one arm round her neck and stop her mouth with his hand.

The coach stopped at one of the gloomiest houses in the Birdcage Walk.

The front door of that house was in Queen Street, but there was an entrance through a garden from the Park.

" There's your guinea, my man," said Sang to the coachman ; " and I would advise you to get another fare as soon as you can, to drive this one out of your head "

The driver of the coach quite understood what the extraordinary fare of a guinea was paid for ; and pocketing his share in the little bit of villany, he drove off

" Now, my dear," said Captain Sang after perforce he had lifted Pamela from the coach,—" you may please yourself. Either walk into this house, or I will carry you."

Sang had found out with what abhorrence Pamela regarded him, and that the best way to make her enter quietly his detested abode, was to offer to assist her.

" No, no !" said Pamela, tearfully ; " I can walk, if it must be so. If there is no help for me on earth or in heaven, at least let me escape the pollution of your touch."

" Ha, ha !" laughed Sang, as he opened the gate which led from the Park to the garden, and thence to the house, with a small key which he took from his pocket. " Ha, ha ! my pretty one ! We shall understand each other better by and by."

The Birdcage Walk, at the period of our story, was a very lonely spot indeed : in fact, the whole of St James's Park was in a much more wild condition than modern civilization, and the many buildings around it, have now brought it to.

Pamela looked around her in vain for any help ; and although she would gladly have fled, trusting to her fleetness of foot, yet she had not the opportunity of even that last resource, for Captain Sang kept so close to her, that at the least movement indicative of flight, he needed but to stretch forth his arm effectually to check it.

" I commend myself to heaven," said Pamela, as she crossed the garden.

" Very good, my dear," said Captain Sang ; " the age of miracles is past, and I have no fear of one being revived in your favour. But what is there to look glum about ? Perdition seize me ! I'm a gentleman — a gentleman of good repute—Sir John Pope, you know ! I can surround you with luxury—this is my house— and there's not a lady in the land need be so well off as you. Nay, I will do more than all that ; for if you have any little prejudices that way tending, perdition seize me, if I don't marry you! To be sure, I've two or three wives already up and down; but that don't matter a bit."

While Captain Sang was speaking, the house had been entered, and across a handsome enough hall her captor led Pamela into an apartment which she must have pronounced elegant, had she been in a frame of mind to comprehend or feel anything but the desolation of her postion.

"Hilloa, there!" cried Sang. "Where are you, old snake-skin? Supper, I say—supper!"

"And where are you, wretch and devil-skin?" yelled a hag of a woman, as she made her appearance in a doorway, and looked upon Captain Sang with defiant eyes.

"A plague seize you!" said Sang; "you're in one of your tantrums, I see. But bestir yourself, or I'll find a means to make you. We want our supper—I and Lady Pope that is to be. Be quick about it, or, by the fiend, I'll know the reason why!"

"Quick or slow, as I please," screamed the old woman "I don't care that,"—she snapped her fingers as she spoke,—"I don't care that for your big words and bullying looks!"

Captain Sang ground his teeth together with rage after the old woman had left.

"Useful and faithful to the backbone," he muttered; "but I'm quite sure I shall be the death of her some of these days. And now, Pamela Sharples, for the first time I can speak to you with ease and comfort, and take my own time about it, while you are forced to listen."

Pamela gave a shudder

"Oh, you needn't be afraid—we're at home now; and as you girls, I know, like to hear a love tale, I'll tell you mine."

"No," cried Pamela; "let me speak once and for all! I will forgive and forget the outrage that has brought me hither I will promise that those who would avenge it most bitterly shall likewise forgive and forget it, on condition that this moment you set me free, and allow me to depart in peace."

"Can it be possible," said Sang, in a sneering tone, "that you think so meanly of the intellect of the man who has had the sense to love you? And yet it was not sense! Passion—madness—infatuation! I, too, of all men, to be taken by that doll's face of red and white humanity! I who have run through such a life that sentimental passion should be dead within me—I, of all men!"

He had risen abruptly from the chair on which he had cast himself, and was pacing the room in a disturbed manner, as he uttered these words; then pausing suddenly before Pamela, he spoke with vehemence.

"Girl, it is too late now to inquire how or why it was; but from the first moment that I looked upon you, a wild, mad passion sprung up in my heart, and I vowed that you should be mine. I followed you, and found out who and what you were—the daughter of Jacob Sharples, the coiner; and then I spoke to you, but you scorned me—why, I know not. And then came your apprehension and your conviction, and that peril in which you stood, and from which I could have saved you; but you scorned me still!"

"And still!" said Pamela, as she made an effort to loook into the face of Captain Sang.

He made an impatient gesture.

"Hear me out, girl! I was ten minutes with you in the cell at Newgate, and could have taken you from it with me, and for that ten minutes I paid a hundred guineas to the Governor. I am rich; and I tell you Pamela Sharples, I would have laid down guinea by guinea every one I possessed, if at the end of that time you would but have looked upon me as I saw you look upon a shabby goldsmith's apprentice, and say that you would even try to love me."

"Never!" said Pamela.

"You say so—I hear you—I expected as much; but fate, chance, Providence—call it what you may—has placed you in my power. You cannot escape me. I live

in this house alone, with the exception of that hag, whose defiant insolence I put up with because I know she is mine, soul and body. Look your fate in the face, and make the most and best of it; but, Pamela Sharples, you are mine without redemption. I have sworn it, and I will keep my oath!"

"Have you no touch of pity in your heart—no mercy?"

"None!"

Pamela looked around her despairingly.

"Yes," added Sang, translating the look. "this is your prison. You defy me, and take the consequences. Loving you as I do, you might, Pamela Sharples, mould me to what you will; but do not blame me if you make me what I am, since you will not unbend sufficiently to cast a glance of compassion upon one who—who—— But this is madness! Perdition seize me! I shall turn sentimental Hilloa, snake-skin! Lady Pope waits her supper. Quick, hag, quck! This is a happy night Lady Pope comes home to her husband's house, and waits her supper!"

"Oh, she shall have it!" cried the hag, as she entered the room, and dashed a silver dish upon the table with such force that the cover rolled off on to the floor.

"What hinders me," cried Sang, as he placed his hand upon one of his pistols,—"what hinders me from plastering that wall with your hag's brains?"

"And what hinders me," screamed the beldame,—"what hinders me Captain Sang, villain, highwayman, and wretch,—what hinders me from giving you up to the gallows? Do you hear that? the gallows!"

"That!" said Sang, as, now thoroughly infuriated, he levelled the pistol, the butt of which he had been clutching for some few seconds convulsively, at the head of the hag

Pamela saw the movement, and with a generous instinctive desire to save human life, although that being had not, as yet, addressed to her one word of compassion, she seized the huge cuff of Captain Sang's coat, and forcing his hand upward at the moment he pulled the trigger of the pistol, the bullet lodged in the ceiling of the apartment, instead of, as in all probability it would have done, in the brain of the old woman.

"This, at least," yelled Captain Sang—"this, at least, does not fail me in my hour of need, and miss fire! Ah! foiled, though!"

"Would you commit murder?" exclaimed Pamela.

The white smoke of the discharged pistol curled up to he ceiling of the room.

White as death itself, the old hag confronted the highwayman.

"This is the second time," she said—"the second time, John Sang. that you have attempted my life!"

"The third ought to be lucky, then," cried Sang, with a brutal laugh. "I have warned you time out of mind not to try me too far, but you will do it—you will do it!"

"I was wrong."

"Be off. with you, and bring the wine. Perdition seize me! I'm crossed at every turn!"

"I know I was wrong," said the old woman; "so I forgive this pistol shot, as I forgave one before. But the pretty young lady is tired, and there are tears in her eyes You will come with me, Lady Pope; and by the time Sir John has trimmed his beard and washed his hands—for it seems to me, as it ever seems, that there is blood upon them— you can come back to supper more cheerfully. Come with me, poppet. Why, you are but a child, after all!"

"Let her be!" said Sang, as he involuntarily glanced at his hands, to see if indeed blood was upon them—"let her be, I say! And yet—— Well, be it so. Come back with brighter eyes and a fairer colour in your cheeks. I, too, am somewhat apparel-stained; but I will wait here. You see, Pamela, how indulgent I am to you if you will but permit me to be. Take her with you, old snake skin, if needs must, and bring her back to me in a better spirit. But beware!"

"Oh, be under no fear, John Sang," said the old woman. "When did I ever play you false?"

"Never. I admit that. But you have the temper of twenty fiends in one."

"And what temper have you?" yelled the old woman. recovering all her former vehemence—"what temper have you, robber and murderer?"

"Oh, do not—do not," implored Pamela, as she held by the arm of the old woman,—"do not begin this tempest of words again, or worse will come of it. Do not, I implore you!"

Captain Sang had sprung to his feet, and looked flushed with rage; but the old woman yielded to Pamela's remonstrances, and drew her out of the room into the hall again, closing the door upon Sang, and immediately as she did so placing her finger on her lips, to signify to Pamela to be silent

At the end of the hall was a wide, winding staircase, and up this the old woman led Pamela, and so into a room on the first floor, much darkened by Venetian blinds at the windows, but which Pamela could see was a bedchamber, and that of the most costly description.

"Speak, girl," said the hag, "and tell me what brings you here?"

"Force"

"Nothing but force? Is it possible that he—that John Sang should endanger his existence by a folly like this?"

"Force alone, indeed, has brought me hither," replied Pamela. "I was seized by this odious man, who from my inmost heart I abhor and detest, in the public street. He dashed his cloak about my head and face, so that I could not cry for assistance; and scattering gold about him, he found ears that voluntarily closed themselves against my moans and feeble cries—he found eyes that would not see the outrage he was committing. And as my strength could not cope with his, I am here a prisoner, with but one resource."

"What resource?"

"Death!"

"Then you would sooner die than stay with Captain Sang?"

Pamela's tears flowed freely.

"It is hard to die," she said, "but it seems that there has been nothing presented to me so repeatedly of late, and in such a variety of shapes, as death; but I shall welcome it in any shape, if it free me from this monster."

"That makes two," said the old woman.

"Two what?" faltered Pamela.

"You will be the second who has preferred death in this house, to the companionship of John Sang. But you are the first who has raised a hand to do me a service Alas! alas! a service do I call it? How strange it is that in the midst of every misery we cling to life? You do not understand this, you who are young; and that makes it stranger still. The young seem ever ready to set their life on any cast; while age, without hope, without joy, and burdened with a thousand distresses, clings to existence, because I suppose it is a last possession."

"He would have murdered you."

"He would—in his rage, he would. You saved me, and I must needs be grateful. Girl, I know not who and what you are, but you shall not be sacrificed to John Sang!"

Pamela uttered a cry of joy as she flung herself upon the breast of the old woman and clasped her in her arms.

———

CHAPTER XXXVII.

CAPTAIN SANG FINDS THAT HE IS NOT QUITE "OFF WITH THE OLD LOVE BEFORE HE WOULD BE ON WITH THE NEW."

PAMELA clung to the old hag-like woman, who seemed to be the only breathing thing with an air and aspect of humanity about her at Captain Sang's house, as some wrecked mariner might cling to the frail spar which alone separates him from eternity.

"Save me! save me! Oh, in mercy, save me!"

"Hush! He will hear you!"

Pamela's voice was stilled in a moment. That was the only invocation that could have induced her to be silent at such a time.

She shook like some one whose mortal life had received too rude a shock ever to recover; and the look of painful anxiety that she bent upon the face of the old woman was terrible to see.

That ancient face was a map of many passions. Hate, —fear—revenge—remorse—all seemed to be struggling the one with the other upon the countenance of this housekeeper of Captain Sang.

It seemed doubtful which of these various feelings would obtain the mastery. But yet she had promised to save Pamela; and the young girl clung with joy to the fair words of hope.

Pamela was as yet too young and too little versed in the ways of the world to be very suspicious, and she fully believed in the promises of the old woman, notwithstanding the evidence of contending emotions which were manifest in her face.

Insult, ill-usage, and degradation had sapped the intellect of that poor lost soul; and there were times when the demon of insanity found a ready home in the seared heart.

Revenge against Captain Sang would then degenerate, and expand, and grow into revenge against the whole of the human race.

She had suffered much, and there would arise in her mind, then, a feeling of intense and mad delight in the idea that any one else could be made to suffer.

That was Pamela's danger.

If one of those moods should take possession of the mind of the hag, it was more than likely that Captain Sang might yet rejoice in the success of the villany that had brought poor Pamela to his house

The grasp of the hag tightened upon the wrist of Pamela.

She spoke in deep, strange accents, having in them, likewise, such a wail of grief that they would needs melt any heart to pity.

"She was fair—fair even as thou art! Oh, she was fair, and good, and bright as the morning, when his hateful glance fell upon her! And what is she now? Oh. what is she now?"

Nothing could exceed the agony of tone in which these last words were pronounced.

"Of whom spoke you?" said Pamela, faintly.

The old woman uttered a faint cry. It was half a scream, half a shout of defiant indignation

"Of whom should I speak but of my own child? Of whom should the bereaved, mad mother speak but of the child she loved?"

Pamela shrunk back with terror.

The door of the room close at hand was dashed open, and Captain Sang appeared.

"What is all this?" he cried. "Are you still in your mad fits, Jezebel?"

"Oh, save me—save me! Mother, save me!" mourned Pamela

The appalling look upon the young girl's face—the tears that streamed from her eyes—the one touching word, mother, that she had uttered, she knew not why, all combined to cast oil upon the troubled ocean of the mind of the infuriated woman.

The storm of invectives which she had commenced hurling at the head of Captain Sang died away.

"Wretch! monster! murderer! Who do you dare call Jezebel? Blood on your head, your hands, your heart and your lips! You—you—I—no—John Sang —John Sang! Be patient She is but a child—nearly a child! You will leave her to me for a short time, and I will speak to her! Go—go now to your own rooms—to your supper. I will see to her, and—and—when—when I knock on the floor, then you can come, John Sang, you can; and who shall say that you may not utter words of love to the ears of beauty? Ha! ha! ha! Oh, heaven, have mercy upon us all!"

The old woman clasped her hands over her face, and the wild hysterical laughter was more painful to her than the deep, heart-felt sobs that succeeded it.

Sang looked at her for some few moments in silence, then, turning on his heels, muttered to himself as he went, " Be it so—be it so! There is some reason and some sense in that; although, on my faith, I think she's more mad than ever !"

It was an immense relief to poor Pamela to feel that she was once more alone even with that poor bereaved spirit.

With a natural feeling of kindness and affection which nothing could ever eradicate from the mind of Pamela, she cast her fair young arms around the neck of the aged woman, and spoke words of comfort to her.

" Ah, do not weep—do not weep! Bethink you that there is a heaven above which sees all."

The hag looked through her tears into the sweet young face.

How like a pitying angel Pamela looked.

" And do you feel so much for me?"

" Indeed and in truth I do."

" And will you pray for me?"

" With all my heart, I will."

" Whatever may happen, and whatever may be my guilt, will you say one good word and shed one pitying tear for me in heaven?"

" Alas! alas! do not speak so! I belong not to heaven, but am, even as you are, of this earth, and have many faults; but I will pray for you "

The old woman drew a long breath.

" Then that is the mercy at the last," she said. " Come, dear child, come. You are safe; and John Sang shall not profane by his blood-stained touch one ringlet of that fair hair."

She smoothed gently with her old, rugged hand the fair hair of Pamela, and a look of unutterable human affection beamed from her eyes.

Then the old hag—nay, she was no longer an old hag, for there was the divinity of kindness in her eyes—took Pamela gently by the hand, and led her to the door of a room in that house which was painted of one uniform and deep black.

Pamela shuddered.

There was something suggestive of death and of the grave in the dull, heavy colour of that door.

But the young heart of Pamela felt a sensation of sickness come over it, as, upon looking closer by the light of the candle that the old woman carried, she saw that the lock of that door was covered over with black crape.

" You see—you see," said the old woman, in low, agitated tones — " you see, dear child, that this is the chamber of death !"

" Of death ?"

Pamela drew back a pace.

" Alas! dear child, it is not the dead that will ever harm you, but the living."

" Yes—oh, yes! I know. And yet—yet what ?"

" You shall see—you shall see. This door has not been opened for four long years. Oh, so long—so long! It has seemed to be an eternity of suffering to me !"

The old woman took a key from some secret pocket in her apparel, and removing the crape from before the door of the lock, she opened it.

Pamela's feelings were so much excited, that she would not have been surprised if some fearful spectacle had presented itself at the moment that the door was opened.

But there was nothing but darkness.

" Enter! enter!" said the old woman. " It is a vault !"

" A vault ?"

" Yes. And yet, I say, she was as fair as thou art now."

The old woman took hold of Pamela by the sleeve of her dress, and led her into the room. She held up the light calmly and steadily, and its rays fell upon an object in the centre of that apartment which was well calculated to fill her young heart with dismay.

That object was an unmistakable pall of black velvet, with its deep white bordering !

Beneath that pall was the sharp, angular outlines of a last home of poor humanity. A coffin, whether tenanted or not, was most undoubtedly there.

Some wreathed flowers—flowers shrunk up to a few hard, dry leaves—lay upon the pall; and yet Pamela thought that their fragrance lingered in the air of that apartment.

But we must take one glance at the other contents of that room in Captain Sang's house.

It was a bed-chamber.

Rich, rare, and beautiful were the various appointments of that apartment. The toilette was covered with all those little adjuncts to beauty which even the young and the fair do not despise.

The whole place, indeed, bore the aspect of lavish expenditure. It was such a room as some fond heart might have wished in which to enshrine some being whom it loved devotedly.

But there, in its centre, was that terrible object so suggestive of the end of all earthly things.

The pall and the coffin !

Pamela feared to speak. The old woman had placed the candle upon the pall close to the dried flowers, and with both her hands pressed tightly upon her heart, she was looking around her like one who, after some long sleep, had awakened in a strange land.

Then tears came to her relief.

Happy, fortunate tears; for they washed away some of the wild fever of that poor vexed brain.

She was able to speak calmly.

" I have spoken of my child; and she of whom I have so spoken is here."

The old woman bent her head forward until her forehead rested on the coffin and the pall, and then her tears rolled down the black, soft velvet, and reached the floor.

But she continued speaking.

" I have called her my child, but she was not quite that, except to my heart and love. She was my child's child."

" Your daughter's child ?"

" Yes, she was that. She is but sixteen years of age now—she will never be but sixteen years of age—so young, so bright, so beautiful—for Angela cannot surely grow old and look as I am !"

Pamela took one of the hands of the old woman in both her own.

" Tell me—oh, tell me, what sad fate overtook one so good and so young ?"

" It was an infatuation—a strange infatuation. This man Sang pretended that he loved her, and he persuaded her that he did. As Sir John Pope, which name and title he had assumed, he won her childish heart, by attentions, and by presents, and by flatteries. She was then but fifteen years and six months old She had no mother—ah, yes, she had—she had! She had me; but you comprehend that her actual mother was no more, and poverty had stepped in at our door, and I had to toil early and late to support the dear child."

" And she loved you ?"

" Loved me? Oh, yes—yes! Such love! But let me tell you all You will listen ?"

" With all my soul !"

" This man, then—this Sir John Pope, as he called himself—came as a pretended benefactor. He either had actually known the father of my dear grandchild, or he found out sufficient about him to seem to have known him well; and that was his introduction to us."

" And that father, too," said Pamela—" that father was no more ?"

" No more. He found a grave in the deep sea, whither he went a long and perilous voyage to the Gold Coast, with hope of bringing wealth home for his child. That was a mercy."

" A mercy ?"

" Yes—it was a mercy of heaven, that; for if he had come home, what would he have found ?"

" Yes, yes—I comprehend now. It was a mercy."

" It was—it was! Well, I did not like the man—

Sir John Pope, I mean. I suspected no evil, though, of him; and it came upon me like a thunder-clap to receive a cold note, one day, on my return from some work I had obtained, informing me that my dear child was his wife, and could be found at this house."

"His wife, was she?"

"You shall hear. I hastened to this place, and found my child. I soon found, by questioning her, that Sir John Pope had imposed upon her by a false marriage. I taxed him with it, and he laughed aloud. I reproached him bitterly—no doubt, most bitterly—and he struck me. I was ill for more than three long months, and when I recovered I found myself still here, and my child still beautiful, but like the shadow of her former self."

"She regretted?—she repented?"

"Both—and he, too!"

"He regretted and repented?"

"Oh, no; he got tired of her. He used her like a dog. No, no; worse than that. A hound would have turned and bitten him. One day, then, he struck her on the brow, and—and—she was killed!"

"Oh, heaven!"

"Yes, she died of that blow—I was sure of it; and then I went mad—mad at times. I do not know how or why it was that I did not rush into the open streets and denounce him to the law, but I think it was because I was always meditating some more terrible retribution than any process of law would visit him with, and because I wished to be so deeply revenged. Time has run on, and I am as yet not revenged at all."

Pamela could quite comprehend how this insatiate spirit of revenge had defeated itself. She was about to make some reply to what the suffering woman had said to her, when the furious ringing of a bell sounded through the house.

The old woman's eyes lighted up with the flame of insanity, as she spoke: "Ha! ha! Sir John gets impatient!—Sir John Pope gets impatient!"

CHAPTER XXXVIII.

PAMELA ESCAPES FROM SIR JOHN POPE'S HOUSE, AND THE LONG-DELAYED VENGEANCE OF THE BEREAVED MOTHER IS ACCOMPLISHED.

THE bell rang again violently.

Pamela trembled in every limb.

"Oh, he comes!—he comes!" she said. "He will come here, and I am not saved from him!"

"Hush! Be calm; he will not come here."

The old woman left the room, and Pamela could hear a loud altercation of a few minutes' duration taking place over the staircase, and then all was still; after which, a door in the lower part of the house was closed violently.

Pamela had been alone with those sad memorials of death about five minutes, when the old woman returned to her.

"He will wait," she said.

"Thank heaven! and you can then permit me to leave this house?"

"Yes, but it must be in my way. A few more words places you in possession of all I have to tell of her."

With a tearful expression, the poor, sad woman indicated whom she meant by placing a hand on the pall; and then she added, "When she was no more, and he saw that it was the face of the dead that he looked upon, the slight feeling of apparent compunction that took possession of him was compounded of fear and superstition. He was more afraid of the dead than the living."

"Indeed?"

"Yes; it was so. He left the house for a time; that is to say, until I, in as expensive a manner as I chose, should get rid of the dead. When he returned I told him that I had done so; but I could not part with the sad remains; and in conjunction with a friendly man who was to have had the conduct of the funeral, I arranged that the seeming corpse that was carried from this house in its coffin should only be some billets of wood, while the real remains of my child's child were left here to me."

"A sad memorial!"

"It may be so, but it is the only thing that has kept me in life. I seemed to feel that I was not quite separated from her."

"But what did he—what did this fearful man Sang say to such a course?"

"He never knew it!"

"Could you successfully keep it from him?"

"Yes; most successfully and easily I have told you that he was superstitious, and perhaps that is the only fear, properly so called, which belongs to his disposition. This room, then, in which his poor victim has breathed her last, was, of all others, the one which he would most avoid entering."

"I comprehend that."

"Yes, it was so: he left me undisturbed possession of it, and never even suggested that I should surrender to him the key of it. When I had the door painted black, as you have observed; and when I covered the lock with crape, he never made the slightest remark—looking doubtless upon those acts as wild fancies springing out of my grief, which it were far better to indulge than to seek to thwart. But we will this night stir up a mortal terror in the heart and brain of this villanous Captain Sang, which shall drive perhaps even him to madness."

The old woman, as she spoke, opened a wardrobe, and with a deliberate earnestness that showed that she was intent upon some well-arranged purpose, she took from it a riding-habit of the most costly materials, and trimmed in a most peculiar manner about the neck with fur of a rare description.

"Take this," she cried: "here, too, is the hat—here the veil. These gloves, too, with their pendant tassels of bullion—oh, nothing was spared to adorn the victim for the sacrifice—these all belonged to her who sleeps yonder so calm and so still, with the red stain of Captain Sang's brutal hand upon her brow. Let me array you in these garments, as I have often arrayed her; and to the guilty imagination of that fiend in human shape, Captain Sang, you will seem as one arisen from the dead to drive him to despair."

Pamela began now to understand how it was that there was a possibility of her escaping from the house of this pretended Sir John Pope, personating his poor deceased victim, and so terrifying him into becoming a probably submissive spectator of his exit from the mansion

Rather—much rather, however, would she, with the connivance and good-will of the old woman, have left the house there and then.

But without that connivance and good-will she felt how impossible it would be to do so; and escape under any condition was too blissful a thought to be trifled with in regard to its terms.

Faintly and gently only did Pamela suggest how easy it would be to let her go at once, and seek for safety in the open park or the open streets.

"Dear kind heart, she said, "that has taken pity upon me, take further pity still; and sparing me from being an actress in this arena of retribution, let me go—oh, I pray you let me go!"

There was a gleam like a lightning flash from the eyes of the old woman.

"It is well—it is well!" she said "Self, self—ever self! And am I to have no vengeance? Do I not suffer? Is it too much, girl, for you to look for one moment into the eyes of Captain Sang for my sake, when possibly I encounter death for yours?"

"No, no!" exclaimed Pamela. "Do not say that! I am not—will not be ungrateful The course you suggest, I will pursue. Guide me—mould me as you will —but only save me from that man!"

With feverish and eager haste the old woman attired her in the riding habit She arranged her hair as well as she could on the urgency of the moment in a particular fashion. She made her assume the riding hat and the gloves, which latter were of themselves things to be identified specially—being of some foreign make, and loaded with ornamentation rarely seen in England.

Then the old woman, with clasped hands, bowed down before the image she seemed to have herself created

Her scared heart flew back past those years of misery to the time when she had been the tender, kind, and affectionate nurse and mother to that beloved grandchild who now slept the sleep of death.

"Back to me—back to me!" she cried; "you have come back to me! Death has unloosed his grasp, and the grave has given up its victim!"

Pamela was deeply affected at this burst of feeling, and could not forbear crying out aloud—"I am not the dear one you have lost; but for this night's protection and goodness, I will love you even as she loved you "

Then, before the old woman could reply, that loud, clamorous bell which Captain Sang had rung before in his passionate impatience, sounded through the mansion.

The old woman tottered to her feet again, for she had sunk down in an attitude of prayerful supplication close to Pamela.

She uttered a faint cry compounded of exultation and of alarm, as she seemed to come back again to the realities of her present position.

"He will wait no longer!—he will wait no longer!" she cried "When once the demon of rage and impatience is aroused in his heart, he will listen to nothing!"

"I am lost!—I am lost, then!" cried Pamela, clasping her hands despairingly.

"No, you are saved! Follow me, and all will be well!"

Pamela stumbled for a moment over the skirt of the riding habit—for she was unused to walk so encumbered; and then, with a natural grace, which no art could have attained to, she held it more closely about her, and was able to follow the old woman on to the principal staircase of the house.

That staircase led direct to the hall, from which opened the suite of rooms specially in the occupation of Captain Sang.

There he waited that promised signal of the knocking on the floor, which should summon him to his victim; but he had drunk deeply.

The fumes of wine were in his brain, while remorseless passion sat brooding in his breast.

He kept up a perpetual and violent ringing of the bell, which, in that still, solemn, and almost uninhabited house, seemed to awaken hundreds of strange echoes, and to be the only sound possible to be heard within its walls. But soon another sound mingles with the sharp ringing of the bell.

A heavy, dull series of blows upon the flooring of the room immediately above that in which Captain Sang is sitting.

Pamela hears it.

Captain Sang hears it.

The sound of the bell ceases, and those heavy blows upon the floor take its place.

The change was startling and great, and poor Pamela as she stood upon the staircase, some few steps only from the landing at the top, felt as if each of those dull, heavy sounds were struck upon her own heart.

The period that ensued was one of fearful suspense.

Three separate actions were going on in that house—performed by three separate actors, each one of whom probably felt more intense excitement than had ever before, perhaps, accompanied any former action of their existence

Poor Pamela was full of a thousand hopes and fears —all connected with a possibility of escape from that dreaded place; for she had no means of estimating if the effect of her disguise would be sufficient to overcome the dreaded opposition of Captain Sang.

That poor, broken-hearted woman, who had suffered so much, probably thought that the long-delayed hour of vengeance had now arrived, and that the retribution she had abstained from seeking at the hands of the law—lest it should fail to be sufficient—would that night overtake the monster of ingratitude and cruelty who had blighted the existence of one she loved with almost more than mortal affection.

And Captain Sang himself was not the least interested party in the proceedings of that night

We are aware with what an infatuation—for it can be called by no other term—he had pursued Pamela

For once in his life, that man of many evil passions seemed to have been touched to his heart's core by the rare beauty of the orphan girl.

We have heard how he was wont to assail her with supplications even in the public streets.

We have heard how, in a cell of Newgate, he prayed her to choose him and his love in preference to death; and how even the latter had appeared to her the most grateful and endurable fate of the two

And so it was, that when Captain Sang heard that beating on the floor, and in it recognised the signal which the old woman had promised him—that old woman who, in respect for her feelings, we can no longer call a hag—he sprang to his feet, and a wild, exultant look flashed from his eyes.

"She is mine!—she is mine!" he cried. "She shall, and she must, love me! I have wealth and I will lavish it upon her! I am not yet so hardened and indurated by the world but that there are still some soft spots on this heart, on which she may repose! It may be madness, this terrific love; but it is a madness that brings with it the delights of twenty existences! She is mine!—she is mine! and no power on earth—no, nor in heaven—shall wrest her from me!"

The knocking continued.

Over the dark features of Captain Sang came a blood-red flush.

He held up one hand before his face, and it shook convulsively.

"Steady!—steady!" he cried. "She is mine!—and why am I thus agitated?—mine, now, and for ever!"

The knocking continued.

"Do I still tremble? Why, this is the folly of some brain-sick boy! Pamela, I come!—I come! One bumper more of this bright, red wine, and I am calm! Ah, yes! that is new blood! Cease, hag!—cease that ponderous noise!—it seems to shake the very house! I hear you, and obey the signal!"

If the last bumper that Sang drained to its dregs inspired him with more courage than he had before possessed, it certainly, at the same time, had the effect of producing a state of incipient intoxication, that was sufficiently manifest in his walk as he left the apartment.

There was scarcely an object of furniture between him and the door against which he did not contrive by some sort of fascination to lurch heavily.

Then he made a great effort, and straightening himself up, he seemed to shake off some portion of the effects of the strong potations he had indulged in.

And so he passed through the outer room of the two he usually inhabited, and reached the hall.

The knocking on the floor had ceased. The old woman had been lying with her ear close to the carpet, and she had heard the murmur of Sang's voice, and the devious and uncertain manner in which he had left the room below.

She flew to the stair-head, and there, crouching down precisely behind Pamela, she held up the light she carried, but not sufficiently high that its flame could be seen, although it threw the form and figure of the young girl into startling relief.

There was an oil lamp in the hall likewise, and that sent a sufficient radiance up the staircase to fall on the figure of Pamela, and define it.

As she there stood, trembling with emotion, wondering and fearful what might next ensue, that poor Pamela seemed to enshrined in light—not strong and sunlike, but faint and spectral—for the candle carried by the old woman had burnt low in the socket, and was near to extinction.

"Mine!—mine!" shouted Sang. "The only being I ever loved! Mine, now, after all dangers and difficulties, at no cost but my own courage and perseverance!—mine now—mine once—and mine for ever!"

He rushed across the hall.

He made a dash at the staircase, clinging to the balustrades as he went; and it was a thousand wonders that Pamela retained her position, as, without casting his eyes upwards, until he was close to her, the man the most dreaded upon earth came raging towards her.

Then he saw her.

But for a moment.

He flung his arms above his head, and, with one terrific yell, he fell backwards down the staircase.

CHAPTER XXXIX.

DICK DOUBLEDAY AND HANDSOME JEMMY HAVE SOME ADVENTURES ON THE ROAD.

"Dick," said Handsome Jemmy, the highwayman, as he reined up his horse on a little eminence which overlooked Ealing Common,—"Dick, what do you mean to do?"

Dick Doubleday was troubled; he passed his right hand over his brow twice before he replied to his friend the highwayman; and when he did speak, his manner was despairing both as to tones and gestures.

"I am lost—I am lost! I know not what to do!"

Handsome Jemmy looked towards the east. A bright and beautiful glow was in the sky—the morning was coming.

"Dick!"

"Yes, Jemmy?"

"Look at that, and tell me, now, what right you have to despair? It seems to me that there is a sort of night in your breast, and that you think it never will be morning again! Tell me if you could see such a sight as this from a cell in Newgate?"

"Alas, no!"

"Alas, no? Well, I like that! Perhaps you would rather be back there than here. with this sweet, free air blowing about you, and——Hark! That is a blackbird! Was there ever a sweeter gush of music to welcome in the dawn, and——There again! That's a lark! Up he goes!—up—up—up higher still! Dick, you are ungrateful!"

"Jemmy, I have but one word to say to you in reply, and that is one in which all my griefs and heart-bitterness are summed up."

"And that word?"

"Is Pamela!"

"Worse and worse!" said Handsome Jemmy,—"worse and worse! Why, Dick, if I had such a sweet, dear, pretty young creature half so fond of me as she is of you, I should think myself the luckiest fellow under the sun!"

"Ah, me!"

"Ah, you! Come, come, Dick!—there is the first gleam of the morning sun; and it won't do exactly for an owl like me to be caught in the broad daylight. And, besides, I am so far human as to feel confoundedly sleepy just now; and so, Dick, taking one thing with another——"

"Hold, Jemmy! What does that mean?"

"What, Dick?"

Dick Doubleday's attention had been directed, while Handsome Jemmy was speaking, towards the common, across which, at rather a slow pace, there had travelled a large, old-fashioned family coach.

The peculiarity of the coach was, that it was not driven, as might have naturally been expected, by some

servant in livery, but by a man who had all the appearance of a gentleman, so far as his clothing was concerned.

The coach stopped on the very verge of the common, close to some ancient oak palings, which enclosed an estate; and then the man who was acting the part of coachman scrambled on to the roof of the vehicle, and looked from that elevated position warily about him

"What does all that mean, Jemmy?" asked Dick Doubleday.

Handsome Jemmy shook his head.

"Can't make it out, Dick! But suppose we keep as far back as may be among these elm trees, and watch."

The highwayman dismounted as he spoke, and led his horse by the bridle completely into the shadow of the trees.

Dick Doubleday followed his example, and their position was so far improved, that while they had no difficulty in keeping their eyes on the movements of the mysterious man on the top of the coach, they were themselves effectually hidden from observation.

At that very early hour of the morning, too. no one was as yet abroad in the meadows or among the hedgerows; so that Dick and his friend Jemmy, and that coach on the common, looked as though they had the whole world to themselves.

In a few seconds the man dismounted from the roof of the coach.

They saw him go to the door of the vehicle, and look into it; and by the animation of his gestures, they could guess that he was addressing some persons who were inside the vehicle.

Then the coach door opened, and two men and a female got out. Two of those men went to the horses' heads, and held them, while the rest of the party walked rapidly towards the old oak palings.

Some heavy blows as of iron upon iron were struck, but what with, or upon what, Dick and Jemmy could not see. They soon, however, were able to guess what the blows meant, for the man who held the horses' heads that drew the coach suddenly led them along, and horses and coach both disappeared within the park palings.

"That's it!" said Jemmy.

"What?" asked Dick.

"Why, don't you see, Dick? They have opened some old, disused gate in the oak fence, either by knocking it off its hinges or its lock, and in they have gone!"

"But with what object, Jemmy?"

"That remains to be seen, Dick; but if you will mind the horses for a few minutes, I will try and get a nearer look at what they are all about down there."

"Do so, Jemmy—do so. I would propose going myself, as there may be some danger, only that I feel sure you will find out more in five minutes than I should in an hour."

"Experience, Dick, experience—that is all. I'll soon be back; and if anything very contrary should happen while I am away, just pull the trigger of one of the holster pistols, and I will soon be with you again."

"I will—I will!"

Handsome Jemmy took all the advantage possible of the ground, and by skirting a tall and luxuriant hedgerow, he was able to get down from the somewhat elevated position he and Dick Doubleday had occupied, right to the little common, without much risk of observation.

Then Jemmy saw something to interest him, although he was by no means able to explain what he saw.

The oak palings, through an old disused door in which the coach and horses had been taken, enclosed an estate, which was "To let or to sell."

A large board, nailed to a tree. and which seemed to have suffered a good deal from wind and weather, testified to this condition of the property.

What, however, the coachful of company could want in such a place, he, Jemmy, could not divine.

But of one thing he felt certain.

CAPTAIN SANG IS REMINDED OF A BYGONE CRIME.

No. 13.—FELON'S DAUGHTER.

The object, be it of what precise nature it might, was not an honest one; for if it had been, there could be no difficulty in finding some entrance to the estate in a less secret manner than it had been effected.

But Handsome Jemmy soon had another surprise awaiting him.

From within the palings there came four persons—three men and one woman—the same number as he had seen with the coach.

But were they the same persons?

That was the question.

Now, the three men and the woman who had accompanied the coach, had all, so far as their attire went, the aspect of people in a tolerably good position in the middle class of society.

But the three men and the woman who now emerged from what may be called the estate side of the park palings, were very different persons.

To the eye, they were veritable gipsies.

The woman had on a tattered scarlet cloak. Her coal black hair hung in light ringlets down her deep brown cheeks, and her shoes looked old and dirty, as from long travel.

The men wore the shabby habiliments of the gipsy race, and their ragged slouched hats half hid brown faces and glaring eyes.

These people brought with them their stakes, which they set up in the ground in the true gipsy fashion, and beneath which they lit a fire.

Over the fire they then suspended an iron pot, and then, assuming various lazy attitudes, they lounged upon the grass and among the bushes close to the oak palings.

How like a party of gipsies they looked!

Yes, that was it. Like gipsies, but not gipsies in reality.

Handsome Jemmy, from the first moment that he cast his eyes upon them, felt quite convinced that these four people were acting.

What was the object?

Who and what were they?

He could see that they were conversing with each other in low tones, but he was too far off to catch the slightest sound of what they said.

A burning desire to come at the root of all this mystery took possession of Handsome Jemmy.

But how was he to do so?

At one moment he thought that he would boldly present himself to them, and stay by them, embarrassing them by his presence, so that they would be compelled, rather than give up what they were about, to make him a confidant.

But, upon reflection, Handsome Jemmy gave up that little scheme.

He had thought of a better.

What was to hinder him from getting over the oak palings of the estate at some distance from these mysterious people, and so creeping towards them, shielded by it?

No sooner had this mode of operations suggested itself to Handsome Jemmy, than he proceeded to put it into operation.

Over the park palings clambered the agile highwayman, and alighted among a quantity of ferns that grew in the damp shadowy ground in great luxuriance on the other side of the fence.

A few moments' progress brought him to the coach, which was to all appearance completely abandoned.

The two horses were eating the sweet grass and herbage at their feet.

Then Handsome Jemmy heard the voices of the pretended gipsies; and, creeping closer still to the palings, he was soon able to detect what was said.

"It must and will succeed," said a voice. "I have set my life upon it, and it shall succeed!"

"And if we fail," said the woman,—"if we fail, we can but die! I would rather fail and die twenty times over than think that such a prize was actually within our grasp, and we let it go by us!"

"No, no!" exclaimed the man whose voice Handsome Jemmy had heard first,—"no, no! It shall not go by us. He is certain to come this way, and then no earthly power can save him!"

There was a suppressed kind of vehemence about the tones of these people, which sufficiently indicated that some very strong passions were at work within them.

Indeed, if their words might be translated to mean what they indicated, they would seem to point to murder!

That was the suggestion which they awakened in the mind of Jemmy.

But he was destined to hear more, and that more was of a much clearer character than what he had already listened to.

A voice took up the conversation that had not yet spoken—at least, while Handsome Jemmy had been a listener.

"It shall—it must be done! A peerage and a fortune of thirty thousand pounds per annum are not things to be trifled with! We are brothers and sister, and we shall be true to each other! If the information we have is correct—and we have no reason to doubt it—he must come this way; and one lucky shot makes me Baron Malvern, of Malvern Leys, and all of you rich and happy!"

"Happy, did you say?"

That was the voice of the third of the men who had not, in Handsome Jemmy's hearing, spoken.

"I did say happy."

"Ah! On! Well, I don't feel very well. I hope it will all go right, I'm sure; but there are moments when—when——"

"When what?"

"When I almost wish that I had not joined in the matter."

"Coward!"

"Well, don't make a noise about my ears if I don't happen to be quite so foolhardy as all of you. I always was a little more cautious; and I don't like, and never did like, to put my head in the way of getting it broke, if I could help it."

"Coward!"

"Don't go on saying that. I'm here, and what would you have more? I'm here disguised as a gipsy, and have come with you all to help to murder——"

"Hush! hush!" cried all the others.

"Oh, that's it! You don't mind doing it, but you don't like to speak about it!"

"Silence! On your life, silence!"

The whole four persons assumed attitudes of listening, and Handsome Jemmy placed his hands upon his pistols, for, from what he had heard, he felt pretty well convinced that some person was expected to pass that way, whose life was inimical to the interests of these four individuals, who had apparently prepared a deliberate plan of assassination.

The highwayman did not hesitate for a moment as to what he intended to do, for although he would have been glad to have had Dick Doubleday with him on that occasion, yet he was so truly courageous that he would not risk losing his share in the adventure by any attempt to leave the spot, in order to rejoin his young companion.

But it was a false alarm.

Probably some accidental stamping of either Dick Doubleday's horse, or that of Handsome Jemmy, had led the pretended gipsies to the conclusion that their victim was upon the road.

The total silence, however, that now ensued dissipated that idea, and, as some distant church clock struck the hour of five, one of them spoke again, in a low tone.

"It is nothing—it is nothing. He will not—cannot be here yet; but it was well for us to reach this spot by an early hour. The fire will burn, and the iron pot will boil. We shall look more like veritable gipsies an hour hence than we do at present."

Handsome Jemmy was thinking and cudgelling his brains to ask himself where on earth he had heard this name of Malvern before; for it came with a familiar sound to his ears, and he felt certain that he must have heard it, and that at no very distant period.

It was with a flash of recollection that he suddenly remembered Lord Malvern to be the very name and title of the eccentric young nobleman who had so inopportunely recognised Dick Doubleday in Bedford Square, and succeeded in lodging him in Newgate.

"By Jove!" said Handsome Jemmy, to himself, "that must be the very man, unless there are two lords of the same title, which is not over likely. He's not a bad fellow, by all accounts; and if he were, I don't see why he's to be quietly knocked on the head in this kind of fashion."

Handsome Jemmy's reflections were brought to an abrupt close now by the unmistakable sound of horses' feet, and looking, as well as he could, slantways through some of the crevices of the oak palings, the highwayman was able to see, coming at a slow pace down the declivity towards the walk, a mounted man.

One glance was sufficient for Handsome Jemmy. In that mounted man he recognised the foppish young nobleman with whom he and Dick Doubleday had already had such curious adventures.

It was none other than Lord Malvern himself.

The young nobleman rode a superb horse, which the eyes of Handsome Jemmy regarded with eyes of covetous admiration. The eternal eye-glass was held as usual by muscular contraction to one eye; and as Lord Malvern came quietly along, he presented all that careless, indifferent, lethargic aspect which surely sprung from the affectations of one who was agile as a chamois, could run like a hunter, and who knew not the sensation of fear.

CHAPTER XL.

A SCHEME OF MURDER AND VILLANY IS DEFEATED, AND DICK DOUBLEDAY MAKES A FRIEND OF AN ENEMY.

IT was quite evident to Handsome Jemmy that the young nobleman, Lord Malvern, who was approaching on the road from the high ground down to the common, was the person for whom the pretended gipsies were lying in wait.

That their intention was murderous he felt as certain as that he saw in the foppish young lord the object of their attack. Handsome Jemmy's mind was soon made up upon the subject; or rather, we should say, that it required no making up at all.

That he would frustrate the projected villany, and save the life of the young nobleman, was to be expected on the part of the highwayman. But he paused yet for a few moments, since the danger, although imminent to Lord Malvern, would not actually have to be met until he was somewhat closer to the spot where the sham gipsies had their encampment.

Jemmy, too, watched to discover, if possible, what would be the precise mode of attack upon Lord Malvern, and how it would be carried out—whether by one or the whole of the sham gipsy party.

With his right hand, therefore, upon the hilt of one of his pocket pistols, the highwayman watched the course of events for a few anxious moments.

And slowly onward came Lord Malvern.

The horse he rode appeared to be abandoned to his own devices, both in regard to the pace he chose to adopt, and the route he chose to take.

Lord Malvern himself, with the eye-glass still at his eye, was surveying the wide, open landscape before him, and listening to the carol of the birds about him in the trees and hedges.

Then, as he approached step by step, there was a visible commotion—visible to Handsome Jemmy, who kept his eyes upon them—among the pretended gipsy party.

"Pile more sticks on the fire!" said one. "With all

his pretended carelessness, there is not a more observant man in all the world than Sydney, Lord Malvern!"

"Get your pistol ready!" said another.

"Kill him quickly!" said the woman. "Do not half do this painful, but necessary act!"

"It shall not be half done by me!" exclaimed the man who had driven the coach, and who seemed to assume a sort of mastery over the others. "What I do, I do effectually. The hours—nay, the minutes—of Lord Malvern—are numbered!"

"They may be!" said Handsome Jemmy to himself. "They may be, and probably are; but not by you, my fine fellow, if I can in any way help it!"

Jemmy very cautiously threw up the pan of the pistol he held now fairly in his hand, and shook the powder in it; for he knew not upon what contingency the life of the young nobleman might hang, and a miss fire might be fatal.

The noise of this action on the part of the highwayman was very slight; but still it was not possible to prevent a light snap of the spring, and the attentive ears of the sham gipsy party heard it.

"What is that?" cried one. "Did you not hear something, Edward Riley?"

"Confound you!—and if I did," was the impatient reply, "is that any reason why you should blab my name even to the wild birds of the air, or the croaking frogs in this ditch, close at hand?"

"It slipped out at the moment, unawares."

"Did it? I thought one of the principal things we all decided on, before coming on this enterprise, was, that by no accident were we to be induced to name each other?"

"It was! it was!" cried the woman; "but is this a time in which to quarrel?"

"No, no!"

"There was a noise!"

"Most probably, one of the horses!"

This gave Handsome Jemmy a hint, which he was by no means slow to improve upon. Feeling at his feet, among the mud and grass, he found a pebble, which he flung at one of the horses in the coach. The creature immediately stamped and shook its harness. The sound was not like that made by the opening and shutting of the pan of the highwayman's pistol, but it, at the moment, satisfied those who heard it.

"There! there!" said the man who had just spoken; "it was the horse!"

"He comes! he comes!" said the woman, in agitated tones.

"Hush! hush! The moment approaches! We have now but to be true to each other."

"You will shoot him?"

"I will."

"Oh, how often you have boasted of your skill! Show it now, and we shall all be rich, and you will be the possessor of a title!"

"I would take a dozen such lives for such objects. Look, all of you, as busy and as indifferent as you can, until he is exactly opposite to this spot; and then do you call out to him abruptly, by name. On the impulse of the moment, he will be sure to come to a halt; and then he is a dead man—for I cannot miss him!"

These words were addressed to the woman who was thus expected to play her part in the contemplated tragedy of that early morning.

Handsome Jemmy could just manage to see this woman's countenance through a chink in the park palings.

How deadly pale it was!

But the highwayman had been intensely occupied during the past few moments in lengthening and widening that same chink in the oak fence through which he had made his observations.

His object was to get it of sufficient size to enable him to protrude the barrel of one of his pistols through it; and that he had succeeded in doing.

And now came an anxious moment—one, indeed, so

anxious, that the excitable temperament of Handsome Jemmy could hardly be controlled to bear it.

Lord Malvern, or his horse, it was hard to say which, appeared to have been attracted by some object a considerable distance off At all events, the horse had come to a stand-still; and Lord Malvern seemed, with that eye-glass still at his eye, to be looking miles ahead of the spot in which his steed had paused.

The woman spoke.

"Now!" she said—"surely, now! You could do it now that he has stopped of his own accord, and I might be spared the part in the transaction you have designed for me!"

"No!" was the brief reply.

"I pray you to do so! On my knees, I pray you to do so! The boasted skill you have in the use of the pistol surely will suffice at this short distance?"

"No!" said the assassin again, as he crouched low down by the fire that had been made in imitation of the gipsies. "No! I am resolved that you shall have a share in the affair; so I will not anticipate you."

The woman uttered a low moan.

Lord Malvern put his horse, or the horse put himself, into motion again, and slowly came on as before.

"Now!" said the man with the pistol.

"Now, then!" said Handsome Jemmy. "I am ready, if you are!"

The woman sprung to her feet. She called out aloud, "Sydney, Lord Malvern! Sydney, Lord Malvern, you are wanted!"

"Eh? Who wants me, eh?"

The horse was now undoubtedly stopped by Lord Malvern himself.

"Die!" shouted the man with the pistol.

He raised his arm. No doubt his finger was upon the trigger, and he intended to take deliberate, though rapid, aim at the young lord.

But there was one who was beforehand with him.

Before he could pull the trigger of his pistol—before, even, he could get his arm and hand up to the level of the aim he wished to take—a sharp report of the discharge of a fire-arm awoke the echoes of the morning air.

That was the pistol of Handsome Jemmy.

A yell of pain from the assassin testified to the success of the highwayman's shot. He dropped his own pistol from his nerveless grasp; although, in the very act of dropping it, he discharged it.

The couple of bullets with which it had been charged whistled high over the head of Lord Malvern.

Handsome Jemmy had made a lucky shot, and just the one he wished to make. Nothing in the world would have been easier for him than to have sent a bullet into the brain of the would-be assassin; but he had preferred doing what he did, which was to send one exactly through his wrist.

The highwayman did not then wait for any action on the part of Lord Malvern; but he sprang over the oak fence at once, and spread consternation among the party of mock gipsies, as he cried out, "Murderers, you are foiled, when you thought yourselves most secure! My Lord Malvern, help me, and we shall have them all!"

"Aw! By Jove!" said Lord Malvern.

With a scream, the woman started off, and fled with amazing swiftness over the common.

"Catch her—catch her, my lord!" cried Jemmy. "I think I can manage the others!"

"Aw! She wuns well, but I can wun—aw! It's wewy odd; but wunning is one f—aw!—the things I can do—aw! I'll soon bwing her in—aw!"

Lord Malvern had, in his lazy, careless way, dismounted; and now, as Jemmy caught hold of the wounded man and another of the party, and held them securely, the foppish young lord set off at a swinging pace after the woman.

It looked like a race for a life.

Never had anything feminine run so fast before, except, perhaps, in some far-off island of the soft Pacific,

where female huntresses may be found capable of running down the fleetest game.

But in this case it was fear which added wings to the feet.

Yet she had no chance from the moment that Lord Malvern fairly took up the chase. As he himself said, "One of the things he could do was to run;" and run he did, like a roebuck.

The woman heard him coming. She shrieked aloud—she fell! Lord Malvern must have trampled upon her, but that, when he got close to her, he took a flying leap, and went far beyond where she lay.

Then he brought himself to a pause, and, without the least apparent want of breath, and with the eternal eye-glass still at his eye, he stepped back and looked at her.

Handsome Jemmy could not, at the distance, hear what was said between them; but, by the gestures of Lord Malvern, he could see that he was expressing surprise in his easy, quiet way.

Then he left the woman, to go or stay on the common, as she pleased, and came back to Jemmy, without once looking behind him.

The highwayman thought that very indiscreet conduct on the part of Lord Malvern; for if that woman had been in possession of a pistol, she might, after all, have carried out the object of the plot and the ambush, by shooting him.

Lord Malvern looked rather pale as he came up to the sham gipsy encampment.

"My lord," said Handsome Jemmy, "I'm afraid you have let escape one of the worst of the culprits!"

"Aw!—no! I—aw!—don't know exactly what they wanted to do; but—aw!—if it was to kill me, she has not got away—aw!"

"Why, my lord, there she goes!"

Lord Malvern did not even turn his head to look, but, letting the eyeglass drop from his eye to the end of the ribbon by which it hung, he said, "No, no! Aw! She may seem to get away, but—aw!—she carries with her the knowledge of what she meant to do, and that I know her!"

There was a look of calm dignity about the foppish Lord Malvern, as he uttered these words, which impressed Handsome Jemmy with far more respect for him than he had ever had before.

The man with the pistol-shot through his wrist lay, now on the grass, groaning with pain.

The other one was held firmly in the grasp of Handsome Jemmy.

"Aw!" said Lord Malvern. "My good friend, there is—aw!—another of these fellows somewhere—aw! I'm sure I saw three of them."

"By Jove, yes, my lord!" exclaimed Jemmy, as he looked around him anxiously,— "there were three!"

"Aw!—yes! By Jove—aw!—I saw three!"

The man who appeared to have succeeded in effecting his escape was the one who had been taunted with cowardice by his companions.

CHAPTER XLI.

LORD MALVERN RIDES TO TOWN IN DOUBTFUL COMPANY, AND SENDS FOR THE COURT PHYSICIAN.

HANDSOME JEMMY and Lord Malvern looked about them with some curiosity for the third man who had taken part in that atrocious conspiracy to murder.

But the search was fruitless for a time.

"Aw!" said Lord Malvern, "I think we will take this rascal to town."

"With all my heart, my lord," said Handsome Jemmy. "I daresay your lordship will be able to manage it."

"Aw—yes! But you will come too?"

Jemmy shook his head.

"I don't think that the air of London is just now, my lord, good for me. Perhaps your lordship does not recollect me?"

HANDSOME JEMMY SAVES LORD MALVERN'S LIFE.

"Aw—yes; I never forget anybody. Aw—that's one of the things I can do, like wunning. I can wun, and I recollect always everybody."

Jemmy looked at Lord Malvern, and smiled as he said, "Then I still think the air of London not good for me, my lord."

"Aw—why?"

"Because, in my case, it is apt to be confined air, you see."

"Aw—I comprehend; but I'll see about all that. Come with me, and I don't think anybody will interfere with the friend of Lord Malvern. If—aw—anybody does, why—aw—by fair means, or—aw—some other means, we will—aw—get rid of him—aw! What the deuce is that?"

A tall chesnut tree, close to where Handsome Jemmy and Lord Malvern were holding this little discourse, was crowded with chesnuts, and one of them at this moment came with rather a sharp crack upon the hat of Lord Malvern.

The great green envelope of the chesnut burst open, and the bright brown fruit fell about his lordship, and rolled to the ground.

Handsome Jemmy glanced up to the tree involuntarily, and so did Lord Malvern.

Then they both looked at each other, and as their eyes met, a smile was upon each face, and a look of intelligence passed between them.

They were both of opinion—of most decided opinion that some one was in the tree.

Who could that one be but the third man of the mock gipsy party, whom they had in so sudden and unaccountable a manner missed?

"Aw," said Lord Malvern, "it's very provoking to stand under a chesnut tree, and have chesnuts coming down on your head."

"Very!" said Handsome Jemmy, drily.

"Aw—I think it's some crow."

"So do I."

"In the tree."

"That's just my idea. Some ugly crow in the tree."

"Then—aw—I'll soon dislodge him. I can wun, and I can shoot!"

As Lord Malvern spoke, he took from his saddle a pistol, and levelled it up towards the tree.

A yell of fear came on the instant from some one amid the thick foliage of the old chesnut.

Bang went the pistol of Lord Malvern, at the same moment; and then, accompanied by a complete shower of chesnuts, and leaves, and broken branches, the third man of the mock gipsy party fell to the ground.

"Murder! murder! Help! I'm a dead man! I'm shot! I'm killed! I'm a dead man!"

"Aw—there you are, are you, Mr. Jones!" said Lord Malvern.

"Oh! oh! oh! I'm shot and killed!"

"Well, if you are, you need not make such a wow about it."

"Oh! oh!"

"My lord," said Jemmy, "do you know this man?"

"Quite well."

"And the others?"

"All of them. Those two men and that woman are my cousins. One of them—that man with the dark hair —is the next in succession to the title and estate of Malvern, if I should die without children. This man, Jones, is a more distant relation of the family—aw!"

"Then, my lord, the plot as against your life is quite clear?"

"Yes, wewy clear indeed!"

"Mercy! mercy, my Lord Malvern!" said Jones, now crawling towards the feet of the young nobleman, despite the assertions he had made that he was shot and a dead man. "Oh, have mercy upon me! I was drawn into it by the others—indeed I was; and always felt sorry at the idea of any harm coming to your lordship —indeed I did!"

Lord Malvern looked down at the trembling wretch with ineffable contempt.

"Get up," he said.

"Yes, my lord, yes; anything you wish, I'm sure! I'm only too happy to obey your lordship's orders in anything."

"Aw! and so you disapprove of my murder?"

"Yes, my lord, I do! With all my heart I disapprove of it; and I'll be evidence against all the others with pleasure, and help your lordship to take them up to London, and give them up to justice."

"You hear that—aw?" said Lord Malvern, turning to the other prisoners.

They had heard it, and they all spoke together: "I will be evidence!" "No, I will!" "No, no! Take me, my lord! Let me be the evidence!"

"Aw—now you have overdone it, all of you. If any one had had the courage to say nothing, but to stand to the consequences of his crime with anything like courage, that one should have gone free."

"Oh, my Lord Malvern!" said Handsome Jemmy, "could you expect any courage or nobleness of mind in people who could deliberately plan your assassination?"

"No; you are right. And yet I feel too much contempt for them even to prosecute them."

A flash of joy came across the countenances of the prisoners.

"But they shall have a wun for their lives," added the eccentric Lord Malvern. "The common is wide; they shall each and all have a wun across the common, and if I can hit one or all of them with a bullet, down they will go; but if I miss, why then they get off scot free. Aw—that is what I will do!"

The guilty men looked pale as death.

"It is murder!" said one.

"Dare you talk of murder?" said Handsome Jemmy. "But it is quite clear, my lord, they prefer the cells of Newgate."

"No, no!" cried two of the men; and then the female, who, by her presence, made that plot to commit murder ten times more hideous than it could otherwise have been, added the word "No!" to the others, and looked pale and defiant.

The man who had been found in the chesnut tree was, however, of a different opinion.

With yells, cries, and shouts for mercy, he besought Lord Malvern to let him go, without the chance of being shot.

His lordship lost patience with this man, and cried out angrily, "Aw—if you don't be off at once—aw—I'll begin firing at you as you are here now. Off with you! You shall have a fair start, while I count twenty. One, two, three, four, five, six, seven, eight, nine, ten——"

The whole party of would-be murderers started off at wild speed across the common.

The man who had fallen from the chesnut tree scrambled along for some distance on his hands and knees; but then finding he was left far behind in consequence of practising that species of locomotion, he sprung frantically to his feet, and with shouts of terror ran over the common.

Lord Malvern went on counting.

"Eleven, twelve, thirteen, fourteen, fifteen, sixteen, seventeen, eighteen, nineteen, twenty!"

Crack! went the first pistol shot.

Handsome Jemmy was infinitely amused, for he could see that Lord Malvern purposely took no aim at the fugitives.

Crack! crack! went two more shots, and at the report of each, the whole four of the assassins fell down on the turf of the common, as though they had been shot, and had great difficulty in scrambling to their feet again.

The most cowardly of the lot went right into a ditch, from which he emerged covered completely with that green vegetation which is so much admired by ducks.

Jemmy was so well pleased and amused at this affair, that he handed Lord Malvern his own pistols, as soon as those of his lordship were discharged, so that there were no less than six shots fired after the fugitives before they got fairly over the common.

Then they disappeared.

"Aw—I think that will do!"

"Not a doubt of it, my lord!"

"Aw—who is this?"

Dick Doubleday had got into a state of dreadful impatience and anxiety at the protracted absence of Handsome Jemmy, and when he heard all this pistol-firing, he could control that anxiety no longer, but at once rode forward and appeared upon the scene of action.

The sight of him was quite a surprise to Lord Malvern, who, refixing his eye-glass in his eye, from which he had temporially removed it, looked at Dick Doubleday as if he rather doubted the evidence of his own senses.

"What is the matter, Jemmy?" cried Dick. "Is there danger?"

"None, Dick! There was, but there is none now."

"Aw—young man, will you be so good as to say—aw—if you ever wun away from Bedford Square with somebody who could wun a little faster after you—aw?"

"Yes, my lord!"

"Aw—I thought so—aw!"

After this, Lord Malvern did not seem to care how or by what chance Dick Doubleday was there on the open common, in freedom; but Dick Doubleday spoke further, and added, "Yes, my lord; I am that person whom your lordship pursued and caught; but I hope that now —now——"

Dick did not know very well what to conclude with, and Handsome Jemmy took up the speech by saying, "We both hope, my lord, that the past will be forgotten."

"Aw—do you? By Jove! but it won't, though! Do you think I'm game or vermin? Aw—I'm not going to forget that you saved my life, and that you are the friend of—of—aw—the man who has so saved my life. Come with me back to London. I'll take good care no harm comes to either of you—aw! They shall put me in limbo before they shall you—aw!"

Handsome Jemmy and Dick Doubleday exchanged glances, and Jemmy said, "I rather think we had better thank Lord Malvern, and go our way, Dick, while he goes his."

Dick Doubleday made but one short reply to these words. He stretched out his arms in the direction of London, as, in a voice of emotion, he uttered the one name of "Pamela!"

There was no mistaking the action, and what was uppermost in Dick Doubleday's thoughts. Now that he might go to London again and search for Pamela, his whole soul was bent upon so doing.

The highwayman did not seek to oppose the operation of this feeling.

"Dick, you are right," he said. "But I——"

"Oh, pray do not say what I fear you are going to say; but come with me. I shall soon be lost without you."

Jemmy shook his head.

Lord Malvern looked from one to the other of them while this little conversation went on, wondering what it was all about.

"Aw," he said—"I don't think there can be much danger. I'll make you a present of the horse and the coat. I'll withdraw the charge, and say—aw—it was all a joke—a bet—a wager—aw—and that will settle the whole affair."

"Then, Dick," cried Handsome Jemmy, "I am with you, lad, in life or to death!"

Dick Doubleday pressed the hand of the highwayman gratefully; and Lord Malvern, through his eye glass, looked at the process as he said, "Aw—can I be of any use—aw—in any way in London?"

"I think," said Jemmy, "you ought to tell Lord Malvern, Dick, all about Pamela."

"I will—I will! My lord, as we ride along, will you care to hear my story?"

"Go on—aw—I'll listen to it—aw—with all my ears, as the man in the play says—aw!"

Upon this, Dick Doubleday, in as few words as possible, made Lord Malvern acquainted with the whole of the sad and eventful history of poor Pamela, and of the many perils that had surrounded her, and which. for all he could take upon himself to say to the contrary, surrounded her still.

When he had concluded, Lord Malvern let his glass fairly drop from his eye, and said no less than five times, "By Jove!"

Then his lordship faced about to Jemmy, and said, "I know this Doctor Haslem quite well—aw."

"You do, my lord?"

"Yes—aw—oh, yes! He attends my family and me. Not that I ever want a doctaw; but—aw—I mean if I did want a doctaw, which—aw—I don't—for a fellaw who can wun as well as I can don't want a doctaw; but if I did—aw—well, I mean—aw——Eh? Aw—I've lost the thwead of—aw—what I did mean; but you know, perhaps?"

"Oh, yes—yes!" said Jemmy.

"Quite well," said Dick.

"Aw—then that's all right By Jove! you shall both of you come home to my house in Park Lane, and I'll send for Doctaw Haslem, and he will think that there is something the matter with a fellaw; and then I shall say to him, 'Doctaw—Doctaw—by Jove, Doctaw!' I shall say, 'where is—is——' Eh? What did you say her name was?"

"Pamela!"

"Aw—yes. I shall say, 'Doctaw, by Jove! where is Pamelaw?'—aw—aw!"

CHAPTER XLII.

DETAILS WHAT BECAME OF PAMELA AND OF CAPTAIN SANG AFTER THE NIGHT ADVENTURE ON THE STAIRCASE OF THE MANSION IN THE BIRDCAGE WALK.

CAPTAIN SANG fell backwards down the stairs at the sight of Pamela.

He was a tall man—a stout man too, for his height; and going over upon his heels as he did, the fall he got was a terrific one.

His head did not happen fairly to strike upon the edge of a stair; if it had done so, he must have been killed at once.

But he fell rather obliquely, and then rolled the remainder of the distance into the hall.

There he lay quite insensible.

There could be no doubt but that at sight of Pamela in that riding habit, he thought he saw the apparition of his former victim—the granddaughter of the old woman who kept house for him.

Heated with wine as he was, and his brain in a state of abnormal excitement, no doubt his imagination on the moment provided every accessory that was wanting to make the illusion of the figure perfect.

The success of the old woman's stratagem was, therefore, complete.

At the fall of Captain Sang, she rose up from the crouching position she had assumed behind poor Pamela, and uttered a shout of gratification and triumph.

Pamela, who was not aware that the old woman was so close to her, was more terrified at that wild exultant cry behind her, than she had been at the yell that came from the lips of Captain Sang

It was only by grasping the balustrade of the staircase suddenly and impulsively, that Pamela saved herself from falling down the whole flight.

"Revenge!—revenge!—revenge! Revenge! I have revenge at last!" shouted the old woman.

"He is dead!" said Pamela.

"No, no—not dead. John Sang is not dead yet. That would be to baulk me! Surely he is not dead yet, I do not want him dead."

The old woman darted past Pamela on the stairs, and took her way to the hall below, where she laid her ear to the breast of Captain Sang, to know if his heart still beat.

It did.

"No, he is not dead: John Sang and I have not done with each other yet. Girl, you are free—free as air! Descend and leave the house at once for it is one of death—one of triumph—and one of despair?"

The old woman—she almost looked like a "hag" again to the eyes of Pamela—fairly stood upon the prostrate body of Captain Sang, as she addressed these words to the terrified young girl, whose most ardent wish was to get leave to quit that house as soon as possible.

That the poor bereaved creature, who had suffered so much by her connexion with the brutal and infamous Captain Sang, was now quite in a state of frenzy, there could be no doubt.

But Pamela was too young, and too inexperienced in the ways of the world, to know what steps she could take, or aught to take, under such circumstances.

All she felt, was the burning wish to get out of that house as soon as possible.

And so she hastened to avail herself of the kind of permission—half permission, half command—to leave it, which was implied in the words of the old woman.

Pamela therefore hastily divested herself of the riding-habit, and then descended the stairs.

It was with a shuddering horror that she felt herself compelled to step over the feet of the prostrate Captain Sang, on whose breast the old woman still stood.

"Oh, let me thank you!" said Pamela—"let me thank you for more than life."

"Go!" screamed the old woman. "You are not wanted here!"

"I will pray ever for you!"

"Go, I say!"

"I will speak to those who can, and who will, befriend you."

"Away! away! I want no befriending!"

"But you may still know peace. If happiness be denied you because you will not be able wholly to forget the past, you may still know serenity.

The old woman uttered a hoarse cry of anger, and making a rush to the door, she flung it open.

The cool night-air came gratefully from the open expanse of the Park beyond, to the senses of Pamela.

"Go, I say—go!" cried the old woman once more,— "go, lest worse befall you!"

Pamela made an effort to take her hand and press it to her lips as she passed the old woman, but the latter tore it from her; and the young girl, with a heart full of gratitude for her escape, passed out of the house.

The gate that led fairly into the Park was only on the latch, so that Pamela was, to all intents and purposes, free.

What a joyful sensation that was!

With what a healthful, bounding impulse the blood coursed through her veins.

It seemed to her that the cool, fresh air had never before been so full of vitality; and the few stars that looked down upon her from the somewhat dull and vapoury night-sky, appeared to her to be unusually bright and beautiful.

She wandered round the Park in the direction of St. James's.

Where was she to go?

With whom was she to seek a refuge?

How lonely she began to feel in the vast city, without one to whom she could turn with a certainty of finding a kindly welcome—for she knew not where to find Dick Doubleday.

She knew not where to look for Handsome Jemmy, the highwayman.

And she did not wish to return to the house of Doctor Haslem.

Gradually, she had contracted the idea, that with all his kindness to her, the Court Physician had designs and objects inimical to Dick Doubleday; and so there was Pamela, not far off from the Palace, wondering where she should go and what she should do.

And she, so young and so fair, all alone in mighty London—although, at that time, the great city slept, and it was only faintly that at times the sounds of life would rise up from the streets, as some late and noisy roysterers took their way home from the tavern.

Then Pamela was struck with the feasibleness of an idea that came across her mind.

What if she should go to Long Lane, and endeavour to find out, from Dick Doubleday's uncle, where he was to be met with?

Nay, it was possible that Dick might be there; and if so, she could have no hesitation in at once putting herself under his protection. At least, there was the chance of hearing something of him at that house.

It was a positive relief to Pamela to lift her mind, so to speak, out of the perfect chaos of uncertainty which had beset it; and the mere fact that she had now a kind of destination, seemed to strip her position of many of its terrors.

"Yes," she said, "I will go there—I will seek that house which has been the home of him that loved me for so long; and even if I meet with but a cold and repulsive reception, some chance word may give me all the information I seek."

There was no difficulty in leaving St. James's Park at such an hour—although, probably, admittance to it might have been refused by the sentinels.

But Pamela was very oddly attired—for she still wore the hat and gloves which had formed part of her disguise in the house of Captain Sang; and, quite forgetting these things in the pre-occupation and excitement of her mind, she was rather surprised at the steady stare of curiosity with which the sentinel at the gate of Spring Gardens regarded her.

But Pamela gave this circumstance only a passing attention, and went her way with what speed she could towards Smithfield.

Her acquaintance with the streets of London was much greater—speaking topographically—than might have been supposed for a girl of her age and experience; but that arose from the peculiar use which Jacob Sharples, the coiner, had made of her youth and innocence, by sending her on many an expedition to different parts of London, ostensibly to make small purchases, but, in reality, to get change for spurious coin, while he remained at home in safety.

Thus was it that Pamela, all alone as she was, and with nothing to sustain her but her own innocence and gentleness, was able, without much wandering from the true path, to make her way towards the house of Dick Doubleday's uncle.

She heeded not the soft rain which began to fall, but, in the course of half an hour, felt herself almost beneath the shadow of old Newgate again.

Then it was that a terrible terror came over the heart of the young girl, and she feared that some hand would be outstretched to seize her, and drag her into the abode of misery.

She no longer thought that Dick Doubleday was an inmate of the prison.

A change had come over her ideas on that head, for she had reasoned herself into a belief of the impossibility of one whom she loved, and who loved her, committing any act which would consign him to a cell in that dreary place.

And, moreover, that first impulse which had tempted her to seek the dismal prison, to discover his fate, had passed away; and, with returning reflection, Pamela had come to the conclusion that the way to serve Dick Doubleday, even if he were confined under some baseless charge, was certainly not to knock at the prison gate.

This conclusion was all the more rational and reasonable, inasmuch as she herself had suffered so much from a false accusation, and, for all she knew, might still be at the mercy of the so-called ministers of justice.

Taking, then, a devious course round the old prison, and shrinking down under the shadow of doorways and archways as she went, Pamela took a circuitous route towards Long Lane.

Faint and exhausted, then—for it was long since she

PAMELA ESCAPES FROM CAPTAIN SANG.

No. 14.—FELON'S DAUGHTER.

had tasted food, and she had gone through much fatigue and excitement—she stood upon the threshold of old Zachariah's door, with but a faint hope of there procuring a refuge, or of there hearing any news of Dick Doubleday.

With the exhaustion and weakness of her physical frame, the first brightness of the hope which her idea of visiting Zachariah's house had engendered, faded away.

And now that she stood upon the very doorstep of that wretched, dingy abode, which, however, was hallowed in her eyes as having been the home so long of one who had loved her so truly and well, she felt almost inclined to ask herself what had brought her there.

Perhaps it was fate.

But, being there, she would still make the experiment, and arouse old Zachariah, if it were possible, to answer the question she desired to put to him.

And now, unwillingly, we must leave Pamela for a few seconds on that doorstep while we enter the house of Zachariah; and making our way to that wretched, gloomy apartment at the back of the shop, in which, like some ancient spider in a far-off corner of his web, Zachariah waited for his victims, we shall there look upon two persons.

These two persons are no other than Zachariah himself, and Jacob Sharples.

A miserable rushlight, the gradual consumption of which Zachariah beheld with deep regret, and testified to by groans, was on the table between them.

The feeble light fell upon the faces of the two men, and it would have been hard to say which looked the most haggard, old, and careworn.

Yet these men were both rich.

But what a price they had paid for their riches!

They had bartered for gold, health, strength, fame, and safety.

Jacob Sharples was considerably the younger man of the two; but in looks he was fully equal in age to Zachariah.

They were conversing in low tones, and their thin, fleshless lips seemed to curl and snarl at each other, although, in truth, they were perfectly in accord as regarded the subject of their conversation.

That subject was money—gold; how to conserve and make the most of that which they had, and how to add to it as much more as possible.

There was a deep wound upon the forehead of Jacob Sharples, and one of his arms was in a sling made of an exceedingly dilapidated, old cotton handkerchief. Down the side of his face, too, was a stain which looked like a burn; and, take him for all in all, a more wretched object than Jacob Sharples, the coiner, could scarcely have been imagined.

Old Zachariah, on the other hand, looked cold, white, and crafty, as usual; and was every moment indulging in a habit which was peculiar to him, of plucking his white, bushy eyebrows as far over his eyes as possible, while he peered through them as though gazing with difficulty through a bush.

Little did poor Pamela suspect that the first rap she should make at the door of Zachariah would reach the ears of Jacob Sharples, to whom, and for whom, she could have no other feelings than those of detestation and terror.

But so it was. Pamela's perils were not yet over.

———

CHAPTER XLIII.

PAMELA FALLS AGAIN INTO THE HANDS OF JACOB SHARPLES WHO STRIVES TO MAKE HIS OWN TERMS WITH THE PHYSICIAN.

IT was quite evident that in the conversation, if it could be called such, that was taking place between Jacob Sharples and old Zachariah, the latter had very much the advantage.

The coiner spoke in tones which at times were full of entreaty, and then again he would raise his voice into threatening accents.

But neither of these moods or conditions had any effect upon Zachariah.

Still cold, white, sarcastic, and determined, he treated the coiner as the inferior person over whom he had power.

"Say at once—say at once," cried Sharples, as he dashed his hand on the table, so as to make the rushlight jump again—"say at once what you will give me for the jewels?"

"Nothing!" was the cool response of the old man.

"Nothing? Nothing? Do you say that to me?"

"I do."

"But — but, Zachariah, it is your trade, your business, your calling to buy such things, and to buy them of such men as I am."

"Eugh! Eugh!" coughed Zachariah. "My good friend, permit me to remark that you have taken leave of your senses."

"As how? As how?"

"Why, you come here, and you talk of jewels, of rings, and brooches, and a bracelet, which you want me to buy, and in the same breath you tell me you have them at home; as if a man like me ever bought such things of a man like you, without seeing them!"

"You—you want to see them?"

"Of course I do. Eugh! Eugh!"

"Zachariah!"

"Well?"

"You are an old man."

"Not so old. I am only seventy-two. Not so old, Master Sharples."

"And that cough has a sound as of the hollow and echo of a church-yard about it."

"Eugh! Eugh! I have had it for forty years."

"You are rich, too. Come now, Zachariah, I have a proposal to make to you."

"What is it?"

"I will take good care of you and your money for the remainder of your life. You shall come with me to some foreign country, where the soft and genial climate will give you a new lease of existence, and with all your money we can both live like princes!"

"I am not deaf!"

"Well, what say you?"

"No!" roared old Zachariah. "Get out—get out! Thief!—robber! You want my poor, hard-won savings —I know you do! You have no jewellery to dispose of —you never had! You are Jacob Sharples, the coiner, and that is all you are; but there is a price upon your head—a hundred pounds reward for you—and it will be well-earned money!"

Sharples sprang to his feet.

"You would betray me?"

"You would rob me!"

"Wretch!"

"Villain!"

The two men—Jacob Sharples, with the use only of one hand, since the other was badly hurt and in the sling—and the old lapidary, with both hands, it is true, but a weak and nerveless grasp, grappled with each other.

But the moment they did so, they both seemed to feel the impolicy of a disturbance that might bring the constables upon them.

They released each other simultaneously; and then they glared in each other's faces with excited aspects; and Zachariah spoke with agitation, as he said, "Jacob Sharples, Jacob Sharples, we know too much of each other to quarrel!"

"A great deal too much!" said Sharples.

"And so—and so I will buy your jewellery of you; but I must see it; and I feel quite convinced you have it about you."

"You are right, Zachariah; I have it here."

"Good—good! Now, Jacob Sharples, let us be friends again—good friends again! Eugh! eugh! Why should we quarrel, except in a friendly way?"

As he spoke, old Zachariah made a weak effort to trim the rushlight, the wick of which was of portentous length.

Then, slowly and reluctantly, Jacob Sharples took from his pocket a leather bag, from which he produced the articles of jewellery he had mentioned. He averted his own eyes, and shuddered as he regarded them; for he could not help recollecting where and how he had procured the costly gems.

It was from the poor fugitive wife on the Thames, in the midst of that storm of rain and wind, when she had fled from the house of the physician, in Bedford Square—from the mother of Pamela it was that he had taken those jewels; and he fully believed that the cold, heaving waters of the river rolled over all that remained of the victim of his cupidity on that sad and eventful night of terror.

"Take them—take them, Zachariah!" he said, as he averted his eyes from those evidences and remembrances of his guilt—"take them! Give me what price you can for them, and never let them meet my eyes again!"

Whatever baleful effect these jewels had upon the eyes of Jacob Sharples, it was quite evident that they were objects of pleasure to those of old Zachariah.

"Right—right!" he cried. "You are right, Jacob Sharples! Never keep things like these, that remind you of the past! I will give—I—I will give—let me see—I will give forty—that is to say, I mean thirty-five—or suppose we say thirty pounds for the lot?"

"Villain!"

"Eh?—what? A bad name, that, Jacob Sharples!"

"But a deserved one! For the sum of one hundred pounds, these trinkets are yours! Attempt to get them of me for less, and they shall sink as deep in the Thames as—as—she who once wore them!"

"You are mad!"

"Perhaps so! Good night."

"Stop! stop!"

"One hundred pounds!"

"No—I——"

"Farewell!"

"Stop—one moment! You are wilful; but an old customer and an old friend ought to be sometimes humoured, even at the cost of some money; and so—and so——"

"You will buy them?"

"I—I suppose I must."

"The money! Quick—the money! I shall be far away from London by the dawn of another day! The air of the City is hateful to me! Give me the money, Zachariah; and let me go at once!"

It was at this moment that poor Pamela made her first appeal to the knocker on the shop-door of old Zachariah.

Both the—what shall we call them?—thieves—yes, both the thieves started at the sound; for it was not one of those signal raps which were well known by those who were in the habit, at all hours of the day or night, of bringing stolen plate and other portable valuable plunder.

The feeling of quarrelling between these two men passed away on the instant before the common danger that possibly was at hand.

"Who is that?"

"Who can that be?"

They both listened intently. The knock was repeated; and then it would seem that Pamela had seen a bell-handle, and had more faith in that procuring her some attention than the knocker.

The sharp tinkle of the bell smote on the ears of the two criminal men alarmingly.

"It is time for me to go," said Jacob Sharples, in a low tone—"it is time for me to go!"

"Hold! hold!" said Zachariah. "If—if, my dear old friend—if——"

"If what?"

"If the—the officers—the runners—the—the constables should be after you,—if they have traced you

to this door, and—and—if they should, despite all we can do, take you—I—I have only one thing to say——"

"In the fiend's name, what is it?"

"It will do you no harm——"

"Speak! What is it?"

"No harm in the world. You may as well let me have the reward, which I shall get, if they come in, and see my hand upon your collar!"

"Put it there only for one half-second, Zachariah, and you are a dead man!"

The ring at the little bell was repeated.

The wretched old woman who formed the only member of Zachariah's domestic establishment had been peremptorily ordered to go to bed some time since, so that there was no one but Zachariah himself to answer the bell.

"You are violent!—you are violent, Jacob Sharples!" he said. "You are violent and headstrong, without reason! I will go to the door."

"And I with you."

Old Zachariah took the rushlight in his trembling hand and went along the gloomy passage to the private door of the house.

Jacob Sharples followed him as closely as foot could fall.

Zachariah rapped with his knuckles upon the inner panel of the door, as he cried out, in his thin, croaking voice, "Who is there?—who is there? Speak! Who are you that knock and ring at a quiet, respectable house at such an hour as this?"

"Ah, sir!" replied a soft, gentle voice; "you are Richard's uncle, I think?"

"Good gracious!"

"Ah! it is the girl! It is—it is Pamela!" said Jacob Sharples.

The two men looked at each other dubiously for a few moments, during which they were calculating what advantage or what change could result from this visit of Pamela.

"She is mine," said Jacob Sharples—"she is mine! I shall now hold a hostage as against fortune. The girl is mine!"

"But, Jacob, there is——Oh, dear! oh, dear! there is——"

"What do you mean?"

"A reward for her, too. If that be Pamela Sharples on the other side of the door, you know that since it has been found out she was not really pardoned by the King, there has been a reward of a hundred pounds for her, too; so that—so that——Oh, dear me! This is very perplexing—very!"

"What is?"

"I—I—don't know what to do—I don't know what to think. A hundred pounds on each side of the door; one for you, and one for her. Oh, Jacob Sharples, Jacob Sharples! for once in a way be friendly. Do, do! You are sure to be taken some day, and as well now as then. Let me give her up, and get that hundred pounds; and let me give you up, and get the other. Do, do! Jacob Sharples, Jacob Sharples! It will be all the same to you in the end."

"You—you old scoundrel!"

"Nay, now don't be angry. It will be all the same, don't you see?"

Jacob Sharples pushed the old man on one side, and although he had but the use of one arm, he yet managed to get the better of Zachariah, who was much the older man of the two.

"Make any alarm at your peril!" said Sharples. "I will open the door and speak to the girl."

Jacob opened the door.

By the dim light even of the rushlight, Pamela might have seen who it was; but the draught of air that came into the narrow passage at once extinguished it, and all was darkness.

The voice of Jacob Sharples, however, smote upon her ears with terror; and but that he had the skill to render his first few words deeply interesting to her, she would have fled from that ill-omened place, and he would never have set his guilty eyes upon her again.

"Pamela! Pamela!" he said. "Dick Doubleday is at my house, and I only linger in London to restore you to him and him to you."

Pamela heard these words, and it is needless to say that they sounded grateful y and pleasantly enough in her ears.

She had one objection to them, and that was that they came to her in the accents of Jacob Sharples.

But he was quite right in supposing that they would act as a spell to stop her from any instant flight from the door of Zachariah's house.

She shrank back as far as the pavement extended, and in a voice of entreaty she spoke.

"Jacob Sharples—Jacob Sharples! can I, ought I to believe you?"

"Not believe your own father, Pamela?"

"That delusion is dispelled—that terror has passed away. Too well do I now know that you are not my father."

"Girl!—girl, you are mad!"

"No, no! I was surely mad, or too little versed in the ways of the world, when I ever believed that you were my father!"

"Well—well, I—a—I —— Well, I say, we will not dispute about that. All I wish now to do is some act of kindness—of goodness—of justice, before I leave England for ever; and that I would fain do by uniting you with Dick Doubleday. He is satisfied, and why should you not be?"

"How is he satisfied?"

"He is at my house now. He has commissioned me to seek you."

"No, no, no! Richard Doubleday would seek me himself!"

"Not if the myrmidons of the law kept watch for him. Do you not know that?"

This was a haphazard sort of speech on the part of Jacob Sharples, but it happened to tally well with the information that Pamela had already become possessed of regarding the fortunes of Dick Doubleday. She hesitated if she should venture to put any trust in what Jacob Sharples said or not; and then it was a terrible idea to her to abandon the hope or the chance of rejoining Dick if the statement of the coiner were indeed true.

"Swear to me!—swear to me by some holy word or name!—swear to me, Jacob Sharples, that what you say is true, and I will trust you; leaving to you the guilt of the deceit, if deceit there be, and to me the despair which, after all, shall not be so acute in suffering as the agony of a perjured heart!"

It took even Jacob Sharples an effort after this to speak as he did.

His voice was hoarse and strange as he said, "I swear to the truth of what I have said to you, Pamela!"

"In the name of heaven?"

"In—the name—of—of—heaven!"

"Then I will trust you."

Jacob Sharples felt sick at heart as he tottered rather than walked over the threshold of Zachariah's house, and took hold of Pamela by the arm.

"No, Jacob Sharples," she said, with a shudder—"no; touch me not! Walk with me, and lead the way, but touch me not!"

"Watch! watch! Police! police!" screamed old Zachariah, at this moment, making his way half out into the street. "Police! Watch! I claim the reward! I give up two hundred pounds—no, I mean I give up two people with two hundred pounds reward for them, and I claim the money! Watch! watch!"

Something glittered for a moment in the hand of Jacob Sharples, and then descended like a flash of light upon the breast of Zachariah.

The old man fell with a groan upon the threshold of his door.

"Wait for me one moment, Pamela," cried Jacob Sharples, "or you will never look upon Dick Doubleday again!"

He darted back into Zachariah's house, over his prostrate body, to the room in which they had so lately held their guilty conference; and snatching from the table the articles of jewellery concerning which he had been bargaining, he dashed out of the house again, and rejoined Pamela in the street.

"Come, come, Pamela!" he cried; "come with me now at once, and gladden the eyes of Dick Doubleday by your presence!"

"You have sworn!"

"I have—I have! You heard me. Come at once, or the treacherous cries of this old man may yet bring danger upon us!"

"I will follow you!"

CHAPTER XLIV.

PAMELA IS MADE A PRISONER IN THE HOUSE OF JACOB SHARPLES, AND DISCOVERS SOME OF ITS MOST TERRIBLE SECRETS.

IT did not appear possible to Pamela that any one in this mortal life, with a single shadowy hope beyond the grave, could perjure themselves as Jacob Sharples had done to her that night.

And yet—yet there was a fluttering at her heart as she followed the coiner, which served to warn her against some fearful treachery.

And Jacob himself appeared to suspect that such would be the case, for more than once as they proceeded through the rain, which was now falling freely, he pronounced the name of Dick Doubleday, as the spell which would still keep the fair girl in his power.

"Dick Doubleday will be anxious!—Dick Doubleday will be impatient!—Dick Doubleday will think us long in coming!"

Such were the specious sentences by which Jacob Sharples kept the mind of Pamela from thoroughly comprehending and appreciating all his possible treachery, and so she followed him.

Followed him to that gloomy street in Clerkenwell; to that wretched house where for so long he had held his abode, and where the reader has already seen him in the midst of his fears and his miseries.

What but fear, and what but misery, had the evil courses of Jacob Sharples brought upon him as yet?

Well did poor Pamela know the route to that dismal abode, which she had thought never to have looked upon again.

Well might she shrink with a sickening tremor as she reached its threshhold.

"Oh, Jacob Sharples!—oh, Jacob Sharples! if, despite the oath you have taken, you are deceiving me, and leading me here with any other purpose—with any other hope than that which has induced me to follow you, surely I shall have need to pray for your forgiveness!"

"Peace, girl, peace! You speak wildly! Why should I deceive you?"

"Alas, I know not!"

"Dick Doubleday is here!"

"Ah, you pronounce his name again, and I must needs follow you!"

They crossed the threshold of the wretched house.

The coiner closed the door behind them.

Pamela sighed deeply.

"Let me call to him!—let me call to him!" she said; "he will know my voice!"

"No, no! abstain from doing so for a moment! There may be danger—danger to him!"

"Danger here?"

"Ay, even here! Follow me closely! There are rooms in this house which you have never seen—never visited, and it is in one of them that I have made a secure hiding-place for him whom I can well perceive you love truly and fondly—Dick Doubleday, I mean This way—this way, Pamela; and you—ha! ha!—you will soon find whether I have deceived you or not, my girl!"

There was something ferocious and terrible in the hideous laugh of Jacob Sharples.

Well might the innocent and gentle girl, who had been lured to that house, shrink from it with terror.

But she had gone too far to retreat; and the name of Richard Doubleday, which had been the spell to bring her to that place, still lingered in her ears as the faint echo or remembrance of music will linger upon the senses after the sound itself has died away.

Jacob Sharples conducted her to that gloomy and wretched apartment where he had been found by Dr. Haslem on the occasion of the visit made to him so recently by the physician.

It was a familiar place to Pamela, and she felt that she could almost see, through the eyes of memory, every well-known object in the squalid room, even before Jacob Sharples procured a light, which shed a faint glimmer upon the scene.

"At home—at home once again!" said Sharples, in tones of repressed exultation. "So you're at home once again, my girl!—at home in the old place, my pretty Pamela! Why—why it seems an age—quite an age since we talked together beneath this ancient roof! And so they nabbed and caged the pretty bird, did they?—and all for trying to spend a guinea that did not happen to be current gold!"

"Jacob Sharples!" said Pamela, while an undefined terror gathered at her heart—"Jacob Sharples! I will not listen to this!—I did not come to listen to it! Remember your oath, and conduct me to Richard Doubleday!"

"Oh, yes, certainly—certainly! But who would have thought it?—who would have thought so fair a bird would ever have wandered again into a cage like this? But follow me!—follow me! In good truth we waste time! Oh, believe me, your pretty face will soon gladden the eyes of Dick Doubleday!"

Jacob Sharples led the way from the room, and Pamela followed him to the end of the gloomy passage, where there was a black and cavernous-looking staircase conducting to the lower regions of the house, and more resembling in its foul aspect the deep and dangerous entrance of a well, than any flight of steps down which a human being might descend with safety.

"Take the light—take the light," said Sharples,—"take the light and descend! You will find him there."

"Oh, no, no! I will call to him, and he will come up to me! Not into that gloomy place—where neither you nor I, Jacob Sharples, ever penetrated before. At the first sound of my voice he will come up to me, if he be in truth there. Richard! Richard! Richard Doubleday! It is I—it is Pamela who calls to you! Richard Doubleday, come to me! I am here to seek you!"

"You do but vex him," said Jacob Sharples, with a grim smile.

"Vex him? What mean you?"

"Just this. He was accused of—of I know not what—some real or fancied crime, and the pursuit was hot!"

"They took him—they lodged him in Newgate!"

This was news to Jacob Sharples; but he had tact enough at the moment to adopt the information in a style that led Pamela to suppose he had been perfectly aware of it.

"Oh, yes—of course! As you say, they lodged him in Newgate, from which he escaped, or he would not now be here. Escaped at great peril and risk of his life; and, indeed, with such hurts and wounds——"

Pamela uttered an exclamation of grief and despair.

"Such hurts and wounds," added Jacob Sharples, "that had I not received him and tended him carefully, he must needs have been a dead man; and were you to cry to him with ten times the voice you have to do so, he could not reply to you, although his heart might break in the effort!"

Pamela snatched the light from the hand of Jacob Sharples.

There was a world of reproach in the glance she cast upon him, as she cried out, in anguished accents, "And you did not tell me this—and you did not tell me this! You have kept me here lingering, debating, doubting, and fearing, while he—who is more than life to me—may be dying! Richard, Richard! I come to you—your Pamela comes to you! Live yet for her, for she loves you still—loves you still as ever!"

Holding the light aloft, so that its star-like rays created a dim twilight in the cavernous place into which poor Pamela descended, she seemed to skim down that gloomy staircase more like a bird upon the wing than aught human.

"Richard, Richard!" she cried again—"speak to me, if it be but faintly. It is your Pamela who calls to you!"

Jacob Sharples craned his neck over the dismal opening from the passage, and looked at the faint light and flying figure of the young girl as they receded from him.

Then he raised a shout of triumph.

It was a half scream, half yell with which he congratulated himself on the success of a stratagem which he believed would perfectly ensure his own safety, and immunity from every evil consequence of his previous acts.

"Caged! caged!" he cried—"caged at last! I have now a hostage, which will be redeemed at any price! Remain there, Pamela, until I come to you; and no mortal power can rescue you till that hour arrives!"

There was a door at the head of that staircase—a door that opened wide, and laid itself very flat against the wall. Rust and decay had done their work upon its hinges, and the sounds with which they did their long unaccustomed work were harsh and grating.

But Jacob Sharples put his shoulder to the door, and it closed with a loud clang.

An iron bar swung pendant to the wall, and had but to be lifted into a niche prepared for it, to make that door secure.

This Jacob Sharples accomplished on the instant, although he was in profound darkness.

Then there came upon his ears a stifled shriek.

It sounded miles away, as if deep down beneath the earth's crust.

He trembled and listened.

He placed his ear flat against the door, with the hope to hear that cry again; for it would at least assure him that nothing fatal had happened to Pamela,—for, if she were to be valuable to him as a hostage, it must be in life, and not in death.

But all was still.

A cold feeling came over Jacob Sharples. Terror might have killed that young and fragile being, whom he could not but notice had looked pale and delicate, as if from exhaustion, before she had descended to that gloomy region.

He searched in his pocket for some coin, with the sharp edge of which he might make a sound against the door.

A penny piece answered the purpose, and with that Jacob Sharples kept up a clipping noise upon the iron bar; and then he called out aloud, "Pamela! Pamela! Pamela! No one seeks to harm you, and there is no danger! The rats, the mice, and the beetles will fly from you! I know who and what you are, but it is necessary for my own safety that I should have some high price to offer to those who have the power to assure me of that safety, and that high price must be you, Pamela!"

He listened, but there was no reply.

He tapped again with the penny piece on the iron bar, and the sharp sound echoed through the dismal house. But Pamela spoke not.

"A trick—a trick!" muttered Sharples to himself. "She thinks to frighten me—to alarm me to opening the door again, and setting her free; but no, no! that will not do for Jacob Sharples. I've a game to play that must be played out. She won't hurt till morning—she cannot hurt till morning! It is almost morning now, and then I will seek this Court Physician, who sets such store by the bright eyes and fair face of his long-lost child. I will seek him, and I shall care not what he says or what he thinks! All threats of retribution for the past will scatter themselves into the idle air. I will ask for safety—the assurance of full and complete pardon for the past, which he, by his influence, can procure, and the price shall be the restoration of Pamela!"

Jacob Sharples could not prevail on himself entirely to leave the passage without again listening at the door.

Not the faintest cry from below rewarded him.

"Be it so—be it so!" he said, somewhat angrily. "Let her take her own course, and I take mine. Be it so, I say! I will sleep—sleep, for much I need it. No, no! I cannot sleep. When did I sleep last? When shall I ever sleep again? When I close my eyes, I seem to see myself again in that boat upon the river. I hear a cry for life—a cry for mercy! It rings in my ears, and I wake bathed in a dew of terror. No, no! No sleep—no sleep, yet, for me! What's that?"

Jacob Sharples listened.

"It is but the rain—it is but the rain. It beats this way, and patters against the door and doorstep. It comes in at yon broken fan-light. I feel the spots now upon my head—upon my brow—upon my face. They are grateful and cool, and I see a faint grey light which tells me that the morning is at hand. I will go out into the rain—out into the rain. I like it! It calms and stills the fever of my veins; and so soon as the hum and stir of active life rises from the city, I will visit this great, rich, haughty Court Physician, and I will say, 'Pardon, complete, full, and perfect, for Jacob Sharples, and the price is Pamela!'"

CHAPTER XLV.

JACOB SHARPLES VISITS DOCTOR HASLEM, AND FINDS MORE COMPANY THAN HE EXPECTED

CROUCHING down, to escape the fury of the rain and the wind that assailed him at every corner, as though it would drive him to his own dismal house in Clerkenwell, Jacob Sharples made his way towards Bedford Square.

He persevered in his design of calling upon Doctor Haslem.

Fain would Jacob Sharples have done something to put an end at once and for ever to the terror of the life he was now leading. All had been gloom—all despair and darkness; but now he thought he saw the daylight of hope.

Surely the Court Physician would redeem his own long-lost, much-loved child, at any price.

"Pardon for the past, and competence for the future."

Those were the words that Sharples kept repeating to himself as he neared the house of the Court Physician.

The calculation that the coiner made in those two particulars was not a bad one. It was more than probable that Doctor Haslem would be willing to pay any price, and to make any sacrifice, for the purpose of procuring the restoration to his heart and his home of that daughter who was all that fate had left him now in the world to love.

And so it was that, drenched with rain, and presenting altogether a most deplorable aspect, Jacob Sharples stood on the door-step of the Court Physician's house.

There was a light in the hall.

A faint gleam had seemed to come from one of the windows on the first floor.

Jacob Sharples, with his habitual cowardice and caution, paused several minutes before he knocked at the Doctor's house, and even after he had done so he shrunk aside, and hid himself, as far as it was possible, behind one of the plain columns that supported a balcony over the entrance.

The door was opened promptly enough. A rush of cold wind and rain found its way into the hall, and along with them went Sharples, the coiner.

"Doctor Haslem!" he said harshly.

"Not at home to anybody."

Sharples laughed.

"Oh, yes, he will be at home to me, be it in the night or the day—in bed or at board, he will be at home to me, if you go and say to him that there is one here who can speak to him of Pamela."

"Oh, dear, no! The Doctor is busy."

"Indeed! Well, I sit here and wait for him; and when you feel disposed—ha! ha!—not one moment before, mind you; because, if you delay long, you will lose your place; and I don't care whether you do or not—you will take him this ring, and say that the man who brought it waits."

So many odd things had happened of late at the Doctor's house, and so many strange people had crossed its hall, that the porter began to fancy there was probably some truth in what the wretched drenched figure before him said.

He took the ring from the long bony finger of Jacob Sharples, and looked at it doubtingly.

"Well?" said Sharples.

"It is what they call a turquoise."

"It is. The Doctor will know it, perhaps, although he has not set eyes upon it for many a long, long day and night."

Jacob Sharples sat down in the hall, and rested his head upon his hands.

"Safe! safe!" he said; "oh, quite safe! No one can have the least notion of where she is; and so long as I keep my secret until I have made the conditions I require, I am as safe as an archbishop on his throne."

It was an odd comparison for Sharples to make, and he smiled at himself as he muttered the words.

The hall-porter had left the hall with the turquoise ring; and while he is gone, we may very briefly state what had become of the Court Physician when he left Newgate in such a state of despair from his fruitless inquiries for Pamela, and with only the vague information that he might get some news of Dick Doubleday and his friend Handsome Jemmy, at some place in Field Lane, which went by the name of "Coles's."

Physicians are accustomed to penetrate into the most obscure places of London society; and when he, Doctor Haslem, reached Field Lane, it was not the aspect of the dingy, criminal thoroughfare that frightened him so much as the dim and death-like look of the particular house, to which a ragged urchin directed him as being Coles's.

The Doctor knocked—knocked as well as he could with a stone that he picked up from the roadway, for knocker or bell there were none.

"Who's the pal?" asked a voice coming from he knew not where, but it sounded above his head.

"I want to ask for some information, for which I will pay handsomely."

A low whistle sounded.

"Do not mistake me," added the Physician; "it is not an unfriendly inquiry."

The whistle sounded again.

Then the voice spoke.

"What's the news wanted?"

"I will give any reasonable sum if you can tell me where I can find one Handsome Jemmy, and—a—well, I may as well use the word, and say that I believe he is a highwayman."

A strange laugh came from he knew not where, and then he thought he heard a sound, as if of the striking of a gong in some underground place.

All this was not very promising as regarded the information he wanted, but he did not exactly associate it with danger to himself.

The Doctor was not for long, however, kept in doubt upon that point.

The previous silence of Field Lane, which had been so profound you might have fancied yourself in a city of the dead, was suddenly broken.

The solitary voice that had addressed the physician, no longer appeared to be the only one it was possible to hear in that thieves' haunt.

With yells and shouts, oaths and imprecations, there came, from every cellar and from every house-door—and, indeed, dropping out from some of the windows as well—the motley and degraded population of the pestiferous place.

It was then a woman, who, looking out at one of the first floor windows, seemed to be seized with a sudden compassion, and called out, "Fly! Fly for your life! The police spies never escape from this place, if they delay a moment when the gong sounds!"

Then Doctor Haslem began to comprehend his danger.

At first, he thought he would stay and expostulate, and declare that he was no spy, and had nothing to do with the police; but he soon saw how useless would be such a course, and that his only safety would be in flight.

A rush was made towards him.

Several squalid hands grasped at his coat. He was struck right and left, and but for the number of his assailants he would have come badly off at once. Those very numbers, however, saved him, for they impeded each other.

The Doctor began to have the courage and the strength of despair; and he fought his way, with some success, through the motley crew about him.

The throng did not consist of very formidable persons individually: the real business men of the locality were not there.

The stalwart footpad, the burglar, the pickpocket, the highwayman—they were not there, for it was the time when they were plying their different vocations; but all the strange crew that lived upon the criminality of those persons were at home.

Beggars, who haunted the thoroughfares of the city in the daytime—cripples, past work of any kind—old men who had lost their activity and their strength—youths not yet fairly admitted as members of any particular branch of the "family"—and women, presenting the feminine nature in its worst possible aspects.

All these were there, because they were the constant home population of Field Lane.

And of such were the assailants of the Court Physician, whose unprofessional mode of knocking at "Coles's" door had awakened such a storm of suspicion and rage against him.

His apparel torn, and blood upon his face, the Doctor at length found his way to the Holborn end of Field Lane.

"Watch! watch! watch!" he cried aloud.

And then the strange crew that had attacked him disappeared as if by magic.

They had no wish to come into collision with the watch, or to extend their foray beyond the precincts of the "Lane," as it was familiarly called.

If Doctor Haslem had fallen, or if he had happened to be further up the dangerous thoroughfare than he was, there is very little doubt but he would have met his death, and been thrown down one of the traps or gullies that communicated with the Fleet Ditch below.

As it was, he escaped; and bleeding and bruised, he was thankful for a hackney coach to take him home.

What should he now do to discover the retreat of Pamela?

Whither should he now go, in all the, to him, wilderness of London, to search for that dear one, who was now his life and hope?

Alas! he knew not!

Bitterly and dearly did the Court Physician now rue the circumstances which, so long ago, had induced the hasty steps that had cast a blight upon his home.

Happier—far happier did he now think that brother, who lay in death so still and calm, than he was himself, amid all the bitterness of remorse and continued hopeless existence.

He flung himself on the floor of one of the reception rooms; and the strong man—the man of skill and science, who was so celebrated for calmness and courage—sobbed himself to sleep like a child.

The morning dawned and the day waned again before Doctor Haslem awakened.

He had locked the door of the room in which he had repaired the waste of mind and body by that long repose, and his servants had believed that he was out, and had taken the key of that apartment with him.

When he did open his eyes again, he felt much calmer and more collected.

A blessed vision had greeted his sleeping dreams.

He thought that he was walking down a fair garden path fringed with roses on both sides, and that she came to meet him with outstretched arms and a smile of forgiveness on her face—his long-lost wife.

Tears were in his eyes when he looked up from this dream, but they were not altogether tears of despair.

A hopeful feeling had sprung up in his heart, and he was, so to speak, a new man in comparison to what he had been the day before.

Then he went to his dressing-room and attired himself in a completely new suit; and to the surprise of his servants, he appeared in the breakfast-room, and asked for some tea.

Some cards were on the table, and some letters.

One of the cards bore the name of Lord Malvern; and written underneath the name, in pencil, were the words:—

"Will call on Doctor Haslem, on urgent business, some time this evening."

The Doctor then ordered his carriage, and went at once to the Secretary of State. His name procured him admission to the cabinet of the Minister, and it was in agitated tones then—for when he spoke of his lost wife and Pamela, he could not preserve the calmness he wished—that he spoke.

"By the memory of a friendship that has now lasted some years, although originally based merely upon professional acquaintance, will you permit me to ask one favour?"

"Certainly, Doctor. What can I do to oblige you?"

"It is an errand of mercy that I come upon."

"Mercy—for whom?"

"I want a pardon, free, complete, and unconditional, for a young girl, who is as innocent as you or I of what has been laid to her charge, and whose innocence in the course of time can be made to appear; but at present it would harass both her and those who look upon her with affection, if she were to fall into the hands of the administrators of the law."

"Who is she?"

"She is known as Pamela Sharples."

"What! The coiner's daughter, who was condemned to death for passing bad money, and who made one of the most audacious escapes from custody that was ever attempted! True, I am informed she has baffled the authorities; and how, or by what means, she does it, I cannot guess. Oh, Doctor! you have a kind heart, no doubt, and some tale has been told to you which has awakened your sympathies for an unworthy person."

"No, no—not an unworthy person!"

"The daughter of a criminal."

The Doctor bowed his head.

"We are all criminal in the eyes of omnipotent goodness and justice; but she of whom you speak is not the child of Sharples, the coiner."

"Whose, then?"

"Mine!"

"Good heaven!"

"Yes, my own child, stolen from me—long lost to my yearning heart. Oh, save her—save her!"

"I will seek an interview with the King at once on the subject, Doctor Haslem; but it is right that I should inform you—although, perhaps, you know it as well as I do—that his Majesty is very obstinate on such matters."

"I do know it, and shall exact from your sympathy and kindness no more than you can well perform"

"Then depend upon my doing my best. I will call upon you this evening at your house, after I come home from Kew Palace."

CHAPTER XLVI.

HANDSOME JEMMY MAKES A RESOLVE THAT IS EXCESSIVELY IRKSOME TO JACOB SHARPLES.

THE Doctor, then, was at home when Jacob Sharples reached his house in Bedford Square, and sent up to him the turquoise ring.

Too well he knew it.

It was one of those that had belonged to his poor wife, and had been taken with her on the night of her terrible and mysterious disappearance.

But Doctor Haslem was not alone on this occasion.

The light which Jacob Sharples had seen shining from one of the windows of the front floor of the mansion, came from a lamp which shed its lustre upon the faces and forms of three persons.

A fourth person was so much in the shadow, that only dimly could he be observed.

That was Doctor Haslem himself.

The other three persons were Lord Malvern, Handsome Jemmy, and Dick Doubleday.

Lord Malvern was speaking.

"Aw, you see, Doctaw,—aw—a fellow can only say what—aw—he thinks, you see, Doctaw; and if you have hid the girl—aw—why—aw—it is a trick not at all worthy—aw—of a doctaw!"

The physician was resting his head upon his hands, but now he looked up, and although very pale, he spoke with some firmness.

"It is necessary that I should no longer conceal from all the world who the young girl, named by mistake Pamela Sharples, really is. She is my own dear child; and along with that information, take my most solemn affirmation before heaven that I know not where she is!"

Dick Doubleday clasped his hands together, and looked the picture of despair.

Lord Malvern screwed up his mouth into the form necessary for whistling.

Handsome Jemmy only smiled.

"Aw, Doctaw,—aw—"

"What would you say, my lord?"

"Aw—I suppose—aw—that all of us have—aw—our little foibles! Aw—I hope you did the handsome thing by the girl's mothaw—aw!"

"My lord, Pamela's mother was my wife!"

"Lost! lost!" exclaimed Dick Doubleday. "Lost—lost, then, to me for ever!"

"Why so?" said Handsome Jemmy—"why, Dick? I do not see that in the same light that you do, at all!"

Dick Doubleday looked imploringly at Doctor Haslem, and sighed deeply.

"How can I hope," he said, "that the daughter of the Court Physician, Doctor Haslem, will be ever bestowed upon the homeless, almost nameless——"

"Hold!" said Handsome Jemmy. "I cannot hear my friend speak in that way; and I feel quite sure that Doctor Haslem thinks differently. The man who could risk his life, as you have done, Dick, for Pamela, while you only supposed her to be the daughter of Jacob Sharples, is worthy of her best love, were she to turn out to be a duchess!"

"Aw—young man," said Lord Malvern—"aw—it appears to me that—aw—that's a very pwoper wemark—aw! What do you think, Doctaw?"

It was at this moment that a light tap at the door of the room announced that some one wished to see the physician.

A servant appeared, bearing on a salver a small object which Doctor Haslem could not make out at the moment; but when the servant spoke, he raised his eyes, and he saw the ring which was spoken of.

"Sir, if you please, the man who brought this ring is in the hall, and insists upon seeing you."

Doctor Haslem uttered a cry which almost made Lord Malvern, impervious as he was to ordinary impressions, start from his chair.

Without a word, then, of explanation, the Court Physician dashed from the room, and was making his way down the stairs, when he met Jacob Sharples half-way.

The bereaved husband thus stood face to face with the coiner.

A gleam of intelligence had passed through the mind of Doctor Haslem at sight of the turquoise ring; and he began to believe that in Jacob Sharples he saw the murderer of his innocent and much-suffering wife, as well as the harsh gaoler of his child for so many years.

The Doctor grasped Jacob Sharples by the breast. He shook him to and fro, as though he had been but a reed in his hands.

"Villain! Wretch! Monster! Tell me all, and no longer perjure your soul with untruths! Tell me—are your hands red with the blood of the innocent?"

Jacob Sharples was terrified.

All the coward instincts of his soul prompted him to fly; but the Doctor's grasp was upon him, and he felt that he was powerless.

Then he recollected the errand that had brought him to that house, and what a power he was in possession of, by being the sole depository of the secret of where Pamela was to be found.

This thought—this recollection—which for the instant had been submerged in the fears that came over Sharples—gave him courage and confidence.

"Beware! beware!" he cried. "For your daughter Pamela's sake, beware!"

The Court Physician uttered now another cry, but he still kept his hold of Jacob Sharples; and when Lord Malvern, Handsome Jemmy, and Dick Doubleday reached what might be called the scene of conflict between the physician and the coiner, they found them both bent nearly double upon the staircase, and Doctor Haslem apparently intent upon his destruction.

"Let him be, my good sir," said Handsome Jemmy. "I know the rascal well."

"Jacob Sharples here!" exclaimed Dick Doubleday.

Now, when Sharples saw Handsome Jemmy and Dick, his heart sank within him.

It was Doctor Haslem alone that he had wished to see in that house.

It was the excited, pained heart of the bereaved father that he wished to play upon.

Strangers—that is to say, strangers to the excess of feeling and passionate grief which had found a home in the breast of the Court Physician—might be able to cope with him, Sharples, in a different fashion.

He began to wish himself out of that house again, with much more excess of anxiety than he had wished himself in it.

But there was no retreat now for Jacob Sharples.

Handsome Jemmy took him quietly by the collar, and handed him, with a power that he felt it was in vain to attempt to resist, into the room where the little party had been sitting.

Lord Malvern fixed his glass to his eye, and looked at the coiner, as if he had been some new species of animal only just discovered.

"Aw—that's the wascal, is it—aw?"

"Yes," replied Handsome Jemmy, "and a greater one never disgraced the form of man."

"Pamela! Pamela!" half screamed Dick Doubleday; "I ask you, Jacob Sharples, for Pamela!"

"My child! my only one! my daughter! my fair and innocent child!" cried Doctor Haslem, "I demand at your hands, infamous villain that you are!"

Jacob Sharples was ghastly pale.

He looked from Dick Doubleday to the physician, and then back again at Dick Doubleday; and then a covert smile, that had no mirth in it, but a world of hate, cunning, and ferocity, curled his lips.

He folded his arms across his breast.

He burst into a short, hyena-like laugh.

Yes, Jacob Sharples was, or fancied he was, the master of the situation.

"Speak, ruffian!" cried Dick Doubleday.

"My child! my daughter!" screamed the Doctor.

PAMELA DISCOVERS THE BODIES OF THE OFFICERS.

"Brandy!" said Jacob Sharples.

Jemmy, the highwayman, shook his head

"Yes," he said, "that is just it Doctor, and you, Dick, allow your feelings to carry you away, and so this man gets an advantage of you. It is well that I am here to cope with him."

"Ha! ha!" laughed Sharples. "I am strong enough to cope with you all, and you know it. I, and I only, know where Pamela Haslem is; I, and I only, can restore her to you! The secret is here! here! here!"

He struck his breast as he spoke.

Doctor Haslem sprung upon him, and grasped him by one arm, as he shouted, "Speak! speak! It is a reward you want? Name the sum, and I will coin my heart's blood into gold, if the transmutation be possible, to satisfy you! Only give me back my child!"

"Now you speak sensibly," said Sharples.

"No," said Handsome Jemmy—"no. And yet, perhaps, my lord, it will be as well to hear what the rascal has to say."

"Aw—yes. Don't hold his arm, Doctaw—he can't wun away; and if he does, I can wun after him. I can wun! That's one of the things I can do—aw!"

"I don't want to run away," said Sharples. "What I came here to say, I will say; and if I had not intended to come, I could have easily staid away. Pamela is in danger!"

"Danger!" echoed Dick Doubleday.

The Doctor groaned.

"Great danger," added Sharples—"but I can save her; I can rescue her; I can restore her to your arms; and I will, on certain conditions."

Both the physician and Dick Doubleday were about to speak, but Handsome Jemmy motioned them to silence; and Jacob Sharples, whose restless, eager, ferret-looking eyes were upon everybody, and noted everything, proceeded.

"On conditions, I say; and those conditions are a full, free, and complete pardon for all the past, which I have no doubt the influence of the Court Physician can procure me; and such a sum of money down, or such a well secured annuity, as shall make me easy and comfortable for life."

"Both—I consent!" cried Doctor Haslem.

"No, Doctor, no! you are hasty," said Handsome Jemmy; "you are by far too hasty. Do you not know, Jacob Sharples, that you have stepped into the lion's den, and that it is a very absurd thing of you to make conditions?"

"Do your worst!"

"Do you know what that would be?"

"Yes—you could give me up as Jacob Sharples, the well-known coiner, with a reward upon his head for his apprehension."

"Nothing else?"

"Nothing! And there is one thing that will be interesting to you, Doctor Haslem, to know as a doctor; and that is, that your child—your daughter, Pamela, is now without food, and will remain so as long as you please to detain me! The most savage natures are subdued by want of food—what, then, must be the effect of long starvation on one so fair, so young, and so fragile?"

"Hold, Doctor!" cried Handsome Jemmy, as the physician was about to speak. "Let me settle this little affair with Jacob Sharples."

"And I'll settle it with him—aw!—in half a minute!" said Lord Malvern, as turned up one cuff.

Handsome Jemmy made imploring signs to them all three to let him have his own way.

"Jacob," he said, then, "you asked for brandy?"

"I did!—I parch for it!"

"Would you like any other refreshment as well?"

"With it? Yes, I would. I have not eaten nor drank for I don't know when. Ho! ho! You too, my fine fellow, will come to terms, I see! Well, gentlemen all, I rather think Jacob Sharples is a match for all of you!"

Handsome Jemmy had rung the bell, and when a servant appeared, he said quickly, "Bring a tray with some refreshment, as quickly as you can, and some brandy."

Jacob Sharples settled himself in the chair in which he sat, and laughed aloud.

The tray with the refreshments was brought. A cold fowl—a Westphalian ham—some delicate tarts—and a decanter with sherry, and another with brandy.

"Good!" said Sharples. "I——"

"Stop a moment!" said Handsome Jemmy. "Allow me!"

He poured out a glass of the brandy, and handed it to the coiner, who eagerly raised it to his lips. But at that moment Handsome Jemmy gave the glass and the hand that held it a blow; and the brandy, with the crystal vessel that contained it, fell to the floor.

"No, Jacob Sharples," he said, "not one drop shall you ever drink again in this world—not one morsel shall you eat, until Pamela is in the arms of her father! And to make sure that this sentence which I pass shall be carried out, I will remain by your side, if it take a week to kill you; and like your shadow, I will be a constant companion, not to be shaken off! Come, Jacob Sharples; food and drink, on condition that you restore Pamela to us free and uninjured—if not, starvation and death!"

CHAPTER XLVII.

PAMELA MEETS WITH SOME TERRORS, AND YET ESCAPES A GREAT DANGER, IN THE CELLARS OF JACOB SHARPLES'S HOUSE.

ALAS, poor Pamela!

She heard the clang of the iron bar that Jacob Sharples swung over that door, which was the only apparent outlet of escape from the dreary regions below the ground floor of his house, to which he had consigned Pamela.

She heard the mocking, screaming tones in which he exulted over her capture and imprisonment.

But yet she could not, with all those evidences of treachery, quite convince herself that Dick Doubleday might not, even as he, Sharples, had said, be in that wretched place, wounded and in danger.

She still called aloud to him by name.

"Richard! Richard! my Richard! It is your own Pamela who calls to you! Speak, if you be here, and assure me that you live!"

Her own voice, in the echoes that it awakened in the dreary place, formed the source of the only answer she received.

Pamela paused—faint and terrified, she paused and listened.

The strange, tapping sound that Jacob Sharples produced by means of the penny piece against the iron bar, came plainly to her ears.

She could not tell what that sound portended, but a terrible fear came over her in the dismal region to which she was consigned.

If, indeed and in truth, her Richard was there, he was dead!

Of that she felt assured; for if one spark of life had lingered at his heart, it would have sprung into a flame at the sound of her voice, and enabled him to reply to her.

But there was no such reply; not the faintest moan reached the ears of Pamela.

Then she felt that she was very desolate indeed, and all the terrors of loneliness in such a place came over her young imagination.

It will be recollected that she had passed much of what should have been a pure, beautiful, and happy childhood, in the company of Jacob Sharples, in that wretched house, among the slimy foundations of which she was now a prisoner.

Many and many a time had he almost stilled the beating of the young heart, and filled the gentle child-intellect with terror, by vague threats of imprisonment in that gloomy place.

And now, when she had come of an age to feel the pangs of mental terror, combined with those of loving sympathy for another who was dearer to her than life itself, she found all the old threats of Jacob Sharples fulfilled, and that she was a prisoner in that loathsome place, which she had always regarded with an undefined apprehension.

"Help! help!—oh, help!"

She uttered those words aloud, but then her own voice alarmed her.

It sounded so hollow and so dismal in those dreary cellars.

She had made her way far from the staircase, in her intense anxiety to discover Richard Doubleday, and she had some difficulty in making her way back.

When she did so, Sharples was gone.

He had set down to obstinacy the silence that had followed upon his attempt to speak to her.

He was gone, and she was alone in the dreary house —alone in the dreariest part of it.

She struck with her fair hand upon the heavy door, and she called to him by name.

"Jacob Sharples! Jacob Sharples! What have I done to you that you should thus persecute me? Have you no mercy in your heart—not one gleam of compassion? What have I done to you, O Jacob Sharples?"

Surely, if the coiner had heard those words he would have been moved to compassion, and even his brutal and obdurate nature would have shrunk before the suffering he was inflicting upon that young and innocent girl.

And now, when poor Pamela had for some time made an unsuccessful appeal at the door at the head of the staircase, that shut in the prison so dark and drear to which Jacob Sharples had consigned her, she turned again, and looked down into the deep, cavernous-like abyss.

The very look of that intense darkness has terrified her.

In imagination, she was able to people that space down below with strange grotesque images, so that to descend and mingle with them appeared an effort far beyond any ordinary human courage.

She shrunk down on the top step of the steep stairs, and strove to disarm that darkness below of its terrors

But the more she gazed, the more those terrors increased.

She thought she saw strange, uncouth-looking shapes rolling and tumbling over each other, and now and then great eyes would glare forth that could not belong to aught human.

Pamela was still young.

She had none of that kind of knowledge and kind of logic, which would have enabled her to successfully battle against these impressions.

What she saw, or thought she saw, became to her facts and realities. The knowledge that seeing is not believing in all cases had not been imparted to her.

She was rapidly reaching a height of fear which would have gone far to turn her brain, and she uttered a scream, as at length she thought she saw something—a shape she could not define, but something most ungainly and horrible—begin to crawl up the stairs.

It was but a fancy.

The scream scattered it.

That shrill sound of her own voice seemed to bring her back to the world again and all its realities; but now she held her breath, in her intense desire to listen to some sound she thought she heard from below.

She was struck instantly by the real, substantial difference between imaginary sounds and real ones.

In regard to the former, there is always a doubt of their existence.

The latter are seized upon by the mind at once, and recognised as real.

So on this occasion, when Pamela, from her position at the head of the stairs, heard a low, faint moan, as of

some person at the point of death, she had no doubt of the fact; and her intense listening was in the expectation of hearing it again.

Was it an answer to her scream? Was it the last appeal of some expiring prisoner in that gloomy place, to attract attention and awake compassion? Was it Richard Doubleday; and had Jacob Sharples, after all, spoken the truth, when he said she would there find him?

Pamela in an instant cast to the winds all her imaginative fears. The real honest human feeling that resided in her heart did successful battle with them; and, forgetting all but her intense desire and hope to save him, she streamed down that dismal staircase again like a spirit.

"Richard—Richard, I do hear you! I am here—I, your Pamela!"

She paused at the foot of the staircase—paused to listen; but for some time she could hear nothing but the beating of her own heart.

Then—then, when she had almost given up the hope of doing so, she heard the low moan again.

There could be no possible doubt about it now.

Guided by the sound, Pamela, with her hands outstretched before her, lest she should in the darkness encounter some unexpected obstacle, ran forward.

"Speak—oh, speak to me! Let me hear your voice, Richard Doubleday! It is your Pamela who seeks you, and who would rather die with you, if you must die, than live without your love!"

She paused again.

She had penetrated far beneath the basement of Jacob Sharples's house.

And then she heard a voice, but it was not the voice of Richard Doubleday.

"You may perhaps save him yet if—if you have compassion. Go—go to the police—the police! My comrade is dead, and I am dying!"

"Who?—who?" cried Pamela, as she panted with excitement. "Who are you?"

"The police!" moaned the voice again. "I and my comrade! He is dead! We came to arrest Jacob Sharples. He betrayed us to this dreadful place! I fear I am killed! If—if only I could raise my head——"

"Alas! alas!" said Pamela. "Can you tell me anything of one Richard Doubleday?"

There was no reply.

A terrible fear came over Pamela that she had heard the last words that would ever come from those mortal lips, and that she was alone with the dead.

But in a few seconds the moan came again.

"Ah!" she cried. "You live still?"

"I live still—I live still!" said the sorely-wounded officer,—"I live still! Yes, I have one hand free! If —if I could only reach the—the——"

"Reach what? Speak plainer, if you can!"

"I have the means of getting a light—we—we are never without those means—if I could reach the matches! Oh, what pain—oh, what agony! Yes—yes! You cannot help me—it is so dark—dark!"

By almost a superhuman effort, the officer did contrive to get from his pocket the match-box that would enable him to get a light.

A faint blue flame illumined the dreary cellars for a moment; and then lighting up, as the wood-work of the match faintly ignited, the terrified Pamela was able to look at the fearful spectacle before her.

The two officers who had come to that house of gloom and of mystery to arrest Jacob Sharples, had both, as the reader is aware, been precipitated down the broken staircase into those vaults below.

One was dead.

His companion lay, desperately hurt, partially over his body.

And now that that other, in whose form the breath of life still lingered, contrived to light the match, Pamela saw him, and the sight was one of terror.

He was much disfigured. His worst enemy—if he had a enemy, ever so full of malignancy—must there and then have pitied him, had he seen the sad spectacle he presented.

The effort to procure the match, and light it, was the last that the nerveless hands could perform.

The little mimic torch fell upon the breast of the dying man as his hands refused to hold it longer.

There lodging, in some accidental fashion, in an upright form, it continued to burn, with a small, bright flame, while, perhaps, you might have counted eight.

And during that time Pamela looked upon the form of the dying man. She saw that awful change creep over it—that shadow from the valley of death which may well affect humanity; and at the moment that the little match-light went out, the last breath came with a faint puff from the blood-stained lips of the officer.

Pamela then knew that she was alone with the dead.

She knew, too, that there was no help there, but she could not resist the cry for aid that rose to her lips.

Then she paused abruptly and listened.

Some new sound mingled with the echo of her own cries.

A person knocking at the door of Jacob Sharples's house.

Bang! bang! bang! bang!

Whoever there knocked, certainly did not come in secrecy or silence. Was it a friend or a foe? What was she to do? Was she still amenable to the law? Would it be still safe, or otherwise, for her to throw herself upon human aid; or was it better that she should remain there in silence and in safety with the dead?

Those were fearful questions for a young heart, like Pamela's, to put to itself!

The knocking continued. Then there was a loud crashing sound; and whoever had so furiously demanded admittance to the house of the coiner, had evidently determined upon an entrance, and had broken a way in.

Pamela could hear heavy footsteps in the passage far above her. The sound of harsh voices likewise came upon her ears.

She made her way with some difficulty to the staircase. She flew rather than walked up it, and with her ears close to the panel of the door at the top, and her fair hair, so beautiful in its disorder, streaming far and wide down to the stairs, she listened.

The persons who had forced their way into the house of Jacob Sharples were not at all disposed to be secretive or silent. They spoke quite loudly and plainly of what they came about.

"I don't believe it, and didn't from the first," said one; "but it's all as well to try to find her. It's a good round sum, the reward."

"It is, Bill," said another voice; "and if so be as we catches her, we shall get on to the blessed 'stablishment at the Stone Jug, and no mistake!"

"It's almost a pity, though, after all," said another, "to hang a young girl like that, even if she did pass a few spangles with the gilt on, for real guineas."

"What's that to us, I should like to know?" remonstrated another of the men. "If we can't get the reward without Pamela Sharples swinging at Tyburn, why, what are we to do, I should like to know, but try and give her the swing, eh?"

Pamela shrunk back.

These men—officers—informers—or those wretches—themselves always the worst of criminals—who take up the trade of amateur constables, were, then, after her! She crept gently down the stairs, for she no longer dreaded the company of the dead.

CHAPTER XLVIII.

JACOB SHARPLES FINDS THE STATE OF AFFAIRS DECIDEDLY UNPLEASANT, AND TRIES TO COMPROMISE MATTERS.

THE calm, cool, resolute look with which Handsome Jemmy regarded Jacob Sharples, filled him with despair.

Had that most uncomfortable speech which the highwayman had made to him, been uttered by any one else, Sharples would have scarcely believed in it; or, at all events, he would have thought it possible in some manner to avoid its meaning.

But it was very different with Handsome Jemmy.

Jack Sharples gave himself up, so far as regarded the carrying out of his scheme of purchasing safety for the future, and immunity for the past, at the price of the surrender of Pamela.

But rage as well as despair found a place in his heart and brain.

With busy ingenuity, he began to ask himself how he might be revenged—revenged upon them all, even if he himself should fall a victim to the circumstances he might bring about.

But he was surrounded by those with whom he could make no successful fight.

They knew him well; and no cajolery, no specious tale that he might invent, would have the slightest effect upon them, in regard to their treatment of him.

It was Doctor Haslem that he would have liked to deal with, if he could have done so alone.

The father's heart would have given way to any conditions that would speedily have returned to him his child.

Or he would have dealt with Dick Doubleday, the young lover, who in his heart's agony, lest one hair of the beloved one's head should be injured, would, no doubt, have committed himself to some promise, that would have saved Jacob Sharples.

Handsome Jemmy, however, and Lord Malvern were in the way of all compromises.

The coiner looked about him from face to face, and his own turned paler and more wan as he so looked.

It seemed as if the process of starvation that the highwayman had promised him, had began.

"You are mad, all of you," said Sharples, "to take such a course as this."

"You will be, if you continue," said Handsome Jemmy.

"You will destroy her whom you wish to save," added Sharples, as he licked his parched lips.

"She will then ascend to heaven, as one of its angels," replied the highwayman, "while you, Jacob Sharples, lie howling."

The coiner shook in every limb.

Doctor Haslem watched him, and he saw that dark circles began to show themselves under his eyes. The struggle between life and death with such a man would not be long.

Lord Malvern then spoke.

"Aw, Doctaw—aw—I think that we—aw—need need not keep this fellaw company. I, for one, should—aw—have no objection to some suppaw."

"Nor I, Doctor," added Handsome Jemmy. "Suppose we shut up this rascal here. There is a bell in the room, and when he is disposed to give in, we will come to him on his ringing. No—he can't get away!"

The highwaymen, as he spoke, had been going the round of the room, and glancing from the windows, to be sure that there were no facilities for the escape of Jacob Sharples.

"Save your own life, Sharples!" cried Dick Doubleday; "save your own life, and restore to us Pamela!"

"My Lavinia!" moaned the physician.

"Save her yourselves!" said Sharples. "I have named my conditions—pardon for the past, and prosperity for the future!"

"But the tables are turned," said Handsome Jemmy. "It is we who are in the position to name and insist upon our conditions—a life for a life!—yours for Pamela's!"

The door was closed and locked upon Jacob Sharples, and then Handsome Jemmy, addressing the Doctor, said calmly, "Sir, I don't want supper; I only spoke of food, to keep alive the tantalizing idea in the mind of Sharples. Let me have a chair, and I will keep guard here outside this door; for I will keep my word, and, practically, I will be by the side of Jacob Sharples till the last."

"I too! I too!" said Dick Doubleday.

"Very well, Dick; I will not say but that I shall be glad of your company."

As Handsome Jemmy spoke, they all plainly heard the crash of glass in the room they had left, and where Sharples was a prisoner.

"He has broken the window and no doubt intends to call for help from it," said Doctor Haslem.

"Oh, no, no!" replied the highwayman; "that is the last thing that would ever come into the mind of Jacob Sharples. The dread he has of apprehension can never be sufficiently overcome by any other fear, to induce such an action on his part. You find that all is still."

All was still.

But there was an uneasy look upon the face of the physician, and upon that of Dick Doubleday.

The bell that Jacob Sharples had been told he might ring then sounded sharply through the house.

Handsome Jemmy raised his hand in a warning attitude as he said, in a low voice that could not reach the ears of Sharples through the door, "I pray you all to permit me to deal with this tricky scoundrel."

Handsome Jemmy then opened the door.

"You rang, Jacob Sharples!"

"I did!"

"Well, what would you say?"

"I ask only for justice."

"You shall have it."

"Stop—stop and listen to me. The officers of police are after Pamela. Her escape from the cart which was on the route to Tyburn has angered the officials. She is still as one condemned to death. What if, while you hold me here a prisoner—here, to starve me—she be taken and lodged in Newgate? What then?"

"Oh," said Handsome Jemmy, "I am quite surprised that you should ask such a question!"

"What then?—what then, I say? What good will you get, then, by detaining me?"

"None!"

"Ha! ha! You then release me?"

"Yes, so far as we are concerned; but the police will, of course, hold you fast; and we shall make, through my Lord Malvern here, a statement to the Secretary of State, to the effect that, as we give up in you the real criminal, there need be no prosecution of the innocent Pamela."

Jacob Sharples uttered a cry of dismay.

He flew to the window that he had broken, and, regardless of the jagged edges of the splintered glass, he looked out.

Then he uttered another cry.

He saw a man pick up a piece of folded paper, and, eagerly opening it close to the nearest lamp, read it, and then hurry off out of the square.

"Lost! lost!" cried Sharples, as he fell flat on the floor; "lost! lost! I am baffled at every turn!"

Now all this was quite inexplicable to Handsome Jemmy, the highwayman; but a very few words will suffice to explain it to the reader.

When Jacob Sharples found that all his calculations had failed him, and that he was a prisoner in the house of the Court Physician, he bethought him, not what he could do to escape, for that he did not think possible—but what he could do to be avenged.

The bitterest feelings rankled in his breast, and if he could have done anything that would have involved Pamela, Doctor Haslem, Dick Doubleday, Lord Malvern, and Handsome Jemmy in one common destruction, it would have given him the greatest delight.

He fancied, then, that he had the means of heaping anxiety—perhaps despair—upon them all, and he set about the plan.

He wrote upon a scrap of paper, which he folded up, the following words:—

"The girl Pamela, who escaped by a forged order of release from execution, is to be found concealed in the house of Jacob Sharples, in Clerkenwell."

He did not wish that the paper should fall into any stray hands, who would, perhaps, rather release Pamela than arrest her, and therefore was it that he put so vague an address upon it as merely Clerkenwell.

The police authorities, he was well aware, knew his house perfectly well, and that they would eagerly seize upon Pamela, he believed. Then he thought she would send to Doctor Haslem; and when it was found she was no longer in his custody, there would be no motive—at least, that was the idea of Jacob Sharples, until he was enlightened on the subject by the highwayman—there would be no motive in detaining him longer.

To break a pane of glass, and cast the folded scrap of paper into the roadway close to the front of the physician's house, was Jacob's next act; and then he rang the bell.

The few words that Handsome Jemmy had spoken to him seemed like the oracles of fate.

A terrible destiny appeared to be overwhelming the coiner; and he began to think now that he was on some fearful downward course, and that whatever he said or whatever he did only accelerated his descent.

Clasping his hands together, he looked in the face of the highwayman with the expression of a maniac.

"No, no!" he then screamed; "do not say that!—do not do that! I see before me the cart for Tyburn—the coffin, and the cold, hard, thin face of the man who, for gold, kills his fellows at the fatal tree! Mercy!—oh, have some mercy upon me! Fly, if you would save Pamela! She is—she is ——"

Handsome Jemmy made a step forward.

Those frantic words, too, of Jacob Sharples had reached the ears of the persons on the landing outside the door; and their anxiety and impatience would not permit them to be still.

"Where, where is my child?" cried the physician.

"Where is Pamela?" said Dick Doubleday, in imploring, anxious accents.

Lord Malvern only fixed his eye-glass more firmly in his eye, and looked sternly at the coiner.

Jacob Sharples paused.

Was it possible for him yet to alarm them into some compromise with him; to make them come to terms—perhaps his own terms—yet?

"Pamela is in the greatest danger," he said. "If you would save her, you must at once release me; for I only can step between her and death."

Both Doctor Haslem and Dick Doubleday were about to speak; but Handsome Jemmy, so to speak, intercepted the words upon their lips.

"Oh," he said, "that is the old story, Jacob Sharples; and it is one that I do not believe. You must be hungrier and thirstier yet, before we get the truth from you."

Jacob Sharples yelled with rage. He flung himself to the floor, and rolled over and over on the carpet, and seemed to give himself up to all the agony of disappointed malice.

Suddenly becoming calm, then, he said, "I give in—I am beaten! Be it so! You can have no real motive in betraying me to the law. Go to my house. You, Jemmy, and you, Dick Doubleday, both know the way. Go there, and you will find Pamela in the cellar beneath it."

"Wretch! villain!" shouted Dick Doubleday; "if you have harmed her——"

"I have not; she is safe—that is to say, if you hasten. But if you do not, you will be too late!"

"Too late! Oh, heaven!" cried Doctor Haslem.

"Not too late," added Jacob Sharples, "as you take my words. Not too late to see her in life; but she will be in Newgate. Go at once, and take this information from me as a something for which you will owe me a recompense some day. Do not trouble to go into the house to look for her; but any one of you will find no difficulty in lifting the first stone that forms the door-step. Immediately beneath that you will find a grating that opens with a hinge. Beneath that are the cellars, and there you will find Pamela."

The Doctor, Lord Malvern, and Dick Doubleday dashed down the stairs of the house.

Handsome Jemmy was not in such a hurry. He took from round his waist, where it was snugly put away, a coil of stout twine.

Jacob Sharples fell to his knees.

"Oh, do not tie me up! Do not leave me here a prisoner! Have some mercy! I have told you all the truth, and more than I need have told you! For the extra information, have some mercy upon me!"

"On one condition, Jacob Sharples"

"Name it—name it! I consent beforehand!"

"It is that you accompany us to your house, and make no effort to escape by the way."

"I—I consent."

"Very well. Come on, then"

Handsome Jemmy had rapidly constructed a running noose in the cord he had taken from his waist; and now, to the intense horror of Jacob Sharples, he flung it round his neck, and drawing it rather tight, he held the other end.

"In mercy, take it off!—oh, do!"

"Pho! pho! It is nothing. Jacob, to what you will feel when your time comes at Tyburn, as it most assuredly will."

"No, no!"

"But I say yes, yes! So come along."

Handsome Jemmy gave a tug to the cord, and Jacob Sharples was compelled to follow him. The highwayman called over the balustrades of the staircase, to the rest of the party, that he was coming, and they paused a little for him.

It looked, then, a curious group of persons that left the house of the Court Physician, in Bedford Square, and hailing a hackney coach, desired to be driven to Clerkenell Green.

CHAPTER XLIX.

PAMELA FALLS INTO THE HANDS OF THE OFFICERS, AND JACOB SHARPLES MYSTERIOUSLY DISAPPEARS.

PAMELA paused half-way down the stairs leading to the cellars in Jacob Sharples's house, for she heard the men who evidently were searching for her above, arrive at the upper door with the iron bar across it.

The voices came but confusedly to her ears, but the consciousness that they would soon be in close pursuit of her came strongly to her imagination. She fled down the remainder of the stairs with that hopeless feeling which, although it does not impede flight, lends it the element of despair.

She heard the iron bar removed.

She heard the rough, harsh voices, and the heavy footsteps.

"Here, then, if anywhere," cried one.

"Then light the link," said another.

There was a moment's pause, and then a dull red glare of light seemed to pursue poor Pamela, and to pass her amid the dreary gloom of the dungeon-like place

She fled onwards now, fleet of foot, and yet knowing not whither she fled. The instinct of self-preservation came strongly upon her. She saw, in fancy again, if she should fall into the hands of those men, the prison cell, the cart that was to carry her to death, and all the terrors from which she had so narrowly escaped on the occasion when Handsome Jemmy and Dick Doubleday interposed between her and a fearful and ignominious death.

The darkness—the gloom—the uncertainty of where her steps would carry her, and the certainty that those cellars contained objects the sight of which might well appal a stouter heart than hers—all sank into insignificance before the dread of falling into the hands of those who sought her life judicially.

The clatter of descending footsteps on the stairs had come faintly upon her ears. The dull red light of the link no longer shone upon her and past her into the obscurity.

And still, as she fled onwards, she kept repeating to herself the name of Richard Doubleday, as though it were possible she might yet invoke his presence to save her.

She was astonished at the extent of these cellars beneath the house of Jacob Sharples, for it appeared that she must have proceeded for a very considerable distance.

Pamela, however, in the darkness and uncertainty that surrounded her, did not keep a straight path; and, moreover, as she paused and half-turned to listen to the distant sounds that heralded the approach of her pursuers, she no doubt altered her course.

Then she came to some steps.

Fortunately, there were but two of them, for she fell the limited height of them. But she regained her feet on the instant, and rushed on.

On—on, she knew not where; while her heart, which had been wildly beating by the excitement of the moment, for a brief period seemed to suspend its pulsation.

She heard the voice of Jacob Sharples.

"Here, I tell you—here! Lift the stone, and lift the grating, and she is yours!"

Where was the voice?

On the right—the left—above or below?

"She is yours, I tell you!" added Sharples's voice; "and as I give her up to you, so do I expect you to release me!"

Those words, to the ears of Pamela, could have but one import.

She was to be given up to the hands of the constables, as the price of the safety of Jacob Sharples.

She shrunk back from where she had stood while hearing so plainly the name of Sharples, that it was only in a confused fashion that she heard other voices in reply to him.

Oh, Pamela Pamela! why do you not remain to hear those other voices as plainly as you hear that of Jacob Sharples?

Would they not have been to your senses as the sweetest music?

The voice of the handsome highwayman—your true and fast friend—you would have heard.

The voice of the Court Physician, your father.

The voice of Dick Doubleday, to whom you have given your young and peerless heart

But no! you heard them not. It was only the tones of the betrayer that came to your ears.

Unhappy Pamela!

"What shall I do—oh, what shall I do?" she exclaimed.

Danger was before her, as she thought

Danger was behind her, she knew; for she heard the sounds of pursuit through the dreary, darksome cellars

A faint flash of light—so faint that, whether it represented some artificial light, or was a gleam from the fair sky of a new day, she could not tell, but it came from the direction where she had heard the sound of Jacob Sharples's voice, fell upon her eyes.

She heard his voice again.

"Pamela, Pamela!"

"No; any fate but to be betrayed by him. Anything but to be cooped up a prisoner in that place, and then sold as the price of his safety."

A feeling of indignation came over the mind of the young girl.

If she must be taken—if she could not save herself, at least she would not be serviceable to the man who had shown himself so cruelly selfish as to be her worst enemy, for no other purpose but his own conservation.

She turned, and retraced her steps.

"I am here!—I am here! My name is Pamela!"

With a shout of exultation, she was the next moment surrounded by half a dozen men, all of whom bore a link.

"Hilloa, my lass!" cried one. "You have led us a pretty dance in this underground place!"

Pamela was deadly pale. She seemed to be on the

point of saying somethil g, but then to correct the impulse, and to leave it unsaid.

"By my faith, she is a pretty one!" said another of the men.

"It's a thousand pities," added another, "that we cannot get as much for letting her alone as for taking her to the Stone Jug; but as it is, little one, why, come on, for there is no help for it."

Then Pamela did speak, for she heard behind her now, in the direction that the hated voice of Jacob Sharples had come from, some light sounds, and she made sure that he was approaching, and bringing with him the men who, from what he had said, appeared to be holding him in custody as a hostage for Pamela.

"Take me away anywhere," she said, "so that you take me at once, or it will be too late "

"Too late? What do you mean, my lass, about being too late?"

"Listen!"

Pamela held up her hand in a listening attitude, and then her captors heard the same sounds of approaching footsteps that she was cognisant of.

Those sounds alarmed them to the full as much as they did her.

They might—they must, indeed, mean one of two things in that place.

They were either friends of Pamela's, with whom there might be a troublesome contest, or they were men who would seek to share the profits of the capture with them.

In either case they were most unwelcome; and the object of the persons whose hands Pamela had fallen into, was to get out of the cellars, and out of the house with her as soon as they possibly could.

There was only one real constable among them, and he was the man who, in Bedford Square, had picked up the little memoranlum that Jacob Sharples had flung through the broken window in the physician's house.

By way of making the most of the information it contained, he had brought with him, not brother offizers, but the men who, for an agreed-upon stipend, were willing to aid him.

It was the constable, then, who, grasping Pamela by the wrist, cried out, "Now, my lass, I will trouble you to run along with us as quickly as you ran from us; for I don't want, and, what is more, I won't, share the reward with anybody."

"I am willing," said Pamela. "Anywhere but where he is."

The constable did not take the trouble to inquire at the moment who the "he" was that Pamela was so anxious to avoid, but still keeping hold upon her wrist, he turned her towards the staircase that led up to the house.

Oh, if she could but have guessed that she was flying from Dick Doubleday!

But she had no such idea. It was Jacob Sharples whose voice she had heard, and whom she fled before as from a pestilence.

"All right!" cried the officer. "Don't put out the links yet. That will do!"

The top of the staircase was reached. One man whom they had left there as a sort of guard seemed delighted to see them, for he had a half-scared look about him, as though he had seen an apparition.

"What's the matter?" asked the constable, sharply.

"I don't know, but there has been all sorts of odd noises; and I went along the passage, and looked out over the door through the old broken fanlight, and what do you think I saw?"

"What? what?"

"I saw some men—I don't know how many, or that they were men at all, though they had the look of human beings; but you may believe me or not, as you like, when I say that I saw them sink down into the earth bodily through the stone door-step "

"Stuff! you have been asleep. Come on now, my lass I don't know, Pamela Sharples, if you are aware that there is a hundred pounds offered for you?"

Pamela shook her head sadly.

They hurried her down the passage of the house, and then the officer, as he opened the outer door, cried out to one of the men, "Stevenson, just come back, and put up that iron bar again to the door at the head of those stairs. I don't know who may be in the cellars, but I'm quite sure I heard somebody."

Pamela was upon the point of saying that she could tell them who was in the cellars, and that it was none other but Jacob Sharples, the coiner. She abstained, however, from giving the information, from the same motive that had inclined her to fly from him, and actually surrender herself a prisoner — namely, that her inevitable capture should not be serviceable to him.

So Pamela was silent when she might have spoken, and with all the misconceptions of her real position that had beset her during that fearful night, she was hurried out of Jacob Sharples's house.

Dick Doubleday was at the top of the stairs leading to the cellar, making vain efforts to open the door and penetrate by that way into the coiner's house, at the time that his Pamela was silently leaving it.

Within one hour, Pamela was in Newgate.

A brutal under female warder pushed her into a cell, and struck her as she did so.

Pamela half fell in a huddled-up posture, and clasping her hands over her face, she uttered in moaning accents the name of her lover.

"Richard! Richard! Oh, Richard, how can you save me now?"

CHAPTER I

HANDSOME JEMMY AND DICK DOUBLEDAY CONCOCT A BOLD SCHEME FOR THE DELIVERANCE OF PAMELA FROM NEWGATE

A SEARCH through the cellars of the coiner's house, aided by a lantern, disclosed nothing to Dick Doubleday, Handsome Jemmy, and the Court Physician but the two dead bodies of the unfortunate officers, at the last moments of one of whom Pamela had been present.

It was with the greatest reluctance that Jacob Sharples had been induced to accompany the little party down through the grating beneath his door-step to the cellars.

But he had no resource. Handsome Jemmy, on that point, was inflexible.

He was resolved to stand by the determination he had made, which was never to lose sight of Jacob Sharples, or permit him to eat or drink until he had restored Pamela to them.

So the coiner was compelled to make one of the party to descend into the cellars, with the full conviction that he should confront objects there calculated to fill him with a thousand fears.

His only hope was that Pamela would soon be in the hands of her friends, and that then they would permit him to go whither it might please him.

In that case, all he had lost by that transaction would be what he had calculated upon gaining.

He would be no worse off; and his next mental resolution was, that he would go to old Doubleday, as he sometimes named him, in Long Lane, and thoroughly ransack his house, for he fully believed the old man to be dead.

Then Jacob Sharples had made up his mind that he would get out of England as quickly as possible, he cared not where, so that it was beyond the reach of the arm of the law.

Handsome Jemmy had sprung down the opening beneath the step of the coiner's house first; but Jacob Sharples was compelled to follow him by the persuasion of that piece of cord which was round his neck, and the other end of which the highwayman kept a pertinacious hold of.

The Court Physician carried the lantern.

When they were all fairly on the damp floor of the cellar, Doctor Haslem called out for Pamela, but he used the unfamiliar name of Lavinia.

Perhaps the name Pamela might have travelled to the ears of the young girl naturally, at the time she was half-way up the staircase leading to the passage of the house with her captors.

Then, just as they all distinctly heard the sharp sound of a door being shut rather violently, Dick Doubleday called out aloud, "Pamela, my Pamela, for the love of heaven and of your own dear safety, if you be here, I pray that you will reply to us!"

No—there was no answering cry; nothing to indicate that, well or ill, in safety or otherwise, Pamela was in that place.

Doctor Haslem then turned upon Jacob Sharples, and in a voice that struggled between indignation and grief, he said, "Villain, you have spoken falsely, and she is not here!"

"She was here, I swear it—I swear it! She was here, and should be here still!"

Dick Doubleday uttered an exclamation of horror. He had just cast his eyes upon the two dead officers, and the sight filled him with a thousand vivid apprehensions for Pamela.

Too well did Jacob Sharples guess what sight it was that had met the gaze of Dick Doubleday, and before he was accused, he cried out, "I am innocent! I am innocent! I did not kill them? How could I? Look at me! How could I, small and weak as I am, kill two strong, stout men?"

He trembled in every limb.

Dick Doubleday took the lantern from the hands of Doctor Haslem, and held it close to the face of the coiner.

"Yes," said Dick Doubleday, "you are the murderer! Who that looks in your face can doubt it!"

"No—no, Richard Doubleday—no! I am what you know—I am a coiner, but I do not trade in blood! No, no! And as for the girl, I tell you that she is—she must be here, and safe and sound so far as I am concerned! Pamela! Pamela! Pamela!"

That was the cry, in the hated tones of Jacob Sharples, that poor Pamela had heard, and of course would not reply to.

Then all was still.

The search in the cellars was complete, and Pamela's friends were convinced she was not in that portion of the coiner's house.

Further search then seemed at a stand-still, for the door at the top of the staircase, with its stout iron bar, resisted all efforts to force it.

One of the most curious things to observe during all these proceedings, was the calmness, the utter coolness and absence of all excitement, on the part of Lord Malvern.

With his glass upon his eye, he had gone through with the whole affair as if he had been engaged in the most ordinary transaction in life.

Now, however, when the door at the top of the staircase, leading down to the cellars, resisted all efforts to open it, he spoke.

"Aw! I'll go wound to the fwont, and take down the bar."

"You cannot without a light," said Handsome Jemmy—"you will never be able, my lord, to find your way.

"Oh, yes, yes! one of the things some fellows can do is to find their way in the dawk. I'm a fellow that can do that. I can wun—I can wide, and I can shoot; and I can find my way in the dawk—aw!"

As he spoke, Lord Malvern, who, certainly, among other qualities he possessed, was a complete stranger to fear, left the little party at the top of the steep stairs, and went to find a route, by the way they had come, to the other side of the door.

The grating and the stone that, as well as covering it with a sort of lid, formed the door-step of the house, were both in their places.

Lord Malvern might have added to his many other physical accomplishments that he was a strong "fellaw," for he raised both grating and stone step together, and

emerged in safety at the very time that Pamela, with her captors, left the dismal street in which the coiner's house was situated.

Then finding the door closed, Lord Malvern, with the agility of a harlequin, fairly got into the passage through the broken fanlight.

To find, then, the door at the end of that long, dark passage, and take down the bar, so that the little party on the other side was released, did not take many minutes.

Handsome Jemmy, leading his prisoner, Jacob Sharples, by the cord round his neck, emerged first, but he was closely followed by the Doctor and by Dick Doubleday.

"Now, Jacob Sharples," said the highwayman, "we do not intend to leave one square foot of your house here unsearched!"

"Do you as you please," said the coiner, moodily. "I know not now where she is. I tell you, as I told you before, that I left her in the cellars. There was no harm done to her—I never lifted my hand in anger against her; and now where to look for her I know not. Of course you can murder me, if you like—I am in your power!"

Although Jacob Sharples spoke in this desponding sort of tone, he had not the remotest idea that he stood in any real peril of his life from the persons who held him in custody.

Still, he exhibited a little terror upon Handsome Jemmy saying, "I think that will, after all, be the shortest way!"

"What, Jemmy?" asked Dick Doubleday, sadly.

"To hang Sharples!"

The coiner looked fidgetty.

"And," added the highwayman, "I don't see how he could object, or what it can matter to him. He is sure to be hanged some day, and it may as well be now, as it will save him a deal of trouble!"

The look with which the highwayman accompanied these words, let Doctor Haslem and Dick Doubleday comprehend that he had some design on foot.

As for Lord Malvern, it seemed to him, as no doubt it was, a matter of perfect indifference whether Jacob Sharples were hanged or not.

"I appeal to you, Doctor Haslem, and to you, Dick Doubleday, and to you, my Lord Malvern, as I hear you named, to save me. What good can my murder do you all?"

"I decline to interfere," said the physician.

"And so do I," said Dick Doubleday.

"Aw!" said Lord Malvern. "I can wun, and I can wide, and I can shoot, and I can pull a wope; so if you want a fellaw to give a pull to a wope, with—aw—Jacob what's his name? at the other end of it—aw—I'm the fellaw!"

"Thanks, my lord," replied Handsome Jemmy. "Now, Jacob, if you please!"

"What?—what do you want?"

"Pamela!"

"I know not where she is! On my oath, I swear it! I—I will take any oath you like that I know not where she i—!"

"That's your misfortune," added the highwayman. "If you could tell us, it might save you; but, as it is, hang you must, for I cannot be plagued with you any longer!"

The reader is in possession of information which enables him to know that the highwayman's opinion that Jacob Sharples knew of the place where to find Pamela is erroneous; but Handsome Jemmy fully believed that Sharples could conduct them to the young girl, if he would.

Coolly and deliberately, Handsome Jemmy carried the slack end of the cord, the noose at the other extremity of which was round the neck of the coiner, over the top of a door that led into one of the rooms on the ground floor of the house.

"Now, Jacob," he said, "it will be no amusement to us to see you kicking, so you will be so good as to get

JACOB SHARPLES IS THREATENED WITH SUMMARY PUNISHMENT.

No. 16.—FELON'S DAUGHTER.

on the inner side of the door; and as I perceive there is rather a large space above it, I can draw you up nicely from this side."

Jacob Sharples started, and a sudden change came over his countenance. He assumed a dogged, obstinate look

"You dare not do it!" he said.

"Oh, that's your calculation, is it?" replied the highwayman. "I'm afraid, Jacob, that you deceive yourself!"

As he spoke, the highwayman pushed Sharples into the dark room, and closing the door, he pulled the cord tight that was round his neck over the top of it, which had shrunk from the framework a good inch and a half.

The coiner kicked on the panel of the door.

"Jacob," said Handsome Jemmy, "where is Pamela?"

As he spoke, he gave the cord a tug.

The coiner kicked again.

"Jacob, where is Pamela?"

Handsome Jemmy gave the cord another tug; but this time the coiner did not kick. The highwayman pulled the cord tighter.

"Jacob Sharples, where is Pamela?"

There was no reply.

"I fear," whispered Doctor Haslem, "that he is choking!"

"Aw!" said Lord Malvern. "I think—aw—there is—aw—something odd about the fellow!"

Lord Malvern opened the door as he spoke, to look on the other side of it, and see what state the coiner was in, while Dick Doubleday held the lantern for him; and then he turned his eyeglass towards Handsome Jemmy, and said, "I's a bwass hook—aw!"

"A what, my lord?"

"A bwass hook!"

"Jacob Sharples is gone!" cried Dick Doubleday.

"Then it's his own fault, Dick," said the highwayman. "Why did he not speak?"

"But I mean bodily!"

"Ah! say you so?"

Handsome Jemmy swung open the door, and let go of his end of the cord Jacob Sharples was nowhere to be seen; and the noose, which the highwayman had up to that time believed to be firmly round the coiner's neck, was attached to a brass hook in the inner panel of the door.

Handsome Jemmy looked chagrined; but he made a rush into the room, as he cried out, "The lantern, Dick,—the lantern!"

Dick Doubleday held up the lantern; but there was little or nothing to be seen but the bare walls. A few squalid-looking pieces of furniture were certainly there; and in one corner was an old flock mattress; but there was nothing to indicate how Sharples had contrived to escape.

"Confound the fellow!" said Jemmy.

"Aw!" said Lord Malvern, "that's—aw—what I call wather clevaw—aw!"

"Ah!" cried Handsome Jemmy. "Now I know all about it! Jacob Sharples, your blood be upon your own head! Hold the light, Dick!"

"Yes, yes!"

The highwayman drew a pistol from his pocket, and fired it up the chimney.

A volley of soot was the only response.

Then he fired another pistol at one of the old wainscot walls.

But there was not the least sound indicative of alarm from some hiding-place of the coiner.

"Bravo, Sharples!" cried Handsome Jemmy.

"Aw—he's quite a clevaw fellaw!"

"But," said Doctor Haslem, in a voice of agonized impatience, "can nothing more be done?"

"Oh, yes, Doctor; but it's an extreme measure."

"What is it?"

"I intend to have down the house."

"And perhaps Pamela in it!" shouted a voice at this moment, which they all thought came from the

passage, and which was recognised as belonging most unquestionably to Jacob Sharples.

The highwayman made a rush to reach the passage, but the door of the room they were all in was fast; and although by a second dash at it he fairly burst it open, and reached the passage, when he did look about him there, by the aid of the lantern, no vestige of Jacob Sharples was to be seen.

But the outer door was open, and the cold night-wind blew keenly into the house.

"Foiled and baffled; and by such a fellow as that, too!" said Handsome Jemmy, in tones of mortification.

There was a rapid rush of footsteps in the street, and directly following that sound, some half-dozen officers of the police crowded the doorstep.

"Caught in a trap!" said Handsome Jemmy.

"No," remarked Lord Malvern—"aw—it's only vermin that—aw—are caught in traps."

He stepped forward as he spoke, and the light from several lanterns, carried by the constables, flashed upon his face.

The foremost of the constables then touched his hat as he said, "I think I have the honour of seeing my Lord Malvern? I was born on your lordship's father's estate. My name is Biggles, my lord."

"Ah, well, Biggles, what do you want here?"

"Why, my lord, the young girl your lordship may have heard of, who was cast for death for passing bad money, is in Newgate, after her strange escape; and as she was apprehended in this house, I am sent to search it."

"In Newgate!" exclaimed Dick Doubleday; "Pamela in Newgate?"

"That's the name, sir—Pamela Sharples!"

The officer looked curiously at Dick Doubleday and Handsome Jemmy; but Lord Malvern took an arm of each, and said, quietly, "Friends of mine; and—aw—this is Doctor Haslem—aw!"

The officer stepped aside, and the little party left Jacob Sharples's house in safety.

CHAPTER LI.

JACOB SHARPLES VISITS THE HOUSE OF DICK DOUBLE-DAY'S UNCLE, AND HAS A RACE FOR HIS LIFE.

THE mysterious disappearance of Jacob Sharples at the time when Handsome Jemmy, the highwayman, thought that beyond a doubt he had him completely in his power, was still a fact that puzzled and perplexed the little party who left the coiner's house under the protection of the kind-hearted and eccentric Lord Malvern.

Like many other mysterious circumstances, however, which seem to confound the judgment, this one is easy of explanation.

Jacob Sharples was well acquainted with the secrets of the house, which, before he inhabited it, had been in the possession of a band of coiners, whose operations had assumed the most extensive character.

In order to baffle the, from time to time, researches of the police, these men had, with great care and diligence among themselves, without calling in the aid of workmen, constructed various hiding-places in the house.

Some secret means, too, of getting from one of these hiding-places to another were not forgotten; and although it is possible enough that even Jacob Sharples was not fully aware of all the resources of the old house, yet he knew enough of them to ensure his purpose, so soon as he got fairly out of sight of Handsome Jemmy and his friends.

In the first instance, the highwayman had fastened the hands of the coiner behind him; but at the intercession of Dick Doubleday he had suffered him to be at liberty so far.

That little concession was all that the coiner wanted, and from the moment that he obtained it, he considered that he was virtually a free man.

He had got rid, too, of his principal fears; for whereas he thought at first that Handsome Jemmy had really taken it into his head to hang him, he now had no such notion.

As soon, then, as a door—a thick, palpable door—was interposed between Jacob Sharples and the highwayman, the coiner set to work.

A small knife which he had in a waistcoat pocket released him from the cord round his neck; and he took good care, at the same time, to hold it tight, so that Handsome Jemmy should not be sensible of any diminution of the strain upon it.

Then to tie a new loop, and hang that loop over one of the hooks at the back of the door, was, to the long, nimble fingers of the coiner, the work of a few seconds.

Jacob Sharples was free!

Free from the cord, but not yet, however, free from those persons who were only separated from him by a couple of inches of wood-work.

He soon altered that state of things.

Darting lightly to one side of the room, he by a touch, exactly where he knew how to apply that touch, moved a portion of the skirting-board of the wall to the extent of about eight feet or more.

That piece of skirting-board turned upon invisible hinges, and immediately beyond was, not a secret passage—not any staircase or winding way between the walls—but simply a long, narrow cavity, into which a person so thin and attenuated as Jacob Sharples could easily push himself.

Lying down, then, the coiner rolled himself after an odd fashion into the cavity.

On the inner side of the hinged skirting-board there was a strap of leather, which was looped so that it could be pulled firmly from within.

Jacob Sharples placed his fingers in the loop, and pulled the skirting-board towards him as he lay in the cavity.

There was a slight snapping sound as it fastened itself by a kind of latch. Then all was safe!

The walls might be tapped for hollow sounds, the floor might be searched for trap-doors, and the ceiling might be carefully examined; but without previous indication or suspicion of the hiding-place of the coiner, it was a thousand to one that it would pass completely undiscovered and unsuspected.

It was not a pleasant place to be in.

The space was small.

The darkness was profound.

The feeling that was likely to come over any one there hiding would somewhat resemble that of being buried alive.

So coffin-like and cramped up were the sides of that narrow hiding-place.

But it answered the coiner's purpose.

With a feeling of exultation he heard his foes depart —baffled completely, when they thought they had him so completely at their mercy.

Then he waited for some time, and was about to emerge from the cavity in the wall, when he heard the fresh arrival of officers of the police, who came to look for him.

He drew back again in some affright.

But, in reality, he had nothing to dread. What the officer considered, and justly so, a thorough search, was made of the premises; and then they left the dingy, miserable-looking house, tolerably convinced in their own minds that the coiner was not there.

Jacob Sharples then emerged again slowly and cautiously from his hiding-place.

He lay for some time in the place, and listened for the faintest noise which should indicate the continued presence of any enemy.

No! All was still. He had that old house to himself, and he resolved to profit by the opportunity.

Jacob Sharples was a miser.

He had commenced making spurious coins, and getting them into circulation having good solid gold and silver change brought to him for them by poor Pamela, with the idea of accumulating some considerable amount of money, and then enjoying it.

Probably that is the first idea of all misers.

But the habit of accumulation—the disposition of mind which commences the system of hoarding, soon assumes another phase.

The pursuit of gold becomes the pleasure.

The mere possession of it—the sight of it—the jingle of piece against piece—the gradually day by day increasing hoard of the precious medium of exchange, becomes a delight.

A delight of a feverish, anxious character, which sharpens the visage, fades the eyes, and fills the whole soul of the man with a thousand apprehensions.

The idea of parting with any of the precious spoil flies from the gold-dazzled heart.

Such was the case with Jacob Sharples.

He had become a miser, and although he would often picture to himself some prince-like life that he was some day to lead, with the produce of all his criminality, that day never came.

In poverty—almost real poverty, because he would not use the gold he had—Jacob passed his days. In the midst of squalor and discomfort he lived. Denying himself more and more the comforts, and even the necessaries of life, as his means absolutely increased of procuring them, he existed, rather than could be said to live, in that wretched house.

And he was rich!

Yes, the ragged, squalid, half-starved-looking Jacob Sharples was rich!

He had a secret store in that house, which in imagination he was always gazing at, and counting and recounting over and over again.

Now he proposed to himself to take that store with him, for he could not conceal from himself that his career, in London, at least, was over.

Formerly, he had had a notion that it would be in some foreign country that he should find peace, and spend his ill-gotten wealth; but of late he had changed his purpose.

In the far-off country parts of England he began to consider that he would find as much safety, and perhaps more comfort.

"Yes!—oh, yes!" he said, as he now emerged from the cavity in the wall; "oh, yes, I shall be very, very happy! What do I care for Pamela, or Lavinia, or whatever her real name may be? And let her be hung or saved now, what does it matter to me? I can make myself prodigiously welcome, go where I may, with the gold that I have."

He listened again, but all was still.

Up the crazy staircase he went—that staircase which was a peril of no common character to ascend at all, but which he, the coiner, knew so well, that he was able to place his foot upon the points of support.

Up to the attic he made his way, and opening a narrow casement of diamond-shaped little panes of old, green glass, he looked out into the night.

The stars were now shining down upon the vast city through deep, long rifts in the night clouds.

A cool, refreshing air fanned the wan, feverish cheeks of the coiner.

"Oh, yes, yes!" he said; "I have time yet—I have plenty of time yet! I am only fifty years of age! What is that? I may live to eighty! Thirty years of peace, of enjoyment, of serenity! Yes, I am yet a fortunate man; for I shall, by virtue of my gold, have beauty, excellence, wit, talent, power. Ha, ha!"

The coiner scrambled out at the window.

There was a leaden gutter exactly on the side of the parapet close under the window. It looked old and undisturbed, but Jacob Sharples felt along it until he came to a join in the lead where a small portion stood up like a lip.

With rapid fingers he pulled up the whole of the edge of the thin lead, and then he rolled it back for the space of about three feet.

Immediately beneath, there was a space in the brickwork, in which lay a dark-looking bundle.

It was a something carefully wrapped up in oil-cloth

of a black colour—a something heavy, suggestive of value.

Jacob Sharples gathered up the dark-looking bundle out of the cavity, and lifted it within the attic window.

It was his money.

His precious gold.

All gold, too ; for he had, of course, found no difficulty in changing gold silver into gold.

The weight was something to think of—perhaps about fifteen or sixteen actual pounds in weight ; but when did any one of the frame of mind of Jacob Sharples think that gold was too heavy to carry ?

No; had the weight been twice what it was, Jacob would only have been too happy to burden himself with it.

He was afraid to have a light, although he would have been well pleased to feast his eyes upon the sight of his beloved gold ; but he felt them when he had opened the oil-cloth. His hands revelled among the guineas and the half-guineas—he let them pour from one hand to the other in a golden shower, and, as he did so, he listened with delighted ears to the pleasant jingle they made.

What music was equal to that ?

None—none in all the world !

Then Jacob Sharples made the gold up into a bundle that was about four feet in length, and rolling it up in the oil-cloth, he tied it round and round with many a wind of cord, until he had the whole secure.

His object was to place the money round his waist. Then he should be sure to feel its presence, and its weight would not harass him. He would have the free use of his arms, too, although one of them was still weak and somewhat painful.

"Now," he said —"now I have but one thing more to do, and it is a thing I cannot leave undone. I must search the house of old Doubleday, in Long Lane, on the chance of finding some hoard of his. What if the board should contain jewels—diamonds, pearls, bright rubies ? Yes; I know that he has dealt in such for many a long year, and I must have them. Who knows but this gold that I now carry about me may sink into insignificance before the wealth that I may find yet before the sunrise ?"

He crept down to the passage.

He listened long at the street-door, before he could make up his mind to open it, and then he sallied forth.

He fell over some one on the very door-step !

Jacob Sharples uttered a cry of despair.

"Hilloa ! What's that ? Oh, to be sure ! You are my prisoner !" cried a voice.

It was a constable, who had been left there on the watch, but who had fallen asleep upon the door-step of the coiner's house.

He caught Jacob Sharples by the leg.

There was then a scream of anguish. A lifeless body rolled off the step. The coiner was free again, but the unfortunate officer, with a deep and fatal wound in the neck, lay on the jagged pavement, close to the old house.

A few casements were opened, and curious faces looked out, to endeavour to discover the cause of the death-cry ; but as all was still again, the casements were closed.

Jacob Sharples fled at the top of his speed, and his route was towards Smithfield—towards the house of Dick's uncle.

CHAPTER LII.

LORD MALVERN QUARRELS WITH THE SECRETARY OF STATE, AND PAMELA IS HELD TO A FATHER'S HEART IN A CELL OF NEWGATE.

LET us leave Jacob Sharples to carry out, as best he can, his designs upon the secret hoards of old Doubleday, while we follow the party, consisting of the Court Physician, Lord Malvern, Dick Doubleday, and Handsome Jemmy from the house of the coiner.

Not one person of that party tasted the sweet repose which Nature demands on that night ; and as by the earliest dawn the news that poor Pamela was in Newgate was thoroughly authenticated, the feelings of Dick Doubleday may be imagined, but can hardly be described.

The desire to rush to the prison—to batter at its gates —to make vain and frantic efforts to pull down its walls —to accuse himself—anybody—all the world, so that he could procure the release of Pamela, came over the frantic heart of the young lover with such rushes of painful anxiety, that Lord Malvern, for some time, kept his eye-glass at his eye, and could do nothing but look at Dick.

It was eight o'clock in the morning when Lord Malvern rose from the early breakfast he had partaken of at the Doctor's house, and with his usual coolness spoke : " Aw ! I am going—aw—over to the Secretary of State, to speak about Pamelaw. I shall say, ' My lord, the girl is innocent—aw—and she must, by Jove—aw—be let go—aw—you see ; and I pledge my honour to wun after Jacob Sharples, who is the weal bad fellow, and catch him—aw !"

" Heaven prosper you on your errand, my lord," said the Doctor. " The death of the Princess Amelia has deprived me of all influence with the King."

" Aw ! never mind ! Death is a fellaw that when he chooses—aw—to wun after anybody—aw—he is sure to catch him, in spite of the Doctaw !"

With this sententious sentiment in his mouth, Lord Malvern left the Doctor's house, in Bedford Square, and made his way westward, to the private residence of the Home Secretary.

The name of Lord Malvern admitted him at once to the breakfast-room of the Minister, who was snatching an early meal while he read some newspaper reports and despatches.

" Oh, Malvern, I am glad to see you ! Pray sit down. Have you breakfasted ?"

" Aw ! yes. I have come to talk about Pamelaw !"

" About who ?"

" Pamelaw—the young girl who was going to be hanged, but providentially—aw—got away. Some fellaw has put her into Newgate again—aw—but she is quite innocent—aw—and I want you to wecommend a fwee pardon at once—aw !"

" My dear Malvern, look there !"

" Aw ! Where ?"

" At that report. I will just finish this despatch while you read it. It is the metropolis night report, as it is called, and which is laid upon my table every morning at eight o'clock, as a report of everything particular that has taken place."

" Aw ! What's it about ? Aw—I see ! The body of the smugglaw, who hanged in chains, at Greenhithe— aw—has been cut down—aw !"

" No, no ! That is not it ! Further on ! A little lower down !"

" Oh, aw ! ' The young girl, Pamela Sharples, who was condemned to death for passing bad money, was apprehended at the house of the notorious Jacob Sharples, her reputed father, with, in her possession, a quantity of spurious money.' "

" There, my lord !" said the Secretary of State ; " what do you think of that ?"

" It is not—aw—at all necessary to think—aw ! It's a lie—aw !"

" But, my lord, the report is signed by the head of the London police !"

" Aw ! It's a lie !"

" Really, Lord Malvern, I—a—hardly know what to say to you ; you are so—so very eccentric."

" Look here ! You know as well as I do that this girl Pamelaw is not the daughter of Jacob Sharples, but the child, long lost, of Doctaw Haslem. She was stolen by Sharples, and in her child-like manner—aw— was made to go about changing his bad money into good—aw !"

" But she had money still found in her possession. What do you say to that ?"

JACOB SHARPLES MURDERS THE CONSTABLE.

"Why—aw—that those who apprehended her lacked pity—aw! I only wish I had been among them—aw! I say that if some bad coins were found on Pamelaw, they placed them where they were to be found—aw!"

"Oh, my lord, you are a warm advocate!"

"Aw—yes—I am ; or no advocate at all—aw!"

"Well, my lord, I will now read you a few words from my private diary of yesterday, which relates to an interview I had with the King."

"About Pamelaw?"

"Not specially, but about miscellaneous business; during which, in pursuance of a promise I had made to Doctor Haslem, I mentioned her. There it is, my lord ; I trust you with it "

"Twust—twust? Do you think—aw—I am going to wun away with your diawy?"

"No, no !"

"Because—aw—if I did, you would never catch me; as wunning is—aw—one of the things I can do!"

"No doubt of it, my Lord Malvern! I have often heard as much. But be so good as to read what you will find there."

"Aw—well, I will !"

Lord Malvern, in low tones, read the diary :—

"An interview with the K two hours—spoke of Pamela Sharples, now said to be the long-lost daughter of Doctor Haslem. K quite decided not to grant pardon except on conviction of Sharples. K possessed with idea that the girl can give up the coiner, and point out depositories of spurious money, and expose system generally. Absolutely refuses pardon, and recommends rigour."

Lord Malvern looked up.

"Aw! Is that all ?"

"Not quite, my lord ! Pray, read on."

"K added that Pamela ought rather to have been hanged, innocent or guilty, than set the bad example and scandal of escaping the law."

Lord Malvern threw down the diary.

"You see that I have done all I can, my Lord Malvern ; and I am afraid the girl will still have to suffer."

"Suffaw—suffaw? Not if I know it !. Aw—you have the power to do one thing ; and that is, to grant an order of conditional release to Pamelaw, on my security !"

"No, my lord !—oh, dear, no !"

"Yes. It has been done, on the judge who pwesided at the twial agweeing. If Jacob Sharples is not in Newgate in ten days, I pledge myself that Pamelaw will give herself up again, and take the chances of what may happen."

"It cannot be done !"

"Then—aw—look here ! I mean to save her ; and —aw—I will !"

"My lord ?"

"Well?—aw—well ?"

"I cannot listen to such language ! Pray do not repeat it, I beg of you ! In my position, I ought not to hear it ; and hearing it, I ought to repeat it to the Privy Council, considering who your lordship is !"

Lord Malvern rose, and bowed.

"As you please—as you please !" he said. "But of one thing—aw—you may make quite sure : I will not leave upon your soul the sin of the—aw—judicial murder of that innocent young girl !"

The Secretary of State bowed.

Lord Malvern bowed

The Secretary rang the bell, and Lord Malvern was with all ceremony shown out of the house.

The moment he was fairly gone, there came from behind a screen in the breakfast-room one of the strangest-looking men that mortal eyes ever looked upon.

Tall, gaunt, and haggard—pale, and bleared about the eyes with blood, some surgical plasters upon his face, and one arm in a sling—this man presented all the appearance of one who had sustained most terrible injuries, and had only escaped with his life.

He stepped up to the table at which the Secretary sat, and struck it heavily with his hand

The Secretary of State, with a cry of fright, sprang to his feet.

Another moment, and the bright barrel of a pistol was pointed at his head ; and the man of many hurts spoke in a low, hoarse voice.

"Sit down, my lord ! I am the highwayman who stopped you on Kew Green, and took from you the small green despatch-box, last Tuesday evening."

"Ah !"

"Yes. My name is Sang—Captain Sang !"

"Villain !"

"Yes, by heaven, that's true !"

"Help !"

"Ah! will you? Another such cry, and I will plaster that gay wall behind you with your brains ! Hush! some one comes ! I will sit down here. Hand me a cup of coffee. I am a mad, half-killed, reckless man, and your life is in my hands ! Hand me a cup of coffee, I say, and call me Sir John Pope ! Quick ! or you are lost ! Call me ' My dear Sir John Pope !'"

"But ——"

"What now ?"

"The servants will wonder how you came here !"

"Let them wonder, and be hanged !"

Captain Sang—for it was indeed that ruffian who, by little short of a miracle, had escaped from the perilous situation in which Pamela had left him at his house in Birdcage Walk—sat down opposite to the Secretary of State.

He placed a table-napkin lightly over the pistol with which he had threatened the Secretary's life ; and then, with a hideous grin upon his blood-dabbled visage, he held out his hand for the coffee.

The door of the room opened. A servant looked respectfully in.

"Did your lordship call ?"

"No—yes ; that is, no ! Take a cup of coffee, my dear Sir John Pope !"

"Thank you Go !"

The astonished footman retired, and closed the door after him.

"Excuse me one moment, my lord," said Captain Sang, as he rose from the table with difficulty, for he was badly hurt—"excuse me one moment "

"What—what for ?"

Sang nodded, as much as to say, "You will see ;" and then lifting a heavy plate from among the breakfast things, he went to the door, and opening it suddenly, he brought down the plate with a crack upon the head of the footman, who was, as he (Sang) had guessed, immediately outside, listening at the panel, with his ear close to it.

The heavy plate was dashed to pieces, and the discomfited footman nearly rolled down the adjacent staircase.

Captain Sang had taken good care to carry the pistol with him.

Even if he had not, it is doubtful if the Secretary of State would have had presence of mind at the moment to take advantage of it.

"Now, my lord," said Sang, as he re-seated himself, " we must come to an understanding."

"What do you mean ?"

"Oh, it's very simple ! I took from your lordship, on Tuesday evening last, on Kew Green, a despatch-box !"

"I was stopped on that evening, while alone in my carriage, and robbed."

"Just so."

"You, then, were——"

"The robber ! I admit it—I confess it ! In the despatch-box was one letter, marked ' Private and confidential,' from Vienna——"

"Stop !" said the Secretary of State.

"What for ?"

"Because I now quite understand you! You bring that letter to sell to me; and you are right! I will give any price in reason for it. What do you demand?"

"That is not quite all."

"Say on, then! But at one thing I am lost in wonder!"

"What is that?"

"It is as to how you got here!"

"Oh, that was easy! The next house to this, which was so many years in the occupation of my Lord Porchester, has, since his death, been empty. I got into that with ease; and from that, into this!"

"I see!"

"Of course you do. And now as regards the letter from Vienna."

"Yes. What do you ask for it?"

"Nothing."

"Nothing! Can you—can a man of your ferocity—of your profession—be so generous?· Give it to me, at once; and if—or, I ought to say, when—the law lays hold of you, I will consider what can be done for you, if the case should happen not to be a very black one."

"Oh, you are too kind, my lord; but I am afraid you do not comprehend me! I will not part with that letter but with my life—and perhaps not then; but I will keep its contents and its existence a secret from all men, on one condition."

The Secretary bit his lip.

"No, no." he said; "you will sell it! Money must be what you want, or perhaps safety! Come, shall I say to you 'Give me the letter, and from this very moment be a free man, with a thousand pounds in your pocket?'"

"No! Ah! who is that? Some one comes! Hand me some of those anchovies!"

CHAPTER LIII.

CAPTAIN SANG MAKES HIS OWN TERMS WITH THE SECRETARY OF STATE, AND ASTONISHES THE GOVERNOR OF NEWGATE.

THERE came a respectful tap at the door of the breakfast room in which Captain Sang, *alias* Sir John Pope, was holding so singular and agitating a conference with the Secretary of State.

"Come in!"

A slim young man of aristocratic bearing appeared.

"Quick!—the anchovies!" whispered Sang. "Who is that?"

"My secretary. My dear Sir John Pope, will you take some more anchovies?"

The young man, who filled the most honourable post of private secretary to the Minister, looked annoyed, as well he might.

"I am afraid I intrude."

"No, no! Oh, no!"

"Some despatches."

"Keep them in your own room, if you please, till I come to you."

The secretary bowed, and retired.

The Minister of State bit his lips with vexation as he looked at Sir John Pope, *alias* Captain Sang, and said, in suppressed tones, through which the rage that was at his heart could well be heard, "What in the name of all that's—that's—infernal, sir, do you want?"

"A mere trifle."

"Name it, sir—name it! Every moment of mine now is precious, and the important occupations of the day commence at once! Name it, sir! What is your price for that most unfortunate letter?"

"I think I had the honour of saying that I put no price upon the letter at present."

"Then, what do you mean; and what do you want? Are you mad; or am I?"

"I can answer for myself that I am perfectly sane, although somewhat hurt, as I happened to fall into the hands of an old she-dragon, from whom I escaped as by a miracle."

The Secretary of State sat fretting and pining; and Sang continued.

"Look you, sir! I have two hopes and two good expectations from that 'Vienna' letter. If I consent, on my honour and word, to keep it a secret, I ask a mere trifle of you in return. When I consent to actually give it up to you, I shall ask something of more consequen e."

"Speak plainly."

"I will. What I ask for keeping the secret is, the life—the release of Pamela Sharples."

"Ah!"

"Exactly so. When I do give up the letter actually into your hands, so that it can be of no further service to me, it will be when I want to ask the life and the release of a more important personage still."

"Who?—who?"

"Sir John Pope, *alias* Captain Sang, the highwayman, Mr. Secretary."

"Villain!"

"Pho! pho! It was but now you told me how precious your moments were; and now you waste them with such idle trash, as well as call me names!"

"What on earth can it matter to you whether this girl, Pamela Sharples, is hanged, or set free?"

"Fancy! fancy! A mere matter of fancy; that is all!"

"But—but——"

Sang put on a look of demoniac gravity, and he dashed his fist on the table with a force that started from it on to the floor some of its contents.

"Hark you, sir! I will not be trifled with. I—I—— Well, much as I dislike the word, I use it——I love the girl! I am maddened at the loss of her; for I have lost her, seeing that she was once in my possession—in my house! But I was fooled, tricked, cozened. Ha! ha! I will not be so again!"

The Secretary of State turned pale.

"And, then, I am to comprehend that the price of your silence as regards the letter you stole from me is, that I should give up to your evil passions a young, and, by all accounts, innocent girl?"

"That's it!"

"You avow it?"

"Of course I do! Be quick now! Be quick; for I am half mad!"

The Secretary turned paler; and then, as if some happier thought had occurred to him, the colour began slowly to revisit his face.

"Do you mean, Captain Sang that I am, in defiance of all law, justice, and practice to give you an unconditional order to take Pamela Sharples from Newgate?"

"Just so."

"But how can I justify it? What can I say when the transaction is spoken of, and challenged, as it assuredly will be, in both Houses of Parliament?"

"That's your affair!"

"Very well; I cannot help it. You shall have what you require."

"Of course I shall!"

Sang kept his eyes on the Home Secretary, who wrote on some official paper, and sealed it with his office seal, the following words:—

"Secretary of State's Office.
"To the Governor of Newgate.

"Sir,—These are to require you to surrender to the bearer, Sir John Pope, the young girl named Pamela Sharples, now in your custody, without question or hindrance; and these shall be your sufficient warrant for such a purpose.

"G. MINTORN."

"There, Captain Sang! Will that do?"

"Capitally! I have the honour, now, to bid you a good morning! Ha! ha! The next time you hear from me, you will get the letter; for then I shall have to ask for my own life and liberty; and if that time should never come, you will never hear of it again, nor will mortal man!"

Captain Sang, with these words, left the room, with as much a swagger of his gait as he could, and was soon out of the house of the Minister of State.

From the window, the Secretary saw him descend the steps of his house; and then he turned sharply to the table he had just left, and touched a hand-bell

The private secretary appeared.

"Quick!" said the Secretary of State. "A matter of life or death! A despatch to the Governor of Newgate, instantly! There it is!"

Almost as he spoke, the Secretary of State had written, on a sheet of letter-paper, the following message to Newgate:—

"To the Governor.

"Sir,—You will obey an order that will be presented by Sir John Pope, relative to Pamela Sharples; but you will, on one excuse or another, manage to delay his departure from the prison till eleven o'clock.

"Yours obediently,
"G. MINTORN."

The private secretary, with the hastily-written and hastily-sealed note to the Governor of Newgate, vanished from the room.

The moment he was gone, the Secretary of State wrote another note:—

"My dear Lord Malvern,—If you will kindly come here at once, I will put you in the way of pleasing yourself, and obliging your friends, by the release of the young girl from Newgate of whom we were speaking this morning.

"Believe me to be,
"My dear Lord Malvern,
"Yours very truly,
"G. MINTORN."

One touch at the hand-bell on the table brought a servant, to whom the Secretary handed this note.

"Let this be delivered to Lord Malvern as quickly as possible! If he be from home, let him be sought out wherever he can be found, and say that I shall not leave here until I see him, or until it be past eleven o'clock, in which case an interview is useless!"

The servant bowed, and a messenger started with the letter in two minutes.

Then the Secretary of State paced his rooms to and fro, and ever and anon struck his brow with his open hand.

"Curses on my own folly," he said, "to carry such an epistle about with me! Oh, why did I not hide it in some inaccessible place, where no eyes but mine could even look upon it! If discovered by my political opponents, it would ruin me for ever! That I, a minister of the Crown, was carrying on a private correspondence with a foreign Court! But if I breathe maledictions on my own incaution, what shall I say of the obstinacy of the blood-thirsty old maniac, who fills the throne of these realms, and who——"

A tap came at the door of the room.

"Come in!"

"My Lord Malvern!"

The Secretary of State, with some difficulty, suppressed a cry of pleasure

The appearance of Lord Malvern so very promptly after he had been sent for was so utterly unexpected, that the Minister could scarcely believe his own eyes.

"Is it possible, my lord, that my message could have been so quick, and your lordship so prompt?"

"Aw—I have the lettaw."

Lord Malvern held in his hand the open letter of the Secretary, who still looked puzzled about the question of time, till the servant, who was still at the door, said, "The messenger was fortunate enough to meet my Lord Malvern at the corner of Whitehall Yard."

Those few words solved the mystery at once to the mind of the Secretary.

He made a sign, and the door was closed upon him and Lord Malvern, whom he then, with some slight confusion of manner, addressed: "My lord, the earnestness with which you desired to be of service to the young girl, who, you tell me, is Pamela Haslem, and not Pamela Sharples, set me thinking of some plan by which, without sacrificing ministerial etiquette, or incurring awkward responsibilities, I might aid you."

"Aw—yes."

"Well, my lord, what is the time now?"

"Aw—it wants five-and-twenty minutes—aw—to eleven."

"Then there is ample time. I have but one question to ask your lordship and on your answer to it hangs the fate of Pamela."

"Aw—well, what is it?"

"Will your lordship consent to adopt, without hesitation or question, what will appear to be a very odd and unaccountable mode of being of service to the girl?"

"Yes"

"That suffices Your lordship's word is all-sufficient, and cannot be doubted."

"Aw—you say so much—aw—about it, that one would think—aw—you did doubt it—aw!"

"No, no; not for the world!"

"Well, what about Pamelaw?"

"If your lordship will go to the Old Bailey, taking with you a proper force, and keep your eyes upon the wicket-gate of Newgate, you will see come forth, about eleven o'clock a man, with Pamela."

"Aw—with Pamelaw?"

"Yes. That man is a notorious villain—a highwayman of the worst possible class—and all you will have to do, will be to rescue her from him; and as to Captain Sang, the highwayman, give him in charge to the authorities of Newgate as a capital felon, and they must keep him. Then you can take Pamela away with you, and I hope to heaven I may never hear her name again."

Lord Malvern looked at his watch.

"Aw—a quarter to eleven!"

He turned on his heel, and without another word to the Secretary of State, he went out of the house, and mounting his horse, which was at the door, he bent low in the saddle for a moment, and made some slight alteration in the harness; and then giving the horse a slight pat on the neck, he started for the City at a gallop that left all things, horses, men, and carriages, far behind him.

It was four minutes and a half to eleven o'clock when Lord Malvern reached the top of Snow Hill, and beheld Newgate, grim, cold, and stern, in all its stony face, before him.

He fixed his eye-glass to his eye.

There was no time to think of getting any one to help him. Indeed, he was not the sort of man to care about help, so self-reliant was he, and accustomed to rely upon his own resources.

A coach was at the door of Newgate.

A common hackney vehicle it was; and, by the look of the disreputable man who sat upon the box, it seemed as if it was one of those night vehicles that generally, at the approach of day, disappear with their old jaded horses and thieves of drivers; for, notwithstanding the fact that many, and, indeed, most of the old hackney coach drivers were respectable men, who had been servants of the gentry and nobility, the facilities which the thieves of London found the possession of a hackney coach afforded them for carrying away booty, made many of them set up the trade, to the great scandal of the more decent members of the fraternity.

Doubtless this is the case at present.

This coach, then, was drawn up close to the door of the prison.

The disreputable coachman was half asleep on his box.

MOTHER BENDYDYKES SURVEYS THE FEATURES OF THE CORPSE.

No. 17.—FELON'S DAUGHTER.

Lord Malvern rode into the inn yard exactly opposite to the prison gate, and, dismounting, he said to the first ostler he saw, "Aw—take care of my horse—aw!"

The horse was a hunter, worth a couple of hundred guineas; and Lord Malvern himself was so evidently a gentleman, that his orders were obeyed respectfully.

CHAPTER LIV.

A STRANGE SCENE TAKES PLACE AT MOTHER BENDYDYKES', AND MORE PERILS SEEM TO BE IN STORE FOR PAMELA.

WE regret to leave Pamela, even for an hour longer than necessary, in Newgate; and we regret to leave Captain Sang and Lord Malvern on the eve of the collision that seemed fated to take place between them; but circumstances compel us to request our readers' attention to a strange scene which was taking place at the house of the mysterious woman who went by the name of Bendydykes, and who resided in Blackfriars.

For a brief space, it had seemed that this woman had disappeared.

No one had been able to obtain entrance to the house. The cats and the old sorceress herself seemed all bodily to have taken their departure from the place, and silence and desolation apparently reigned there instead.

There were, however, more mysteries in connexion with that place than met the eye; and it is one of these which it is necessary now, to the progress of our story, we should lay before the reader.

It is midnight.

The midnight of squall, rain, and storm which saw that visit, of anxiety mingled with hope, of Doctor Haslem, Handsome Jemmy, Dick Doubleday, and Lord Malvern, to the house of the coiner, at Clerkenwell.

That midnight on which Jacob Sharples had played so clever a trick, and eluded the vigilance of Handsome Jemmy.

A high tide in the Thames brought the dingy, pestiferous water right up to the back steps of the old house.

The wind blew gustily about the chimney tops, as if it contained within itself the dismal sighs and groans of the many victims whose bones lie rotting deep down in the mud of the Thames.

In only one room of that house is there a light.

By that light might have been seen old Mother Bendydykes herself, with that odd and most mysterious cowled cloak she was in the habit of wearing drawn closely about her.

She was tending, or making a fire.

One cat stood on the chimney-piece that was just above her head, and kept spitting and sputtering as the fumes from the fire came up to her sensitive eyes and nostrils.

Another cat was on the back of old Mother Bendydykes; and with great skill moved about, as she sometimes stooped and sometimes stood more upright, so as to keep her place.

The fire burnt badly.

The wood was damp.

The dampness of the grave was upon it; and more than once, with an old pair of short tongs, such as were commonly in use in chemical furnaces, the hag drew out nails from among the embers of the fire, and kept muttering to herself, "Fine times—fine times! So he must needs play the fool at last, eh? Well he has paid for it! Has he not paid for it, my chicken?"

The cat on the chimney-piece, who was an ancient specimen of the feline tribe, and who, either from some scald or from age, had no hair on its head, uttered a snarling reply, and spat down upon Mother Bendydykes.

"Yes, my chick," she added, "you know all about it—of course you do; and so do you, my Pretty Ghoul!"

Pretty Ghoul seemed to be the authorized and well-comprehended name of the other cat who was on her back, for that one uttered a horrid howl.

"Pretty—pretty!" said Mother Bendydykes. "I was always fond of music!"

She then suddenly started.

A strange, wailing sound came from the direction of the river.

Then there was a low whistle.

The old hag almost stood erect, so that the cat on her back had to dig its claws as deep as it could to hold on.

"Ha, ha!" she laughed "Another—another!"

The whistle sounded again.

Mother Bendydykes took up the old rusty shovel from the firegrate, and struck it with the poker three times.

"That will do!" she said—"that will do, if it would; and if it ain't, why it will do no harm; but I fancy it is Mould!"

With this rather enigmatical speech Mother Bendydykes made her way across the room, and lifting a curtain that shut off either another apartment from it or a portion of that one, she approached a window.

The shutter was closed and barred, but she flung it open.

A cold gust of wind from the river blew into the place, and she saw how nigh the tide was—in fact, it lashed, and rippled, and broke into eddies against the back wall of the house.

"Hilloa!" said a voice. "Is that you, old Mother Bendydykes?"

"And what if it is, owl?"

"All's right! I have brought one!" added the voice.

"I don't want it!"

"Oh, come, come, you know you make a handsome profit, besides having the coffin wood to burn!"

"I tell you, Mould, I don't want it! Go and make the handsome profits yourself!"

"Don't say that! You know as well as I do that I can't do it! I have been in trouble once before for body-snatching, and very nearly lost my situation as sexton of the new burying-ground in Tottenham Court Road. But by bringing the bodies to you, and taking half-price, it answers my turn, and you make a profit! Come now, old Mother Bendydykes, you know any of the young City doctors will be glad to buy it of you!"

"No, no! I won't—I can't! I'm dead—dying—anything you like! Be off—be off, I say!"

"Well then, after all my trouble, I must sink it in the Thames."

"And yourself with it, if you like."

"Come, come!—that's rather too bad, after all our little dealings. Shall I tell whose body it is?"

"No, no! what care I?"

"Well, but it's all fair, because you see it's one of the doctors themselves, I take it, or as good as one of them; for this is the body of the brother of Doctor Haslem, of Bedford Square, who was buried this day, or rather, I ought now to say, yesterday. I have got it up, and you can have it, coffin and all, for seven guineas. Come, now!"

The hag uttered a shriek.

She clung to the window-sill, and screamed out into the night air.

The criminal sexton, who thus disposed, for the purposes of dissection, of the dead from the then new burial-ground which was under his control, was so terrified at these cries from Mother Bendydykes, that he began to paddle away with his boat as quickly as he could.

She heard the sound of the retreating boat.

She saw it gliding off from under the window, with the long, dark-looking object within it.

"Stop! stop! Oh, God, if you be human—be—be——Did I say God?"

The sexton stopped.

"Good gracious, Mrs. Bendydykes, have you lost your senses? Do you want to bring the whole neighbourhood about us? What are you at, to go on in that way?"

"Stop! stop!"

"Well, I have!"

"What—what—what did you say?—or was it only some voice out of my own crazed heart, that spoke? What did you say? Whatever it was, say it again—oh, say it once again!"

"There's no objection to that, Mother Bendydykes, only don't fly out in that kind of way"

"Go on—go on! Say it—I listen!"

"Well, all I said was, that this was the body of the brother of Doctor Haslem, of Bedford Square, who died suddenly, they say."

"Oh, heaven!"

Mother Bendydykes fell upon the window-sill, as if she, too, had then and there died suddenly.

It was but dimly that the sexton of the new burial-ground in Tottenham Court Road could see her, but he was astonished at the effect the intelligence had upon her.

"Perhaps," he said, "you knew the gentleman, and, in that case, would rather not?"

"Peace! peace! groaned the hag. "I will give you the money!"

"Come, that's business!"

Mother Bendydykes disappeared from the window, but it was only for a few minutes, after the lapse of which she returned, bringing with her a long, sloping plank, about the thickness of a floor-board.

In fact, it was one which, for the purpose she was now applying it to, she had taken up from one of the rooms of the house. This board she projected from the window into the boat in a slant direction, and upon it the sexton slid the coffin.

Mother Bendydykes got hold of one of the handles, and drew the receptacle of the dead slowly towards her.

Some portion of the board projected into the room, so that as soon as the principal weight of the coffin came upon that portion, and past the point of support afforded by the window-sill, the board tilted slowly up, and the coffin was deposited in the room without further trouble.

"Wait a moment!" said the hag.

She was absent from the window about two minutes, and when she returned, she cast into the boat a folded paper containing money.

"Go, now," she said—"go, now, and return no more, for I shall not be here."

"Very well, Mother Bendydykes. Good night!"

"Good night!"

She found it easier to push the plank right out at the window into the water, than to draw it back into the room, so she did so, and then closed the window and the shutter.

She tottered back to the room, or part of the room, where she had a fire, and she lit a wretched rushlight, with hands that trembled so excessively that she could scarcely manage to accomplish the task.

Uttering, then, low moans, she went back to the coffin.

She bent over it, and held the light close to the plate.

She shrieked aloud.

The alarmed cats, with yells and screams, fled from her.

She fell forward on the coffin, and the light was extinguished, as it slipped from her nerveless fingers.

She had seen on the plate the name of the physician's brother.

Mother Bendydykes must have had some lingering hope that the sexton had purposely or ignorantly deceived her in regard to the identity of the corpse, or she never would have so completely lost all consciousness when she read the name upon the coffin-plate.

For more than an hour she remained in a swoon.

Then there came a shudder over her frame, and then she looked up.

"Where am I? what has happened?"

All was darkness.

The only sound she heard was the sighing of the wind without, for as the tide of the river began to ebb the wind did not blow quite so furiously.

Then she recollected all that had happened.

But the fierce flush of feeling had passed away, and it gave place to a cold, dismal feel, that seemed to be making war against life.

She slowly rose to her feet

"A light! a light! I will see him once again, although in death!—once again, for he has made me what I am, and I have made him what he is! A light! a light!"

Again she made her way towards the fireplace. The smouldering remains of the coffin-wood that for years had formed the only fuel she burned, were deep down in the grate, but there was no difficulty in getting up a flame with some paper that she flung upon those embers.

She fanned them with an old coffin-plate. A flame came, and she lit another piece of candle, and approached the coffin

The cats followed her.

One sprang on her back.

Another sat on the coffin-lid.

Mother Bendydykes, with a skill that sufficiently showed she was used to the work, began to force open the lid of the coffin

She sighed and groaned, and now and then uttered faint shrieks, as she worked.

CHAPTER LV.

PAMELA DISCOVERS ONE OF THE SECRETS OF NEWGATE, AND IS NEARLY SUCCESSFUL IN EFFECTING AN ESCAPE.

IT is midnight.

Pamela is in Newgate.

With a faint reverberation through the thickness of the walls, she hears the hour struck by the gigantic bell of St. Paul's

She hears it as though faintly echoed by the clock of St. Sepulchre's Church.

Then all is still. It is not the stillness of repose or of serenity—not that stillness which comes over the vexed or faded heart, as if air from heaven had gently swept aside all the dull vapours of earth; but the stillness of despair, the mute agony of those against whom the stony portals of hopelessness had closed for ever.

There was nothing peculiarly connected with the cell into which poor Pamela had been flung to warrant the idea that took possession of her, but the sensation she felt was one as if she could not breathe.

The air appeared to be either too thick and heavy for human lungs, or too little of it to afford vital sustenance.

And yet along the gloomy stone passage from which the cells opened, there blew a cold, damp blast.

That artificial current of air whistled and moaned as it made its way under the cell door, and though the close bars of a narrow grating that was as high up as the low ceiling of the cell would allow of its being constructed in the solid stone wall above the door.

But still Pamela found it difficult to get rid of the choking sensation.

It was the consciousness of imprisonment that gave rise to it.

She knelt down on the cold stones and the damp straw, and prayed.

She prayed for strength yet to overcome the oppression of her sad fate; and although some strength did come, as it ever will, from the act of prayer, yet there lingered still sufficient sadness and hopelessness at her heart to make her very sad indeed.

Who could aid her now?

How was that young, good, generous and loving heart, that was all her own, to reach her in that dreary prison-house?

With a deep sigh, she breathed the name of Richard

Doubleday ; but for all that, she knew he was far away, and she might never look upon his face again.

Then Pamela began to weep.

Her sobs, she thought, were surely the only sounds which disturbed the profound stillness of the prison.

Alas ! she knew not in how many of the then wretched cells of Newgate, innocence, even such as her own, might be sobbing and shrieking for the mercy and the succour which came not.

Then she heard the sound of one o'clock from St. Paul's, and its echo from St. Sepulchre's.

The sounds had scarcely ceased, when her attention was attracted by another kind of interruption to the stillness of the night.

A strange, half-tapping, half-scratching noise came, as she thought at the moment she first heard it, right into the cell in which she was.

So perfect was the delusion, that Pamela shrank back as far as the wall would permit her, and, amid the darkness, held out her arms before her, lest any one should encounter her and do her some injury.

"Who is it?—who is it?" she cried. "Speak!—oh, speak! Who is here?"

The low tapping sound ceased on the instant, but there was no reply to her inquiries. In vain she strove to pierce the darkness with her eyes, and to detect the presence of something or somebody in the cell.

All she saw was what imagination conjured up out of the thick gloom.

Strange, grotesque faces—bodies without heads, and heads without bodies—all those chimeras of the disturbed fancy which seem to people any space into which no wandering ray of light is permitted to enter.

Then, after a pause of about half a minute, the scratching, tapping sound came again.

This time, Pamela did not so far mistake it as to suppose that it was in her cell, but she felt tolerably certain that it was beneath the floor of it.

What could it mean ?

That floor was composed of slabs of stone, each about a foot square ; and beneath them, surely, there was nothing but the solid earth.

And yet, the more Pamela listened, the more she felt certain that it was from beneath the floor the mysterious sounds came from.

She resolved to make no further inquiries by word of mouth, but to listen to what sounds might be repeated with all the power of attention she could command.

The noises now, after another pause, commenced again, and continued without any intermission.

There could be but one explanation of them.

Some one was at work beneath the cell—some person, probably, who was burrowing among the foundations of old Newgate with a hope of escaping.

By dint, then, of great attention, Pamela was able, so to speak, to localize the sounds—that is to say, she heard them at one particular spot.

She felt sure that she had found the special square stone in the floor of her cell beneath which the sounds could be heard most distinctly.

Of what use she could make this information, Pamela could not say, but all speculation on the subject was put an end to by a sudden flash of light into her cell.

It came, that flash of light, through the grating in the wall, above the door.

To the perception of Pamela that light was as mysterious, if not more so, than the knocking and scratching beneath the floor of the cell.

Slowly the reflection of the iron grating traversed the ceiling of the cell, so that it was evident the light was moving onwards down the stone passage without ; but, listen as she might, Pamela could not hear the faintest sound of any footstep.

What could it all mean ?

A superstitious dread for a short time began to take possession of her, and a feeling something akin to that which had come over her in the cellars of Jacob Sharples's house began to take possession of her heart again.

But such sensations, in the healthy intellect of Pamela, were not likely to last long ; and she felt certain that it was from the material world that all the phenomena by which she was surrounded came.

The scratching and tapping sound beneath the floor of the cell continued.

But the light had now become stationary.

Partly on the ceiling, and partly on one of the walls of the cell, was the reflection of the iron grating, exaggerated in size as it borrowed expansion from the radiation of the rays.

Pamela then crept to the door of the cell and listened.

She placed her ear close to the panel, and then she heard whispered voices.

At first they were too indistinct for her to make them into words ; but the extreme caution with which they were uttered gave way a little, after a time, and she was quite sure two men were speaking.

"Why don't he come then, and have done with it?" said one.

"I don't believe in it," said the other.

"Oh, there's no sort of doubt about it ! He's trying that dodge, and it will be all the worse for him, and for whomsoever gave him the tools !"

"Well, perhaps so. It won't do to let folks get out of the Stone Jug that way !'

"I should think not ! Garnish is the word, and plenty of it !"

"To be sure—to be sure ! It's setting a bad example to let anybody go without the proper price being paid."

"Keep dark, Jem ; I hear the Governor coming !"

"All's right !"

The reflection of the grating on the ceiling and the wall of the cell suddenly disappeared, and the disappearance was accompanied by a faint sound, which Pamela translated into being that produced by the closing the slide of a dark lantern.

She had seen such things in the possession of Jacob Sharples.

But still she listened.

The men continued speaking.

"Who's here, in number nine?"

"Nobody."

"Ain't there, though?"

A violent push was given to the cell door—a push before which Pamela recoiled, although the door remained as fast as a rock.

"Yes, there is, though ; and I can tell you who it is!"

"Who, then?"

"Why, that young girl who gave the 'nibbing cheat' (gallows) the slip so cleverly, and has been green enough to let herself be nabbed again ; and swing upon nothing, she will !"

"Hush ! here's the Governor !"

Footsteps now sounded upon the flagstones of the passage, but they were light, and evidently modified by the desire to make as little noise as possible.

By this time, however, Pamela had begun to have a suspicion as to the exact facts of the case.

To her ideas, all that was taking place might be explained on the supposition that some unfortunate was attempting an escape from the cell next to hers by working a passage beneath the cells.

If such were the case, a fellow-feeling, prisoner as she was, prompted her to make the endeavour to warn the unhappy prisoner of his approaching danger.

She immediately left the door, and made her way to the stone slab beneath which she had heard the tapping and the scratching.

She eagerly rapped with her hand on the stone.

The sound, however, that she so produced was of too faint and dead a character to reach any one below. With the assistance, then, of a small tortoiseshell comb that she took from her hair, she was able to make an acuter sound on the stone.

The tapping and scratching ceased on the instant

Pamela put her lips close down to the stone it was quite a forlorn hope that she could make herself heard.

MOTHER BENDYDYKES AND THE RESUSCITATED CORPSE.

"Save yourself—you are discovered!"

The stone moved.

Pamela put her hands down to it and tried to raise it. She succeeded to a slight degree, and then she heard a voice, in muffled accents, say, from beneath it, "Good heaven! where am I?"

Before Pamela had time to utter a word in reply, there came a loud shout from the adjoining cell.

That shout was echoed by a scream from the escaping prisoner beneath the floor, and the stone slab in Pamela's cell fell at once into its place again.

"Come out! come out!" shouted a voice, and then a pistol-shot was fired; and to the horror of Pamela, who was compelled to be a helpless listener to all that was taking place, she heard a fearful struggle—a struggle of life and death—in the adjoining room.

There were oaths, cries, prayers, and maledictions, and then all was still.

The cell door was shut with a crash, and she could see again the reflection of the iron bars coming slowly across the ceiling of her cell, as one voice cried out, "Bring him along! What care I? It's always a justification for anything to stop an escape. Bring him along!"

She heard the footsteps pass her cell-door, and she was certain that along with them was dragged some heavy, inert body.

CHAPTER LVI.

MOTHER BENDYDYKES RECOGNISES AN OLD FRIEND AND PROVES HER SCIENTIFIC SKILL.

MOTHER BENDYDYKES did not get the coffin of the Doctor's brother open quite so quickly as she was in the habit of performing that operation

Her hands shook so excessively, that she was almost helpless at times. A strange, spasmodic kind of start, too, would every now and then almost jerk her to the floor.

But she persevered.

The coffin-lid was removed. She looked upon the face of the dead.

It was some few seconds, however, before she could gather courage to look at that face otherwise than in a slant, oblique kind of fashion; and when at length she fairly held the light, and looked at it, as one might look at a picture that merited examination, the convulsive, spasmodic movement that had come over her increased fearfully.

Her features appeared as if they were, from some involuntary cause, forced to assume every variety of expression, from the most grotesque to the most hideous.

She tried to speak, but she had no power to utter a word.

The last look that came over her face, then, was one of alarm. Perhaps she thought that death was about to seize upon her as its next victim, and that she would soon fall down in "cold obstruction" by the side of the coffin.

She dropped the light.

She tottered rather than walked to a cupboard in one corner of the room, and from it she, with difficulty, produced an ancient-looking flask, in which was some compound which was not altogether alcoholic, although, from the odour it gave forth, such formed some portion of its contents.

She drank freely, and then she fell to the floor as if all her limbs, all the muscles, all the sinews, all the powerful levers and pulleys of self-support, had succumbed beneath some terrible pressure.

The flask broke.

Mother Bendydykes lay on the floor for a good hour, in a trance that looked like death.

Then she moaned twice or thrice, and then she slowly rose to her feet.

The strange, alarming, convulsive movement of her face and limbs had passed away, and as she made two steps towards the open coffin of the Doctor's brother, she seemed calm, and cool, and collected.

But she looked years older than she had done one hour since.

She clutched the side of the coffin, and uttered a cry of surprise.

The corpse had moved in its narrow hearse, and was half lying on its side, while one of its arms was over the edge of the coffin.

"He lives! he lives!" cried Mother Bendydykes. "He lives! he cannot die yet! Until my time, too, comes, he cannot die!"

Overcoming all repugnance if, indeed, she had any, she seized the body in the coffin by the shoulders, and sat it upright, propping the ghastly head against the wall of the room.

She then flew to the cupboard from which she had taken the flask, the contents of which had thrown her into the seeming trance which had been a period of recovery for her.

But it was not there.

She was not conscious that it had fallen from her hands, and was lying on the floor, broken into fragments.

"The flask! the flask! Oh, what fiend has been here and stolen it? Ah!"

She trod upon a portion of it.

The crackling of the broken glass under her feet aroused her attention to the fact; and then, with a cry of despair, she held the light, which she had re-lighted, downwards, and saw what had happened.

Slowly the body of the Doctor's brother swung over to one side, and fell, with a sickening blow, upon the side of the coffin.

"Hold! hold!" cried the hag. "Live but a moment more! Preserve, for that brief space, the mystery of vitality! Here! here! here!"

The flask, it is true, was broken—it lay upon the floor in fragments, but the circular bottom of it had come off entire, and that still contained about a tablespoonful of the contents of the vessel.

Mother Bendydykes seized upon those few precious drops, as some drowning wretch might seize upon the friendly plank launched for his preservation.

"Live still!—oh, live still!" she shouted, as though she fully believed the occupant of the coffin would hear her, and make some strange and terrific struggle yet for existence.

She flew to the corpse, and caught the apparently dead head by the hair as it hung over the side of the coffin.

"Breathe again—speak again—think again—and suffer again!" she shrieked, as she poured upon the livid lips some portion of the accidentally saved contents of the flask.

At first, no effect ensued.

Then a convulsion shook the corpse.

Mother Bendydykes clapped her hands, and cried out still louder, as if she, by the vehemence of her speech, could arrest the fluttering soul in its passage to eternity.

"Come back—come back again! Live yet; for you have yet some work to do!"

The convulsion continued.

The apparently dead body became endowed with a terrible vitality. It rolled from the coffin, and fell heavily upon the floor.

The hag had laid down the little bit of convex broken glass, but she now seized upon it again; and kneeling by the prostrate form of the Doctor's brother, she forced the remaining few drops of the liquid between his lips.

Then, with an awful groan, he opened his eyes.

"He lives! he lives!"

"Oh, heaven!"

"No, no! No heaven for you! Live yet! Some joy, possibly; and then—extinction! Live—live for me! I have saved you; and you are mine, now, at once and for ever, while the blood shall flow, and the spark still kindle in the human heart!"

She propped him up against a chair.

She wrapped around him a coarse rug; and as she flitted to and fro before his dazed and shrinking eyes, he seemed as though in vain striving to identify her.

She tore off from her head some of the wrappers in which it was enveloped.

Some scanty locks of fair hair fell down from a long, long confinement. The woman was evidently younger than she had seemed to be. She dipped the end of a linen rag in some water, and cleared from her face some stains, and smears, and artificial wrinkles.

A load of years seemed to vanish from her.

She leant forward, and spoke in high, shrieking accents—

"Do you know me now?—do you know me now?"

"Anna!"

The name came in gasping accents from the parched lips of the man who had been numbered with the dead.

"Yes," she added, "my name is Anna; although, in the service of Doctor Haslem, your brother, I was, as you well know, known by another name! I am Anna—the Anna who found out how madly you loved your brother's wife—the Anna who aided and assisted you in that terrible tragedy by which you sought to be revenged of her scorn of your suit! The Anna who did all that——"

"For gold—for gold!" gasped the Doctor's brother—"for gold! The Anna who soiled her soul with such a world of guilt for gold!"

"No!" thundered the hag—"no!"

"It was so!"

"False—false as your own heart, is the imputation!"

"I paid the price!"

"And there it is!"

Mother Bendydkes tore up a small portion of the flooring of the room which turned upon a hinge. It was not a space larger than a foot in length, and only comprehended the width of one floor-board; and from the cavity beneath she extracted a bag which she flung at the feet—indeed, on the feet—of the Doctor's brother.

"There is the gold!"

"Woman—woman, you are mad!"

"I know it!"

"Help! help! I sinned for passion! I obeyed the mysterious instincts of those human passions that providence——"

The hag burst out into a screaming laugh.

"He talks of providence!—he, the liar—the suborner of false evidence—the perjurer—the murderer!"

"No, no!—oh, heaven!—no!"

"I say 'murderer;' for who is it that sleeps the sleep of death beneath the dark waters of the river?"

"Forbear!—oh, forbear!"

"Your brother's wife——"

"Mercy!"

"The beautiful, the innocent, and the true! A miracle—a miracle from heaven, if there be a heaven—saved the child—saved Pamela, your niece!"

"But you had the gold?"

"It is here!"

"You hoard it, as a miser gloats upon his wealth, and finds his joy more in its continued possession, than in its exchange for all that gold can produce;—you hoard it, and gloat upon it!"

"It is gone!"

She lifted the bag of gold—for such it seemed, and such doubtless it was—and flung it crashing through the casement. It fell into the high tide of the river with a sullen splash.

"It is gone! Does the miser cast away his hoard?"

The Doctor's brother now held up one of his hands, and looked at the thin, tendonous fingers as he said, moaningly, "Why snatch me from the trance of death, which would so soon have been death in all its reality? I felt nothing—I knew nothing—the pang was past!"

"I know not! It was to be! We are all the creatures of a fate which may not be resisted! It was to be, and so it is! But you say you sinned from the mad suggestions of human passions?"

"I do—I do! I loved that woman! Oh, she was exceeding fair! I loved her, and the hopeless passion eat into my soul, and drove me mad!"

"Be it so! Now listen!"

"Listen to what? To more reproaches?"

"No; to a confession! There was one who loved you—even as you loved your brother's wife—with a wild, unholy passion! You saw it not; for your whole mind and heart were wrapped up in the divinity you have shaped out of the woman you adored! She then—that is to say, the one who loved you, but who never by word, or gesture, or look, procured from you a glance of tenderness to light up the gloom of her heart—she then bethought her of what could be done to separate you from all humankind!"

"Separate me from humanity? Could any one who loved wish that?"

"Yes; because—because she, and she alone, then would cling to you, and you would be all her own in your isolation!"

"I see!"

"You only begin to see! The charm which was to shut you off from all men was to be one of guilt; and when you yourself proposed to me to help you in your schemes to blast for ever——"

"You?—you?"

"To turn from house—home—husband—child—the innocent wife, I aided you, to make you that isolated, crime-stained wretch that only I would cling to!"

"You?—you?"

"Yes! I, too, loved; my acts, like yours, were born of human passions and despair!"

The living man, who had been rescued so strangely from the grave, wrung his hands and groaned.

"Yes," added the hag; "we are now equal, you perceive! We both loved—were both scorned—we both took counsel of our evil passions, and both committed crime! Now, at the last, we meet, and are on equal terms! What say you to me now?"

The Doctor's brother struck his breast, and uttered strange cries.

"Speak—oh, speak to me—Joseph Haslem, speak to me!"

He looked at her wildly.

He looked down at himself, arrayed as he was, in the grave-clothes; and then he wept like an infant.

"Speak to me, I say—oh, speak!"

"You have saved me!"

"From death? I have! What is to be my reward for that?"

"Let us fly—away—far away from England, at once and for ever! My brother—all who knew me—all the world believe me dead! Let me be still dead to them all, and I will fly with you!"

The hag seemed to be choking; she tore at her throat for a few seconds with both hands; and then she fell to the floor in a swoon.

"Help! help!—oh, help! No—there is no help here!" cried Joseph Haslem. "No, no! She is dead! Alive and dead! I dead, and she alive; and now a new life to me, and death to her! What shall I do?—what can I do! May heaven——She has no belief in life beyond the grave; but I have—yes, I have—I have belief and dread! There is—there is a heaven above us!"

"Hilloa! hilloa!" shouted a voice from the direction of the river. "Hilloa! Mother Bendydkes! Hilloa, I say!"

CHAPTER LVII.

PAMELA FINDS HER WAY OVER NEWGATE, AND MEETS WITH A FRIEND AND AN ENEMY.

PAMELA listened with agonized attention to the retreat of the Governor and the turnkeys along the stone passage outside her cell, as they bore along with them what she had too much reason to suppose to be the dead body of one of the prisoners of Newgate.

Little idea had she, in the simplicity of her mind

of the real prison life which was passed by the sad souls that found their way into that gloomy house.

And far was she from guessing that murder was a thing that could be, and was but too often, accomplished within those cold and terrible stone walls. only to be flimsily excused on the plea of necessary violence to prevent an escape.

A cold feel was at her heart, and she felt as if all strength had departed from her, carrying with it even the desire to live.

But Pamela was young.

The life-blood that flowed in her veins might, by the hardships she had endured, and the terrors that had encompassed her, be diminished in quantity, but what there was of it was fine and light.

It soon revisited her pallid cheeks, and she felt that she was still of this world, and had yet much to do with all its affairs—its hopes, its fears, its dangers, and its successes.

Then, as all became so profoundly still about her—as she began to feel that she was indeed alone again, and to look upon any other disturbance of the silence of that part of the prison for many hours as not probable, —new ideas found a home in the brain of the fair young girl.

She remembered how close to her had been that mysterious tapping on the stone slab that formed a portion of the flooring of her cell.

The few words, too. that she had overheard were all-sufficient to point to the conclusion that some prisoner, who had been in solitary neighbourhood to her, must have made some progress in working his way beneath the gloomy walls of Newgate

Curiosity urged her to some action.

A faint hope, too, of escape, sprung up in her heart

It was a very faint hope, that—faint as that mysterious glimmer which now and then, in the darkest night, will seem to illumine the night-clouds as though with a promise that day was at hand, long before the first rays of the sun could possibly show themselves.

But it was a hope.

Pamela approached the stone slab. She strove to move it.

The stone shook, but still it seemed deeply embedded in the earth.

The reflection of a few moments now enabled Pamela to hit upon a means of furnishing herself with a tolerably efficient tool to work with.

The water that was allowed her in her cell—and which was one of the things that even the bitterest malice of the worst governor that ever carried out his private ends in Newgate dared not deny to a prisoner—was in a coarse, common, brown pitcher.

Pamela thought that if she broke that pitcher, it might furnish her with some piece or pieces handily shaped for use in clearing away the trodden earth of the cell around the moveable slab of stone.

The idea was reasonable enough.

The pitcher was easily broken against the stone walls.

But Pamela took good care to fortify herself for work by a good draught of its contents before she destroyed it.

Then she felt piece after piece, and looked at them too, for the dim night lantern in the corridor that the cells opened from—although the amount of light it sent into those cells, through their narrow gratings, was something.

It is said, and no doubt truly, that those who for many years have been confined in the darkest dungeons. will at length become so accustomed to the atmosphere about them, that they could see to pick up the smallest pin from the dark, noisome floor.

Pamela had not been long enough the inmate of a prison to test this fact, but she had certainly got accustomed to the dim light of the cell.

Her young eyes served her well, and she could see all things darkly.

Armed, then, with a peculiarly shaped piece of the broken pitcher, Pamela set to work upon the floor of her prison.

She did not find much difficulty in clearing the mould and rubbish from around the stone slab; and as, from time to time, she felt that it lay most decidedly looser to her touch, she was encouraged to continue her work.

Then the stone made a sudden movement, as though it were about to fall down into some cavity beneath.

If it did so, all her labour would be in vain.

With the energy of despair, Pamela took both her hands to it, and on the impulse of the moment she raised the stone.

Perhaps, in cooler moments, it would have been beyond her strength; but as it was, she cast it aside on to the floor of the cell.

Beneath was a hole or cavity, some three feet in depth

What could it mean?

Whither could it lead?

Pamela felt all round the sides of this cavity, and she found that in one direction only was it free and open.

That direction was towards the cell in which she had heard the fearful tumult so short a time since

Then Pamela comprehended that she was at the end of a channel that with infinite labour had, no doubt, been worked by her neighbour from one cell to the other.

She did not stop to ask herself a multitude of questions, not one of which she could have replied to satisfactorily—such as, what object a prisoner could have had in trying merely to get from one cell to another?—but commending herself to the protection of heaven, she made up her mind, if it were possible so to do, to explore the passage for herself.

It was not an easy task.

But still, by one so light, so slim, so active as that young girl, it might be done.

The heart of poor Pamela beat fast as she made her way thus mole-like in the earth—but the distance was short.

A welcome gush of cool air came upon her brow.

Another minute, and she emerged in the next cell.

The door was open.

The careless warder had not thought it necessary to close and fasten the door of a cell which had no inhabitant.

Pamela stepped out into the narrow corridor beyond the range of cells, with a feeling of infinite relief.

And yet what had she accomplished?

How far could she say she was towards the free, open air outside those dreadful walls?

Hope almost died within her as she stopped to listen for any sounds in the prison that might direct her where to go.

No—all was still!

Pamela pursued the corridor in the direction past her cell door until she came to an iron grating.

It was locked.

A bunch of keys, however, were on the other side, one of which was in the lock.

The grating was composed of stout upright bars of iron, interlaced with wire of some strength and thickness

No man's hand could have passed through the small meshes of the wire. But those who constructed that gate had not calculated upon so small and flexible a hand as Pamela's having a desire to pass it.

The long, slender fingers passed through with ease, and not only was the iron gate speedily unlocked, but Pamela got possession of a bunch of keys that might be of the greatest service to her.

It was with a strange, mystical sort of feeling now that Pamela took her way through Newgate

She had not the slightest idea of whither in the prison the route she had taken would lead her. It might be to freedom—it might be to still deeper and more stringent imprisonment.

Like some fair spirit which has lost its way through the blue ether of the universe, and alighted on some strange planet the existence of which was unknown

PAMELA UNEXPECTEDLY MEETS WITH THE POST-MESSENGER.

No. 18.—FELON'S DAUGHTER.

before, Pamela wandered onward with the heavy bunch of warder's keys in her hand.

She came to another grating.

The same key that had opened the former one opened that.

She came to a flight of steps. It was a gratification to her that they ascended, instead of descending.

The process of going upwards seemed to lift her above some of the cares and turmoils of her position.

Mechanically, and she knew not why, she counted the steps.

There were thirty-two.

A closed door was at the top of them, and it was some time before Pamela could find a key to fit it. At length she did so, and for the first time in her peregrinations through old Newgate, on that occasion she trod upon boards.

She was getting to the ordinary habitable part of the prison.

Another surprise likewise was in store for Pamela.

She found it was daylight.

From the time that Pamela had heard the sound of midnight boomed forth from old St. Paul's and echoed by the bell of St. Sepulchre's, it seemed to her to be but a few fleeting hours—perhaps two, at the utmost, but in reality that night in Newgate had passed away.

The light that came on to the stair-head, on which she found herself, was not bright, but still it was the blue light of day.

Pamela paused now, for the first time since quitting her cell, to try to come to some conclusion in respect to her route.

There were two paths open to her.

The top of the staircase was but the commencement of a long corridor, that seemed to go the whole width of that portion of the prison; but close at hand there was another flight of stairs, carpeted, and apparently conducting to some of the best apartments of the building.

Which course should she take?

Pamela decided upon the carpeted stairs, and fled up them like a bird upon the wing; for she was getting impatient and anxious now that she saw the daylight.

At the top of the stairs, before she could sufficiently recover herself to stoop down, even with the poor hope of avoiding any one, she was met by a man carrying some letters.

Pamela uttered a half-shriek.

The man indulged in an exclamation, and dropped some of his letters.

Then Pamela did not attempt to escape; she made no show of resistance, but, picking up the letters, she handed them to the bewildered-looking messenger, as she said, "Oh, sir, will you not have some pity for me, in case some child of your own should chance to be so persecuted and so unhappy as I am?"

CHAPTER LVIII.

PAMELA SEEMS TO BE HOPELESSLY ABANDONED TO A TERRIBLE FATE.

WE left Lord Malvern at the precise moment when he had delivered his horse to the care of the ostler at the inn-yard opposite Newgate, and while the disreputable hackney coachman was nodding on his box at the gate of the prison; but, anxious as we are to inform our readers of what Lord Malvern, the bold and the eccentric, did on that occasion, we must still keep him waiting for a brief space, while we follow the fortunes of our poor Pamela in Newgate.

The man with the letters looked astonished and terrified.

"A child of my own?" he cried. "Great heaven, I have one, my dear!"

"Ah!—then you will pity, and, perhaps, befriend me?"

"Gracious me!—what can I do?"

"Save me—save me! Show me a route out of this dreadful prison-house; for, although I am here, I am, indeed and in truth, innocent!"

It would have required a person of very strong sensibilities indeed, to believe that anything in the shape of guilt could reside in such a face as that of the fair Pamela.

"My dear girl, you terrify me! I am only the post-office messenger that comes every morning with the letter-bag for Newgate!"

"Where am I? I mean in what part of the prison am I?"

The good-hearted post-messenger would no doubt have replied to Pamela's question readily enough; but at the moment he was about to do so, a door not far from where he and Pamela stood was flung open, and a man put out his head, crying angrily, "Am I to have no letters this morning? Where is the post-messenger? Jones!—Jones, I say?"

"Down—stoop!"

Pamela crouched down below the top step of the staircase, while the post-messenger stood so as to hide her from the eyes of the man, who was no other than the Governor, who had looked through the doorway so angrily and so abruptly.

"Here are your letters, sir."

"Then why the deuce don't you bring them to me, idiot? How do I know what important communication may be there?"

"Here—here—here!" cried the agitated post-messenger, as in his eagerness to prevent the Governor from even getting the chance of a sight of Pamela, he made a kind of butt at him with the letters as though he were an enraged bull, and meant to toss him.

The Governor, who was not a courageous man—a fact that might be easily guessed from the fact that he was a confirmed bully—retreated backwards into his room, and fell over a chair.

"What do you mean?—what the deu—the—a—deuce do you mean, sir?"

"Nothing, sir—nothing! That's all, sir! No more letters, sir. Shall I shut the door, sir? Yes!—oh, dear yes—I don't mind trouble! Shall I lock it, if you please, sir, on this side?"

"Mad, mad—he is mad!" cried the Governor. "Help, help! Clap a pair of handcuffs on him! The fellow is as mad as a March hare! Help, help!"

The Governor's hand was upon the bell-handle in his room when the post-messenger ran up to him and stopped him, saying, "Oh, sir, have some mercy—some consideration! Let me make to you the same appeal that reached my heart! Have you a child?"

"A what?"

"A child of your own?—a young girl, say about sixteen years of age, so beautiful—so innocent—so despairing——"

The Governor was more than ever convinced that some accession of insanity had come over the poor post-messenger.

"What do you mean, sir? I a child—I a daughter? No, thank heaven!"

"Then she is lost! There is no humanity in the heart of one who cries 'Thank heaven, he has no child to love him!'"

The post-messenger turned and fled from the presence of the Governor, with the intention of warning Pamela to make good her retreat as quickly as she could, in any direction but that one; but the Governor's suspicions were thoroughly awakened, and as he was no longer prevented from ringing the bell, he did so, in the short, impatient manner which betokens some alarm.

"Fly, fly, my dear girl!" cried the post-messenger, hastily.

Alas! he only brought immediate danger upon Pamela by the injunction. A couple of turnkeys came tearing up the staircase at speed. She must encounter them or the Governor. It was a more natural impulse for her to fly before those two men, than to go to meet them; so she made her way to the top of the stairs, and was greeted by a shout of surprise, as the Governor recognised her so soon as he set eyes upon her.

The young girl drew herself proudly up, and shook off the touch of the Governor, as he tried to catch her by the wrist.

"Yes, I am Pamela; but not Pamela Sharples The villain who has brought distress and danger upon me, thank heaven, is not my father!"

The poor post-messenger was wringing his hands in grief.

The two warders, who had so hastily replied to the Governor's alarm-bell, stood irresolute at the top of the stairs, awaiting some orders.

A dark smile came over the Governor's face, and he made a mock bow of respect to Pamela, as he said, smilingly, "Oh, I'm sure, I beg your young ladyship's pardon! I thought you were Pamela Sharples, the felon's daughter; but if it's all a mistake, why, pray walk into my room, and we will put it to-rights."

Pamela hesitated.

The Governor beckoned to the two warders, and made a sign to them. They rushed upon Pamela, and she was carried to the Governor's room with a celerity that set resistance at defiance.

"Go," said the Governor, "but be within call! Pamela Sharples, or Pamela anything else that you like to call yourself, or that people like to call you, I believe you are a girl of spirit, and I have a proposition to make to you!"

Pamela looked into his eyes to see if the promised proposition had any of the elements of mercy in it. But she did not reply to him.

"Come now," he added, "I know how you and I can make our fortunes—ay, that we can, and by a much easier mode than passing bad money, my girl! What say you? The City is full of rich old merchants, who have gold in ingots stored away in their great tall mansions in the back slums and lanes, and only want a little coaxing to part with any amount of it! You shall be my wife! You shall then do the coaxing, and we will share the plunder; for your beauty does nine-tenths of the business without a word!"

The innocence of Pamela prevented her from fully appreciating the infamy of this proposal, but she shrank with an instinctive feeling of evil from the man who made it.

"Now! now!"

"You refuse?"

"Absolutely—now and for ever!"

A dark scowl came over the Governor's face.

"My lass, did you never hear of Jasper Browne's cupboard?"

Pamela shook her head.

"Very likely you never did. Well, Jasper Browne was Governor of Newgate in the time of Queen Anne; and as he had no end of Jesuits, and traitors, and such like folks in Newgate, when the Tower was full, he had a cupboard made in this room with a marble floor, which could be let down to one of the most noisome dungeons of old Newgate, or wound up again at pleasure, so that he could make what terms he chose with his prisoners Now, I am the Governor, in place of Jasper Browne, and it is my cupboard now. What do you say to that?"

"I have nothing to say to you. If I am accused of crime, as it appears I am, although heaven knows how falsely, I at least desire to be tried by the judges of the land"

"Oh, indeed! I thought all that little process had been gone through. You are condemned, girl; and all that need be done now is to bring you before the justices, and identify you, and you can be hanged without further trouble."

Pamela shuddered.

"But," added the Governor, "I still hold my little proposal open to you, or—behold!"

He flung open the door of a cupboard in the room, and casting an ambiguous glance at Pamela, he added, "This is Jasper Browne's cupboard."

Pamela glanced through the narrow doorway that was opened in the wall, and she could not forbear a slight expression of fear as she pictured to herself the possible terrible descent through some chimney-like channel in the gloomy walls of Newgate.

The Governor wished to improve upon the occasion, and raise Pamela's fears to the highest point He assumed an air of determined brutality.

"Decide, girl, and decide quickly, for I have no time to waste even on such as you."

Pamela, alarmed by his gestures, retreated behind a chair, to the back of which she clung.

"You are human," she said, "and even your heart must know some touch of heavenly pity."

"Pity? No! It is a short word that I know nothing about. You may cry out, and show fight if you will; nobody cares for such things here. And as for the reward which that Doctor offers for you, it sinks into insignificance compared with what I mean to make by you. It is your fate, girl, I tell you, and resistance is useless"

There was a strange light in the eyes of the Governor, as he made two steps towards Pamela, who could not forbear a shriek of dismay, and then there came two sharp raps on the outer panel of the door, which was opened at the same instant, and a loud voice cried out, in the monotonous tones in which visitors are announced "Sir John Pope!"

The Governor uttered a malediction.

Pamela shrank down out of sight behind the chair; for, of all the names that could be uttered by human lips, there was not one that brought with it such fearful associations as that of Sir John Pope, *alias* Captain Sang, from whose baneful clutches she had so recently escaped by what might almost be considered a miracle.

With that same ghastly aspect which he had presented in the breakfast-room of the Secretary of State, the villain Sang made his appearance.

Darting one glance of sharp suspicion round the apartment, he approached the Governor, and handed him a folded paper, without uttering a single word.

The Governor took it in ominous silence, and as the door of the room was closed by the turnkey who had announced Sir John Pope, it was evident that these two men kept wary eyes upon each other's movements, as each felt convinced he beheld an assassin.

"Sir John Pope!" gasped the Governor.

"Why not?"

"I heard—that is, some one said there was a report that—that you were hurt—killed!"

"You see the contrary. I have nine lives—six of them only are expended."

The Governor glanced at the written paper, and turned pale.

"Well, sir," said Captain Sang, "is it your pleasure or not to comply at once with the order I have the honour to bring you?"

"This paper," muttered the Governor, licking his parched lips as he spoke, "purports to be an order from the Secretary of State for Home Affairs to deliver to you the girl named Pamela Sharples, who was in my custody."

"Was!" cried Sang, as a livid look came over his countenance. "Is, you should say, Mr. Governor! She could only pass from your custody to the gallows, without such an order as this! Surrender her at once; and you shall not find it the worst morning's work that this week may present to you!"

"She has escaped!"

"False!—false as——"

"Nay, Sir John Pope; restrain yourself. I will send a turnkey with you to the very cell she inhabited, and if you find her there, take her, in the name of heaven; for she seems to be more trouble than profit to Newgate!"

"I need not go so far," said Sang, as in two long strides he reached the chair behind which Pamela had a temporary refuge; "she is here!"

Pamela sprang to her feet.

The Governor dashed the Secretary of State's letter to the floor, and stamped his foot upon it.

"Mine!" said Sang, as he made an effort to seize the arm of Pamela.

She fled from him with a shriek of dismay.

The mysterious inlet in the wall, which the Governor called Jasper Browne's cupboard, met her eyes Any fate was preferable to falling again into the hands of the villanous Sang.

"Let me descend then to the lowest depths of Newgate! Let me find companionship with the reptiles that crawl in its most noisome dungeon! Any fate is preferable to companionship with thee!"

Pamela fully expected, from what the Governor had said to her, that the floor of that seeming cupboard would descend with her, but it remained immoveable.

The Governor, however, made a rapid movement to a portion of the wainscoting adjoining, and crying out in a defiant voice to Sang, he said, "The girl's fate is in my hands! You may have her, Sir John Pope, but not in life!"

"Ah! say you so?" cried Sang, as passion made the blood rush to his face, giving him that awful aspect from which he had acquired his name of Sang—"say you so? Then take your reward in full!"

The villanous highwayman must have had a pistol concealed in the ample sleeve of his coat, or it never could have reached his hand with such celerity as to enable him to discharge it full in the face of the Governor of Newgate.

The report, in the rather small apartment, came with a stunning effect upon the ears of Pamela, and before she could see how it had fared with the Governor, Sir John Pope had flung the door of the room open, and lifting the Secretary of State's letter from the floor, he called out aloud, "Who will disobey the order of the highest authority in this realm, under the Crown?"

Several turnkeys and warders of the prison appeared on the threshold of the apartment with wonderful celerity.

The smoke cleared away, and they saw the Governor sitting in a chair, looking ghastly and blackened about the face, from the discharge of the pistol.

"It was only powder," said Sang. "We had a slight disagreement Who among you has authority sufficient to act upon an order from the Secretary of State? Or rather, I should ask who among you has audacity sufficient to dispute it?"

The turnkeys looked at each other with indecision.

"I am shot through the head! I'm a dead man!" said the Governor.

"Pho, pho!" said Sang; "a little warm water will see you to-rights."

"Villain!"

Sang shrugged his shoulders.

"A hard word, Mr. Governor; but we shall have abundant opportunities of settling our little difference in time to come. Pamela Sharples, you are my prisoner!"

"Save me! save me! Oh, if you be men, save me from this fiend in human shape!"

Summoning all his latent strength to his aid, Sang flung his left arm round the slender waist of Pamela Sharples. and flourishing the Secretary of State's order in his right hand, before the eyes of the warders and turnkeys of Newgate, he cried aloud, "Dispute my passage at your peril! There is not one of you whose place is worth a word of contradiction to this imperative order! Pamela Sharples, you are mine! It is fate."

CHAPTER LIX.

HANDSOME JEMMY REACHES MOTHER BENDYDYKES AT AN OPPORTUNE MOMENT.

THE course of our eventful narrative now compels us for a brief space to leave Pamela at this crisis of her varied fortunes, and to assume a presence with those whose vices and passions have surrounded that fair young heart with such an atmosphere of danger, and evoked, so to speak, Pamela's Perils!

We left the Doctor's brother in the house of that strange, mysterious woman who had rescued him from the grave at the moment that his own cries and lamentations were interrupted by a voice from the river.

They both knew the voice.

It was that of Handsome Jemmy, the highwayman, and the sound of it seemed to awaken the hag from the swoon into which she had fallen, and which, to the eyes of the physician's brother, looked so like death.

She raised her head and listened.

She dashed aside that long hair which she had so nimbly liberated from its disguise and confinement, and an expression of terror came over her face as she bent forward towards the window, to be certain that it was a human voice which she heard.

The Doctor's brother, who had been so strangely snatched back again through the portals of death, was not less alarmed than the hag.

And yet, surely, he was free now from all dread of human retribution? He had nothing to fear from the laws or from the opinions of his fellow-men, since by all who knew him, or who could speculate upon his guilt, but that one who had been instrumental in restoring him to life, he was believed to be quietly sleeping the calm sleep of death in the burying-ground of the new chapel in Tottenham Court Road.

But still he looked terrified.

"Hilloa!—hilloa, Mother Bendydykes! Open—open! I must and will see you!"

There were several blows struck upon the window.

All was darkness now in the room where the hag, the Doctor's brother, and the coffin were; and, from the outside, it would be exceedingly difficult to see any of the contents of the apartment.

The dense clouds that had swept up during the night from the south-west, and had brought under them the squally fitful gale that had bred such a commotion on the river, still hung heavily between earth and heaven.

The water still beat high against the old house of Mother Bendydykes.

Whoever it was that sought her on that night, from that direction, must have a boat; and it was probably with one of the oars that Handsome Jemmy, the highwayman, struck at the window.

But neither Mother Bendydykes nor the Doctor's brother, whom she had rescued from death, spoke.

It was probably from very different mental sensations that they kept silent.

The hag was fearful that this visit from the highwayman portended her no good in relation to some of the past acts of her life.

The Doctor's brother, Matthew Joseph Haslem, as was his real name—his brother calling him always Matthew, and the hag preferring the name of Joseph—shook in every limb, and seemed to have a terrible dread of the appearance of Handsome Jemmy.

But the dashing highwayman was not a person to be easily put aside or baffled when he chose to see any one, let the difficulties be what they might.

Again he struck at the back window of Mother Bendydykes' house.

Again he shouted aloud from the boat he had on the high tide of the river.

"Hilloa! house! house! Mother Bendydykes, unless the devil has been and claimed his own, and you are no longer here, I will see you!"

Then a pane of glass—it was about the only whole one left—was broken in the window.

Purposely or accidentally, Handsome Jemmy had committed the act; but be that how it may, he was enabled to get close to the window-sill, and so look into the room.

When the glass was broken a sharp cry of alarm came from the lips of Matthew Haslem.

The hag echoed it

But she had not wholly lost her presence of mind.

She seized the coffin from which the Doctor's brother had been so short a time since rescued, and dashed it on one side.

HANDSOME JEMMY PAYS A VISIT TO MOTHER BENDYDYKES.

By almost the same action, she released the folds of a thick, heavy. black curtain, which, like some huge snake, was coiled up close to the ceiling.

It fell in rapid convolutions to the floor, cutting off a portion of the room of about four feet in depth

"Hide!—hide!" whispered Mother Bendydykes to Matthew Haslem. "Hide yourself until I can rid us of that man!"

Matthew Haslem did not need to be urged twice to do as Mother Bendydykes advised, but he shrunk behind the black curtain, with a feeling of great relief that it was between him and the unexpected and most unwelcome visitor.

The hag went to the window.

"Who calls? A curse, a blight, and a desolation fall upon you, whoever you are!"

"Oh, spare your breath, mother!" replied Handsome Jemmy. "I care not for your curses; and, besides, you know as well as I do, the old proverb."

"Away!—away with you! I want neither you nor your proverbs!"

"Curses are like young chickens," added Handsome Jemmy: "they come home to roost."

"What want you? Wretch! what want you here? Say your say, and begone!"

"I want to say a say that cannot be said all in a moment."

"Then come some other time!"

"No time like the present. My horse waits for me at the 'Wheatsheaf,' in Whitefriars, and I don't want to waste time."

"I am busy—I am busy!"

"So am I; and, therefore, if you don't open the window, so that I may step in, I shall be busier still for the next few moments in breaking it down bodily."

A cracking sound about the window frame sufficiently showed that Handsome Jemmy was quite inclined to be as good as his word, and that, too, as quickly as possible.

There can be little doubt but that Mother Bendydykes had in her house—ay, and in all probability, quite ready to her hand—the means of taking the life of any unwelcome intruder; but there was a something about the bold, high spirit of the handsome highwayman which prevented her from proceeding to such extremities with him.

"Advance another inch in your violence, and you are a dead man!"

"Stuff!"

"I swear it!"

"Nonsense, mother, nonsense! You are by far too fond of me to send me floating down the Thames a corpse! Come, come! I am on no uncivil errand Let me in, and I will not detain you long."

"In the name of all that is merciful, now, what do you want?"

"To speak to you about somebody who I am sure you know well, for more than twice or thrice have I seen him darken your doorstep with his shadow!"

"Who?—who?"

"The brother of the Court Physician in Bedford Square!"

"Ah!"

"Yes, that is the man!"

With, then, that recollection ringing in his ears, Matthew uttered a deep groan.

"What is the matter now, mother?" said Jemmy. "That was not a healthy groan!"

"It was not I!"

"Who then?"

"Hush! You are yet of earth, and those who have passed the gates of death do not choose to be questioned!"

"Pho, pho! Don't think, Mother Bendydykes, to frighten me! I am one of those sort of fellows who deny nothing because they know nothing, but who, at the same time, fear nothing!"

"Beware!"

"Ha, ha! Come, now, if you have any ghost on hand, let me see him! I would put my horse to his mettle, and gallop him within half an inch of a broken wind, only to look for half a moment into the face of a real ghost!"

"You would?"

"On my faith, yes!"

"Come in, then!"

The hag undid the window, and, without a moment's hesitation, Handsome Jemmy stepped into the room.

"Now, what have you to say of Matthew Joseph Haslem?"

"Ah! Matthew Joseph! Is that his name?"

"It is."

"Humph! M. J. H."

"Those are his initials."

"A light! a light, good Mother Bendydykes! I want a light!"

"No! No light here!"

"Why not?"

"You might see those your mortal eyes would fail you in looking upon!"

"What folly! Look you here, mother! I come to ask you some questions, not because I think you have any dealings with another world that may be supposed to know and communicate to you the secrets of this one, but because I know you to be a clever, shrewd woman, who from time to time has had many things communicated to you by people who came to consult you."

"Say on."

"Then, in the first place, I should like a light, because I have something to show you."

"What?"

"A locket, edged with pearls, and attached to a Venetian gold chain, as the particular pattern is named. That locket I was not aware could be opened, until Mr. Matthew Haslem, the Court Physician's brother, opened it."

A deep groan came from behind the curtain.

"What or who is that?" asked Jemmy.

"Heed it not, but say on."

"Well, since then I have made a very careful and strict examination of the locket, and I find on it the initials—very small, yet sufficiently legible—of M. J. H."

The groan came again.

"Come, come, Mother Bendydykes, you are playing some of your common-place tricks upon me. that, no doubt, frighten common-place people. Attend to me, and answer me, if you can."

"I made no sound."

"Well, I don't care about it. Am I to consider that those initials of M. J. H. mean Matthew Joseph Haslem?"

"You may."

"You may!" echoed a deep, hollow voice, that seemed to come from the tomb.

That was the voice of the Doctor's brother from behind the black curtain. He did not intend to speak, but he found himself impelled to do so, as if from some power that it was not in mortal nature to resist

"Then," said Handsome Jemmy, "putting this and that together, I am led to the conclusion that Matthew Haslem knew something about me, and as it is possible that he was what I may call an intimate of yours, you know it likewise."

"No."

"Do not say no! The grave has closed over him, as you well know. I don't feel able to explain to myself how it was, but as I passed to-night the iron railings of the grave-yard in which he lies, my heart seemed to be weighed down with an unaccountable sense of oppression; and tears, hot scalding tears, came to my eyes, so that—so that I was compelled to say to myself more than once, 'What is this dead man to me, that I should weep for him?'"

There was a tone of emotion about the highwayman which made a deep impression upon Mother Bendydykes; and after the pause of a few seconds, she spoke to him in low, but gentle tones.

"Tell me all, and I will do my best to answer you. Tell me how you came by that locket, and speak freely of your life."

"In good faith, I have little to tell. At the age of two, I was found on a door-step, with the locket round my neck; and the only other remarkable thing that I can recollect is, that there was rather a deep cut or scratch on the back of my left hand, the scar of which still remains."

A shriek burst from the lips of the Doctor's brother.

Handsome Jemmy stepped towards the window, and placed his hand upon one of his pistols.

"Ware that! ware that!" he cried. "Whoever interferes with me, will catch a Tartar!"

"Peace! peace!" cried Mother Bendydykes. "What does all this mean?"

The black curtain was violently agitated.

"Light! light!" moaned Matthew Haslem. "Light! I had little doubt, but it is all removed now! Light! light!"

"Peace! Are you mad?"

"No, no. But I shall be, if—if——"

"If what?"

"If I am not permitted, before I die, to look upon the face of my son!"

CHAPTER LX.

CONTAINS THE PARTICULARS OF A FEARFUL CATASTROPHE THAT OVERTOOK MATTHEW HASLEM

As Matthew Haslem uttered these words, he seemed to fall against the black curtain, so that he emerged somewhat from it, sufficiently for his head and one arm to be clear of it.

"What is all this?" shouted Handsome Jemmy. "Am I alive—am I awake or asleep—or is there indeed such a thing as listening to the voice of the dead, after the ground has seemed to close over them for ever and for ever?"

Mother Bendydykes was fearfully agitated.

She had now all the disposition in the world to procure a light; but such was the trembling that seized all her limbs, that she was unable to do so.

Two such romances, with all their exciting and agitating particulars, as had occurred to her in that one night, were more even than her iron nerves could stand.

She made vain efforts to compose herself sufficiently to reach the materials for getting a light.

But all was in vain.

She sunk in a huddled-up posture to the floor.

The highwayman could but dimly see her.

He had, for once in a way, no matches himself, although he was, professionally, generally provided with them; so he did the best thing he could, which was to fling the casement wide open, and get into the room, along with air in abundance, as much of the lingering night-light that the clouds would afford, as possible.

That was but a small amount.

Fortune, however, favoured the acquisition of a faint illumination.

On the opposite side of the river, some furnace door of a factory of some kind was suddenly opened, and a broad red gleam of light came over the water.

It shone into that gloomy apartment at Mother Bendydykes' house, tinting everything and everybody with a crimson glow.

Then Handsome Jemmy could see about him tolerably well.

Mother Bendydykes was on the floor, in the huddled-up position she had assumed; but it was not upon her that the handsome highwayman cast the most of his regards, but upon a terrible face and figure which had now completely emerged from behind the black curtain.

Somebody attired in grave-clothes, which, with the red light upon them that came over the river, had the strangest appearance conceivable.

It was Matthew Haslem.

The dreadfully agitated and weakened condition of his nerves deprived him at that moment of the power of articulation. All he could do was to stretch forth his arms, and clutch at the empty air, as if he longed to hold something in his grasp, and yet could not move a pace forward to reach it.

Was it his son that he wished to hold to his breast, if it were but for one fleeting moment, before his fainting spirit fled to the realms of the unknown?

Ah, yes! Even that man, so stained in iniquity, had, deep in his sinful heart, a love for his child!

His own son!

But Handsome Jemmy was in no hurry to cast himself into the embraces of such a seeming spectre.

Keeping as far towards the window as he could without actually stepping out of it, the highwayman warded off the seeming red apparition in grave-clothes, as he cried, in accents of mingled horror and curiosity, "Speak, if you be mortal; or if you be of another world, still I will not fear!"

Matthew Haslem made an effort at articulation, but for some seconds more it was a vain one. Then he did manage to make his words, so far as mere words were concerned, comprehended.

"Son—son! Father—son! Own—own son! Oh, heaven—heaven!"

"Speak again!" cried the highwayman. "Your voice is that of Mr. Matthew Joseph Haslem! Are you —were you my father?"

"Father!—father!—father!"

"And—and you come from the grave to tell me so?"

"Yes, from the grave!—from it—from it! But I live —snatched from it to live—to hope—to weep! Oh, if I could only weep! To kneel at the feet of my own son! I am—I am your repentant—your sinning, wicked father!"

"Good heaven!"

Matthew Haslem tried to kneel at the feet of the highwayman; but the effort was too much for him, and he fell forward on his face.

The fall of flesh and bones was of too substantial a character for Handsome Jemmy to doubt for a moment the corporeality of the seeming vision before him. He darted forward, and raised Matthew Haslem from the floor. He placed him in an old arm-chair, and then he cried out, almost menacingly, "Woman—woman, rouse yourself! You see we are in darkness once again! Let us have light, or I will awaken the neighbours to procure it! Quick—quick!"

The furnace door on the opposite side of the river had been suddenly closed, and the red light that shone into the room of Mother Bendydykes was gone.

This appeal to the hag seemed to rouse her from the state of helpless depression into which she had fallen.

She rose up and tottered across the room, and in a few seconds a faint light from a match flashed through the darkness.

Jemmy the Highwayman then saw the necessity of closing the window again, if he expected any flame to live in the air of that room, and he did so.

He then saw that it was not in the power of Mother Bendydykes, in consequence of the trembling of her hands, to apply the match successfully to the candle.

"Let me do it!—let me do it!" he cried, as he sprang towards her just in time to save the match.

With some difficulty he lighted the little miserable rushlight that the old woman held in her shaking hand. The flame required a little coaxing and shielding from the still slightly agitated air of the room.

But that process did not occupy many seconds.

It was very provoking, though, that the moment Handsome Jemmy turned round with the light, the casement should swing wide open again, and a gust of wind should extinguish it on the instant.

"Another match—another match, Mother Bendydykes! We shall never see about us till day-dawn!"

The second match was lighted. The hag herself closed the window, and stood by it holding it, for the fastening had been dashed off, and it was a door casement.

Handsome Jemmy relit the candle.

Perhaps the whole process had occupied three

minutes—certainly not more—and then he turned to Matthew Haslem.

The chair was empty.

"Gone!" cried Jemmy.

Mother Bendydykes uttered a scream.

"Then it was a vision!"

"No, no! Flesh and blood!—flesh and blood! Ah, look, look! Oh, behold! There! there! Now gone and for ever!"

Mother Bendydykes had let the casement fly wide open, and she pointed towards the river, where Handsome Jemmy saw for one fleeting instant something white gleam on the surface of the tide, and then disappear, never to be seen again.

"Lost! lost!" he cried. "Is this the end? Was that man my father, and am I never to look upon his face again?"

"Never!" said the hag.

The light had again gone out, but Mother Bendydykes could see, although dimly, some sad and despairing gestures of the highwayman.

"All is over now!" she said. "Peace, and I will tell you all!"

"All? all?"

"Yes! That was your father! He—he had a wife."

"My mother?"

"Yes, mother! He never loved her. She died of—what shall I say?—a broken heart and desertion. I saw her once a mendicant in the streets, with a little infant at her breast."

The handsome highwayman uttered an exclamation of anguish.

"I heard that she was dead, and the infant with her. I know that she herself passed away, but I did not know that you were spared. You are that infant. There can be no doubt you are the son of Matthew Joseph Haslem; and you have seen your poor mother only with the eyes of early childhood; while your father has but stepped from the grave to look upon your face, and let you for a brief minute behold his!"

"A dream—a dream! It is all nothing but a hideous dream!"

"Would it were so!"

"It is—it is!"

"Nay; I will give you proof. Can you see what that is?"

The hag drew aside the black curtain.

The coffin was dimly visible.

Handsome Jemmy stooped and felt it.

"A coffin!"

"Yes; your father's coffin!"

"My father's?"

"Yes. He was quietly interred in that sad narrow home in the graveyard of Tottenham Court Road. A man who trades with the living for the dead brought him here. I found that he lived, and that his recovery was all but certain when you arrived."

"Alas! alas!"

"You know all. Make the most of your knowledge, or anything or nothing. I care not; for before to-morrow's dawn I shall be far away. The remainder of my life may be a desolation and a blight, but it shall not be passed beneath the skies of Britain!"

A kind of stupor seemed to come over the handsome highwayman for a few minutes. Then rousing himself from it, he sprang from the open window into the boat which had brought him to that house.

"Farewell!" he said,—"farewell! I know not whether to thank you or to curse you; but your own heart and conscience will tell you which I should do, and whichever that is, accept either the thanks or the curses!"

"Both!" said Mother Bendydykes.

Handsome Jemmy bent to the oars, and the boat soon shot out into the stream, where he paused, and looked long and anxiously over the swelling waters.

No, not a trace of Matthew Haslem, in his grave-clothes, could be seen.

"That is over!" said Handsome Jemmy; "and I

am——Well, I am just what I was, with the addition of a painful remembrance!"

"Pull away, my lads, and you have him!" shouted a voice.

"Ah," said Jemmy, "that is a Thames police galley! Look out for sport!"

CHAPTER LXI.

CAPTAIN SANG OVERAWES ALL RESISTANCE, AND CLAIMS HIS VICTIM.

THE hour of eleven struck as Captain Sang, *alias* Sir John Pope, reached the vestibule of Newgate with Pamela.

No one had opposed him.

It was his coach that stood at the door, and which had been noticed by Lord Malvern, when he put up his horse at the inn yard just opposite to the prison.

What pen shall now depict the despair of Pamela?

What words shall suffice to convey to the reader the true aspect of that young and ingenuous mind, when it found itself engulfed in such a whirlpool of despair?

She was once again in the power of the terrible Captain Sang.

It seemed as if heaven had deserted her, and some malignant fate had taken a delight in surrendering her into the hands of that most infamous man of many crimes.

And yet, in her progress to the vestibule of old Newgate, she had to pass many prisoners, not one of whom, perhaps, had any real sympathy with her, although there was not one who could do otherwise than guess the dreadful fate that Sang intended for her.

Those prisoners were human, but habit, and their profession, had indurated their habits.

The show of authority, under which Sang acted, discouraged any attempt to interfere with him; and, still flourishing the order of the Secretary of State, he reached that small apartment which is exactly within the arched gate of the prison.

His victim was still in his grasp.

"Make way!—make way!" he cried. "Who shall dare oppose me? Make way, I say!"

A stout, burly turnkey was on the lock.

He took his key out, instead of turning it to open the wicket.

Sir John Pope, *alias* Captain Sang, or Sir John Pope only, as he was known, or thought to be, in Newgate, saw the action.

He set Pamela on her feet for the first time since he had rushed through the prison from the Governor's room with her.

Pamela uttered a scream, and then dropped to her knees. She thought she saw a gleam of pity in the face of this stout turnkey.

She thought she saw significations of opposition to the domineering and violent progress of her captor.

"Oh, save me!—save me! Oh, for the love of heaven, save me from this man!"

"He dare not!" said Sang, as he looked pale with rage, and confronted the stout turnkey. "He dare not!"

"I shall do my duty, sir!" said the man.

"To God—to heaven—to justice!" cried Pamela.

A hideous smile flickered over the face of Sang.

"We have nothing to do with heaven or justice here. There, my man, if you can read—and I suppose that is a qualification for your post—you will see that I am armed with an authority you dare not disobey!"

Sang held towards this man "on the lock" the Secretary of State's order.

The man shook his head.

"I have nothing to do with that, Sir John Pope. Somebody from the Governor must give me my order to let you take any one out of Newgate."

"Wretch! Why do I not brain you on the spot?"

"Because you can't."

The stout warder put himself into an attitude of defence, with his massive keys in his hand.

PAMELA ENTREATS THE CHAPLAIN OF NEWGATE TO SAVE HER.

No. 19.—FELON'S DAUGHTER.

Captain Sang was a coward.

He fell back a pace.

He knew that the Governor was not likely to aid him, and he cried out in a loud voice, "The clerk of Newgate! Where is he? I want the clerk of Newgate!"

A man in black stepped forward, and said mildly. "Sir, will you permit me to ask what all this tumult is about?"

"Who are you?" demanded Sang fiercely.

"I am the chaplain of Newgate."

"I, then, Mr. Chaplain, am Sir John Pope, a friend of the Secretary of State. Be so good, reverend sir, as to look at this order, and tell the pig-headed man with the keys that it must be obeyed."

"Oh, no, no!" cried Pamela, in an agony of grief: "it is an iniquitous and cruel order, if a true one Save me! Oh, save me!"

The chaplain looked at the order.

"Young woman——"

"Oh, you will save me—you will protect me?"

"Young woman, one of the most valuable lessons we should all of us learn, is to bow down with very submission to those in authority. Hem! It seems to me that the gentleman is in possession of an order from the Secretary of State, who is, of course, a high authority. Hem! Therefore, you should humbly and most thankfully obey."

"Sir!"

"Hem! That is my opinion. The Secretary of State, who has many valuable Church livings, and who is the brother-in-law of the Lord Chancellor, is a kind of master, and should be obeyed. Hem! That is my opinion."

"And a capital opinion, too," said Sang. "Reverend sir, I will come and hear you preach some day."

"Sir, you are very good."

"Ha! ha! am I? Now, Pamela, you are mine!"

"Oh, no—not yet! Oh, reverend sir, surely you will obey your higher and mightier Master!"

"What do you mean, girl?"

"I mean your Master who is in heaven above us, and He will order you to succour the distressed, to lean to the side of those who are wrongfully treated, to save the innocent!"

"Oh, stuff—stuff! Here is an order from the Secretary of State, who is brother-in-law to the Lord Chancellor, and you want to argue me into saying anything against it. Pooh! pooh! Young woman, you are in a bad frame of mind. Mr. Warder, the order is quite sufficient."

"Then I must have a receipt," said the stout man at the lock, doggedly.

"A receipt for what?" roared Sang.

"For the young girl you take with you!"

"Bah! Bo!"

"Oh, you may go on saying 'bah!' and 'bo' as much as you like; but I don't put my key in the lock till you give it me."

Sang uttered a howl like that of some wild beast in a wood, who is trapped or baulked of its prey, and then he dragged Pamela with him to a table that was always in the vestibule of Newgate, with writing materials, and hastily scrawled—

"I, Sir John Pope, Knight, have taken with me Pamela Sharples from the prison of Newgate, by virtue and authority of a special order from the Right Honourable the Secretary of State!"

"JOHN POPE"

"There! there is your receipt. Perhaps we may meet on some occasion, when I shall remember that I owe you something, which I will take good care to give you, without troubling you for a receipt at all."

"I think I can take care of myself, Sir John Pope," replied the turnkey, as he slowly opened the wicket.

"Oh, heaven!" cried Pamela. "Is it possible that I am to be surrendered up to this dreadful man?"

"Come!"

"No—no!"

"Young woman!" said the chaplain, "you are committing the sin of resisting lawful authority."

Pamela wrung her hands in despair. The horror of being, as an alternative, carried by Captain Sang, made her follow him, but she called out aloud, "I proclaim to all here present that this is Captain Sang, the highwayman! He is not Sir John Pope! He is himself a criminal—a murderer! Oh, look at him, and see the confirmation of my words in his face!"

The horrible blood-red tinge that had given Sang that nickname, came now about his eyes. With an angry growl, he flung his left arm around the slender waist of the fair Pamela, and darted down the steps of Newgate with her.

The stout turnkey looked compassionately after her.

"Jennings! Jennings!" he cried, "will you relieve me on the lock? I will do as much for you another time."

"All right!" said another warder, as he approached the wicket.—"all right! Do you want to go out into the world?"

"Yes, yes!"

It was a kind of slang term in Newgate, "going out into the world," which was in use among the warders and turnkeys when they left the prison.

The stout turnkey surrendered his keys to Jennings and ran down the steps.

Captain Sang's coach was still there.

The coachman, when he saw Sang, was going to dismount, but the villanous captor of poor Pamela cried out firmly, "Keep your seat, and be ready to drive off at once! Keep your seat!"

With his disengaged hand he opened the coach door.

Pamela, as he pushed her into the vehicle, impeded his sight, and he did not make any effort to look past her into the coach, which he could not have the least idea was otherwise than empty.

"Go in—go in!" he yelled. "You are mine, and no power now on earth shall save you!"

Sang dashed into the coach after Pamela.

Then he uttered a half stifled cry, and his head began in a very mysterious manner to go bump, bump, bump against the frame portion of the vehicle immediately behind the coachman.

Crash went the glass in that direction; and still Captain Sang's head kept repeating those bumps against the frame-work.

Pamela was for a few seconds perfectly transfixed by surprise and by the hope that sprung up anew in her heart.

Some one was in the coach.

Some one had been there waiting patiently for Captain Sang, and that some one had him by the throat, and with a grasp of iron held him and bumped his head in that extraordinary manner against the vehicle.

Who could that be but the eccentric Lord Malvern?

When he had put up his horse at the inn yard opposite Newgate, and saw the coach at the door, he knew that he was not too late.

The whole attention of the disreputable-looking driver, who no doubt was some special emissary of Captain Sang's, was directed towards the vestibule of Newgate, where the dispute with the stout warder was going on.

Lord Malvern had not had the least difficulty in opening quietly the coach door which was next to the road, and stepping into the vehicle.

He closed the door again from the inside, and then, without the least impatience or perturbation, he fixed his glass in his eye, and waited for Sang.

He waited, too, for Pamela.

The voices in the vestibule of Newgate were all quite loud enough to reach the ears of Lord Malvern, so that he had an opportunity of ascertaining what the precise views of the chaplain were in regard to temporal authorities.

Lord Malvern only spoke to himself once.

"Aw," he said, "that is Pamelaw! Aw—I am in time to wescue Pamelaw!"

And so he waited.

Pamela was quickly aided in taking a seat in the coach, by the left arm of Lord Malvern. With his right he met Captain Sang.

The villanous Sang thought for a moment or two that his neck had been caught in some vice that was worked by some piece of well-constructed machinery; so rapidly did he find himself moved to and fro, while those bumps took place at the back of his head.

"Murder!—murder!"

"Aw—no, not yet; and—aw—when it is—aw—it's only manslaughter, or—aw—I should say justifiable homicide!"

"Help!—help!"

"Hoorah!" cried a voice.

The stout turnkey was looking in at the coach door.

"Aw—aw— you are a constable?"

"Yes, sir. Go it, sir!—don't mind me—go it, sir!"

"Aw—I am glad to mind you You will —aw—take this man into custody—aw! I give him in charge for a felony—aw! He is a highway robber!"

"Is he, yer honour?"

"Aw—yes. Sang is his name!"

"You don't mean, sir, to say that you know this man is Captain Sang, the highwayman?"

"Aw—yes. Dwat the fellow! He has made my glass fall out—aw—from my eye!"

At this moment the coachman, who had been so thunderstricken by all that had so suddenly taken place, that he had lost his faculties, recovered them sufficiently to begin whipping his horses to put them in motion.

"Aw—stop him!"

"That I will—rather!" said the stout turnkey.

With a vigorous pull at what the turnkey called his near leg, he brought the coachman to the pavement on his back, and the hackney coach horses were only too glad to stand still.

The stout turnkey, then, with a dash, that, considering his size, was something wonderful, made an assault upon Sang, and tore him out of the coach.

"I've got him, your honour!"

"Stop! stop! What is all this?—what is all this about?" shouted a man, who, with his face all black and smeared with gunpowder, ran out of the vestibule of Newgate.

That was the Governor.

At the same instant, there turned into the Old Bailey from Ludgate Hill a splendid carriage, all gilt and emblazonments, with a couple of footmen behind and a coachman on the box, wigged and cocked-hatted to a marvellous extent.

This carriage, at a brisk pace, rolled up to the door of Newgate, and only stopped when its pair of tall, strong horses were face to face with the two miserable hacks in Sang's hackney coach.

"The Sheriff!" cried the stout turnkey.

"The Sheriff!" cried Jennings, who had taken his place "on the lock."

The Governor made an effort to wipe his face with the skirt of his coat, and only made the smears of the gunpowder so much the worse.

Lord Malvern looked out at the coach window with his glass at his eye.

CHAPTER LXII.

LORD MALVERN DISCOMFITS CAPTAIN SANG AND SAVES PAMELA.

THE state of affairs at the door, or the wicket gate, of Newgate was interesting.

The stout turnkey had Captain Sang in his grasp, and the villain, what with the treatment he had received at the hands of Lord Malvern, and the anything but gentle manner in which the stout turnkey had taken him from the coach, was past the power of active resistance.

Pamela was still in the coach, with her hands clasped, and smiles contending with tears upon her fair face.

Had she not been saved from a fate that was infinitely worse than death?

The whole of the warders and turnkeys who were off special duties in the interior of Newgate thronged to the wicket gate

The two footmen, in all their gorgeous array, at the back of the Sheriff's coach, got down and opened the door of the gilt and emblazoned vehicle.

The Sheriff stepped out.

"Gracious! What is all this about?"

"Aw—how d'ye do?" said Lord Malvern.

The Sheriff rapidly turned round.

"Have I the pleasure and the honour of seeing the Right Honourable my Lord Malvern?"

"Aw—yes. How d'ye do? Aw—Mr Sheriff, will you be so good—aw—as to let that wascal be well looked after in Newgate?"

"Certainly, my lord, certainly! What rascal? Oh, the rascal with the black face?"

"No! I daresay—aw—that is a wascal, too; but he isn't—aw—the wascal I mean just now—aw!"

"I'm the Governor!"

"You the Governor!" exclaimed the Sheriff—" you the Governor, and with that face!"

"Yes, Mr. Sheriff; it was—an—an—an accident, that's all."

The Governor caught the eye of Captain Sang fixed menacingly upon him, and he knew that he was so far in Sang's power that that now discomfited individual might make some very troublesome revelations concerning him and his conduct in regard to Pamela.

"Dear me!" said the Sheriff, "I seem to have arrived in the midst of all sorts of accidents!"

"Aw—yes—aw! That's the wascal with the wed face."

Lord Malvern gave a side-long jerk of his hand in the direction of Sang.

"You charge him, my lord."

"Aw—yes. He is Captain Sang, the well-known and—aw—universally detested—aw—highwayman!"

"Captain Sang! cried the Sheriff. "Secure him instantly!"

"Aw—that will do. Good-bye—bye, bye! How-de-do?—aw—bye, bye!"

Lord Malvern looked at the prostrate coachman, and then turning to the stout turnkey, he said "Aw—my fwiend, will you pick up that man, and put him on the box. I want to dwive to Bedford Squaw, and may as well give him the job—aw. And do you see that dwover with the cattle, just turning the corner of—aw—I think it is Giltspur Street—aw? Give him this guinea—aw—and ask him for that stick he has with the—aw—bradawl at the end of it—aw!"

"Yes, my lord!"

Captain Sang had been given into the hands of two or three constables, who hustled him into Newgate at once; and while the stout turnkey went for the drover's cattle goad, and while the coachman clambered sulkily on to his box, Lord Malvern beckoned to the Sheriff, and spoke to him.

"Aw—the Governor of Newgate will let Captain Sang escape if he can—aw. I saw it in his eyes—aw—through the glass. I can generally judge what a fellow is going to do by his eyes—aw!"

"I'll stop that, your lordship," said the Sheriff. "Mr. Governor!"

"Yes, your honour!"

"If Captain Sang escapes, I will recommend your removal!"

The Governor bit his lips.

"He shall not escape, your honour."

"Very well; look to it that he don't."

"Aw—thank you—aw! I see that is the cattle goad. Now, Pamelaw, where do you want to go?"

Poor Pamela's feelings were too much to allow her to speak for a few seconds—she could only clasp her hands in great thankfulness, and sob.

Lord Malvern spoke again.

"Aw—Pamelaw—the Court Physician—Doctor Haslem—who wesides in Bedford Squaw—you know him?"

"Oh, yes, yes!" faltered Pamela.

"Well, he—aw—has found out that you are his child—aw!"

Pamela's tears flowed afresh. They were partly tears of mingled emotions, and partly those of joyful feeling.

"I cannot say," she replied, "that I have not, from all the circumstances that have occurred, been able to tell, my lord, that that is perfectly true!"

"Then—aw—will you go to Bedford Squaw?"

"Yes—oh, yes! You have saved me gallantly—nobly,—saved me from the villain Sang; and if—if you——Yet I ought not to ask you!"

"What is it, Pamelaw?"

"There is one——"

"Aw—so there is—I forgot him! The rascal is driving slow on purpose!"

"Oh, no, no!"

"You—aw—mean the coachman?"

"No; I mean Dick Doubleday!"

"Never mind! Aw—a little quickaw, please!"

Through the broken front window of the coach, Lord Malvern dealt the confidential coachman of Captain Sang such a dig with the drover's goad, that he uttered a shout of pain, and increased the pace of his horses considerably.

"Now, Pamelaw, we will talk about Dick—aw—Doubleday—aw! You see I know him—aw!"

"You do, sir?"

"Yes—aw—he and Handsome Jemmy, as—aw—I find he is called, stopped and wobbed me on the highway!"

"You?—you?"

"Aw—yes! I was the man, and they were the fellaws!"

"Oh, sir, can you forgive them?"

"Aw—I have! You will find—aw—Dick Doubleday at the Dootaw's house—at least——No, I am wong!"

"Wrong, sir?"

"Aw—yes. I ought not to say so; I—aw—ought only to say that I left him there. Get on!"

The coachman uttered another yell as the goad admonished him to speed.

In this manner the distance from Newgate to Bedford Square was performed; and the moment Lord Malvern alighted at the door of Doctor Haslem's house with Pamela, the coachman got down, and, caring nothing for either coach or horses, he darted off, and disappeared round the first corner.

"Aw—he's a good widdance!" said Lord Malvern. "Is the Doctaw at home?"

"Yes, my lord."

"Come along, Pamelaw!"

Pamela's heart beat fast as she followed Lord Malvern into the drawing-room, where Doctor Haslem was.

With a scream of joy, he rushed towards her; and then, when within a few paces of her, he dropped to his knees.

"My child—my own child—my Lavinia, so long estranged from me! Can you forgive your poor, unhappy father for all the past?"

"Ah, sir!" said Pamela, "that word 'forgive' should never be used from a parent to a child in this sense. Let me forget all but that I have a father!"

Pamela, with the most charming air in the world, approached Doctor Haslem, and rested on his breast.

"Aw—bye, bye! How-de-do? Bye, bye!" said Lord Malvern.

"No, no, my lord!" cried Doctor Haslem; "I pray you not to go!"

"Aw—family affairs—aw! But, before I do go, I want to see Dick—aw—Doubleday."

Doctor Haslem looked confused.

"Is he not here?" asked Pamela. "Oh, father, to him, and to his friend Handsome Jemmy, I owe this happy home; for, but for them, your child would, ere this, have met with an ignominious death; and even now——"

Bang! came a hard knock at the door of the Doctor's house.

Pamela shrank towards, not her father, but Lord Malvern, for protection.

Bang! came the single heavy knock again.

"Aw—who is that?"

A servant opened the door of the room.

"If you please, sir, Mr. Simms says he would be glad to see you."

"I know no such person."

"But you will now, sir!" cried a stout, coarse man, in top-boots, who pushed into the room past the servant. "Oh, that's my little creature! Pamela Sharples, I arrest you as an escaped felon!"

"Aw!" said Lord Malvern, as he placed himself between Pamela and the officer,—"there is no such person as Pamelaw Sharples. This young lady is Lucinda Haslem!"

CHAPTER LXIII.

HANDSOME JEMMY EFFECTS A FORTUNATE ESCAPE FROM THE POLICE-GALLEY.

WE left Handsome Jemmy in some peril.

He could not doubt for a moment but that the galley that pursued him on the Thames was manned by the police-officers.

How they had succeeded in getting upon his track he knew not, but there they were; and he felt that all his energies now would have to be exerted to escape from them.

The night was passing away.

Already the surface of the water began to reflect the first faint flushes of the dawn.

The situation was a critical one; and Handsome Jemmy, after a few moments' reflection, resolved to adopt the only course which presented to him any chance of escape; namely, to try for the shore as quickly as he could.

The nearest place was the Temple Gardens, by the Terrace Walk.

It was, however, by no means an easy matter to make such a landing; for, although the tide was certainly high, yet it was a good bit lower than the stone coping of that old historical Terrace Walk.

But, as we have said, it was his only chance, and therefore must be attempted, let the difficulties be what they may.

With vigorous strokes of his oars the highwayman pulled straight for the Terrace.

In a few moments—a very few moments, indeed—the officers in the police-galley saw what was his intention.

A loud voice shouted the order to "give way."

The whole of the rowers in the galley went to their work, and shot through the water with a tremendous rapidity.

It was a wonder that the little boat could distance it at all; but a stern chase is proverbially a long chase; and in this instance the proverb was not belied. The small boat kept its distance wonderfully; and then, when about a hundred yards from the Terrace, the highwayman seemed as if he had changed his purpose, and suddenly made for the stairs at the side of the Temple.

"Give way, lads!" cried the chief officer in the boat. "He will escape us yet!"

"No, no, sir!"

The police-galley was pulled round in the direction that Handsome Jemmy went; and when he saw that they had fairly accomplished that manoeuvre, he, by one

THE GARDENER AT THE TEMPLE ATTEMPTS THE CAPTURE OF HANDSOME JEMMY.

brisk stroke of an oar, shot the much smaller boat he occupied close under the Terrace wall.

Before the large police-galley could turn again, Handsome Jemmy was in the Temple Gardens.

The officers were furious.

"Stop him! stop him! A hundred pounds reward! A highwayman! a highwayman!"

An adventurous gardener who heard the cry of "A hundred pounds reward," made a blow at Handsome Jemmy with a rake.

The next instant the aforesaid rake was twisted out of his hands, and Jemmy caught him by the back of the neck with its teeth.

"Something for you to do, my fine fellows," he observed to the officers on board of the police-galley, and rake and gardener were floating in the river.

But some half-dozen persons made a rush into the gardens by one of its gates.

Handsome Jemmy saw his danger, and he saw likewise a door open, which led up one of the common staircases conducting to various suites of chambers.

It was all chance work for Jemmy—he tried the first door he came to, and then knocked at it sharply.

The inhabitant of that set of chambers was slow in answering the summons for admission, so the highwayman ran on to another door.

Yes, that was open!

Handsome Jemmy, without the least ceremony, rushed into a room, the whole walls of which were surrounded by books.

A table in the centre of the room was piled up with books—books were on the floor—books on every chair.

At the table, in a very dreamy kind of condition, was an elderly gentleman, with the gown of a counsel on him, and the wig, and bands, which would enable him at any moment to rise and repair to one of the law courts.

"Doe on the demise of Buggins!" said the old lawyer, in an abstracted way.

"Sir!" said Handsome Jemmy. "Sir!"

"The plaintiff Strangeways was the lessor of Grubaway——"

"Sir!"

"Eh?"

"If you please, sir, have you a cupboard, or any convenient place that one man may hide in, who, I suppose, by this time is pursued by fifty?"

"Eh? Are you the plaintiff?"

"No; the defendant."

"My dear sir—I am glad to see you. Do you admit the forfeiture of the lease or leases, as a consequence of the laches of Buggins?"

"I will admit anything in half a moment."

"My dear sir!"

Handsome Jemmy knocked down a great stack of books, and opened the door of a cupboard in a corner of the room. It only had a couple of old dusty bandboxes in it.

"But, my dear sir!"

Rat-tat-tat! came at the door of the chambers.

The knock was a hasty and defiant one.

Handsome Jemmy had very little doubt indeed, if he may be said to have any at all, that the knock was the signal of the approach of his enemies.

"Sir," he said, as with two strides he reached the chair from which the old lawyer had not risen, but which he had moved half round upon its castors, to enable him to look at his strange visitor—"sir, I am beset. Will you help me?"

"My dear sir!"

"It is a case of necessity."

"A case?"

"Yes. I ask you to save me!"

"My dear sir, if you can show me any precedent for such a thing——"

"Twenty!"

"Then I will do it. I will do anything in the world, always provided there is a precedent for it; and I would not stir to save society if there were none."

"Come this way."

"Yes—yes."

"Your wig—your gown—your bands!"

"Eh?"

"Quick!"

"But I'm quite sure there is no precedent!"

"There is."

"Where?—where? Tell me where?"

"In Jemmy Haslem's Reports, volume one, page twenty-two!"

"Good gracious! I never heard of Jemmy what's-his-name's Reports."

"You do now—that will do. Good-bye!"

With amazing celerity, Handsome Jemmy had dispossessed the old lawyer of his silk gown, his wig, and his starched chest bands, and put them all on. A slight push sent the old man, without any sort of precedent at all, into the cupboard, against which Jemmy pushed up the pile of books again.

Rat-tat-tat-tat—bang!

Whoever was at the door was getting impatient.

It was well that the latch did not attract the attention of the officers. Or perhaps they were a little delicate about intruding upon the eminent King's counsel who they knew inhabited those chambers.

"Knock away, my fine fellows!" remarked Jemmy to himself: "you can come in as I did when you are tired of ceremony."

Handsome Jemmy had just seated himself in the old counsel's chair, and put up the reading glass to his eye, which he found lying before him, when the door of the chambers was opened.

"Beg pardon, Sir William," said a man with a constable's staff in one hand, and a pistol in the other. Beg a thousand pardons, Sir William Mansfield, but there is a highwayman in the Temple."

Handsome Jemmy looked up from beneath the wig that he had drawn down close to his brows in an abstracted manner.

"A highwayman, sir, if you please."

"A what?"

"A great rascal, sir, in the Temple!"

"Go along—go along! As if I did not know there were many great rascals in the Temple!"

"Well, Sir William, that may be; but it's my duty to apply at all the chambers. If so be, sir, you have been here, you must have seen him if he had come in here!"

"Yes—yes—go along!"

"You have not seen him, sir?"

"No, no; I don't know what you want! Stay—ah, yes! Now I think of it, I am glad you have come?"

"Indeed, sir! Then you do know something, Sir William?"

"Of course I do! Here!—what's your name, sir, eh? Come, now, don't prevaricate—what's your name?"

"Lor', sir! all London knows my name, sir! It's Bellingham!"

"Will you swear that?"

"In course, sir!"

"Very good; then fetch me that topmost book yonder, with all the dust on it, and then be off—that's all I want of you. I am glad you have come, though you say you are a highwayman!"

The discomfited officer fetched the book.

"But, Sir William, if you please, I am not the highwayman!"

"Well, well, my good man; don't you see you are wasting your own time and mine too?"

"By Jove, so I am!"

The officer left the chambers at once, and Handsome Jemmy heard him say on the landing, "He ain't in there, I will take my oath any day!"

The search through the entire house was continued, but was, as a matter of course, quite unproductive; and Handsome Jemmy, when he heard the officer descend from the chambers, went to the cupboard to release the ancient counsel, who he now knew to be the Sir William Mansfield for whom he had been so successfully mistaken.

The old lawyer did not seem to be in the least discomposed by his slight imprisonment.

"Young man," was all the remark he made, "your ideas of the liberty of the subject are in a very wild state."

"They may be, sir; but you have saved me perhaps from death. Take your gown, and wig, and bands again, and I hope you will not think that they are any the worse that they have been the means of saving a human life. I was a highwayman, but I am one no longer, since now I know who I am."

"Indeed!"

"Yes; till within the last hour, whatever suspicions I might have had, I was practically a nameless wanderer in the world. I know now that my name is Haslem, although I shall never again look into my father's face."

All the strange exciting scene at Mother Bendydykes' came again vividly before the imagination of Handsome Jemmy, and his voice shook with emotion as he uttered the last words.

"Haslem! Haslem!" said the old counsel. "Did you say Haslem?"

"I did, sir!"

"Matthew Joseph Haslem, do you mean?"

"Ah, sir! Matthew Joseph were the names of the father, I think, whom I never fairly saw until this night; and then I saw him but to lose him again as quickly."

"You could not see him to-night young man—he has been dead two or more days; and these papers now before me are sent by the family solicitor of Doctor Haslem, of Bedford Square, who was his brother, in order that I may unravel from them what seems to be a strange episode in Matthew Joseph Haslem's life, in which a marriage with some one, afterwards described, seems to have taken place."

"My mother!"

"Your mother?"

"Yes. Oh, let me tell you all, sir! This is providential! Will you listen to me, sir?"

"Assuredly."

Briefly, and with a perspicuity that quite charmed the old lawyer, Handsome Jemmy related all that part of his history which it was necessary to know in connexion with the long-kept secret of his birth.

The scene that had taken place only that night at Mother Bendydykes' greatly interested the old counsel.

Handsome Jemmy produced the little locket likewise, and then Sir William Mansfield, as he looked up at him, said, "Sir, the evidence you produce, and the corrected narrative you tell, will be sufficient to convince the most sceptical. Ah! some one knocks!"

The door of the chamber was slowly opened and a head was put in.

"Beg pardon, sir, but Mr. Billington left me on duty and I thought I heard a strange voice, sir."

"You heard this gentleman," said Sir William Mansfield "His name is Haslem!"

CHAPTER LXIV.

JACOB SHARPLES FANCIES HIMSELF AT THE SUMMIT OF FORTUNE.

It will be noticed by the observant reader that both Pamela and Handsome Jemmy, who turn out to be first cousins, were saved in much the same manner from the grasp of the officers of the law.

In Pamela's case it was Lord Malvern who had foiled the officers, by giving his word that she for whom they sought as Pamela Sharples was named Lavinia Haslem.

And so in like manner so high a legal authority as Sir William Mansfield passed his word that Handsome Jemmy was a Mr. Haslem.

And now, leaving Pamela to the care of her father and Lord Malvern, and the handsome highwayman to that of the old lawyer of the Temple, we feel constrained to follow the fortunes of one in whom the reader may feel an interest, although of a far different character to that which is inspired by the good and the true.

We mean Jacob Sharples.

At the period of his career when the reader last looked into the haggard face of the coiner, he had a chance which his evil genius prevented him from embracing.

A chance of escape!

He had money!

From that sure hiding-place on the roof of his house he had possessed himself of the large sum that he had saved from his illicit transactions in regard to the coin of the realm.

That large sum he had coiled about him.

It was in truth coiled, for was it not the serpent that had betrayed him, and made him what he was?

And so, if Jacob Sharples had had the sense, the judgment, the common intellect to see his position fairly, he might have escaped.

But he would not.

Or he could not.

It was not to be. That man was born first to be the relentless enemy of others, and then his own.

The cupidity that was the reigning principle of his existence had pictured to him the possibility of some day ransacking the hoards of Dick Doubleday's old uncle.

He could not—he did not even attempt to resist the temptation.

Old Doubleday was dead!

He, Jacob Sharples, had himself committed the crime that had sent him to his account, and was he not to seek to profit by it?

In after-time was he to remember how he had rushed out from the old house in Long Lane, and chased the old man out of his path; and was that to be all?

No, no! A thousand times, no!

Jacob Sharples had often, in his secret heart, contemplated the possibility of taking the life of old Doubleday, and having the disposal of his secret hoards.

Well did the coiner know that it was the habit of old Doubleday to shut up his shop for days, while he went on various errands of iniquity, no doubt, so that the neighbours were not likely to feel any alarm at the non-appearance of the old man.

Was it so in this instance?

Should he find all quiet at that wretched house in Long Lane, and nothing but the dead to interfere with him?

Such were the questions that Jacob Sharples asked himself, as he struggled through the rain and the wind, on that night of storm and tempest when he left his own house at Clerkenwell in search of the hidden treasures, if such there were, of old Doubleday.

Stooping down so low, as the rain and the wind beat him in the face, that it seemed as if at last he would grovel on to the very roadway, Sharples revolved in his own mind, as he went. the circumstances under which he had last left old Zachariah.

He had stabbed him on the threshold of his own house.

Half into the street, and half on the step, he had fallen

Then the anxiety of Sharples to make his escape with Pamela had prevented him from taking any steps to conceal his crime. He recollected that he had stepped over the body of the old man when he came back with the jewels.

But that was all.

Beyond that he knew nothing.

As, therefore, he approached Long Lane, he slackened his pace and shrunk along closer to the houses.

Jacob began to see the necessity of caution

He would reconnoitre the neighbourhood and the house before taking any very active steps.

And so, shrinking from doorway to doorway, from

one court to another, Jacob Sharples finally stood opposite to old Zachariah's house, in Long Lane.

How dismal it looked!

Jacob Sharples knew that it had a tendency to lean on one side, but he never thought it so one-sided as it now appeared to him.

The shop was closed—closed as usual—and from top to bottom of the old tenement there was not the faintest vestige of a light to be seen.

Long Lane, too, for all the signs and relics of human presence about it at that hour, might have been a desert

Jacob Sharples had it all to himself.

He crossed over the way.

He placed his hand upon the door.

It was fast.

Jacob Sharples was a good hand at picking a lock. Now, one of two things must have happened. The door was either locked from the outside, or made fast in some way from the inside.

If the former, his task would be easy enough.

A pick-lock would soon do its duty in getting out of the difficulty.

Jacob Sharples tried one.

Yes, the door yielded—that is to say, it yielded after a fashion; for a cold perspiration broke out upon the brow of Sharples as, after he had pushed the door open a few inches, it was forced shut again from the inside.

Yet not a word was spoken.

Jacob Sharples was over the way in a moment, and he had uttered one sharp cry of alarm.

Then he crouched down and watched.

The door remained still; no one came out. There was no sound—no alarm. What could it mean? What was he to think?

Jacob Sharples was puzzled, and well he might be. The thing was altogether inexplicable. If any one were lying in wait for him, why did they not come out? If not, why did the door close in that mysterious fashion?

"Past two o'clock, and a cloudy night! Move on! Oh, it's a post! Very good!"

A half-asleep watchman passed on without seeing Sharples.

The coiner began to have a feverish anxiety to try the door again. It was possible enough that he had let his imagination deceive him, or that some vagaries of the currents of the night-air had produced the effect.

He crossed the way again.

He pushed the door.

It opened a short way, and then a something heavy fell down in the passage.

Jacob Sharples shrunk back. No, it came to nothing. No one spoke. The door yielded a little further, just about sufficient to enable Sharples to go into the passage if he chose.

But he did not choose.

Not till he had got a light—the light of a thieves' match, with which he was always provided.

He peered into the passage.

He uttered an exclamation of terror.

Lying down immediately behind the door was the dead body of old Zachariah Doubleday.

The whole mystery was now clear to Jacob Sharples.

The old man, after being stabbed, had, instead of calling for help, made an effort to get into his house and close and fasten the door.

He had died with his hand upon the lock.

It was the mere weight of the dead body that had made the door swing close again after Jacob Sharples, the coiner, had opened it with his skeleton key.

Jacob Sharples did not like the dead, but he was not half so much afraid of them as he was of the living.

He stepped over the dead body of old Zachariah, and closed the door. Lying extinguished in the passage was a rushlight, in a wretched old japanned, or what had once been a japanned, stick.

Jacob Sharples lighted it with a thieves' match, and looked about him.

A feverish sensation of triumph came over him.

CHAPTER LXV.

THE PLUNDER OF THE OLD HOUSE IN LONG LANE
DAZZLES THE EYES OF THE COINER.

JACOB SHARPLES felt himself sole master of old Zachariah's house. Who was now to oppose him in his search for the secret hoards of the receiver of stolen property?

No living soul!

The dead he persuaded himself that he feared not, and yet there was a vein of strong superstition in the mind of Sharples, which circumstances might at any time work upon.

The only passion or feeling of the mind that could be set up in opposition to that superstition, was cupidity.

In the present instance that feeling was upon him in its full form.

He had always had vague ideas, and on that account exaggerated notions of the wealth of old Zachariah, and now what was to hinder him from getting possession of the whole?

Nothing! nothing!

The house was deserted.

The old woman who had waited upon Zachariah was either dead, or had betaken herself away to a more wholesome region.

He was monarch of all he surveyed.

Into that gloomy little back parlour of Zachariah's shop, where he had had the last interview with him, on the occasion of the trafficking for the jewels, Jacob Sharples made his way.

The candle he had lighted shed a dim, uncertain radiance about it.

But it was enough for the coiner's purposes. He would have dreaded a much brighter light, for, the reflection of it might reach unfriendly eyes from without, through some cranny, or crevice, or window pane, ear.

Sharples even shaded that small light with one hand occasionally, as though he dreaded too ample a diffusion of its rays

Then he set his back against the wall of the dingy room, and as he held the light a foot above the level of his head, he said in deep, husky accents, " Where now should I hide money in the place ?"

As he spoke he ran his eyes over the wretched room.

The furniture was of the most ancient and ricketty description. It seemed as if one well-bestowed kick would be sufficient to send any article in the place to atoms.

In the chimney was piled up quite a mass of old paper and straw, and what looked like odds and ends of old cloth.

"At the bottom of all that," said Jacob Sharples.

He set down the light, and cleared the chimney and the grate.

No, there was no hoard there to be found. Jacob was puzzled.

There was a piece of furniture in one corner of the room, that looked like an old bookcase.

Sharples did not think it likely that such a man as Zachariah would choose so inartificial and commonplace a receptacle for his money, but still there was a chance.

The house had had what is called "a settlement" at that corner—that is to say, the foundation had there sunk down a few inches.

The consequence of this was that the old bookcase had a one-sided, dissipated looking aspect.

Jacob Sharples gave it a good shake.

His shoulder pained him, but it was wonderfully

JACOB SHARPLES IS PURSUED BY THE DROVERS.

No. 20.—FELON'S DAUGHTER.

better. The extreme frugality of Sharples no doubt helped him over any physical hurt much more quickly than other people would have recovered from such an injury.

The old bookcase creaked fearfully.

One side of it was loose.

The back was loose.

It swayed and strained so, that the locked drawers opened of themselves, and then it went all on one side with an ominous lurch.

Jacob Sharples heard a jingling sound: one of the drawers slid out about half a foot.

Sharples raised a small shriek of delight. Truly he was successful, and it was the hidden produce of all old Zachariah's villanies, extending over many years, that he saw before him.

Some small, symmetrical looking bags suggestive of coin.

Yes, there they were.

One, two, three.

A tempting little row of wealth.

A wooden bowl, too, was in that drawer, in which was loose copper and loose silver.

How very indiscreet of Old Zachariah—the cunning, artful, close-fisted, and deep old Zachariah—to have his money so easily accessible as that.

It transcended belief.

And yet seeing was believing in a matter like that. There it was. Jacob Sharples lifted up the wooden bowl, and shook it.

There were about five shillings there, in copper and silver.

A look of contempt crossed the features of Sharples. He put down the bowl, and then took up one of the little bags. Yes, silver was there. Another—the sight ravished him !

Gold ! gold !

He had found what he sought—unless, indeed, some secret hoard of jewels was to be hit upon.

Old Zachariah was one of the finest judges of jewels in Europe. He had dealt in them largely. Stolen jewels came to him in a natural kind of way, like iron filings to a magnet.

"Surely," thought Sharples, "there will be some in the house?"

But no other possibility of hiding anything in that room appeared. There were, however, apartments above—apartments which he, Sharples, had never seen, and which old Zachariah never permitted any one to penetrate to.

We have said the house was an old, broken-down concern. It was one of those ancient, little, low edifices with a long sloping roof, in which there were little windows like eyes, suggestive of small, inconvenient attics.

These attics comprised all that there was in the way of accommodation, such as it was, above the ground-floor.

But, doubtless, it was in one of those that Zachariah slept ; and it might be that in one of those he, Sharples, might find jewels.

He stowed about him the little bags—one of silver and one of gold. He took the light and opened the door that led into the passage.

He listened, for he thought he heard an odd sound. Where did it come from ?

" The next house," said Sharples to himself.

What a convenient thing a " next house " is as a general explanation of all unusual noises in the night! The tired, half-awakened sleeper hears something that, if he lived in a detached house, must rouse him up with thoughts of robbery or fire; but he only turns on the other side, and composes himself to sleep again. It is only in the next house!

And so it was that Jacob Sharples comforted himself that a mysterious noise he heard was in the next house.

It sounded as if it came from the kitchen—that awful underground, gloomy abomination called a kitchen, so common in London houses—that melancholy cellar in which cooking is performed, as if the light and the air were things to be avoided on all possible pretences.

But Jacob Sharples could not muster nerve enough to go down there and look about him.

He passed the head of the dark staircase that led to that lower region, and made his way upwards.

The staircase creaked and groaned.

It was almost in as bad a state as his house in Clerkenwell. It ought to have fallen down any time these twenty years past; but in some mysterious way these old, ricketty houses hold together.

They tumble on one side—they collapse behind—they bulge out in front, but there they are still. What holds them up?

Jacob Sharples reached the attics.

It might have been called the first-floor—it was the first and the last. What little dens they were !

In one there was a kind of bedstead, made from some sacking stretched across two trussles. A chair, in a very dilapidated state, made an extemporized washhand-stand, for the brown earthen basin fitted it cap'tally.

A triangular piece of old looking-glass, which itself had a crack that divided it into two pieces, was held to the wall by bent nails.

Old Zachariah when he looked into it must have had the advantage of seeing two reflections of himself at one and the same time.

Jacob Sharples was so startled at this optical effect that he nearly let fall the candle.

Then he shaded it with one hand, even as he had done down stairs, and looked about him carefully.

No, no! There was nothing there that could be in the least suggestive as a hiding-place.

But he recollected that he had hidden his own money out at the window of an attic.

Might not old Zachariah have done the same thing ?

Sharples hid the light on the landing, and merely closed the door of that attic, and then he opened the window, which was in one of the sloping compartments of the roof.

That roof or ceiling of the attic, we should before have stated, was ingeniously contrived, so that go where you would you were sure to butt your head against some peak, or projection, or slant surface.

Jacob Sharples had given his head a good half-dozen hard raps since he had been in that attic.

But now he looked out at the window into the night. The rain had left off for a space, only to come again harder than ever. It pelted in at the open window.

One look was enough for Sharples. There was no hiding-place on the sloping tiles without.

He withdrew his head and closed the window. Then he saw that there was a visible crack in one of the beams that went across the ceiling.

To get the light, and take a good close look at that beam and that crack, was the work of a few seconds.

Sharples could have uttered a shout of delight. He was confident the beam had a hollow place in it. Yes, there it was. He pushed out a piece of wood about half a yard in length. There was a cavity.

In that cavity was an old silk purse of large size. It was heavy at both ends.

Jacob Sharples did raise a sharp, short cry of delight.

Diamonds, pearls, rubies, emeralds—a good handfull in each end of the old silk purse.

" Found! found!" cried Sharples. " Oh, idiot, to think that such silly hiding-places for gold and jewels would escape the observation of such a man as I am !"

He had no further disposition now to remain longer in old Zachariah's house. He had found his two hoards —his gold and his jewels. Why should he stay ? Ah ! what is that ? The noise again !

Jacob listened.

The sound came from below.

The utmost stretch of imagination could not resolve those sounds now into the next house.

He crept to the head of the stairs. He leaned his head and neck over the ricketty balustrade.

Yes; some one was below.

Perhaps more than one.

Jacob Sharples blew out the light he had instantly.

A faint gleam like moonlight came up from the passage below.

He heard a voice.

"Bless us, yes, my dear Nick, to be sure! The old wretch is murdered, and it were that villain Jacob Sharples as did it; but he runned off like an 'unted hare, and so we may as well as not, my dear, have the money and the jewellery. Nobody knows but me where they is, but I watched him through the keyhole many and many's the time."

"Hold your gab, mother, and let's be quick about it," growled a man's voice.

Jacob Sharples felt cold and hot by turns.

He was certain that the female voice belonged to the old woman who had waited upon Zachariah.

The man, by the way in which she spoke to him, seemed to bear the relation of son to her, and by his language to be anything but one of the brightest or gentlest of human beings.

CHAPTER LXVI.

JACOB SHARPLES HAS TO FLY FOR HIS LIFE, AND TAKES A COURSE SET DOWN BY FATE.

JACOB SHARPLES was afraid to creep down even one of the stairs—they would creak so.

But he longed to look upon these two people who at so inopportune a time for him had made their way into the house, and who were doomed to be disappointed by his success.

How were they to find the gold and the jewels of old Zachariah, when he had both so snugly in his pockets?

He must pass them and escape. He must leave them to their disappointment and rage. Ha, ha! How he would laugh when far away with those little bags of money, and that deep, old, silken purse, with the jewels. Ha, ha!

Jacob Sharples won'd have liked to laugh aloud if he had dared, but he restrained the impulse, and when he felt convinced that the old woman and "Nick" had gone into the little room at the back of the shop, he determined upon risking the descent of the stairs, let them creak as they would.

Chance favoured him.

One of those terrible machines upon wheels without springs, which we might suppose were a copy of the first cart ever made, went along Long Lane.

Bump! bump! bump! Rattle! rattle! rattle! Bump and rattle!

The execrable noise was enough to alarm a whole city, but it was at that moment very welcome to Jacob Sharples

Under cover of it, he stepped down the old creaking stairs without being heard. Nay, such was the noise without, that if he had rolled down before him a beer barrel, it could scarcely have been heard by mortal ears.

And so he reached the passage.

The door of the back room was slightly open.

Now Jacob Sharples might have stepped along the passage—stepped over the dead body of old Zachariah—opened the street door, and got away; but he heard a few words from the old woman in the little back room that made him pause.

"Goodness gracious! they have been, as he always said they would some night, and been took in, as he meant they should!"

What did these words mean?

A vague something sprung up in the mind of Jacob Sharples that he was, in the language of the woman, "took in."

"Oh, bother!" growled the man. "Who cares, so as we get the swag? Come, be quick about it, now!"

"He! he! he!"

"What the deuce are you sniggering at there—eh?"

"Nothing, my dear—nothing; only they have been took in!"

"How do you mean?"

"Why, you see, Nick, when you was so cruelly transported——"

"Bah! Don't go back to that again. I have got back, and here I am! That's enough for you, and me too!"

"Well, I was only saying that then being a lone female, I took service with this Zachariah, and I watched him. He put some copper and some silver in that old bookcase, as he used to say on purpose for thieves, and a bag of gold, too."

"Gold?"

"He! he! he! It looked like gold; but it was only a few handfuls of Jacob Sharples's bad money—all gilt, you know. Did you know Jacob Sharples, the coiner, Nick?"

"No."

A cold feel crept from the heart to the brain of Sharples. What had he done? Robbed the house, not of gold, but of a bag of his own spurious pieces! Then, as he thought of the purse and the jewels, he very nearly betrayed his presence by a scream of despair. What if they were placed where he had found them on purpose "for the thieves?" What if they were spurious likewise?"

"Well, well!" said Nick; "it don't matter what he left for others. What am I to get?"

"The real gold!"

"Where is it?"

"Ay—where is it?" whispered Jacob to himself; and he shook with anxiety as he placed his ear close to the crevice of the room door.

"You see," said the old woman, "that old pickle-jar without a lid?"

"Yes."

"And you see that little cask with the red herrings?"

"Well, what then?"

"Then the real money!"

Sharples groaned.

The pickle-jar and the red herring barrel were both carelessly placed in the room, and no one would think of looking into either of them. Old Zachariah then was not the fool they took him for. The prize had escaped him to fall into other hands.

What should he do?

What was in his power to do?

"Ha, ha!" cried Nick. "Here are the spangles sure enough. Well, mother, you said the old man had sparkles of different sorts, as well as spangles."

Jacob Sharples knew now that it was to a professional burglar he was listening.

"Yes, my dear; and he got ever such a lot of imitations in coloured glass, and put 'em into a puss."

"A what?"

"A silk puss."

"Oh, ah! go on. You should have said a tassel bag—that's what we calls 'em."

"Well, my dear, he had that in his room up-stairs, so that if he was beset by thieves he would pretend to give all up to them, and laugh at them all the while."

"'Coloured glass!'" moaned Jacob Sharples—"'laugh at them all the while!' Her ghost, if there are ghosts, is laughing at me now!"

"But where are the real jewels, mother—that's what I want to know?"

"He! he! he! Why, here, in this drawer; done up in brown paper, with a ticket on 'em, my dear; and on the ticket it says, 'Coloured stones, at ninepence-half-penny a dozen.'"

"And those are the real stones?"

"To be sure they are. I've seen him kissing of 'em, and mumbling, and chuckling over them many a time."

Jacob Sharples was getting desperate. He felt for his knife.

"Can I," he thought,—"can I kill them both? Thieves that they are—can I kill them both?"

"Well, mother," said the burglar, "you have done

your part. Is there anything in the shop worth the taking?"

"Nothing."

"Then let's be off."

Jacob Sharples was in a perfect agony of bitterness, disappointment, and rage. He could not—let the risk to himself be what it might—he could not allow these two people to walk away with the substance of Zachariah's wealth, and leave him the shadow.

If he could not get it, they should not have it.

He crept along the passage.

He stumbled over the dead body of old Zachariah.

"Who's that?" shouted the burglar.

Jacob Sharples, with his long, nimble fingers, opened the street door in a moment and sallied out. He closed it with a loud bang, and then he shouted, in high, screaming accents, "Thieves!—thieves!—thieves!"

Old dead Zachariah's housekeeper and her criminal son perhaps at that moment felt some of the pangs they had made him (Jacob Sharples) suffer.

"Thieves!—thieves!—thieves! Watch!—watch!—thieves!"

There was a rush of footsteps, a springing of rattles, and loud shouts from both ends of Long Lane.

The door of Zachariah's house was dashed open, and the burglar sprang out.

Jacob Sharples struck at him.

The old woman ran out of the house after her son, and the moment she saw Jacob she shrieked out.

"Murder!—murder! There is the murderer of my poor old master!"

Sharples had done all he meant to do, now, and he fled up Long Lane.

The burglar wisely stood still, and pointed after the retreating figure of Jacob, as he said, "That's the man!—that's the man! He has murdered old Mr. Zachariah, and robbed the house! That's the man!"

"Yes!" screamed the old woman; "and it's Jacob Sharples, the coiner, too!"

Half a dozen watchmen ran up Long Lane after Sharples.

He was running, and looking behind him as he did so. His escape would have been tolerably easy but for that. As it was, he ran with terrific force against a post, and fell half-stunned and bleeding to the ground.

The instinct of self-preservation, however, did successful battle against the sensation of physical injury. Jacob Sharples struggled to his feet and ran on.

But he was bewildered by his fall, and had not half the power he before possessed.

Several chance passengers in the streets took up the chase. Some dogs joined in it; and by the time Sharples reached St John's Street Road he was followed by at least fifty people.

"Stop him!—stop him! Knock him down! Take him up! Whoop! Hilloa! A murderer! Stop him! Stop thief!"

At the corner of the City Road a herd of cattle was passing.

Jacob Sharples made his way among the beasts, with frantic speed.

"A hundred pounds reward!" cried some one "Stop him!—stop him! A hundred pounds reward!"

The drovers left their cattle and ran after Jacob.

Dogs, men, boys, a man on horseback, all joined in the pursuit.

Jacob Sharples tore along up the High Street of Islington like a hunted hare. One dog got hold of his skirts, and he had to drag him at his heels. The man on horseback headed him, and struck at him with the heavy handle of his riding-whip, but Sharples avoided the blow, and the horseman overbalanced himself, and fell from his saddle.

Jacob tore on, and the mob followed closely at his heels.

A man-hunt.

One of the drovers caught him.

Jacob turned like a tiger at bay, and plunged his knife into the man's neck.

He was free again. He dashed down a lane. Islington, at that time, was a much more suburban and rural district than it is now. The lane was overhung by tall trees, and for a moment or two those who hunted the coiner seemed at fault as to whether he had gone on or turned into the lane.

That was owing to the shadowy character of the spot.

Jacob profited by that moment's hesitation, and scrambled through a hedge. He fell among a bed of roses on the other side, and lay for a moment or two panting and exhausted.

CHAPTER LXVII.

THE MAN-HUNT CONTINUES, BUT THE COINER BAFFLES HIS PURSUERS.

IT was the pertinacious dog that had for a time held on to Jacob's skirt till it came off, who found out that he had gone down the lane.

With a yelping eagerness the animal led the pursuers of the coiner on the scent.

Sharples crouched down among the roses. The sweet perfume surrounded him like an atmosphere of that famous "attar of roses" which in the voluptuous East is so much esteemed.

Panting, almost breathless, his heart beating with fearful velocity, Jacob waited to see what fortune had in store for him.

Would that terrible dog pass on, or would he, too, come among those fair flowers and seized upon him?

That was a question which Sharples found soon decided.

The dog rushed through the fence in a moment, but that moment was his last.

The coiner had dropped his knife, but rage and the excitement of the moment lent him strength, and he caught the dog, as good luck would have it, by the neck, and held him as though in a vice.

If he could only maintain that hold long enough, the dog must die.

Jacob Sharples did retain it with a terrible pertinacity. The dog kicked, writhed, and tried to yell, but it was of no use. Death took possession of its limbs; the creature soon became an inert mass in the hands of the coiner.

Then, by a great effort, Sharples flung the dog over the hedge into the lane some distance from the spot through which he had made way.

There was a shout from the people who had followed Sharples thus far, and he saw through the thick herbage the gleam of lanterns.

Another dog came close to the hedge, and began yelping and barking.

That drew attention to that part of the leafy fence; and Jacob felt that that place was no longer tenable for him.

He rose up from among the roses, and fled again.

Fled for his life!

With shouts and cries his pursuers were again on his track.

"Stop him!—stop him! A murderer!—a murderer! Stop him!"

They did not actually break a way through the hedge into the garden to get at their victim, but they ran to a high-gate that was close at hand, and clambered it quickly.

Sharples ran forward, he knew not whither. Over some flower beds—diagonally across a gravel path—and then across a lawn again; and then he came to some dwarf iron hurdles, which he almost rolled over.

A light shone in his eyes.

It came from the windows of a house close to him—the house no doubt, that the grounds through which he had passed with such frantic speed, and so recklessly as regarded their arrangement, belonged.

There was a raised terrace at about the height of four

THE DROVER'S DOG ATTACKS JACOB SHARPLES.

feet from the garden walk, and on to that terrace opened some four or five windows.

It was from three of those windows that the light came.

Sharples was in too great a state of excitement, and in too great danger, to stand upon any ceremony.

Just at the moment that he saw one of the windows opened, and a female form step half out on to the terrace, he darted forward, and flinging himself at the feet of the person who appeared, he cried out, " Oh, save me —save me! Be merciful to me, and hide me from those who seek my life!"

What could induce that man of many crimes to ask for mercy, or to suppose that any human being ought to interpose between him and justice, it is hard to say.

Perhaps the whole act was purely impulsive, and had no reasoning for its basis.

But be that as it may, the tone of agony in which he spoke seemed to touch the heart of the female, be she whom she may.

" God forbid," she said, " that I, of all persons, should refuse succour to any human being in distress!"

" Ah! you will save me? you will try to save me?"

" Assuredly."

" But you hear them coming. They have hunted me as man was surely never yet hunted! Hark! they come—they come!"

" This way! this way! Follow me! I do not—I will not ask if you are a man of crime, or if you be wrongfully thus pursued; I will only feel that you are in distress."

" Thanks—oh, thanks to—to——"

Jacob Sharples felt that the word heaven stuck in his throat; he could not say it.

But he followed the lady.

As he did so, the pursuers came rushing through the garden. They reached the terrace.

Sharples flung himself down flat on the floor of the room to which the window led. He then crawled under a table, the cloth of which hung low, almost to the floor.

Then he crouched down, trembling so excessively that he almost shook the room with his emotion.

The lady stepped back again to the window.

Two or three persons sprung on to the terrace.

" What is all this?" she said, with that calm dignity of manner which always awes the most turbulent people.

" A murderer, ma'am, if you please—we are in chase of a murderer; and we fancy he made his way into these grounds."

" A murderer!"

" Yes, ma'am; it is our duty to find him if we can."

" Doubtless—you have my free permission."

The lady still stood at the open casement.

No one had the temerity to put the question directly to her whether or no the fugitive had passed her and gone into the house. The idea was apparently too preposterous for them to entertain, so calm and so destitute of all excitement did she appear.

" Then we will take a good look over the garden, ma'am."

" Do so—do so!"

" Perhaps, ma'am, some of the servants may have seen the fellow?"

" It is possible. The servants' entrance is on the other side of that clump of shrubs."

" Thank you, ma'am—thank you!"

The garden was well searched; the lower part of the house, with the exception of that one drawing-room in which the lady sat, was looked at.

She did not speak to Jacob Sharples

She did not look around her to see where he was hidden.

But she felt conscious that the hunted man was there

The man who had been called a murderer!

She was sad; but she could not bring her mind to give him up.

The atmosphere of the room seemed strange to her by his presence; and that he was beneath or behind some piece of furniture, she was sure.

But she would not look for him.

By the light of a lamp that was shaded by a pale green glass, the lady sat at work.

A strange object for very great regard was in the work-box that stood open before her.

It was a child's shoe.

And yet with what loving eyes the lady regarded it!

Only a shoe—a little infant's shoe, of pale blue morocco; and there it lay deep in the work-box, so that by the slightest rise of the head and the eyes she could see it.

And often and often did she so look at it.

And as often as she did, her eyes would become suffused with tears.

Deep sighs would come from her labouring heart.

At length she laid down her work, and rested her head upon her hands as she murmured forth the words, " Why to-night? Why this night, of all others, am I thus deeply affected by the sight of this sole relic of the past? I thought I had subdued the acute expression of my suffering to the calmness of sadness, along with the hopes that lie beyond the grave!"

Then came the sound of footsteps outside the door.

She heard them, and looked up from her contemplative attitude.

Jacob Sharples, too, heard them from beneath the table.

He looked out. He clasped his hands.

" Oh, in mercy, say nothing! Do not—oh, in mercy, do not betray me!"

" Hush!" said the lady.

She took up her work again, and strove to appear quite calm

A tap came at the door.

" Come in!"

The door was opened, and an elderly female servant appeared with a light.

Immediately behind her were several men, one of whom held in his hand a constable's staff.

" If you please, madam," said the elderly servant, " these people are after an escaped criminal, and they have looked all over the house but here!"

" Yes, ma'am," said the man with the constable's staff. " we feel quite sure he came into the grounds, and perhaps made his way into the house."

" Well?"

" Well, ma'am, we have looked in every room but this."

" I have been here, for the last two hours, and have never left the room for a moment during that time."

" Oh, if that's the case, ma'am, then we must not trouble you "

The lady gently inclined her head.

" And we are sorry, ma'am, to have troubled the house at all; but duty is duty, you know, ma'am, and we had to do ours."

" Certainly."

" Good night, ma'am, and many thanks!"

" Good night!"

Jacob Sharples was for the time saved. The door of the room was closed, and the lady at the work-table was again alone with the coiner—the murderer!

CHAPTER LXVIII.

JACOB SHARPLES THINKS THAT HE SEES THE DEAD RESTORED TO LIFE

THE constables who had taken up the chase of Sharples from London to Islington were at fault, but they were far from being satisfied with the result of their search in the grounds of the villa.

It was just possible that Sharples might have passed the house, and made his escape out of the gardens by the other side; and yet the officers did not think so, for one of the first things they had done had been to send some scouts round the place in that direction.

But they were foiled, although they knew not exactly how.

A more minute investigation of the garden with lanterns was of course fruitless, so they placed sentinels on watch about the villa and its grounds, and resolved to wait till morning.

The lady went on with her work.

Jacob Sharples, half dead with fright and anxiety, was still under the table.

Half an hour elapsed.

Sharples then resolved to speak.

"Madam! madam! Oh, how can I thank you?"

"Hush!"

She slowly rose and went to the door of the room. She looked out into the hall beyond. All was still. She felt satisfied that no one was lurking near to listen, and she came back and resumed her seat.

Then she said gently, "Come forth—come forth! If I have saved you, let it rest in your mind as the work of that gracious heaven which is more anxious that you should repent than that you should be punished."

Jacob Sharples was not disposed to quarrel with the ground on which the lady of the villa chose to put his preservation.

He mumbled out something that might do duty for an assent to the proposition, and then put his head out from beneath the table-cover.

"I am here!"

"Be quiet, yet!"

Jacob Sharples drew back his head in a moment.

The lady had fancied she heard a slight noise at the window.

She slowly walked to it, and opened it, as she had done before, when Jacob Sharples arrived at it.

A little pet spaniel of her own was on the terrace.

"What, Flora! is that you?"

The little dog bounded into the room, and found out Sharples in a moment.

A furious barking testified to the fact.

Jacob Sharples registered a vow of enmity against all dogs in his mind, for as long as he should live.

"Quiet! quiet! Down, Flora, down!" said the lady.

The dog crouched down at her side, but was still uneasy at the presence of the stranger.

"All is safe, I think," said the lady in a low voice. "I cannot say positively what those persons who have been pursuing you are about, but as far as I can judge, all is safe now."

Jacob Sharples looked out again from beneath the table.

The little pet spaniel got into a dreadful state of mind. It was as much as the lady could do, with all the powerful control she had over the creature, to quiet it.

"Come forth," she said—"come forth! There must be something more than this done, if you are really to escape!"

Jacob Sharples crawled out from under the table.

The lady took off from the lamp the green shade, so that a white light was in the room.

Jacob Sharples gathered himself on to his feet on the other side of the table.

The lady rose at the same time.

The lamp was nearly between them—not exactly, but so far only on one side, as to shed a good clear light upon each of their faces.

These two persons then, who up to that moment had not looked at each other, met, so to speak, face to face!

Eyes to eyes!

They knew each other then!

The lady turned pale and faint.

Jacob Sharples uttered a gasping cry, and, but that he clutched the edge of the table for support, he must have fallen backwards.

His eyes dilated—a look of horror was in them. He tried to speak. He seemed choking. He tore at his throat, then, with one hand, as if that action would relieve him, and then he gasped out, "Death has come! death is near, since—since my mortal eyes have looked upon one who comes to me from beyond the grave!"

"No!" said the lady, and her colour slowly came back again, though her lips still trembled,—" no, I live!"

"Live?—live?"

"Yes, by God's mercy!"

"You—you! From the rank, slimy bed of the Thames!—from death—death! No, no, you cannot live!"

"I do live; and I am the wife of Doctor Haslem, the Court Physician!"

Jacob Sharples slid, rather than sank, to his knees.

"And you," added the lady—"you are the man who, one night, many years ago, took me and my little child in a boat on the Thames, and robbed and murdered both, as you thought!"

"No, no! Oh, heaven, no! I can say heaven now, because——"

"Because what, O impious man? Because what?"

"Because you live, and because—I—I saved the child!"

The lady uttered a shriek, that found many an echo in the room.

The door was flung open, and the elderly servant appeared on the threshold in a state of the greatest possible alarm.

"Oh, madam—madam, what is the matter? What has happened to you?"

"She lives! she lives!"

"Lives, madam? Who? what?"

"My child—my own child—my Lavinia—my little darling—my heart's love—its light—its life! Oh, God, this is, indeed, a mercy—a reward for all! To Thee, thanks; to Thee, the gratitude—the outpouring of all the tenderness of this poor heart! She lives! she lives! My own—own child!"

She rushed to the workbox.

She snatched the little blue morocco shoe from it, and kissed it frantically.

Jacob Sharples, still on his knees, cowered down before this tide of rapturous feeling, as though it passed over his head with the force of a tempest.

The elderly servant, whose tears ran down her cheeks in profusion, could only clasp her hands, and repeat the words, "Lives? The dear child lives still—the little Lavinia?"

"Yes—oh, yes! Ask that man!—ask that man! You will hear it from his lips, and I, too, shall hear the welcome news once again!"

"Heaven bless you, sir, for such good—such happy news!"

"No, no!" said the lady; "he—he is not one upon whose head we should call down the blessings of heaven yet."

The old servant shrunk back from Jacob Sharples.

"You know my story," added the lady—"you, who have been my friend more than my servant for so long. You know all my story, and you know that there was a man in a boat—who—who—"

"Oh, gracious!"

"Yes. You remember! That—that is the man!"

Jacob Sharples cowered down lower still. If the finger with which the lady pointed to him had had the power of emitting a spark of fire from its extremity, which had scorched his heart, he could not have shrunk from before her with greater fright.

"The villain! the robber! the murderer!" screamed the old servant.

"No, no!" said Jacob Sharples. "No, no! I tell you the child lives!"

"Where—oh, where is my little one? Tell me where I can seek her, and I will freely forgive all the past."

Jacob began to feel his power now, and he rose to his feet again.

"Yes; I know where she is. I, only—I, only,

know where she is! I saved her—I took her home on that night—I thought you were—that is to say, you—you were drowned accidentally!"

"Murdered!"

"No, no! Don't say that! I don't think—that is to say, I feel quite sure that such was not my intention; but I saved the child!"

"Bring her to me! Oh, no! let me fly to her! Man, I will reward you—pay you! The plunder that was your temptation on that fearful night is nothing to what I will give you now freely, if you will let me feel that I have my own child once again in my arms."

Jacob Sharples drew a long breath of relief.

He began to find himself the master of the situation.

He looked about him at the handsomely furnished drawing-room, and began to calculate upon how much he might expect as his reward for not murdering Pamela.

"Madam, as I say, I saved the child; and in safety, in honour, and—hem!—in great respectability, I, at considerable charge, brought her up."

"You? You?"

"Even I! She is a young woman now!"

"A what?"

"A young woman, madam; and as beautiful as she can be."

The bereaved mother looked at the little child's shoe she had in her hand, and which, up to that moment, she had identified with her lost little one; and then her thoughts flew back to the distant period at which she had last looked in the eyes of her darling, and she remembered that it would be no longer the little girl for whom that shoe would be suitable whom she could now see.

"Ah!" she cried; "I shall not know my own Lavinia!"

"You will," added Sharples,—"you will, for she is wonderfully like you, as well as like her father!"

"Her father! Oh, heaven, her father!"

"Yes, she is like you both; and I am the only an in all the world who can tell you where she is!"

"Where—oh, where?"

"Speak at once, wretch!" cried the old servant.

Jacob Sharples bent a scowling glance upon her.

"Ill names are not the best means to get any man to speak. But you, madam, said something about a reward?"

"I did! I did!"

"What will you give?"

"All I have—everything—this house, and all it contains—everything, to the last farthing, for one look into the eyes of my child!"

"Indeed!"

"Oh, my lady, you are rash!" said the old servant.

"No, no, I am not rash! What is all the world—what are all the goods of the world, and all its wealth, compared to such a restoration? Oh, it is a new heart—new life—a new soul! I tell you, man, that you shall have all, if you will take me to my child!'

"Agreed!" cried Sharples, as he clapped his hands together,—"agreed! It is a bargain, then?"

"Oh, yes, yes!"

"Not quite, my dear madam!" said a deep, quiet voice, as the door of the drawing-room opened, and a young and most gentlemanly-looking man, in black, walked into the room.

CHAPTER LXIX.

JACOB SHARPLES GOES FROM BAD TO WORSE, AND FINDS HIMSELF IN PRISON.

JACOB SHARPLES uttered a shout of fear, and darted to the window to escape, but the young gentlemanly-looking man in black caught him by the wrist, and held him with the tenacity of a vice.

"No! You remain here! Sit down, sir!"

Jacob Sharples found himself forced into a chair, as if this operation had been performed by the action of some irresistible machine.

"Who—who—who are you?"

"I am the Rev. James White, curate of Islington Church."

"The—the—the Reverend—a Reverend?"

"Yes, I am what I say; and it is my duty, as well as my pleasure, to protect this lady from renewed affliction at your hands. Already I know sufficient to enable me to find a reason for your presence here, and to know that the injuries you have already done her are such as the repentance of a life can scarcely atone for."

"My presence here?"

"Yes; you are here, because it has been, and is, the will of providence that you should not pass away from this mortal life without meeting her whom you thought you had murdered!"

"Murdered?"

"Yes. Do not trifle with me, or with her, or with yourself. You know now, as well as I can tell you, that this lady is the wife of Doctor Haslem, the well-known Court Physician; and you know, too, that you were one of the agents of the man, be he whom he may, who induced a too ready belief in the mind of that gentleman of the criminalities of one who, by her pure, blameless life, has set a pattern to her sex."

"Oh, no, no!—not that!" sobbed the lady of the villa at Islington, who we now ought to call Mrs. Haslem.

Most undoubtedly was she that long lost wife of the physician in Bedford Square.

Most truly was she the lady who, in the small boat on the Thames so many years before, had attracted the cupidity of Jacob Sharples to a sufficient extent to make him think that he had taken her life, in order to possess himself of the jewels that then adorned her.

And she was the veritable mother of our heroine, the gentle, the good, and the beautiful Pamela!

What a weight of guilty remorse ought to have been lifted from the soul of Jacob Sharples upon these discoveries.

Was it so?

Alas, no!

He only seemed to feel an increase of terror.

The disposition of Jacob Sharples was so intensely selfish, that he would rather have endured all the pangs that conscience, at moments when it might be partially awakened, could inflict upon him, than meet his victim face to face, along with power on the side of that victim to punish him.

Sharples looked at the Rev. James White askance and with fright in his eyes.

The young clergyman took good care to keep between Sharples and the windows.

"Now, sir," he said, "you owe all the reparation in your power to this much-injured lady. What have you to say?"

"Her child lives! As I have said, I saved the child, and she lives!"

Mrs Haslem looked faint and ill.

"Ought I—oh, ought I to believe this man?"

"I think so," said the Rev. Mr. White. "He shall gain nothing by a suppression or perversion of the truth, but he may gain by speaking it."

"I do—I will speak the truth!" cried Sharples; "and, upon a promise that I shall be protected, held free of all consequences, and handsomely paid——"

A look of contempt came over the face of the young curate.

Jacob Sharples was trying to play the same game there, at that villa at Islington, that he had tried at Doctor Haslem's house at Bedford Square.

He thought it possible actually to trade upon the consequences of his own iniquity and villany.

But he was again mistaken.

The young curate, probably, had not quite so much knowledge of the world as Handsome Jemmy, the highwayman; but, in all other respects, he was quite a match for Jacob Sharples.

"No!" was the prompt reply. "It is for us to make

THE INTERVIEW BETWEEN THE KING AND CHIEF JUSTICE HOLT.

No. 21.—FELON'S DAUGHTER.

conditions with you, not for you to dictate them to us."

"What conditions?"

"In proportion as you show an inclination to atone for the past, so shall be your fortune in the future."

Jacob Sharples probably did not put the same construction upon these words exactly that the Rev. James White did, but at all events they had to him a disagreeable sound.

"What—oh, what," he cried, "would you have me do?"

"Confess and atone!"

"I do not comprehend you."

"Go to Doctor Haslem, and so far as you know the facts, declare to him the innocence of this injured lady!"

"Yes—yes."

"You will do so?"

"Gladly—most willingly. I will go at once; only assure me that I am not beset outside this house by those men who have hunted me hither!"

"That," said the young curate, "cannot matter."

"Not matter?"

"Not in the least. The repentance and atonement we require are not what may arise from fear of prosecution. It is in the furnace of affliction that the heart of such a man as you must be purified."

Jacob Sharples began to find that he was in what he called bad hands.

But the experience he had already had of the personal powers of the young clergyman let him see that an attempt to escape by force would be out of the question.

He assumed a dogged tone.

"In my hands," he cried, "is the life of the child of this lady and of Doctor Haslem. I will let it be sacrificed, or I will myself be saved!"

"We shall see!" said the Rev. James White. "I am decided! Dear madam, I will speak to you soon, and seek your sanction for what I am about to do."

"You have it—you have it," sobbed Mrs. Haslem. "I know that in better, and purer, and stronger hands than yours I cannot leave all my hopes!"

The young curate bowed.

Then he turned to Jacob Sharples, and spoke coldly and firmly.

"On condition that you say at once where the daughter of this lady is to be found, you shall *not* be delivered up to the constables, who, I have no doubt, are still within call."

The tables were turned with a vengeance. Instead of making terms that would be to his advantage, he found that he was only to reap some negative good from the information he pretended was in his hands.

He groaned before he spoke, and then he uttered the word "Newgate."

Mrs. Haslem uttered an exclamation of grief and horror.

Jacob Sharples found a pleasure in making somebody suffer.

"Newgate," he repeated,—"she is in Newgate, and is convicted of uttering base coin, and will perish yet on the scaffold!"

"Oh, my child! my child! Oh, heaven, save her!"

"Hush!" said the curate. "Let me still speak to this man."

He fixed his eyes on Sharples, who, after a vain effort to withstand the earnest gaze and out-face him, quailed beneath the look.

"Tell me," said the young clergyman, "is the girl innocent or guilty?"

"Innocent or—or guilty of—of what?"

"Of the crime laid to her charge."

"Guilty, of course."

"Then nothing can save her?"

"Nothing—nothing!"

"Oh, heaven, do not say that. Let me not hear such dreadful words!" cried Mrs Haslem.

The young curate held up his hand to demand silence.

"Dear madam," he said, "the laws of the land in which we live may be open to criticism, but they should be obeyed, and we should all seek to aid them, unless we should positively see that some great good will arise from even shielding a malefactor; for better is it that ten guilty persons should escape, than one innocent heart be unjustly condemned."

"But my child—my own dear little one, into whose eyes I have looked and fancied there was no heaven more fair!"

"Hush! Oh, hush!"

Jacob Sharples was slowly rubbing his hands one over the other.

He rather fancied that at last he was getting the better of the young clergyman.

The coiner was mistaken.

"You say," added the curate, "that she is guilty. There, then, can be no object in screening you, since there is no chance in saving her."

"Eh?"

"And, therefore, I shall surrender you at once to the officers!"

"No, no!"

"Yes! What has already taken place will be quite sufficient to convince Doctor Haslem of the entire innocence of his wife! Come!"

The curate took Jacob Sharples by the collar, and fairly held him up on his feet.

"No, no! She—she is not guilty. She had no guilty knowledge that the gold she changed was base. She is innocent—innocent!"

The young curate let go of the collar of Sharples.

The coiner fell huddled up to the floor.

In solemn words, then, the Rev. Mr. White repeated what he had before said in reference to Sharples and Pamela.

"Better than ten guilty should escape, than one innocent perish. You shall have mercy so far as it can be extended to you, for the sake of that innocent girl."

Jacob began slowly to rise to his feet.

"Be still!" said the curate.

He sunk down again to the floor, like a beaten dog.

The curate hastily wrote on a piece of paper the following words:—

"I declare that the young girl named Pamela by me, and who has been convicted of uttering base coin, is entirely innocent, and I consent to a voluntary detention in the hands of the Rev. James White, until steps can be taken to prove such innocence."

"Read, and sign!" said the curate.

"But——"

"Nay, if you have any objection, the constables are without."

Jacob Sharples signed the paper.

Then the curate, turning to Mrs. Haslem, said gently, "Hope for the best. Trust in heaven and all its mercies. And now tell me if in this house there is any room which will make a strong, secure temporary prison for this man?"

"The loft!" cried the old servant. "The old loft at the top of the house. It is only reached by a trap-door and a ladder."

"I think that will do. The house is a detached one, and so from such a position he cannot well escape."

To the great discomfiture of Jacob Sharples, then, he was introduced to a low apartment in the roof of the house, which was, when a ladder was removed, cut off from all communication except with a very awkward staircase through a trap-door.

There he was left alone with a jug of water and a loaf of bread, and recommended by the Rev. James White to pray.

Jacob Sharples, we are very much afraid, did the other thing.

The young curate spoke many words of comfort to Mrs. Haslem.

"Out of all this evil," he said, "shall spring good. I

can see, as in a glass, that happy days are in store for you, and that all will be well. I have a second sort of cousin who is a nobleman, and who, although somewhat eccentric in his ways and habits, has a good heart in the right place. To him I will go by the earliest hour in the morning I can hope to see him, and seek his help."

"Ah, how can I thank you?"

"Not at all—not at all! If any thanks are due, let them be given to a higher power than any on earth Now go to rest; I will watch here, for you have a dangerous guest in this house."

Mrs. Haslem was completely subdued by grief and excitement. She could only find words now to ask the name of the distant relative to whom the young curate meant to apply, that she might remember it too in her prayers.

The reply was brief, and will be more full of meaning to the reader than it was then to Mrs. Haslem.

"His name is Lord Malvern."

CHAPTER LXX.

CAPTAIN SANG APPEARS YET TO HAVE A CHANCE OF ESCAPE FROM NEWGATE.

IF ever a human being felt all the agonies of rage and despair, that human being was Captain Sang, *alias* Sir John Pope.

The formidable and bloodthirsty reputation that the name of Sang possessed in Newgate made his capture one of the most pleasant and desirable episodes of any day's work that could then possibly be done.

A perfect host of warders and turnkeys fell upon Sang, and he was heavily ironed at once.

In one of the condemned cells he was flung, like a sack of rubbish, for he had raved and blasphemed, and bitten, and kicked, and plunged, until the officers were tired of him.

So they left him to himself, one of them informing him that if, at the end of an hour, when they came to him again, he was not a little more composed, he would be subjected to the prison fare in such cases—namely, repeated pails of water thrown over him, till he was in a rational, quiescent state.

"Wretches! devils! Let me go! I will kill you all! I will pay you all!—I will make you as rich as you like! I will cut all your throats! Murderers, scoundrels all—let me go! Give me a club—a mallet—anything, with which I can cleave all your skulls!"

The warders laughed, and left him.

With blood upon his face, the Governor of Newgate crept down to his private room on the ground floor, and summoned the head warder, for already he had heard something of what had taken place.

Hardly, however, had he time to make an inquiry of him, when a handsome private chariot drove up to the Governor's house at Newgate.

A footman in plain clothes got down from behind the carriage, and in the most respectful manner took some orders from a person within the vehicle.

Then he knocked at the Governor's house.

All this little manoeuvring, so to call it, had passed under the observation of the turnkey whose special duty it was to attend at that part of Newgate, so that the door of the Governor's house was opened while the echo of the knock of the servant out of livery still reverberated in the hall.

"A gentleman to speak to the Governor!"

"What's his name?"

"Only a gentleman."

The style of the equipage, and the look of the person within the coach, combined to give the turnkey an idea that the visitor was of importance.

The visitor was admitted, and in three minutes was ushered into that private room in which the discomfited Governor sat.

The disposition of the Governor was to be rude to visitors who did not bring with them the power of some name or title that he felt compelled to bow down to.

But there was a quiet kind of dignity about this visitor that baffled him.

The Governor bowed in spite of himself.

"I perceive, Mr. Governor," said the visitor, "that you do not know me?"

"No, sir."

"I am the Secretary of State for the Home Department."

The Governor, upon this intimation, was quite ready to bow down to the dust, and to kiss the shoes, if that were necessary, of the high authority.

The Secretary continued, "You have by this time a prisoner here, who has been given into your custody as Captain Sang, the notorious highwayman."

"Yes, my lord; but—but——"

"But what?"

"I was going to say that I myself have not been for more than five mortal minutes in possession of that news."

"That is of no consequence."

"But, my lord, how is it possible that you can know it?"

"It is the duty of persons in my position not only always to know what has happened, but in many cases to know what is going to happen."

The Secretary of State made the speech with so much gravity that it fairly imposed upon the Governor.

He bowed again.

"Certainly, my lord, certainly. It is so, no doubt; and Captain Sang, after coming here and trying to murder me, is in one of the strong cells."

"What came he here for?"

"Why, my lord, he brought an order from your lordship for the liberation, into his hands, of one Pamela Sharples."

"Indeed?"

"Oh, yes; and it was because I could not at the moment take upon myself to say that such a strange order was genuine, that the rascal fired a pistol right into my face, and the ball must have missed me by a perfect miracle."

The Secretary of State shook his head.

"Well, my lord," added the Governor, "if I did not miss it, it is in my head still."

"I do not allude to that circumstance, but to the pretended order for the liberation of a prisoner. I cannot believe it."

"But, my lord——"

"Nay, it transcends belief."

"Then, my lord, here it is!"

"Ah! Indeed!"

"Yes, my lord; one of our men picked it up on the steps of Newgate."

The Governor handed to the Secretary of State the very order which the Secretary had written at his own breakfast-table for Sir John Pope.

"Ah! I perceive it is an impudent forgery, and so I shall retain it."

Right glad was the Secretary of State to put into his pocket so singular and dangerous a document.

"But, my lord!"

"What now?"

"I understand from my men that some one else has been here and taken away the same prisoner, by virtue of another order."

"Mr. Governor!" said the Secretary of State, with a sly look.

"My lord!"

"Mr. Governor, it seems to me that the affairs of Newgate are conducted in a very lax manner; but as I do not wish to injure any man in an official position, I shall say no more on that head."

"I assure you, my lord——"

"Silence!"

"My lord, I——"

"Silence! I require to see this man who is called

Sir John Pope, *alias* Captain Sang, the highwayman I happen to know something of him, and for the ends of justice I require to see him."

"Certainly; you lordship has but to command here."

"As quickly as possible, then!"

"Will your lordship go to his cell, or will your lordship see him here?"

"Here, by all means! No cells for me! But I want to see him alone. All I require is, that assistance, should I need it, will be within call."

The Governor bowed with an air of reverence to those orders; and in the course of ten minutes, Sang, in a very miserable plight and heavily fettered, was ushered into the room.

The Secretary of State stood in the shadow of the door, so that until it was shut and he advanced, Sang did not see him.

When the ruffian highwayman did cast his eyes on him, he uttered a howl of rage.

By putting this and that together, as the saying is, Sang was able pretty well to come to a correct conclusion in regard to the causes of all that had so recently befallen him.

The first words of the Secretary of State, if he had had any doubt upon the subject, would quickly have resolved them.

Those words were but two.

"Check mate!"

Sang made a rush forward. He had forgotten the fetters that cramped and confined his limbs, and he fell heavily to the floor.

Heavily at the feet of the Secretary, who took advantage of the event to deal his prostrate foe a hearty kick.

"Up, scoundrel!"

Sang yelled with rage.

A warder looked in.

"Anything amiss, sir?"

"Oh, no, no! I will call when I want you. Never mind how high you hear his voice."

"Very good, sir!"

"Now, scoundrel!" said the Secretary, in a low tone. "What have you to say for yourself? It is my turn now! Did you imagine for half a moment that you had wit enough to criminate me?"

"Master!" said Sang.

"Oh, you own it?"

"I do! I do!"

"Then that will make things all the easier. I demand the letters you took from me on the highway, and for them you shall have life and liberty; but you must promise—ay, and keep your word—to leave England for ever!"

CHAPTER LXXI.

THE SECRETARY OF STATE IS STILL BAFFLED IN HIS PURSUIT OF THE PRIVATE LETTERS.

CAPTAIN SANG, *alias* Sir John Pope, heard the words of the Secretary with which we concluded our last chapter with something of the sensation of a drowning wretch, in whose ears echo the cry, "Here's a plank!"

He felt that he was saved.

He scrambled wholly to his feet, and as well as he could he clasped his hands together as he said, "It is a bargain!"

"Very well; carry it out, then! You recollect that this morning, at my house, I told you that things would come to this pass?"

"You did!—you did!"

"Well!—the letters?"

"You shall have them! Let me go and fetch them, and they are yours!"

"No!"

"No, say you?"

"I do say no!"

"But—but——"

"Nay, hear me out, Sang—for that you are the veritable Sang I make no doubt in the world! Before one of those manacles are removed from your limbs I must be in possession of those letters!"

"You cannot!"

"Why not?"

"Because they are hidden!"

"They can be found!"

"No, no!—a thousand times, no! They are so securely hidden in my house in the Birdcage Walk, at Westminster, that no human being but myself can find them!"

The Secretary smiled.

"But yet," said the Secretary, "it is a little different to the story you told me this morning at my house!"

"Different?"

"Yes! I fancy you have had a tap on the head during the day's proceedings, which has confused your perceptions somewhat. If those letters are so well hidden that no human hand can find them, and if I have you sent to the gallows, why, all will be well!"

"No! no!"

"Why not?"

"I can direct persons where to look for them, and will do so!"

"Direct me, then!"

Sang groaned.

Whatever he said, and whichsoever way he turned, fresh difficulties seemed to start in his mind.

"I own it!—I own it!" he cried. "I am foiled! I own it! Make now what conditions you will, and I give in to them!"

"Well, you are reasonable. Direct me where to find the letters, and upon my getting possession of them I will pledge my word that you shall be a free man!"

Sang looked with a wild, troubled expression into the face of the Secretary of State, but he felt that he had no resource now but to trust him.

"Be it so, my lord!" he said; "be it so! Go to my house. Force a way in, for I have lost the key, and there is no one to admit you. Take down a portrait of King Charles the First, which hangs in the front room on the ground floor. It is a framed and glazed print: behind it, and between the backboard and print you will find the letters!"

"Very good! Ho! warder, ho!"

A couple of the prison officials immediately advanced.

"Call the Governor!"

"Mr. Governor," said the Secretary, "I have some reason to doubt if the prisoner is Captain Sang, the highwayman. I am about to go now somewhere for the purpose of resolving those doubts one way or the other, and shall be able to let you know in a couple of hours."

Sang drew a long breath.

There was hope in these words—hope that the Secretary of State would really keep his word with him.

"In the meantime, I suppose my lord, we must keep him safe?"

"Most certainly!"

"I am willing—I am willing!" said Sang. "It is all a mistake, and it will be found to be such. It is all a mistake; but I am willing to be kept in custody—oh, quite willing; because I feel sure that it will be found out to be all an error, and that I am in reality Sir John Pope."

The Secretary slightly inclined his head, and left Newgate.

Sir John Pope's house in the Birdcage Walk, by St. James's Park, had a gloomy and melancholy aspect.

Every blind was down.

Every shutter was shut.

It did not seem to be a very easy matter to get into it at all; but the Secretary of State was resolved that he would not go home till he had got into it; and he, in as calm a manner as he could assume, ordered his coachman and footman to find some mode of entrance.

A window on the ground-floor seemed to be the most probable way, and a pane was broken, and the shutters forced.

The Secretary entered the house quite alone.

Yes. In that very room was the portrait of King Charles the First that Sang had mentioned to him, and by the light of day that came in at the window he took it down.

As he did so, the backboard fell out. The print followed it. The glass was loose, and likewise fell to the floor. The Secretary held the frame, denuded thus of all its accompaniments, in his hand, but letters there were none.

The polite, aristocratic coolness of the Secretary gave way, and he uttered some expressions that would have been heard with the most intense surprise in the drawing-rooms of St. James's.

"Foiled! foiled! The rascal has lied, after all!"

A second thought, however, modified the opinion thus hastily formed.

The state of the picture-frame and the picture showed that some tampering had taken place with it. What if Sang was right? and what if some one else had found out the secret, and got possession of the concealed papers?

It might be so.

That some one else might be in the house, for all he knew.

The Secretary drew the dress sword that he wore, and dashing open the door of the room which led to the hall and to that staircase down which Sang had had so horrible a fall, he stood and listened.

Not a sound could be heard in the whole house.

The fanlight above the outer door let in plenty of light from the Park to the hall, but there was some coloured glass in that fanlight that cast strange shades upon the hall.

One of those shades, however, was so much deeper than any of the others, that the Secretary touched it with his foot to ascertain if it really proceeded from the stained glass of the fanlight or not.

It did not.

He trod upon some slippery, humid substance.

It was coagulated blood!

A feeling of terror took possession of the Secretary, and he was out of the ill-omened house in a few seconds.

Mortified and disappointed, he drove home, deeply cogitating as he went what he should do.

A poor old woman, apparently in the last stage of poverty, sat on the doorstep of his mansion.

At sight of him, as he stepped out of his carriage, she cried out aloud, "Is that the great lord? Is that the great lord?"

"Yes," said a servant, "that is his lordship If you please, my lord, this old beggar woman pretends she has something to say to you."

"Yes, I have!" screamed the old woman, as she flung herself at his feet. "Yes, I have! Have mercy, and compassion, and charity on a poor, lone, old, destitute woman?"

"Out of the way, hag!"

"Oh, do not spurn me! Have some mercy upon me!"

"Out of the way, I say! Take the old hag to the Round-house!"

The Secretary strode almost over the old woman into his house.

Then she burst into screaming, frantic laughter, as she shouted, "It is done! It is done! I did but try him! Ha! ha! ha! He shall not have them! No, no! He shall not have them now! He knows not what he has lost!—lost!—lost!"

The hag rose to her feet, and pushing through the throng of servants, who, to tell the truth, were much better pleased that she should run away than that they should have the trouble of carrying her to the Round-house, she disappeared from the street.

And, as she went, she clutched something that she had hidden in the breast of her apparel.

That something was a packet, and that packet contained nothing less than those important letters which the Secretary of State had already consumed all his morning in trying to possess himself of.

And who was this old hag, but the housekeeper of Sir John Pope, *alias* Captain Sang.

She had left the house of the highwayman, believing that its once master lay a corpse in the hall; but she had taken with her those papers which she had, through the keyhole of that door, seen him hide behind the portrait.

The Secretary of State, therefore, after being within arm's length of the documents he wanted, went into his house with a troubled look, while the old hag rapidly increased her distance from it.

The Secretary then sent, by his own messenger, a note to the Governor of Newgate.

"The Secretary of State presents his compliments to the Governor of Newgate, and has to state that he is not yet in a position to speak positively to the identity or otherwise of the man said to be Captain Sang, *alias* Sir John Pope; and therefore he, the Secretary of State, desires that the prisoner should be kept in strict custody, for which this shall be a sufficient authority."

The Secretary wanted time to think.

Captain Sang had plenty of leisure for the same mental exercise, in the silence of his cell.

The Secretary's thoughts were not very prolific of events, but Captain Sang's were.

What those events were, we will now proceed to detail.

CHAPTER LXXII.

A FAMILY PARTY ASSEMBLES AT THE DOCTOR'S HOUSE, AND DICK DOUBLEDAY IS HAPPY.

BY a careful investigation of all his pockets, Captain Sang found that he had the sum of sixteen guineas about him.

His eyes were getting accustomed to the gloom of his cell, and as he looked at these sixteen guineas, he felt that they, at least, were sixteen friends whom he could trust.

He waited with impatience for some indication of the approach of the news of his release. The two hours that had been mentioned by the Secretary had certainly passed, and no one came near him with the welcome tidings that there was some mistake, and that he was a free man.

Those were the tidings he expected, provided the Secretary did not betray him, and forfeit his word.

But they came not.

Sang, when about four hours had passed away, got furious.

He banged the earthen pitcher that contained his allowance of water against the door of the cell.

He roared and shouted.

A warder came.

"What now, eh?"

"Ill—sick!"

"Not allowed."

"Mad!"

"It's agin the regulations."

"I have sixteen guineas!"

"Oh, that's all right, and quite another thing! How are you, Captain Sang? Can I do anything for you? Always willing and ready to oblige a gentleman with sixteen guineas, I'm sure!"

The turnkey held out his hand, and Sang felt that he could do no better than hand him at least half of the gold.

"Tell me," said Sang; "has any order come about me from the Secretary of State?"

" Yes."

" Ah!—it has ?"

" To be sure; and it is that you are to be kept fast!"

" The treacherous villain!"

" Oh, I know nothing about that!"

Sang felt how useless it would be to take his money's worth in abuse of the Secretary of State, so he suddenly assumed a calmness he was very far from feeling.

" Look you here!" he said. " I want to write a letter, and get it posted."

" All's right! That's a guinea!"

" Very well; I have given you——Let me see!—yes, I have given you eight."

" Oh, they are gone!"

" Gone ?"

" Yes, into my pocket. You didn't say a word about a letter when you handed them out."

" True, true! You are a man of business!"

" Rather!"

" Then take another guinea, and get me the means of writing a letter, as quickly as you can!"

Writing materials on these terms were soon supplied to Captain Sang, and he wrote the following letter:—

" To Chief Justice Holt.

" My Lord,—The young girl, named Pamela Sharples, who was condemned to death for uttering bad money, has escaped again from Newgate, and is in the keeping of Lord Malvern. Is justice to be defeated to shield the paramour of a nobleman, who has always been in opposition to his Majesty's Government?

" These few lines come from one who need not put his name to them, because the slightest inquiry will suffice to substantiate their truth."

The letter was duly posted, and Captain Sang waited the result.

The result was just this.

The Chief Justice was at Windsor on audience of the King at the time that letter, with some dozen others, was sent after him, as was the custom, by a special post messenger.

Now the escape of Pamela from Newgate had been duly notified to the King; and he, with that disposition to push criminal punishments to the greatest extremity, which he had, was extremely mortified upon the subject.

It was almost a matter of daily reproach to the Lord Chief Justice, and the King was in the habit of interrupting some more important subject with, " Well, well Holt! I say, what—well—have you caught that young woman who used to pass all the bad money, and then wouldn't be hanged ? Eh ?—eh ?—eh ?"

The invariable " No, your Majesty," of the Lord Chief Justice then provoked some unpleasant remarks, so that it was quite a treat to the judge to be able to say on this occasion, " Your Majesty, while I was in waiting for the honour of this audience, I received a letter about that very young woman who escaped from the hands of justice and the gallows at Tyburn "

" What ?—what ?—eh ? The young woman who made and passed all the bad money—eh ?"

" Yes, your Majesty."

" Pamela Sharples—eh ? Never forget people's names. Might have have taken a bad guinea ourselves—eh ?"

" It is possible, your Majesty."

" To be sure it is! Well—eh?—caught her, have you, Holt ?"

" No, your Majesty; but here is a letter which affects to give information of her, and which I will do myself the honour of reading to your Majesty, if it is your royal pleasure."

" Yes, it is!—yes, it is! Go on! Read away! What is it. Always like to read letters, particularly other people's—eh?—what? No, don't mean that! Go on! So! Hilloa! A pretty thing! My Lord Malvern! Know him quite well! Obstinate man, very! Opposition peer! Won't put up with it! Hang her! Should like to hang him too! What's to be done, Holt ? Eh ? eh ?"

" The first thing, your Majesty, will be to ascertain the fact."

" Well, well!—what then ?"

" Then, unless your Majesty should feel inclined to interpose with your royal pardon—"

" Royal what? Royal fiddlestick! Pardon? No, not if we know it, Holt! Oh, dear, no! Hang her? Hang her!"

" Then all that can be done is that she be apprehended, and identified in Court, when she can be again left for execution."

" To be sure! Do it—do it! That will be settled then! Might be put off some day with a bad guinea ourselves, you know, Holt—eh? eh?"

The Lord Chief Justice was in duty bound to take action about the affair, and he placed it in the hands of the Sheriff, who again empowered the officers to act, and the danger of Pamela soon became imminent again.

But what is she about now, that she is no longer an inhabitant of one of the gloomy cells of Newgate ?

And what is the kind, warm-hearted and eccentric Lord Malvern doing, now that he has so gallantly rescued Pamela ?

Where now are the two sworn friends, Dick Doubleday and Handsome Jemmy, the highwayman ?

And how fares it with the sad, afflicted heart of Doctor Haslem, the much-envied and fashionable Court

Alas! how little the world really knows of those whom it envies!

We shall see, however, something of all these persons if, at exactly twelve o'clock on the morning following the release of Pamela from Newgate, we look into the principal drawing-room of Doctor Haslem's house in Bedford Square

The Doctor himself is seated on a couch.

On a low ottoman at his feet, with both hands clasped in his, is poor persecuted Pamela.

All that had required explanation was explained now, and Doctor Haslem felt indeed that it was his long-lost child into whose fair face he looked.

But it was through tears he gazed at her.

He was still under the impression that it would need to be amid the mud and slime of the river that he would have to search for all that remained of his poor lost wife.

Oh, what a thought of agony was that!

How it dashed the joy-cup from his lips, which otherwise, on the recovery of his daughter, would indeed have overflowed with nectar!

He was speaking tearfully and tremulously.

" In the midst of our greatest joys we shall ever find our greatest griefs! Our truest and dearest affections bring with them ever our most heartrending anxieties! The seeming pure gold of human happiness is never without its alloy! I ought to be happy with you, dear, dear child; but my heart and soul is full of recollections of your mother, and there is no abject wretch on all the earth so unhappy as your poor, poor father!"

" No, no! Oh, do not say so!" sobbed Pamela. " Heaven is merciful and just, because it is so just to be merciful! Human frailty will not then be confounded with human guilt, and we shall all yet be happy in the sunny presence of everlasting life! Father, dear father, all will be forgiven!"

The door of the room was gently opened, and Lord Malvern appeared, leading in two gentlemen.

One is a thin and handsome gentleman.

The other a man of commanding presence, and a model of masculine beauty, if we may use the word.

" Mr. Doubleday—aw—and Mr.—aw—Haslem—aw—desire to pay wespects to you, Doctaw, and to you, Pamelaw. Excwese me—aw—calling you Pamelaw still; when—aw—I think a fellaw ought to call you Laviniaw."

" Dick!" cried Pamela, as she sprung to her feet. " My own dear Dick!"

" Pamela!"

In a moment, she was in the arms of Dick Doubleday.

"Oh, father," she then cried, "he was so good, so gentle, so affectionate, tender, and mindful of your girl, when she had no one else that she knew of in all the wide world to love her, that you must not be angry with me for flying to his arms! But for him, where should I be now, and what would you be?"

"Aw—that's twue—that's twue! Come, Doctaw—I ask the hand of Pamelaw for my pwivate secwetawy—aw—Mr. Wichard Doubleday—aw!"

"Is it possible," said the Doctor, "that I can say no to any request of yours, Lord Malvern? And if that be impossible, how much more must it be so that I can place myself in opposition to the happiness of this dear child? What right have I?"

"Father! father!" cried Pamela, "you must not speak so. Your child must be happy with your sanction, or not at all!"

"Or not at all, sir!" said Dick Doubleday, as he knelt with Pamela at the feet of her father.

"Be happy, then, my children both; and may existence in its fairest, sunniest aspect ever be yours. May it never know the clouds which have obscured the better part of my life!"

"Aw—that's wight—that's wight! And now, Doctaw do you know this gentleman—aw—Mr. Haslem?"

"Mr. Haslem?"

"Yes; he was—aw—Handsome Jemmy, but he is now your nephew, and the son of your brother who is dead—aw. He will tell you—aw—all about it, and—aw—convince you of the facts while we—aw——Look out at this window—aw! Eh? what do those fellaws want here?"

As Lord Malvern looked from the window, he saw a strong party of police officers, who made no concealment of their red waistcoats and small staves of office, gathering about the door-step.

Alas! Pamela's perils are not yet quite over!

CHAPTER LXXIII.

PAMELA IS ONCE MORE IN THE HANDS OF THE OFFICERS, BUT SHE DOES NOT DESPAIR.

HANDSOME JEMMY had no time to tell his story to his uncle, Doctor Haslem, before he was attracted to the window of the drawing-room by the remark of Lord Malvern to the effect that the house was beleaguered by constables.

He strode to the window at once.

One glance of his practised eyes was more than sufficient to let him see the exact state of affairs, and he felt that either his liberty or Pamela's was threatened—perhaps both, and possibly that of Dick Doubleday likewise.

"Danger!" he cried, as he turned from the window.

A sharp knocking at the outer door of the Doctor's house, mingled with this utterance of the word "Danger!" by Handsome Jemmy, whom we feel hardly yet inclined to call by his new name of Haslem.

The little party in that fair and handsome room looked in each other's faces with something like dismay

Doctor Haslem clasped both the hands of Pamela in his own; for he seemed to feel instinctively that if there were real and actual danger, it would be to his beautiful child, whom he had but just recovered.

Dick Doubleday, too, had a similar feeling; and he stood close to Pamela, looking rather pale, but with a determined expression upon his face, which should have been more than sufficient to convince any one that there was danger brooding at his heart to all who by word, look, or action should seek to interfere with her whom he loved better than his life.

Lord Malvern settled his eye-glass more firmly in his eye.

It was Handsome Jemmy alone who took another long look from the window; and then, turning to the little party in the room, he said, "They are Bow Street runners; but to which of us here present they bring danger and trouble it is hard to say."

"To none, let us hope," said Doctor Haslem.

Handsome Jemmy shook his head.

"We will all," added the Doctor, "stand or fall together. No power on earth shall now wrest from me my child!"

"Nor from me my life!" said Dick Doubleday.

As he spoke, he sufficiently indicated what he meant by his life, by stepping a pace in front of poor Pamela.

She was terribly agitated.

What a sad fate it would be at such a time to be torn from all those who had loved her so well and so truly!

From the new-found father!

From the lover who had been so constant and so true under all circumstances!

No wonder that the heart of Pamela sunk within her, and tears rose sparkling to her eyes.

The knocking at the outer door of the Doctor's house had ceased.

It was not possible to hold that mansion closed, as though it were in a state of siege.

The servants had promptly enough responded to the vigorous appeal of the constables.

They rushed into the hall.

The man who led them was a constable who was always on special duty about the Chief Justice, and who generally followed him wherever he went; but on this occasion he had been given the command of the important party that had been sent to capture Pamela.

That capture that seemed so easy after the information contained in the epistle from Captain Sang.

"You, Brett, and you, Jackson!" cried the officer in command, "keep guard in the hall!"

"Yes, sir!"

"Don't let a soul leave the house!"

"All right, sir!"

"Now, comrades, follow me, and we will take things easy."

What this officer meant by taking things easy, was not to make any inquiry whatever for his victim but to proceed in a systematic way to look for her in that house.

The system consisted in looking carefully into every room on the ground floor, and then locking the doors one after the other and taking possession of the keys

By this plan of operations, the officers, by the time they ascended the staircase, had quite a bunch of keys in their possession.

There was but little time in which to think of any mode of procedure that should promise safety to Pamela.

Unfortunately, the room in which they were was not that one which communicated by the secret passage to the apartment which possessed so many terrible memories for Doctor Haslem.

But there was a large Indian screen in the room, and although it was not likely that the officer would omit to look behind it, yet it afforded a temporary safety for Pamela.

By the advice of Handsome Jemmy she retired behind it.

The door, then, was unceremoniously opened and the throng of constables appeared.

Pale and trembling in every limb, and looking much older than he really was, Doctor Haslem advanced.

Yet there was about his white hair and grief-lined face an aspect of dignity that for the moment had its effect upon the officers.

The foremost took off his hat involuntarily, and then clapped it on his head again as he said, "Are you Doctor Haslem, sir?"

"I am."

"Very good! Then, from information we have received, we are of opinion that a young girl of the name of Pamela Sharples is in this house."

"There is no such person."

"It's all very well, Doctor, for you to say that, but we are the sort of men, you see, who don't take an answer; so we will, if you please, look for ourselves."

Lord Malvern stepped forward.

"Aw—do you know me, fellaw?"

"No."

"Then—aw—I am Lord Malvern!"

"Why, then, my lord, you are just the man we expected to find here. It is the smart little wench that your lordship has in keeping that we want."

Lord Malvern tightened the glass in his eye, and made a slight movement to clear his right wrist well of the cuff of his coat.

"Aw—fellaw!"

"Well, my lord?"

"Will you—aw—say that again?"

"To be sure I will. We want the smart little girl that——"

"Stop! I will give you credit for the rest of it—aw—and now I beg to tell you that there are a few things —aw—that I can do. I can wun—I can shoot—I can swim, and I can knock down a fellaw that tells an insulting lie of a young lady—aw!"

Out flew the right fist of Lord Malvern as if it had been a battering-ram, and crash it came exactly on the nose of the officer, who fell backwards among his men as if he had been hit by a cannon-ball.

"Murder! murder! Call out the military!—read the Riot Act! Oh, oh! Murder!"

"Now—aw—if any more of you want anything," added Lord Malvern, settling his eye-glass, which had been a little deranged by the blow, "come on, and don't —aw—mind giving me a little trouble!"

The officer shrunk back.

"My lord," said one, "we don't want you."

"Aw—I don't suppose you do."

They helped up their chief, who glared at Lord Malvern through tears and blood, as he said, "Very well, my lord, you will have to pay for this!"

"Aw—I suppose I shall; but one of the things—aw —that I can do is to pay—aw!"

"Go your ways," said Handsome Jemmy to the officer; "don't you see you are not wanted here, and the object of your search is not present?"

One of the constables looked hard at Handsome Jemmy, but he bore the scrutiny without the least flinching.

"Beg, pardon, sir: I don't know who you are, sir; but if you wasn't a gentleman, I should say you were Handsome Jemmy, the Highwayman."

"Indeed! Perhaps some of you will recognise us all one after the other."

"Yes," said another of the officers, "and that young gentleman in black, there, looks as like Dick Doubleday, who was concerned in the rescue of Pamela Sharples from the procession to Tyburn, as one pea looks like another."

Dick smiled.

"Aw!" said Lord Malvern; "that is my pwivate secwetary—aw!"

"However, I'll take him!" said the officer, who had spoken.

"No, no! he is innocent!" cried Pamela, as, in the agony of the moment, at thinking Dick Doubleday would be dragged off to a prison, she lost all perception of her own danger, and rushed from behind the screen.

"Ah!" cried the officer, who had been so adroitly knocked down by Lord Malvern, "that's our bird!"

"Pamela! Pamela!" cried Dick Doubleday, in a reproachful tone.

"Oh, heaven!" ejaculated Doctor Haslem.

The officers did not like the looks of either Dick Doubleday, Handsome Jemmy, or Lord Malvern, and they at once produced their pistols.

The chief of them likewise took from his pocket a slip of paper, which he held aloft, as he cried out, "This is the warrant, under the hand and seal of the Lord Chief Justice, for the apprehension of Pamela Sharples!"

"This is not Pamela Sharples," said Doctor Haslem.

"You may call her whatever you like, sir, but she is my prisoner!"

"Never!" said Dick Doubleday.

"Never!" cried Handsome Jemmy.

"Then the bloodshed be upon your own heads!" said the officer; "for, come what may, I must and will do my duty!"

"Aw—stop!" said Lord Malvern.

All parties looked at him.

"Stop! Constables, you will lose nothing by one hour's delay."

"Can't think of it, my lord!"

"Yes, you will think of it. I pledge myself to be absent only one hour, and to pay you fifty guineas among you for that hour, provided you stay here, and do not attempt, in that time, to molest your prisoner."

The constables looked at each other.

"Then—aw—that is agreed?"

"Well, my lord, to oblige a nobleman——"

"That will do. Wait!"

Lord Malvern at once left the room with the intention of seeking a noble relative of his who was a member of the Privy Council, and who could demand an audience of the King.

Lord Malvern was not aware how bitter and exasperated the feelings—if they may be called by such a name—of the King were against the poor innocent young girl who had been so wrongfully doomed to death.

If his lordship had but been fully aware of the sort of language used by the King to the Lord Chief Justice Holt in relation to Pamela, he would scarcely have thought it necessary to attempt anything in that quarter.

But, as it was, the eccentric but warm-hearted nobleman went down the staircase of the Doctor's house three steps at a time, and reached the hall with a speed that astonished the servants and the two constables who there stood on guard.

"My horse! Where is he?" cried Lord Malvern.

"Aw—I left him at the kerb!"

"Beg pardon, sir!"

"Eh?"

"Beg pardon, sir! Don't know who you may be, sir, but we can't let anybody leave the house till Mr. Webbles comes down!"

"Eh?"

"Mr. Wobbles is our chief officer on this here hoccasion, you see, sir," said the others; "so we must say no, sir, you sees!"

Lord Malvern eyed them with scorn.

"Who do you come here for?"

"For Pamela Sharples."

"Am I Pamela Sharples?"

"Oh, dear, no, sir; but you see orders is orders; and so we can't let you go, sir, till Mr. Wobbles comes down, sir!"

Lord Malvern made but one spring at this officer, and caught him by the throat. Dashing his head on one side, he hit the other officer such a bewildering blow on the mouth with his comrade's skull, that they both slipped from their feet as though they had been upon ice.

"Help! help!"

"Aw—you will be so good as to get out of the way —aw!"

Lord Malvern opened the street door himself, and ran right into the arms of some one who had at that moment just ascended the step, and had his hand up to knock.

"Aw—get out of the way, do!"

"My lord!"

"Eh?"

"Don't you know me, Malvern? I have been to your house, and your man, Smithers, told me you would be found here."

"Oh, don't! Get out—aw—I don't mean get out, but I can't speak to you now, White."

"Nay——"

"Indeed, I can't! You are a good fellow, and my

CAPTAIN SANG COMMITS HIS LAST CRIME.

No. 22.—FELON'S DAUGHTER.

cousin; but if you were twenty good fellows, and twenty cousins, I must be off just now."

"Excuse me, Malvern," said the Rev. James White—for it was none other than that single-minded and courageous young curate, who had just reached Doctor Haslem's house,—"excuse me, Malvern, but it is a matter of life and death."

"What?"

"I want to speak to you of some one."

"Aw—look here! If you will speak to me, White, there is only one way."

"What is that?"

"You must get up behind me on my horse, for I won't and can't wait."

CHAPTER LXXIV.
PAMELA SURRENDERS TO THE LAW BY THE ADVICE OF ALL HER FRIENDS.

THE proposition to get upon the horse that Lord Malvern's groom now, at sight of his master, trotted up to the door of the Doctor's house, was not a very palatable one to the Rev. James White.

He drew back.

"If such is the case then, Malvern," he said, "I must needs wait your whim."

"In an hour."

"Be it so."

Lord Malvern sprung on his horse's back.

"One moment more," said the Rev. James White: "is Doctor Haslem at home—for what I want to speak to both you and him about is the means of saving the further persecution and the life of his long lost child, Pamela?"

Lord Malvern looked astonished.

The glass dropped from his eye.

"Do you mean to say that it is about Pamelaw you come to speak?"

"It is. I have in my custody one whose testimony will shield her from all harm, and I will take good care that testimony shall be given."

"Aw—what one?"

"Jacob Sharples."

"Tally-ho! whoop! yoicks! stole away! tally-ho!" cried Lord Malvern.

The Rev. James White was astonished at this ebullition on the part of Lord Malvern, and the groom was so frightened, thinking his master had gone mad, that he widened his distance by several yards.

"Why, Malvern," said the curate, "you seem to be greatly interested in what I say."

"Aw—I am."

"How so?"

"Come in! come in!"

Lord Malvern flung himself off his horse as rapidly as he had mounted it a moment before, and flinging the bridle to the groom, he caught his cousin, the young clergyman, by the arm and conducted him into the house of the Court Physician.

The doors of all the lower rooms were locked, and Lord Malvern wanted to get into one, so he put his shoulder to it, and, with a sudden move, he forced it open.

"One of the things I can do," he said, "is to bweak open a door."

The Rev. James White was not altogether so much surprised as he might have been at the proceedings of Lord Malvern, because from long acquaintance with him, since they were boys together at the same school, he was pretty well accustomed to his eccentricities.

Lord Malvern then took hold of his cousin by the arm and forced him into a great arm-chair, and standing by him he said, "Now, James, what have you got to say? and if it's nothing I'll knock you over."

The young curate smiled.

"No, Malvern, you won't knock me over, for it is something. Listen!"

"With all my ears."

The Rev. James White then, in the clearest, shortest, and most concise manner, told Lord Malvern the whole story of Mrs. Haslem, and how on the evening before, this very man, Jacob Sharples, who had robbed and attempted to murder her, so long ago on the Thames, had actually sought and obtained a shelter in her house.

To say that Lord Malvern heard the tale with interest is to say little. The attention he gave to it was of the most absorbing character, and when the curate concluded by saying, "And so I hold the rascal in custody, and he promises that he will appear in court and clear Pamela," Lord Malvern fairly embraced his cousin.

"Bwavo! bwavo! Then it's all wight—aw! Bravo! Pamela shall go to Newgate!"

"To Newgate?"

"Yes. Don't you see?"

"Hardly!"

"Why, she will then be brought before the Lord Chief Justice, and we will have that fellow Jacob Sharples there, and then, in the open face of day, she will soon be free."

"But it is a hard case, Malvern, that the young girl should actually if she be now at liberty, be delivered up to captivity."

"No; it's all the better. Come up-stairs. She is there."

"Here? In this house?"

"Her father's house."

"Then they have come together?"

"To be sure they have—aw—and there is quite a a gang of constables up-stairs along with them. Stop a moment, let me think."

"Of what?"

"Of Pamelaw's mother."

"Oh, do not think of her; but let us lose not one precious moment in reuniting her to her long-lost child."

"Very good; but we must not be too hasty If Pamelaw has to go to prison, even for a day and a night, why should she have the agony of, during that time, thinking she might be united to her mothaw, eh?"

The young curate saw the drift of Lord Malvern's argument instantly.

"You are right," he said—"you are extremely right. It would indeed be cruelty rather than kindness so to play with the best feelings of either the mother or the child.

"Aw—so I think."

"Let it be so, then, my dear Malvern. Let Pamela know no more than she knows at present of her mother until she is quite free of the charge that hangs over her head."

"Aw—just so."

"And let the mother know nothing further of her child until she can be conducted to her arms."

"Aw—that's it! Only—aw—as you are used to preaching—aw—and all that sort of thing, you know how to put it—aw!"

The Reverend James White smiled; for he knew perfectly well what his cousin, the eccentric Lord Malvern, meant—which was, that he was so in the habit of preaching, that he used a great many more words in his private discourse than were necessary.

But, in good truth, that was not a reproach to which the young curate was fairly liable.

"Come on now," added Lord Malvern, as he looked at his watch, and found that he had consumed just half the hour he was to pay the officers the promised fifty guineas for—"come on, and you shall see Pamelaw."

"I long to do so."

"She is as pretty a girl as you will see—aw—on a long summer's day—aw!"

"Her poor mother, notwithstanding all the years of grief she has suffered, has still all the remains of wonderful beauty."

"Aw—has she? Well, that's all wight! But Pamelaw hasn't the wemains, but the beauty itself—aw! This way."

Lord Malvern led his young relative up the stairs to the room where Pamela, her father, Handsome Jemmy, and Dick Doubleday were to be found.

The officers, with the exception of their chief, had left the room, and stood grouped on the top of the stairs.

"Here I am, you see," said Lord Malvern; "and the hour has not passed away."

"All right, my lord."

The officers officiously opened the door for him—for already had they, in imagination, spent some of the fifty guineas which they were to have among them for that one hour's delay, and they were delighted to see him come back.

"Aw—a fwiend of mine—the Reverend James White!" said Lord Malvern, as he stepped into the handsome apartment.

The look upon the face of Lord Malvern was so serene and contented, that Doctor Haslem, Handsome Jemmy, and Dick Doubleday, and Pamela herself, anticipated nothing else but that he had succeeded in giving quite a different turn to affairs.

And so, indeed, he had; but not in the way they anticipated.

It was with the greatest suspense that they listened to him as he spoke in his odd way.

"Aw—I have been thinking that—aw—the very best thing to do will be for Pamelaw to go to Newgate at once!"

"Oh, save me!" said Pamela.

"My child to Newgate!" cried the Doctor.

"Not yet; for I still live!" said Dick Doubleday.

"Yes," added Lord Malvern; "and the reason is just this. My cousin here, the Reverend James White, has found out a testimony to the perfect innocence of Pamelaw."

"And is that a reason why she should be torn from this, her proper home, to a prison?" exclaimed Doctor Haslem.

"Yes—aw—that's the reason."

"Permit me," said the Reverend James White, in that quiet, calm, gentle voice in which he always spoke, and which was so pleasant to listen to.

"Aw—yes—you explain."

"In order that this young lady should be really free, and in order that her perils should be really over, she must be released in due course of law; and the only way that can be done is for her to surrender to the law, and then the man whose testimony shall save her will be forthcoming."

"Aw—that's it!"

"What man?" said Dick Doubleday.

"Jacob Sharples!"

"Sharples!" said Pamela. "He save me!—he give testimony of my innocence! Oh, no, no! He is the last!"

"He shall be the first," added the Rev. James White. "He shall come forward, and he shall depose to the truth, which is that you had no guilty knowledge of the spurious character of the coins he sent you to change, about London."

"Indeed, and in truth, I had not," said Pamela, sadly.

"No one who has taken the pains to look into the case can doubt that, but it requires the direct testimony of Sharples."

"Who will believe him?" said Handsome Jemmy.

"All the world, I think, when that testimony will convict himself."

Pamela stepped up to the young curate and looked him in the face.

"Sir," she said, while the tears flowed from her eyes, —"sir, you are a man of God—you will not, I am sure, deceive me."

"Not for the whole world's dominion!"

"Say, then, what shall I do?"

"Surrender to these officers."

"I do! I will!"

"Pamela!" cried Dick Doubleday.

"Lavinia—my child!" shrieked the Doctor.

"There is no danger," said the Rev. James White. "Let her go—let her go on the route to liberty, and to that peace of mind which neither she nor any of you who love her can ever know while the terrors of the law are hanging over and about her."

"I see what all this means," said Handsome Jemmy. "The course of proceeding will be, that our dear Pamela will be brought up to-morrow before the Lord Chief Justice for identification, and then will be the time for Jacob Sharples to be produced."

"He shall be produced," said the Rev. James White.

"Then I, too, counsel you, Pamela, to go with the officers."

"But not alone," said Doctor Haslem. "Where my child goes, I go."

"Aw—and I, too," said Lord Malvern.

CHAPTER LXXV.
CAPTAIN SANG CONGRATULATES HIMSELF UPON HIS SUPPOSED SUCCESSFUL VILLANY.

SANG laughed in his cell.

"I am at least avenged!" he muttered. "I am avenged upon them all! Pamela may not be mine; but who will fight and struggle for the cold corpse from the gallows? Ha, ha! I am avenged! I may fail in my intentions, but my failure shall be as terrible to others as my success!"

As he was thus congratulating himself on the probable misery he should produce, he heard the sound of the massive key in his cell door.

He roused himself to listen.

A turnkey approached.

"You are wanted."

Sang sprung to his feet as well as his fetters would allow him; for after the specimen the authorities of Newgate had had of his vicious disposition, they were quite resolved to keep him out of mischief.

"Wanted! Who wants me?"

"Oh, a gentleman—that's all."

"Ah! the Secretary of State?"

The turnkey laughed.

"Well, that's about the oddest idea I ever heard in the old Stone Jug! The Secretary of State, indeed! Ha, ha! Well, come on; you are wanted; and I don't know who it is that does want you."

"I am a free man!"

"Are you?"

"I shall be. Lead on, and I will come after you."

"Oh, dear, no! We don't do things in that sort of way, in the old Stone Jug! You will go first, and I will come on. I like to see mischief before me."

The push with which the turnkey accompanied those words admitted of no further argument upon the matter.

Much to his disgust, Captain Sang was driven along the gloomy stone passages of Newgate like some wild ox, the turnkey every now and then dealing him an admonitory tap on the head with his keys.

These rather harsh proceedings in regard to Sang arose from the fact that the Governor of Newgate was so thoroughly enraged at the attempt Sang had made upon his life, that in the vestibule of the prison he had made a little speech about the sanguinary prisoner.

"I look upon that rascal Sang," said the Governor, in the hearing of all the turnkeys—"I look upon that rascal Sang as quite a wild beast; and it would not in the least surprise me—although, of course, I am bound to say that I disapprove of any severity—if the warders and turnkeys were to push him about like a mad bull."

This was quite sufficient.

Captain Sang was, after that expression of opinion on the part of the Governor, to receive no quarter.

Hence, then, the turnkey who now conducted him to the attorney's room kept up the little exercise with the keys on his head all the way.

The villanous Sir John Pope, alias Captain Sang, by

the time he reached the room where the gentleman was waiting for him, certainly merited his name of Sang.

There was blood upon his brow, which trickled down in crimson streaks over his face, making him look as though he gazed from behind bars of that colour.

"There you are!" said the turnkey, as he gave Sang a kick, when they reached the threshold of the room, which sent him nearly headlong into it.

Sang was furious.

He turned and bent a ferocious look upon the turnkey.

"Wait!—wait!" he said; "I can wait, and so will you! My time may yet come!"

The turnkey laughed.

Little did he care about the vindictive threats of a man whom he looked upon as doomed to death.

Captain Sang then turned his attention to the person who had "wanted" him, and at a glance he saw that it was not his old acquaintance, the Secretary of State.

The personage was a little slim man, attired in black with a care and precision that indicated his pretensions to belong to one of the learned professions, although which one Sang could not determine.

The highwayman was not left, however, long in doubt upon that point.

"Hem!" said the prim-looking personage—"I am a member of the bar!"

"Ah! a lawyer?"

"Well, you may say a lawyer, if you like! I have no objection to be your lawyer, if you are a reasonable man."

Sang saw at once that something was wanted of him, and he was prepared to be as insolent and exacting as possible, accordingly.

"And well, Mr. Lawyer," he said, "what do you want with me?"

"Oh, it is very simple! Can you say clearly and distinctly where you got certain letters from, which were addressed to a certain Secretary of State, and along with which were in his handwriting drafts of his replies?"

The sumptuously attired little individual held his head on one side, and looked inquiringly into the face of Captain Sang.

He guessed well enough of course that the inquiry had to do with those letters which were of such great importance to the Secretary of State; but the character of the inquiry itself it was that baffled his comprehension,

"What do you mean?" he said.

"You know——"

"May I be hanged if I do!"

"Hem!—the probability of your being hanged is strong enough, and if you don't know what you are wanted to know, it will be a settled thing!"

"What, in the name of ——"

"Hush! I don't like violent language!"

"Then what the——"

"Will you be civil?"

Sang had difficulty in speaking without the use of some rather strong expression, but by a great effort he controlled himself, and added, "What, then, sir, am I expected to reveal?"

"Just this! You are wanted to know that you had certain letters direct from the noble and illustrious individual who now fills the office of Secretary of State for the Home Department!"

"Why, he knows I did!"

"Did what?"

"He knows, and can tell you perfectly well, that I had them from himself, and that is one of the reasons why he was so anxious to get them back again!"

"Ah!"

The lawyer pondered over this reply for some few moments, and then he said, "Captain Sang, I fancy you are labouring under some misapprehension."

"What?"

"You fancy that I came from the Secretary of State in question?"

"Of course you do."

"Certainly not! I came from a noble personage who is his political opponent, and into whose hands those letters have accidentally fallen."

"Ah!"

"It is so. I am fond of candour, so I will tell you at once how it was. There was an old woman—a wretched hag—a beggar ——"

"Had she a scar on her brow?"

"She had."

"I know her."

"Of course you do; for she could not know you so well without your knowing her."

"Go on—go on! What of her? I thought she was dead!"

"Ah!—a little mutual mistake. She thought you were dead. But be that as it may, she came to the door of my client, the exalted political personage, to beg, and my client was on the point of stepping out. He gave her a crown-piece, and then she immediately took from her bosom a packet, which she, in a frenzied kind of way, handed to him, saying, "I will keep my oath! Into the first hands that are held forth in kindness to me I will place this secret of the villain Sang!"

"Indeed!"

"The villain Sang!"

"You said that before, sir."

"I wanted to impress it upon you."

"Go on—go on!"

"Well, my worthy and exalted client did not know who the villain Sang was, and he spoke kindly to the old woman, whose strength was so far gone that she fell upon the doorstep; but my exalted client had her conveyed into the hall of his house."

"What then?"

"She died."

Sang drew a long breath of relief.

"Dead! dead! What care I, then? But how—if those were the letters—how did she become possessed of them? Did he miss them? Did he find nothing behind the picture? Did that old witch watch me? Is all lost?"

In this disjointed manner Captain Sang reasoned upon what had possibly happened; and as he did so, the lawyer, with his little head on one side, and his keen eyes fixed upon him, devoured every word. He said, "Well, Captain Sang?"

"Sir," said Sang, "you have either said too much, or you must say more."

"I will say more. The old woman died; but before she did so, she said that she had found the letters behind a picture in the house of Sir John Pope, alias the notorious Captain Sang, in his house in the Birdcage Walk."

"She said that?"

"She did; and then expired. My exalted client, thereupon looking at the letters, found that they much concerned another exalted personage; and he wants to know what you can say to show that the letters were ever actually in the possession of that other exalted personage, so that he may not be able to say that they are mere forgeries which he never saw."

A light broke in upon the mind of Captain Sang.

He comprehended, now, the posture of affairs. The old hag had got possession of the letters so essential to the peace of mind of the Secretary of State, and from her they had passed exactly in the way the little lawyer stated, to some high political opponent.

"And if I supply the wanting link in the chain of evidence?" said Sang.

"If you do——"

"Well, what then? What am I to get?"

"Life, liberty, and a couple of thousand pounds."

"Done!"

"You accept the terms?"

"I do—I do!"

"Good! Then all I have at present to say is, that you will hear from me soon, and that I wish you a happy deliverance."

"Hold, sir!"

"What now?"

"You speak of life and liberty. How are you, or your exalted personages, to find the power to bestow such boons upon me?"

"There will be a change of Ministry. The exalted personage for whom I act will be the next Home Secretary, and then he will keep his word with you."

Sang looked blank.

"Then all I have to trust to," he said, "is the word of an exalted personage?"

"That is it; and a most ample security it is."

Sang laughed.

"You play with me," he said. "You and your exalted personage have no such letters as you mention. It is all a sham—all a delusion! There is some purpose in your visit, but you have no such letters."

"You are wrong."

The lawyer was one of the most cautious and undemonstrative men in the world; but by one of those involuntary movements which human nature may give way to at the best of times, and in the most cautious of persons, he slightly touched the breast of his coat.

That slight action was enough for Sang.

"There are the letters," he said to himself. "He has the letters in that pocket, and they shall be mine again!"

—

CHAPTER LXXVI.

CAPTAIN SANG SEEMS TO BE THE MASTER OF THE SITUATION.

THE lawyer smiled, and tried to leave the room.

He thought he had managed the interview with the highwayman capitally. He was prepared to go a great deal further in promises to Sang, if the life and liberty and two thousand pounds did not suffice; but as they had been apparently sufficient, he was well pleased.

The tone in which he now said "Good day, Captain Sang," was that of a man on the very best terms with himself.

It is seldom that a man goes out of the world in the midst of so much mental satisfaction.

But this professional man did so.

Sang, with the stealthy spring of a tiger, sprung upon him.

Lifting both his manacled arms, he brought them down with a crash upon the top of the head of the lawyer.

There was not the slightest cry—not a moan—not a sigh!

The professional man lay dead upon the floor of the room!

The smile of self-satisfaction was still upon his lips! The expression of self-gratulation at having managed the business he came upon cleverly was still about his eyes!

But he was dead.

Sang pounced upon the body, like some carrion-crow, and tearing open the vest he at once found the letters.

Those very letters which he had taken originally from the Secretary of State on the road—which he had then, without the least idea that he had been watched, hidden behind the framed and glazed panel in his house—the letters which he had sold for his life, but which the Secretary missing to find, had got back to him now after so strange a fashion.

But what was he now to do?

Murder, then, in that room, was added to his other offence.

Where should he hide the body?

Where should he hide the letters?

He knew that he was not likely to be left alone for long. He knew, too, that if he were taken before a magistrate he should be searched, with all the skill that practice gave the warders of Newgate, beforehand.

He glared about him like some wild animal who has caught his prey but hears the hunters at hand, and feels the necessity of for a time concealing it.

The room was bare enough of furniture. One table and one chair, that was all.

There was a fire-place, but no fire.

A sudden thought took possession of Sang—a thought of escape. He peered up the chimney: could it be ascended? He felt up it as far as he could reach. No; there was no hope there. A couple of strong iron bars were set into the solid stone-work in the chimney shaft, about six or seven feet from the grate.

They formed an effectual barrier against climbing that chimney in old Newgate. But the presence of those bars suggested another scheme to Sang.

He saw by their use the way to dispose of the dead body of the lawyer.

He felt that he had no time to lose. He did not want to complicate his case in Newgate by such a self-evident murder. At any moment a turnkey or a warder might put his head in at that room door.

It was a nervous time for Sang.

He stripped the neckcloth, which went at least three times round the neck of the little prim attorney, from his throat. He tied one end of it once only round his neck. Stretching his arms then up the chimney, Sang passed the other end of the noose once over one of the iron bars.

He then drew up the body.

It disappeared in the chimney.

Sang had a good deal of difficulty in making fast the other end of the noose, but he did so to a portion of the clothes of the dead man.

Then nothing could be seen of him.

The letters he carried about him.

"If I can only get back to my cell," he thought, "I will hide them in the earth most effectually until I want them."

The door was opened.

"Ready to go, sir?" said a warder.

"What do you want?" growled Sang.

The warder looked round the room in surprise to see that only Captain Sang was there.

"Why, where's the visitor?" he said.

"Oh, none of your jokes," said Sang; "you ought to know! One of you came some time ago, and let him out, and then slammed and locked the door in my face; but it don't matter to me."

The turnkey looked incredulous.

"Hoy, hoy! Bennett!" he cried. "Did you let Mr Mathews out of here?"

"No!"

"Did you, Ingram?"

"Not I!"

"Well, he's gone."

The three turnkeys stood at the threshold of the door, and looked in on Captain Sang, who put on, as far as he could, a look of injured innocence, as he said, "It don't become any of you to make game of a fellow in this kind of way, because he happens to be nabbed! I want to write another letter, and here's the money for it. Let me do it, and it will be all the better for all of you."

"But where's Mr. Mathews?"

"Oh, bother! don't plague me! What kind of a joke is this? I don't see anything funny in it!"

The officer did not see anything funny in the matter either; but there was the fact that the lawyer was gone; and then arose a little circumstance which put an end to all further trouble on the subject.

The warders began each to suspect the other of playing off this pretended mysterious vanishment of Mr. Mathews as a kind of practical joke the one upon the other.

That settled the matter.

They all laughed and jeered at each other; and Captain Sang, by paying his guinea (the Newgate price), was soon accommodated with the means of writing a letter.

The epistle was to the Secretary of State, and ran as follows :—

" Sir John Pope presents his compliments to the Right Hon. the Secretary of State, and begs to say that he is aware there was a little disappointment in regard to what was to be found behind the picture-frame in his house at the Birdcage Walk; but at the same time, Sir John Pope feels himself in a condition to say that he can still place in the hands of the Right Hon. the Secretary of State the documents in question —*or in any other hands.*"

The last five words of this epistle were what Captain Sang prided himself upon.

With a grim smile, he despatched the letter; and then he waited, as calmly as a man of his temperament could wait for anything, the accomplishment of his villanies.

" Yes," he muttered to himself, " all will go now as I wish—that is to say, as I wish now. It is true that I have failed in some of my plans; but I shall succeed in others !"

He rattled his chains, and tried to sing.

It was a dreary effort, that.

Captain Sang had been a buccaneer at one time. He had formed one of a ship's crew of those relentless men who cruised on the Spanish Main.

The song that he tried to sing was of a seafaring character, but he broke down in it; and in the loneliness of his cell, he began to feel all the horrors which such men dread more than they do actual danger.

But the time wore on.

The day passed away; and the dim, the very dim light that found its way into the cell of the highwayman faded away.

While that light lasted, though, he had managed to dig a hole, about a foot deep, in the floor of his cell, into which he placed those letters which were so uncomfortably incriminative of the Secretary of State.

In those bits of paper, Captain Sang felt, consisted his preservation.

Without them he was but a dead man.

Then the night came, and the last visit of the turnkey who had charge of that cell took place.

Captain Sang heard his footsteps on the stone passage, and the moment the door was opened he called out to him.

" Speak ! speak ! Let me hear the sound of a human voice !"

" What, Captain, have you got the horrors? I thought you were too seasoned a bird for that !"

" No, no ! But—I feel lonely ! Could you—will you—if I pay you well—get me some brandy ?"

The turnkey shook his head.

" I will give you a guinea a glass !"

" Hum !"

" Come, what say you ?"

" Well, you shall have half a bottle. It holds—let me see—half a bottle holds fourteen glasses !"

" Impossible !—five you mean !"

" Oh, well, if you say impossible, Captain Sang, why there is an end of the matter !"

" No, no !"

" You agree, then, that half a bottle of brandy reaches sixteen glasses !"

" You said fourteen !"

" No, no ! Seventeen !"

" Good gracious! what will you get too at last ?"

The turnkey laughed.

" Will you have it ?"

" Yes, yes ! I have still the money to pay for it. It is a wise principle that lets a man who is brought into Newgate keep his own money. Fetch the liquor ! I shall die without it ! Quick !—oh, quick !"

" Twenty guineas !" said the turnkey, when, after a good half-hour's delay, which seemed an age to Captain Sang, he came back with a bottle which was about a third full of brandy.

Sang paid the money with a groan.

" Come, now," said the turnkey, " I will give you a piece of news that will be worth all the gold ?"

" What is it ?"

" Pamela Sharples is again in Newgate !"

" Ah !"

" It is true ! But I can't make out what is going on ! She is lodged in the Governor's house, and waited on like any lady in the land !"

" No, no ! And yet—yet—no !—she will—she must—hang ! Nothing can save her ! She is already condemned ! Nothing but the self-crimination of Jacob Sharples could now save her; and from what I have heard of him he is just as likely to do a thing of that sort as—as I should be !"

" You are about right there, Captain," said the turnkey, as he slammed shut the door of the cell, and locked it for the night.

The information that had been conveyed to Sang by the turnkey regarding Pamela was quite true.

She was in Newgate—but Lord Malvern had shown good reason both in the shape of gold and argument to the Governor.

Both he and her father, the Court Physician, remained that night in Newgate.

At the earliest dawn there came a note to the prison from the Secretary of State. Its purport was interesting to Captain Sang, and it ran as follows:—

" The Secretary of State for the Home Department begs to state that upon more perfect recollection he is quite prepared to identify Captain Sang, *alias* Sir John Pope, as the man who robbed him in his dwelling house.

" The Secretary will be in attendance at Bow Street, by the hour of one, precisely.

" The Secretary thinks the notorious criminal in question had better be informed that if he has any memorial, praying for consideration or mercy, it had better be sent to the Secretary at once, that it may reach his, and not *any other hands !*"

There was something so mysterious about the latter part of this note, that the Governor desired it might be read to Sang.

He understood it.

" No," he said—" no; I have nothing to say, now. Nothing to send."

And so these two men, one of whom was in reality not a whit better than the other, as regarded their moral depravity, played fast and loose with each other even to the last.

Sang felt that hanged he certainly would be so soon as he said a word to any one else about the treasonable letter.

The Secretary felt that he dared not actually let a rope be put about the neck of Sang, so long as he had those letters hidden somewhere.

We shall see how these two personages still tried to outwit each other, and what in the end became of it.

Our business is now with the fair Pamela.

——

CHAPTER LXXVII.

PAMELA IS BROUGHT BEFORE THE CHIEF JUSTICE FOR RE CONDEMNATION.

It is early morning in Newgate.

In the private house of the Governor sits three persons—we were going to say, enjoying a breakfast ; but, in good truth, there was little enjoyment in it.

Pamela — our Pamela, who has passed through so many perils—is one of the persons.

Lord Malvern and Doctor Haslem are the two others.

The Governor politely spared them the infliction of his society.

Pamela is pale.

The Court Physician has a look of intense, painful anxiety in his face.

Lord Malvern looks just a little flushed, as if some unusually interesting affair were in progress, but there is a confident gleam in his eyes, which the Doctor keeps looking at and envying.

They can hear, where they are sitting, the clock of St. Sepulchre's strike, and it now gives forth the hour of nine.

Doctor Haslem involuntarily draws his chair a little closer to that of Pamela. She smiles, and holds out her hand to him.

"Father, all will be well."

"Yes, yes! All well—all must be well! Oh, my child—my own dear, dear Lavinia!"

Doctor Haslem had suffered so much, that his heart was weak, and the tears were ready to gush forth from his eyes at any moment.

"Aw," said Lord Malvern, "it's all wight, and there need be no appwehension. When James White, my ecclesiastical cousin, says things are all wight, why, all wight they are."

"You have great faith in him, my lord," said the physician.

"Aw—yes, I have So, as he has said it's all wight, why—aw—it is all wight."

There came now a respectful tap at the door of the room.

"Aw—come in!" cried Lord Malvern.

Mr. Purcell announced a turnkey.

Doctor Haslem sprang to his feet, and half stood before Pamela.

"Oh—aw—it's all wight; Mr. Purcell is our family solicitaw. I told him to come. It's all wight!"

Mr. Purcell, who was one of the most eminent solicitors in London, made his appearance, and was soon seated at the breakfast-table.

"Aw—Purcell?"

"Yes, my lord."

"You know all about Pamelaw, and what ought to be done; and I want you to tell the Doctaw that it's all wight, you see, Purcell."

"Yes, my lord. You need be under no apprehension whatever, Doctor Haslem. I have been put into communication with the Rev. James White by Lord Malvern, and this morning, before I was up, I received this note from that rev. gentleman."

Doctor Haslem took the note eagerly. It simply contained the following words:—

"Dear Sir,

"I will be in the Criminal Court of the Old Bailey at eleven o'clock, with Jacob Sharples.

"Yours truly,

"JAMES WHITE."

"Aw—that is wight. Oh, yes; after that, it's all wight. It was all wight before that, and now it's all wight again."

"Then, sir," said the Court Physician, "you think my child will be saved?"

"Most undoubtedly."

Doctor Haslem looked into the eyes of his beautiful Lavinia, and joy shone in his face.

"You see, Doctor Haslem," added the solicitor, "as this young lady has been already condemned to death for passing bad money with a guilty knowledge, the course of procedure will be that, as she has been out of custody, she must be brought into court to be identified."

"Yes—oh, yes."

"Then the judge must, so to speak, re-condemn her; but he will ask if she has anything to say why the sentence that has already been passed upon her should not be carried out; and then the eminent counsel that I have retained on her behalf will state that there is proof of her innocent participation only in passing the spurious coin; and if Jacob Sharples can be produced, and be made to swear that fact, it will not be possible to make this young lady suffer."

"She will be free?"

"Not at once."

"How so, sir, if innocent?"

"Truly, she should be; but, having been formally condemned, she must be pardoned by the Crown—merely, in this case, as a form, you see."

"Let them do as they like, so that my child is saved to me!"

"Aw—it's an odd thing," said Lord Malvern, "to pawdon a fellow or a girl who has done nothing! It's —aw—a sort of thank-you-for-nothing sort of—aw— pwoceeding!"

Then came another tap at the door.

"Aw—come in!"

"The Sheriff!"

"Aw—Mr. Shewiff, how de do?—how de do, eh? All wight? Aw, Doctaw, the Shewiff is good enough to intewest himself about Pamelaw!"

"It is both a duty and a pleasure, Doctor Haslem," said the Sheriff, "on my part to do all I can for your lovely daughter, who, I am assured, is innocent. What a strange, romantic fate hers has been, to be sure! But we must not delay now, if you please; for there is no man on the face of the earth more punctual than the Lord Chief Justice, and I'll warrant he is in Court now."

As the Sheriff spoke, he offered his arm to Pamela.

Doctor Haslem had hold of her hand, and he hesitated to give her up to anybody.

"My dear sir," said the solicitor, "all this, now, only amounts to a matter of form. Let her go with Sir Samuel, if you please, and we shall all the sooner get this little affair over."

"Yes, father, I feel now that all will be well," said Pamela. "Let us part for a short time, in order that we may part no more!"

Doctor Haslem bowed his head.

"Be it so—be it so! Heaven hold you in its holy keeping, my innocent child!"

Pamela went away with the Sheriff, and the Doctor, with Mr. Purcell, at once repaired to the Criminal Court.

And now, during this short space of time, when Pamela is on her route to the bar where it has became necessary she should appear before the Lord Chief Justice, we will take a glance at what is taking place at that villa at Islington, where Jacob Sharples is a prisoner.

At the same time that Pamela, her father, and Lord Malvern sat down to breakfast in the Governor's house at Newgate, the Reverend James White crossed the lawn of the villa, and entered its hall.

Mrs. Haslem, who had been up since the dawn, flew to meet her.

"My child!—my Lavinia?"

That was all she could say.

"Well and happy!" was the prompt reply. "She has been told that she will soon be free; but she has not yet been told that a greater joy still will follow that freedom, by being permitted to rest on the heart of her long-lost mother."

"And—and—he—he—my husband?"

"I have seen him."

"And told him——"

"Nothing, as yet. Sufficient for this day, or at all events for the commencement of it, is the load of anxiety about his newly-found daughter."

"Yes, yes—oh, yes! How—how does he look?"

The Reverend James White shook his head.

"I never saw a man yet who bore about him the expression of so much grief."

"Alas! alas!"

"His thin, white hair——"

"Thin?—white? Has he so changed—so—so suffered?"

Mrs. Haslem leant her head upon her hands, and wept bitterly.

"Oh, let me go to him at once! Let me tell him that all is forgotten—all forgiven!"

"Nay, allow me to persuade you not to be too precipitate. Let this terrible day as regards Lavinia pass over, as no doubt it will, all well. Lord Malvern, my cousin, put me at once into communication with his solicitor; the most eminent counsel is retained; and the Lord Chief Justice has had a report of the case sent to him; so all will go well."

"But do you—can you think that that man, Jacob Sharples, will really criminate himself to save my child?"

"No; certainly not. Not to save your child, or any one's child, or all the children in the world; but he will depose to enough to save Lavinia, in the hope that it will afford him a chance of escape, and on the promise that the grave charge you could produce against him will not be mentioned."

"Then I may hope?"

"You may, indeed. So now I will go to him, and he shall at once proceed with me to town, and play his part."

The Reverend James White then went to the top of the house, where Jacob Sharples was imprisoned.

The coiner had made some desperate efforts at escape, but had been foiled by the precautions that the Reverend James White had taken. He looked like some wild animal that had been caught in a trap on which he had exhausted all his fury in vain.

On the appearance of the young curate, he made a dart at him as though he would strike him.

"You had better not, Jacob Sharples!"

"Why had I better not? You are my foe—my fate—my mortal enemy!"

"Because if you so much as touch me with the tip of your finger, I will knock you down."

Jacob Sharples was cowed.

"Now, sir," added the curate, "you will come with me to the Criminal Court of the Old Bailey."

"No, never!"

"Oh, yes, you will! When there, too, you will, on your oath, depose that not only was the young girl you named Pamela ignorant of the character of the spurious coin you sent her to change in different parts of London, but that you took the utmost care that she should not have the remotest suspicion of the fact, because you knew that if she had, nothing in the world would induce her to do so."

"I will not."

"You will not what?"

"I will not make such a deposition. I refuse it, utterly and entirely. Let her hang!"

"Very well."

The manner in which the Rev. James White said "Very well!" rather surprised Jacob Sharples.

"Ha, ha! Let her hang, and so I spoil you all!"

"Oh, no! she will not hang! We should prefer slaiming her in the open face of day; but if you will not do so, she will not hang. The King has placed in the hands of the Archbishop of Canterbury the power of actually pardoning once a-year any condemned person; and he (the Archbishop) has not this year used up his privilege, but he will in favour of Pamela—or, rather, of Lavinia Haslem."

Jacob Sharples looked wild and agitated.

The Rev. James White went to the top of the ladder that led into the loft, and called out quietly, "Martha! Martha!"

"Yes, sir," replied the old servant of Mrs. Haslem.

"At the corner of the lane, Martha, you will find two men. Tell them I want them."

"Yes, sir."

"Stop!" bawled Jacob Sharples. "Who are they?"

"Constables."

"Well, it don't matter. I should be given into charge in the court, if I were fool enough to go and criminate myself as a coiner."

"But I do not mean to give you in charge as a coiner. It is for the attempted murder, and the actual robbery, of Mrs. Haslem, on the Thames, that you will be given in charge here; and I think that is an offence that will effectually shut the gates of human mercy against you."

"No, no! Stop!"

"Stop what?"

"I—I will rather take my chance of—of the charge of coining."

"It is too late—the servant has gone."

"No, no—not too late! Do not say that! Save me from the other charge—save me from that, and I will go with you to the court! Help! Oh, have some mercy upon me!"

"Come, then."

The Rev. James White took Jacob Sharples by the collar, and led him down the ladder, and out of the villa, as quietly as a lamb. In the garden they met Martha with two men.

"I shall not want you, I think," said the curate; "but if you will kindly get a coach and come with us, it will be as well."

Jacob Sharples trembled in every limb, for he saw that these men were veritable constables. The coach was procured, and into it got Jacob and the curate. One of the constables rode on the box with the driver; the other got up behind.

"To the Old Bailey," said the Rev. James White. "I want to get there by eleven o'clock precisely."

CHAPTER LXXVIII.

THE CONCLUSION.

Some sort of *bruit*, or report, that a case of more than ordinary interest would come before the Criminal Court of the Old Bailey on that eventful morning must have got abroad, for the court was crowded in every part.

It was with some difficulty that Doctor Haslem and Lord Malvern found places; but at length, by the assistance of Mr. Purcell, they got seats at the attorneys table.

The Lord Chief Justice had taken his seat on the bench. One of the trials was commencing. A poor wretch had picked a pocket, and was soon condemned.

Then a slip of paper was handed up to the judge, and he spoke to the Sheriff, who was on the bench.

A communication was made to the Clerk of the Arraigns, and the crowd in the court saw that something unusual was about to take place.

A counsel with a very florid face rose and spoke.

"My lord, I have to pray the judgment of the court."

"In what way, brother Nicholls?" asked the Lord Chief Justice.

"My lord, a condemned criminal, named Pamela Sharples, escaped from custody pending her execution, but has been recaptured. I have to pray that she may be brought into court and properly identified before your lordship, and then surrendered to the Sheriff."

"Be it so!"

There was a stir among the crowd, and some commotion, as people tried to get better places, and then Pamela was placed at the bar.

Doctor Haslem would have sprung to his feet, but Lord Malvern held him down.

"It's all wight—it's all wight! The baw is only a bit of wood, and we are on one side of it, and Pamela is on the other—that's all!"

Poor Doctor Haslem could not take this philosophical view of the bar, and he was deathly pale. But Pamela looked towards him and smiled gently: she was serene, and so he was happier, or not so unhappy.

The florid-looking counsel then cried out, "John Skinner!"

A man got into the witness-box, and was sworn.

"What are you?"

"Chief warder of Newgate."

"Look at the prisoner at the bar, and say if you know her?"

"Yes. That is Pamela Sharples, who was condemned last sessions to death for passing counterfeit coin."

" That will do."

The florid-looking counsel sat down. The Lord Chief Justice looked at Pamela.

" Prisoner, have you anything to say why the sentence of the law should not be carried out?"

Pamela had been instructed what to say, and she replied in her sweet voice, " By my counsel, yes, my lord."

Then the eminent lawyer who had been retained by Mr. Purcell, rose.

" My lord, the prisoner at the bar was convicted, very properly, no doubt, on the case as it then appeared, of uttering counterfeit coin, with a guilty knowledge. Since the trial and the condemnation, evidence has been found which clears her of the guilty knowledge; and in that case, if such evidence should be satisfactory to your lordship, I am sure your lordship would not deliver the prisoner to Mr. Sheriff."

" God forbid!" said the Lord Chief Justice. " Produce your evidence, brother Hotham."

" Jacob Sharples!" cried the counsel.

The clock of the Court at that moment struck eleven.

There was a commotion at the entrance to the court —a pressure of people—strange cries and ejaculations A small knot of persons appeared to be making way through the throng. The officers of the Court cleared a passage as well as they were able, and then the Reverend James White, with the two constables who had come with him from Islington, and Jacob Sharples, appeared.

Sharples appeared.

White as a sheet, and such a trembling in all his limbs that he could scarcely stand, Sharples was placed in the witness-box.

" Your name?" asked the counsel when he was sworn.

" Jacob Sharples."

" Are you related to the prisoner at the bar?"

" No, I——."

" That is enough. Did you send her to pass spurious gold, and bring you the change?"

" I—did."

" Had she any knowledge of the spurious character of the gold?"

Sharples licked his parched lips for a moment or two, and then he replied.

" No—she had no such knowledge. If she had even suspected it, no human force would have prevailed upon her to go!"

The counsel looked at the judge, who, in a voice of emotion, spoke.

" After this testimony—which surely is sufficient, seeing that this man who tenders it places himself, by so doing, in the hands of the law—I shall allow the prisoner to go at large on bail, and take upon myself to say that the royal pardon shall be immediately procured."

A shout of applause rung through the court.

Pamela was free!

In the arms of her father—carried through the crowd to his carriage—home then to Bedford Square—in the arms of Dick Doubleday—in the arms of her cousin, Handsome Jemmy—oh, how happy was our Pamela!

It was the Rev. James White, who then, after a glance from the window of the room, which showed him that a plain chariot was at the door, spoke to the Doctor.

" Doctor Haslem," he said, " the ways of Providence are not our ways, and we cannot take upon ourselves to question them. There has been a great deal of misery for many years past in your heart, and there is, I am told, a room in your house which you have kept closed."

" I have! I have! Never again shall it see the light of day. Alas! there is in my heart a dark chamber which will never see light."

Handsome Jemmy, at a sign from the curate, had left the room.

Then the Rev. James White added—

" Doctor Haslem, I spoke to you, I hope, with a certain authority. I ask you—nay, I tell you—that you should on this day go to that room and open its shutters, draw

up its blinds, for it is now the will of heaven that the dark chamber in your heart should know once more the light of day. Go, sir!"

There was a tone and manner about the young curate that awed Doctor Haslem into compliance. Like a man walking in a dream, he left that room, and went to the one which had above the chimney-piece the secret route to the closed boudoir.

Dare we—ought we to attempt, by the skill of any mortal pen, to describe what took place in that room when the Court Physician found his long-lost wife, the mother of his dear Lavinia?

Ah, no! Let the human hearts that feel for the woes and the joys of the personages of our story, imagine for themselves the tears, the sobs, the cries to heaven of gladness and thanksgiving of that blessed meeting.

An hour has passed away.

During that hour, though, Lavinia—we ought now now to call our heroine Lavinia—was then informed of all the sad story of her poor mother's fate, and in the end informed, too, that she was now beneath that roof.

Upon that news, Lavinia would hear no more, but she rushed from the room, calling out aloud, " Mother, mother—my own mother! Mother, mother! it is your child who calls you."

There was a crash of a broken down door, and Doctor Haslem appeared with his wife on his breast.

With a scream, Lavinia was in her mother's arms.

* * * * * * * * *

Pamela's perils are over.

Once, now, for good and for all. That day week there was quite a grand wedding from the house of the Court Physician in Bedford Square.

The bride was Lavinia Haslem.

The bridegroom, Dick Doubleday.

And now all we have to say is that Jacob Sharples was duly convicted of coining, and that he died in prison, which was a great relief to everybody.

What became of Mother Bendydykes, nobody ever knew. She disappeared.

Captain Sang was duly hanged; for being removed into another cell, in consequence of some repairs to the foundation of Newgate, the letters he had hidden were mixed up with rubbish, and stone, and mortar, and never saw the light; so that although he mentioned them on his trial, the account he gave, as they were not found, was treated as an idle and malicious fable, and the Secretary of State escaped the consequences of his treachery and treason.

Nay, he became so virtuously indignant at the charge, that his friends and admirers were compelled to present him, at a grand banquet, with a service of plate, to soothe his wounded feelings.

The Court Physician and his wife lived long enough to take a delight in the innocent prattle of their dear daughter's children; and the pleasantest room in the whole house became that long closed up apartment with its secret route through the walls.

Lord Malvern was a constant guest at Bedford Square, and in his odd way he always called Mrs. Doubleday, Pamela.

If ever a moral duty presented itself at the close of an eventful narrative, surely it is to be found here, when we have carried over Pamela as we may truly name her, through such a sea of troubles. Has she not shown that purity, constancy, and that innocence and singleness of mind and purpose, which is the heritage of the best and the purest, are amply sufficient safeguards against all that the most crafty and designing hearts can devise?

So full of gentleness; so true in her affection; so utterly without guile was Pamela, that the most consummate hypocrisy felt itself no match for the simplicity of that young soul.

And if, in the case of Pamela, we find that there is

" A divinity about virtue,"

which carries it safely through all perils, do we not, in the case of the Court Physician's brother, perceive that there is a mortal retribution, which, come it soon or late, is as certain as that any bright sunset we may look upon at the close of a day is the harbinger of a dawn upon the morrow.

The circumstances attending the condemnation of Pamela went far towards the amelioration of that cruel and barbarous penal code which disgraced England and outraged humanity. In that way, likewise, did the sufferings and the dangers of our heroine bear holy and grateful blossoms; and out of all the evil that was actually inflicted upon Pamela, and all the destruction that was threatened, was evolved some of those lessons of humanity which from that time entered into the administration of the criminal laws.

And who was more certain to rejoice and look back with pleasure, rather than pain, at all she had gone through, seeing that such was the result, than Pamela?

THE END.

9 781535 812665